FIONA McINTOSH

THE SCRIVENER'S TALE

BOOKS BY FIONA McINTOSH

TRINITY
Betrayal (1)
Revenge (2)
Destiny (3)

THE QUICKENING
Myrren's Gift (1)
Blood and Memory (2)
Bridge of Souls (3)

PERCHERON
Odalisque (1)
Emissary (2)
Goddess (3)

VALISAR
Royal Exile (1)
Tyrant's Blood (2)
King's Wrath (3)

The Whisperer

FIONA McINTOSH

THE SCRIVENER'S TALE

HARPER
Voyager

THE SCRIVENER'S TALE. Copyright © 2012 by Fiona McIntosh. All rights reserved. Printed in the United States of America. No part of this book may be used or reproduced in any manner whatsoever without written permission except in the case of brief quotations embodied in critical articles and reviews. For information address HarperCollins Publishers, 10 East 53rd Street, New York, NY 10022.

HarperCollins books may be purchased for educational, business, or sales promotional use. For information please write: Special Markets Department, HarperCollins Publishers, 10 East 53rd Street, New York, NY 10022.

This book was originally published in 2012 by HarperVoyager, an imprint of HarperCollins*Publishers* Australia Pty Limited.

FIRST WILLIAM MORROW PAPERBACK EDITION PUBLISHED 2013.

National Library of Australia Cataloguing-in-Publication entry:

McIntosh, Fiona, 1960–.
  The scrivener's tale / Fiona McIntosh.
  ISBN: 978 0 7322 9245 4 (pbk.)
A823.4

ISBN 978-0-06-223730-9

13 14 15 16 17 OV/RRD 10 9 8 7 6 5 4 3 2 1

PROLOGUE

He stirred, his consciousness fully engaged although he was unable to recall the last occasion anything had captivated his interest. How long had he waited in this numb acceptance that a shapeless, pointless eternity stretched ahead, with boredom his only companion? He was inconsequential, a nothingness. Existing, but not in a way that had worth or even acknowledgement … suspended between now and infinity. That was his punishment. Cyricus laughed without mirth or sound.

He was in this limbo because the goddess Lyana and her minions had been victorious several centuries previous, crushing the god Zarab. It had been the most intense confrontation that he could recall of all their cyclical battles, and Zarab's followers, himself included, had been banished from the spiritual plane to wander aimlessly. He was a demon; not as powerful as his god, Zarab, but not as weak as most of the disciples and certainly more cunning, which is probably why he'd evaded being hunted down and destroyed. He and one other — a mere disciple — had survived Lyana's wrath.

Cyricus remained an outlaw: a life, but not a life — no longer able to move in the plane of gods and never able to return to it, but he'd never given up hope. One day, he promised himself, he would learn a way to harness the power he needed, but not yet. He was not nearly strong enough and must content himself to exist without substance on the edge of worlds, and only his fury to keep him company.

But it was ill fate that he had recognised a fantastically powerful force emanating from the mortal plane; that force, he learned, was called the Wild. It sprawled to the northeast of an unfamiliar land called Morgravia. He'd been drifting in his insubstantial form for what might have been centuries, finally unwittingly veering into northern Briavel toward the natural phenomenon known as the Wild. It had sensed his evil and his interest long before he'd fully recognised its power: with the help of its keeper, Elysius, the Wild had driven the spirit of Cyricus and his minion into the universal Void. He could do nothing now but watch, bored, over more centuries, while mortals lived and died their short, trivial existences.

And then a young woman in Morgravia had done something extraordinary, fashioning a powerful magic so sly and sinister, so patient and cunning, that if he could he would have applauded her. It dragged him from disinterested slumber to full alertness, amusement even. This village woman, still languishing in her second decade, had crafted an incantation so powerful that she gave it an existence of its own: it had no master but it appeared to obey a set of rules that propelled it toward a single objective. Most curious of all, rather than cursing the man she loathed, Myrren had instead gifted her dark spell to his enemy, a boy.

Cyricus set aside his own situation and yearnings and gleefully focused his attention on the boy — plain, red-headed, forgettable if not for his name and title. He was Wyl Thirsk, the new hereditary general of the Morgravian Legion — forced to accept the role at his father's untimely death — and he had no idea that his life had just taken a deviant path. Even Cyricus had no idea what the magic could do, but he could see it, shifting as a dark shadow within Thirsk. What would it do? What could it do? And when? Cyricus was centuries old; he was patient and had learned through Lyana's punishment how to remain that way. Whatever magic it was that the young woman Myrren had cast, he was sure it would, one day, show itself.

It took five annums — a mere blink to him — before Cyricus could see the effect of Myrren's gift. When it finally quickened within the young man and demonstrated its capacity, Cyricus mentally closed his eyes in awe.

It was a beautiful magic answerable to no-one.

And it was simple, elegant, brutal.

Wyl Thirsk moved haplessly, and savagely, through different lives while the magic of Myrren raged, always seeking that one person its creator hunted. Cyricus watched, fascinated, as the magic wreaked its havoc: changing lives, rearranging the course of Morgravia's, Briavel's and even the Razor Kingdom's history.

And then at the height of his amusement it stopped. The spell laid itself to rest as abruptly as it had begun, although the land in which it had raged was an entirely changed place. Four kings had died in its time — two of those directly because of it — and a new empire had emerged. And the target of Myrren's gift — and her curse — was finally destroyed.

In spite of the disappointment at his entertainment being cut short Cyricus had developed a respect for the magic. It was not random, it was extremely focused and its goal had been reached ... revenge on King Celimus of Morgravia had been exacted in the most fantastic of manners.

The magic eased away from its carrier, Wyl Thirsk. However, it could never die once cast, of course, and Cyricus watched it finally pull itself into a small kernel until it was barely there, drifting around as he once had, attached to no-one and nothing — or so he thought — until his tireless observation refuted that presumption.

The magic did belong somewhere and it wanted to return there — to its spiritual home. But it was not permitted. And almost like an orphaned creature he could sense its longing, he could feel a kinship — they were both seemingly evil, both lost and unwanted, each unable to have substance, and yet both unable to disappear entirely into death.

He felt empathy! A unique moment of awakening for Cyricus.

In following Myrren's gift, his gaze fell upon the Wild once again, and what he now discovered brought new fury, a rage like he had not felt since he was first defeated alongside Zarab. He learned that Myrren had been the child of Elysius! Her magic was born of him! The Wild protected them! But it repelled her savage, killing magic that she'd designed with only darkness in her intent.

Suddenly Cyricus had a purpose and it was Myrren's cursed gift that gave him an idea: he would escape this prison of eternal suspended existence. The magic was there — homeless, idle, useless, ignored. He would lure it — make it notice him, welcome it even and then harness it. But he needed help.

He would need Aphra, his willing slave and undeniably adoring minion. He had longed for her carnal ways if not her vaguely irritating company. She had always worshipped him. He had toyed with her when it suited, had controlled her utterly. She would still do anything for him —

3

torch, maim, pillage and kill for him. He liked her pliable emotions, her cunning — which, though no match for his, was admirable — and now he finally had good use for her. She'd been calling to him for decades — so many years he'd lost count and hadn't cared to know. He'd had no reason to communicate.

But now he could see that dear love-blinded Aphra was his way back into some sort of life. She would provide him with what he lacked once he had captured the magic, understood it and moulded it to suit his needs. Myrren's magic was his priority; the rest would fall into place.

And so Cyricus remained close to the three realms and began to plot while they became one; he watched the empire rise and flourish, and then begin to wane as factions within its trio of realms erupted to start dismantling what Emperor Cailech and his Empress Valentyna had given so much to achieve. Cyricus couldn't care less. They could all go to war and he would enjoy watching the carnage ... they could limp on, remaining allied but hating one another and it would make not a jot of difference to Cyricus.

All that mattered to him was being able to return to substantial form again — he wanted to be seen again, for his voice to be heard again. And he wanted to make this land — and the Wild that protected it, that had flicked him into the Void — pay for his suffering. His patience knew no bounds and while he tirelessly worked toward his aim he watched as heir upon heir sat on the Morgravian throne, unaware that theirs might be the reign that felt the full impact of his hungry revenge.

ONE

In the stillness that came in the hour before dawn, when Paris was at its quietest, a dark shape moved silently through the frigid winter air.

It landed soundlessly on a balcony railing that was crusted with December frost and stared through the window, where the softest glow of a bedside lamp illuminated the face of a sleeping man. The man was not at rest though.

Gabe was dreaming, his eyes moving rapidly behind his lids as the tension within the world of his dream escalated. It was not his favourite dream of being in the cathedral but it was familiar all the same and it frightened him. He'd taught himself to recognise the nightmare whenever and without any warning he slipped into the scene; only rarely did its memory linger. Most times the details of the dream fell like water through his fingers. Gone in the blink of surfacing to an alertness of his reality.

Here it was again: *You're in the nightmare, Gabe,* his protective subconscious prodded. *Start counting back from ten and open your eyes.*

Ten ...

Gabe felt the knife enter flesh, which surrendered so willingly; blood erupted in terrible warmth over his fist as it gripped the hilt. He felt himself topple, begin to fall ...

... six ... five ...

He awoke with a dramatic start.

His heart was pounding so hard in his chest he could feel the angry drum of it against his ribcage. This was one of those rare occasions when vague detail lingered. And it felt so real that he couldn't help but look at his hands for tangible evidence, expecting to see them covered with blood.

He tried to slow his breathing, checking the clock and noticing it was only nearing six and the sky was still dark in parts. He was parched.

Gabe sat up and reached for the jug and tumbler he kept at his bedside and drank two glasses of water greedily. The hand that had held the phantasmic knife still trembled slightly. He shook his head in disgust.

Who had been the victim?

Why had he killed?

He blinked, deep in thought: could it be symbolic of the deaths that had affected him so profoundly? But he also hazily recalled that in his nightmare death had been welcomed by the victim.

Gabe shivered, his body clammy, and allowed the time for his breathing to become deeper and his heartbeat to slow. Paris was on the edge of winter; dawn would break soon but it remained bitingly cold — he could see ice crystals in the corners of the windows outside.

He swung his legs over the side of the bed and deliberately didn't reach for his hoodie or brushed cotton pyjama bottoms. Gingerly climbing down from the mezzanine bedroom he tiptoed naked in the dark to open the French doors. Something darker than night skittered away but he convinced himself he'd imagined it for there was no sign once he risked stepping out onto the penthouse balcony.

The cold tore at his skin, but at least, shivering uncontrollably, he knew he was fully awake in Paris, in the 6th arrondissement ... and his family had been dead for six years now. Gabe had been living here for not quite four of those, after one year in a wilderness of pain and recrimination and another losing himself in restless journeying in a bid to escape the past and its torment.

He had been one of Britain's top psychologists. His public success was mainly because of the lodge he'd set up in the countryside where emotionally troubled youngsters could stay and where, amidst tranquil surrounds, Gabe would work to bring a measure of peace to their minds. There was space for a menagerie of animals for the youngsters to interact with or care for, including dogs and cats, chickens, pigs, a donkey. Horse riding at the local stables, plus hiking, even simple cake- and pie-baking classes, were also part of the therapy, diverting a patient's attention outward and into conversation, fun, group participation, bonding with others, finding safety nets for the wobbly times on the tightropes of anxiety.

It was far more complex than that, of course, with other innovative approaches being used as well — everything from psychodynamic music to transactional therapies. Worried parents and carers, teachers and government agencies had all marvelled at his success in strengthening and fortifying the ability of his young charges to deal with their 'demons'.

Television reporters, journalists and the grapevine, however, liked to present him as a folk hero — a modern-day Pied Piper, using simple techniques like animal husbandry. It allowed his detractors to claim his brand of therapy and counsel was not rooted in academia. Even so, Gabe's legend had grown. Big companies knocked on his door: why didn't he join their company and show them how to market to teens, or perhaps they could sponsor the lodge? He refused both options but that didn't stop his peers criticising him or his status increasing to world acclaim. Or near enough.

Fate is a fickle mistress, they say, and she used his success to kill not only his stellar career but also his family, in a motorway pile-up while on their way to visit his wife's family for Easter.

The real villain was not his fast, expensive German car but the semi-trailer driver whose eyelids fate had closed, just for a moment. The tired, middle-aged man pushed himself harder than he should have in order to sleep next to his wife and be home to kiss his son good morning; he set off the chain of destruction on Britain's M1 motorway in the Midlands one terrible late-winter Thursday evening.

The pile-up had occurred on a frosty, foggy highway and had involved sixteen vehicles and claimed many lives, amongst them Lauren and Henry. For some inexplicable reason the gods had opted to throw Gabe four metres clear of the carnage, to crawl away damaged and bewildered. He might have seen the threat if only he hadn't turned to smile at his son ...

He faced the world for a year and then he no longer wanted to face it. Gabe had fled to France, the homeland of his father, and disappeared with little more than a rucksack for fifteen months, staying in tiny alpine villages or sipping aniseed liquor in small bars along the coastline. In the meantime, and on his instructions, his solicitor had sold the practice and its properties, as well as the sprawling but tasteful mansion in Hurstpierpoint with the smell of fresh paint still evident in the new nursery that within fourteen weeks was to welcome their second child.

He was certainly not left poor, plus there was solid income from his famous dead mother's royalties and also from his father's company. In his mid-thirties he found himself in Paris with a brimming bank account, a ragged beard, long hair and, while he couldn't fully call it peace of mind, he'd certainly made his peace with himself regarding that traumatic night and its losses. He believed the knifing dream was symbolic of the death of Lauren and Henry — as though he had killed them with a moment's inattention.

He thought the nightmare was intensifying, seemingly becoming clearer. He certainly recalled more detail today than previously, but he also had to admit it was becoming less frequent.

The truth was that most nights now he slept deeply and woke untroubled. His days were simple. He didn't need a lot of money to live day to day now that the studio was paid for and furnished. He barely touched his savings in fact, but he worked in a bookshop to keep himself distracted and connected to others, and although he had become a loner, he was no longer lonely. The novel he was working on was his main focus, its characters his companions. He was enjoying the creative process, helplessly absorbed most evenings in his tale of lost love. A publisher was already interested in the storyline, an agent pushing him to complete the manuscript. But Gabe was in no hurry. His writing was part of his healing therapy.

He stepped back inside and closed the windows. He found comfort in knowing that the nightmare would not return for a while, along with the notion that winter was announcing itself loudly. He liked Paris in the colder months, when the legions of tourists had fled, and the bars and cafés put their prices back to normal. He needed to get a hair cut … but what he most needed was to get to Pierre Hermé and buy some small cakes for his colleagues at the bookshop.

Today was his birthday. He would devour a chocolate- and a coffee-flavoured macaron to kick off his mild and relatively private celebration. He showered quickly, slicked back his hair, which he'd only just noticed was threatening to reach his shoulders now that it was untied, dressed warmly and headed out into the streets of Saint-Germain. There were times when he knew he should probably feel at least vaguely self-conscious about living in this bourgeois area of Paris but then the voice of rationality would demand one reason why he should suffer any embarrassment. None came to mind. Famous for its creative residents and thinkers, the Left Bank appealed to his sense of learning, his joy of reading and, perhaps mostly, his sense of dislocation. Or maybe he just fell in love with this neighbourhood because his favourite chocolate salon was located so close to his studio … but then, so was Catherine de Medici's magnificent Jardin du Luxembourg, where he could exercise, and rather conveniently, his place of work was just a stroll away.

He was the first customer into Pierre Hermé at ten as it opened. Chocolate was beloved in Britain but the Europeans, and he believed particularly the French, knew how to make buying chocolate an experience akin to choosing a good wine, a great cigar or a piece of expensive jewellery. Perhaps the latter was taking the comparison too far, but he knew his small cakes would be carefully picked up by a freshly gloved hand, placed reverently into a box of tissue, wrapped meticulously in cellophane and tied with ribbon, then placed into another beautiful bag.

The expense for a single chocolate macaron — or indeed any macaron — was always outrageous, but each bite was worth every euro.

'Bonjour, monsieur … how can I help you?' the woman behind the counter asked with a perfect smile and an invitation in her voice.

He wouldn't be rushed. The vivid colours of the sweet treats were mesmerising and he planned to revel in a slow and studied selection of at least a dozen small individual cakes. He inhaled the perfume of chocolate that scented the air and smiled back at the immaculately uniformed lady serving him. Today was a good day; one of those when he could believe the most painful sorrows were behind him. He knew it was time to let go of Lauren and Henry — perhaps as today was his birthday it was the right moment to cut himself free of the melancholy bonds he clung to and let his wife and two dead children drift into memory, perhaps give himself a chance to meet someone new to have an intimate relationship with. 'No time like the present', he overheard someone say behind him to her companion. All right then. Starting from today, he promised himself, life was going to be different.

Cassien was doing a handstand in the clearing outside his hut, balancing his weight with great care, bending slowly closer to the ground before gradually shifting his weight to lower his legs, as one, until he looked to be suspended horizontally in a move known simply as 'floating'. He was concentrating hard, working up to being able to maintain the 'float' using the strength of one locked arm rather than both.

Few others would risk the dangers and loneliness of living in this densely forested dark place which smelled of damp earth, although its solemnity was brightened by birds flittering in and around its canopy of leafy branches. His casual visitors were a family of wolves that had learned over years to trust his smell and his quiet observations. He didn't interact often with them, other than with one. A plucky female cub had once lurched over to him on unsteady legs and licked his hand, let him stroke her. They had become soul mates since that day. He had known her mother and her mother's mother but she was the first to touch him, or permit being touched.

Cassien knew how to find the sun or wider open spaces if he needed them. But he rarely did. This isolated part of the Great Forest had been his home for ten summers; he hardly ever had to use his voice and so he read aloud from his few books — which were exchanged every three moons — for an hour each day. They were sent from the Brotherhood's small library and he knew each book's contents by heart now, but it didn't matter. It also didn't matter to him whether he was reading *Asher's Compendium* about medicinal therapies or *Ellery's Ephemeris*, with its daily calendar of the movement of heavenly bodies. He was content to read anything that improved his knowledge and allowed him to lose his thoughts to learning. He was, however, the first to admit to his favourite tome being *The Tales of Empire*, written a century previously by one of the Brothers with a vivid imagination, which told stories of heroism, love and sorcery.

At present he was immersed in the *Enchiridion of Laslow* and the philosophical discourses arising from the author's lifetime of learning alongside the scholar Solvan Jenshan, one of the initiators of the Brotherhood and advisor to Emperor Cailech. Cassien loved the presence of these treasures in his life, imagining the animal whose skin formed the vellum to cover the books, the trees that gave their bark to form the rough paper that the ink made from the resin of oak galls would be scratched into. Imagining each part of the process of forming the book and the various men involved in them, from slaughtering the lamb to sharpening the quill, felt somehow intrinsic to keeping him connected with mankind. Someone had inked these pages. Another had bound this book. Others had read from it. Dozens had touched it. People were out there beyond the forest living their lives. But only two knew of his existence here and he had to wonder if Brother Josse ever worried about him.

Cassien lifted his legs to be in the classic handstand position before he bounced easily and fluidly regained his feet. He was naked, had worked hard, as usual, so a light sheen of perspiration clung to every highly defined muscle ... it was as though Cassien's tall frame had been sculpted. His lengthy, intensive twice-daily exercises had made him supple and strong enough to lift several times his own body weight.

He'd never understood why he'd been sent away to live alone. He'd known no other family than the Brotherhood — fifteen or so men at any one time — and no other life but the near enough monastic one they followed, during which he'd learned to read, write and, above all, to listen. Women were not forbidden but women as lifelong partners were. And they were encouraged to indulge their needs for women only when they were on tasks that took them from the Brotherhood's premises; no women were ever entertained within. Cassien had developed a keen interest in women from age fifteen, when one of the older Brothers had taken him on a regular errand over two moons and, in that time, had not had to encourage Cassien too hard to partake in the equally regular excursions to the local brothel in the town where their business was conducted. During those visits his appetite for the gentler sex was developed into a healthy one and he'd learned plenty in a short time about how to take his pleasure and also how to pleasure a woman.

He'd begun his physical training from eight years and by sixteen summers presented a formidable strength and build that belied how lithe and fast he was. He'd overheard Brother Josse remark that no other Brother had taken to the regimen faster or with more skill.

Cassien washed in the bucket of cold water he'd dragged from the stream and then shook out his black hair. He'd never known his parents and Josse couldn't be drawn to speak of them other than to say that Cassien resembled his mother and that she had been a rare beauty. That's all Cassien knew about her. He knew even less about his father; not even the man's name.

'Make Serephyna, whom we honour, your mother. Your father must be Shar, our god. The Brothers are your family, this priory your home.'

Brother Josse never wearied of deflecting his queries and finally Cassien gave up asking.

11

He looked into the small glass he'd hung on the mud wall. Cassien combed his hair quickly and slicked it back into a neat tail and secured it. He leaned in closer to study his face, hoping to make a connection with his real family through the mirror; his reflection was all he had from which to create a face for his mother. His features appeared even and symmetrical — he allowed that he could be considered handsome. His complexion showed no blemishes while near black stubble shadowed his chin and hollowed cheeks. Cassien regarded the eyes of the man staring back at him from the mirror and compared them to the rock pools near the spring that cascaded down from the Razor Mountains. Centuries of glacial powder had hardened at the bottom of the pools, reflecting a deep yet translucent blue. He wondered about the man who owned them … and his purpose. Why hadn't he been given missions on behalf of the Crown like the other men in the Brotherhood? He had been superior in fighting skills even as a lad and now his talent was as developed as it could possibly be.

Each new moon the same person would come from the priory; Loup was mute, fiercely strong, unnervingly fast and gave no quarter. Cassien had tried to engage the man, but Loup's expression rarely changed from blank.

His task was to test Cassien and no doubt report back to Brother Josse. Why didn't Josse simply pay a visit and judge for himself? Once in a decade was surely not too much to ask? Why send a mute to a solitary man? Josse would have his reasons, Cassien had long ago decided. And so Loup would arrive silently, remaining for however long it took to satisfy himself that Cassien was keeping sharp and healthy, that he was constantly improving his skills with a range of weapons, such as the throwing arrows, sword, or the short whip and club.

Loup would put Cassien through a series of contortions to test his strength, control and suppleness. They would run for hours to prove Cassien's stamina, but Loup would do *his* miles on horseback. He would check Cassien's teeth, that his eyes were clear and vision accurate, his hearing perfect. He would even check his stools to ensure that his diet was balanced. Finally he would check for clues — ingredients or implements — that Cassien might be smoking, chewing or distilling. Cassien always told Loup not to waste his time. He had no need of any drug. But Loup never took his word for it.

He tested that a blindfolded Cassien — from a distance — was able to gauge various temperatures, smells, Loup's position changes, even times of the day, despite being deprived of the usual clues.

Loup also assessed pain tolerance, the most difficult of sessions for both of them: stony faced, the man of the Brotherhood went about his ugly business diligently. Cassien had wept before his tormentor many times. But no longer. He had taught himself through deep mind control techniques to welcome the sessions, to see how far he could go, and now no cold, no heat, no exhaustion, no surface wound nor sprained limb could stop Cassien completing his test. A few moons previously the older man had taken his trial to a new level of near hanging and near drowning in the space of two days. Cassien knew his companion would not kill him and so it was a matter of trusting this fact, not struggling, and living long enough for Loup to lose his nerve first. Hanging until almost choked, near drowning, Cassien had briefly lost consciousness on both tests but he'd hauled himself to his feet finally and spat defiantly into the bushes. Loup had only nodded but Cassien had seen the spark of respect in the man's expression.

The list of trials over the years seemed endless and ranged from subtle to savage. They were preparing him but for what? He was confident by this time that his thinking processes were lightning fast, as were his physical reactions.

Cassien had not been able to best Loup in hand-to-hand combat in all these years until two moons previously, when it seemed that everything he had trained his body for, everything his mind had steeled itself for, everything his emotions and desires had kept themselves dampened for, came out one sun-drenched afternoon. The surprise of defeat didn't need to be spoken; Cassien could see it written across the older man's face and he knew a special milestone had been reached. And so on his most recent visit the trial was painless; his test was to see if Cassien could read disguised shifts in emotion or thought from Loup's closed features.

But there was a side to him that Loup couldn't test. No-one knew about his magic. Cassien had never told anyone of it, for in his early years he didn't understand and was fearful of it. By sixteen he not only wanted to conform to the monastic lifestyle, but to excel. He didn't want Brother Josse to mark him as different, perhaps even unbalanced or dangerous, because of an odd ability.

However, in the solitude and isolation of the forest Cassien had sparingly used the skill he thought of as 'roaming' — it was as though he could disengage from his body and send out his spirit. He didn't roam far, didn't do much more than look around the immediate vicinity, or track various animals; marvel at a hawk as he flew alongside it or see a small fire in the far distance of the south that told him other men were passing along the tried and tested tracks of the forest between Briavel and Morgravia.

Cassien was in the north, where the forest ultimately gave way to the more hilly regions and then the mountain range known as the Razors and the former realm beyond. He'd heard tales as a child of its infamous King Cailech, the barbaric human-flesh-eating leader of the mountain tribes, who ultimately bested the monarch of Morgravia and married the new Queen of Briavel to achieve empire. As it had turned out, Cailech was not the barbarian that the southern kingdoms had once believed. Subsequent stories and songs proclaimed that Emperor Cailech was refined, with courtly manners — as though bred and raised in Morgravia — and of a calm, generous disposition. Or so the stories went.

He'd toyed with the idea of roaming as far as the Morgravian capital, Pearlis, and finding out who sat on the imperial throne these days; monarchs could easily change in a decade. However, it would mean leaving his body to roam the distance and he feared that he couldn't let it remain uninhabited for so long.

There were unpalatable consequences to roaming, including sapping his strength and sometimes making himself ill, and he hated his finely trained and attuned body not to be strong in every way. He had hoped that if he practised enough he would become more adapted to the rigours it demanded but the contrary was true. Frequency only intensified the debilitating effects.

There was more though. Each time he roamed, creatures around him perished. The first time it happened he thought the birds and badgers, wolves and deer had been poisoned somehow when he found their bodies littered around the hut.

It was Romaine, the now grown she-wolf, who had told him otherwise. *It's you*, she'd said calmly, although he could hear the anger, her despair simmering at the edge of the voice in his mind. *We are paying for your freedom*, she'd added, when she'd dragged over the corpse of a young wolf to show him.

And so he moved as a spirit only rarely now, when loneliness niggled too hard, and before doing so he would talk to Romaine and seek her permission. She would alert the creatures in a way he didn't understand and then she would guide him to a section of the forest that he could never otherwise find, even though he had tried.

For some reason, the location felt repellent, although it had all the same sort of trees and vegetation as elsewhere. There was nothing he could actually pin down as being specifically different other than an odd atmosphere, which he couldn't fully explain but he felt in the tingles on the surface of his flesh and the raising of hair at the back of his neck. It felt ever so slightly warmer there, less populated by the insects and birds that should be evident and, as a result, vaguely threatening. If he was being very particular, he might have argued that it was denser at the shrub level. On the occasions he'd mentioned this, Romaine had said she'd never noticed, but he suspected that she skirted the truth.

'Why here?' he'd asked on the most recent occasion, determined to learn the secret. 'You've always denied there was anything special about this place.'

I lied, she'd pushed into his mind. *You weren't ready to know it. Now you are.*

'Tell me.'

It's a deliberately grown offshoot of natural vegetation known as the Thicket.

'But what is it?'

It possesses a magic. That's all I know.

'And if I roam from here the animals are safe?'

As safe as we can make them. Most are allowing you a wide range right now. We can't maintain it for very long though, so get on with what you need to do.

And that's how it had been. The Thicket somehow keeping the forest animals safe, filtering his magic through itself and cleansing, or perhaps absorbing, the part of his power that killed. It couldn't help Cassien in any way, but Romaine had admitted once that the Thicket didn't care about his health; its concern was for the beasts.

None, he'd observed, from hawk to badger, had ever been aware of his presence when he roamed. With Romaine's assistance, he had roamed briefly around Loup on a couple of occasions. Cassien was now convinced that people would not be aware of his spiritual presence either.

Only Romaine sensed him — she always knew where he was whether in physical or spiritual form. The she-wolf was grown to her full adult size now and she was imposing — beautiful and daunting in the same moment. Romaine didn't frighten him and yet he knew she could if she chose to. She still visited from time to time, never losing her curiosity for him. He revelled in her visits. She would regard him gravely with those penetrating yellowy grey eyes of hers and he would feel her kinship in that gaze.

He straightened from where he'd been staring into the mirror at his unshaven face and resolved to demand answers from Loup on the next full moon, which was just a few days away.

TWO

Gabe strolled to the bookshop carrying his box of cakes and enjoying the winter sunlight. Catherine gave a small squeal and rushed over to hug him as he entered the shop.

'Happy birthday!' And not worrying too much about what customers might think, she yelled out to the rest of the staff: 'Gabe's in, sing everyone!'

It was tradition. Birthday wishes floated down from the recesses of the shop via the narrow, twisting corridor created by the tall bookshelves, and from the winding staircase that led to the creaking floorboards of the upstairs section. Even the customers joined in the singing.

In spite of his normally reticent manner, Gabe participated in the fun, grinning and even conducting the song. He noted again that the fresh new mood of wanting to bring about change was fuelling his good humour. He put the giveaway bag with its box of treats on the crowded counter.

'Tell me you have macarons,' Cat pleaded.

Gabe pushed the Pierre Hermé box into her hands. 'To the staffroom with you.' Then he smiled at the customers patiently waiting. 'Sorry for all this.' They all made the sounds and gestures of people not in a hurry.

Even so, the next hour moved by so fast that he realised when he looked up to check the time that he hadn't even taken his jacket off.

An American student working as a casual sidled up with a small stack of fantasy novels — a complete series and in the original covers, Gabe noticed, impressed. He anticipated that an English-speaking student on his or her gap year was bound to snaffle the three books in a blink. Usually there were odd volumes, two and three perhaps the most irritating combination for shoppers.

'Put a good price on those. Sell only as a set,' he warned.

Dan nodded. 'I haven't read these — I'm half-inclined to buy them myself but I don't have the money immediately.'

Gabe gave the youngster a sympathetic glance. 'And they'll be gone before payday,' he agreed, quietly glad because Dan was always spending his wage before he earned it.

'Monsieur Reynard came in,' Dan continued. 'He left a message.'

'About his book. I know,' Gabe replied, not looking up from the note he was making in the Reserves book. 'I haven't found it yet. But I am searching.'

Dan frowned. 'No, he didn't mention a book. He said he'd call in later.'

Catherine came up behind them. 'Did Dan tell you that Reynard is looking for you?'

Dan gave her a soft look of exasperation. 'I was just telling him.'

'And did you tell Reynard that it's Gabe's birthday?' she asked with only a hint of sarcasm in her tone.

'No,' Dan replied, but his expression said, *Why would I?*

'Good,' Gabe said between them. 'I'm —'

'Lucky I did, then,' Catherine said dryly and smiled sweetly.

'Oh, Cat, why would you do that?'

'Because he's your friend, Gabe. He should know. After all —'

'He's not a friend, he's a customer and we have to keep some sort of —'

'*Bonjour, Monsieur Reynard,*' Dan said and Gabe swung around.

'Ah, you're here,' the man said, approaching the counter. He was tall with the bulky girth of one who enjoys his food, but was surprisingly light on his feet. His hair looked as though it was spun from steel and he wore it in a tight queue. Cat often mused how long Monsieur Reynard's hair was, while Dan considered it cool in an old man. Gabe privately admired it because Reynard wore his hair in that manner without any pretension, as though it was the most natural way for a man of his mature years to do so. To Gabe he looked like a character from a medieval novel and behaved as a jolly connoisseur of the good life — wine, food, travel, books. He had money to spend on his pursuits but Gabe sensed that behind the gregarious personality hid an intense, highly intelligent individual.

'*Bonjour,* Gabriel, and I believe felicitations are in order.'

Gabe slipped back into his French again. 'Thank you, Monsieur Reynard. How are you?'

'Please call me René. I am well, as you see,' the man replied, beaming at him while tapping his rotund belly. 'I insist you join me for a birthday drink,' he said, ensuring everyone in the shop heard his invitation.

'I can't, I have to —'

Reynard gave a tutting noise. 'Please. You have never failed to find the book I want and that sort of dedication is hard to find. I insist, let me buy you a birthday drink.'

Cat caught Gabe's eye and winked. She'd always teased him that Reynard was probably looking for more than mere friendly conversation.

'Besides,' Reynard continued, 'there's something I need to talk to you about. It's personal, Gabriel.'

Gabe refused to look at Cat now. He hesitated, feeling trapped.

'Listen, we'll make it special. Come to the Café de la Paix this evening.'

'At Opéra?'

'Too far?' Reynard offered, feigning sympathy. Then he grinned. 'You can't live your life entirely in half a square kilometre of Paris, Gabriel. Take a walk after work and join me at one of the city's gloriously grand cafés and live a little.'

He remembered his plan that today was the first day of his new approach to life. 'I can be there at seven.'

'*Parfait!*' Reynard said, tapping the counter. He added in English, 'See you there.'

Gabe gave a small groan as the man disappeared from sight, moving across the road to where all the artists and riverside sellers had set up their kiosks along the walls of the Seine. 'I really shouldn't.'

'Why?' Cat demanded.

Gabe winced. 'He's a customer and —'

'And so handsome too … in a senior sort of way.'

Gabe glared at her. 'No, I mean it,' she giggled. 'Really. He's always so charming and he seems so worldly.'

'So otherworldly more like,' Dan added. They both turned to him and he shrugged self-consciously.

'What's that supposed to mean?' Gabe asked.

19

'There's something about him, isn't there? Or is it just me?' Gabe shook his head with a look of puzzlement. 'You're kidding, right? You don't find his eyes a little too searching? It's as though he has an agenda. Or am I just too suspicious?'

Cat looked suddenly thoughtful. 'I know what Dan means. Reynard does seem to stare at you quite intently, Gabe.'

'Well, I've never noticed.'

She gave him a friendly soft punch. 'That's because you're a writer and you all stare intensely at people like that.' She widened her eyes dramatically. 'Either that,' she said airily, 'or our hunch is right and Reynard fancies you madly.'

Dan snorted a laugh.

'You two are on something. Now, I have work to do, and you have cakes to eat,' he said, 'and as I'm the most senior member of staff and the only full-timer here, I'm pulling rank.'

The day flew by. Suddenly it was six and black outside. Christmas lights had started to appear and Gabe was convinced each year they were going up earlier — to encourage the Christmas trade probably. Chestnuts were being roasted as Gabe strolled along the embankment and the bars were already full of cold people and warm laughter.

It wasn't that Gabe didn't like Reynard. He'd known him long enough. They'd met on a train and it was Reynard who'd suggested he try and secure a job at the bookshop once he'd learned that Gabe was hoping to write a novel. 'I know the people there. I can introduce you,' he'd said and, true to his word, Reynard had made the right introductions and a job for Gabe had been forthcoming after just three weeks in the city.

Reynard was hard to judge, not just in age, but in many respects.

Soon he approached the frenzy that was L'Opéra, with all of its intersecting boulevards and crazy traffic circling the palatial Opéra Garnier. He rounded the corner and looked for Reynard down the famously long terrace of the café. People — quite a few more tourists than he'd expected — were braving the cold at outside tables in an effort to capture the high Parisian café society of a bygone era when people drank absinthe and the hotel welcomed future kings and famous artists. He moved on, deeper into the café, toward the entrance to the hotel area.

Gabe saw Reynard stand as he emerged into the magnificent atrium-like lobby of the hotel known as Le Grand. He'd never walked through here previously and it was a delightful surprise to see the *belle époque* evoked so dramatically. It was as though Charles Garnier had decided to fling every design element he could at it, from Corinthian cornices to stucco columns and gaudy gilding.

'Gabriel,' Reynard beamed, 'welcome to the 9th arrondissement. I know you never venture far.'

'I'm addressing that,' Gabe replied in a sardonic tone.

'Isn't it beautiful?' Reynard said, gesturing around him.

Gabe nodded. 'Thank you for inviting me.'

'Pleasure. I have an ulterior motive, though, let me be honest,' he said with a mischievous grin. Gabe wished he hadn't said that. 'But first,' his host continued, 'what are you drinking? Order something special. It is your birthday, after all.'

'Absinthe would be fun if it wasn't illegal.'

Reynard laughed. 'You can have a pastis, which is similar, without the wormwood. But aniseed is so *de rigueur* now. Perhaps I might make a suggestion?'

'Go ahead,' Gabe said. 'I'm no expert.'

'Good, I shall order then.' He signalled to the waiter, who arrived quietly at his side.

'Sir?'

'Two kir royales.' The man nodded and Reynard turned back to Gabe. 'Ever tasted one?' Gabe gave a small shake of his head. 'Ah, then this will be the treat I'd hoped. Kir is made with crème de cassis. The blackcurrant liqueur is then traditionally mixed with a white burgundy called Aligoté. But here they serve only the kir royale, which is the liqueur topped up with champagne brut. A deliciously sparkling way to kick off your birthday celebrations.'

The waiter arrived with two flutes fizzing with purple liquid and the thinnest curl of lemon peel twisting in the drinks.

'*Salut*, Gabriel. *Bon anniversaire*,' Reynard said, gesturing at one of the glasses.

'*Merci. A la vôtre*,' Gabe replied — *to your health* — and clinked his glass against Reynard's. He sipped and allowed himself to be transported for a moment or two on the deep sweet berry effervescence of this prized apéritif. 'Delicious. Thank you.'

'My pleasure. It's the least I can do for your hours of work on my behalf.'

'It's my job. I enjoy searching for rare books and, even more, finding them. You said there was a favour. Is it another book to find?'

'Er, no, Gabriel.' Reynard put his glass down and became thoughtful, all amusement dying in his dark grey-blue eyes. 'It's an entirely different sort of task. One I'm loath to ask you about but yet I must.'

Gabe frowned. It sounded ominous.

'I gather you were … are … a clinical psychologist.'

The kir royale turned sour in Gabe's throat. He put his glass down. At nearly 25 euros for a single flute, it seemed poor manners not to greedily savour each sip, but he knew he wouldn't be able to swallow.

He slowly looked up at Reynard. 'How did you come by this information? No-one at work knows anything about my life before I came to Paris.'

'Forgive me,' Reynard said, his voice low and gentle. 'I've looked into your background. The internet is very helpful.'

Gabe blinked with consternation. 'I've taken my mother's surname.'

'I know,' is all that Reynard said in response. He too put his glass down. 'Please, don't become defensive, I —'

'What are you doing looking into my past?' Gabe knew he sounded annoyed but Reynard's audacity made him feel momentarily breathless, its intensity bringing with it the smell of charred metal and blood. He had to swallow his instant nausea.

'Let me explain. This has everything to do with your past but in the most positive of ways.' His host gestured at the flute of bubbling cassis. 'Why don't you drink it before it loses its *joie de vivre*?'

'Why don't you explain what you want of me first?'

'All right,' Reynard said, in a voice heavy with a calming tone, all geniality gone from his expression. 'Do you know what I do for a living?'

Gabe shook his head. 'I don't do searches on my clients.'

'Touché,' Reynard said evenly. 'I am a physician.'

He hadn't expected that but betrayed no surprise. 'And?'

'And I have come across a patient that I normally would not see but no-one else is able to help. I think you can.'

'I don't practise any longer … perhaps you'd noticed?'

Reynard smiled sadly as if to admonish him that this was not a subject to jest about. 'She is willing herself to death. I think she might succeed if we can't help her soon.'

'Presumably she's been seen by capable doctors such as yourself, and if they can't —'

'Gabriel. She's a young woman who believes she is being hunted by something sinister … something she believes is very dangerous.'

'That something being …?'

Reynard shrugged. 'Does it matter? She could be afraid of that glass of kir royale. You of all people know how powerful irrational fears can be. If she believes it —'

'Then it is so,' Gabe finished for him.

Reynard gave a nod.

'Why did you search for my background in the first place?'

His companion sipped from his flute. 'Strictly, I didn't. I was researching who we could talk to, casting my net wider through Europe and then into Britain. Your name came up with a different surname but the photo was clearly you. I checked more and discovered you were not only an eminent practitioner but realised you were my bookshop friend here in Paris.' He shrugged. 'I'm sorry that you are not practising still.'

'I'm sure you can work out that my life took a radical turn.'

Reynard had the grace to look uncomfortable. 'I am sorry for you.'

'I closed my clinical practice and don't want to return to it … not even for your troubled woman.'

'I struggle to call her a woman, Gabriel. She's still almost a child … certainly childlike. If you would only —'

'No, Monsieur Reynard. Please don't ask this of me.'

'I must. You were so good at this and too within my reach to ignore. I fear we will lose her.'

'So you've said. I know nothing about her. And frankly I don't want to.'

'That's heartless. You clearly had a gift with young people. She needs that gift of your therapy.'

Gabe shook his head firmly. 'Make sure she has around-the-clock supervision and nothing can harm her.'

Reynard put his glass down, slightly harder than Gabe thought necessary. 'It's not physical. It's emotional and I can't get into her mind and reassure her. She is desperate enough that she could choke herself on her own tongue.'

'Then drug her!' Gabe growled. 'You're the physician.'

They stared at each other for a couple of angry moments, neither backing down.

It was Gabe, perhaps in the spirit of change, who broke the tension. 'Monsieur Reynard, I don't want to be a psychologist anymore. I haven't for years and I've no desire to dabble. The combination of lack of motivation and rusty skills simply puts your youngster into more danger.' He picked up the glass and drained the contents. 'Now, that was lovely and I appreciate the treat, but I'm meeting some friends for dinner,' he lied. 'You'll have to excuse me.' He pulled his satchel back onto his shoulder, reaching for his scarf.

Reynard's countenance changed in the blink of an eye. He smiled. 'I almost forgot. I have something for you.' He reached behind him and pulled out a gift-wrapped box.

Gabe was astonished. 'I can't —'

'You can. It's my thank you for the tireless, unpaid and mostly unheralded work you've put in on my behalf.'

'As I said earlier, I do this job because I enjoy it,' he replied, still not taking the long, narrow box.

'Even so, you do it well enough that I'd like to thank you with this gift. Your knack for language, your understanding of the older worlds, your knowledge of myth and mystery are a rare talent. It's in recognition of your efforts. Happy birthday.'

'Well … thank you. I'm flattered.'

'Have you begun your manuscript?'

Gabe took a deep breath. He didn't like to talk about it with anyone, although his writing ambition was not the secret that his past had been. 'Yes, very early stages.'

'What's it about?' At Gabe's surprised glance, he apologised. 'I'm sorry, I don't mean to pry, but what I meant is, what's the theme of your story?'

Gabe looked thoughtful. 'Fear … I think.'

'Fear of what?'

He shrugged. 'The unknown.'

'Intriguing,' Reynard remarked. He nodded at the object in Gabe's hand. 'Well? Aren't you going to open it?'

Gabe looked at the gift. 'All right.'

The ribbon was clearly satin the way it untied and easily slipped out of its knots. Beneath the wrapping was a dark navy, almost black, box; it was shallow, but solid. It reeked of quality and a high price tag.

'I hope you like it,' Reynard added, and drained his flute of its purplish contents. 'I had the box made for it.'

Gabe lifted the lid carefully. Lying on navy satin was a pure white feather. He opened his mouth in pleasurable astonishment. 'It's exquisite.' He meant it. He fell instantly in love with the feather, his mind immediately recalling its symbolic meanings: spiritual evolution, the nearness to heavenly beings, the rising soul. Native Americans felt it put them closer to the power of wind and air — it was a sign of bravery. The Celts believed feathers helped them to understand celestial beings. The Ancient Egyptian goddess of justice would weigh the hearts of the newly dead against a feather. He knew the more contemporary symbolism of a feather was free movement ... innocence, even. All of this occurred to him in a heartbeat.

Reynard smiled. 'I'm glad you like it. It's a quill, of course.' Then added, 'You British see it as a sign of cowardice.'

Gabe was momentarily stung by the comment that he wasn't sure was made innocently or harking back to his refusal to see Reynard's patient. Too momentarily disconcerted to find out which, Gabe noticed that the shaft of the feather was sharpened and stained from ink. Now it truly sang to his soul and the writer in him as much as the lover of books and knowledge.

Reynard continued. 'It's a primary flight feather. They're the best for writing with. It's also very rare for a number of reasons, not the least of which is because it's from a swan. Incredibly old and yet so exquisite, as you can see. Almost impossible to find these days.'

'Except you did,' Gabe remarked lightly, once again fully in control.

Reynard smiled. 'Indeed. You are right-handed, aren't you?' Gabe nodded. 'This feather comes from the left wing. Do you see how it curves away from you when you hold it in your right hand? Clever, no?' Again Gabe nodded. He'd never seen anything so beautiful. Very few possessions could excite Gabe. For all his money, he could count on one hand the items that were meaningful to him.

'Where did you get it?' he added.

'Pearlis,' Gabe thought he heard Reynard say.

'Pardon?'

'A long way from *Paris*,' Reynard laughed as he repeated the word, and there was something in his expression that gave Gabe pause. Reynard looked away. 'Apparently it's from a twelfth-century scriptorium. But, frankly, they could have told me anything and I'd have acquired it anyway.' He stood. 'Have you noticed the tiny inscription?'

Gabe stared more closely.

'Not an inscription so much as a sigil, in fact, engraved beautifully in miniature onto the quill's shaft,' Reynard explained.

He could see it now. It was tiny, very beautiful. 'Do we know the provenance?'

'It's royal,' Reynard said and his voice sounded throaty. He cleared it. 'I have no information other than that,' he said briskly, then smiled. 'Incidentally, only the scriveners in the scriptorium were given the premium pinion feather.'

'Scriveners?'

'Writers … those of original thought.' His eyes blazed suddenly with excitement, like two smouldering coals that had found a fresh source of oxygen. 'And if one extrapolates, one could call them "special individuals" who were … well, *unique*, you might say.'

He didn't understand and it must have showed.

'Scribes simply copied you see,' Reynard added.

'And if you extrapolate further?' Gabe asked mischievously. He didn't expect Reynard to respond but his companion took him seriously, looked at him gravely.

'Pretenders,' he said. 'Followers. Scribes copied,' he repeated, 'the scriveners originated.'

Again they locked gazes.

This time it was Gabe who looked away first. 'Well, thank you doesn't seem adequate, but it's the best I can offer,' Gabe said, a fresh gust of embarrassment blowing through him as he laid the feather in its box. He stood to shake hands in farewell, knowing he should kiss Reynard on the cheek, but reluctant to deepen what he was still clinging to as a client relationship.

'Is it?' Reynard asked and then smiled sadly.

Gabe felt the blush heat his cheeks, hoped it didn't show in this lower light.

Reynard looked away. '*Pardon, monsieur,*' he called to the waiter and mimicked scribbling a note. The man nodded and Reynard pulled out a wad of cash. '*Bonsoir,* Gabriel. Sleep well.'

Something in those words left Gabe feeling hollow. He nodded to Reynard as he headed for the doors, toying briefly with finding another bar, perhaps somewhere with music, but he wanted the familiarity of his own neighbourhood. He decided he would head for the cathedral — Notre Dame never failed to lift his spirits.

Clutching the box containing his swan quill, he walked with purpose but deliberately emptied his mind of all thought. He'd taught himself to do this when he was swotting for his exams 'aeons' ago. He'd practised for some years as a teenager, so by the time he sat his O levels he could cut out a lot of the 'noise', leaving his mind more flexible for retrieval of his study notes.

By the time he reached his A levels, he'd honed those skills to such an edge he could see himself sitting alone at the examination desk: the sound of the school greenkeeper on his ride-on mower was removed, the coughs of other students, the sounds of pages being turned, even the birdsong were silenced. At his second-year university exams, the only sounds keeping him company were his heartbeat and breathing. And by final exams he'd mastered his personal environment to the point where he could place himself anywhere he chose and he could add sounds of his choice — if he wanted frogs but not crickets he would make it so. Or he could sit in a void, neither light nor dark, neither warm nor cold, but whatever he chose as the optimum conditions.

He was in control. And he liked it that way.

Curiously, though, when he exercised this control — and it was rare that he needed it these days — he more often than not found that he built the same scene around himself. Why this image of a cathedral was his comfort blanket he didn't know. It was not a cathedral he recognised — certainly not the Parisian icon, or from books, postcards, descriptions — but one from imagination that he'd conjured since before his teens, perhaps as early as six or seven years of age. The cathedral felt safe; his special, private, secure place where as a boy, he believed dragons kept him safe within. And at university he believed the cathedral had become his symbol — substitute even — for home. As he'd matured he'd realised it simply represented all the aspects of life he considered fundamental to his wellbeing — steadfastness, longevity, calmness, as well as spiritual and emotional strength. However, in the style of cathedrals everywhere it was immense and domineering, and if the exterior impressed and humbled, then the interior left him awestruck.

Gabe had sat for his Masters and then finished his PhD, writing all of his papers from the nave of this imaginary cathedral. The pews he deliberately kept empty to symbolise his isolation from others while he studied. The only company he permitted in the cathedral was that of the towering, mystical creatures of stone, sculpted in exquisite detail. They supported the grand pillars rearing upwards to the soaring roof and each was different and strange.

A curiosity was that he knew what they were, although he'd never seen them in life. He also allowed that his cathedral — when he wasn't within its care — was regularly populated by worshippers and knew that every person who entered the cathedral belonged to one of the fabulous creatures. Pilgrims didn't have to know before they entered which was their totem. They could walk into the cathedral and one of the creatures would call to them ... talk to their soul. Gabe had no idea how he knew this, for he had never seen anyone in the cathedral.

But which creature did he belong to? That was the single image he couldn't evoke. He couldn't summon a scene in which he saw himself entering the cathedral and feeling the pull of his creature. He was either outside the cathedral admiring it, or within it ... but he couldn't participate in the life of the cathedral. It had never mattered though — the cathedral of his mind had protected him and given him peace and space.

Gabe hadn't needed the cathedral in a long time. In fact, tonight was the first time in possibly as long as three years that he had thought about his old haven. Was he feeling threatened by Reynard — is that why the cathedral was in his thoughts and why he was drawn to Notre Dame this evening? Gabe understood the clever machinations of the mind — how it could trick and coerce, manipulate oneself and others. And somewhere during the course of this evening he had been left feeling 'handled'. Gabe gave a soft growl.

He'd been skirting the Tuileries; gorgeous on summer nights, but a little too dark for comfort on a winter eve like tonight. Cars whizzed down the wide boulevard of the rue de Rivoli but he barely noticed them. He was looking for one establishment and there it was, next to the equally celebrated hotel Le Meurice. Angelina was an early 1900s tea salon and café, once known as Rumpelmayers. The rich and famous had frequented it and still did, although these days it was on the pathway of the tourist stampede. It was closed though tonight. Gabe was deeply disappointed, especially since he could already taste his first sip of the famous Chocolat L'Africain and now would have to go without. He strolled by the Louvre, hauntingly lit and knew the cathedral was not far away now.

Notre Dame loomed, floodlit and imposing — especially tonight with the moon so bright and the Seine waters reflecting their own light back onto the structure. Gabe walked around the building; he was particularly fond of the flying buttresses about the nave but he always found something new to enjoy about the gothic structure. Tonight it was cold enough to move him along faster than usual and he was quickly heading for the Petit Pont, the bridge that would take him across the river onto the Left Bank. Perhaps he'd head for Les Deux Magots for the second-best hot chocolate in Paris.

High above, hiding behind one of the structures that Gabe had been admiring moments earlier, the same dark figure that had studied him this morning while he dreamed now watched his retreating back until he was lost in traffic and the darkened streets beyond the river. It blinked, looking into the night, as still as one of the famous 'grotesque' sculptures that decorated the cathedral. After a long time the watcher stirred and hopped back along the buttress and onto the part of the building that housed the choir, disappearing into the blackness of the night. No-one saw or heard it. But it had marked Gabe … and now it knew him.

THREE

The next morning at the bookshop passed slowly, but Gabe kept himself busy in the office catching up on paperwork. Eventually his rumbling belly told him it was nearing lunchtime. He emerged from the office stretching, wound his way down the rickety staircase and saw that the shop was all but empty.

'I'm just ducking out for a baguette,' he said. He didn't offer to pick up for anyone else. Didn't want that becoming a habit.

The day had not improved with age. It was overcast and drizzly. He zipped up his jacket. He didn't walk along the river, as the cafés here tended to ply their trade — and their prices — for hardy tourists. Instead he walked deeper into Saint-Germain unaware that he was being followed.

'*Bonjour*, Gabriel,' he heard a familiar voice call after him.

He turned. Reynard waved to him. He was not alone. Standing alongside, dwarfed by the tall physician was a fragile-looking girl. Gabe could hardly ignore them. He smiled weakly.

'*Bonjour*, Reynard … *mademoiselle*.'

'This is Gabriel, whom I've mentioned,' Reynard said to her.

Gabe noticed how Reynard held the girl's arm. There was something possessive in his stance. Reynard was nervous, too. Gabe took all this in with a brief gaze at the man and then shifted his attention to the reason they were surely paused in a damp, narrow street of Paris. She turned her dark and solemn eyes on him, but said nothing. He felt his breath catch slightly. She looked like a piece of exquisite porcelain; her skin was almost translucent it was so pale. Her ebony-black hair cut bluntly in a bob only accentuated her alabaster complexion as it skimmed the line of her jaw. It was a severe style yet she seemed to wear it with ease, and the texture was shiny and slippery like silk. In that moment he wanted to touch it.

He cleared his throat. 'Forgive me, I hadn't expected to meet anyone,' he said, cutting a look at Reynard.

'Gabriel, could you spare us just five minutes of your time?' the man began, and when Gabe started to shake his head Reynard put a hand up. 'A quick coffee,' he appealed. 'Two minutes … if you could just …' His words ran out as he gestured at his companion.

Again the dark eyes of the girl regarded him. How odd. He'd thought they were dark brown, but now he noticed they were the smokiest of greys, brooding and stormy … and troubled. In a moment of hesitation, he recalled Reynard's fear that the girl might kill herself. He felt suddenly obliged.

Just a few minutes couldn't hurt. The smell of grilling meat and spices of cumin and coriander, anise and cinnamon wafted over from the kebab shops in the narrow streets around Place Saint-André-des-Arts, reminding him he was hungry. His mouth began to water at the thought of lamb with tzatziki, perhaps some tabbouleh and hoummos wrapped in a warm pita. It would have to wait. A swift coffee first.

'Sure,' he said, shrugging a shoulder and noticing at once how Reynard's anxious face lit with surprise. Nevertheless, he appeared tense despite his relief at Gabe's decision.

'Over here's a café,' he said, pointing, then guiding his companion.

Gabe followed Reynard noticing that his charge was as uninterested in her surrounds as she was in her companions.

He sat down opposite the odd pair and smiled at her.

'We haven't been introduced yet,' he said, but as he'd anticipated, Reynard answered before she could.

'Oh, my apologies. Gabriel, this is Angelina.'

His mind froze momentarily as though he'd been stung.

'Gabriel?'

'Sorry. Er, like the famous tea salon,' he muttered. Then took a breath and smiled at them. 'I was only staring at its sign last night.'

She said nothing but fixed him now with an unwavering look. Her expression didn't betray boredom or even dislike. He felt as though he were being studied. He'd experienced such regard before and allowed her to fixate without showing any discomfort in his expression.

'Do you believe in coincidence?' Reynard asked him in English.

Gabe remained speaking in French to let Reynard know that he had no intention of isolating Angelina, if she didn't understand English. 'Do I believe in coincidence?' he repeated. 'Well, I know it happens too often to not be a reality of life, but I would never count on one, if that's what you mean.' He noticed Reynard was trying to catch the attention of the waiter. 'Er, with milk for me,' he said.

Reynard nodded, conveying this to the waiter before returning to their conversation. 'I meant,' he continued, now in French, 'do you believe in coincidence or do you believe in fate?'

'I've never thought about it. But now that you make me consider it, I think I'd like to believe in predestination rather than chance.'

Reynard raised an eyebrow. 'That's interesting. Most people would prefer coincidence. They don't like the notion of their lives already being mapped out.'

'You can change life's pathway. I'm testimony to that. But then the question was hypothetical. I like the notion of fate. It doesn't mean I believe it's what runs our lives or that chance doesn't have a lot to do with what happens to us.' He returned his attention to Angelina, feeling highly conscious of her penetrating gaze. The winter sun was filtering weakly into the café and lighting one side of her face. The other was in shadow and just for a moment he had the notion that her spiritually darker side was hidden.

The waiter arrived to bang down three coffees and their accompanying tiny madeleine biscuits.

'Do you enjoy Paris?' he tried.

'I should tell you that Angelina is mute,' Reynard said. 'She is not unable to talk, I'm assured, but she is choosing not to talk.' He shrugged. 'It's where you come in, I hope.'

She hadn't shifted her gaze from Gabe and now — as if to spite Reynard — shook her head and he realised it was in answer to his earlier question. He persisted. 'If you could be anywhere, where would you go?' He reached for his coffee.

She blinked slowly as if she didn't understand the question. Then turned to Reynard and pointed at the sugar up on the counter. Reynard looked in two minds. He cast a gaze around to nearby tables but it seemed sugar wasn't routinely left on them.

Gabe frowned. 'Er, I think you'll have to go to the counter,' he suggested.

It was clear Reynard didn't want to get up. Angelina pushed her coffee aside suggesting she wouldn't drink it without the sugar. It was done gently but the message seemed forceful enough. As a couple, they were intriguing. Gabe felt a tingling sense of interest in unravelling the secrets of the relationship before him.

Reynard rose. 'Back in a moment,' he said.

Angelina was astonishingly pretty in her elfin way but she shocked him as his gaze returned from Reynard to her. 'Help me.'

He coughed, spluttering slightly with a mouthful of coffee. 'So much for being mute,' he remarked.

'You have to get me away from him,' she urged, fumbling for his hand beneath the small table. 'Don't look at it now. Just take this,' she said, pressing a small note into his hand.

Reynard was back. 'There you are,' he said, sliding a couple of sticks of sugar onto the table.

Gabe was in no small state of shock at her outburst. The girl was obviously frightened of the physician.

'So,' Reynard began, sipping his drink, 'Angelina will not mind me saying this, I'm sure, but she is suffering a form of depression. She has feelings of persecution and —'

'Wait,' Gabe interrupted. 'If she's mute how can you know any of this?'

'Previous notes from previous doctors,' Reynard answered. '"Delusional" is the word that has been used time and again. Her muteness is a recent affliction. Remember, she's choosing not to speak.'

'Since you began treating her, do you mean?'

Reynard sipped his coffee slowly and didn't give any indication of offence. 'She's not prepared to communicate with doctors anymore. I don't think it's directed specifically at me.'

Gabe flicked a glance at Angelina and the surreptitious look she gave him over the rim of her cup contradicted Reynard's claim.

'Angelina is frightened and capable of harming herself,' Reynard continued, unaware of the silent message. 'But if, Gabriel, you can be persuaded, I think you might be the right person to guide her through this.'

'This what?' Gabe asked.

Reynard looked at him quizzically, his silvery eyebrows knitted together. 'This period in her life, of course. You're my last hope. If I can I'd like to find her family, get her reconnected and hopefully out of enforced care — which is all that she can look forward to unless we can fix this.'

Gabe put his cup down deliberately softly to hide his exasperation. 'When you say "last hope", Reynard, what exactly do you mean?'

Reynard sat forward. 'I've saved her from mental health hospitals. I've taken her on as a special case with a promise that I will find the right doctor for her. Soon she'll be returned to the care of institutions and become a ward of the state … and you know what that means. She'll be lost to the corridors of madness. They'll drug her, labelling her schizophrenic or bipolar, and they'll move on to the next youngster. She'll be tied to a bed, kept like a zombie for most of her waking hours, they'll —'

'I work in a bookshop,' Gabe appealed. 'I'm writing a book,' he added, his hands open in a helpless gesture, a desperate attempt to avoid this task.

'Ah, yes, the scrivener,' Reynard replied. 'It's your distance from your previous profession, perhaps, that makes you all the more valuable. You haven't forgotten how, surely?'

Gabe sighed. 'No. I haven't forgotten.'

'So you'll see her?'

He recalled standing opposite Angelina's last night — it was an omen. He remembered the note crumpled in his left fist, which was now plunged into the pocket of his jacket. He shifted his gaze back to her. In her look was a plea.

'Yes, I'll see Angelina.'

'Excellent. Oh marvellous, thank you, Gabriel … I —'

'There are conditions —'

'I understand,' Reynard said, barely hearing him, Gabe was sure.

'Don't be too hasty. Hear me out first. I insist on seeing her alone,' Gabe said, knowing it would not go down well.

Reynard's face clouded. 'Oh, I'm afraid that won't be possible.'

'Why?' he asked reasonably.

'I am responsible for Angelina … for every moment that she is out of hospital.'

'Are you suggesting she's in danger with me?' Gabe asked, without a hint of indignation.

'Not at all. She's unpredictable, Gabriel.'

34

They both glanced at Angelina, who had in the last minute or so seemed to tune out of their conversation. She was staring through the window but with unseeing eyes. Her coffee was cooling, untouched; crystals of sugar were scattered around from her opening the sachets carelessly.

'Unpredictable?' he queried, returning his attention to Reynard.

'Dangerous,' Reynard replied.

Gabriel tried to school his features but he wasn't quite quick enough to shield Reynard from the slight slump of his shoulders that clearly conveyed his mistrust of this diagnosis.

'I don't feel threatened by her,' he said as evenly as he could. 'And Reynard, this is not a request, it's a condition of me doing the assessment for you. You're the one asking the favour.' How quickly that firm note came back into one's voice, he thought, privately impressed. So many times in his working life he'd had to adopt that calm but implacable stance with parents, guardians, teachers, even other doctors.

'Where?' Reynard asked sounding reluctant.

'It will have to be my studio, I suppose. It is neutral for Angelina. It is also spacious and quiet. You can wait downstairs in the lobby or you're welcome to sit on the landing outside. But I want to speak to her without interference of any kind.'

'I will wait on the landing as you suggest. When?'

Gabe shrugged, surprised by Reynard's continuing possessiveness. 'It's my day off tomorrow. Let's say eleven, shall we?'

'That's fine.'

Gabe stood. 'Bring a book. The landing offers no diversion,' he said, his tone neutral. He looked at the girl. 'Bye, Angelina.' She ignored him. Reynard began to apologise. 'Don't,' Gabe said, 'it's okay. We'll talk tomorrow.'

'Thank you,' Reynard said.

Gabe left without another word, unaware of how Angelina's gaze followed long after most people's vision would have lost him to the blur of street life.

Brother Josse opened the door to the calefactory and felt the change in temperature. It was the only chamber, other than his private room, where a fire was permitted. But he invariably went without setting a fire

35

in his living quarters as he believed in leading by example, and though his bones were weary — when he lay down these nights his muscles seemed to lock themselves without his permission, then the aches and pains would arrive — and his eyesight failing, he would not capitulate and give himself more comfort than the rest of the Brothers.

The warmth enveloped him like a blanket and he sighed with silent pleasure. He regarded the back of his visitor, who was looking out of the window onto the herb gardens. Spare and small-framed, the man turned at the sound of Josse closing the door.

'I didn't hear you arrive,' the stranger said, soft of voice but with a warm and ready smile.

'That's the point, I believe,' Josse replied, equally genially. All in the Brotherhood could move in silence. 'It has been a very long time.'

'It has,' came the reply. 'You were not much more than a lad last time we met.'

Josse nodded. 'And you said one day you would need my help, that you would come,' he said, taking in his guest's straight bearing beneath the simple grey robe, the neat hair shot through with silver, but the face surprisingly unlined for one so old. How could that be?

'I have kept my promise,' the visitor said gently.

Josse knew he was staring, trying to make sense of the man's presence. He finally gathered his wits. 'Er, will you break bread with me?'

'Thank you. My tastes are uncomplicated though, Brother Josse. I eat no meat.'

'Ah, that's right. No living creature; I remember you telling me all those years ago.'

The man smiled again, the echo of its brightness sparkling in his eyes. 'I think the fruits and vegetables forgive me though,' he said with a shrug.

'I have followed in the same steps.'

Surprise registered on the man's face. 'Truly? I'm impressed.'

Josse laughed. 'I believe I've been in awe of you since childhood.'

'I don't know why,' came the reply and even the tone was modest.

Josse shook his head. 'Even now you surprise me with your own humility and yet I know that you are —'

'Please,' the man said, 'do not treat me with any deference. I am, as you see, a simple soul with simple needs.'

'May I offer you a cup of gleam?'

'Certainly, it would be a treat. I haven't tasted the spicy wine in many years. It will loosen our tongues for we have important matters to discuss.'

Josse felt a thrill of excitement. He didn't know why this man had taken such an interest in his life when he'd been brought to the priory at the age of nine. He remembered him not much differently than how he stood here now: the hair was a little less silvered perhaps, but beyond that the eyes were still sharp and bright, pierced by a curious shot of gold around the pupils.

The jug of gleam arrived, and although they seated themselves by the fire, Josse was sure that his guest did so only out of cordiality rather than need. Josse had asked for them not to be disturbed, and so now they sat opposite one another, but not really in a comfortable silence — because Josse felt nervous.

Josse grabbed his opportunity. It was now or never. 'May I ask, um … forgive me, I don't know what to call you. I have never known your name.'

The man smiled and it was as though new warmth filled the room. 'How remiss of me. My name is Fynch.'

'Brother Fynch,' Josse repeated the name, as though testing it on his tongue.

'Just Fynch,' his guest said mildly.

Josse took a breath. 'May I ask another question, er, Fynch?'

'By all means.'

'You were a friend of our great King Cailech.'

'I was.' He paused to smile in private memory. 'And of his queen, Valentyna,' Fynch added.

'Yes, indeed.' Josse hesitated, but then decided he had to clarify this or he would die wondering. 'Um, and yet I am in my winter years and you look like spring.'

They both chuckled at the metaphor.

'Looks can be deceiving, Brother Josse. I can assure you I am much older than you.'

'But —' and something in the look Fynch gave him told Josse to leave it. There was no reprimand, no irritation in Fynch's expression, just a soft glance that seemed almost painful to behold, so Josse looked away and accepted that the mystery would always remain so. 'Well, you are an inspiration.'

Fynch smiled. 'I'm sure you would like to know why I'm here after all this time.'

Josse sat forward, placing his half-full cup of gleam on the small knobbly table that sat between them. He noticed Fynch's gleam was untouched. 'Yes, I would. I'm intrigued.'

'I need the aid of the Brotherhood.'

Josse looked surprised. 'But you know we are here only in the service of the Crown?'

'I do.' Fynch eyed him now and the golden glints in his eyes seemed to glow even brighter. 'Tell me about the man in the forest.'

'Cassien? Of all our men, why him?'

'Because you were asked to prepare him.'

Josse looked astonished. 'But those were secret instructions, from the desk of —'

'The royal chancellor. Yes, I know and I'm sorry for the stratagem. It would have prompted too many questions had I approached you directly on this matter when you took over as Head Brother.' Fynch gave a small shrug of a shoulder. 'I know it's confusing, Brother Josse. Tell me all you know about him. And then I'll tell you why he is so important to me.'

Josse sat back and took a deep breath. 'All right. Cassien came to us as an infant … an orphan. His mother was a slattern.' He paused as Fynch smiled tightly at the polite word. Josse cleared his throat. 'She was nonetheless incredibly beautiful, and it was said rich men from far and wide would journey to see and partake of this woman's … er …'

'Services?' Fynch offered.

'Yes,' Josse agreed, relieved to discover that his guest was not stuffy about these things, even though he'd always thought of him as something of a holy man. 'She lived and worked in Pearlis, not far from the cathedral. She died neither young nor old — in her prime perhaps you might say, ravaged by a disease that no-one had any knowledge of, or cure for. It is believed the sickness was brought from across the oceans, and her body was burned as it frightened everyone so. Cassien knows none of this. He believes his mother died soon after childbirth. She gave him to us when he was little more than nine months. I have to say her attitude sounds cold, but I met her and she was a warm, laughing individual who wanted the best for her son, which she knew she could not give him. I never visited her. She accepted no money for him, asking only that she be allowed to glimpse him from time to time.'

'And did she?'

'Every moon until she died. We would take Cassien through the market and past a designated spot where she would be watching him from a close distance. I always felt sorry for her, even though she'd given her child away. There was only ever tenderness and love in that beautiful face of hers. I gave her my word that her son would never know.'

'The father?'

'According to her he was a traveller, a wastrel. She loved him, apparently. He was rarely home from what we learned. Again, I never met him.'

'There were brothers, weren't there?'

'An elder brother,' he corrected. 'I never saw him and I have no idea of his life.'

'Go on.'

'Well, the young Cassien charmed us all from his arrival. He was an agile, bright-eyed infant with great curiosity and the sharpest of minds. We all loved him. I most of all, I suspect. I taught him all that I could and ensured that he had the best training. He didn't disappoint. As he grew he showed himself to be the most adept and willing student. Everything he turned his hand to he did well.' Josse reached for his spiced wine again. He knew it had cooled but he didn't mind. His voice became scratchy when he talked for long periods. Fynch's drink remained untouched.

'The Brotherhood has a knack for finding each of its members' special talents, does it not?'

'Indeed, Master Fynch. We pride ourselves on it. Some of our Brothers become specialists at negotiation, while others are skilled poisoners; some have a talent for inciting political instability, while a few down the years have shown a gift for subterfuge and all manner of clandestine activity from spying to assassination.' He shrugged. 'It just depends on the individual. We nurture all skills and then we choose which to focus on for a particular individual.' Josse sighed. 'Only a few know of our existence — most think we are a small religious sect — but we are at the

Crown's disposal, always ready to meet its needs. We are looked after by the Crown.'

'And yet you live quietly as monks … frugal, spiritual even.'

Josse nodded. 'It cannot be any other way or these skilled men could be turned to the wrong side for money or status. Emperor Cailech set us up in this manner. His aim was for us to Opérate as a religious Brotherhood, and ensure our members make their commitment to the Crown as a monk might make his to his god. It is definitely a spiritual undertaking.'

'Yes, Cailech was inspired in this creation. And you have not let him down.' Josse nodded his head, pleased with the compliment. 'And what of Cassien?' Fynch continued. 'What is his speciality?'

'Ah, he could have gone several ways. However, Cassien has become something of a one-man army.' Josse laughed but there was no mirth in it. 'He is a living, breathing weapon.'

'Please explain that to me, Brother Josse.'

'Quite simply: I defy any man to be his equal in combat. He can run faster, longer, harder than anyone in the empire, I suspect. He can take uncharted levels of pain. His stamina, thinking speed and range of thought are immense — and by that I mean his strategic decisions are usually always right and they are made in a blink, even under pressure. He is strong, flexible and supple; light as air if he needs to be. If you blindfold him, he can still "see" because his senses are so finely tuned. He has developed a method of bouncing sound off hard objects to gauge his nearness to them.' Josse gave a tight smile. 'Just as a bat might,' he added and frowned.

'What is it, Brother Josse?'

'There is something else about Cassien that I don't know how to explain.'

Josse watched Fynch lean forward slightly. 'Yes?'

He shook his head. 'It's an intangible skill. One I cannot put competently into words, but it's as though he possesses an otherworldly sense that the rest of us don't know or understand. I know he keeps it secret.'

'You mean it is an inherent part of him.'

'Exactly. He alone owns it, wields it, but I know not when or how. He has only admitted once to me of its existence, when he was a child, and even then he could barely explain it. I suspect he's forgotten ever mentioning it.'

He watched Fynch's eyes blaze now. 'Magic?'

Josse felt genuinely uncomfortable. He cleared his throat, sipped his gleam. 'There is no other explanation, I suppose.'

'When did you last see him?'

'Me? I haven't seen Cassien for a decade. Our man, Loup, visits him each new moon to put him through various, shall we say, tests. And he is certainly rigorous, Master Fynch.'

'And?'

'He is astonishing. Two moons ago Cassien bested Loup for the first time. Loup tells me he now believes our charge to be near enough invincible in a one-on-one fight. We believe he could do a lot of damage to any enemy if he was sent in alone. One of his strengths is his quiet presence. Loup says there are times when …' Josse trailed off, unsure how to say it, for it sounded so far-fetched.

Fynch's head snapped up from where he had been staring thoughtfully at the fire. 'When what?'

'Er … well, when he believes Cassien is somehow not entirely of this world.'

He watched Fynch straighten, his chest swell as though it was being filled with anticipation and excitement. 'This is very good news, Brother Josse.'

'Is it? Frankly, it frightens me, this talk of magic.'

'One must not fear magic, Brother Josse.' His guest stood, contemplating. 'Good …' Fynch murmured. 'Very good.'

'So, this mission you mention suggests the Crown has a specific use for him, Master Fynch?'

'It does.'

'Then by all means ask the palace to —'

'No. This is the most secret mission that any of your men will ever undertake because they will do so without the knowledge of the Crown.'

Josse shook his head. 'I don't understand.'

'You don't have to. I promise you, he will be working for the good of the realm, for the empire it is part of and for the young royal who presides over it.'

Josse blinked.

'You trust me, Brother Josse?'

'I do,' he replied without hesitation.

'Thank you. I will personally brief Cassien.'

'Of course. You will need a guide. Loup will take you.' There was a soft knock at the door. 'Ah, perfect timing. We can offer a hearty vegetable stew with chesil manchets baked here in our own bakery. We prefer the grainiest of bread … I hope it suits.'

Fynch smiled. 'Bread is a rare treat in whichever form it is given to me. Thank you.'

Josse pointed to a basin nearby and heard the sound of Fynch washing his hands as he opened the door to young Turc, who brought in two bowls of stew, vapour rising enthusiastically from the brew, and bread still so warm he could smell its escaping steam. A chunk of butter he knew had been churned only the previous day was scattered with salt flakes.

His guest was taking an inordinately long time to dry his hands and Josse realised Fynch did not want to be seen.

'Leave the tray, Turc. Thank you, lad. I can take it from here.'

FOUR

Gabe had half an hour to kill before Reynard arrived. He paused at the sideboard where the swan quill sat in its box and traced a finger over the feather, watching the individual spines part and then flick back into a soldierly line.

He remembered that Angelina had a sweet tooth and realised he had time to nip out and grab some simple fruit pastries drizzled with white icing, plus a new bag of his favourite coffee beans. He liked a strong roast that hinted of chocolate and licorice, and having invested in a 15-bar Italian coffee machine, he enjoyed the ritual of making his coffee to order.

He thought again about Angelina and Reynard's peculiar possessiveness about her. And then he remembered the note. *Hell!* He'd left the café yesterday and hurried back to the shop, only to get sucked into a black hole of new stock and paperwork, and had forgotten about Angelina's piece of paper, which she'd pushed into his hand surreptitiously.

As soon as he was back at the apartment he threw down his packets from the bakery and dipped into the pocket where the note had been stuffed. He smoothed it out on the kitchen table and read it.

Don't trust him! He is lying to you! Trust only me and what I say!

The three exclamations made her warning look desperate. So her fear was about the physician. *He is lying to you!* Why would Reynard lie? Lying about what? He presumed he was soon to find out more.

He set out the pastries and put some background music on very softly. It was melodic guitar music, nothing too Latin and upbeat but nothing melancholy either.

At just a minute or so to eleven he heard the security buzzer sound.

'Reynard … Angelina?'

43

'Good morning, Gabriel,' Reynard's disconnected voice said through the loudspeaker. 'Thank you for your emailed directions.'

'Just push the door,' Gabe replied and hit the button to let them enter. He walked outside his flat to the landing, where he'd put a chair for Reynard. It was cold and, even though it felt churlish, he didn't care. He was not permitting the physician inside while he was assessing Angelina. He leaned over the elegant wrought-iron railing that twisted serpentine-like around the shallow white marble stairs between floors and heard the lift crank into use. The lift took its time in its creaky ascent but finally it opened and there they were, the oddest couple.

Reynard was dressed in his habitual pinstripe suit while Angelina looked wan in a short skirt, ankle boots, thick tights, a duffel coat, scarf, gloves, beanie … it was as though she was a child being dressed by a protective grandmother against the elements.

'Hello again, *Monsieur* Reynard, Angelina,' he said warmly to both, but looking at her.

They stepped out of the lift.

'So how do we do this?' Reynard asked. He looked nervous.

'I've put a chair here,' Gabe said, gesturing toward the landing's window. 'It's cold but you're well wrapped up, I see. Did you bring a book?'

'I'll be fine,' Reynard replied. 'How long?'

'I'd say we need at least forty-five minutes undisturbed.' He gave a sympathetic grin but his tone was firm. 'I can offer you coffee?'

'I understand. And no, but thank you. I've recently had one,' Reynard said.

'Angelina, will you follow me, please?' Gabe offered. She nodded.

Reynard touched his arm. 'Be careful, Gabriel. Remember my warning,' he whispered.

Gabe looked over his shoulder with a quizzical frown. 'We'll be fine,' he assured Reynard. He closed the door on the physician and turned to the young woman. 'It's warm in here so feel free to take off your coat and put it down over there,' he said, pointing to the sofa. He left it entirely to her. But it pleased him to see that she began peeling off her heavy garments. It was a good start. He turned away. 'Now, how about a decent coffee?'

She shook her head, dark eyes regarding him far from suspiciously. In fact, he'd describe her look as hungry but not for food. He convinced himself he was imagining it and decided that she was probably relieved to be away from Reynard's supervision.

'This is not jar coffee,' he insisted, mock offended.

Angelina's face broke momentarily into a grin. She pulled off her beanie and shook out her hair; again, he had the desire to touch it. Without her bulky coat on she looked so vulnerable.

Helena, a female colleague at university during his PhD, was doing her thesis on personality types with regard to romance and/or sex. She had used Gabe as one of her test subjects and had surprised him with a summary of the sort of woman he was most attracted to. He'd argued it, of course, and he'd seen many women since who didn't fit that bill, but, curiously, Angelina ticked many of the boxes: small, dark, not a chatterbox, someone who seemed slightly remote from the mainstream. She would have to be very pretty, Helena had assured him with a wry smile, but not traditionally so. How thoroughly annoying, he thought now, as he looked at Angelina, that Helena could have been so accurate … or more to the point, that he could be so predictable. He cleared his throat as Angelina stepped closer.

'I don't like caffeine in any form,' she said, and there was lightness in her tone that he had not heard before. He took a private pleasure in thinking that Reynard had probably never heard her voice.

'Don't like caffeine?' he repeated with feigned despair. 'How do you cope?'

'I manage,' she murmured, almost playfully. She ran a hand over the coffee machine. Her nails were trimmed blunt, but neatly, with perfect half-moons above the cuticles. They were free of varnish but still they shone. He was one of those people who noticed. Unbitten, trimmed, buffed and well-kept nails spoke droves.

'You have lovely hands, Angelina,' he said, before he could censure himself.

'I'm not vain but I do take care of them,' she said, looking at her nails briefly. She gave a rueful laugh that sounded like a soft sigh. She walked away from the coffee machine and him.

'Are you warm enough?' he asked solicitously.

She nodded over her shoulder. He didn't want this time to drift into awkwardness. They'd begun well and he needed to keep that positive energy bouncing between them if he was to make progress with her.

'Angelina, today we're just going to talk. Like a couple of old friends, having coffee and,' he pointed to the small table, 'sharing some pastries.'

She looked so small and alone he felt an urge to hug her as extra reassurance. It was obvious the young woman was starved of affection, but it was not his role to provide it. Instead he opened his palms to her. 'Can I get you a soft drink? Mineral water?'

She eyed him gravely. 'I'm fine, really. Do you want me to sit down?'

He nodded and looked at the comfy chairs by the window. 'I'll just finish this.'

She turned away but paused at the sideboard to look at his boxed quill. 'This is very lovely,' she said. 'May I touch it?'

'Be my guest,' he said over the sound of grinding the beans. He watched her pick up the quill and weigh it in her hand before she held it out to admire it in the light. 'It's old.'

'Antique, apparently,' he replied.

'Older,' he thought she said.

'It's from a swan, can you believe?' he called over the noise of the machine gathering steam. He tamped down the coffee and locked the bar handle into place, then pressed the button. The machine responded with its routine noises as the pump now wound up the pressure. He walked away from the groans and grinds for a few seconds so he could hear her properly.

'Only scriveners are given the swan quill.'

Gabe was astonished by her remark.

'How would you know that?' he said with a smile as he returned to the machine to test that it was ready to froth the milk. A burst of steam wheezed. 'Oh, Reynard, of course,' he said, before she could reply. It made sense that Reynard would have told her about the quill.

Gabe glanced over and noticed her short skirt ease higher up her stockinged thighs as she sat and stared out of the window. Angelina had a far more voluptuous body than he'd imagined beneath all those layers.

'Voilà,' he murmured to himself as he poured the milk into the shot of coffee.

Gabe sipped as he moved to join her, and sighed as he finally seated himself opposite. He put the coffee on the table between them before he leaned back and nonchalantly crossed a leg. It was a series of deliberate actions to make her feel comfortable, to show that he was relaxed and that she should feel the same. At the same time he was thinking how she was beautiful in an almost ethereal way.

'It wasn't Reynard,' she said, brushing some invisible lint from her skirt.

'Sorry?' He wasn't sure what she meant.

'The swan quill. It wasn't Reynard who told me. Everyone knows a scrivener needs the quill of a swan,' she said airily, as though it was of no further interest to her. 'It's nice here. How long have you been in this apartment?'

Everyone? He didn't. But she'd moved on, he could tell. He would think on the quill later. Gabe looked around the apartment. 'Er … let's see … it must be coming up to four years. I'm glad you like it. I enjoy living here.'

'You obviously live alone.'

'I do. Not even a goldfish for company.'

He thought she might have smiled but her gaze only became more intense. 'Do you get lonely?'

'I suppose I should, but I choose this lifestyle. I'm perfectly happy living alone with my coffee machine and working in a bookshop. How about you?'

'What do you mean?'

'Would you like to have a family, friends, a home?'

'No,' she murmured.

That surprised him. His gaze narrowed. 'You want to change your current situation though, I'm sure.'

'Is that a question?'

He smiled at her dry tone. 'Do you remember anything about your life before the hospitals?'

'I remember everything. I just don't want to share it with doctors.'

Gabe realised too late that he'd reacted far too obviously in sitting forward with a confused expression. Angelina had the grace to look away … far away out of the window.

'Do you have a family?' he asked, unable to help the question. The accepted rule was to avoid such directness at the outset, to approach all probing as obliquely as possible. He was so rusty.

'No,' she said, unfazed.

Well, if she was happy to answer … 'So where is home?'

'A long way from here.'

Before the session had begun, Gabe had not had any intention of going beyond winning her trust. But now he wanted to know everything about her; she was as intriguing as she was seductive. The more he looked and listened to her the more he realised that Angelina was needful, but not needy. It was physical help she was after, he now suspected. She wanted his help to get away from Reynard and the doctors, otherwise she'd never have allowed him to know she was not mute.

She was, however, disarmingly charming and desirable and he was vaguely embarrassed at how she aroused him.

He cleared his throat again. 'Angelina —'

'My friends call me by a different name.'

Gabe was ready for her this time. He didn't react. 'Tell me about them?'

'They're elsewhere.'

'Have you a plan to return to them?'

Her eyes blazed. His question had fired some hidden desire deep within.

'Yes,' she replied, and for the first time since he'd set eyes on Angelina, she gave him her complete attention. Suddenly, it was as if no-one else existed in the world, just the two of them. 'Are you going to help me?' she asked.

He realised he was nodding. He hadn't meant to make any commitment beyond this single hour. But now he was under her spell.

'Will you tell me why you're scared of Reynard?'

There it was, the question he'd promised himself he wouldn't ask. His task was to give Angelina's doctors a glimpse into the world in which she lived, not explore her fears in this opening session.

Again, she felt none of his unease and replied with candour. 'I know you think he cares about me, but he doesn't.'

'What do mean by that?'

'I mean that you're putting your trust in the wrong person. He's trying to stop me getting home.'

'Why would he do that?'

'Because he's scared of me.'

'Why should he fear you?'

'His fear is for you.'

Gabe had to repeat that in his mind. *Fears for me?* he said silently with incredulity.

He had to backtrack. 'Firstly, why do you scare him?'

'Because of what I can offer.'

The meaning of her response was clouded, but it was also highly suggestive.

'And what is it that you offer?'

'Eternity,' she replied, a little dreamily.

He didn't show his irritation at her response but decided to refocus her and deliberately reached forward to pick up his coffee. He sipped slowly, saying nothing, waiting for her attention to return. It tasted terrible. He was off his game. As he knew it would, his silence won her notice.

She blinked, looked at him. 'What?' she asked, sounding as though she had missed what he'd said.

'You wrote me a note. I have it here,' he said, putting his glass down and digging in his pocket.

'I know what it says.'

'Will you explain it to me? Let's return to the beginning. I mean, why you're so frightened.'

'I'm not when I'm here with you.'

'Good. Why is that?'

'Perhaps you've noticed how he watches my every move? He doesn't let me out of his sight.'

Gabe shrugged. 'Well, that's because he's your physician and responsible for —'

'No, Gabe. Can I call you Gabe?' He wasn't sure what to say but she'd taken his hesitation as permission. 'He's frightened of me leaving.'

'Leaving?' He frowned. 'Paris?'

Angelina threw out her arms. 'No, here.'

'My apartment,' he qualified.

She smiled as though he was simple. 'This world.'

He deliberately paused, allowing her comment to float around them for a few moments so that she could explain herself.

'Are you surprised?' she asked.

'You demanded that Reynard not accuse you of being delusional. I have to wonder how you think you sound when you say something like you just did.'

'I realise what I say is hard to grasp. It doesn't mean I am delusional,' she replied without hesitation. Her gaze was unswerving. 'I'm far more sane than Reynard, who, by the way, is out of his mind with fear. Especially today because I am now closer to my goal than I have been in a very long time.'

'Your goal. To leave Earth, you mean?' he said, working at sounding reasonable. Yes, indeed, his skills definitely needed brushing up. This sort of interested tone used to come so easily.

'Not Earth, Gabe. This world,' she corrected.

'Sorry,' he said. 'So your goal is to reach a point where you can exit this plane,' he offered, believing that sounded catchy but also succinct.

'Not reach a point, but the person who would take me away.'

'Pardon,' he said, more confused.

'I've been looking for someone.'

'And?'

'I've found who I've searched for.'

'Oh, good.' Now he just sounded patronising. He wasn't ready to dive back in like this. It made him feel and sound amateurish.

'You don't understand, do you?'

'Explain it to me,' he encouraged.

'I've been looking for *you*, Gabe.'

He blinked with consternation. 'For me?' She nodded slowly. 'But until yesterday you didn't know me.'

'When we met I knew it was you I had been seeking.'

'Angelina, forgive me, but do you realise how odd this seems and why people are concerned about you?'

'I cannot help that.'

'Yes, but people like Reynard are trying to help.'

'He's using you.'

'Why would that be?'

She smiled and just for a blink he sensed an old cunning.

'Angelina?' he prompted, waiting for her to explain.

She glanced toward the door. 'Reynard is becoming impatient.'

He frowned. 'I told him to wait.'

'Any moment the phone will —'

The phone began to ring.

He looked at it startled, then back at Angelina, who was staring out of the window again as if lost in deep thought. He resisted answering it and finally the machine whirred into action. He listened to his automated message being politely trotted out, waited for the caller to speak. The line went dead.

'He won't let it be,' she warned dreamily.

Gabe felt his mobile phone vibrate against his thigh. He ignored it. The main phone rang again. It sounded even more shrill, demanding his attention with an *I know you're in there!* screech.

'Excuse me,' he said. He stood up and grabbed the receiver. 'Hello?' he said, sounding irritated.

'Gabriel, this is Reynard.'

She turned to give him a slight 'told you so' glance and then immediately looked away.

'Er, yes, Reynard. I thought we had an arrangement about being left quietly.'

'It's been forty-five minutes.'

'I said *at least* three-quarters of an hour.'

'I was worried.'

'For whom?'

'Are you finished?'

'We are now. You interrupted us.' He sighed. 'I'll let you in.' He put the receiver down and walked over to the door to unlock it.

The man came in hesitantly. He gave a small embarrassed smile. 'Well. How did it go?'

'We'd barely begun,' Gabe admitted. 'I can't just leap in, Reynard. I'm playing with someone's life. It has to be approached with caution and a genuine regard for Angelina's state of mind and what she wants to reveal at this stage.'

'And what has she revealed?' Reynard whispered.

'Nothing I can give any credence to.'

'It's hard when she doesn't speak, I know.'

Gabe shook his head. 'There is nothing to tell and I must pay attention to her wishes and rights too. This is a therapist–patient session — or so it has turned into.'

'What *can* you tell me?' Reynard demanded.

'She needs a sense of safety and to be around a therapist she trusts. I'm not sure anyone you've chosen so far is providing the confidence for

51

her to open up.' They walked over to Angelina, who was now ignoring both of them. 'She's an intelligent person and needs respect.'

'Don't lecture me, Gabriel,' Reynard snapped. It was the first time Gabe had seen anything but the genial personality of the man. 'We're dealing with a girl who can't express herself in —'

'Wait. I'll stop you there,' Gabe said reasonably. 'Reynard, you should know that Angelina has spoken to me.'

He watched the colour drain out of Reynard's face.

Gabe continued. 'She speaks as easily as you and I are conversing now.'

Angelina was dressing in her warm clothes as she stared outside, entirely unisinterested in the pair of them. He would be lying if he didn't admit that he was hooked.

They were still standing by the door, blocking any run for freedom she might suddenly decide to make. 'Reynard, why are you so scared of Angelina?' he said, softly enough for their hearing only.

'Scared?' Reynard growled, cutting him an incredulous look.

Gabe realised he needed to temper his approach. 'Perhaps I should say that you are overly anxious for her. Talking briefly with Angelina today she seems, um … "airy" for want of a better word, but not insane and certainly not dangerous.'

'Then you are seeing a different Angelina. She believes herself threatened by some outward force and would rather kill herself than be hunted down.'

'How has she told you this?'

'She wrote it.'

'Wrote it?'

'Not once, Gabriel, but hundreds, thousands, maybe a million times. She wrote it on paper, her walls, her floors, her clothes, her skin! She even wrote it on a hamster, a pet of one of our patients at the clinic. She never stops writing it. The girl is unbalanced and definitely suicidal.'

Gabe shook his head, absolutely certain of what he was about to say. 'She is *not* suicidal. I assure you.'

'You have no —'

'Reynard, you asked for my professional opinion and now you have it. What you do with it is your business. I have done what you asked. In my reckoning, Angelina is thinking clearly and not about death. However, she is moving in a world of her own. I don't want to call her delusional because it smacks of crazy. She is convinced of a threat, but not the one you think, and she is no danger to herself, let me reiterate that.'

'I cannot believe she is speaking with you.'

'Believe it. I'm not shocked. Many youngsters choose their moment to reveal themselves. Sometimes it's with the most unlikely partner. She obviously feels safe here.'

Reynard stared at him. 'And your advice is?'

He shrugged. 'Bring her back. I was on the brink of learning more when you interrupted. Let me have a second session with her and see what can be achieved.'

Reynard looked tired and old suddenly. Gone was the pleasantness and confidence of the previous evening. Now he looked intense and worried.

'It's entirely up to you. If you want me to see her again, I will. But I won't push.' Reverse psychology, Gabe thought.

'All right. When?'

'Thursday. It will have to be the evening. I'm sorry that I can't offer more convenient sessions.'

'I understand. In two days then.'

'Seven okay?'

Reynard nodded. 'We'll be here. Remember my warning, though, Gabriel. It is not given lightly. Come then, Angelina.'

She drifted over to them like a child with her attention riveted in her own thoughts.

'Why don't you say a proper farewell. I gather that you can,' Reynard said with only a hint of sarcasm.

She looked at him with loathing. A quick glance was all Gabe was given but it was enough. He saw only humour in it.

'Thank you,' Reynard said to him, trying to smile but failing. 'I can't be sitting out in a draughty hallway each time,' he added.

'Well, you could just trust me with Angelina,' Gabe replied.

Reynard pulled Gabe aside and dropped his voice. 'It's not about trusting you, Gabriel. It's about not trusting her.'

'There you go again. What are you so frightened of?'

'She will bring you harm,' Reynard hissed in warning as they watched her hit the lift button.

Gabe shook his head. 'Not on my watch, she won't.'

'Well, see you Thursday,' Reynard said.

Gabe was tiring of him. 'You can read the papers or just people-watch in the café across the street. No interruptions this time. You must trust me.' He looked at Angelina. 'See you soon.' He watched the light flash to say the lift was imminent. 'Ah, wait. Hold the doors,' he urged, dashing back into the apartment to grab the pastries, which he threw back into their bag. He returned just as the lift doors opened. 'Take this for a sugary hit later,' he said, winking at Angelina and noticed the glimmer of a smile touch her eyes.

He wondered briefly if he should charge a fee for this work. He decided he wouldn't. He would regard it purely as a favour and then he owed Reynard nothing — they were square. Gabe closed the metal doors and watched the lift jerk before its captives began their descent.

He turned back into the apartment and was surprised to see a crow seated as still as a statue on the tall tree that reached up to his apartment. Its winter-bare branches clawed the air but provided good purchase for the crow. He'd never seen one in this neighbourhood previously; they tended to show themselves in and around the main tourist traps. He stepped closer to the window. It didn't so much as blink.

And it had a lightish grey end to its beak, not at all like the highly glossy beak of the crows he was familiar with, and it was smaller. It seemed to be staring through his window and right into his soul.

He clapped his hands. 'Shoo!' he exclaimed. He stepped forward and banged on the window.

It jumped into the air at his yell and with an almost slow-motion beat of its wings, effortlessly dragged itself away from his building. The winter light caught its feathers and he saw a purple glow shine off its back, which was oddly beautiful. His interest piqued, Gabe immediately opened his laptop and searched the net for 'crows', unexpectedly becoming fascinated by the family Corvidae.

He finally found what he was looking for. His spy had not been a carrion crow as he'd first thought. He was now sure that the visitor was a raven, which had feathers that were described as iridescent. His bird's beak was definitely curved, as the information said it should be, and it certainly had shaggy plumage at the throat. He'd noticed the bird's feathers at the low point of the neck were pale, near enough to grey. Yes, definitely a raven.

Odd that it was alone, for apparently these birds moved like wolves, with certain laws of the pack guiding their lives. Perhaps it was a sentinel? His reading told him that while others trawled for food at lower levels, a few of the birds stayed higher in trees to keep watch.

And yet this one seemed to be watching him, not its companions, if there were any.

Gabe lost himself in an hour of research on ravens, strongly attracted to these mysterious old-world birds, once commonplace in Europe during the Middle Ages, now less so. He noted in particular their place in myth and legend, especially their association with death as escorts to the departing soul.

It never occurred to him to recall the death dream.

FIVE

Loup arrived silently at dusk but Cassien was waiting, sitting quietly on the stoop of the hut; he had sensed the man's approach long before. He felt a flutter of nervous energy at what he planned to say, wondering if Loup could write an angry response fast enough. He didn't plan on taking 'No' for an answer.

Loup nodded at Cassien's wave.

'Good evening, Loup. Welcome back.'

The man stopped at the edge of the clearing where Cassien's hut stood. 'It's always good to see you, Cassien,' he said.

Cassien's mouth dropped open in astonishment as he stared at Loup, who gave him a sheepish look.

'I'm sorry.'

'All these years,' Cassien murmured, shock racing through him.

'I half wondered if you might sense it.' Loup looked down at his big hands. 'They were my orders.'

'Brother Josse must be so proud of you.' He was disgusted at the deception and wanted this man to know it.

'As he is you,' Loup said, still not coming nearer.

'I wouldn't know,' Cassien replied.

'I am as obedient and committed as you are, Cassien,' Loup grumbled.

Cassien stood abruptly and turned away. 'There's food in the pot,' he growled over his shoulder. 'Forgive me, I need to be alone.' And then he was gone, grabbing his dagger and bow, blending into the forest in a blink and running silently, as far from Loup as possible.

It never failed to impress him that Romaine could know his mood. Many times she had suddenly appeared out of nowhere when he had found himself particularly unhappy, or hurting deeply from his injuries. Romaine would come, sometimes across many miles. She would lick his wounds and sit close to him, allowing Cassien to hug her, bury his face into her thick fur if he wept. The training had so often felt as though it had no purpose and now he felt betrayed. Loup — his one connection with the world outside the forest — had been lying to him. He was walking now, had stopped running as soon as he'd distanced himself from the man.

He heard a soft growl and Romaine emerged from the darkness. Light was fading from the day anyway, but here, this deep into the forest, it was almost always dark. Her pale coat looked luminous in the faint light.

'Romaine,' he whispered.

She whined softly with pleasure as he crouched down to embrace her.

'Oh, those cubs are close,' he said, forgetting his troubles and gently touching her swollen belly. 'But you came to find me anyway, didn't you, girl?' Now he stroked the broad, almost arrow-shaped head, which tapered to her nose and pale grey muzzle.

She ran a large, dry tongue over his face in welcome as he dug his fingers into the bushy fur at the base of her head; she welcomed his rough scratching around her neck and ears.

'You are so beautiful. You never let me down. How are you feeling? When will you have your family?'

She whined in response.

'Soon, I think,' he answered for her.

Romaine had always stood out from her small pack — not just because of her affectionate attitude toward him, but more particularly because of her colouring. Most of her kind were nondescript grey with a darker stripe of fur running the length of their back. Romaine was a creamy grey, lightening to a near-white around her flank. But each hair seemed to have a black tip, which gave her the extraordinary colouring of smoke.

Her yellow eyes looked deeply into his and he absently stroked her forehead.

'I've been tricked,' he moaned in answer, and went on to tell her of Josse's orders and how angered he was by Loup's deception. 'It's the final insult,' he continued. 'We are Brothers, raised to be loyal and that loyalty is our religion. You know how it is with your pack. You all trust each other. Without that to rely on, I don't think I want to be part of this family any longer.'

She growled again, as if she wanted to convey a message.

'Romaine is warning you that your decision may not be wise,' said a voice.

At the first word, Cassien had flipped backwards and was on his feet in one agile move, which included drawing his dagger from its sheath. He was poised, crouched slightly, tensed and ready to strike in less than a heartbeat.

'Who are you?' his scratchy voice echoed back from the trees, inwardly seething that he hadn't heard or picked up any stray sound or smell. Why hadn't Romaine warned him?

'No-one you should fear,' came the reply. The voice was mild and friendly.

'Where are you?'

'Here.' A small, spare man stepped out from behind one of the great oaks and stood beside Romaine. He touched her head and Cassien was astonished to see her lean against his leg as though they were long-time companions. Her mouth parted and she panted in that happy way of hers, her tongue lolling slightly. These two *were* friends.

Cassien backed away a few silent steps to rapidly gauge his surroundings. His senses strained to hear and see what threats might have accompanied the stranger.

The man seemed to know what he was thinking. 'I am alone, unarmed.'

'You came with Loup,' Cassien accused, frustrated by Romaine's easiness around this stranger.

'Yes.'

'To kill me?'

The man smiled. 'May we sit? My name is Fynch. Loup knows to leave us be.'

The stranger called Fynch looked as relaxed and unthreatened as a person could be.

'Please,' Fynch urged, 'sit with me.'

Cassien lowered himself fluidly in one movement to sit cross-legged. He could throw the knife accurately from a seated position; the man would get no more than half a step before it was lodged in his throat.

'Thank you,' Fynch said. 'I'm sure you have questions but I come to ask for your help.'

58

'Help,' Cassien repeated.

'A mission.'

'Does Brother Josse know?'

'He has sanctioned it. If it helps to ease your burden, he was sending Loup for you anyway … to bring you back to the priory because your testing is over. You are ready. I happened to come along the evening before Loup was due to leave, with a proposal.'

Cassien cleared his throat. All this talking was making it sound even grittier. 'What sort of proposal?'

'The secret sort,' Fynch said. 'Our new queen is under threat.'

'We have a queen?'

Fynch's grin broadened. 'They haven't been fair to you at all, have they?' he replied, referring to Cassien's isolation. 'Lucky you have Romaine, if just for company.'

Cassien's expression clouded further. 'That's my name for her. How do you know it? Loup doesn't.'

Fynch stared at him. 'She told me.'

Cassien blinked. 'You and my wolf talk,' he said, his tone acerbic.

'You and *my* wolf are friends. I respect that. But yes, she and I talk.'

Cassien shifted his gaze to the wolf as she leaned even harder against Fynch's legs. There was no doubting the bond between the stranger and Romaine. He felt hollow. Even his wolf was in on the betrayal.

'Romaine is loyal to you,' Fynch said, as though he'd listened in on Cassien's thoughts. 'I am her spiritual leader, you could say, and she has been known to me since she was still in her mother's womb. I gave her to you. She has looked out for you and kept me informed of your progress.'

'Romaine is a spy?' he qualified.

'No, Romaine is your friend and guard. She would never let anything bad happen — other than Loup and his fists and weapons,' Fynch said, his tone tinged with regret. 'She hated how he hurt you and it took all my reassurance to urge her to let it be … that the injuries would heal.'

Cassien shook his dark hair with disbelief. 'What are you?'

Fynch shrugged. 'An old man, as you see. A loyalist to the imperial throne. I called Emperor Cailech friend. I knew him when he was a youngster with red hair and freckles. His great-granddaughter is therefore like family — certainly someone I care deeply for — and I will do all in my power to protect her and the Crown.'

Cassien evaluated what had just been said. None of the paintings of Cailech he'd seen as a child had shown red hair. The great King of the Razors of yesteryear and emperor of the three realms had been a fierce, towering bulk of a man with golden hair ... not a freckle in sight. But more confusing was the claim that this slight man, old but not aged or infirm, knew Cailech in his youth and was still alive decades beyond his time.

'I know what you're thinking,' Fynch said.

'Do you?'

'I believe I do. Let me ask you this. Do you believe in magic, Cassien?'

It was the last question he could have possibly imagined being asked. Something in the man's look demanded he be honest. 'Yes.'

Again Fynch nodded, this time thoughtfully and as though pleased.

'Do you?' Cassien threw back at him.

'Without question,' the older man replied. 'I am surely living testimony to it,' he added with a wink.

'I need that explained.'

'I'm sure. You may go, Romaine. I feel your time is far closer than even you realise.'

Romaine obediently departed, first licking Fynch's hand affectionately before trotting over to lick Cassien's face as he bent down to ruffle her fur. It felt like an apology.

'She is now the lead female in her pack,' Fynch continued conversationally, as they watched her dark tail disappear between the trees. 'She must keep the family going. Her pups will be the only litter for this year. But then I'm sure you know the salient facts — being so attuned to life in the forest.'

'Her mate is the big dark wolf. All others fear him for miles around here. But he is as tender as any lover to Romaine.'

'As he should be,' Fynch said, 'or he would answer to me.'

'I'm not sure I understand why he would.'

'I know. There is a lot to tell you in a short time. Are you hungry?'

'No.'

'Then we shall begin,' he said, seating himself comfortably on an ancient fallen tree. 'You know my name, you sense my age is impossible and I have informed you of my connection to the royals. Do you trust what I have told you?'

He didn't have a choice but also, if he were honest, there was only one answer. 'Yes.'

'Why?'

'Because as much as I don't like it, Romaine trusts you. What are you?'

'That is probably the hardest question to answer.'

'Then let's get it out of the way,' Cassien offered.

Fynch gave a wry, brief smile. 'Who is the king of all the beasts in your estimation?'

'Folklore would say the dragon.' Cassien frowned. 'No, wait, I must qualify that. It's not just folklore. It is at the heart of spiritual belief in Morgravia. The dragon is the beast closest to Shar in our estimation. Plus, the dragon is the creature that belongs only to royalty.'

Fynch nodded his encouragement as Cassien thought back to his early education. 'All the creatures in the world pay homage to the dragon in the same way that the people in Morgravia would pay homage to their king.'

'Or queen,' Fynch corrected. 'Indeed. The dragon is a fearsome, splendid, majestic beast.'

'And one of myth,' Cassien added.

Fynch raised an eyebrow. 'You haven't seen one?' he asked playfully.

'Have you?' Cassien challenged without hesitation.

'Seen, ridden, know well. What's more, I am bonded to the dragon in a way that no other can be.'

Cassien gave a mirthless snort. 'I don't understand.'

'Let me put it another way to you. The dragon and I are one … spiritually and to some extent physically.'

'Physically?'

'I ache to be away from him. I also suffer physically. He pines if I'm not near. We are of one flesh almost … not quite.' Again the apologetic smile. 'We are Shar's servants but we are closer to Shar than any other. Why do you think that is?'

Cassien decided to go with the line of thinking and see where it led. 'The spiritual story we learned from birth is that Shar gave a bone to the dragon.'

'And the dragon gave a tooth to every other creature,' Fynch replied.

'And scales to those without teeth,' Cassien finished.

'So?'

It was like being back in one of old Brother Bellamee's religious instruction classes. 'So the dragon is of Shar and all the other creatures of the world are of the dragon, hence their homage.'

'Good.'

'But you said you were of the dragon and thus Shar.' Cassien looked at him puzzled, unsure of what to think of this.

'Correct again. How can it be, I presume you're asking? All I can say is that it is. In the reign of the king known as Celimus — do you remember hearing of him?' Cassien nodded. 'Well, my loyalties were to his enemy. His enemy's name was Wyl Thirsk.'

'Thirsk,' Cassien repeated. 'Should I know it?'

'Only if you're a scholar of history. The Thirsk family were the celebrated soldiers of Morgravia. Each son became a general to his Morgravian king. Wyl was general, briefly, for King Magnus before the heir Celimus wore the crown, but the Thirsk ancestral line died with Wyl. His sister died young and in unfortunate circumstances.'

'He never married? Had children?'

'He did both. What I'm about to tell you I have not uttered previously to any person.'

Cassien frowned. 'Why? Is it a secret?'

'Yes. It is also dangerous knowledge.'

'But you trust me with it.'

'I do but only because you believe in magic.'

'Why me?'

'Because I am going to make you part of that secret.'

Fynch stared at him and Cassien felt impaled by the golden gaze. Twilight would be closing in on the forest but he was struck by the notion that the man seemed to glow with an internal light.

'Wyl Thirsk's life was profoundly changed by a powerful magic. It matters not the whys and wherefores to you — only that it existed. He unwittingly became King Cailech and ultimately emperor of the three realms of Morgravia, Briavel and Razors, through that magic's curse. It's Wyl and Valentyna's descendants who are our current generation of royals: Magnus, Florentyna and Darcelle.'

An owl hooted once in the distance and Cassien could hear animals bumbling around not far from where Fynch sat. His sharp sense of smell picked up an aroma that he suspected was gobel … probably a pair.

Fynch continued. 'The heir, Magnus, a fine young, healthy prince, died as a result of an accident, which was a shock to everyone. He left behind two sisters, one barely out of childhood, both of them groomed to be excellent wives — although I daresay Florentyna would go slit-eyed on me to hear it.' He put a finger in the air. 'That said, Florentyna has accepted her role with strength and energy.'

'So where is the problem?'

'Her sister, Darcelle. She is younger than Florentyna by five years, the spoilt child of the family, but she is quick and smart, fiery and very beautiful.'

'She sounds like a perfect woman.'

Fynch shook his head. 'Far from it. She demonstrates more of the arrogant, brutal brilliance of the mountain king's ancestry than the subtle and more modest strength of the Thirsk blood that runs so strongly in Florentyna. Darcelle is cunning and capable. With Magnus dead and the way open for a queen to rule, an empress's role to play — well, Darcelle suddenly fancies herself in that part. Up until Magnus's death, I'm uncertain whether it had occurred to her that a woman might rule. Perhaps the possibility was too far away from the third child for it to concern her.'

'Exactly how cunning is she?'

'Enough to potentially consider regicide.'

Understanding erupted across Cassien's expression. 'I see.'

'And she would make a terrible ruler. I suspect Darcelle is capable of some atrocious decision-making as long as it serves her needs. And with the wrong people pushing her she could be convinced to make the worst decision of her life.'

'So you want me to protect Florentyna.'

Fynch glowed. 'Yes. Protect her from her sister and those who would see her ousted. But here is the problem, Cassien. Florentyna will not hear a bad word against her younger sister.'

'Do we have any sense of timing on the danger?'

His older companion shrugged. 'It is present and immediate. Florentyna has not had much luck. She was promised to the eldest prince of Tallinor. He became king a few years ago and the wedding ceremony — a mere formality — was to take place at the cathedral.'

'Let me guess. He was murdered.'

Fynch shook his head. 'Close enough though. The king's ship was accidentally sunk en route, smashed onto rocks during a storm. Two hundred souls were lost that day. Florentyna was deeply withdrawn for her moons of mourning. She is a sensitive girl but don't let that fool you into believing she doesn't possess a will of iron when required.' Fynch pointed a bony finger. 'Test it by saying something negative about her sister.'

'Does Darcelle have a match?'

'A mighty one, the King of Cipres. The power it brings in so many hidden ways can't be ignored. Darcelle must marry King Tamas and here's the most interesting part of all.' Cassien looked over at him. 'He's fifteen years her senior and Tamas seemingly adores her as much as she adores the notion of being Queen of Cipres. In his presence she is almost gentle and genuinely fond of him.' Fynch laughed. 'A match made by Shar.'

'And of course she would return to Cipres.'

'If Darcelle goes to Cipres, I no longer have to fret about the threat from within.'

'So where is the hurdle?'

'Darcelle may not want to leave Morgravia just yet. The empress is not encouraging her to rush away. Her stepmother, whom she is very close to, wants her to have this Ciprean crown but again I think they're clinging to their youngest.' Fynch stood. He shrugged. 'I can't second-guess women. Walk with me. It is time to return to Loup.'

'I don't understand why you need me especially.'

'I need your fighting talents and especially that magical skill you possess that you don't speak of to anyone.'

Cassien halted abruptly. 'What do you know?'

'Only what Romaine has told me, for we both know that you have hidden this aspect from your fellow Brothers. Oh, Brother Josse knows there is something rather special about you but he doesn't really know much at all. He believes you can "see" things. Puts it down to being in tune with the spiritual world.'

'And you?'

Fynch urged him to move forward, his look gentle and reassuring. 'Romaine has spoken of the magic you call "roaming" as dangerous to the forest creatures but that you're careful.'

'I shall have words with Romaine about her loose mouth.'

'I must assure you that she was torn between her loyalty to you and her duty to her king. Be assured, she loves you, Cassien.'

'So tell me how you want me to protect the queen? Should I call her a queen or an empress?'

Fynch nodded. 'Confusing, I agree. In Morgravia she is addressed as its queen. But she also sits on the imperial throne and is an empress by right, although that increasingly seems to be in title only. The union of the three realms, so strong under Cailech, has been whittled away gradually. She hasn't travelled enough to each for people in Briavel or the Razors to know their empress.'

'How is she addressed?'

'In Morgravia as Queen Florentyna.'

'And surely she has an army to command,' Cassien retorted.

'She does. But no number of mortal men can fully protect Florentyna. The Crown needs the aid of skills that go beyond.'

'Why?'

'Darcelle is only the closest threat but by no means the most fearsome. The greatest danger to Florentyna will come from the spiritual world, where gods and demons play.'

Cassien stopped walking. 'I'm very confused.'

Fynch chuckled and Cassien heard a soft note of underlying despair. 'I have seen the signs. No-one is better placed than I who straddle the two worlds of men and spirits. The threat is real. The enemy is hungry. The queen is vulnerable ...' Fynch trailed off.

Cassien could see the soft drift of smoke coming from the hut's rudimentary chimney. 'What does the enemy want?' He still didn't understand what this was all about.

'Oh, the usual. Destruction, damnation.'

'Why?'

'I suspect because magic was unleashed into Morgravia a long time ago — a very powerful magic that disrupted the natural order of life decades previously.'

'Wyl's magic?' he wondered aloud in a blind thrust.

'Wyl didn't possess magic and he didn't wield it. That was the tragedy of his life. He was a good man, who never sought power or wealth or status; all seemed to find him. But it was brought about originally by a curse being set upon him as a young man by a witch called Myrren.

From thereon he was a puppet, dancing to the tune of her sinister magic. It controlled him. He moved through several lives, not by choice and each death he brought — including his sister's — was heartbreaking in its own way. He tried to avoid it, but lives were given so Myrren could take her revenge on Morgravians.

'The curse's dark path was finally cut short when he entered the body of King Cailech and became sovereign.' Fynch gave a sad smile. 'I know I say that casually and I know it requires a lot more explanation but we don't have time now. Wyl died of old age as Cailech.'

'So it's over? The curse I mean.'

Fynch frowned. 'Myrren's curse has ended but that dark style of magic may not be. I don't know where the threat is coming from and I don't really know why I feel it, but I do feel it … even as removed as I am in the Wild. All the signs are there.' Fynch looked up from the leaf he'd been studying and fixed Cassien with a firm, disconcerting gaze. 'The magic is alive.'

Wednesday night closed in early and Parisians knew winter had surely arrived as the icy cold wrapped its claws around the city. A ripe yellow moon was intermittently shuttered by heavy clouds drifting across its face and threatening rain. Gabe couldn't wait to close the shop. He'd promised himself an indulgent risotto and on the way home had resisted the urge to take the shortcut; instead, wrapping his scarf tight around his mouth to keep out the chill, he ran to the nearest Monoprix to grab his fresh ingredients.

The clouds burst while he was paying for his groceries and he'd forgotten his umbrella; he pictured it on his desk at the shop and remembered that Cat had distracted him as he was packing up to leave. Cursing his luck, he had to walk home in the rain, but rather than allow himself to slip into misery at being cold and wet, he pictured himself turning on the fire, sipping a glass of wine as he chopped leeks and garlic, the intoxicating aroma spreading as both began to warm in the olive oil and release their fragrances and flavours. His mouth watered. Gabe delved into his coat pocket for his house keys and hit the stairs outside his building, taking them two at a time, and nearly tripped over her at the top. He only just managed to stop himself from sending the bag of food sprawling across the landing.

'Angelina?'

She pushed herself to standing on the stair. 'Sorry,' she murmured but didn't seem embarrassed; more amused if anything.

'What are you doing here?' Gabe asked, quickly adjusting his voice from surprise to a neutral tone. 'Are you all right?' he asked gently, suddenly worried for her.

She shrugged.

He looked around. 'Where's René?'

'Not here,' she answered and he heard defiance.

Gabe's lips twisted slightly in thought. 'You'd better come in,' he said, making up his mind. He opened the front door of his building and looked over his shoulder. 'Come on, unless you want to sit here all night. It's too cold to sit in the hallway.'

'Not for René, though?'

'Cruel guardians don't count,' Gabe answered with a wink.

'He's not my guardian,' she said quickly.

'All right. How would you describe him?' he said. 'I prefer the stairs to the lift,' he warned.

She shrugged as if it mattered not to her and followed him.

'Go on, how do you describe his relationship to you,' he encouraged as they made their ascent to his apartment.

'Keeper is too gentle a word. Jailer is probably too harsh.'

'Supervisor?' he offered helpfully but equally wry in his tone. 'Minder?' he added, flicking through his bunch of keys for the right one to open his door.

Angelina shook her head as she arrived alongside. 'Guard.'

'Guard?' he repeated as the door opened. 'Odd word. What is he guarding against, I wonder?' She shrugged again as he tapped in the alarm code and deactivated the security. 'Get that wet coat off,' he suggested, letting the topic go for now. He dumped his groceries on the kitchen counter and flicked on the gas fire. 'I'm just going to dry off.'

He strode to his bathroom and closed the door, reaching for a towel to dry his hair. As he dragged it across his face he caught sight of himself in the mirror and paused, only his eyes visible over the top of the towel.

'What are you doing?' he murmured to his reflection. 'This flies against everything you know to be correct protocol.' He took a deep breath, knowing he had to make a decision. He finished drying off his hair, neatened it with his fingers by pushing it behind his ears and nodded at himself. 'It's your funeral,' he said, echoing a favourite threat he and his wife used to throw at each other when one was in disagreement with the other's decision.

He emerged. 'Okay?'

She smiled back. 'Fine.'

Gabe watched her from the corner of his eye as he unpacked his groceries. Angelina had taken off her coat and stood with her back to the fire looking around his room as though seeing it for the first time. She didn't appear in the least uncomfortable or embarrassed to be here with him alone.

'So are you going to tell me?'

'What?' she said, turning to gaze at him with her smoky, dark eyes so full of promise that Gabe found himself clearing his throat. Today she was wearing a pair of narrow, tight jeans that clung to her petite, beautiful shape with vigour. Her mauve cashmere knit top was short and tight, revealing a few centimetres of bare midriff and accentuating her full breasts. He tried not to stare but this garb was entirely different to her almost childlike clothes of the previous day. For so long, women he met had not excited him in this way ... now, suddenly, there was Angelina.

She found a lighter on the mantelpiece. 'May I?'

He shrugged. 'Of course.'

Angelina began to light the candles he'd put around the room months previously simply because they looked good. She switched off overhead lights as she continued around the room touching her flame to the wicks, making sure he had plenty of opportunity and time to watch the graceful movements of her lithe body. Six were burning by the time she returned to the fireplace and the space had already begun to fill with the rich perfume of earthy, fresh sandalwood and sweet, heady frankincense.

Control seemed impossible now. He wanted to hold her, feel the contact of her skin against his, his lips on hers, his hands on her —

She broke into his guilty thoughts. 'Do you have a lover?' Angelina asked, eyes glittering in the low light.

The question was so brazen the corkscrew he'd just placed on the wine cork slipped and stabbed into his left thumb, slicing it open.

'*Merde!*' he growled.

He heard her gurgle with laughter behind him, guessing at what was happening.

'Idiot!' he added.

'Let me help,' she said, gliding over.

He didn't want her to touch him, but she was already close enough for him to smell her perfume — violets, he thought. The whole situation of candlelight and blood, pain, comfort: it was all dangerous and wrong.

Angelina had reached for a tea towel and was pressing it onto the cut.

'It's not deep,' she assured him, still amused.

'I'll look after it now,' he began, awkwardly reaching to take over.

'No-one's watching, Gabe. Relax. Let's just stop the flow of blood,' she said, preventing him from pulling his hand away.

'You're very different when René is not around.'

'You haven't answered me.'

He remembered her question. 'Why would you use the word "lover" when most people would say "girlfriend"?'

She looked up at him now and he felt his throat tighten. 'It's clear to me you don't have a girlfriend,' she replied with the utmost confidence. 'Lover strikes me as more accurate.'

'How do you know I don't have a girlfriend?'

'There'd be signs of her around here. And don't look at the scented candles — they don't fool me,' she giggled.

Angelina was being witty. Perhaps the slashed thumb was worth it.

'What's wrong with the word "lover", anyway?' she challenged.

'Nothing … it's just intimate.'

'And that disturbs you?'

'It doesn't disturb me,' he defended, hearing the lie in his hollow tone. 'It's a confronting word for want of a better description.'

'Confronting?'

'Too direct. It became an impolite question because of it,' he cautioned.

She laughed at him. 'You're intimidated by a word.'

'I'm not intimidated,' he replied.

Angelina smiled. 'Aren't you?' she said. 'I'm usually good at reading people. My mistake. So answer my question then.'

He took a breath, feeling vaguely ridiculous as she held his hand. 'No, I am not romantically involved with anyone at present.'

She cast a glance over his ingredients. 'And yet this is such a romantic dinner you're making for yourself.'

'It's a risotto.' He could hear the defensiveness in his tone.

'But risotto is a meal to share, to savour with another. There's nothing lonely or selfish about a risotto. Risotto is a meal made with love because it takes time; a meal that speaks of love to the person you share it with because you have taken that time over it.'

Gabe swallowed. Surely it wasn't that complex?

'Such a tactile dish,' Angelina continued. 'Lots of attention,' she said, mimicking stirring the pot. She rubbed her belly but there was something suggestive in it. 'And so warming.' She unwrapped the tea towel from around his hand as she spoke. They both watched as the blood sprang again to the surface and oozed through the cut. It was hardly flowing but it was bright and glossy. 'Glutinous ... sticky ... wet,' she murmured and then shocked him by raising his hand to close her lips around his thumb.

He could feel her tongue licking at the blood and instantly he felt an erotic rush of blood elsewhere. The risotto was forgotten — as was the bleeding thumb and the still unopened bottle of wine.

Like a helpless schoolboy his face guided itself to her mouth. He vaguely registered the smell of violets on her breath before drowning in the desire to pull her as close as humanly possible. She was so petite he had to bend to hold her properly. Before he knew it, she had clambered up onto him as a child might, her supple legs wrapped around his hips, her arms around his neck. She was light and tiny, but her body was all woman.

The kissing was mind-blanking. He was robbed of all thought, all awareness of anything beyond desire. His traitorous fingers began exploring her body. Somewhere deep horror resonated that he was taking advantage of a vulnerable patient, but the patient was now rhythmically moving against him and moaning softly.

He was supposed to be a man entirely in control and yet here he was ... like putty, suddenly incapable of resisting when she made her body so available — soft, compliant, eager. He blamed his new mood to change his life, he blamed the return of the cathedral — his mind palace — back in his thoughts. He wanted to blame the raven that had unnerved him — in fact anything except being a vulnerable man in the presence of an erotic young woman.

Suddenly they were on his bed and he was pulling off his clothes and hers. Gabe knew he should but he didn't want to exercise control. He wanted Angelina. He needed this. His inner voice assured him as he pulled at her buttons. *She's adult, she's consenting ... she's —*

... your patient! reinforced another — René's — but he ignored that caution.

Angelina never let go of him. There was always some part of her connected to him — mouth, hand, breast. It was as though she knew that to break the connection was to break the spell.

And then their bodies joined as one and Gabe was lost to it, riding a wave of unbelievable joy that he had found something he'd not thought possible to ever find since Lauren and Henry had died. It wasn't love — he knew that. It wasn't even affection because they'd barely paused to consider any fondness which might exist between them. He couldn't call it emotional ... there hadn't been time to build this relationship.

It was purely the physical closeness to another that he'd denied himself for so long. She was unlocking years of pent-up need. There was nothing else but Angelina in his hollow, sterile life. Only her — beneath and above him. She was suddenly his sun, his sky, his earth, his sea. And he travelled with her now, drowning in her depths and soaring to her heights.

Did it last for eternity or was it just a brief interlude? Gabe lay confused and ashamed. The candles still blinked and guttered softly from a draft somewhere; the bloodstained tea towel still lay on the floor where it had dropped. His thumb had stopped bleeding now but he could see smudges of blood on the sheets. He glanced at the clock next to the bed. It was only just coming up to nine. He'd arrived at his building at around seven-forty he guessed. So he'd lost not even an hour and a half of his life and yet it felt as though he'd been absent for days.

He turned to gaze at Angelina, sleeping as still as a corpse next to him with her lips parted. There was blood smeared on her cheek where he'd held her face to kiss her, and seeing the blood reminded him of René's warning. *She will bring you harm.* He leaned close until he could feel her breath against his lips, smell that curious hint of sweet violets on it. Her skin looked lilac-blue in the low light, except that her cheeks had a small pinch of colour, as though they alone held the memory of their passion. He swung his legs to the floor and held his face.

'*Insensé!*' he cursed beneath his breath. '*Vous êtes fou!*'

She stirred. 'Who is mad?' But she rolled over and her mumbling dissipated.

Gabe watched her for a moment, struck again by her ethereal beauty, the dark almost black hair such a contrast to the pale skin. He smiled in spite of himself — she was irresistible and he could only imagine what René would think if he could see this scene.

René. There had to be fallout from this. The man so jealously guarding Angelina was hardly going to take this event on the chin and with a grin. Gabe sighed again.

He padded over to the coffee machine and flicked it on. All he knew was that the myriad sensations of being with Angelina had swept away years of pain. As he ground the coffee beans, heedless of whether it disturbed his guest, he saw movement from the corner of his eye. Turning around, he was alarmed to see the raven sitting on the balcony, backlit by the streetlight so that a halo of gold surrounded its menacing shape. It made no sound. Gabe was speared by its gaze, and Angelina's arrival into the kitchen area nearly made him yell with fright.

'Hello,' she said sleepily.

He snapped his fear-filled attention from the bird to her. 'Evening,' he replied, as casually as he could. He glanced back to the window but the raven was gone.

'What time is it?' she asked, yawning.

'Well past nine. Toast? Coffee?'

She shook her head with a smile. 'But thank you.'

'Do you ever eat?'

Angelina laughed. 'I suppose I'd better go.'

He wasn't sure what to say and watched her turn away. He took another worried look at the window. The bird was definitely no longer there but he felt rattled by its presence. Neighbours hadn't mentioned ravens. He would have to make some enquiries.

Gabe sipped his espresso before moving after Angelina. She was pulling on her clothes. She'd never looked more desirable than now, half-dressed, her hair tousled and a bit sleepy still.

'You don't have to leave, you know.'

Angelina paused. 'I'll be missed.'

'You never did tell me how you slipped René's watch.'

'It doesn't matter. I just feel lucky I've had this chance to be alone.'
She shrugged.

'Does he lock you up?'

She shook her head. 'I've never disobeyed him.'

'I've noticed. You've had opportunities to slip him even in my presence.'

'No point.'

'Why?'

'Because here is where I want to be.'

He frowned. Didn't understand. Angelina was behaving in an obtuse manner.

'Here? But you don't like Paris, you said you wanted to leave … and go home. A home that was far away.'

'I'm glad you paid attention.'

'You're hard to ignore.'

She pulled on her sweater, a small strip of her belly showing at its lower edge. And once again he felt a pulse of desire. Not again, he told himself.

'I'm pleased to hear it,' Angelina remarked and sat on the bed to pull on her boots.

'Except what we did was wrong.'

'Why?' she asked conversationally, not even looking at him.

'I mean, what I did was wrong.'

Now she gazed up at him. 'I had some say in it, you know.'

'Yes,' he sighed, all too aware of how patronising he was sounding. 'I'm trying to say that the blame is mine, not yours.'

She looked at him unimpressed. 'Oh, I don't know. It looked very much to me like I was seducing you.'

'Yes, but —'

'And men are so predictable in this regard,' she added, echoing his earlier thought.

'We're simple creatures,' he said in mock apology.

'Not you, Gabe,' she said.

He gave a low snort. 'I'm as simple as the next man.'

Angelina stood and walked over to him. He loved the way she moved. Silent and as though she glided over the surface of his carpet. 'You underestimate yourself.'

'And you know so much about me,' he gently rebuked her.

'You'd be surprised how much I do know.'

'Angelina, don't go.'

'Why?'

'Because it's late. It's freezing outside. It's …' He paused to glance through the window, half-expecting a raven to leap at him. 'It's turning frosty so you could slip on the wet, icy pavement. Not very nice people use the cover of darkness to be abroad.'

'Abroad?' She laughed. 'What a quaint phrase. How thoroughly medieval of you.'

He frowned. 'Stay. Why don't we revisit the conversation that René interrupted?'

'Back to psychologist and patient?'

He didn't respond immediately. Then sighed. 'Why not? It's what we are.'

'Half an hour ago we were something rather different.'

He felt himself blush. 'All right, I deserved that. What I mean is that it's a perfect opportunity for us to talk without René breathing down our necks. Whatever trouble happens, it's not going to happen for a few more hours. We have time.'

She nodded and let out a sigh, sank back onto the bed. 'Ask your questions.'

Gabe swallowed his coffee, put the small cup down and sat beside her. 'You feel safe here … in this apartment,' he began. 'That's what you meant by "here", I take it?'

'I meant with you.'

'You feel safe with me, then.'

'No, I have found what I came to find. You.'

He gave her a searching look. 'Let's leave that for now.' She smiled and once more he had that sense of an old cunning. 'You said René is fearful.'

'He's scared of both of us now, particularly that the two of us might be alone together like this. If he knew this was happening, he would try and kill you.'

Gabe blinked in astonishment. 'Well, there's an overreaction,' he said, unable to mask the sarcasm.

She stared back at him. 'You think I jest?'

'I know you do.'

'Shall we call him and see his reaction?'

'No. I want to know why you believe he is scared of me.'

'Because of what you're capable of.'

'Can you be more specific?'

'Yes, but you wouldn't believe me.'

'Try me.'

'You have the capacity to bring down an empire.'

'An empire?' He tried not to laugh but the amusement was evident in his expression.

Angelina's remained grave. 'I need you to kill me, Gabe.'

'What?' he roared.

She flung her arms around him, staring gravely into his eyes. 'Kill me. Release us.'

'Stop it,' he said, trying to unwind her arms, then her legs as they snaked around him.

'Only death will free me.'

'Angelina, where has this come from? You're acting delusional again.'

'I'm as sane as you. Remember when we were making love? Do you recall seeing anything?'

He shook his head. 'My mind was blank.'

'No, it wasn't, Gabe. Think!' She kissed him. Her tongue softly licked his lips and stimulated every part of him. He remembered now. *The cathedral* ... from his mind palace. And then he was outside it, looking around for the first time. He could see it belonged to a huge city, but no city that he recognised. Angelina suddenly pulled away.

'I know you saw it. I saw it too. The Great Cathedral of Pearlis.'

'Pearlis?' he stammered. The word reminded him of the name Reynard had murmured in connection with the quill. Gabe had heard Pearlis, and yet Reynard had quickly adjusted it to Paris.

Angelina nodded. 'I know you used to visit it often but only in your mind. I can take you there, Gabe. I can give you the Great Cathedral of Pearlis.'

'What are you talking about?' he said, trying again to loosen her arms from his neck.

'I can give you so much, Gabe, but you have to trust me. René is no friend of yours. He is the enemy.'

'Enemy,' he repeated, lost.

'He wishes only harm. He wants me dead, but he knows he can't kill me. Not yet anyway, and not here.'

'Angelina, you're speaking in riddles.'

'The raven. I know it has found you.'

Gabe choked at the mention of it. She let him loosen her hold on him, and he almost jumped away, running a hand through his unbound hair.

'You've seen it too?' he said, suddenly feeling haggard.

She shook her head, moving into a kneeling position on the bed, following him with her gaze. She began to undress again. 'I've felt it. The other day when I was here I could feel its taint. I can keep you safe but you have to trust me.'

'Safe.' He laughed scornfully. 'I don't understand any of this.'

'Kiss me again. I want to show you something,' she said.

He couldn't resist her. He sat down and she moved to encircle him with her arms and legs as he kissed her.

What Gabe saw shocked him rigid.

SIX

Loup led them back toward the priory.

Leaving the hut hadn't been difficult. Cassien had been dreaming of this day. Leaving Romaine had been another matter. Fynch had shown him where her nesting burrow was and Cassien had been amazed that her mate — the one he called Flint — permitted them to approach. Even in his wildest dreams Cassien would not have attempted to get past Flint unarmed. But with Fynch present the huge male wolf had sat back on his haunches. Fynch scratched the back of his ears while Cassien stepped forward to hug Romaine farewell.

'I'll be back when these cubs are grown,' he promised in a whisper.

He watched with affection as the four fat, sleepy cubs snuggled closer. Blue eyes would yellow in the coming moon. Three of the cubs were dark like their father but the third, the smallest, resembled her mother. In his mind he called her Felys and, as the name formed and stuck, she stirred and he saw her tiny tongue lick at his finger. His heart swelled and he blew softly on the cub's face. Cassien was sure it was an old wives' tale, but he had been told that if you blew into the nostrils of a puppy, the dog it grew into would always be loyal to you and you alone. The baby blinked blindly but he glimpsed her pale blue eyes and smiled. She knew him now. And he already loved her nearly as much as her mother. He turned to Romaine and gave her a kiss on her forehead.

'Thank you for being my friend,' he whispered and stood.

Fynch had nodded. 'Let's go.'

The smells had changed as the forest gradually thinned. He was excited but it was nonetheless daunting to know that he was going to be amongst people again. He'd have to teach himself how to integrate, how to converse easily, how to be friendly even if he didn't feel friendly, how to be polite despite his mood, how to cope with noise.

The reassuring perfume of the trees, the aroma of the damp earthiness of the forest floor, the daily meal — a soup usually — of vegetables he could forage for, were all comforting smells that would no longer be part of his daily life.

Initially, these had given way to the intoxicating scent of baking bread and he'd forgotten how heavenly it was and how it made his belly rumble in anticipation. But there were soon other smells that assaulted him — far less pleasant … the metallic, tangy blood of slaughtered animals mixing with the fouler smells of urine and dung from the local tannery. There was a yeasty smell of ale and a vapour of smoked plants that someone was using for healing. However, the all-pervading aroma was of people: sweat, perfumes, cooking …

'Where are we again?' he asked. Loup had obviously led them a less direct way to the priory.

Fynch paused. 'I asked Loup to bring us through Barrowdean.'

Cassien nodded. He'd never heard of it.

'I'm not sure why,' Loup admitted. 'Farnswyth is more direct.'

'Because, Loup, this is where we shall part company,' Fynch replied.

Loup blinked. 'But I thought …'

Cassien looked between his two minders uncertain of what this impasse meant.

'Yes, I know,' Fynch said evenly, 'but I will guide Cassien from here. We look obvious enough as a pair, but as a trio we draw far too much attention.'

'Brother Josse didn't say anything to me,' Loup replied, his brow furrowing deeply.

'Brother Josse knows he is being paid for Cassien's services, Loup. He gave me the freedom to set up Cassien's mission — that he is aware of — as I choose. He made no stipulations.'

'This is very unusual. He always briefs me. And he said nothing other than to take you into the forest to Cassien and then to bring you both back.'

'Bring us both back to where I required,' Fynch corrected. 'I agree it's probably unusual but then this is a very unusual mission. So, thank you, Loup, for bringing us to this point. I can recommend the Jug and Hare for a night's rest.' He extended a tiny jangling pouch to Loup. 'This coin should cover your stay and a very good meal with plenty of ale. You have earned it.'

Loup stared at it, nonplussed. Cassien would have been surprised if Loup had taken it. No member of the Brotherhood was motivated by money.

'You can journey to Hambleton tomorrow.' Still the man didn't move, but raised his gaze to Fynch and Cassien saw a hint of defiance in it. 'This is beyond your control now,' Fynch continued, with gentle caution, his voice just fractionally firmer, but no louder. He didn't jangle the pouch, or push it any further forward.

'Loup,' Cassien began, feeling obliged to get involved, 'you know where my loyalties lie. They've never been in question and I hope you don't question them now. I am told this is for the Crown. We must assist. It is our purpose in life.' He put a hand on the man's thick shoulder. 'It's what you've trained me for. Let me do my work.' He eased the pouch from Fynch's outstretched palm into Loup's reluctant one, believing that his conferring of the money might make it easier on his Brother's conscience. The move seemed to work. Loup looked down at the tiny sack in his hand and didn't move or speak.

Cassien turned to Fynch, who nodded. They walked away, not in a hurry, but also not dragging their heels. Neither looked around, although Cassien didn't have to in order to know that Loup watched them until they had long disappeared.

'That was well done,' Fynch admitted.

'Did you think he wouldn't let us go?'

'It crossed my mind. I didn't want any attention drawn to us.'

'Why do I think you didn't discuss us coming to Barrowdean with Brother Josse?'

'Because you are intuitive,' said Fynch.

'So is Loup.'

'But Loup is obedient.'

'So am I.'

'But you live by your instincts. Loup doesn't. He does *only* what he's told. He can't deviate.'

'Except today,' Cassien said, feeling a sudden surge of guilt.

'Forget Loup. From now on you need to assume that everyone is your enemy.'

Cassien scoffed. 'That's dramatic.'

'I can't tell you from whom the threat might come.'

Cassien frowned as they walked, skirting the town, struggling with the noise, the dusty air and the new smells most of all.

'You'll have to get used to it,' Fynch remarked and when Cassien threw him a glance, he added: 'Your expression says droves, but you need to adjust quickly. I can't have you staring in wonder at everything, or looking as shocked or disconcerted as you do, or you'll be noticed.'

Cassien nodded absently, well aware that while his life had been slowed to a crawl, the rest of the world had clearly sped up. There were many people on the move, lots of yelling and frustrated carters angry with people in their way, while other people tried to weave around the disruptions, busy with their own chores. He saw a young woman lugging a basket as big as herself, full of linen. His inclination was to help her carry it but he knew by the set of her mouth how independent she obviously was. Dogs barked and gathered in groups, a bit like the old men sitting outside the dinch-houses grumbling about younger men and ogling the women who passed. There were so many people, so many horses and carts, wheelbarrows and activity. It made him feel dizzy.

'Look at that,' Fynch remarked, nodding toward the men clustered around their steaming pots. 'We didn't even know what dinch was in my time. Now we have watering holes dedicated to it.'

'Really? Even I know dinch,' Cassien replied.

'You're a lot younger than me,' Fynch said with a wry smile. 'It came over with the travellers and merchants. I gather the Penravens are particularly fond of their dinch and guard their recipes zealously. Would you like to take some with me?' Fynch guided him to a table outside another dinch-house.

A serving girl was at their side immediately. She grinned at Cassien, who blinked.

'I'll have a pot please,' Fynch said.

'And for you, handsome?' she said winking at Cassien.

'The same,' he said, amused by her saucy manner.

She bent down to place a jar of honey on their table, making sure that Cassien enjoyed a generous view of her breasts. 'Right back, sirs,' she said, casting him a jaunty smile before taking her next order. 'Going to the bathhouse later?' she quipped.

Cassien was too busy hungrily watching her to register her comment and it was several long moments before his wits came back and he turned to Fynch, realising how quiet it suddenly was. Fynch was smiling at him.

'Sorry,' Cassien said.

'Don't be. How long is it since you've been with a woman?'

He was not ready for such a direct question.

Fynch grinned and just for a moment Cassien glimpsed a boyish innocence. 'Was that too direct?'

'Er … it just took me by surprise.'

Fynch chuckled, genuinely amused. 'I wanted to put you at your ease so you don't have to apologise for enjoying the sight of a pretty girl. Did the priory make provision for your … needs?'

Cassien's brief gust of a laugh was answer enough.

'Ah,' Fynch said, 'that explains the phiggo root I noticed in your hut.'

He stared at the older man, confused. 'I was instructed to brew a liquor from it each week and drink a spoon of it daily.'

'Yes, I'm sure you were and I'm also sure that Loup checked on that brew and your supplies regularly.'

Cassien nodded. 'He was quite particular. Assured me it was for strength, good health.'

Fynch sighed. 'It's traditionally used by armies to keep the men focused on their soldiering. It's why you haven't gone mad with pent-up lust.'

Cassien looked at his companion, astounded by this information. It made instant sense but that didn't lessen the shock. 'They drugged me?' he murmured, shaking his head.

'How else could they keep a virile young man in the forest without companionship for so long?' Fynch nodded at the approaching serving girl. 'Anyway, I'm sure you'll rectify the situation soon enough, although perhaps it should wait until we reach Pearlis.'

Fynch hurried the serving girl on with a bigger than usual tip. He gently tossed the moneybag and a second one he'd dug from a pocket across the table. 'You've had no need of coin in the past. But you will need it from here on. Tie those to your belt, although I do think we should kit you out with some fresh garb.'

Cassien looked down at his clothes. They were certainly the worse for wear. Dun, colourless, shabby.

'Have we time?'

Fynch nodded. 'Plenty. You could use a shave, a haircut, too. Drink up, Cassien. And while you do, I'll talk.'

He took his first sip of dinch sweetened with honey, although sparingly, knowing all of these rich new substances hitting his belly might bring him some grief. He could taste flavours of cinnamon and shir, and something else he couldn't identify. The taste was complex and delicious. He sipped slowly and paid attention as Fynch looked away, lost in his thoughts, before beginning to speak. Gone was the light-hearted tone of their previous conversation. His voice was grave now and his expression sombre.

'I told you I don't know what the re-emergence of the magic means, but it was a cynical, sinister and destructive magic when it was first cast so I can't imagine that part of it has changed. There is a demon called Cyricus who is likely to be its puppeteer but I don't know who will be its host. I warned her majesty of it more than fourteen moons ago. I felt it stirring then. The Wild is like that. It is highly sensitive to changes, not just in our world but in the spiritual world that surrounds us. My experience with Wyl Thirsk and the evil curse on his life meant I would always know the taint of the same magic.'

Cassien didn't like to interrupt but couldn't help himself. 'You said you warned the royals.'

'As best I could. The chancellor believed me, or at least in taking seriously any threat to Florentyna, magical or otherwise. He supported my efforts to have an audience. Darcelle, I learned, sneered at the suggestion; regarded me as some sort of senile herbwizard. The queen gave me a fair audience but she couldn't countenance the threat of a demon.'

'Does she trust you?'

'That's tricky. I sensed she wanted to but demonic threat is hard to prove ... and she wanted proof.'

'So?'

'We decided to find it.'

'We?'

'The chancellor and I. He offered his help and I took it.'

'What of Briavel? Every little morsel of news I could glean from Loup I would turn over in my mind for days, trying to piece it together with other titbits he'd give me. I got the impression that Briavel's and Morgravia's relationship was strained.'

'To say the least,' Fynch admitted. 'While Cailech and Valentyna unified their realms, their grandchildren allowed the strong bonds to slip. Briavel became touchy when much of its rich farming land was given to members of the Morgravian aristocracy and Briavel's nobles didn't seem to warrant equal generosity. There were high hopes for the great-great-grandson, Magnus. He was fond of a very senior and beloved noble's daughter from Briavel. It was exactly what the empire needed; a marriage between those old realms and their families to reinforce the imperial bond. But when he died so did our hopes.' Fynch shrugged with a soft sigh of despair. 'It could all break down quickly because the union was only ever as strong as the royal couple that led it.'

Cassien noticed Fynch had not touched his dinch, just as he had not eaten a morsel since they'd met. There was clearly something otherworldly about the man, if indeed he could call him a man. 'All right, that's in the past,' he began, finding it easier to leave that confusion behind. 'Obviously you believe there is hope for the empire or you wouldn't be conscripting help.'

Fynch nodded, pushed his untouched dinch forward. 'Help yourself to more,' he said absently. 'I do believe in the empire. We can only have this conversation once, Cassien, so you need to understand all that you can now. Once we get deeper into the capital, there are ears listening everywhere, and I also don't trust how long we might have. So with that in mind let me quickly sum up what you need to know. I believe our hope is Queen Florentyna.'

'So you want me to protect the queen from any potential threat from her sibling or from an otherworldly attack,' Cassien concluded.

'Her life is paramount — there are no heirs other than Darcelle.'

'How old is Florentyna?'

'Twenty-two summers. She thinks like Cailech, looks like Valentyna, has all the dash and daring of her Briavellian line, and the courage, agile mind and determination of her mountain king forebear. And she has the green eyes of Wyl Thirsk. When I looked into them, I saw him there. I know he lives on through her.'

'But what of the threat of Cyricus?' Cassien demanded.

'Indeed. Who sits on the throne is only one half of our frightening equation.'

'Fynch,' Cassien began, his voice hard, looking directly at the older man, 'explain precisely to me what you believe Cyricus aims to achieve?'

Fynch took a deep breath. 'The magic that was once the witch Myrren's is, I believe, returning in a more dire form. It was formerly focused on revenge, Myrren finding a way from the grave to punish Morgravia for her torture and burning, but particularly its nastiest son, King Celimus, for his part in her demise. This time I think it will be used directly against the imperial Crown.

'I have seen Cyricus in my dreams and in my spiritual wanderings. I don't know from where he comes but he is an old, old mind. He is not of this region. He was ancient even when Myrren was casting her curious magic. I was too young, too caught up in the curse on Wyl Thirsk to notice Cyricus. But he was there — an interested bystander you could say, watching us. And I suspect his curiosity was pricked by her unique, twisted magic.'

'What is he?'

'A demon, as I told you,' Fynch said, standing. 'I think we should give you a chance to bathe, to get new clothes.'

'But what about —?'

'I realise I have given you a sense of urgency but in this matter we must show a little patience,' Fynch said, raising a hand. 'Now, you are wrinkling your nose at the smells of the town but I can assure you, the other travellers are going to pinch theirs when they get a whiff of your particular aroma.' Fynch beamed Cassien the bright smile that lit up his eyes and warmed anyone it touched.

Cassien sniffed the sleeve of his leather jerkin.

'That bad?'

'Eye-watering,' Fynch assured. 'You're going to meet a queen. We want you at your best.'

Cassien found himself immersed in an oaken barrel of hot water. He was mesmerised by the feel of the soap's slipperiness on his skin, and the sensual pleasure of having someone wash his hair, rubbing his scalp clean. The fact that it was the bark-smoking Wife Wiggins with her black teeth and gravelly voice, rather than a pretty young woman like the inn maid, didn't matter. It was heavenly.

Wife Wiggins was not in the least moved by his nakedness; she'd raised her eyebrows in disdain at Cassien's bashfulness and cast a sigh over her shoulder towards Fynch. Nevertheless, Cassien emerged from the depths groaning with satisfaction.

'I'm surprised you have no lice,' she remarked, 'you're so grubby. Make sure you use the soap on your —'

'Thank you,' Cassien said, cutting off her advice. 'I can manage now.'

She looked at Fynch, who nodded. 'Right then, I'll leave you to it,' she grumbled. 'I suggest you soak for a while. You seem to have leaf mould growing out of your ears, young man.'

'I'll see to it. Thank you again for the clothes,' Fynch said.

'Yes, well, you've paid handsomely. And I'll be burning those old rags he wore when he walked in here.'

'Do we tip the water out or —'

'Tip it out?' she cried from the doorway of the barn she called a bathhouse. 'Are you mad, sir? I'll wash three more men in that water before it gets tipped. Just leave it as you found it.' She left, pushing the bark smoke back between her lips.

Cassien blinked. 'What a scary woman.'

Fynch's eyes sparkled with amusement. 'You can just imagine the array of men who pass through her tubs. It started out as a service she offered the tanners but now she has to run ten tubs, and in high season can bathe fifty men a day. She doesn't usually scrub them down herself, I must admit, but you're special.'

'Fynch, I must know more about this demon. It's as though you hesitate.'

'Maybe I don't want to accept it as real and by getting you involved I must fully accept the reality of his threat.' He sighed deeply. 'I told you Cyricus has been watching us from afar for decades.'

'And you have been watching him.'

'I have watched you too. You are suited to the role.'

'What role?'

'To kill the demon when he presents himself. You are all we have. Your killing skills and your very special magic.'

Now, finally, it made sense. Fynch was after the weapon of his mind. He could see in Fynch's open face that the old man knew Cassien understood that.

Fynch sighed. 'Cyricus will come to Morgravia in the guise of a man, of that I'm sure. He must travel in that form in order to walk our land, otherwise he has no substance.' Fynch held up a long, slim finger. 'But as flesh he is also vulnerable in the way a man is.'

'How will I know him?'

'You won't. But he will attack the Crown. That will be part of his plan. To bring it down. He will seek to destroy first the royals and then seize power.'

'Why would he want to?'

'Because he can,' Fynch said in a weary tone, handing Cassien a linen, signalling it was time for him to clamber out of the tub. 'Because he is bored. Because he enjoys stirring trouble, bringing problems. He sees an unsettled people and he wants to spice up the discontent. And because he has reason to destroy a single region of the empire that I will not, cannot permit.'

'And where is that?'

'It's called the Wild. It is our bad luck that his attention has been attracted and focused on our empire but it's no good bleating. We must act.'

'Surely an army is better than a single man?' Cassien stood with the linen wrapped around his lower body, water pooling around his feet. He knew Fynch's story sounded far-fetched, and yet because Romaine trusted him Cassien felt compelled to follow suit.

'An army against another army perhaps,' Fynch replied. 'But an army is no match against a foe it can't see, or doesn't know is there. What's more, I have no desire to give Cyricus warning that we know of his presence. Right now he believes himself unknown — and to most he is. But I know him. I feel him. I smell him. I taste him and his hungry interest on a bitter wind. One day I may hear his cries for mercy or touch the dead body he chooses to inhabit, but right now surprise is my only defence … and you and I the only people who stand in his way.'

'Has our world faced a demon before?'

'Not to my knowledge, although Myrren's curse on Wyl Thirsk could be viewed that way. But, while I might be old, this demon is as ancient as the Razors, maybe older. He comes from the east, I believe.'

Cassien pulled on the ill-fitting pants and shirt, posing for Fynch, who made a face of amused resignation. 'That will have to do for the moment.' As Cassien continued dressing and tidied his hair, Fynch finished what he could of the story.

'Cyricus was astonished, excited by the power of the Wild when he discovered it, and sought to use it. The magic within the Wild repelled him, bouncing his acolyte, the sycophantic Aphra, out of our plane to another, trapping her and weakening Cyricus. This is very ancient history, mind you,' Fynch warned, 'long before my time. Cyricus did nothing until the scent of the magic of Myrren reached him centuries later, stirring him from whichever depths of thought he lived in.'

'And being cautious now he simply watched?'

'Exactly,' Fynch said. 'Ready?' Cassien nodded. 'Then it's time to call on the tailor,' Fynch said, looking up as they departed Wife Wiggins's barn.

'How do you know all of this information about Cyricus?'

'I told you I'm old. I've mentioned I've travelled — and not just in this plane. On this you must trust me. I've had a talent since childhood for gathering, memorising and being able to collate vast amounts of what might appear to be unrelated pieces of information. And the beasts of the world are far more attuned to the natural order of things, especially if they are disrupted in any way. They know he is coming.'

Fynch guided Cassien to a small lane that dipped down and led to the centre of the town. 'We don't have to go all the way in. Just a few doors down is Master Zeek.'

'You said he needs a host,' Cassien wondered aloud.

'He will inhabit a mortal to gain power before he begins to lay waste to the forests and the Wild as well as its creatures.'

Fynch had his hand on the door-knob of a shop doorway.

'This is the tailor. We must stop our discussion now. I know you have more questions but there are only two points that matter in all that I've said.' He raised a finger. 'Your role to protect the new queen with your life.' He raised a second finger. 'And to find a way to slay Cyricus when he presents himself ... and he will.'

The door was opened and Cassien had to bite back the flood of new thoughts because a smiling, rotund man emerged from behind a small curtain.

'Master Fynch, welcome back. And this must be your nephew.'

The small shop smelled of endless rows of fabric, slightly oily and earthy and pleasing to Cassien. It was quiet too, which he appreciated after the bustle of the small lanes they'd walked to get here. Bolts of linens were piled high behind the smiling tailor in towers of colours of all hue; others lay on the ground in smaller heaps and others still, the finest cloths, were in glass cabinets.

Cassien watched Fynch smile warmly at the man. 'Tailor Zeek, this is him, yes. Do you think we made a good fit between us?'

Zeek's waxed moustache twitched as he appraised Cassien with a knowledgeable look, his head cocked to one side. 'Indeed, Master Fynch. I doubt few, if any, adjustments may be required to what I made up on your instructions. Shall we try?'

Fynch turned to Cassien. 'Would you care to try on some new clothes?'

'They'll scratch at first,' Zeek warned, 'but this particular yarn from the senleng plant softens like no other. You'll barely know you're wearing the garments in a moon or two.'

Cassien looked between the pair of them, realising that Fynch had had these clothes made for this moment, had obviously decided some time ago to steal Cassien away from beneath Loup's nose and Josse's rules and the Brotherhood's care, and had planned their escape. 'I'll be glad to try them on,' he replied, and stepped into the back of the shop.

'I shall hang them here,' Zeek said, placing a shirt, vest, trews and cloak on a hook nearby. 'Take your time, young man.' He disappeared to the front of the shop and Cassien could hear the men talking in low voices.

He regarded the clothes. The trousers were dark … the colour of scorched wood. The shirt was a lighter hue, but not by much, while the cloak was soft wool, black as the forest night and whisper-light. Each item was cut and sewn together beautifully. He'd never handled such fine garments before and could barely believe they were for him. Guiltily he climbed into them, amazed by their nearly perfect fit.

He came out from the back area and Zeek cast an appraising eye up and down, getting Cassien to turn this way and that.

'Those trousers are not snug enough around the waist.'

'Yes, I think you might have worked a little harder in the last few moons, Cassien, than I calculated,' Fynch admitted, regarding him.

'They fit like a dream,' Cassien replied, unsure of what they were both unhappy with. He turned to stare at himself in the tall mirror on one side of the shop and blinked. He'd not seen himself from the chin down in a long time.

Fynch sidled up. 'Recognise yourself?'

Cassien looked with surprise at the man staring back at him from the mirror. He was familiar with the face but the frame that these new dark clothes hung from was surely too tall, too hardened beneath the linens. He could see muscles outlined on a chest he'd never realised was that broad. He'd arrived in the forest as a youngster and he'd left it as a man. His hair was darker than he ever remembered it, even despite its dampness.

'Now,' Zeek continued, 'as per your instructions, Master Fynch, I had these made in a town in the far north. Only recently delivered — I was worried, I'll admit,' he said, reaching behind his counter and straightening, holding an odd contraption of leather straps.

'This is for you, Cassien,' Fynch said. 'I'm sure you'll work out its use.'

Cassien studied what now lay in his hands, knowing instantly what it was. Fynch had obviously commissioned a special holster, not just a belt for a sword, but with straps that wrapped diagonally across his body and over his back so that he could also carry two concealed daggers on his back. Except he'd not brought any weapons. Loup had taken them.

Even so, he was thrilled to tie on the holster and marvelled at how its colour matched the shirt so as to blend in and almost disappear.

Zeek came up behind him and placed the hooded cloak around his shoulders, tying it at his throat. 'This covers everything, but you should find it light enough that if you need to draw your weapons it can be flicked aside.'

'I can see you are happy,' Fynch said to him.

'I am privileged,' he remarked, unsure of what to say. 'Thanks to you both.'

'Well, there's more, Cassien,' Fynch continued. 'All of that leatherwork is useless without its weapons. I presume you have my parcel, Master Zeek?'

'Oh yes, indeed. I have kept these hidden and am very glad to finally pass them to their owner. They are fearsome. I hope you never have to use them, sir,' he said to Cassien. He disappeared once again behind the shop.

Zeek returned, this time carrying a box. 'Impossibly beautiful craftsmanship, Master Fynch, as only Orkyld knows.'

Fynch nodded. 'Master Wevyr is a magician with weapons,' he admitted.

Zeek placed the box with great care on the counter and Cassien, holding his breath, peered in. He could barely believe he was looking at the most beautiful set of sword and daggers he'd ever laid eyes on.

'Aren't you going to hold them?' Fynch asked.

He tore his gaze away and turned it on Fynch. 'These are truly for me?'

'I can't handle them, and I know Master Zeek is a wizard with a needle and thread, but a sword?' Fynch shook his head in mock despair. 'We are old men.'

'I couldn't even swing that more than once, Master Fynch,' his co-conspirator, Zeek, agreed. 'My shoulders aren't what they used to be.'

Cassien reached in, holding his breath, and reverently lifted the two daggers first. 'Caronas,' he whispered.

'Wevyr said you'd know them.'

'Matching. Ancient styling. Perfect balance. To be drawn as a pair over each shoulder.'

'Hence the special holster,' Zeek remarked rather unnecessarily, but it seemed all three men were under the spell of the beautiful blades.

Fynch gave some explanation as Cassien ran his fingers over the metalwork of the throwing daggers. 'The metal on all of these has been forged personally by Master Wevyr of Orkyld. Wevyr said he'll discuss them if you pay a visit. For now I'm to tell you that they contain three metals each, and one additional ingredient that is a secret only Wevyr and I know is in the sword. They have been heated and cooled, hammered and re-heated many times. Their strength is unrivalled but within that strength is a flexibility you will appreciate. That pattern on the blade you see …'

Cassien touched the exquisitely expressed symbol of the Brotherhood — a twisted knot — that ran the length of the blades in a lighter metal. 'Beautiful,' he murmured.

'No other sword or dagger will ever bear that marking again. He said he has done this for you alone.' Fynch smiled. 'He called this the Cassien Collection.'

'Master Fynch, they must be worth a fortune,' Cassien said, shaking his head.

'Indeed, and if Master Zeek wasn't such a reliable man I would have to ask you to use that blade on his throat right now to ensure secrecy.'

Zeek gave a soft squeal of horror. The weapons possessed a presence of their own — frightening in a quiet, elegant way. Fynch chuckled to reassure Zeek that it was a jest, but Cassien frowned. It was the first time that he'd heard a note of insincerity in Fynch's laugh; he wasn't so sure that Fynch had been jesting. In that moment, he saw the toughness, the spine that Fynch possessed; beneath the kindly façade was a man on a mission.

Zeek laughed nervously. 'Oh, Master Fynch, you know I would never discuss private business matters,' he assured him.

Cassien noticed what would be invisible to most people … tiny beads of perspiration on the man's forehead.

'Did you get the boots as I asked, Zeek?' Fynch continued.

'Yes, yes,' he said with forced merriment. 'Let me fetch those too. I hope they will fit.' He disappeared once again.

'He's lying.'

Fynch regarded Cassien. 'Why do you say that?'

'Small signs betray him.'

Fynch had no time to ask more, for Zeek was back, his forehead patted dry of its telltale beads, although Cassien's keen sense of smell picked up the tangy dampness of fresh sweat. He was sure now.

'Here we are,' the merchant said brightly. 'Boots, as you asked, Master Fynch.'

Fynch forced a smile at Cassien. 'Hope they fit.' He could smell the leather that creaked beneath his touch; it was soft yet held the shape of the boot perfectly. He knew they would be comfortable and this was proved as soon as he slipped them easily on to each foot.

'Once again, perfect. Thank you, Master Zeek.'

'Expensive, but worth it. I'm afraid I have no money to return to you, Master Fynch. But then we did —'

'Yes, we did,' Fynch agreed. 'Have you kept any record of the transactions, Zeek?'

'None at all,' the tailor replied, scratching his head. Then he busied himself with clearing away the string that held the boots together. He began talking about the onset of bad weather. 'I hope you don't have far to travel, Master Fynch. There could be a storm in the region.'

Fynch ignored the small talk. 'And you spoke to no-one else about the weapons or the belts, the boots or the garments … or of my presence?' he pressed.

'No, no,' Zeek protested, his tone defensive. 'I am as good as my word,' he said, irritation beginning to crease his face but Cassien saw that his gaze never lighted on Fynch.

Fynch glanced at his travelling companion, but Cassien's attention was drawn abruptly to the mirror … which held the image of Romaine. It was as if time stood still, just for a heartbeat.

He can describe you. He must be dealt with.

Her image shimmered away. He blinked, confused. Fynch was still looking at him.

'Must be time to go,' he said.

Cassien nodded. 'Thank you, Master Zeek.'

'Oh, any time, any time,' he prattled, coming around the counter to show them out. 'Watch that storm now. Farewell to you both,' he said, hurriedly closing the door behind them.

Once outside and out of the shop's line of sight, Cassien pulled Fynch into a small alley. 'He can point me out, lead the enemy to either of us.'

'You're sure?' Fynch pleaded.

Cassien nodded. He chose not to mention Romaine. 'You impressed on me that surprise is our real weapon.' He nodded toward Zeek. 'No matter how innocent, he could have already ruined that.'

'Who could Zeek have told that would trouble us?'

'Does it matter? He's talked, that much is obvious. I have to find out who to and then kill him.'

Fynch's gaze dropped and he seemed to sag like a sack of flour. 'I saw Romaine. I was not privy to what she shared, but I know she was present. She agrees, doesn't she?'

'That he must be dealt with, yes.'

'I've known him a long time.'

'Master Fynch, I've had to take you at your word, trust your instincts, believe all that you claim. I am even having to ignore orders from the Brotherhood.'

'I have no reason to lie to you. Even letting Brother Josse in on this plan was dangerous, and by that I mean it endangered his life. Right now Josse doesn't even know what you look like. He can't describe you. No-one can.'

'Zeek can.'

Fynch nodded. 'Make it silent and clean.'

Cassien heard the familiar soft buzz behind his ears that arrived just before one of Loup's tests. It spurred him on. He spun on his heel and walked back into the shop. It was deserted as before, but this time he didn't wait, easily jumping the counter and pulling back the curtain where he found Zeek clearly packing up.

The tailor turned and gave a soft, terrified shriek. 'Please, I didn't mean to bring any trouble,' he begged.

Cassien took a deep breath. The man was confessing before he'd even exchanged a word. 'Who have you told?'

'No-one important, I promise.'

'Who?' Cassien's arms were relaxed at his side although Zeek's gaze kept flicking to them in case he suddenly moved to draw the weapons that the tailor had just seen him strap on.

'You were sworn to secrecy.'

'Yes,' the man whispered, trembling.

'You were paid handsomely for that secrecy, as I understand it.'

'I was. More than I dared dream of.'

'So why, Master Zeek?'

He shook his head. 'I've never seen so much money at once. I drank too much. I went to the brothel and probably said more than I should. But she was just a whore. What can she do?'

'What did you tell her?'

Zeek began to moan. 'I can't remember. But it wasn't the local brothel. It was the one at Orkyld, when I picked up your weapons. She probably can't even remember the fat, blathering drunk who fell asleep on top of her,' he wept.

Cassien moved closer to the tailor and felt sympathy for him as he shied away. 'She may not mean to but she could pass on information to any number of others. There are men who would want these weapons.'

'You look like you can defend yourself,' Zeek bleated.

'Yes, I can. It's not that. It's the knowledge being out there that I have them. You have marked me by your loose mouth. What is her name?'

'Name?' He shook his head. 'How should I know? I was drunk.'

'Think. It will help your case.'

Encouraged by the titbit of pity, Zeek strained to remember, closing his eyes. He shook his head, his cheeks wobbling. 'I can't remember. Oh, please, I'm sorry.'

'Try harder. Any clue?'

Zeek reached hard. 'Pila? ... No. Petal?' He held his head. 'I can't recall. Something like that. I'm nervous, forgive me.'

'Describe her,' Cassien suggested.

'Flame-haired, arresting eyes. Very popular.' He sighed. 'I was her tenth that day, she said. I know she won't remember me or my ramblings.'

Cassien nodded.

'I will give you the money, whatever remains,' the tailor tried.

He knew it was hopeless. Not only was this man unreliable and untrustworthy, he was also a coward and he would beg on his knees to anyone who came around asking questions about Fynch or his so-called nephew, or the weapons.

'You see that out there, Master Zeek,' he said gently, pointing to the window.

Zeek frowned in spite of his fear and obediently looked ... and it was in that moment of distraction that Cassien acted. In a heartbeat he had wrapped the man up into a hold favoured by the Brotherhood known simply as 'the Tomb'. It was an effective death-hold that depressed a pressure point in the man's neck rendering him unconscious. As soon as Zeek went limp in his arms Cassien laid him gently on the ground.

'I'm sorry, Tailor Zeek,' he murmured and then silently recited the Prayer of Sending that all the Brothers accorded their victims. It was short, committing Zeek to Shar's safekeeping and acknowledging himself as the killer but on Shar's authority to protect the Crown.

'Search your heart until you see it as pure, Brother Cassien,' Josse had said in parting on the day Cassien had been taken to the forest. 'You cannot undertake the work of the Brotherhood until you have no conscience about it.'

'How can we take a life coldly and absolve ourselves of any crime, any responsibility, any remorse?' he'd queried, feeling angry. He recalled his mood well because Brother Josse had snapped at him.

'You don't absolve yourself. Shar does! But that's not the point. You take responsibility for the killing because you are safekeeping the Crown and for no other reason. It is the law that guides us.'

'Outside of the priory we'd be put on trial as murderers. Why are we any different?' he'd argued.

Josse had regained his patience. His voice had been gentle when he spoke again. 'Cassien, our work is on behalf of the royals alone. The ancient royal house of Morgravia that absorbed Briavel and the Razor Kingdom to form its new imperial throne decades ago was the seat of the dragon. You understand this, don't you?' Cassien had nodded. Of course he knew it. The sovereigns of Morgravia — and *only* those of royal blood — were linked with the dragon as their motif, the spiritual power that guided their reign. 'The imperial throne answers only to Shar. Do you understand that too?'

'Of course,' he'd replied, trying not to sound exasperated.

'Then the work of the Brotherhood, which is exclusively on behalf of the imperial throne, answers to no-one other than the imperial ruler. We are above all other courts or claims. It is not our collective conscience that should be troubled.'

Josse had made it sound reasonable. Since then — in the short space of not a decade — the empire's structure had crumbled. The three realms that had been unified had since pulled apart with their quarrels, and now each had local governments and had settled into a loose triumvirate. The imperial throne was still acknowledged as Morgravia but any semblance of empire had fractured. Empress Florentyna had a long road and hard task ahead of her to rebuild what her father had allowed to slip.

He looked down at the unconscious Zeek. He could still walk away and the man would regain his wits shortly. But he was obliged to protect the Brotherhood as much as himself and Fynch. Besides, he'd already said the Prayer of Sending.

He smothered the tailor soundlessly. It would look as though the older man's heart had given out. Cassien quietly overturned a chair to make it appear as though the tailor had simply fallen as his heart failed. He double-checked for any signs that he and Fynch had been in the shop, quickly gathering up the old clothes that Wife Wiggins had supplied and he had discarded. He knew there would be no written record of any of the transactions involving him.

He left silently via the back door but his mind was already reaching toward the next step of damage control. He found Fynch sitting on a low wall just beyond the alley, his head turned toward the sun. He thought the man was smiling but as he drew closer he saw that Fynch was grimacing.

The spry old fellow opened his eyes. There was sorrow reflected. 'Is it done?'

'Yes. No-one will suspect anything other than that his heart gave up.'

'Then our secret is safe.'

'Not quite. There's a whore. He told her things. I don't know how much she knows or whether she could even be bothered to pay attention, but I'm not inclined to gamble.'

'A whore,' Fynch repeated to himself, staring at the ground, although he didn't seem surprised. 'Does it end there?'

'I hope so. But there's more bad news.'

Fynch looked up.

'Her brothel isn't local,' Cassien continued. 'It's in Orkyld.'

Fynch closed his eyes as if in pain.

'We can't undo it, but we can fix it.'

'Quite right,' Fynch replied with resolve.

'I think we should ride, rather than take the coach. It will be faster. I can take us on a more direct route through the forest on horseback.'

'Fine. Go to the stables and organise the horses — you have plenty of coin. I will get some supplies.'

'This Wevyr, he's reliable?'

Fynch snorted. 'We have nothing to fear from Wevyr. The brothers Wevyr, in fact. They understand secrecy — were raised on it. I'm afraid your shave and haircut must wait.'

SEVEN

As their lips touched, Gabe felt as though he had become entirely disconnected from the world. Most of his senses simply shut down. He could hear the whoosh of his own blood pulsing in his head, nothing else. All the subliminal noises of his apartment — the drone of the fridge, the whirr of his computer, the beep from his coffee machine cycling through its stand-by phases — disappeared. Even the more persistent sounds of the building's lift, voices from the street, the horns and general groan of traffic … all of it had been silenced.

Neither could he see his apartment anymore, or anything familiar. What had, at first, been a blank Void began to stir and change: the grey nothingness seemed to swirl and move as though reshaping itself, but even before it had fully formed, he knew what the dreamscape was showing him. He tried to pull back but he was trapped. Angelina's lips held him, and he was sure if his ability to smell or taste were available to him, he would be surrounded by the fragrance of violets on her breath. The scene continued to sharpen. He wanted to scream but could not.

He mentally shook his head. Did not want this. Did not want to face the memory of the wreckage of his car because that would mean confronting the wreckage of his wife and son trapped inside. Dying, if not already dead.

'Release me!' he was sure he pleaded.

But just as the smell of petrol fumes and the tang of spilled blood assaulted him and he felt a cry of anguish racing to his throat, the scene changed. In a heartbeat, he was in the calm of his cathedral — or so he thought. It felt right, the atmosphere was right, but he saw in the shadow a man.

It looked as though it could be him but the figure had his head thrown back in agony.

The link was cut and Gabe snapped back to reality to find himself staring into the smoky eyes of Angelina. Her legs were still wrapped around his hips. She was smiling guiltily, knowingly.

'What did you see?' she asked, unable to mask the smug tone.

'You ... you promised the cathedral.'

'I decided to let you choose and demonstrate just how connected we truly are. You seem upset, Gabe,' she said softly, sounding offended now as she gently touched his cheek. 'Are you frightened by the vision?'

'Did you see it too?'

She nodded. 'I don't understand it though — it's obviously something very personal to you. I smelled petrol. I assume the image was of the motorway accident that killed your family ...' He didn't want her to say another word about it, and perhaps she sensed this. 'Who is the man in the second vision?'

'I don't know.'

'He's your dream.'

'That may be. But I still have no idea.'

'It's obviously very powerful if it can override not only your nightmare of the accident, but more importantly, what I intended to show you,' she remarked.

He frowned at her. 'What are you?'

'I am what I am. I have skills.'

'Skills,' he repeated evenly, gently disengaging her arms from his neck. She obliged by releasing her legs and sitting back on the bed. 'Explain them,' he said, deliberately getting up and walking away from her.

'I can't.' Angelina shrugged, wrapping her arms around her knees, looking like a child again, and uncaring of her nakedness. 'But it's a reason why Reynard keeps me under such close guard.'

Gabe picked up the quill at the mention of Reynard. He stroked the soft swan feather and once again wondered at its significance. 'I don't understand,' he said to her but also to himself about the strange gift.

'No,' she said in a slightly bored, dismissive tone, 'but that's because you're not really listening to me.' Her expression flared into something simmeringly close to anger, and she got up to pace near him. 'I am not of this world, Gabe. You should trust that now. How else can I take you into your world of dreams and nightmares? I can take you to the cathedral in your mind palace. But you need to believe me when I tell you that it's not just a dream or a fiction. It is not of your own mind. It is real. And it's calling to you.'

'And all I have to do is kill you,' he said, flatly, his tone now dripping with disdain. 'Are you aware how your request sounds to any sane person?'

'You see? You don't respect anything I say.'

'Angelina —'

'Well, Reynard can have me then. That's his plan. He will kill me and he will travel to Pearlis.'

'Then why did he involve me?'

'He needed your skills to unlock what he believes is my mute mind and make it possible. He's a fool if he thinks he can outwit me. He's using you, Gabe, not just to provide "access" to me but making sure he can trust my magic. If you now tell him what you've seen, he'll know it's Pearlis. But he doesn't want you to be the one to travel. He wants to go. *He* will be the one who has your cathedral. And the raven spy will have you!' she snapped viciously, as she turned away from him.

It was too convoluted and so little was making sense. He grabbed her, the quill still in his hand. He didn't want to lose her even though all of this was wrong; everything about Angelina and his relationship with her was wrong and yet he didn't want it to end — not like this.

'Wait! I need to understand, to know about you.'

Before he could say another word, she was holding him again, kissing him again; hard this time and angrily. But the sensation of his lips being bitten and bruised disappeared as he was thrust into the frantically busy market square surrounding … no, it was impossible. *Impossible!* Yet Gabe stared in hungry wonder at the huge doors and the façade of the cathedral he knew so well.

He felt the instant calm of close proximity to it. It was real. He realised he was walking up to it, desperate to lay his fingers on the stonework but his hand passed through its soft grey shimmering walls. Drifting through the open doors, he found his familiar place. *The safe place.* He had sat in here so many times in his mind. But it had never been real. Now he could actually feel the worn timber of the pew he sat on, hear the click of the flagstones beneath him, feel the cool of the grey stone around him. It wasn't imagined. He was actually here! Gabe looked around in awe, but just as his thoughts turned to the famed mythical creatures, he was yanked rudely back to his apartment as Angelina's lips withdrew from his.

'Do you believe me now?'

In spite of himself, he nodded, lost for words, staring at her as though she were an alien.

'I can take you there. I can put you physically into the cathedral you yearn for.'

He shook his head like a child trying to blot out a nagging parent. 'I built that place. Its architecture is mine! My specifications … simply to please me.'

'No, Gabe! If it was just a product of your imagination, how can I know it so intimately? You have never discussed it with anyone, have you … least of all me?'

'It is private,' he murmured.

'Exactly!'

'I don't know,' he bleated, confused, frustrated.

'How can I know exactly the scene of your car pile-up if I was not able to tap into your mind?'

He shook his head. He could feel a migraine coming on and dropped the swan quill onto the bed. He rubbed at his temples.

'Touch me,' she demanded, pulling one of his hands to her and placing it on her chest. He could feel her breastbone and her heart thumping. 'Do I feel real?'

'You are real,' he answered.

'You're a sane, smart man, Gabe. You know I'm real so I can't be in your imagination. Even if you think *I'm* delusional, you know you're not. How can I show you what I just have and not be telling you the truth? I have no reason to lie to you.'

'Let me be clear about this … I will not be killing anyone or anything, Angelina,' he said, flicking her hands away.

'It's ridiculous!' he snapped, coming back to himself, regaining his equilibrium. This wasn't the way to speak to a patient, but then neither was being naked alongside her. He'd broken every sacred rule of being a clinical psychologist.

Gabe hadn't realised he'd aired this thought aloud.

'Gabe, I seduced you. You didn't ask me to do anything that I wasn't already planning to do with you,' she said in a soft tone, snuggling close.

Angelina had a knack for wrapping herself around him in such a way that he felt owned by her.

It may have been a hollow reassurance but he was grateful to hear it all the same. Its effect was momentary, though, for he could feel a sinister and familiar sense returning, bringing with it all those old feelings of despair that he'd kept at bay for so long.

'What's wrong?' she shook him.

'It's happening again. I'd escaped the accident, rebuilt my life, walked away from it all,' he said, drawing back from her. He ran a hand through his hair again and stood in his apartment, naked and trembling — but not from the cold.

'Gabe, I can make it all go away.'

He flicked his gaze to her, filled with mistrust and a new sense of loathing as she offered herself to him. He wished Angelina had never come into his life, but even now, he felt desire stirring. She was impossible to resist ... for him, anyway. 'All I have to do is kill you, right?' he said scathingly.

'It is my way back.'

'Your way out, more like,' he sneered.

'Your raven has returned,' she taunted him, pointing out the window.

True enough, the bird was there, black as night, staring at him as it perched on his tiny balcony's railing. It fleetingly occurred to him to wonder precisely how she knew the family of Corvidae. Most people would have called it a crow.

'What does it *want?*'

'He's your enemy. He's keeping you under observation.'

'My enemy,' he said, with a cold smirk. 'Now I must fear even the birds. Why is he my enemy, Angelina?'

'He's following you. It's his role. He is the observer ... the messenger.'

'You're amazing. Do you just make things up as you go along?'

'You don't believe me,' she said, disappointed.

'I know *you* believe it, and I know how powerful that can be. I'm sorry that I can't see what you do. I live in Paris, you live in a world of your own making.'

'Is that so?'

He shrugged. 'We should never have had sex. It's my fault —'

It was Angelina's turn to laugh and it sounded bitter. 'I'm not talking about sex, you fool.' She crawled forward on the bed. 'I'm talking about knowledge. Things that can't be explained, like showing you your own dreams.' Gabe began to shake his head and he could see it infuriated her. 'All right, what if I told you that in three seconds the phone will start to ring, there will be a banging on the door and you'd —'

She didn't finish. His mobile began to vibrate loudly on the kitchen counter and a heartbeat later there was a loud rapping at the door.

Gabe blinked. 'How could …?' he said, staring at the door and then back at her.

'Both are Reynard,' she said calmly. 'He knows you're in here. He will now tell you that he knows I'm here too.'

'I know you have Angelina with you, Gabriel!' Reynard obliged.

Gabe stared open-mouthed, astonished.

'He'll bang again,' she said. 'Twice.' Reynard did just that. 'I shall have to call in the police,' she mimicked in his manner.

'I shall have to call in the police,' Reynard repeated precisely and then simultaneously with Angelina mimicking the gesture, he rapped loudly on the door. 'Open up!' she said silently, but in perfect sinister synchronicity with Reynard. It was as though his deep voice had become hers. Angelina put her hand to her mouth and mimicked a cough in tandem with Reynard. She smiled mirthlessly at Gabe.

'She is trying to escape! Don't help her, Gabriel,' Reynard urged, while Gabe watched her mouth forming each word also. It was chilling. How was she doing this?

'How am I doing it?' she asked, as though she could now hear his thoughts as well as Reynard's. 'I have skills that defy your understanding,' Angelina said, moving toward him as though floating on air. 'But not his,' she sneered, pointing at the door. 'Oh, definitely not. Reynard knows what I'm capable of. He was sent to keep me close, keep me from my mission.'

Reynard's banging and the constant vibration and beeping of the phone's message system began to fade and only Angelina's voice was clear.

'I was sent to guide you to a place called Morgravia. The bird is your enemy. Reynard was sent to stop you making the journey — he is also our enemy. But you and I must look out for one another. I am your protector, Gabe. I can take you to the cathedral, where I know you feel safe. And because I'm not real in the way you accept, you can't kill me. It will be like a dreamscape. My death will *not* be real.'

She was playing with words. No longer making sense. Hitting all the right buttons to confuse him … his mind was becoming fuzzy. He could still hear Reynard, the phone, now the bird cawing at him. He could see it, flapping outside and leaping at the window. He could hear the thump of its body connecting with the panes of glass, the scratch and tap of beak and claws, as it desperately tried to keep his attention. He was being plunged back into the fear and the loathing, the old terror that haunted him after losing his family. And now here was Angelina handing him a knife. Where did that come from?

He tried to speak, but it was as though his mouth was suddenly filled with sawdust. His voice had slowed down and sounded deep and robotic, as though a machine was filtering his words. 'What are you doing?'

'Making it easy, Gabe.' Her voice tinkled like crystals moving against each other. 'Come, travel with me. I will take you to the cathedral. To safety. To peace.' She leapt at him like a cat, fast and lithe; he heard her groan, wrapping her legs around him. He stumbled and they fell awkwardly onto the bed.

He could feel her flesh against his. It was cool and smooth, like marble, and then her lips were on his, her tongue searching, her body moving against him. Reynard, the phone and even the sounds of the raven disappeared. He was back in the Void, waiting for its movement — was he holding his breath? — then the swirling began, and what had been nothing but a grey mist a moment ago began to sharpen into the contours and colours of the scene he most craved.

He was far more exquisitely aware of Angelina this time. He could feel her touch, her skin, her warmth, whereas before, when she'd allowed him to glimpse this place, he'd been aware of nothing. Now all of his senses were his again. It was as though the scene was deepening into reality, while at the same time he could feel Angelina becoming slack against him and a wetness against his belly. For a moment there, he thought his desire to see his cathedral had twisted into something erotic — and who could blame him, with a naked woman wrapped around him?

Without warning, hard on the heels of the sensation of wetness, he felt himself toppling, falling, spinning without control. There was no pain, no flailing about; he didn't know which way was up, but in his mind's eye he was travelling closer to the cathedral. He heard Angelina's voice in his mind.

Let go, Gabe, she whispered. *Let go of Paris … of the world.*

And he did, but as he did so his hand felt something familiar. *The quill.* It was all he had to anchor him and he wrapped his fingers around it, feeling its softness and its solidity. It helped him to focus on one final notion: that to let go fully would be dangerous. It was something in his subconscious, perhaps something from his training as a psychologist. Clutching the quill, in the midst of his confusion and dislocation, Gabe felt a part of him hold back as he began to fall into whatever new dreamscape Angelina was forming for him.

It was the kernel of strength and self-possession and even self-awareness that had brought him through his darkest hours; it was the part of him that urged him to breathe, forced him to wake up and accept the day and to find a way through each new one until the pain of his failure and loss of his family began to diminish into the background of his life. He knew from his counselling work that many people didn't have this special private place in the core of their being to draw upon, to rely upon. It couldn't be taught. Couldn't be bought. Couldn't be acquired. It simply had to be discovered within. He believed everyone possessed this special 'force' and he had encouraged his patients to find it, hunt it down. Many had succeeded, with his help.

He was sure his elders didn't think he possessed any deep strength; they'd viewed him as a coward for running away from confronting the reality of his life, offering wisdom that, in his grief, he couldn't stomach hearing.

The accident was a random event. It's not your fault. Except it was.

You can't be in control all the time. You can. He shouldn't have looked away from the road.

You aren't the enemy. He felt like the enemy.

You can't save everyone. You're a psychologist. Not a god.

Or his personal favourite. *You have to move on.*

He knew they meant well; knew these soothing words worked for some people, but to him they were sickening placations.

And so now as he travelled toward his haven, wondering whether he was dead or alive, he held back the one last part of him that he exercised total control over and no-one else could touch … not even Angelina, with her erotic, irresistible manner. He closed himself around the kernel of his most private self — his soul, as he liked to think of it. He rolled it up tightly, every bit of himself that was truly him — character traits, personality, ideas, memories — and wrapped them in a separate sphere that was no longer connected to his body but hovering invisible within it, and he clung to this sphere ... this new embodiment of himself. It was his only link with the reality he knew. The cathedral was a dream. He couldn't be convinced otherwise but, oh, how he wanted it to be real ... to live it, touch it, smell its scented candles, taste on the back of his palate the fragrance of herbs crushed underfoot.

The scape before him was shaping into brilliant colour; he could hear muffled sounds beginning to sharpen, a faint aroma begin to reach him. This had not happened before. The cathedral began to soar before him in all its imposing, soft grey beauty, every aspect of it coming into sharper focus.

He hadn't been aware of himself as flesh since Angelina kissed him but now he was aware of her body more than his own. And she was pulling away from him in a slow, gentle slump. Her once beautiful dark, smoky greyish eyes gave him a listless gaze in return and he could see the life leaching from them. Her grip around his waist was loosening but all the while the wetness that he recalled feeling, was increasing. It was not his desire ... it wasn't even hers.

It was blood.

He could see its red brightness, gleaming and glistening. He'd been stabbed! Angelina's blade. She'd stabbed him and his hands were covered in his life's blood. As he thought this, he became acutely aware of Angelina's naked body becoming entirely limp as it fell away from him. There was a soft smile playing about her generous lips that had been kissing him so deeply just moments earlier.

And he realised with deeper shock that it was Angelina who was dead. And the knife was in *her* belly ... it was *her* bright blood, *her* life taken.

He had killed her, just as she'd asked.

He looked around, desperate for help, the name of Reynard springing to his lips, but he was no longer in his apartment and he was no longer near his cathedral. He was nowhere at all that he recognised.

Reynard burst through the door of Gabe's apartment with an anxious-looking concierge following hot on his heels and making loud protests.

The small man fell instantly silent when they saw what was lying on the bed.

The ghastly scene and the iron smell of freshly spilled blood combined to make the concierge gag and he rushed for Gabe's kitchen sink, retching helplessly before raising his head, his complexion ashen and expression filled with horror.

'This is monstrous,' he wailed. 'I'm an old man, I shouldn't have to —'

'Go downstairs and call the police now!' Reynard ordered him.

The man obeyed blindly, staggering out of the apartment.

Reynard approached the body of Angelina, her belly ripped open like a macabre smile. Blue-grey ropy intestines spilled in a glistening, gelatinous mess from the gash of the fleshy grin. Her eyes were open, distant, as though looking a long way past the horizon, but they were seeing nothing. He knew that. This was simply the corpse that some poor bastard would have to clean up and he could imagine all the forensics and pathology tests that would now follow. Few questions would be answered. And he would be here for none of it.

Next to her lay the blood-spattered weapon that had inflicted the damage. He nodded, turned away and walked to the French windows. As he moved, his attention was caught and held by the slender box with its navy satin that he'd given Gabe on his birthday. It was open and empty. The quill was removed; he cast a searing gaze around the apartment, but it was nowhere to be seen. Reynard sighed with a relief that felt more like deep sorrow and returned to what he'd set out to do. He pulled the two windows toward him, opening them, and stepped out onto the balcony.

'It is done,' he said to the now silent waiting raven.

It watched him, head cocked to one side as Reynard clambered with difficulty up onto the balcony railings and teetered. Reynard gave a last look at the bird that had been his co-conspirator and nodded with a sad smile. 'Our part is over. I have achieved what I must. I cannot be taken alive by the police. You know what to do.'

The bird leapt at its companion and shoved at his head hard with its feet. It didn't take any more than that to send Monsieur Reynard toppling from the penthouse floor of the apartment building, muttering a strange incantation as he fell to his death.

The raven blinked at the lifeless shape crumpled below, sad for Reynard, who had been brave to the last, before it leapt into the air, flapping its strong wings and lifting itself high above Gabe's apartment to fly with purpose toward Notre Dame Cathedral.

It ascended higher still above the sweeping gothic architecture until it was a dark speck in an overcast sky. Only the keenest of sights would have seen the raven bank slightly and pause for a heartbeat before it began a fast descent, shaping itself into an arrow as though shot from a master bowman. Its target was clear, its aim was perfect. Moments later the bird impaled itself soundlessly on the sharp piece of wood it had previously marked out for this very task.

The raven's last thought, cast toward another world, in the hope that his king would hear him, was a plea to remember the being that was Ravan as a brave member of his flock. And as the bird closed its eyes, its immortal spirit transcended the broken, pierced body of the host and fled.

EIGHT

As Reynard was banging in an apartment door in Paris, Fynch and Cassien had already been travelling north in Morgravia for six hours at a steady clip. Fynch had been determined not to wear out the animals with hard riding, and as much as Cassien urged him to push the beasts to a gallop, Fynch refused.

'If we cover eighteen miles today, it will be a good journey and our mounts will have time to rest, to eat and be fresh for tomorrow.'

'Where will we reach by this evening?'

'By sundown we should crest Vincen's Saddle.' At Cassien's frown Fynch gestured with his hands toward the rise ahead. 'The path leads us up this hill and then another soon after, and from afar the landscape looks like a horse's saddle.'

'From a dragon's back one could be fanciful about any landscape,' Cassien suggested in a wry tone.

Fynch smiled and it was full of affection. 'Indeed.' But that was all. Cassien decided he would not pry further.

'And Vincen?' he said instead.

'No idea.' They both grinned. 'There's an excuse for an inn in the village below. The village is called, rather fancifully I might add, Partridge Vale, and the inn is even more deluded, boasting the name of the Queen's Rest, but the ale is honest and the food passable.'

'I don't eat much,' Cassien admitted. 'I can go without if necessary.'

'Nothing doing. Just don't eat the pigeon pie if it's on.'

'Why?'

'You don't want to know,' Fynch said archly. He slid off his horse and walked it to the stream they'd been following for several miles. Cassien followed suit. It was a lonely road and they'd met few other travellers, certainly none in the last few hours.

He leaned against his horse as it quenched its thirst, and became aware of the new weaponry perched around his body. It was hard to credit how comfortable it felt — as though it had always been there or had been moulded to him. He blinked, realising another aspect about the weapons as he watched Fynch dig out an apple and feed it to his mount.

'Have you noticed that Wevyr's weapons make no noise?'

'I wondered how long that would take,' Fynch replied absently.

'How can metal at my side make no noise?'

'Ask Wevyr.'

'Doesn't it intrigue you?'

Fynch changed subjects. 'You'll need to push yourself to mix with people. Stoneheart is like a small city within the larger one of Pearlis. The palace is going to challenge you in ways you can't imagine and one of the most simple and yet perhaps most daunting hurdles will be feeling comfortable around the endless movement. Stoneheart never sleeps. There are always people working.'

'I'm sure I'll manage.'

'You have to do more than manage, son. I am asking you to infiltrate the life of a queen. It is a tricky task and the politics surrounding her will make you dizzy.'

Cassien nodded. 'It doesn't matter about me. What matters is her life. I'm being sent in to keep her safe.'

'Well said.'

'Tell me, what does the queen think of this notion of a complete stranger walking into her life and shadowing her every move?'

'I don't think she minds the notion yet.'

'Yet?'

Fynch shrugged. 'I don't think she minds just yet because she doesn't know you're coming,' he explained.

'Shar's wrath!'

The older man scratched genially at the close beard that made him look as though he'd been dusted with flour. 'Florentyna will see reason, I'm sure of it.'

'Reason,' Cassien murmured, shaking his head. 'What reason should I go with? A demon is coming to kill you, your majesty, and this man you see before you who, by the way, has just walked out of the woods, is here to keep you safe?'

'Sarcasm is a cheap form of attack, Cassien, or didn't Brother Josse teach you that?' Fynch chided. 'You must trust me. I think Florentyna does. I just don't think most of the people around her do.'

'Who else trusts you? Knows about this?'

'Two others.'

'And you trust them?'

He nodded and his expression became as sombre as Cassien could remember. 'We should keep riding.' He led his horse back to the road and Cassien followed, easily catching the apple that Fynch tossed over his shoulder for Cassien's horse.

'I have entrusted only one man with the information you now know. He is from the court, one of the most senior noblemen and a close advisor to the queen. He was, to some extent, like a father to her after she lost her own.'

'That's a relief. I'll likely need some allies in the palace.'

'He's not in the palace, I'm afraid … not any longer.'

'So how does he help us?'

'He helps by observing someone.'

'Master Fynch,' Cassien said, pausing, 'I'm going to have to ask you to be clearer. You were specific when you wanted me to leave the forest with you and yet you fall back on being vague now.'

Fynch stared at him thoughtfully. 'You're right. But what I have to say you will find hard to believe.'

'Are you sure?' he said, a tone of scepticism creeping into his voice. He heard it and tempered it, schooling his tone to be respectful. 'Given what I've already had to accept perhaps you will allow me to be the best judge of what I find credible.'

Fynch nodded and began slowly. 'Someone I think of as my friend and who was a close counsel to the queen, though astonished by my story, agreed to humour me and introduce me to the sovereign so I could bring her my warnings directly. The queen, though attentive, was dissuaded by her sister, Darcelle, who wields considerable influence.'

Cassien's gaze narrowed. 'Hmm, that does change the complexion of this situation.'

'Yes.'

'Why did Florentyna go along with her sister's decision if she trusts you?'

'Believing she *trusts* me is probably stretching the truth,' Fynch admitted. When Cassien's mouth tightened, he hurried on. 'But she listened without scorn. However, without the close counsel of my ally in her presence — his name was Chancellor Reynard by the way — she was persuaded by the others. Her sister believes I am some sort of mad old fellow who has been chewing the dreamleaf or is in his cups.' Fynch stopped his horse and whispered something to it before he climbed into the saddle.

Quietly, Cassien followed suit.

'You see, Cassien, Queen Florentyna has no idea who I am. She likes me, humours me, perhaps because I'm old, more likely as someone who once knew her father.'

'Why haven't you told her the truth?'

'You admit the only reason you believe me, trust me, is because of a wolf and because I know about your magical roaming. Do you really think a modern young queen — an empress, in fact — such as Florentyna is going to believe in magic?'

'Have you asked her?'

'I didn't dare.'

'Well, surely —'

'And Chancellor Reynard assured me it would be dangerous to permit such talk around the palace. Too many ears. It plays right into the hands of Cyricus. We don't know who our enemies are.'

'Why did Reynard trust you, then?'

Fynch shrugged. 'He comes from a line of courtiers — advisors to the Crown. His great-grandfather — a Briavellian, I think — was an old, old friend of King Valor, Valentyna's father. So Empress Valentyna brought him to her court and enjoyed his counsel. The Reynards have enjoyed royal favour ever since ... I suppose I was able to tell him things about his grandfather, for I remember his grandfather as a very young lad and I was not much older than him. I had followed Wyl Thirsk to the Briavellian palace ... I won't go into it.

'Anyway, we met briefly and talked as lads do. I needed help at the time and all I had as currency was a small token my mother had given me. She had carved her and my initials into a disc of wood that she'd polished and varnished.' He shrugged at Cassien. 'We were very poor, you understand. I showed Reynard's great-grandfather that disc and he liked it. So I snapped it in half and gave him one of the halves, which contained my initial.'

'What did you exchange?' Cassien asked.

Fynch smiled. 'Food for my companion — a dog called Knave. Anyway, I was relating this story to Reynard in the hope that it would convince him that I knew his family. But he did better than I'd hoped. Reynard produced the half-disc. It was a valueless trinket that had been passed down but he had always loved it.' Again Fynch shrugged. 'I could have wept to see it again after so many decades. I was able to show him my half, which joined with his perfectly, and told him the initial he held was mine. He was astonished, shaken, of course. He didn't really want to believe it but could not discredit it. He began to listen and the more I told him, the more he wanted to assist but was almost embarrassed that he believed me. You can understand how far-fetched it all sounds?'

Cassien nodded. If not for Romaine …

Fynch continued. 'Despite logic, he followed his instincts and agreed to throw in his lot with me. He said he'd help but we could not press her majesty again. He offered to attempt the journey of shifting worlds that I spoke of.' Fynch lifted a sad shoulder. 'I don't think he ever believed it would work.'

'How do you know it has worked?'

Fynch's expression clouded. 'I don't but I have faith that the imminent sign — the confirmation — will come.'

'How are you so sure that this demon exists? That he's coming?'

'Because of Aphra. She can't hide herself as well as Cyricus. She leaves a trace.'

'Magical, you mean?'

'Curiously visceral, actually, except it comes to me through ethereal means. Does that make sense to you?

Cassien gave an uncertain shrug. 'Go on.'

'She became suddenly active recently.'

'Here?'

Fynch looked pained. 'No, she's still in another world.'

Cassien took a slow breath but kept his expression even. 'And you know this because …?'

'I could smell violets on the wind. There are no violets in the Wild to yield such perfume.'

Cassien's lips thinned with growing consternation. 'And that's her trace?'

'Yes,' Fynch said softly. 'Breath of violets.'

'And if she's active then so is Cyricus?'

'Cyricus uses her. She is his acolyte and most effective minion. She can be anything to anyone in the female form … her preferred shape. It would take me centuries to teach you all I know, all I've seen, all I've read, all I've gleaned through my long, long life. You have to choose to trust me.'

Cassien breathed out and his shoulders slumped slightly. He scratched at his beard, well aware of needing a shave — he must look a sight, he thought, in fine clothes and ragged chin. 'Right, so you realised Aphra was active,' he repeated. 'What else?'

'I needed her followed. She was our only route to Cyricus … the only connection I could trust.'

'So Reynard agreed to follow Aphra,' Cassien presumed.

'Yes. Reynard was entirely unknown to Aphra or Cyricus. He possesses not an ounce of magic. Only I knew the secret of world travelling. He trusted me, and his fears for Florentyna overcame any dread he might have had of my magic. I sent him, guiding him to Aphra's trace.' Fynch shook his head sadly. 'I can't watch him unless I leave this world but I needed to get you involved. Before you ask, the only way I will know that he has found what we seek is through his death.'

Cassien stared somewhat dumbfounded at Fynch. 'The queen's chancellor has to die to get a message to you?'

'Former chancellor. Yes. It's a special sort of death,' Fynch admitted. 'It allows him to utter words that will be carried across worlds and I will know that he's found Aphra. And if she has effected her death, I will know she's on her way back to our land to meet up with Cyricus, who was trapped here.'

'In the Void,' Cassien qualified.

The old man shook his head. 'I wish it were still so. I blame myself. In trying to protect the Crown, I have made it vulnerable. Over the years I have sent three people out of our world to another, all connected with seeking Aphra. Reynard was the last.' Cassien wanted to ask who each was but Fynch kept talking. 'I considered myself clever … thinking that if I could retain control of events then I could contain Cyricus. I thought it wise to know what the enemy is doing. I designed a way to bring Aphra back to our world and I planned to fling her once and for all into the Void with her demon and then our world would not be troubled by them again. But what I didn't realise is that using the Wild's powerful magic for sendings weakened the Void's hold on Cyricus. He escaped, although he doesn't know why it occurred; his glee is so intense that he isn't questioning it. He doesn't know me, has no sense of me. However, I've set something in motion now that I must stop. He will use Myrren's magic, of that I have no doubt.'

Cassien shook his head at the complexity of Fynch's tale. 'And you'll know it's begun.'

'Exactly. If she has found her way back, she has her mortal host.'

'Wait. You said there was another person you trusted who was helping.'

Fynch straightened. 'Reynard was a man — mere mortal. This second companion is a creature. He is a friend of mine who was once a bird, then a man, and learned he could only be a man in *this* world, but that he could still be his magical bird shape in other worlds.' Fynch smiled sadly in the lowering light. 'It's complicated, Cassien. Suffice to say Ravan is one of the most special creatures I've ever had the privilege to know: formed by a god, answerable to that god, but a friend of men.'

'And?'

'I think when we met on my travels Ravan was a little lost. He needed a purpose. I gave him one. Reynard couldn't be everywhere; I needed him watching Aphra, while Ravan kept her target under observation.'

'The host that you speak of, you mean?'

Fynch nodded. 'Ravan readily agreed to be the second observer.' Cassien gave an encouraging gaze to Fynch. 'Ravan knew he too would have to relinquish his life — in this case, his life as a bird — in order to get back to our world. He will be safe, will walk as a man again. Reynard sadly cannot survive if he sees out his mission.'

They were all meaningless names to Cassien although he tried to sound respectful of Fynch's obvious sorrow. 'If Cyricus is trapped here, what is Aphra doing in her world?'

'If my hunch is right, she's sourcing a carrier to get herself back. It will need to be a very special individual who is somehow in tune — knowingly or otherwise — with other worlds.'

'But you don't even know what this vessel, this man in this other world, looks like.'

He hesitated. 'No,' Fynch then said, 'but Reynard is hoping to mark him somehow. We couldn't plan for something we neither knew nor understood. Fortunately, I *was* able to send him on the trace of the violets almost directly to Aphra, but it was his decision how he would clue me into the carrier from then on.'

Cassien took a long, slow breath as he digested all that he'd learned. He realised they'd crested the second rise that formed Vincen's Saddle and down below them was the village known as Partridge Vale beginning to sprawl outward, perhaps with visions of becoming a town — but not yet. 'Looks like we're here,' he remarked.

'Tomorrow we'll reach Orkyld.'

Cassien was pleased by the sight of softly smoking chimneys and the hint of cooking on the air. 'Can you smell that?' he asked. 'No pigeon pie, Fynch, but roasted chicken, I think. It's been a long time since I've tasted that treat.'

He expected Fynch to smile but his companion looked suddenly troubled. 'Violets,' he breathed. Then looked at Cassien, his gaze raw and intense. 'You smell roasted poultry. I smell Aphra.'

Fynch swayed in the saddle and Cassien leapt down from his horse and rushed to the old man just as he slipped sideways. Cassien's fast reflexes caught him and carried him easily. The man was as light as his namesake.

'Master Fynch!' he cried, looking around for help, but there was none.

He hoisted Fynch over his shoulder and grabbed the reins of both horses to lead them into a nearby grove. After lowering Fynch gently to the leaf litter, he secured both animals. Returning, he noticed that the man he had thought looked so youthful, now suddenly appeared as ancient as the landscape they were traversing and the gnarled trees that shrouded them. His eyes were closed, his features slackening into wrinkles and creases, his skin taking on the look of parchment.

'Fynch!' he called again, rubbing his companion's cold hand.

To his relief the man stirred. 'It is done,' he murmured.

'What?'

Fynch opened his eyes and their light had dimmed: no longer like bright gemstones but more like pebbles on a shingle beach, dashed and rolled around until dulled. He spoke again, croaky this time. 'My friends … their souls have spoken. Aphra is travelling and she's bringing someone with her.'

Gabe woke properly, coming to his senses gasping, hands on knees, to draw breath. There was pain everywhere. He couldn't isolate it. Even his mind hurt.

Be strong, Gabe, said a voice he knew. He straightened with a groan and looked around. He seemed to be alone and had probably imagined Angelina's voice. He was in a shed of some sort … no, a barn but it was huge and full of wheat or barley in sheaves. How quaint. He staggered to the enormous doors and pushed on them. They were solid and heavy, but also barred from outside.

Through a wide gap in the doors he could see beyond to a patchwork of fields — uneven, ragged oblongs of brown and gold, and even pale grey for as far as he could see. There were people working … they were dark specks but he could make out signs of labour. No machinery, just the regular swinging of arms, probably with some sort of tool, he thought. And suddenly a man was approaching. Gabe gave a soft sound of panic and lurched back as the man lifted the bar and unlocked what sounded like a padlock. Sunlight burst in as the doors creaked back. Gabe blinked in the soft rays and saw an elderly man in a black robe regarding him.

'How did you get in here?' the man asked.

Gabe shook his head. 'I don't know.'

'You're naked, man!'

He looked down, only now aware that he was indeed standing there without a stitch on. He cupped himself, embarrassed. 'I'm sorry. I don't know what I'm even doing here. Where the hell am I?'

The man lost his immediate fear and his voice softened. 'Too much cider for you, eh?' he admonished gently. 'Well, I don't know how you got in here, but go on, be gone with you. Quickly now, or I'll have to tell Master Flek and he does so hate for anyone to be in the tithe barn.'

'Who are you?'

'I'm Pel. No-one important.' Gabe stared at him. 'Why do you look so scared? I'm not going to punish you. What's your name?' he asked.

'Gabe … Gabriel. I'm lost.'

'Where do you hail from? Perhaps I can help,' Pel said kindly. 'Is that a quill you've got in your hand, son? I hope you haven't taken that from here?' Gabe shook his head. 'No, I don't recognise it, but even so, a naked man and a fine quill.' He made a small tutting sound.

Gabe's sense of dislocation intensified. *Say nothing!* Angelina snapped and he only now realised she was talking in his mind ... Gabe now felt deeply frightened but urged himself to stay calm, draw on all his counselling skills and practise what he knew. This was some sort of anxiety attack, for sure. He just needed to take a deep breath and be rational.

'Mr Pel. I don't know where I find myself. Forgive me, but I need your help.' He heard Angelina hiss inside his head. 'I'm from Paris.'

'Paris?' Pel asked reasonably. 'I can't say I know that place.'

'Paris ... France,' Gabe insisted.

The man shook his head with an expression of gentle concern. 'No, my boy, I can't bring it to mind. It's obviously not in Morgravia or I'd know. Is it somewhere in Briavel perhaps?'

'Morgravia ... Briavel? Where are these places?'

Pel frowned, his concern clearly deepening. 'Do you need a physic, son?'

'A physic?'

'Perhaps you need a potion to clear your head. You're in Morgravia, west, about two days' ride from Pearlis. Do you mean Pearlis, not Paris?'

'The cathedral,' Gabe bleated, suddenly recognising something of what the man was talking about.

'That's right,' Pel said, his expression now one of relief.

'Mr Pel?'

'Yes, Gabriel?'

'I don't belong here. I don't know how I come to be here. It was magic. One minute I was in Paris, the next moment I find myself in your barn. She worked a spell on me. I don't understand it. I've been brought here to another world from ...' Gabe shook his head as his voice trailed off. He knew he was making no sense, could see confusion reflected in the kind man, who was beginning to lose patience with him.

'Have you been drinking liquor?'

'A little wine, mainly coffee,' he answered obediently, without thinking.

It was the wrong answer. Pel smiled knowingly as if he understood that alcohol was behind Gabe's troubles. 'Hurry now, son,' Pel urged. 'Master Flek isn't nearly as forgiving as I. And it's obvious you haven't stolen anything. Get yourself dressed and be on your way. Everything will make more sense when you've cleared your head.'

The man was not speaking French, Gabe suddenly noticed, and yet he understood the language, though it wasn't one he recognised. Strangely, he seemed to be absorbing the words and their meaning and responding without consciously making any effort.

The stranger smiled. 'You are in the Harpers Riding tithe barn. We're not far from Ramon, but a long way from Pearlis, where I presume you're from.' He went to the door and pointed down the slight incline. 'Head that way, you'll come into the town. If you're from Port Wickel, though, bear left at the ten-mile marker near the crossroads. It's quicker on foot taking that route. But be warned. It's busy as a beehive, what with the royal ship from Cipres arriving.' He walked outside and turned to Gabe. 'I presume your clothes are thrown around. Gather them up and get yourself clad. I'll be back to lock the doors shortly,' he said, but not unkindly. He looked up at the sun. 'Master Flek will inspect after his quart of milk, which he likes to take around now. He's a creature of habit is Master Flek, so he won't be late. Don't be found or he'll have you thrown in the stock, or even irons, without hearing any explanation.'

Gabe nodded, so bewildered he didn't know what else to say. The man disappeared down the hill and Gabe moved further inside the gloomy light of the barn. The shaft of golden light that streamed in through the doors lit a tiny cloud of gnats that bounced and flitted. He swatted at them. What had happened? He had been in his apartment. The phone was ringing and buzzing, a great black bird was beating on the glass of his windows … and Reynard threatening outside the door.

'Angelina!' he called, his voice cracking as it shattered the silence, recalling suddenly a blade and blood … then blackness.

I am with you, Gabe. You must not fret.

He swung around. 'Where …?' He didn't finish, her voice hadn't come from nearby — it had come from within.

I am here. Inside you, she said and he could hear her satisfaction that she'd shocked him.

'Inside? What are you talking about?'

118

You can feel me if you try hard. You brought me with you. I know you are thinking about the knife and all that blood, but it wasn't really me, Gabe. I tried to tell you that. I was never truly of that world ... but then neither are you.

'I don't understand any of this.' He leaned against a tall stand of sheaves.

You released me from that body. Made me free to come here. I won't stay long with you. I will find a new host.

Gabe had no patience for the nonsense in his head and yet couldn't explain Angelina's voice. He was either spiralling into madness — perhaps she'd drugged him? — or, more likely, he was in a nightmare. He had always dreamed vividly. He pinched himself. He felt the bruise of it, but didn't wake — the barn did not disappear. 'Where am I?'

That man just told you. Harpers Riding.

'Where is Harpers Riding?'

He told you that too.

'I heard him. But I am not familiar with these places. I want to know exactly where I am.'

'Not far from Ramon,' said a new voice — a gruff one. It belonged to a huge man carrying a sharp-looking tool. He was dressed in leather motley. 'Ramon is a biggish town in the far southwest of a realm called Morgravia,' he continued. 'Morgravia's capital is Pearlis, arguably the principal city of the triumvirate of Morgravia, Briavel and the Razor Kingdom ... or should I say former triumvirate? To say empire these days is to be hopeful rather than truthful. It teeters on a knife edge.' He smiled.

Gabe was on his guard. Nothing was making sense.

'Are you ... are you Flek?'

'I was. Not any longer.' The man grinned and Gabe could see whiskers of milk at the corner of his mouth. Hadn't Pel said Flek was taking his quart of milk?

'Aphra?'

'I am well, beloved,' Gabe said but while it was his voice, he hadn't spoken. Angelina had. He gagged, coughed.

Flek laughed.

Gabe felt lightheaded. Nothing was making sense: not this conversation, not these surrounds, not the voices talking at him, nor the

119

tithe keeper before him, nor Angelina talking in his head and using his voice.

'You see, Gabriel,' the man continued, shocking him by knowing his name, 'while Flek was handy, he is a dangerous vessel for me because he is known. But you … well, you are "clean", for want of a better word. You can move around Morgravia unnoticed by anyone or their magic — at least for a while.'

'I don't —'

The man stopped him speaking by holding a hand in the air. 'It doesn't matter what you understand.' The words were sympathetic but neither the man's tone nor his expression were. 'We hunted far and wide for you. And of course my beautiful Aphra found you. You're perfect. There's barely a handful of people like you in your world, who dream as you do, but you trespassed into our world because you worked so hard at your dreamings. That cathedral of yours was perfect in every way, except that you couldn't touch it. And the reason it was perfect was because you were seeing it in a different reality. Am I making any sense to you?'

'None at all.'

'Oh well,' Flek said jovially, 'it's of little consequence. Now I need you to kill me.'

'What?' Gabe shrank away, shock trilling through him.

Be calm, Gabe. It's just like before, Angelina, or the voice in his mind that the tithe keeper called Aphra, soothed. *It won't hurt. He is already dead. What you see is simply a shell.*

'Stop it, both of you. Whatever you are, whatever you're doing, it stops now.' His voice shook.

'Run this blade across this man's throat, Gabriel, or I will do it to yours. It's a simple choice,' the tithe keeper threatened.

Gabe realised he was trembling. Vulnerable and naked, he was struck by how many of his patients must have felt a similar fear. Alone, isolated, in danger.

'Let me go back.'

'Too late. Nothing to go back for.'

You're a murderer now, Gabe, Angelina said. *They will have found my body, stabbed with that ugly blade, blood everywhere in your apartment. No, there's nothing in Paris for you. But you can help us. You've always wanted to help me. You've begun by bringing me back — thank you. Now I need you to help my master. You have no choice. Kill or die. Either way, he lives. Your body might as well live, too.*

The body that belonged to Flek advanced on him and Gabe gave a frigid yelp. He was so frightened he couldn't run to save himself. He realised he was still holding his quill, which in an instinctive, defensive gesture, he now held in front of him and felt it press against the chest of his attacker. In his moment of panic, he heard a sizzling sound and the smell of scorched flesh, but then the keen blade of a farm tool he didn't recognise flashed before him.

When Pel returned he was astonished and deeply saddened to see a naked body lying among the sheaves. As he ran over he presumed it was the stranger with the quill. But he leapt back shocked when he pulled at the shoulder of the fallen figure to see someone he recognised. It was Master Flek, the tithe barn manager. Flek's blood was being hungrily drunk by the sheaf of barley the body had been slumped over. A distraught Pel sucked in a breath.

'Shar's pity, Master Flek, what befell you?' he murmured, terrified by the gaping wound at the man's throat. Pel shook his head, ashamed that he'd taken the naked man for a decent one. 'Murder,' he whispered, guilt-ridden. 'But why? What could you give him other than your clothes?'

He ran from the tithe barn as fast as his old legs would move him, down the hill again. He had noted the stranger's features and he would be able to describe him to the authorities. They would catch him, and Pel would stand at his trial and point him out as a cold-blooded killer of one of Ramon's most honest men.

NINE

Fynch could not be persuaded. He was seriously weakened and Cassien was loathe to argue with him.

'Go on alone!' Fynch demanded. 'I am now a liability to you.'

'And where will you go?'

'Never you mind.'

'How will you go if you can't even sit on a horse?'

'That's not your concern. I have my ways,' Fynch said breathlessly. 'Now help me up, please.'

Using Cassien for support, Fynch hauled himself upright and stood there for a few heartbeats, winning his breath back, finding a reserve of strength from somewhere. He looked like all the wind had been punched out of him, his skin was waxy pale and his limbs had a tremor.

'Are you weakened through sadness, or are you physically injured by the news?'

'Both,' Fynch wheezed. 'The message of Aphra travelling is delivered through magic. It sucked all my strength … to reach me, for me to hear it, for Reynard to send it. Ravan will be travelling too. I have no idea where he will emerge but he will not be well for a long time.' He shook his head grimly. 'Cyricus cannot have this land as his playground!'

'Verily!' Cassien replied almost as a chant, using the old language of Shar's scripts to acknowledge something as right or true.

Fynch continued. 'We are fighting an unknown enemy and we don't know his strengths or weaknesses. We are the only two people walking this land who know that he's coming.'

'Then we go to the queen and we tell her,' Cassien tried again.

'And who must she fear? He could be you, he could be me; he could be her wine servant or her page, the stable master or her chancellor. He could be her chambermaid or the cook … her seamstress or the woman who draws her bath. Do you understand the magnitude of our problem?' He coughed, weakened from the effort of speaking.

Cassien nodded unhappily. 'Then what?' he asked, opening his palms in submission.

'This weakness of mine is potent. I didn't foresee it and I am sickening fast.' It was true. In just the last few moments, Fynch's complexion had worsened from pale to sallow, bordering on grey. All the light and geniality had fled, so his face appeared almost a mask of itself. 'I am a burden and a risk because of my magic. I don't know if Cyricus will be looking for it, but I can't take the chance that he is. We must keep him under the illusion of secrecy until we work out who he is.'

'For me to kill.'

'Precisely.'

'If we follow the pattern of Myrren's magic, can he then not just become me?'

'Normally, yes. But you have your roaming magic. This is what makes you so important, my boy.'

Cassien looked at him puzzled.

'Let me sit down,' Fynch said, pointing to a fallen tree. 'I don't have much time.'

'Before what?'

'Before I must leave you,' Fynch said, gasping as Cassien helped him to sit. 'I'm no good to you now. I have the breath only to say this once. Go to Orkyld. Do what you must. Then go to Florentyna and convince her that she must have you as her paladin. She's a queen of her era and doesn't go in for these old-fashioned ideas. I don't care what it takes for you to persuade her. Be at the side of her majesty. Keep her safe.'

'Master Fynch, I don't even know who I'm looking for.'

'Look for whoever has the most to gain. He is a demon and arrogant. While he could easily be the stableboy or the baker, he is likely too proud and would want nobility. I will help if and when I can.' Fynch sighed to himself. 'I wish I had given the possibility of dying some consideration,' he said with a sad chuckle.

'You can't die, Fynch,' Cassien said, sitting next to his companion and taking his hand, which was cool, the skin papery.

'Oh, I can. And I might. But I'm hoping the gods grant that this is not yet my time, although my time is surely overdue. You know all that is important now, Cassien.' Fynch touched his cheek affectionately. 'You are strong here,' he said, moving his hand to Cassien's chest. 'The heart of a wolf. But strongest of all here,' he added, tapping a finger at Cassien's temple. 'Use your magic wisely. Gifts from the gods always come at a price.' He gave Cassien a lingering look before he nodded. 'Now go, my boy. Ride for Orkyld. Ride through the night if you must. You have two horses now, both big-hearted.'

'But you —'

'I have no need of horses,' he wheezed and his voice had dropped to a whisper. He was fading before Cassien's gaze.

'Fynch ...'

'Go, Cassien. Leave me now.' It was not a request.

He stood reluctantly, watching Fynch slump.

'Don't make me beg,' Fynch pleaded. 'He will win if neither of us acts. And our Crown is in jeopardy. That's your path.'

'It's only because of the oath I took to the Brotherhood that I leave you now.' Cassien finally turned on his heel.

The horses whickered as he bound one to the other. He would not be having any roast chicken tonight, he thought with regret. He climbed into the saddle.

'How will I find you?' he demanded, knowing the anger in his voice was worry but wishing it didn't sound so harsh. He hoped Fynch understood.

'I will find you, if Shar permits it,' Fynch said cryptically. He raised a hand slightly but couldn't raise his head. 'Farewell, my boy.'

With his heart hurting and his mouth set in an angry slash, Cassien turned the horses and left without another word. Below him the lamplight from the village twinkled charmingly, oblivious to his fears.

Everything always looks better in the morning. Who said that to him? Was it his mother? No, he couldn't even remember her. Was it Brother Josse? Possibly. His childhood was so blurred, but he remembered he had a brother, if not much else about him. It was his brother's existence he remembered, and his determination that one day they would both make the pilgrimage to the cathedral and discover their mythical beasts. Whatever happened to their family? Why was he given to the Brotherhood in the first instance?

If he survived this test he would find his blood family. It comforted him to think that people might exist out there who belonged to him and he to them. Lost in his thoughts, and with the wind in his face, Cassien didn't hear the soft growl in the distance behind him.

Orkyld, a place Cassien had always wanted to visit, was no small, sleepy town. It felt like a city and all of its noise and colour assaulted him. He was holding his breath as he guided his pair of horses toward its toll-gate until he realised no-one — least of all the toll-man — was paying him any attention.

Cassien flipped the toll-man a coin to enter the thriving town and gave him no time or reason to share words.

The coin was caught nimbly and he heard its soft ring as it hit the rest of the coins in the small sack. Clearly, Orkyld was flourishing. He carefully dismounted his horse, still amazed that the weapons he carried were silent, in order to walk and consider who to ask directions from. Who would be the least interested in him?

He saw a sandy-haired lad with a sack of something that was obviously heavy across his back and shoulders. The youngster was nearly bent double.

'Hey, boy, I'll give you a coin if you'll stop and give me some directions.'

'Where do you need to go?' the boy asked, breathing heavily with the effort of pausing.

'What are you carrying?' Cassien asked, looking at him in amazement. 'You'll break your back.'

The lad managed a grin beneath his load. 'Tapestries, sir. I'm delivering them to one of the noble houses.'

'I hope they pay you well. I'm looking for an inn. But the town looks so busy I don't know where to begin.'

'It's always like this, sir,' the boy wheezed. He reeled off a couple of names and rough directions.

'Thanks,' Cassien said, showing the boy the bronze regent before slipping it into the lad's pocket.

'Of course, sir, most men of your kind stay at the Yew Inn. It's away from the main square, a bit quieter — it's in the centre of the swordsmiths.'

Cassien frowned. Perhaps his clothes were marking him, for the boy surely couldn't see his sword beneath his cloak. 'What makes you think that's where I should be?'

'It's a better sort of establishment. And, with your weapons, sir, I'm presuming you are here to talk to the guild or one of the smiths.'

'You can hear —' He stopped himself. 'What's your name?'

The boy adjusted his load. 'Ham, sir. Er, Hamelyn.'

'Well, Hamelyn, I shall go to the Yew Inn. In that direction, you say?' Cassien said, pointing over his shoulder.

'Follow that street to its end. You'll come to a small crossroads, at its centre a small fountain. Go right and continue … you'll see the smith shops and the inn is along there.'

'Who do you work for, Ham? Wait, let me take that off you.' He dragged the load from Ham's shoulders. The lad visibly sighed before stretching.

'Thank you, sir. I am an errand boy for hire. There are many noblemen who come into the town needing the smiths and they all want errands run. This job is for Lady Hartnell.' When Cassien looked unimpressed, Ham added, 'She's Lord Hartnell's wife and is setting up a country house on the outskirts of town.'

'Couldn't Lady Hartnell have this taken by horse and cart?'

'They forgot this.'

'Ah. When you're done with Lady Hartnell's errands, come and see me. I'll be at the Yew.'

Ham's face lit up. 'Yes, sir. Who do I ask for?'

'I'm Cassien Figaret. Now, let me help you get loaded up again.' They lifted the bundle together and Cassien was astonished at just how heavy the burden was on Ham's back. He was strong. 'All right?'

'Yes, Master Figaret. It's balanced.'

'Call me Cassien. I'll be waiting.' He lifted a hand in farewell but the boy had already turned and lurched off. That was intriguing. How could Hamelyn hear his weapons when they were magically silenced? He looked forward to seeing the lad again.

Cassien found the Yew Inn without difficulty but he took his time and moved slowly through the street of swordsmiths, awestruck that he was actually here. He wanted to visit each of the shops, but Wevyr's, like a beacon, drew him toward it. He could see it up ahead; nothing grand about it and yet it seemed to emanate an aura … silent, slightly sinister, yet not in a way that was alarming. It had none of the traffic that the other smiths appeared to be experiencing. Wevyr's seemed to deter anyone from entering. It clearly didn't take idle enquirers. He smiled. This street — and particularly Wevyr's — was like the high altar for any obedient warrior.

Before he could pay a visit to the famous swordsmith, he needed to get his horses seen to. A man seemed to read his thoughts.

'Are you staying at the Yew, sir?'

'Hoping to.'

'There's room,' the man replied. 'Shall I take the horses?'

'Er, yes, thank you.' Cassien frowned. He could almost imagine this was a scam and then the man would walk away with a fine pair of mounts and laugh with his friends at the idiocy of the stranger in the dark cloak. 'Wait, I'd like to see the stables, please.'

'Follow me, sir. My name is Robb.'

The man led him down a side street and then into a smaller lane that brought him to the rear of what was clearly a busy inn and an equally busy stable. He felt foolish for being so suspicious but reminded himself that not to be might cost him his life. He needed to be suspicious of everyone and every situation, especially while he was familiarising himself with people and city life.

'These horses have travelled a long distance and bravely, because I had to push them. I want them to have the best feed and sweet water. Do you understand, Robb?'

'All our horses —'

'No, Robb. I want these horses to be treated generously and with kindness. I insist. I'm happy to pay you handsomely for your trouble.'

Robb blinked slowly as he digested this. 'I understand, sir.'

'Thank you.' Cassien produced another coin, a silver duke this time. 'Give them a good rub down, too.'

Robb's eyes widened. He clearly wasn't used to seeing silver and reached for it greedily. 'Consider it done, sir.'

'Good. I'll be back later to check on them.'

He wove his way back to the entrance of the Yew Inn. His belly, which he'd ignored since the previous evening, was now howling to be fed. The landlord greeted him warmly.

'A room for you, sir?'

'Please. Two nights,' he said, unsure why he'd need that long. 'Do you have one with a bath?'

'No, sir, I'm sorry. But the baths in Orkyld have few equal, save the public one in Pearlis. I'd wager you'd have a better soak there than in your room.'

Cassien grinned. 'Truly?'

The innkeeper nodded. 'I'd recommend the one favoured by the guild. It's not far from here and tends to be frequented by men such as yourself, sir. We have others, of course, equally good but perhaps not as … discreet.' He smiled. 'And, if you're looking for relaxation of a different nature, sir, there are the brothels, and the better ones have bathing facilities.'

'Indeed. Are there many brothels in Orkyld?'

The man reached behind him to some hooks and found the key he was looking for. 'I've lost count. Orkyld is now the second largest town outside of the capital.' He shrugged. 'That means there's plenty of everything.'

'Innkeeper …?'

'Erris, sir.'

'Good. Erris, what if I wanted to find a particular girl? I promised an old friend I'd look for her … if you get my meaning,' Cassien said, sounding conspiratorial. He winked for good measure.

Erris gave a sly smile. 'I do, sir. Anything you need can be arranged for a price.'

Cassien dug into the pocket where he'd stored some of Fynch's coin. 'How much do I owe you for the room and meals?'

'That would be a crown and six.'

Cassien did a quick calculation. He was having to re-learn how to use money. Six meant regents he recalled. 'I see. And if I wanted that particular errand we've recently discussed?'

'I'd round it up to two crowns, sir, and assure you that it was all included. I can have her sent to your room … er, that is, if you prefer not to visit the brothel and will take your bath in one of the houses.'

'Yes, that would be convenient, Erris, thank you.'

'May I have the girl's name, sir?'

'Well, here's the thing, I've forgotten it,' Cassien lied, making a sound of disgust at himself. 'I was drunk when I was told and all I can remember is that her name is something like Petal, or Pila, perhaps?'

'Ah, no, sir,' he said with a wide, knowing smile. 'It's not Pila. Her name is Penely. Hair like flame, mayhap?'

'That's the one!'

Erris chuckled. 'It's whether she's available, sir. Penely is extremely popular.'

'Do what you can, Erris. I'm keen to meet her, even for a brief time, although tell her I will pay her for a night even if she can only spare an hour.'

Erris regarded him with interest. 'I'll see what I can do, Master ...?'

'Figaret.'

'Figaret,' Erris repeated. 'After your evening meal, sir. Shall we say three hours after sundown?'

'Fine. There's also an errand boy calling for me. His name is Hamelyn. He can probably catch up with me at the bathhouse.'

'Of course, sir,' Erris replied.

Cassien arrived outside the bathhouse, having taken his time getting a feel for this lively town. Ham had been right. The area around the Yew Inn was quieter and somehow more secretive.

He wanted to get the business of the whore behind him. He didn't know what he was going to do yet. Cassien knew that if he had to kill her he'd need to follow her for a few hours and make it appear as though one of her other clients had done the deed. He couldn't have her found anywhere near the Yew Inn or her brothel.

He started to notice a steady trickle of men arriving and realised this would not to be a quiet experience. At the Abbey, the Brotherhood bathed in tubs dragged into a single cold room. The more senior the Brother, the hotter and cleaner the water. Cassien couldn't remember a time when he'd ever bathed in clean hot water, not even at Wife Wiggins's, who swore it was freshly drawn, but Cassien knew she had lied; he'd shared enough tub water to tell fresh from used. He felt a twinge of uncertainty and was fighting a desire to head back to the inn when a familiar voice hollered.

'Master Cassien!' He swung around and could see young Hamelyn running at full pelt. Cassien lifted a hand in relief. The youngster arrived, not even out of breath, and smiling. 'The innkeeper sent me here to find you. Are you taking a bath?'

'I need a shave and hair trim more than a bath.'

'I know someone who can do that better. And even more privately.'

Cassien was impressed. 'How do you reckon I need discretion?'

'Hidden weapons, sir. I hope I'm not speaking out of turn.'

'No, I'm glad you're here.'

'It's not a very elegant establishment.'

'Take me. I no longer care.'

Ham was carrying a sack. 'I brought you this, Master Cassien. The innkeeper is putting it on your tab.'

Cassien peered inside and saw a small loaf and a hunk of cheese.

'I heard your belly growling earlier.'

'Shar's breath, but you're attentive and smart.'

The lad nodded, grinning.

'Thank you,' Cassien said, taking the sack. 'I hadn't realised how famished I was until this moment.' He reached in and took the heel of bread out. 'Here,' he said, ripping the bread in half. 'You look pretty scrawny yourself.'

Ham caught the food nimbly.

'Half the cheese is yours, too. Tell me, Ham, who do you belong to?' Cassien asked, falling in step as the boy led them down a small alleyway.

'Belong to, sir?' Ham asked in between chewing.

'Please, I want you to call me Cassien. In fact, I insist and, as I'm paying, you have to do exactly as I request.' Ham smiled tentatively. 'Yes,' Cassien continued more gently, 'belong to, as in family.'

'I have no-one. I live at the orphanage, share my takings with Master and Wife Bally, who look after the orphans of Orkyld.'

'I see. I was orphaned,' Cassien admitted, 'but I was fortunate to be given a home with a large and generous family.'

'You look prosperous.'

'Looks can be deceiving,' Cassien admitted, 'but I have means, yes. And I would like to employ your services full-time.'

'As what?'

'Ham, you said you could hear my sword.'

'Perhaps I shouldn't have mentioned it.'

'Why?'

'Because a sword that speaks is obviously magical and I suspect that's not something you wish attention drawn to. I know your sword, you see. I watched it being forged.'

Cassien halted. 'I thought Wevyr worked in complete secret on his special jobs.'

'Normally he does. But I heard it. It spoke to me.'

'Now you've got me intrigued.'

'I was making a delivery to Master Wevyr for one of the nobles, at an unusual time. Night, in fact. I didn't want to disturb the swordsmith, but his lordship insisted, paid us both double for the bother. I couldn't find Master Wevyr initially, then I heard a strange murmuring that was half-sung, half-spoken. I thought ...' He shook his head.

'Thought what?'

Ham looked embarrassed. 'I thought the voice called my name. I walked toward the forge. I knew I shouldn't disturb anyone, but the calling felt insistent and it was in my head. Hard to describe, sir,' he said, forgetting himself.

'You're saying it's magic?' Cassien asked quietly.

The boy shrugged. 'I'm just telling you how it felt.'

'So you went inside the forge?'

'No. I found a peephole and spied inside. I saw the iron of your sword being poured.'

'You sound scared.'

Ham took an audible breath. Then lifted a shoulder in a manner that suggested he didn't like talking of this. 'We're here ... Cassien,' he said, pointing to a shabby shop entrance.

'Thank you. Ham, can you hear my sword now?'

He nodded. 'I can hear it making normal sounds of metal as you walk, but I know others can't. I can also —'

'How do you know others can't hear it?'

'Can you hear it?'

Cassien shook his head. 'No.'

Ham said nothing but looked down.

'You can also ... what?'

Again the boy took a deep breath. 'I can still hear it murmuring. It went away for a while but then called strongly to me today. It's how I found you when you arrived in Orkyld.'

'You found me? No. I picked you at random.'

131

Hamelyn gave a sad smile. 'The sword called me to you. It didn't actually say anything in words so much as I somehow knew it needed me to meet you.'

'Shar's balls! What's happening here?' Cassien growled to himself, hating the notion that he was being manipulated. 'What did you see in the forge?'

'I'd rather not say.'

'Why?'

'It was too odd.'

'Tell me, Ham. I have to work out what's going on. We're both involved and we're being coerced.'

'I don't know what that means.'

'It doesn't matter. I need to make sure neither of us is in danger but especially that you are not.'

'Don't worry for me. Besides, the sword is my friend. So are its companions.'

'What companions?'

'The other blades and weapons,' he said in a tone that suggested he was surprised Cassien needed to ask.

Cassien was privately astonished.

'Don't worry, though,' Ham assured. 'I think only I hear them.'

'What did you see?' Cassien pressed, crouching down now, so he was below eye level with Ham. 'Tell me!'

Ham hesitated and then, as if listening to some inner voice, relief appeared to ghost across his expression. 'I saw an elderly man. I knew he was old, but he didn't seem so despite his silvered hair. His movements were easy, his smile even easier and very …' He searched for the word. 'I don't know how to describe it except to say that when he smiled I felt warm inside.'

Cassien blinked. 'Was he wearing simple robes?'

Ham nodded. 'Pale grey. He was almost without colour and yet he possessed —'

'The brightest blue eyes with strange flecks of gold.'

'Yes!' Ham exclaimed, forgetting his former reticence. 'I don't know about the flecks of gold, but from a distance they were bright and blue.'

'His name is Fynch.'

'Ah,' Ham said, his body relaxing in relief, 'that's the name I've been hearing.'

'From whom?' Cassien asked, startled.

'From your weapons.'

Cassien took a deep breath to calm his growing bewilderment and excitement. 'Tell me what Fynch was doing, Hamelyn. Please, it's important.'

'He was bleeding his arm into Wevyr's crucible of molten metal,' Ham replied.

TEN

Florentyna had just finished hearing 'matters', as they were called. It was a duty that Empress Valentyna had instituted during her reign alongside Cailech, taking the view that ordinary people with very ordinary conflicts often needed some formal system of intervention in their disputes.

'If we're going to run a successful union of realms then something as fundamental as rights of possession shouldn't just be for the entitled,' Valentyna was famously quoted.

And so began what was known colloquially as the Court of Hearts. It met each neap tide and Valentyna initiated a trend that ensured the sovereign, or her senior representative, would attend to mediate. To her credit, historical records showed that Empress Valentyna made the effort, often rearranging her formal schedules to be present for at least one session per moon cycle and the people adored her for it; and especially for recognising the need for everyone's conflicts to be given a fair hearing, no matter how inconsequential. The empress organised for each party to have a court advocate, paid for by the Crown. This generosity was based on the premise that whatever the empress, or her representative, decided in each 'matter' was accepted without further debate or claim.

It was a successful experiment and a highly popular one, soon picked up and duplicated in a number of other realms by rulers who saw it as a sign of a progressive nation. Valentyna presided over her petty sessions well into her elder years and one of her deathbed wishes was that the Court of Hearts be continued and taken seriously by her heirs. These days it had grown into a strong court capable of passing minor civil laws.

Even so, Florentyna was growing tired of the Court of Hearts being her most important task. She'd been at the Gathering of Crowns the previous summer; it wasn't her first, but she was still waiting for the senior rulers to take her presence seriously. While people were always interested in discussing strategic union through marriage, few held quite the same enthusiasm for what *she* had to say. It infuriated her but Reynard, her chancellor, had soothed her silent rage.

'Bide your time, majesty. One day they will be falling upon your every word, but for now show your appreciation to King Alred of Grentchen, to the Princes Kerrich and Isgar and their respective realms, and even to the Queen Dowager of Jaspay Seth.'

'We are wealthy, powerful and quite capable of crippling trade on many of their routes if I choose to flex this region's collective muscle,' she'd growled. Reynard had nodded his agreement, his expression filled with sympathy for her gripe. It only fuelled her irritation more. 'What's more, King Alred was being polite simply because he knew my father. The two princes you mention were certainly pleasant, but only because they took time to appreciate the low cut of my neckline and besides they need Morgravia's support as both the realms they stand to inherit are impoverished.' She hadn't finished. 'As for the dowager, she was simply conversing with the only other woman in the room. Her son, the king, didn't bother to attend. Her conversation seemed to be about lace or marriage!' She groaned. 'People only ever want to speak to my elder male counsellors about state issues!'

'And yet each of those four, whom you speak of with disdain, swam against the tide and while others ignored you — or spoke to your counsellors — that quartet paid you the sort of attention a queen of your standing and wealth demands. Reward them. Alred's lands are fertile and his mountains rich with silver. The two princes may be poor now but you have no idea what they're capable of; Kerrich in particular is wily and knows his waterways are rivers of gold because very soon other realms are going to need them for their booming trade. But both are good men of sound values with strong ambitions. As for the dowager, while it might have seemed she was holding forth on subjects that were of little interest to you, don't for a moment believe she wasn't testing you. She is mother to one of the most eligible kings, who happens to be monarch of one of the richest kingdoms. And while he is but a young man now, showing little interest in marriage or anything but sating his more basic desires, that will change. I'm sure she alluded to that while you both spoke. I would quietly caution you never to underestimate the power of a woman's influence or strength, especially a queen.' He had tapped her hand in a fatherly fashion. 'I never do,' he added and smiled affectionately.

Good old Reynard. He'd always managed to say the right thing at the right time to gently show her the errors of her ways and make her feel ten years old again. This occasion was no exception. She was wrong to ignore anyone who might strengthen Morgravia.

And it was true she'd taken a dislike to the young King of Gyntredea, mainly because he'd ignored her. Nevertheless, it had profoundly irritated her that before Reynard disappeared, it was to him that most of the dignitaries cleaved, probably believing her incapable. And now they cleaved to Burrage, who had inherited the role of chancellor, doing a fine job of it and very much a man in the mould of his predecessor — and someone who was formerly in awe of her father, the old king.

And so, on this day's Court of Hearts, when an elderly man calling himself Pel was shown in — escorted by a bewildered Burrage, who went so far as to shrug before saying, 'He has requested a few moments of your time, majesty, saying it concerns a matter he can't explain but needs to share the facts about' — her interest had been piqued.

Pel looked harmless but two strapping soldiers flanked him.

'Should I be scared of you, Master Pel?' she asked.

Pel had already struggled to his knees to bow as low as possible. He seemed reluctant to so much as lift his head to her. 'Oh no, my queen,' he said, his voice muffled . 'I have been searched twice. I swear I come only with information.'

'He says it's about Chancellor Reynard,' Burrage whispered.

This caught her attention fully. She waved a hand at the soldiers, who picked him up, set him back on his feet. She heard both his knees sigh their protest as he straightened.

'Can I offer you a chair, Master Pel?' she asked gently.

He slowly shook his head. 'Thank you, no. Majesty, may I speak privately, please?'

She stared at the newcomer, who gazed at her in earnest. She wanted the information he had brought.

'Clear the court, please, Burrage,' she finally said.

'But your majesty, we have —'

She glanced at him and he promptly covered his lips with a finger as though silencing himself. 'At once, my queen,' he said and went about his business, apologising to other petitioners for the delay, until only he, Florentyna, the soldiers and their charge were left in the petty sessions hall.

'Do we need guards still, Burrage?'

'Yes, I'm afraid I will insist upon that,' he said.

'Then perhaps we can ask them to retreat a way so Master Pel doesn't have to feel like a prisoner.'

Burrage nodded at the men, who moved far enough that Pel could speak without being heard, but not so far that they couldn't cut him down within three strides if he threatened the queen. Florentyna thought the man looked far too weak and weary to be doing much more than sitting down.

She stood, slightly lifted her gown to avoid tripping, and glided gently down the three stairs, not at all threatened by Pel even though Burrage instantly stepped between them and the two soldiers reached to their sides. She lifted a hand to calm everyone.

'Master Pel, where have you arrived from?'

'From the west, majesty. I am curate for the parish of Stowell-in-the-Marsh. I assist Rural Dean Flek. My home is Harpers Riding, where the parish tithe barn is located.'

'I see,' she said, wondering what this might have to do with Reynard.

'And you've ridden here to tell us about Chancellor Reynard, I gather?'

'I rode a day and a night without stopping, your majesty. An event occurred two days ago in our tithe barn.' She nodded but he didn't notice, barely paused to take breath. 'There was a stranger, you see. He looked harmless. Confused actually. I thought he'd slept off a night on the liquor in our barn.'

'And?' Burrage encouraged. 'What struck you as so odd that you have come this far to tell us of it?'

'He was naked, which was curious, but not so disturbing that I was frightened. He seemed bewildered and I suggested he gather his wits, put on his clothes and be on his way before I returned, because Dean Flek is a stickler for the rules, your majesty. His tithe barn is the most successful and well run in the region.'

'Yes, indeed,' she said, remaining patient. 'And what happened next?'

'I returned. It would have been within one bell's period and I thought no more about the man, fully expecting him to be gone.'

'But he wasn't, I'm guessing,' Florentyna said. 'Was it Chancellor Reynard? Do you know him?'

'I don't know him to speak with but he once passed through our region and accompanied Dean Flek on a tour which included the tithe barn. I was introduced to Chancellor Reynard and although we shared but a few words, he was a most charming man. He would not remember me but he is not someone you forget.'

'No,' she agreed, desperate to hurry the story but knowing she mustn't interrupt his thoughts.

'The stranger was not Chancellor Reynard. He was …'

'Was what? Come on, Pel, spit it out,' Burrage urged, no longer as patient as his queen.

Pel looked up and regarded them both with eyes that Florentyna felt looked haunted. 'He was gone but he'd left behind Dean Flek.' He cleared his throat. 'He'd killed him.'

'Rural Dean Flek is dead?' they repeated together, both looking mystified.

He nodded. 'Forgive me, your majesty, but I believe I am still in shock.'

She inclined her head, concerned. 'Burrage, a small cup of brintas, please,' she said, signalling Pel. It was brought immediately and the older man swallowed the slightly spiced wine. It appeared to revive him although he refused more after only two small sips.

'Thank you, your majesty,' he said, slightly breathlessly. 'I feel somehow responsible for Dean Flek's death because I didn't take notice of the threat. Now, on reflection, I can see how confused and troubled the killer was. I thought he was drunk but he could well have been sick or addled in the mind somehow.'

'You're sure the stranger killed him?' Burrage asked.

Pel shook his head. 'I didn't see it happen so no, I am not certain. However, who else could have done this? And the stranger was acting so peculiar that I suppose it now makes sense that he was somehow out of his mind and capable of seeing threats where they may not have been. I thought it was liquor but it was madness. Dean Flek's throat was slashed

138

from ear to ear.' He checked himself in front of the queen. 'It was vicious. No-one of sound mind would do such a thing, surely? What's more, Dean Flek was a stickler for time. He kept to the same rituals, but he was early in arriving at the tithe barn.'

'The newcomer was naked, I think you remarked,' Florentyna said.

'That's the strangest part, your majesty, and why we are taking such caution with whom we share this. There were no clothes. The man had obviously arrived naked — I don't know how; that's another mystery. You see, I closed and locked the barn the previous evening. Master Flek had been with me and we'd been working inside it. It had been locked while we worked, I might add. Master Flek is very strict about these things.'

'So how did the man get inside?' Florentyna asked.

Pel shrugged. 'I can't explain it. The tithe barn is locked securely from the outside. And that lock had not been tampered with. There is no other way into the barn. There are no windows either. The stranger was inside when I unlocked it. I left it open for him to leave. Obviously, Dean Flek broke his rules of the past thirty summers and arrived early, came upon him and the stranger killed him. But why not me? The man had me at his mercy if murder was on his mind.'

'Well, you do come to us with a conundrum, Master Pel,' Burrage said. 'I'd like you to show her majesty what you *did* find. I think she may be interested to see it.'

Florentyna frowned as she watched Pel reach inside his cloak.

'I found this beside some sheaves of barley, your majesty. It must have slipped down. It does not belong to us and certainly was not part of a payment tithe.' He unrolled a length of soft linen. 'The stranger was holding it when we first met.'

Florentyna gasped as she saw a swan feather quill she recognised. 'It's Chancellor Reynard's!' she said. 'I gave it to him. It should have the royal sigil etched into the shaft.'

'Indeed it does and it's why I had to come to the palace. I became terrified that the killer was connected with the royal household, but Chancellor Burrage told me it belonged to Chancellor Reynard.' He reverently handed the quill to Burrage, who passed it to Florentyna. She saw a speck of blood on the pristine white feather and felt her eyes misting. What had happened to Reynard and who was the naked stranger who carried this quill?

'I can't say I know your stranger, Master Pel,' she said, 'but I think we should make every effort to establish who he is because of this quill. Burrage, will you see to it that Dean Flek's corpse is brought to Pearlis immediately?'

Burrage nodded gravely.

'Er, your majesty, I've brought him with me. His family lives in Pearlis.'

'I'll have the body put in the chapel,' Burrage murmured.

She nodded. 'I can't imagine viewing it will reveal much, but we should certainly assure ourselves that no possible clue is ignored. We will have Dean Flek's body delivered to his brother for burial and offer all help.'

Burrage continued. 'Was there anything else, Pel, that this man might have said that we should know about?'

'He was confused. I thought him drunk, as I mentioned, but I smelled no liquor on him. I know he was frightened and very unsure of where he was or why he was in the barn.'

'Drugged, do you think?' Florentyna offered.

Pel looked uncertain. 'He spoke clearly, didn't slur. Didn't strike me as violent or aggressive. He just seemed disoriented and genuinely scared. He asked me where he was and when I told him he looked baffled, as though he'd never heard of Morgravia or Briavel before.'

Both of them stared at Pel, astonished. 'Did he say where he was from?'

'He did, your majesty, but for the life of me I can't remember. I must be honest; I do recall not knowing the two places he mentioned. Neither was from the empire. As you can appreciate, in the church we are well versed with the towns and villages of our lands.'

'Of course,' Burrage said. 'Perhaps it was a tiny hamlet, though, or —'

'I concede that, Master Burrage. But why did he look so bewildered when I mentioned Morgravia and Briavel? In fact, he admitted that he was lost.' Pel frowned. 'I've been thinking about that conversation a great deal, trying to remember it in case it can give me a clue to this stranger. And he said the oddest thing.' They both leaned forward. 'He said he was under a spell. That "she", and I don't know to whom he referred, had brought him to this world from another.' Pel's voice had gradually lowered to a whisper even though they were alone. 'He spoke of magic,' he said, sounding frightened.

Florentyna and Burrage stared at Pel as though he'd just begun talking in tongues.

'From another world,' Florentyna repeated, remembering another stranger with a warning. Neither man responded. 'Did you believe him, Master Pel?'

He looked surprised to be asked such a question. 'At the time I just wanted him to be gone from the barn, my queen, for Master Flek gets deeply irritated if his security is breached. I didn't want a scene.' He gave a mirthless groan of a laugh. 'I was certainly left with one though. I have no idea why he should kill an innocent. I don't know why I found a scrivener's quill with the royal sigil on it, and I don't understand talk about other worlds and magic. I am a simple man; you must forgive me for passing this problem on to the Crown. I didn't know what else to do but to tell you everything I could and return your quill. Oh, I believe his name may have been Gabriel.'

Florentyna listened and nodded. The name could be a lie, of course. 'We're grateful that you came, Master Pel. I'm sorry for your loss,' she said. 'Now, please, let us find you a bed in which to rest and some food. You may return home when you are ready.'

'Thank you, your majesty, you're very kind. I hope the Crown finds him and I will be glad to bear witness against him.'

She nodded and watched the elderly man leave, escorted by Burrage to the door. Florentyna turned away, biting her lip in worry. The talk of magic had prompted a reminder of the man called Fynch, who had told Florentyna of the imminent arrival of a stranger — a magic bearer. She took a deep, steadying breath. She had to speak with Fynch again.

Pel's sinister tale also deepened the mystery surrounding her former chancellor's disappearance.

She wished Darcelle would be a friend and confidante, but it seemed that since the marriage proposal her sister was becoming increasingly bored with life as the spare heir and not especially interested in Florentyna's needs. Darcelle wanted a crown of her own and her new husband-to-be would provide it. And then she would likely consider herself Florentyna's equal. Despite her love for Darcelle, Florentyna knew they had grown apart, especially since the announcement of marriage and particularly with her choice of husband. But Florentyna had refused to dwell on King Tamas and her sister being wed. She would be happy for them, and Cipres was a long way from Morgravia.

Along with Reynard's disappearance, Florentyna was feeling increasingly isolated, to the point where the only trustworthy companions she could call upon were Burrage, in his seventh decade, and Felyx, her champion, who quietly resented his 'nursemaid' role.

'Do you need company?' Burrage whispered, interrupting her thoughts as she began to walk away.

'Just want to clear my head,' she assured. 'I'll be fine.'

'In the grove?'

She found a smile. He knew her too well.

'Felyx will accompany you,' he said, walking to the chamber door. She wanted to be truly alone but knew that was about as likely as two moons appearing tonight. She sighed quietly as she watched Burrage whisper to someone outside the door.

Soon enough, Burrage returned with her nursemaid. Between them they shared one hundred and fourteen summers. Florentyna could use some male company of her own age, as these men always felt the need to advise and counsel, rather than simply listen and let her reach her own conclusion. And there was so much to consider in Pel's curious tale.

Florentyna wished now that she hadn't treated Master Fynch with such indifference. She had allowed others to sway her attitude toward a man she had inherently trusted. There was something about his eyes — so bright and amused, and yet she'd had the impression that the wisdom of centuries lurked behind them. Had he thrown open a window onto something she could not yet see, but was out there?

Magic had been openly accepted as a fact of life in her great-grandfather's time. It could hardly die out, could it, even though she'd read the history tomes that said people had tried to stamp it out by burning so-called witches?

Felyx quietly followed her from the throne room. He was a senior, trusted man from the Royal Blades, a special unit of soldiers set up originally by Cailech to guard his queen.

'Chancellor Burrage says I must return you by midday, your majesty,' Felyx said, catching up with her and interrupting her gloomy thoughts as she left the palace to emerge into the sunlight of the bailey. It helped a little to feel the warmth, thin though it was today. Felyx's sword clanged at his side and his leathers creaked. She was used to it, but today the sounds only added to her annoyance.

'Does he?' she said, although it didn't come out as a polite question. More of a sneer.

Courtiers, soldiers, maids and pages all began bowing as she approached and stayed bent in her wake, but Florentyna uncharacteristically acknowledged no-one. Felyx caught the gate as it carelessly swung back on him then closed it quietly. He was used to this route. It was the queen's most regular one when she chose to escape. She stomped ahead toward the private grove planted by Cailech for his beloved Valentyna.

Gone was the usual cacophony of the great palace known as Stoneheart — apart from the soft 'clank' of Felyx behind her. The noise of people and their daily work was replaced by birdsong and the rustle of trees swaying in the gentle breeze. The comforting, regular gurgle of water ran in a stream that traced a narrow path nearby.

'I'm going to the pool,' she said, somewhat unnecessarily. 'I would like to be alone.'

'Yes, of course, majesty. I'll do a sweep of the grove to ensure all is well. And when I return I will wait for you here,' he said.

'Thank you,' Florentyna whispered and was already moving away from Felyx before he'd finished speaking. She threaded her way through the grove of majestic belaqua, with their huge gnarled limbs and fabulously bright-green heart-shaped leaves, and immediately her burden — whatever it was — felt lighter. She moved to her favourite spot: overlooking a tiny rock pool, away from the foaming rush of the stream that cut through the grove and moved on its busy journey to join the River Tague. That river began in the Razor Mountains and flowed south to separate Morgravia from Briavel.

Before she sank down beside the pool, she snapped a leaf from a low branch and stroked its velvety length, marvelling that its underside could be so rough and hairy. She crushed its tip and let the lemony oil perfume her fingers as she brought the leaf close to her face to inhale the heady scent. Emperor Cailech must have been quite a romantic at heart. There was a tale that he'd hunted all the nine kingdoms to get the most beautiful tree to plant for his Valentyna.

People anticipated a gorgeous flowering tree and yet what he brought home was a strange, dark-looking row of deciduous saplings that were little more than twigs. But they grew fast and they grew strong. They yielded no voluptuous blooms but he was said to have joked that the leaves represented the union of Valentyna and himself: 'the rough north joining with the smooth south'. Then his romantic side had shown itself and jongleurs sang of his claim that each leaf was akin to one of his heartbeats; and each leaf-fall left a carpet of green hearts on the grove's floor that represented a year of heartbeats of his life given in love to his queen. Florentyna had adored the story since she was a little girl and came to the grove because she knew Valentyna had loved this place too.

She wanted love of that nature in her life ... a strong, romantic man who would bind himself to her. She'd never said this to anyone — not even Darcelle — but Florentyna, even as a princess, had never desired a 'prince' with his own realm. She didn't even need a king, even though she was sure Reynard, and now Burrage, had constantly considered options that might offer the right alliance. She already presided over a powerful region — it didn't need to be broadened by marrying another powerful heir or king. It needed to be cared for, nurtured, protected ... just like she did. And what she didn't have was anyone who loved her. It was a pathetic-sounding whine, even for her private thoughts, and she shook her head free of it.

She tossed her leaf into the water and watched it float, drifting gently to the edge, barely disturbing the surface, where she noticed her reflection, caught sight of the droop of her expression. Is this how she appeared to her courtiers, her people? Looking at her image, she saw sadness staring back at her. Just as she was about to dive into self-pity again, she could swear the face of a wolf appeared in the reflection, snarled at her and just as quickly disappeared.

Florentyna sat back, astonished. The beast she'd seen in that flash was magnificent and of such a curious colouring, like cinder toffee. It had possessed glowing, deep yellow eyes; instinctively, she felt it was female.

She shivered, despite her soft wrap of gleaver wool.

When her mother passed away from the shaking fevers that had swept the empire, she and her sister had been put into the temporary care of Twillie — the oldest member of the palace, she was sure. Twillie had been her mother's servant since childhood and, despite her own mourning, had ferociously and happily embraced her role of caring for the girls. Twillie already knew that while the baby, Darcelle, could be quietened with soothing songs or sticks of sugar, the only way her sister would be still was to listen to the old stories. And Twillie had a wealth of them. She was from Tolton Heath in the far northeast of Briavel, one of the villages that dared live close to the border of the Wild.

The people of this area were full of tall tales of magic and mystery, and Florentyna loved Twillie's stories. She learned about giants and small-folk, of dragons that once flew the land, and especially about the dragon king, who was so old he no longer remembered his own name. One story told of how a boy from Morgravia had braved the dragon king and flown on its back. The dragon king and boy had cleaved so close in heart and mind that the child straddled the realms of men and beast as a king himself. According to Twillie, he became the conduit and protector of their empire.

It was a fantastic story that fed Florentyna's imagination. She listened wide-eyed to other tales — of brave men who fought the gilgerbeasts and feisty women who rode the unicorns of old. She trembled at the stories of ogres who roamed the caves beneath the Razors, of great sea serpents who sank ships, and of demons who created havoc to lighten the boredom of their eternal, ethereal lives.

Florentyna knew them all by heart and had argued heatedly with her father, even though she was only eight summers, that they were legend, not myth. These people and creatures *had* existed. As she grew older, she kept her thoughts to herself in this regard for fear of being considered blasphemous in a world that now ignored its former awe and, indeed, fear of magic. Everyone she knew sneered at the notion that magic existed. Florentyna had often wanted to ask them why, then, did the zealous Zerque Stalkers ever exist if not to stamp out magic? Why, even in more recent times, in the reign of King Magnus, were they still burning women accused of witchery? Granted, history told her that Magnus had done much to stop inquisitors, but Confessor Lymbert had still had 'fun' in his dungeon with poor wretches accused of being witches. The last victim recorded was a girl younger than herself. Florentyna knew her only by the single name of Myrren. What a terrible trial she had endured before her burning.

King Magnus died not long after Myrren, and his son, Prince Celimus, ascended the throne. This was a very muddled time as the two great realms of Morgravia and Briavel endeavoured to stop their age-old enmity through the oldest form of strategic alliance. Prince Celimus of Morgravia was to marry Princess Valentyna of Briavel and everyone hoped for the promised peace, but the Razor Kingdom was becoming bolder, and its daring — some said far-sighted — ruler began to believe he would make the better emperor. He also believed he would make the better husband and it seemed Valentyna agreed. When they united the realms, they destroyed the inquisitions and any form of witch hunting. Belief in magic gradually declined and spiritual devotion intensified.

Pearlis Cathedral never lacked for pilgrims, but Florentyna always felt sad that they no longer believed in the power of the creatures which featured so strongly in that cathedral. Florentyna adored the notion that each person was born to one and that it would be their protector. She was born to the dragon, like the royals before her ... *only* those with royal lineage could be allied to the dragon. Did that mean the legendary boy who became the king of the beasts was born to the dragon? How else could he defy it, stare it down, make it his, ride it, love it as his own? She blinked. Had the boy of legend been royal, then? A royal bastard, perhaps?

Perhaps what she loved most about the Cailech and Valentyna story was the vague whiff of magic that seemed to surround them. Historians coldly recorded that King Celimus had died of poisoning and that his chancellor, Jessom, had been murdered, but there were anomalies in the history that were deliberately vague. Florentyna was a gifted student of history, but it did not worry her to have these gaps in the family records because she filled them with her own idea that magic, which seemed to abound in her ancestors' time, had its part to play in their lives. In fact, it fired her romantic notion that Cailech, who had once been considered little more than a barbaric tribesman — and liked nothing more than to dine on his enemies — had employed magic to win his queen. Even the history books attested, in a roundabout fashion, to a personality change once Cailech left the Razors and headed south into Briavel and met Queen Valentyna.

Florentyna smiled thinking about her romantic forebears. When the vision of the wolf came to mind again, she told herself she'd imagined it; of course she had, for when she tentatively leaned over the pool she saw only her dark hair, sensibly pulled back and plaited behind the familiar oval face. She wore no earrings, no necklace, no bracelets or

146

finery, no colour on her cheeks or lips. For a queen she was singularly unadorned. Even her gowns were neat, practical — although like her famous ancestor, Valentyna, she really preferred riding gear — and she had convinced herself she looked best in neutral hues. She left all the frippery to Darcelle. Her sister was the beautiful one — which Florentyna had been told so often as they grew up. Darcelle was the one with the gregarious personality and plenty of suitors; the one who really cared about the family's jewellery and gold vaults, the latest fashions, the best silks.

Everyone knew this. Even the king.

Their father had loved them both deeply, but had admitted that he was glad she was the one who would wear the crown. He thought he'd been saying this privately to Chancellor Reynard, but Florentyna had been in the solar, just outside his main salon.

She'd been permitted in by the king's secretary, who knew he could leave the princess while he ran an errand.

'Does his majesty know you're coming?' he'd asked kindly.

'I want to surprise him,' she had replied in a conspiratorial tone. 'He doesn't know Darcelle and I are back from our trip to Argorn yet and I have a special gift for him.'

'Oh, then if you don't mind waiting, your highness,' he'd murmured, 'I'm sure the chancellor won't be long with your father. Welcome home, highness.'

'I'm happy to wait, Kilryck,' she had assured him, giving him a smile as he'd left.

However, the door had been open and she could hear the two men. She hadn't meant to eavesdrop. Their voices carried. As she heard her name spoken she frowned, moved closer to listen.

'... Darcelle has it all,' her father's deep voice said. 'Looks, personality, desire to be loved. She will be fine. She will be rich and happy as long as everyone dotes on her and looks after her. And in this she is fortunate too, for her elder sister indulges her. Darcelle will not have to inherit a crown to wear one.'

Reynard had always held a soft spot for Florentyna and she mentally hugged him for his sharp reply. 'And you think Florentyna will?'

'It's not like that, Reynard,' her father admonished. 'But you know as well as I that my elder daughter is a plainer, more serious girl and

147

genuinely more suited to rule. She's sensible and intelligent, well read and took her studies seriously. She's done everything right. A sovereign can't expect to be loved as Darcelle is … a sovereign must earn the love that comes with mutual respect. You hear me wrong if you think I criticise Florentyna. She makes me proud and, if not for her intensely romantic nature, I think she's perfect to rule after I'm gone.'

'And yet your praise sounds somehow damning,' Reynard had said sadly. He could get away with it, although her father would tolerate no-one else chastising him so. She heard Reynard continue. 'Your majesty, forgive me, but Florentyna is poorer emotionally for your attitude. The only reason you think your elder daughter is plainer is because Queen Saria has made her so over the past decade. She was an absolutely beautiful child, as I'm sure you recall, and while that beauty doesn't necessarily follow into adulthood, I think you're only seeing the Florentyna she has been shaped to be rather than the one you knew. The beautiful girl with the wide smile and ready affection is still there. It's just been …' She heard a pause as Reynard searched for the right word. 'Well, damn it, my king, it's been all but coerced out of her.'

She heard her father sigh then, heard his soft footsteps and she knew he'd be walking over to the window to look out beyond Stoneheart's huge bailey. 'They've had a difficult relationship, it's true.'

'Except Queen Saria was the adult in that relationship, sire. She came into your daughter's life when Florentyna was just nine and possessed loving memories of her own mother. Your new wife, dare I say, majesty, was not a good friend to the child at a time when Florentyna most needed one to guide her out of mourning and back into life. Florentyna has remained grief-stricken and I have to say it — isolated.' The king must have swung around and glared, because Reynard suddenly sounded defensive. 'You know it's true. Oh, she hides it well, because she knows her place, her role, and because she knows you demand it of her. She's been groomed as second heir since her first breath. But look at her dress and lack of adornment. Her mother has been dead more than a decade, but you wouldn't know it. One could be forgiven for thinking Florentyna's mother died a few moons back.'

'Stop, Reynard,' her father said.

But Reynard didn't stop. He obviously knew how hard he could push his king. 'Meanwhile, your second queen was a role model to the cherubic baby. Darcelle was an infant and easily moulded and Queen Saria has lavished her attention and care on her. She has taught Darcelle brilliantly and look how the girl has blossomed, but Queen Saria has left Florentyna to essentially raise herself in all things feminine. It is fair to say, and we all know it, my king, that the queen dislikes Princess Florentyna. There's no reason for it, other than that she loved her mother so deeply and resembles you and your forebears so keenly but she is a lonely, lonely young woman in a palace full of people.'

Florentyna had felt her cheeks burning with embarrassment, but mostly pain.

She did love her little sister, but she also knew Darcelle was easily impressed, deeply selfish and desperately keen to wear a crown. And while Darcelle made all the right noises toward her as a sister, Florentyna knew that Saria — even from a distance — still enjoyed enormous influence over Darcelle and poisoned her mind as often as she could against Florentyna.

Florentyna stared into the pool, stung by thoughts and memories. Even when her moonblood had arrived, with all of its strange ache and uncertainty, it wasn't Saria who helped, but dear Reynard, for even Twillie had become too old and hadn't been nearby. She'd sobbed in his arms that frightening night, claiming that she was dying. Reynard had carried her, stained and weeping to his rooms and summoned Keely, one of the gentlest, prettiest, most sweet-tempered servants in the palace. And Keely had been left with Florentyna to explain that she was now in a position to bring life into the world. Reynard had quickly appointed Keely as head maid to the princess and, with only a decade separating them, they had become firm friends.

Saria noticed that Florentyna was becoming far too confident and independent. She blamed Keely, having watched Florentyna beginning to blossom under the woman's care. And when Reynard had been away with her father, the queen had cornered Keely and suggested she do a 'tour', as she had called it, to the leper colony on the Isle of Trey. This was another of Cailech's innovations, encouraging his palace staff to show they were not above such things even though they were employed at Stoneheart and enjoyed many benefits as a result.

Keely was quickly pressed into service and even though she went quietly and indeed graciously, it was obvious to Florentyna that Reynard would not have permitted such a close aide to the royal family to be away for so long. Then Keely had become ill; not for a moment did Florentyna believe it to be leprosy, for the talk was simply that Keely was coughing a great deal, but that was irrelevant to Saria, who gleefully and instantly forbade Keely returning to Stoneheart. She was to remain on the island as, according to Saria, she had contracted the suppurating sores of the leper.

Florentyna's blood boiled even now at the memory of it, but she'd been a child and helpless. Her father was distracted on his return and even Reynard would not involve himself in domestic spats despite his disapproval of what had occurred. So Florentyna's life had again turned inward. Some had even begun calling her fey because of her reticence.

She smiled, allowing herself a rare moment of malicious joy as she recalled the moment when she realised what her father's death signified. It had nothing to do with wearing a crown, or ruling, or wealth or status. It wasn't about being the most revered person in the empire or the most powerful. It was quite simply about being in a position to give one particular command.

The king's death was unexpected and traumatic. Pearlis had slipped into shock as quietly as her father had slid from his horse two mornings previously in the bailey soon after mounting up. What had been dismissed as indigestion had been his heart weakening. The king had been immediately confined to his bed and his physics prodded, poked and generally shook their heads at his worsening condition while his breath became laboured and then shallow. His complexion had lost its grey pallor and turned waxy pale. The queen, accompanied by Darcelle, was called back from her sojourn to the famed spa at Tyntar, north of Pearlis, and was at her husband's side that same night, cooing and soothing in a way that made Florentyna feel ill.

As far as Florentyna was concerned, Saria, a widow of a distant cousin on her mother's side, had deliberately set about catching the king's attention and had done so through slyness, cunning and manipulation. Saria was still relatively young at thirty-five summers, still capable of bearing a son. She had been all smiles and friendliness in the early days of their courtship, but once the banns had been called and the echoes of the wedding bells had stopped resounding, Florentyna saw a different and far more ugly side to the new queen she now bowed to.

At the king's bedside, both she and the queen had locked gazes over the sick man. Florentyna remembered well that sudden shift of awareness as the pendulum of power seemed to swing from the queen's side of the bed to hers. And she could all but smell Saria's fear on the other side. Her father was still young by the standard of the day. No-one had counted on him having a weakness of the heart, least of all Saria.

And in that moment Florentyna had realised that Saria was petrified. Florentyna did not want her father to die, but she privately revelled in the uncertainty and terror reflected in the look her stepmother levelled at her as understanding dawned of how life might be about to change for both of them.

To Saria's despair her husband had suddenly awoken from the stupor he'd drifted into in an unnaturally alert state; it was a bad sign. The king spoke briefly to each of his loved ones separately, and then in front of those gathered, he had taken a deep, sad-sounding breath and closed his eyes. Saria had begun to shriek immediately.

Here was Florentyna's defining moment, as Reynard had later remarked. She stepped up to Saria when she could bear the woman's histrionics no more and delivered a stinging smack across one cheek, ignoring Darcelle's shriek of indignation.

'Hold yourself together!' she'd demanded of her elder. Saria was tall in her heels but Florentyna was taller ... without them. She used that height now to intimidate the woman who had been the bane of her life for years. 'Quiet yourself, woman! A hush for the dead, I beg you. Let my father's soul travel to Shar in peace.'

Saria had whimpered and clasped a hand to her shocked face, covering the reddening cheek that bore the mark of Florentyna's fingers. She had become mute, humiliated in front of her audience. Florentyna saw the woman glance at Darcelle but ignored both.

Into the difficult silence the chancellor spoke gravely. 'The king is dead!' he announced at a sombre nod from the head physician. 'Long live Queen Florentyna!'

Florentyna had taken their low bows, working hard to control her breathing, to hold her own tears in for just a while longer. And when each had straightened she'd looked to her sister. 'Master Burrage, would you please see to it that Princess Darcelle is taken to her chambers.' She helped her weeping sister to her feet and kissed her head. 'Go now, dear one. Grieve for our father in private. I will take care of everything and I will see you when I have made the necessary arrangements.'

Darcelle had looked at her with red, watering eyes before turning toward the woman she considered her mother. Florentyna had not given her sister a chance to speak. Until that moment Florentyna didn't know she was going to do anything so swift or decisive, but there was an echo of insincerity in Darcelle's tears that struck a false note.

'And, Master Burrage?'

'Yes, your majesty,' he said, according her the title that had the still stunned Saria looking from courtier to courtier in bewilderment.

'Would you please have someone escort the dowager to the chapel, where I'm sure she will want to grieve for my father.' Florentyna turned to Saria. 'I will have staff wait upon you in the chapel, where I presume you will keep the day and night vigil over your husband's body. From there I will make arrangements for you to be moved to a quiet place for your mourning.'

Saria's mouth moved but no words were formed.

Florentyna masked her sense of satisfaction by looking away as people began to react. 'A quiet word, Chancellor Reynard,' she said softly for his hearing and withdrew to the mantelpiece, as far from the deathbed as possible. She heard people moving behind her and when she glanced back as Reynard approached, she saw her sister and her stepmother being aided from the king's bedchamber.

Reynard drew next to her, staring deeply into her dark green eyes, scattered with warm brown flecks. 'Bravo, Queen Florentyna. I have never felt more proud,' he whispered and bowed again.

She did not smile but a felt a spike of pleasure thrill through her all the same. 'My sister is to be kept apart from our stepmother for the time being. And the dowager, as she is now to be formally addressed, is to be kept under invisible guard. I do not give her permission to leave the palace yet. She is to be kept at the side of my father's body until she has fulfilled her vigil as is required … on her knees, as is also required.'

He'd nodded and she had seen his fierce pride in her actions.

Reynard had then touched a finger to his lips momentarily. 'I'm not certain, your majesty, that the dowager is aware of Morgravia's custom that a wife who outlives her husband must go into mourning for eighteen moons,' he'd whispered.

'No, I suspect not. So Chancellor Reynard, will you make immediate arrangements for her to be removed to Rittylworth Monastery, where she can begin her official mourning as soon as she completes her vigil.'

She remembered how Reynard had permitted himself a tiny smile. 'I will make those arrangements.'

'See to it our most reliable guards escort the dowager to her new abode, won't you, Reynard? Select a team who will remain at Rittylworth as her guard but also our eyes. She is dangerous; I have no doubt about that.'

'You are wise, Queen Florentyna. The dowager will be gone from the palace by tomorrow night.'

Florentyna emerged from her memories at the snap of a twig behind her. 'Is that you, Felyx?' she asked without turning.

'Yes, your majesty.'

'I'm fine. Just a few moments longer, please.'

She heard him retreat and shifted her thoughts to the present. Saria was now unhappily, but securely, entrenched at Rittylworth Monastery. She had nearly completed the period of mourning and Florentyna knew that as soon as she could, the dowager would rush east into Briavel, back to the stronghold of her family's lands at Tamar, northeast of its capital. And from there, Florentyna had no doubt, her vicious stepmother would be out of her black robes and plotting. Not for a heartbeat did Florentyna imagine that Saria would allow her to rule easily. Observers had confirmed that Saria believed a crown had been stolen from her, was even whispering that Florentyna had the healthy king poisoned. It was such abhorrent talk and yet Florentyna knew not to be surprised by it.

'Above all, my queen,' Reynard had advised, 'keep Darcelle close and keep her happy. If Saria is going to make any sort of move against you, she will use Darcelle as her secret weapon.'

Not long after, the strange little man called Fynch had appeared and Reynard had granted him an audience with Florentyna.

'Saria is the least of your concerns, your majesty,' Fynch had said calmly, as though reading her mind, his bright eyes fixing her to the chair in the solar, where she'd greeted him.

She recalled that conversation now.

'You are saying that the empire is under threat from a foe we don't know about and can't see,' she'd repeated, working to keep an even tone in her voice.

'That's my belief,' he'd said softly. 'I have waited for the signs.'

'Signs?'

'Majesty, I am a man with strong spiritual beliefs. I pay attention to … well, shall I call them nuances within the invisible world surrounding our own.' She'd flashed a glance at Reynard. Fynch had seen it but didn't appear to react at her obvious cynicism, and had deliberately turned it back upon her. 'Isn't it true, your majesty, that you believe strongly in the ethereal?'

'My beliefs are not —'

'Your beliefs are everything. You must lead your people and they will follow. Cailech and Valentyna believed in the spiritual world, feared and admired it, paid homage to it … in their own way.'

'What do you know of my forebears, Master Fynch?' she'd bristled.

'Like you, my queen, I am a student of history. And I have lived more than most.'

There was something cryptic in his words.

Just when she'd thought he'd finished, he added, 'If you believe that magic exists, your majesty — and I suspect that you do — then you must also believe it can be put to the work of good or to evil. I believe that an evil magic is loose again.' He shrugged, as if to say he had nothing more to offer.

'Why should we trust this information, Master Fynch?' she'd asked, feeling the weight of his scrutiny.

'Simply because I can speak only the truth to you, your majesty. If I was interested in mischief-making I'm sure there are far more dramatic and indeed easier ways to win your attention. I know it is difficult to place your trust in a stranger but — and this will be even more difficult for you to accept — I am no stranger to Stoneheart or to your family.'

She'd cut him a glance of surprise before she looked at Reynard. 'And why do you trust him so, chancellor?'

'Queen Florentyna, I have nothing other than my ability to judge character upon which to base my trust. I have never been more sure of someone — other than yourself — than I am of this man who stands before you.'

'You're basing your trust on instinct?'

'What else is there, majesty?' Fynch cut in. 'I mean, when logic fails and other sensibilities are removed. We can learn much from the animal realm. Beasts act only upon instinct and rarely make mistakes.'

'Master Fynch, I am mindful of your care for the Crown, but unless you can convince me of your pedigree to be even able to counsel me on such matters ...' She'd shaken her head. 'I don't know who you are or how you might know such things about my family's history.' Florentyna had then fixed him with a hard gaze. 'Every Crown has its enemies —'

'Not like this one, your majesty,' he'd had the gall to quietly interrupt.

Her lips had thinned. It was very difficult for her because Reynard, whom she trusted without question, had a plea in his expression. 'Nevertheless,' she'd continued, 'I want proof. Bring it to me and I will sit down with you, Master Fynch.'

'What sort of proof, your majesty?' he had persisted, frowning.

'I don't know. That's your problem. I'm afraid until there is something real that I can see or touch or even understand, Master Fynch, I shall leave it to Chancellor Reynard to use his instincts and to keep me briefed.' She'd stood. 'Good day, gentlemen,' and she had swept from the room, feeling fractionally hollow for having dismissed him.

Master Fynch began to haunt her thoughts; his warning invaded her dreams; his name resonated deep in her recollections ... back to her childhood to the legend of a boy called Fynch, who rode with a dragon and was friends with an emperor.

And the chancellor had been absent since that meeting, leaving his day-to-day duties to Burrage. It was strange. Reynard had been at her side since she'd begun her reign and now he'd left her without a word. She'd assumed at first that he was attending to imperial matters but it was not at all like him. And then when he had not appeared and could not be found, a sinister pall had laid itself over his disappearance. Privately, Florentyna was certain that Reynard believed in Fynch and was angry at her for not trusting him also. Had he gone off on some journey of discovery of his own — or even with Fynch — to bring her proof of the threat that she had demanded?

When Florentyna had finally broached with Darcelle the subject of the stranger and his claim, her sister had tossed her golden hair and looked at Florentyna as though she'd gone soft in her mind. Darcelle had ridiculed Fynch as a luna-fool.

'He probably howls at the night sky when the tides are high,' she gibed. She'd not let the chancellor off lightly either, taking the opportunity to tell Florentyna exactly what she thought of the interfering old man.

'I'm glad he's finally given you some space to breathe. I know you're very close to him, Florentyna, but perhaps you don't see his oily ways as clearly as others do.'

Florentyna blinked, stung. Her trait was not to react too quickly to criticism so she held her tongue, but Darcelle didn't pause to even take a breath.

'You should banish both, dear sister. Neither is good for you. Everything is well for our land, especially now that I've strengthened our ties with Tamas. I'm the one you should be grateful to. Not silly old men scared of their own shadows and preaching doom and gloom. In fact, I live in your shadow and yet I'm the one doing the work of a queen. I attend the formal occasions that you should, I charm at parties, I deliver your messages in the most eloquent of ways and now I make your realm safe for you.'

Darcelle had clearly forgotten herself but behind this stupidity Florentyna could hear Saria; it was obvious her sister had paid a visit to her stepmother recently. Darcelle loved the role she played for the Crown; it not only gave her purpose but it employed her strengths, showed off her talents. It was beyond belief that Darcelle would complain or consider herself 'used' by the Crown. No, it took a far more devious and malicious mind to come up with that slant.

She'd needed Reynard's counsel but the chancellor had not been seen again and neither had Master Fynch. Had she offended her senior aide or had he met some terrible end? It was a mystery that was increasingly making her feel anxious and she'd begun to convince herself that if she could see a dead body she'd have a better time accepting his wordless disappearance. And what kept returning to her was that something in Master Fynch's gaze had told her he had come as a friend, that he was telling her the truth.

ELEVEN

Cassien was seated in a chair while an old woman with few teeth was sucking her lips and lathering up his face with a huge soft bristle brush and gritty soap.

'Widow Nance is the local herbwoman. She makes up floral charms,' Ham explained. 'She's very busy at the moment.'

'Is there a feast day?' Cassien wondered aloud as she slopped on still more lather.

'Be still,' Nance warned, reaching for a lethal-looking blade.

Her fingers trembled as the blade approached and Cassien baulked.

Ham laughed. 'Don't, Nance. He's new to these parts.'

She cackled, enjoying her joke. 'I can clean up your chin blindfolded with one arm tied behind my back,' she said, slapping Cassien's shoulder. 'Now be still, handsome, and let me get this done.'

'It's blood month,' Ham continued. 'Widow Nance is doing up orders of special red wreaths and posies to hang in all the houses for luck, and especially for food, through the long winter ahead.'

Nance had already trimmed his hair so he no longer looked shaggy and now he could feel the satisfying scrape of the blade over his jaw. Ham had done well to bring him to this place for she was not even vaguely curious about him or his weapons. Soon she was pressing a steaming towel to his face and telling him he was done.

'Well, Ham,' she grunted at the boy nearby. 'You've brought me a welcome one this time. Very tasty, indeed. I'm sure the girls at the brothel will fight over you,' she said, grinning at Cassien. As he opened his mouth, she waved a hand. 'And don't deny it either. All you young bucks head straight there. Although those girls charge a pretty penny now for something you can get right here.' She began to lift her skirts and Cassien leapt from the chair as if stung.

'No, Widow Nance!' he all but begged, and this won a guffaw from Hamelyn and a huge wheeze of a laugh from the old girl.

'I used to be a beauty when I was your age — you'd have accepted me then — but the years have punished me.' She laughed again at his anxious expression. 'Touchy, isn't he? No sense of humour, Ham. You'd better find him one if he's to survive in this town.'

'I won't be staying long,' Cassien assured.

'Then you should take your chances when you can, because I don't make the offer lightly,' she said, again beginning to lift her skirts.

He grinned this time, didn't shrink back and of course she only pulled them high enough to reveal wrinkled knees.

'Now there you are; you learn fast and you're even more likely to win a kiss when you smile like that,' she said. Then switching topics rapidly she poked Cassien in the chest. 'Ham's a good boy. Don't you take liberties with him or you'll answer to me.'

Cassien pressed a silver coin into her crooked fingers, gnarled by the bone-ache, and surprised her again by leaning down and planting a kiss on her hollow cheek. 'Thank you.' Beneath his lips her skin felt leathery but she giggled like a young girl.

'Go on with you, stranger, flirting with an old woman like me.' She gave a tutting sound to match her arch expression.

Cassien smiled wider and rubbed his naked chin. 'You give a good shave, Nance.'

'Don't you forget it. Now go find yourself a young plaything to help you forget the world for a bit. I feel only a gloom in my waters.'

Cassien glanced up from tying on his cloak. 'Oh? Why gloom?'

'Widow Nance has visions now and then,' Ham explained hurriedly. 'Pay no attention.'

'Ignore me at your peril, young man.' She shook a crooked finger at Ham. 'Who warned the village folk in the surrounding hamlets that the mouth rot was coming to their cows?'

'You did, Nance,' he said obediently.

She nodded. 'I saw the death of our king … Shar grant him peace,' she said, touching her hand to her forehead in respect at naming the god. 'It was a shock for the whole realm, the empire even … but not to me. I saw it in my dreams. And now we have a slip of a girl on the throne.'

'Have you seen her?'

His two companions shook their heads.

'Her sister's very beautiful, though,' Ham said, eyes widening in memory. 'She visited Orkyld last summer on official royal business. Golden ... like an angel, she was,' he recalled in a dreamy voice.

'And a heart like ice, child.'

'What makes you say that, Nance?' Cassien asked.

She gave a shiver. 'Oh, I don't know. She has enough beauty for several girls but there was something very cold about her.'

'You spoke about sensing gloom, though.'

She nodded. 'I did. As I say, just a feeling in my water.'

Ham gurgled a laugh.

'He makes fun of me, silly boy. He'll find out soon enough. Watch yourself, Ham. Stick close to this one. He looks like he can handle a blade well.'

But Cassien didn't want to let it go; he knew Fynch wouldn't. 'What's coming, Nance?'

She blinked in surprise. 'No-one ever wants to know what I think. Why should you?'

'Because I trust instincts. They can serve us well. They've been around a lot longer than religion.'

'Ooh, you heathen,' she said, touching both hands to her ears.

Cassien couldn't help but like the quirky old woman. 'I'm not heathen; I simply believe we should all trust what we see and hear, what we can touch, taste ... and especially what we feel.'

She gave him a toothless grin. 'I do too, but most don't set much store by what those of us who are touched by Shar can sense.'

He flipped her another coin. 'Tell me.'

'I don't take payment for my visions.'

'It's not for your visions. I'd like to buy a posy of dried flowers.'

'Then take your pick from those behind you there. As for my instincts, they're telling me a bad wind is going to blow through Morgravia.'

'More of the devil's work?' he asked cryptically, sensing that she preferred to talk indirectly when it came to her visions.

'Perhaps,' she said, glancing at the boy. Her tone said he'd guessed right.

'I'll see you outside, Ham,' he said and the youngster readily obeyed, lifting a hand in farewell to Nance.

'You're a good boy, Ham. Come visit me again soon.'

She returned her attention to Cassien. 'The boy and I have an understanding. We're both touched lightly by something, and so I suppose you could call us kindred souls. But who are you?'

'Someone who doesn't fear the devil,' he said, without hesitating.

Her gaze narrowed as she regarded him.

'Where will this dark wind blow?' he asked.

She shook her head. 'Pearlis, I think, though I see nothing specific pointing there, other than that the dragon has awoken and the cathedral stirs from its sleep.'

Nance was becoming more cryptic by the moment.

'The dragon?'

'Beast of royals. The king.'

'Why has the dragon woken?'

'He knows what's coming. He will warn whomever he can,' she said, her gaze unfocused.

'Is the throne in jeopardy?' he asked, astonished that she was in a similar mindset to Fynch.

She shook her head. 'I can't tell. But if the dragon is involved …' Her words trailed off.

Cassien frowned. 'What do you mean about the cathedral?'

'The beasts awake,' she said tonelessly, her gaze drifting faraway. 'They sense the danger. An ancient danger. A cunning one. They've seen this magic before — the magic that defies death.' She snapped back her attention to him and she was alert again. 'Forgive me, I … I forget myself sometimes.'

'Nothing to forgive.'

'Don't speak of this to the boy … to anyone. Keep him safe.'

'I promise I will. And I have no-one to speak to about what you've told me anyway. I walk alone.'

She nodded. 'Yes, you're him but you're not alone.'

He stared at her. 'Him? Who am I?'

'One of few.'

'I told you, I walk alone.'

'Nevertheless.'

'I don't understand.'

She smiled. 'The dragon has spoken to you.'

In that heartbeat, he thought he saw Romaine reflected in the glass of Nance's tiny window. He blinked and the notion was gone but he was left with a fresh gust of worry for Fynch. 'You're speaking in riddles, Nance.'

The old girl shrugged. 'I told you, no-one pays me any attention. You shouldn't either.'

He frowned deeper, could see she'd shut down in her mind and would give him no more. 'Thank you for telling me.'

She nodded, turned away, looking suddenly fatigued. 'Don't forget your posy,' she said over her shoulder.

He took the nearest one, a tiny heart wreath made of twisted twigs and a few leaves intertwined with red rose hips. He liked its simplicity. It reminded him of the forest and its pristine white wildwood rose.

Emerging from Nance's tiny shop he found Ham kicking his heels in the dust.

'Ready for the inn?' Ham asked. 'Innkeeper told me she said not to be late.'

'I'm ready. Ham?'

The boy turned back.

'Who is Nance? I mean, what's her background?'

'She told me once, said it was not something she shared with others … that I was special.'

'Will you tell me? It's important,' Cassien said.

Ham's forehead creased in concern as he considered the request. He nodded once his decision was made. 'She was a nun, but she fell from grace because she loved a man, had a child with him. The man and the child died soon after its birth. I don't know the details but she said to me that it was her punishment. Shar was making her live her penance, rather than perform it through prayer or good deed.'

'She obviously likes you.'

'She likes few people and she's not terribly popular anyway because she used to share her visions. They were always bleak, so the townsfolk hated it and shunned her. Now she keeps them to herself and shares them only now and then. She was right about the livestock and the king. I don't know how much else she sees. I'm surprised she was so open with you. Maybe she saw something in you.'

'Like she saw something in you, you mean?' he asked carefully.

Ham squirmed. 'She says I'm touched.'

'By what?'

'She's never said,' he replied with a shrug. 'She did tell me that she came to Orkyld because it cleaved to the old ways, accepted magic.'

'Perhaps people who are more in tune with the spiritual world come here because of it.'

'I was born here,' Ham admitted. 'I had no choice.'

Perhaps your parents did, Cassien thought, but kept that to himself. 'Come on then, to the Yew Inn we go.'

'Will your guest be staying the … er, night?'

'No. Are you happy to wait downstairs for me?'

Ham scratched his head. 'Am I now travelling with you?' Cassien stopped. 'I mean, are you employing me to be at your side at all times?'

He smiled. 'Yes, I am. Are you comfortable with that?'

'I'm leaving the orphanage?'

'Do you want to think about it?'

Ham shook his head. 'No!' he said vehemently, startling Cassien. 'I want to travel with you, wherever you go.'

Cassien grinned. 'Right, then. Get yourself some food. Let Innkeeper Erris know you have my permission to put it on my tab. There's a second cot in my room, anyway. I'll pay for the use of it. Here's some coin for you. You should not be without.'

Ham looked at the money as though Cassien had just placed several gold sovereigns in his palm.

'Be my ears and eyes when I'm not around,' Cassien said, his tone grave. 'Tomorrow we go to Wevyr's.' He was intrigued to see the boy squirm. 'Now, we need to hide my weapons. Any thoughts?' He wondered if Ham would be curious as to why. If he was, he didn't show it.

'Wait here,' the boy said and ducked into a nearby stable, returning shortly with a sack. 'Put your blades in here. I'll keep them hidden until you need them. I know the stableboy and checked. That stable is going to be empty for the next two nights on the orders of one of the nobles, whose unfriendly horse is usually stabled there. He's away but pays for that stall to be kept free — it's the end stall. I can hide them under the hay. I can even sleep there if you want.' He shrugged. 'I'm used to it.'

'No need for that.' Cassien frowned. 'You're sure you can keep them safe?'

Ham nodded solemnly. 'My friend Joch can be trusted.'

* * *

As they entered there was no immediate sign of the innkeeper, although the inn itself was filling fast and the sounds dragged him back to his early childhood. He'd forgotten how loud men drinking could be. Sporadic bursts of raucous laughter permeated a convivial atmosphere of talk and the clank of pewter mugs. At trestle tables around the room a few people were already eating and the fire at one end burned steadily. Hanging softly overhead was a thin cloud of smoke drifting from the clay pipes of a few of the older men, who sat closest to the fire, chewing the cud of winters past, no doubt.

'Will you be all right?' Cassien asked.

'I'll eat in the kitchen. I know some of the girls,' Ham said.

Cassien grinned. 'Is there anyone you don't know in this town, Ham?' he said, as he moved toward the back stairs. 'I'll see you shortly.'

'Have fun,' Ham said, and Cassien raised an eyebrow as Ham hastily departed.

'Ah, there you are, sir,' Erris said, arriving from the kitchens and hurrying along three serving girls. 'Those are for the merchants from Briavel.' The first girl nodded and the others pushed past. 'Tell them the ale is with my compliments,' he called after them, returning his gaze to Cassien. 'Your visitor was shown upstairs not long ago.'

Cassien climbed the stairs thinking on the ugly task ahead. If he could depend on her silence he would, but he doubted any whore could be entirely relied upon. He would kill her if he had to. He opened the door quietly, fully expecting to find her rummaging through the room to see if he'd hidden anything beneath loose floorboards or behind the sparse furniture. Instead he found her sitting by a window, her cloak tied around her throat. There was something still about her that immediately captivated him. She cocked her head to one side and regarded him closely.

He might have smiled, if not for feeling suddenly and intensely annoyed. 'I am Cassien,' he said evenly.

'Yes, I presumed that.' Her voice was slightly raspy in a pleasant way.

'You're not Penely, are you?'

She blinked, disconcerted. 'I was told to come here by Innkeeper Erris. I am Penely.'

'You're lying. Please leave.'

'What?' She stood abruptly in a fluid motion and he noticed she was taller than he had first thought, and far slimmer than he'd imagined after gazing at the small window of flesh she'd exposed just beneath the tie of her cloak.

Cassien motioned to the door. 'I said leave.'

'I've given up several —'

He threw her a crown and then a second, which she caught deftly, but also with defiance. 'More than payment for your time. You don't even have to go back to your brothel sore.'

She scowled at him. 'You don't have the manners to go with those looks.' She stepped lightly across the room. 'You missed a good —'

'I don't think so,' he cut in, not meaning it for a moment, but his scornful smile made her bristle.

She pushed past him to the door and Cassien took her arm. The woman hissed, shrank back, clearly afraid of being assaulted. He pulled her closer. 'Tell the real Penely I still want to meet her and that if she doesn't come willingly, I will hunt her. And the next time she wants to send a friend, she should colour her friend's hair with fracca nut. The beetroot and cherlot mix looks far too unnatural. Give her this,' he said, handing out another crown. 'She's safe,' he lied. 'I will only hurt her if she doesn't come willingly.'

'What do you want with her?' she hissed, clearly giving up on the disguise.

The skin tightened around his mouth. 'I have a question. She knew a friend of mine. I also want to know why she's so afraid that she sent you instead.'

He could smell her perfume. It was surprisingly light and subtle. This woman smelled like the fresh grass that he rolled around in when playing with Romaine. Her fragrance distracted him. He blinked.

The woman shook off his grip easily enough. 'I'm her sister. And she's frightened.'

'Of what?'

'Strangers like you, with more money than they should have and throwing it around in her name.'

'She's a whore,' he said, stung with surprise at the accusation. 'How else does she get business?'

The woman prodded him in the chest for the second time that evening. 'She may earn her living by servicing men's needs, but that doesn't give you any right to look down upon her or any of us. Does she bleed? Yes, like any other. Does she have feelings? Yes, just like you. Does she dream? Of course, and it's not about keeping the likes of you happy. She knows nothing about anyone.'

'Do you know every man she's pleasured?'

'Near enough. I told you, I'm her sister, and none of her clients should interest you.'

'Let me decide that. I'm warning you, I can find her anywhere.'

'I'm sure you can, but I'll kill you before you lay a finger on her, stranger.'

Their faces were close together and her teeth were almost bared … and there was that stillness again. She reminded him of Romaine in a woman's form.

'What's your name?' he asked.

'Vivienne,' she said curtly.

'Sit, Vivienne. I've paid for your time. I demand what I've paid for.'

She flung one of the coins at his feet. 'And only my time. Touch me again and I'll scream.'

'I'm sure you will,' he replied. Then added, 'Be assured I have no intention of laying a finger on you.' He said it in a scornful manner, so Vivienne could be left in no doubt that he found her not in the least bit attractive. Cassien decided then and there that he was fast becoming a superior liar.

She looked down the length of his body. 'It's not your finger I'm worried about,' she said, the sarcasm biting.

Cassien stepped away, clearing his throat. Damn her! It had been too long. 'If you sit over there by the window again, then even my massive need can't reach you.'

She laughed, in spite of her mood, and returned to her seat. She said nothing, watching him remove his cloak, but he could tell he was making an impression on her, and it wasn't making her feel any safer. He sat down, placing the cloak in his lap for modesty.

'How is it that you and your sister are prostitutes?'

'How is it you're such a nosy prick?'

He gave a soft snort of exasperation. 'I'm trying to set you at your ease.'

'It's not working. What do you want with us?'

'Are you older than her?'

'Younger.' He was surprised. She seemed to know his next question. 'Penely can wrap most men around her little finger but she needs to be treated like a princess. She's just not …' Vivienne thought about this for a few moments. 'She's just not tough enough here,' she said, pointing to her head, 'for when anyone treats her badly.'

'Isn't she in the wrong line of work if she's that fragile?'

'I can assure you, Penely probably makes more money than most of us girls put together. As I told you, she's exceptionally talented at her work and that means she's the most popular prostitute in the region. She can pick and choose her customers. She chooses not to meet with you.'

'So she sends her little sister?'

'I offered. I am not scared of you.'

'So I see. Vivienne, do you remember a man by the name of Zeek?'

She shook her head.

'Your sister spent a somewhat debauched night with him a few moons back. He was a tailor.'

'Yes, I do remember him now. I didn't know his name. I do recall him but only because he gave her a beautiful shawl of his own design.'

'Well, Zeek is now dead.'

Her poise crumbled slightly. 'Of what?'

'Of murder.'

'Shar's wrath! Why?'

'That's what I'm trying to establish. He died in my arms. He told me he'd recently been with your sister. I want to know what he told Penely.'

Vivienne untied her cloak, slipping it back over her shoulders to reveal wide shoulders tapering to a slim waist beneath large, full breasts. Vivienne's skin was like honeyed milk, smooth and unblemished, but right now her hand was clamped to her throat in anxiety.

She turned back. 'Master Cassien, I can assure you my sister knows nothing about murder. Men talk all the time between the sheets. And girls in our business let it wash right over us like water. They're usually bleating about their wives or their money woes. They all want their mothers! No, not like that,' she hastily assured him. 'They just want to be held for a few hours by someone who won't judge them, someone who likes them in spite of themselves. I'm sure Zeek was like all the others. I seem to remember now that she told me he was desperately drunk, mostly talking nonsense.'

'If she knows nothing, why is she scared to meet me?

She shrugged again, looked genuinely bewildered. 'I probably remember more about their conversation than my sister does. Penely takes the "smoke".'

'The smoke?'

Her expression turned slightly bemused. 'Where are you from?'

'Here and there.'

'But obviously not here. And by here I mean Morgravia, or even Briavel. Shar, even the Razor people know about smoking the embers.'

Cassien cleared his throat lightly. 'I've been away for a long time.'

She regarded him intently before she sighed softly. 'The embers of the lugara. Do you know it?'

He wracked his mind. Was sure it was a bark or plant. She didn't wait. 'It was brought in from the east, I think. Ever since we opened up all these new trading routes we are seeing spices, plants, fabrics, even foods we've never known before. Lugara is a leaf. It takes the pain away.'

'Is your sister injured?'

She gave a low laugh and it sounded kind to him. 'No, she is healthy enough, I suppose. The smoke takes away thoughts … the present you could say. Penely needs escape and the lugara delivers that. Some people have beggared themselves in pursuit of it. But you, clearly, are in no fear of it.'

'No,' he replied, once again reminded of his sheltered former existence. 'Tell me what she said to you of that time with Zeek. Please, Vivienne, it's important.'

'It was all silly girls' talk — nothing relevant, other than a remark she made about some special blades he'd had to commission for a client, but that's it.' She flicked a glance at his hip and he was glad he'd taken the precaution of hiding the weapons. 'The man was very drunk, I recall,' Vivienne continued, 'and Penely was the only one of us who could be bothered with him. He paid very well and lavished her with food and that gift. As I say, I never knew his name until you mentioned it. She called him the tailor.'

Cassien closed his eyes.

'What's wrong?'

'Who else did she mention this to?'

'All of us. It was in the common room. She was laughing about Zeek, showing off his shawl.'

Now Cassien held his head. He'd have to kill them all. 'There was nothing else,' she claimed, her frustration escalating again. 'She's never mentioned him again. Why is this so important?'

'It's not. I'm trying to find the clue to his killer,' he lied.

Vivienne stood. 'Leave her alone ... please. She's —' The woman shook her head. 'Just leave her.'

'She's what?'

'She's dying!' She began to weep and her voice shook. 'The smoke is killing her. It's all she does now — smoke and pleasure men. One feeds the other. Some even pay her with the lugara. It's sickening!'

He took a breath. 'I'm sorry.'

'No you're not. You don't even know her. Like everyone else, you wanted something from her. Well, she's got nothing more to give. Leave her alone. Let her be in peace.'

'How long?' he asked, his tone cool.

Vivienne snatched away a tear. 'I don't know. The physic says no more than a moon. So don't worry, the leaf has done what you came here to do. You can leave with your hands free of her blood.'

Faster than she could react, Cassien leapt up and in a stride had her in his grip. But Vivienne showed no emotion this time. She stood limply beneath his close fist. 'It's what you intended, isn't it?'

'Why do you say that?'

'You're a killer, for sure. I see no weapons but I'm not fooled. Other men would have been happy to have me but you're so obsessed with what you need to discover that you can move past the desire I see in your eyes, trembling through your body. Either you're being paid to do this or you are frightened enough to want to silence my sister. What does she know, you're wondering? You probably killed Zeek.'

'Perhaps I should kill you?'

Her grey gaze looked at him with contempt. 'Well, I can't defend myself, but I have taken some steps for protection.'

He waited.

'Very soon men will come to this door. In fact, they're already lining the stairs and they're outside, if you'd like to check.'

He pushed her away and strode to the window; right enough there were four men looking up at him.

'There's no way out. So if you kill me, they will kill you and the boy you arrived with.' His eyes widened. 'And the woman you visited before you came here. Widow Nance, wasn't it? I may look defenceless, Master Figaret, but no man's strength is a match for a woman's cunning. I am very well liked in this town, and if I am very well liked then Penely is worshipped. It wasn't hard to conscript men to offer me protection while I had this appointment to keep. Now, I think all of us would judge you've had long enough with me for your carnal gratification. They await my safe emergence from your room because I told them I was scared of you.'

He looked down, knowing he had been outsmarted.

'The boy Ham will already be in the hands of the men.'

His eyes snapped up to meet hers. 'You'd better not hurt the child.'

'Who is Hamelyn to you?'

'A friend.'

'What sort of friend? We're wary of strangers who befriend our children.'

'Hamelyn has nothing to fear from me. I have hired his services, that's all.'

'What are you afraid of?' she demanded.

He looked at her with surprise. 'Me?'

She nodded. 'You came to kill my sister, all right, I have no doubt of that. I know you're probably the one Zeek had the weapons made for.'

A fist hammered on the door. 'Vivienne?'

'Yes,' she called and moved back from Cassien, out of arm's reach. 'Don't try anything,' she warned. 'Come in, Murdo.'

Cassien sagged inside.

A huge man stepped in and leered at him. 'Evening, stranger,' he said in a mocking tone. He looked at her. 'You all right?'

She nodded. 'Thanks, Murdo. Ham will keep him co-Operative.'

'What about Nance?'

She shook her head. 'The boy is enough.'

Murdo turned and growled a few low words to the person who was obviously on the other side of the door.

Vivienne returned her attention to Cassien. 'I'm not in the habit of hurting children. I had to be sure. He will be safe, but you will be going with Murdo and his men.'

'I've heard you've got a blade by Wevyr.' Cassien sighed. 'I've always wanted some of Wevyr's weapons,' Murdo baited.

'If I do you'll have to find it first and if you find it, you'll have to win it,' Cassien said calmly.

Murdo laughed. 'And you look like you're in a position to bargain, stranger.'

'Kill the boy, kill Nance, but I can assure you, I can kill Vivienne with a single fist to her face before she can take another step in this room. And if you value her services and she values her life, then you'll agree to a fair fight. You need not threaten a child or an old woman in order to get to me. I will come willingly but I will not willingly give you my weapon. And every man has a right to fight for what belongs to him. A true man of the Razors would believe that.'

It was said quietly but Murdo appeared stung, as if his manhood had been questioned. He looked at Vivienne and she nodded.

'We'll take him from here, Vivienne. You and your sister should be ready for us later. Once we've softened him up, we'll come looking for your pleasuring.'

Vivienne threw Cassien a look and he wasn't sure if there was an element of apology in it. 'I just want you to leave Penely alone. She knows nothing of what you seek.'

Curiously, for all her cunning he trusted Vivienne. Nothing Loup had taught him could prepare him for a woman's wiles. And now she looked sorry for dragging Murdo into their midst.

'Please assure your sister she is safe. I have nothing further to say to her.'

Innkeeper Erris had arrived. 'What is going on here? Vivienne?'

'We were just leaving, Erris,' she said hurriedly.

'Well, begone all of you. I want no scenes or fights in my inn. We run a safe house here. Murdo, you know how I feel about you and your braves picking on my customers. I won't have you or your louts coming into my kitchen. You know where I drew that line last time you were down from the mountains.' He waggled a finger. 'And you've grabbed Hamelyn and terrified my girls.' He shooed at them. 'Come on, out! All of you. Master

Cassien, I'm sorry that goes for you too. I know you've paid. I'll return your coin.' He threw some money onto the bed. 'I can't have this going on or word will get around that I don't have control of my own inn. Take it all outside the Yew and sort out your differences.'

'After you,' Murdo said mockingly to Cassien.

They filed down the stairs. Hamelyn, waiting below, looked at Cassien with wide, frightened eyes. Before he could speak, Cassien did.

'Hide. You know where.'

'What about —'

'Do you hear?' Cassien insisted, his tone angry now.

Hamelyn nodded, pushed past and whispered only for Cassien's hearing. 'He is the son of the Razor king, Metheven.'

'Go,' he said. Then he looked at Murdo. 'Lead on.'

They left by a back door that Erris herded them through. Once outside, Murdo shoved Cassien. 'Follow my men. We're going to use one of those outhouses,' he said, pointing his huge jaw in its direction, not far from the inn.

Vivienne laid her hand on the mountain man's enormous arm. 'Murdo, why don't you come to the brothel now? I have no other customers at the moment. And surely we are done here. I'm not worried about him anymore.'

Murdo shook off her hand. 'Go and wait for me, woman! I want to show this fellow that he shouldn't sneer at Razor men. He might be used to fancy weapons but I'll make him use an honest blade made in the forges of the mountains. But later I'll use my fancy weapon on you,' he promised, and grabbed at her breasts.

She nimbly stepped back and slapped at his hand.

'I have no intention of using any blade against you, Murdo,' Cassien said, irritated by the man's attitude to Vivienne. 'In fact, I have no intention of striking you.'

'What?'

'You heard.'

'Then I shall beat you to a pulp and your fear of me will not stop me striking you.'

Cassien simply smiled. He stole a glance at Vivienne and was surprised to see her staring at him, worried.

Murdo shoved her as he strode past. 'Go bathe for me.'

'Why? You don't bathe for me,' she snapped from behind him.

He swung around and looked confused to see Cassien standing between them.

'Don't touch her like that,' Cassien said evenly.

'I pay so I can do what I like,' Murdo snarled.

'Right now, Murdo, she's on my time. Isn't that right, Vivienne?' He turned to her.

'Yes,' she replied and cut him a look that was half amusement, half gratitude.

'I did say one night, didn't I?' Cassien added, not looking at her. His attention was focused on Murdo.

The pause felt like an eternity. She jangled some coins behind him.

'I believe you did. I'd forgotten.'

Murdo looked stunned. 'You asked us to protect you,' he roared at her over Cassien's shoulder.

'And I paid you! All of you,' she snapped. 'The brothel will expect you, but I can't look after you this evening, Murdo. He has paid,' she lied.

Cassien had to suppress a grin. A glance at Murdo reminded him this was no laughing matter.

'When I'm finished with him, Vivienne, he won't be able to hold his own cock to piss, let alone get it up to fuck you.'

'Let me worry about the rise and fall of my cock, Murdo.'

This brought a roar of laughter from the other men and for this they won a glare from their leader. 'Take him inside,' he growled to them.

TWELVE

Florentyna was ushered silently into the chapel by Burrage. She could see the pale body laid out on the marble plinth while four tall, creamy beeswax candles burned near it: one at his head, one at his feet, and a candle at each side. She was immediately relieved to see that it was definitely not Reynard.

The candle near his right hand guttered and Florentyna noted how the attending cleric reached quickly for his snips to trim the wick; there was so much superstition surrounding bodies and their spirits these days that even the men of Shar paid them heed. She was sure the less people believed in the old magics, the more fearful they became of old superstitions and the greater they intensified their devotions to Shar. These fears seemed to be harking back to the Zerque days, when even a reflection in a puddle of water bore sinister significance.

To Florentyna, however, who took a more pragmatic view, it was simply a flickering candle and nothing to do with spirits — evil or good. Burrage had flinched, however, and looked anxiously at the cleric until he'd achieved a steady burn of the flame again.

She was able to approach the dead man with far less emotion now that she knew it was not Reynard, and as she drew alongside him she experienced a wave of pity on Dean Flek's behalf. He belonged to others: a grieving wife and perhaps some children might miss him; certainly friends — like Master Pel — mourned his passing. Such a waste and such a brutal way to die. She knew death occurred all around her for one reason or another, much of it early and thus cruel, but there was something sinister about this man's demise. There were too many questions surrounding it. Why had an innocent dean been killed so savagely? It wasn't theft, and according to Pel he had no known enemies. Why had the stranger — the presumed killer — been naked? There was even the suggestion that the naked man — Gabriel was the name Pel had tentatively suggested — was of another world.

Burrage may have given a scornful glance, but this last notion is what had unnerved her the most. It was particularly relevant given that Fynch had warned her of this type of threat arriving. But who could she tell? Who would listen to her? Reynard was not here to consult, and she had no idea of how to find Master Fynch.

'Your majesty,' the robed man murmured softly, bowing his head. 'We laid him out, as requested.' He nodded at the open eyes of the corpse.

'Thank you, Morn. Is Father Cuthben about?' she asked the young man, marvelling, as she often did, at his neatly shaved pate as he bent. It suited his small, round head.

'No, majesty. He is at the leper colony for the next two days. I can swiftly organise anything you need.'

She smiled. 'I appreciate it. That will be all, thank you, Morn. We can manage from here.'

He bowed and silently left.

Florentyna returned her gaze to the dead man. He was no longer in his prime but he had surely had a kindly look about him, despite's Pel's claims that he was a stickler for this or that. His once-warm brown eyes were staring sightlessly at the intricately painted chapel ceiling and she briefly looked up at the mural that Emperor Cailech had commissioned to be painted. She had always loved it. The artist, Fairlow, had taken most of his adult life to complete it. It was breathtakingly beautiful, a rendition of the Wild beyond the border where legend had it that dragons flew above the forests and streams, where exotic flowers and other strange fauna abounded. She admired Fairlow's imaginative flair; the lifelike paintings that always made her feel as though the king of the beasts was staring just at her. Not with ferocity, though; more with affection and with joy.

A boy rode the back of the dragon. The legendary Fynch.

That name was haunting her.

'I told the priest not to finalise anything with the body, your majesty, particularly that you had requested seeing it as it was found,' Burrage said.

'And I suppose Pel and other villagers would have been too superstitious to close his eyes anyway.'

'Indeed, majesty. Until prayers were said for him and the name of his killer passed to someone somewhere, they would continue believing his spirit was watching the murderer.'

'Piffle,' she lamented, snapping her attention back to Flek. 'Do you believe that Father Morn or Cuthben might now miraculously give us the name of Flek's killer?'

'No. But even I do feel more comfortable for our spiritual protocols to be followed.'

She sighed and Burrage continued.

'Clearly Pel was so shocked, your majesty, I doubt anyone was prepared to interfere at all with the body.'

She nodded her understanding.

'What are you hoping to see here, your majesty … er, if you don't mind me enquiring?' Burrage asked carefully.

'I don't know. I hoped something would give a reason why Reynard's quill was found with him. Did he steal it? Was he given it?' She didn't wait for Burrage to answer. 'I doubt it was the former. Flek was well liked and known according to Pel. I can't imagine him for a thief.'

'No, majesty,' Burrage said softly in the background over her thoughts.

'So that leaves us with Dean Flek being left with Reynard's quill? Why? Reynard treasured that swan quill. He would never have given it away and even if he did, why to the naked stranger?'

'Perhaps stolen by this Gabriel fellow?' Burrage tried.

She shook her head, irritated that this puzzle eluded her yet feeling conscious of a hidden 'awareness', which some people claimed everyone possessed but rarely tapped into, that this man or at least his death was connected with Fynch's warning.

'Majesty, my head is spinning with all the potential conclusions we could draw. The fact is, unless this corpse can talk, we'll never know.'

She didn't care about Burrage's dizzy head. She knew she was right — the quill was surely meant to be found. The dead man's modesty was protected with linen. Her gaze took in his thick legs before turning to the hands, which were large and sunbrowned. Flek clearly didn't mind working outdoors. She moved to his left and turned that hand over, not at all squeamish about touching the corpse.

It was cool and surprisingly dry, although it had lost its springiness. Florentyna could see the depression of her fingers, which in living flesh would have rebounded immediately.

'If he was left with Reynard's quill perhaps he is a scrivener of sorts?' Burrage offered, clearly feeling redundant. 'We could ask Pel if —'

'No ink,' she remarked briskly. 'Every scrivener I've met had stained hands,' she said, in a vaguely dismissive tone. Then her voice softened. 'No, this man did not write or copy with ink, not even for a hobby, Burrage.'

'You're most observant, your majesty,' he commented.

She gave a mournful smile. 'His death will remain a mystery. The riddle of Reynard's disappearance is now further clouded by the quill's appearance. I'm embarrassed to think that that man Fynch could know more.'

Burrage stared at her stonily. 'He was mild enough, your majesty, but he was stirring trouble. I'll never understand why Chancellor Reynard brought a doomsayer into your life.' He cleared his throat and waited, but when she didn't say anything in response, he asked, 'Why are you thinking of Master Fynch?'

She blew out her cheeks, frustrated. Florentyna shrugged a shoulder. 'He haunts me.'

Burrage frowned. He was standing by the head of the dead man. 'In what way?'

'Something about his manner, some intensity, that demanded I take notice of him.' She could tell from his expression that Burrage thought she was reading too much into Fynch's presence. He began to smile and she interrupted whatever was about to be said. 'Reynard trusted him implicitly. He had shared things with the former chancellor. When I was dismissive, Reynard —'

'Pardon me, your majesty, but claims of magical beings descending on the Crown of Morgravia was really too much for even —'

'That's the point though,' she cut in. 'Our sensible, clear-thinking Reynard handed over his trust and all but demanded I listen to Master Fynch. I don't know what hold he had over the chancellor. What if that hold led Reynard to leave the palace, desert his position and go in search of this threat?'

There! She'd finally aired what had been nagging at her but she could see she wasn't making much sense to Burrage.

'Well, we've found his quill,' Burrage said in a tone of comfort, just pulling up short of patting her hand soothingly. 'Presumably more will turn up if we remain patient.'

The same candle began to gutter again and Burrage frowned. He walked around the corpse to check the wick himself this time. 'Must be one of those woollen wicks. The royal chapel is supposed to have only silk wicks — linen at worst,' he tutted, but she could see he was unnerved at the demented flickering. She knew he was fighting the superstitious notion that it was the soul of the dead man trying to reach out to the living.

He began to fiddle with the wick. 'May I blow this one out, majesty? It shouldn't offend our dead friend here,' he offered.

'Go ahead,' she said. Burrage blew on the flame, coughing quietly as the light winked out, when two extraordinary events occurred.

Florentyna gasped as she saw the shadow on the man's palm. She reached over his body to lift his hand to look more closely and then cried out, spinning through a full circle of fear as she heard the word 'Help' being called, as though carried on the breath of Burrage as he blew out the flame.

Burrage stared, transfixed. 'Are you all right, your majesty?'

'Burrage, did you hear that?'

He looked stunned. 'Hear what? I ... I thought I heard a door in the distance creaking,' he offered.

'No, no, not a door. Did you hear someone speak?'

He shook his head and looked around, clearly spooked. 'Morn!' he yelled uncharacteristically loudly.

The man rushed in through the door he'd left closed. 'Yes, your majesty ... is something wrong?' he enquired, looking between them.

'Is anyone else in the chapel?' the queen asked.

He shook his head. 'I was told to ensure no-one else would be visiting at this time.'

Burrage glanced at her and took up the questioning. 'Have you seen anyone around?'

'We are alone, I swear. The guard passed just a few moments before you called for me. All is calm and quiet.'

Florentyna shook her head distractedly. She moved to the other side of the body to get a better look at what she thought she'd seen in the shadow. Florentyna leaned closer to stare at the man's chest, which was woolly with grey hair.

'There!' she said, astonished.

Burrage peered closer. 'Shar's breath! What is it?'

She recognised it immediately with her sharp eyesight. 'It's the imprint of the royal sigil. And what's more I am sure it's the version of the one burned onto Reynard's swan quill.'

'How do you know?'

'The miniature size … and see the break, there, on the leg of the dragon?' she pointed, excited. 'It's the same on the quill!'

He did not share her glee. Stared at her with frightened eyes. 'How can that be?'

She shook her head, eyes sparkling with intrigue. 'I don't know, Master Burrage. But we can both see it so we know we aren't imagining this. And what's more I heard a voice.'

Burrage now looked petrified. 'Whose?' he asked, sounding reluctant to hear the answer.

'His!' she replied, ruthlessly throwing more kindling onto the fire of his fear.

Burrage gave a squeak, stepping back from the chapel's dead guest.

She looked between the two men, slightly frightened herself, definitely embarrassed that she was nodding her head in such an obstinate way. 'I heard him.'

Morn gave a light sneer, stopped himself before he gave offence to the highest office in the land, and steepled his fingers in a show of quiet superiority. 'Forgive me, your majesty. May I ask did you touch the body?'

'Yes,' she said, just short of snapping. 'I lifted his arm.'

'Ah,' he said, with smug understanding. A look of sympathy flickered into his expression as he adopted the tone of explaining something to a child. 'Quite often when a body is shifted, or indeed even as it lies, air will escape. It's not uncommon to believe the dead are speaking when, in truth, it's simply the body settling. You were mistaken, majesty. Be assured, this corpse did not speak.'

Her lips thinned slightly. Morn had tried but had lost the battle not to sound condescending. She straightened her bearing to show her full height. 'I did not imagine what I heard.'

'Oh, dear me, no, your majesty, I'm not for a moment suggesting you did. It's just that the physics have explained the stages of the decomposing body to me. And I have been around enough to know that odd "sighs" do occur. It can be most disconcerting.'

'It was *not* a sigh, Morn; it was a man calling out. He pleaded for help.'

Morn looked at her aghast.

'Surely, your majesty is not —' Burrage began.

'I know what I heard, Burrage. It was not a door creaking, it was not a dead body settling, it was quite clearly the word "Help".' She glared at each of them, with her mouth set in a firm line, then she moved, speaking as she did so. 'Morn, no-one is to shift or touch this man's body,' she said, reaching the chapel's door. 'Burrage, I want you to find Master Fynch.'

He blinked. 'How?'

She pushed open the chapel door. 'I don't know how and I'm not sure I care. Find him. Have messages sent to every corner of the realm. He was on foot as far as I know so he may still be close. Nail up summons in all the town squares, spread the word among inns. Word travels faster than pigeon or horse but feel free to use every form of communication at your disposal. Get it moving. I want Master Fynch found and brought to me urgently.'

She left both men staring at the empty space where she had stood.

Cassien looked around the small, empty outbuilding that he'd been brought to. In a corner a small brazier burned. It struck him as odd but he didn't think further on it as he was held between two of Murdo's friends. He could smell the liquor coming off their breath.

'I'm going to enjoy fighting you,' Murdo said, dark eyes glittering as he paced before him like a bull pawing at the ground before it charged.

'It won't be a fight, Murdo,' Cassien said. 'I won't strike you back.'

'It's your choice, stranger. I'll just beat you into a pulpy heap, then.'

'I suppose you will and that's easy, given that you have me held between your obedient dogs. It's hardly a fair challenge and far from the courage I'd expect from Razor braves.'

The men holding him showed their offence by pulling his arms harder and further behind his back until his tendons felt as though they might snap, his joints might pop.

'Who are you calling a dog?' one said.

Cassien simply stared at Murdo, his expression unchanged by the stresses on his body.

'Let him go,' Murdo ordered, frowning.

They shoved him forward, no doubt expecting him to fall over but Cassien was far too nimble on his feet and he took a step and twisted back, just in time to miss the blow that Murdo thought he'd land.

Cassien smiled at Murdo.

'Put your fists up, pretty boy, so I can "fairly" smash up that freshly shaved jaw of yours.'

'I don't need my fists,' Cassien replied, already seeing the blow before Murdo could land it.

Murdo punched … and felt only air against his knuckles. He turned to look for Cassien and found him standing behind him. He looked baffled. 'Can't you stand still and fight like a man?'

'Like a man who doesn't know how to fight, you mean? Like you, Murdo?'

Murdo roared and struck with both fists in a round swing meant to box his ears or break his jaw. It was a favourite move of the tough men of the Razors, or so Cassien had learned from Loup. In less than a blink, Cassien had cut both his arms in a sideways movement to block the man's fists. He could hear Murdo's teeth gnash with his rage. The mountain man kicked, again feeling only air against his shin as Cassien neatly leapt over the angry foot and landed lightly with bent knees. He stood up and waited patiently. His breathing rate hadn't changed. But Murdo was snorting like an enraged bull.

Murdo stared with fury, then rushed at him, yelling that fury. Cassien spun one way, Murdo lumbered in his direction, and then Cassien spun in reverse and avoided Murdo's pummelling by rolling over Murdo's back. The mountain man straightened quickly, confused, and roared as his men began to laugh. Cassien waited in an irritatingly patient pose with his hands by his sides, his body relaxed. It wasn't appropriate right now, but he wanted to congratulate the big man. Murdo was sure-footed and not nearly as cumbersome as he appeared.

'Shar curse you!' Murdo roared. 'Fight me!'

Cassien shook his head. 'To what end?'

'Prove which of us is the stronger.'

'You are, Murdo,' he answered. 'Nevertheless, I thought you were going to pulp me.'

'Stay still then.'

Cassien grinned but knew what that reaction would mean. Sure enough, Murdo glanced at his companions.

'Hold him,' he ordered.

Cassien felt his shoulders and arms clamped by Murdo's companions. 'Ah, well done, Murdo, you've entirely outwitted me,' he said dryly. 'Now, with your men bravely holding me down, you can beat me senseless.'

Murdo's grin faltered and his heavy-browed dark eyes became even more hooded as he frowned. 'You're very cocky, given that you're outnumbered.'

Cassien's expression lost its amusement. 'I don't like bullies, Murdo. They need the comfort and bravado of others around them to applaud, to laugh at their jokes, to make them feel like the chieftain they are son to but can't live up to.' The silence that greeted this remark was so thick it felt like a dead weight leaning on Cassien. Nevertheless, he continued to push this needle into Murdo's rapidly deflating ego. 'I'm sure Metheven would be proud to see how far his son has fallen.'

Now the atmosphere of pure taunting turned in an instant to one of a storm gathering. Murdo's stare reflected nothing short of hate.

'Do not dare to mention my father.' His voice sounded like stones grating against each other.

'But I just did,' Cassien said, sounding deliberately breezy and glancing at his two minders.

Murdo walked away, momentarily perplexing Cassien until he saw in which direction the big man was headed. So, fists aren't enough, Cassien thought, and braced himself for what was coming. During Loup's painful ministrations, Cassien had learned how to shrink within himself — how to become so small and distant from the skin he lived in that he believed he became his spirit.

And that was when he'd first heard Romaine talking to him. *Follow me*, she'd said in his mind. He had let his mind wander and it had felt as though he had company within his own body. *You are wolf*, her voice said. *Come to where a wolf in your form pays homage to his kin.*

And within a blink he'd found himself standing in the great nave of the cathedral of Pearlis. He had visited the cathedral only once, as a lad with

Brother Josse to discover his beast. Slowly he had walked down the nave, waiting for one of the massive, beautiful sculpted creatures to call to him.

'How will I know?' he'd asked Josse, wide-eyed with wonder.

'You will know. Your heart will respond instantly.'

'Which is yours, Brother Josse?'

'I am Anguis.'

'The lizard.'

'Well done.'

'What is his peculiarity?'

'Anguis is known for his clarity of thought. The more sight I lose as I age, the more I become like the lizard who looks for the sun, and by that I mean, the more enlightenment I search for.'

'You are always very wise, Brother Josse,' Cassien remembered himself replying and his elder had chuckled.

'Find your beast, know yourself and your strengths,' he'd said. Josse had remained standing before Anguis while Cassien moved on.

Cassien had needed to walk almost the length of the nave before he'd felt his heart begin to race. At one moment it was beating at its normal rhythm and the next it had begun to pound. It had pounded so hard he thought it might tear right through the cage of bones that held it within his chest. And with this racing heart had come dizziness. He thought it was for Lupus. The wolf. Strong, quiet, cunning, proud, fast, loyal. But he was confused.

He'd been looking down when the strange sensations had all assaulted him at once but he'd looked up at the enormous stone head of another: 'Dragon?' he'd whispered, confused, while warmth had suffused his body.

When Josse had arrived at his side and asked the inevitable, he had immediately replied 'Lupus' because in truth he did feel a kinship toward the wolf. He had never returned to the cathedral again, other than in his mind — the first time with Romaine. *We are family now*, she had said, as she'd led him away from Loup's pain and he had found solace in the nave of the cathedral he could conjure in his mind's eye.

She never mentioned his creature. Never asked.

In this spiritual place he could endure Loup's punishments while sitting at the feet of Lupus. Never the Dragon, although he felt its pull. So it was to the huge form of Lupus that he fled in his mind now as Murdo walked back toward him holding a glowing iron.

'I wish this had my family's sigil on its tip so I could burn it into your flesh for taking our name in vain,' he growled. 'Now you will scream your penance to my father … to me.'

Cassien stared at him, the notion that Romaine walked alongside providing comfort. 'You'll hear no sound of capitulation, or anything else, from me. You clearly feel that you are a disappointment to your father or you wouldn't be so touchy about me mentioning Metheven. I certainly took no-one's name in vain but if that's how you see it …' He shrugged.

Murdo's face darkened still further. 'You really are a cocky bastard.'

'I am a bastard, yes, but I simply say the truth.'

'Stop talking or I'll close your mouth properly,' Murdo said, bringing the glowing white-hot tip close to Cassien's lips.

Cassien sensibly remained still but he refused to shrink back as the hot iron came closer. He met Murdo's angry gaze steadily, daring him to use the weapon.

Murdo did just that, lowering the iron before it cooled and touching it against the bared flesh of Cassien's upper chest, where it crackled and hissed, blackening and blistering the skin, laying it open raw. He smiled as he pressed on the iron, but faltered in surprise as Cassien's expression did not change. It was Murdo who flinched as if burned when he realised that Cassien was pushing back against the iron, defying Murdo further.

The Razor warrior ripped the iron back, tearing flesh and even then the newcomer to Orkyld showed no emotion, not even a spark in his eye of the pain he was surely experiencing. Murdo flung the iron and grabbed at Cassien's shirt.

'What in hell's flames are you?' he growled into his face.

'Your conscience.'

'Take back what you said and I'll let you go.'

'Words can't be removed.'

'Then apologise,' Murdo yelled.

He shook his head. 'Not for speaking the truth.'

'Murdo!' came a new voice, breathy and angry. They all looked up to see Vivienne pushing into the barn with Ham at her side.

'You stupid, stupid oaf. What have you done?' she shrieked, eyeing the seeping wound in Cassien's chest. 'Aren't your big bludgeoning fists enough for you?'

Vivienne rushed towards them, but Murdo was now caught in his shame and he struck out as any cornered animal might. His backhanded blow connected horribly with Vivienne, who was sent tumbling backwards, her head knocking against a low beam. She crumpled like a half-empty sack of corn. Hamelyn was equally enraged and leapt onto Murdo's back, pulling at his hair and face, raining down ineffectual blows.

'You're just a big, useless, drunken bully, Murdo,' he railed.

Murdo flicked him away and Hamelyn soon joined Vivienne on the floor. He wasn't stunned as she had been but he was nursing a bruised rib.

Murdo turned back to Cassien but was confronted by a new expression. Gone were the calmness and the almost mocking look. Now his features appeared shrouded in anger; his eyes seemed to lighten from dark green to yellow and in a heartbeat he'd shrugged off his surprised minders, twisting out of their loosened hold and bounding into space.

'Oh, so now you want to fight, do you?' Murdo taunted.

'Anyone who beats up women and children needs to be taught a lesson. And it won't be a fight.'

Murdo howled with contrived glee. 'It won't be fair, I'll give you that.'

'No, it won't. But you won't land a blow.'

Murdo grimaced. 'Take your best shot, pretty boy.'

Cassien jumped into the air. No-one saw the terrible blow coming — least of all Murdo — as Cassien's foot shot out in a powerful, sweeping horizontal kick from head height that connected with Murdo's imposing chin. Murdo's head snapped helplessly to one side, exactly as Cassien had anticipated. He knew the force of the blow, the shock it imposed on the neck and the head, the air that was cut off within that terrible moment of impact, would all conspire to drop Murdo cold. As Cassien was leaping neatly back onto two feet, Murdo was already falling with his eyes rolling back into his head.

Murdo landed heavily as his body crashed, unconscious. His tongue lolled from the side of his mouth and was bleeding where he had bitten it during the impact. His companions looked on, shocked, at their leader's prone, lifeless-looking body.

'You've killed him,' one said.

Cassien glared at the man. 'He's not dead, although he will die if he drinks any more tonight. And that tongue is going to be mightily sore when he comes around. Respect his headache — it is not without its dangers. He needs to be laid quietly in a darkened room for a few hours to recover.' He dusted himself off and walked toward Vivienne, who had regained her wits and was being tended to by Ham.

'Vivienne?'

Hamelyn nodded for her. 'She's all right, I think.'

'What's my name?' he said, snapping his fingers in front of her face.

She batted his hand away weakly. 'Cassien the stupid,' she bleated and then groaned.

'What about you, Ham?'

'I've had worse,' he said, grimacing as he stood.

In a fluid motion he lifted Vivienne easily into his arms.

'What are you doing?' she protested.

'Taking you both away from here.' He turned back to Murdo, who was not yet moving. Cassien could see the rise of his chest and having been knocked out like this himself previously, he knew how it felt.

'Take proper care of your prince,' he ordered the men, 'or I'll pay you a visit and mete out some of the same treatment.'

Cassien walked out into the night with the whore in his arms and a lad trotting alongside him who wore a wide grin.

'I think I must learn how to kick like that,' Ham remarked, his tone reverent.

THIRTEEN

Gabe had remained silent, invisible, since the shock of the arrival of strangers into his body. His sinister companions had no idea that he was present. It had taken him a long time to believe what had occurred, to accept that he was still alive — albeit in a curious form — and also to feel sure that neither of the usurpers was aware of his presence. He had made himself so insignificant that his being alongside them was inconsequential. It was all part of the trick he'd taught himself as a youngster, and practised throughout his life, to go within himself. His defence mechanism and protection from fears.

'Within' was safety and he had spent a long time 'within' after his family's death. He would be silent and think through this extreme and unique situation.

It felt as though an eternity had passed since he'd last seen his apartment and life had felt anything other than blurred. He'd convinced himself to accept that he was not moving through a dream sequence. That's what had taken him the longest time: suspending his own disbelief and no longer praying for deliverance from a nightmare. This was real. The male that now controlled his body was named Cyricus. Angelina's name was revealed as Aphra.

'Why do we travel in one body, my love?' she said now.

'You were travelling in such a handsome shape. Why would I want to remain as fat old Flek when I can be young and virile Gabriel? I like this façade. I may keep it for a while.'

'So we'll travel together?'

'Until I can find you an alternative. I will look for a suitable host for you. One who measures up to your beauty.' He sounded patronising.

Gabe had listened, darkly fascinated by this conversation, from within himself. Cyricus was now fully in charge of his body. What had occurred defied all rational understanding, so he'd stopped drawing on what he knew to be normal and ruthlessly confronted what he had actually experienced.

Cyricus and Aphra were ancient, he knew that much now, and they spoke as lovers. She was every inch the slave. He sensed she was frightened of Cyricus, but found his cunning and power addictive. From their discussion Gabe gleaned that master and slave had been separated for a long time. She'd had been banished centuries ago, from wherever they'd last been together, to wander aimlessly until she'd finally discovered Gabe. He was her 'way back' into the world her demon master inhabited.

'You chose well,' Cyricus had said to her. 'He is without scent or trace of being from elsewhere. No-one will know he is not from this world. I'm intrigued, though. How can this be?'

'As soon as I met him I knew he was the one. He dreamed of Pearlis too. He is an aberration … a gift. I almost believed you somehow sent him to bring me back to you.'

Cyricus had made a soft sound of disdain. 'I wish I could say I had. I admit this is somewhat overly neat. How does a man from one world dream accurately of a cathedral in a world he doesn't know exists?'

Gabe had heard her hesitation and fear. Good. He hadn't even begun to pay attention to the hate that he was feeling for Angelina, but soon he would. No, he reminded himself, she wasn't Angelina. Angelina was some poor young woman whom this vile creature had possessed, using Angelina's body and her own wiles to lure him into her wicked plan.

Cyricus had pushed for more details. 'How has his arrival into this world not caused a disturbance to it, I wonder. Or maybe it has and people attuned to such magic are already sounding alarms.'

Gabe could now feel the tension rising in his body.

'I don't know. It is passing strange,' she replied sweetly, and quickly added, 'but, my love, you know we have experienced where worlds have touched before. You've told me of occasions when people have passed between the worlds.'

'This is true; the most recent I recall was of a man and woman, except those were people *of* Penraven, who returned to it. This man we inhabit is not from our world.'

'No, of course he's not,' she said, sounding worried. 'I found him by chance. We bumped into each other and one thing led to another. I knew he was the one. I knew he could bring me back to you because of his dreaming of the cathedral. You surely don't wish I had stayed lost forever? Perhaps his vision of the cathedral was just a leak from our world. He could only ever dream it, not touch it or move to it. It leaked into his world as a dream and remained his.'

Gabe mentally blinked. That sounded overly simplified.

He heard the demon sigh. 'Gabriel is dead. And with him went any potential magical connection he'd possessed. What's left is his soulless vessel and when the time is right I'll cast it aside. Pity, I like this handsome presence. I will have to make good use of it while I can.'

Aphra gasped as if hurt.

'You misunderstand. Gabriel's good looks and honest face will open doors. Be assured you've always been my favourite. I give you special privileges, Aphra, but when a demon dabbles with mortals, he must be extremely cautious.'

'I know, my lord, that you are being cautious. Gabriel is gone; his body is safe. No-one will be any wiser to your arrival ... or my return,' she'd cooed.

It suddenly hit him. *She had lied to her master!* Gabe's hopes surged ... she wasn't telling Cyricus everything. It was Reynard who had brought Angelina into his life; they hadn't bumped into each other, she hadn't stalked him. Reynard had found him, befriended him and then introduced them.

So Reynard had been telling the truth in warning him about Angelina. But why bring her to him? Did he know what she was? How could he? Gabe reached, as if closing his eyes, straining for the answers. Why had Reynard given him that quill? It meant something — he was sure of that now. And the more he thought about it, the more convinced he became that his customer at the bookshop had known far more than he'd let on.

Had Reynard deliberately set him up? It sounded like madness to think this and yet the notion would not leave him. The more Gabe recalled the way in which Reynard had pushed him and Angelina together, the more he believed the man's protestations at leaving them alone were all a ruse.

It was becoming more credible that Reynard might well have known the series of events that would occur to put him here — Reynard had wanted it to happen, or at least had needed to see it happen. Why? He recalled the raven; it too had been watching Gabe, waiting for something to take place. Was it the death of Angelina and the transference of Aphra into his body? How would it have looked to that bird? One moment he would have been in his apartment naked with Angelina, the next she would be bleeding to death and he would have winked out of existence? His thoughts continued to crash against one another, each one more dramatic and unbelievable than the last. And yet, the more difficult it became to counter these wild ideas, the easier it became to entertain the idea that he had slipped between worlds and the whole event had been staged, carefully planned. Aphra thought she was outsmarting Reynard, but now Gabe firmly believed she was the one outwitted. And he — Gabe — was the stooge, the mule, the courier! Why? Cyricus had just voiced a similar concern. Now Gabe also wanted to know what it was about him that had allowed his body to move between these two planes without creating a disturbance.

There had to be a reason that Reynard had found him, that Aphra had used him. There had to be an explanation for why he had dreamed of a cathedral he'd not seen or known of, but which almost certainly stood proudly in this different world.

He had plenty to learn before he could begin to fathom how to thwart Cyricus and rid himself of his presence. As for Aphra, he hoped they would find a 'suitable host' very soon; he could no longer stand the sound of her voice reverberating through him. She sickened him. Gabe had always thought he didn't possess any capacity for violence and that his calm reasoning would always get him through a situation. Now, his rage was such that he would kill Aphra with his bare hands … if either of them were made of something substantial.

However, he must remain calm and invisible to them. He would sit dormant within his own body, pulling tight any clues to his existence, and he would listen and pay attention. Perhaps he could find a way to get help from the outside. He'd already tried to leave clues. Even in his terrified, mind-scattered state, when he'd been forced into killing Flek, he'd pressed the quill against the man, hoping it would be found and cause questions to be asked.

The demons had missed it because they were so distracted by the transference of Cyricus and their reunion. However, he had sneaked a look when Cyricus had cast a glance through Gabe's eyes at Flek's body. Gabe had seen that a burn mark had been left behind on the man's chest and it seemed to him that the burn resembled the marking he knew existed on the quill. He'd never known what that tiny image represented, but knew that every anomaly and every small connection might help if people were questioning the events surrounding Flek's death.

The other curious moment during the shocking exchange of Cyricus into his body was to use his last remaining gasp of breath to cast the word 'Help' into the dying man's consciousness. If pressing the quill against Flek's chest was a long shot, then pushing the word 'Help' into Flek's dying mouth was just about as far-fetched as things could get. About as fanciful as clinging to the belief that he might have a chance at conquering these interlopers.

Nevertheless, he had given it all of his remaining strength.

In truth, he didn't know why he'd done it, but rationality was not a feature of his landscape at present. It was a desperate moment and he'd regressed to using a game from childhood, except now that he came to consider it, he didn't remember playing any game along those lines while growing up in England. And yet, in that moment of terror, had come the searing clarity of playing a game called 'dead men's whispers' with his brother in a village square, a village square that he saw in that same moment of bleak terror. What brother? Which village? He'd been raised in a city. Even so, the impulse had come to him in less than a beat of his heart and he'd acted, breathing that word as he let go of the shirt of Rural Dean Flek, whose warm lifeblood was spraying his naked body.

It had been desperate, for sure. Who would hear that cry for help from a man who was little more than a spirit himself, via the lips of a dead man? He was truly crazy. But there had been a time in his life when he'd believed in magic, hadn't there? Here it was again, that dim reaching toward a life he couldn't properly recall and yet somehow had flashes of memory, or glimpses into. Was the cathedral at Pearlis one of those glimpses? Aphra seemed to know about the cathedral, didn't she? And here they were in the land where Pearlis existed. His parents had always been awkward when the odd query had come up about his birth, hadn't they? That was over three decades ago though.

Gabriel felt nauseated. Had his parents lied? Had his whole life been a lie, waiting for this moment for him to flip into another world … the world he'd originated from? It sounded feasible, in a sinister way, given his situation. Is that why Aphra had found him to be the perfect 'ride' home? Was it that he would not disturb the fine fabric of the worlds if he were one of Morgravia's own returning? Had she been so blinded by her own desperation that she was risking not telling Cyricus the whole story? Is this why she was so fearful?

Had Reynard known? If so, how? Did the raven know?

And even though his jumbled thoughts crowded in to frighten, disturb and sadden Gabe, this one thought of Aphra's fear of him stood out. It pleased him and he experienced a thrill of pleasure that Aphra was keeping secrets from Cyricus. *Divide and conquer*, he thought.

The wolves surrounded Fynch, deep in the forest, where they had dragged him. Unbeknownst to Cassien, Romaine had sent her kin to range alongside the two men as they'd travelled, staying within the dark shadows, far enough away so the horses did not pick up their scent.

Fynch owed them a debt, for once Cassien had finally — and he knew, unhappily — left him, he didn't have the strength to do much more than die by the roadside. Death! He wasn't ready for it. Surely it would not choose this time to call him, when the Crown most needed his counsel? The pair of wolves had sat, like sentinels, beside him for two days now. He understood they were keeping vigil to watch him slip into death and would stay by him until his body cooled.

The clue that this was not the plan was the sudden stirring of the trees. A strange wind had erupted in the darkest, quietest part of the night when even the owls were still. He heard the leaves flutter above and then felt the air buffet his face. He opened his eyes and, for a heartbeat, he felt a moment's fear that this was it; true darkness had come to claim him. The soft whine of the wolves as they lowered themselves to the ground, and a looming shape above, told him this was not death but life hurtling toward him.

Tree trunks bent, branches snapped, and leaves fell as though it were a different season, as the familiar shape broke through the sparse canopy of this woodland area and landed soundlessly on the forest floor. The beast's colours, like illuminations, glowed and softly spilled a pool of low light about itself.

Fynch blinked, grinning despite his weakness. It had been a long, long time since they had seen one another. 'My king,' he murmured, his spirits soaring to see the great dragon. 'Forgive me for not being in a position to welcome you more elegantly.'

My friend, it replied in his mind, in its usual gracious manner, and dipped its huge head.

Fynch chuckled. 'Far too long.'

Nevertheless, we are always together.

'You've terrified my wolf friends.'

It is the wolves that called to me. Romaine is persistent; she howled her despair for two entire nights. Set my head aching and my whole body on edge, the dragon complained.

'She had me followed!' Fynch complained.

Clearly you can't be turned loose from the Wild before you get up to mischief, the dragon chided.

'Ah, but I wish it were only that innocent. I feel the weight of the world on my shoulders right now, my king.'

It is not your burden to bear.

Fynch shook his head weakly. 'I have pushed it onto the shoulders of others and —'

Look at you, more than old enough to know better than to risk your life, to deliberately spill your precious, magical blood! The dragon gave a soft growl of displeasure.

I think I am dying.

You may have been, but I'm here.

Despite the dark, he and the dragon could see each other perfectly well.

You obviously had good reason to spill the dragon's blood.

'You felt it?'

Every drop. We are of one flesh. You bound yourself to me and I to you.

'So you can heal me?'

My strength is yours to use. But we must leave here.

'Dragon strength,' Fynch wheezed.

Dragon magic. Come, Fynch. He switched out of the language of dragons and spoke to the wolves. *You have guarded him well. Thank you.*

Both stood at his acknowledgement but kept their heads lowered. *Go back into the full safety of the forest now, my sons, and keep the children of Romaine safe. I fear she has other things than mothering on her mind.*

The wolves gave a brief collective howl before each padded over to lick Fynch's hands.

'Thank you, dear ones,' he said, feeling weaker than ever.

They dragged him once again, this time toward the huge clawed feet of their king.

Go now, the dragon commanded.

The wolves melted silently into the shadows and Fynch was alone with his beloved blood-brother.

Back to the Wild, the dragon said, *where you are safe. Let the young learn the way you did all of the secrets behind your life.*

Fynch didn't answer. There had been so much more he should have said to Cassien.

As if the great serpent of the air could hear him, the dragon pushed into his mind. *You have done what you could, put much in place, made enough sacrifice. To leave the Wild again will be to die, Fynch. You must remain within its safety, within its magic. You've defied it three times previously and it has been generous to you. But —*

'I understand,' Fynch said, so weak he could barely form the words.

Under cover of night, flying close to the treetops and landing to hide each time the moon peeped out from behind its cloud cover, the pair moved cautiously until they were far from Morgravia, far from habitation, northeast of Briavel. Not until he saw the welcome sight of the Thicket and felt the life-giving force it pushed into him, did Fynch believe he'd survive this night.

FOURTEEN

Cassien stood over the prone body of Penely. To all intents and purposes she was dead to the world, but the erratic rise and fall of her chest told him she clung to life.

'I'm sorry,' he said.

Vivienne threw a mirthless smile at him. 'Are you?'

They were in a tiny back room of the brothel. He'd followed Vivienne in and had to run a gauntlet of whistles and pinches from the girls on their shift.

'Aren't I good enough?' one had pouted, sucking her finger.

Another lifted her considerable breasts almost into his face. 'These will keep you happy all night, my cherub,' she'd promised.

They were pretty, vivacious women. Vivienne had solid competition. The mistress who ran the brothel had obviously chosen with a discerning eye, and clearly paid her girls well for they looked fed and well kept.

'I'm with Vivienne,' he had replied lamely and duly followed her deeper into the brothel, down two small flights of stairs, until he was far enough below ground that he expected it to feel damp. 'Where are we?' he'd asked as she turned and placed a finger to her lips.

'The cellar is where my Penely's been put. I doubt she'll emerge from here again.'

And now that he was looking at her sister, he had to agree.

'Has a physic seen her?'

'They can't do anything for her now; she's too far gone. She'll die in this state. She's not going to wake up and wish me farewell or smile that bright smile of hers again. She'll just slip away, I've been told. You can see her breathing is very shallow.'

He nodded, feeling sympathy for Vivienne.

'How long has she been like this?'

'A couple of days now. I know you came here to kill her, but you don't have to. It is done, Cassien.'

Vivienne was right. He had no further reason to remain. Both the tailor and his whore were silenced, and he had to wonder if the killing was necessary. He'd been overly cautious. He should have gone south to Pearlis immediately. Perhaps the rules of the Brotherhood didn't apply in this instance. Yes, the Brotherhood would clean up all loose ends when working on behalf of the Crown. His task *was* the Crown. No loose end was not important enough. Had he already failed?

'I shall go,' he said.

'Wait,' she said. 'About earlier with Murdo. No-one's ever fought for my honour before.'

He shrugged. 'I fought for Hamelyn as much as I fought for you.' Her nearness in the cramped cellar made him feel self-conscious again. 'Where is Ham anyway?'

'He said he had something to fetch.' She shook her head to say she didn't know anymore. He guessed it must be his weapons. 'Where are you going?'

'What does it matter?'

She shrugged. 'No-one ever beats Murdo ... other men do their best to avoid him or just give him what he wants. But you defied him and you trounced him. But what's far more unnerving is I watched him burn you and you didn't make a sound. I don't understand that — it frightens me. We also have to dress the wound.'

'I won't trouble you, Vivienne, I promise. And my wound appeared to be far worse than it is,' he lied. 'Just a surface scald.'

Her expression told him she didn't believe a word of it. 'Wait,' she said, touching his arm. 'Don't go yet. Stay with me here tonight.'

He looked at her with curiosity. 'I won't, but —'

'No need to explain,' she said shortly, looking aggrieved. 'It was just a way to thank you ...' She didn't finish and her tone was so tight, it made Cassien feel momentarily breathless.

He let out a sigh. 'I was simply going to say that while I wouldn't remain here, I would like you to come to the Yew Inn with me.' He scratched his chin. 'For what's left of this night.'

She paused before a small sheepish smile ghosted her mouth. 'What about Hamelyn?'

'I'm sure he can stay downstairs. The innkeeper's kind to him, seems to know him well enough.' He waited expectantly, watching her. 'I think when he sees my coin he'll forgive our earlier disturbance.'

She nodded. 'I suppose you have paid me for the night.'

'I have.' He took her hand, inwardly delighting at the feel of a woman's skin again. 'I would prefer you come with me because you want to. There is no obligation. The money I've paid is yours without encumbrance.'

Vivienne leaned forward and kissed him lightly on the lips, but the pressure of her breasts against his chest promised so much more. 'You're very ... polite, aren't you? I'm not used to that. All right, I will spend the night because I want to,' she said staring deeply into his eyes. 'And because you haven't hurt my sister.'

Later, in his room, after Vivienne had assured the innkeeper that all scores were settled, he allowed her to begin undressing them both. He'd been with women in his youth, but it had been far too long since he'd had such tender attention.

Vivienne watched him with a thoughtful frown creasing her face as she undid her bodice.

'Let's have some wine.' Cassien knew once that bodice of hers was undone he wouldn't be able to think straight again this evening.

'Let me get it for you.' She smiled seductively as her blouse fell fully open and he saw her body properly for the first time. She returned with a goblet of the wine that he'd ordered sent up.

Cassien sipped and groaned, closing his eyes. 'That's so delicious.' How long had it been since he'd tasted wine?

'Strike me, I haven't begun yet. Pain first, before pleasure,' she teased, pulling two small vessels closer. One contained tepid water, laced with vinegar. The other was a tiny pot containing a gluey paste he recognised as the ash of burned cotton emulsified with lavender oil.

He gave a brief laugh. 'Vivienne, you need to have walked in my boots to know why this wine, a beautiful woman sitting on top of me and this soft pallet is an incredible treat.'

'Why don't you tell me about the path you've walked in those boots?' she said, unlacing his breeches. 'I'm intrigued.'

'Why?' he said, sipping again and allowing the fruity wine to roll around his mouth.

'Well, let's see. These are fine clothes,' she remarked, fingering his linen shirt, 'and you've handed out money easily today. I heard you speak of Wevyr weapons — those don't come cheap.' She loosened the laces of his shirt. 'You are hardly without …' She stopped talking and her mouth remained open as she stared at his bared chest.

Cassien had known this moment was coming. It couldn't be avoided if he was to live normally among ordinary people. Fynch had asked the old girl who'd helped bathe him in the barrel not to mention it and paid her handsomely for her silence. But with someone like Vivienne — unless he'd insisted on darkening the room — he was never going to escape a confrontation. And every man needed the release that he was about to enjoy. He could wish that her silence was due to the oozing of the burn wound, but he knew he was clutching at clouds.

Embarrassed, he reached to pull his shirt together. Vivienne held his hands away, refusing to let him cover himself.

'Light!' she said, her voice trembling. 'Tell me about that pathway, Cassien. What has been happening to you?'

He covered her hands. 'This is not something I can speak freely of to anyone.'

A tear escaped down her cheek and she stayed silent as she traced a finger over the marks of old wounds, and even older wounds under them, that crisscrossed his body.

'Who did this?' she whispered.

'Someone I know.'

'You permitted it?'

He nodded. 'For all the right reasons.'

'The right reasons? When can anything this vicious be right? Cassien, this is savage. What kind of person does this to another? What kind of person permits it to be done?'

'He was not a bad man.'

'So you asked him to do this to you?' she said and he could hear the loathing in her voice.

'No, but I also didn't have any choice.'

'He tortured you?' He nodded. 'But you didn't have to let it happen?'

'Ah,' he said, feeling trapped. 'There you have me. Don't press, Vivienne. Please. I have now left that part of my life behind.'

'Behind?' she repeated. 'Yet here it is. Travelling with you, wherever you go, for the rest of your life. These scars will always be here.'

'I know this.'

'It looks painful. This scar goes deep.'

'Yes, I can remember that one well.'

She pulled away his shirt fully and began to peel off his breeches, gasping louder.

He stopped her. 'You're spoiling our time.'

'I want to cry for you.'

'No need.' He put his goblet down, took her arms firmly and in a single movement spun her.

Before she could take a breath, Vivienne found herself pinned beneath Cassien. She looked confused, surprised by the speed at which that movement had occurred, mixed with awe at his strength.

'Your wound needs tending.'

'All in good time,' he said.

She gave him a soft look of exasperation.

'Now,' he said, in an ironic tone. 'There is one part of me which is unblemished, extremely friendly and intently eager to wish you good evening.'

She smiled in spite of herself. 'You'd better introduce us, then.'

'Vivienne, it's my absolute pleasure for you to meet …'

The sound of Vivienne's gust of laughter filtered down from the room upstairs to where Hamelyn was curled up near the hearth in the parlour, his arms clasped around the sack containing Wevyr's weapons. In the realm between alertness and semi-consciousness, he smiled as he dreamed of dragon's blood and a stranger crying out for help.

The following day Vivienne woke to find Cassien sitting on the bed watching her.

She opened her eyes to bare slits. 'You're up early,' she croaked, still tasting the wine on her breath. She peered toward the window. 'It's not even slightly light yet.'

'It will be light in moments.'

'Still early for me,' she groaned and dropped her head back onto the bed. 'How is that weeping burn of yours?'

'I've seen to it. It will be fine.'

'It must hurt like merry hell.'

'I dressed it.'

She opened her eyes wider and yawned. 'Not only is your wound dressed, I see you are as well.'

He grinned, shifted a lock of hair that had fallen across her face. 'You're very lovely, Vivienne.'

She shrugged beneath the sheet. 'So you are leaving?'

'Yes,' he said, bluntly, 'today.'

'To where?'

He stared at her with an amused look.

'Is it a secret?'

'No, but I have a creed of not discussing my life ... perhaps you've noticed.'

She nodded. 'I couldn't sleep for thinking on your scars.'

'Couldn't sleep? Really? I thought I might have to leave the room due to your snoring,' he said, in a surprised mocking tone.

She reached behind her and flung a pillow at him. 'And you make love like a man who has hungered too long.'

'Aren't all men hungry for a woman like you?' he flattered.

It didn't work. 'Cassien, is this a religion of yours?'

'I asked you not to press,' he said, his tone instantly low, his expression sombre.

'You did, but I have to know more.'

'Why?'

'Because it's not normal. Hamelyn said he's going to be travelling with you. He's just a lad. We all like him. And ...'

'Ham's in no danger from me.'

'Not from you, no, perhaps not. But with you, maybe he is. What are you?'

He wasn't sure what prompted him to say more, although he was extremely careful. 'There are times in this world when we can't always count on praying to our gods to deliver us from situations.' She frowned. 'Sometimes we need to count on ourselves ... and when the stakes are bigger, to pay others to look out for the common good.'

'You're taking care of the common good?' she repeated, unable to disguise her sarcasm.

'Let's just say my role is as a safekeeper.'

She gave him a look of doubt. 'You were going to kill my sister.'

'Fortunately for me, the gods are doing it on my behalf.'

'No, they're not!' Vivienne snapped. 'She's done that on her own and with the likes of you who pay her so freely for her services.'

He didn't respond but watched her carefully.

'What are you afraid of?' she demanded.

'An angry woman,' he said, standing up and straightening his clothes. 'I must leave.'

Vivienne's expression became dark and clouded. She covered herself with the sheet and refused to look at him.

'What do you want from me?' Cassien asked softly.

'The truth.'

'I've given it to you as best I can. I don't owe you anything.'

That stung. He could see the pinch of it in her eyes when she quickly looked away. 'No, you don't,' she said swinging her legs around and to the floor. 'Maybe you now have to kill me because I know you have secrets. I know you can fight without weapons and still lay Murdo out cold. I know you have a mission, one you are clearly touchy about. Surely I know too much?'

'Again I ask, what do you want from me, Vivienne?'

She shook her head.

'Tell me.'

She lifted a shoulder in a slightly sulky manner. He knew she was embarrassed. 'To know you.' She stood, reached for her clothes and began to slowly pull them on.

Morning had broken and its brightness had begun to slowly creep into the room; its pinkish light touched her skin and seemed to add a fresh glow to its smooth, supple creaminess. He had enjoyed every moment of her generous lovemaking, knowing their connection was more than simply physical. But he had to remain focused on his role for Fynch.

'The problem is mine, Cassien,' she said, turning with a doleful smile. She reached for a clip that he'd pulled from her hair and flung down by the bed at the start of their night's frolic. He watched her clip up her hair and wondered how lovely she would look once that terrible red dye was washed out.

'It's not impossible to imagine we will meet again,' he said, thinking aloud.

'I doubt you'll come back,' she said sadly. She checked her clothes were straight in the small mirror above the single tiny cabinet in the room.

He tied on his cloak. 'The room is paid for. So is food, so please take advantage of that. I never think you should start the day on an empty belly.'

'Or an empty heart,' she said brightly, turning around to smile at him. There was little warmth in it.

'I'm sorry that I've offended you in some way, Vivienne.' He took a step forward and knew he surprised her when he kissed her cheek. 'I hope you will think on me kindly and know that I could never regret that you pretended to be your sister.'

Cassien closed the door behind him and took the stairs two at a time. Hamelyn was waiting for him, sitting in a window not far from the main door, the sack tucked safely behind him.

'Morning, Master Cassien, sir,' he said, straightening immediately.

Cassien shot him a look of mild exasperation. 'Did you sleep all right?'

The boy nodded. 'They even gave me food to break my fast.'

'And you're still going, I see,' Cassien said, nodding at the pear the boy carried in one hand and the small hunk of cheese in the other.

'Waste not, want not, we were told in the orphanage,' Hamelyn grinned and pocketed the food. 'Where's Vivienne?'

'She'll be down,' he replied evenly, 'but we're on our way.'

'Oh,' Hamelyn said, standing, accepting the decision immediately.

'Master Erris. We'll be taking our leave now.'

The innkeeper looked up from where he was stacking some flagons of wine. 'You're all paid, Master Cassien.'

Cassien nodded. 'Um, my guest will be down shortly. I hope my coin covers food for her?'

'Since you haven't partaken of any, sir, we can call it square.'

'Good. May I leave a message for her?'

'Of course, I'll be glad to pass it on.' He looked at Cassien expectantly.

'Er, I thought I might write it down,' he suggested.

The man grinned. 'Vivienne can't read, sir.'

'Right,' he said, frowning. 'In that case, please tell Miss Vivienne that her sister has something to show her.'

The man frowned. 'I'm not sure I understand that message, Master Cassien.'

Cassien grinned. 'I'm not sure you're meant to, Erris. Farewell and thank you for passing that on all the same. Ready, Hamelyn?'

The boy pushed out the door and Cassien followed.

'To Master Wevyr's?' the boy asked softly.

'Yes, but first I need to return swiftly to the brothel. Do you know the mistress there?'

'I do.'

'Why am I not surprised to hear you say that?' he grinned.

At the brothel and wearing his weapons again he was intrigued to discover that Mistress Pertwee was nothing as he'd imagined; she was enormous, amply filling out a long gown that could have happily swamped two, maybe three of her girls. Her hair was white and dragged up into a tight bun and she had to be at least six decades, perhaps more. And yet she possessed a beatific smile, the sort of smile that made the person standing in front of her beam back. Cassien realised he was doing just that as she welcomed him.

'Hamelyn, my boy, I haven't seen you for a while.'

'Mistress Pertwee, this is Master Cassien ... one of your newest clients. He is Vivienne's customer.'

'Nicely done, Ham,' she beamed before turning her bright smile on Cassien. 'Ah, the handsome fellow who bought our lovely Vivienne for a night. The one who put that nasty Murdo in his place.'

Cassien raised his eyebrows. 'News travels fast,' he remarked, bowing gently over her hand, the fingers of which were near enough splayed from the number of thick rings she wore, all sparkling with gems.

She tutted gently. 'Men must beat their chests,' she said, her tone amused as she laid one of her ring-encrusted hands against his heart.

'I prefer to move less ... um ... obviously, than I have in Orkyld, Mistress Pertwee.'

'I'm afraid, sir, looking as you do, you are going to attract attention wherever you go. My advice,' she said, pinching his cheek, as though he were younger than Hamelyn, 'is to embrace that. Walk proud, walk loud.' She waggled a finger. 'You know, sometimes secrets can be kept more easily in public amongst all the noise and colour of open life.' She tapped her powdered nose. 'If you get my meaning.'

'I think I do understand you, mistress,' he replied, 'and I will bear your advice in mind. Now I have a favour to ask of you. It will cost you nothing.'

He smiled and told her what he needed.

'Now to Wevyr's,' he said, clapping Hamelyn on the back as they walked down the street.

'What are you hoping to learn, master ... er, I mean Cassien, if I may ask?'

'I want to know everything about these weapons I carry. There's a mystery to them and it's best I understand it.'

'Are you going to tell him what I saw?' Hamelyn wondered.

'You are not in any trouble. Trust me now and don't worry.'

'It's not me that's worried, Cassien,' Hamelyn replied. 'It's your sword. It's beginning to moan.'

FIFTEEN

Silent as a cloud, Gabe hovered within his own body and watched their progress into what looked to be a market town as he carried his dark companions. He had observed the large number of people on the road herding livestock or transporting their wares in wheeled barrows, while others carried produce on their shoulders. Gabe believed he, and his constant companions, blended in because he was now dressed as a countryman in Flek's simple clothes. No-one asked any questions so he had to assume he had integrated well enough.

'Now that we are together, we could just disappear,' Aphra urged her lover.

'We could. But I choose not to,' Cyricus replied.

'Why, my love?' she asked sweetly. She still possessed the voice of Angelina and it irritated Gabe more than he cared to admit.

They were merging with an increasingly steady stream of people and animals forming a bottleneck at the main gate into the town.

'What are you selling?' he heard the toll-keeper ask the man in front.

'Two bales of wool.'

'Just two?' the toll-keeper smirked.

'Best quality,' the farmer replied. He sounded tired. 'Once they see it, these won't last long and I'll get a good price,' he quipped. He was young. Next to him was an even younger woman, staring forlornly at the ground. She was carrying a small infant. The baby moaned in her arms. The couple looked lean and hungry.

'That'll be a duke.'

The seller baulked. 'I'll only make a few crowns apiece if I'm lucky.'

'Take it or leave it. You know we have the best wool-dyeing in the region. You yourself believe you're guaranteed a sale, young man, and you boasted of a high price. Now hurry up. There's a lot of people trying to get through here.'

The man looked at the woman and she nodded wearily.

'Robbery,' he muttered, digging in his pocket and handing over the coin from the very few that Gabe could see in his palm.

'Next,' the gatekeeper called, his tone indifferent, already looking past the couple and child.

They shuffled forward and he cast his dour look at Gabe.

'Buying presumably,' he said, spitting to his right out of an opening in the toll-house.

'I am,' Cyricus said and Gabe hated that the invader was able to use his voice to answer.

The man's stubby finger pointed them through and Gabe was aware of his body being walked beneath the stone arch that constituted the toll-gate into the town.

'I don't understand why you're bothering with these tiresome people and this forsaken land,' Aphra complained.

'Well, because we have time and because these people bore me I shall give my full attention to explaining why, Aphra,' Cyricus replied with forced patience. 'A long time ago there walked a man by the name of Elysius. As an aside, I should mention that he fathered a woman by the name of Myrren. She was a gifted witch with powerful reserves of magic at her disposal although no-one knew it, for she lived a thoroughly unremarkable life until just before the start of her third decade. She had chosen not to use her magic, preferring the anonymity and pleasure of home and family life as these peasants around us might enjoy.' He sighed. 'What a strange little thing she was to make such a choice. She had untold power and yet her greatest joy of all was being given a puppy. Can you imagine that?

'She never used her power?' Aphra repeated, full of disdain.

'Not "never". She did use it once in her adult life. And when she did she cast out such a mighty and dark spell that it had the capacity to change the course of many lives. In fact, her curse — which it surely was — profoundly changed the course of the land we now walk upon.'

Gabe found himself hanging on the demon's every word.

'What happened?' Aphra obliged him by asking.

Cyricus gave a small chuckle. 'She turned out to be an amazing young woman. Such darkness but such control too. If she had been my daughter I'd have been very proud of her. Myrren offended a noble, choosing not to give up her virginity to the fumbles of a drunken duke who happened to take a fancy to her as he passed through her village. Her anonymity might have been preserved had her eyes not been two different colours. The scorned duke, who had the ear of the royals, was able to leverage that quirk of Myrren's and have her arrested as a witch. This was a time when people were frightened of anything that might seem different or smacked of something they couldn't understand.' He sighed. 'The Morgravians were a superstitious lot.' Cyricus gave a sound of disgust. Gabe noticed they were leaving the main street, presumably leading into the central market square, and were veering off into a quieter part of the town.

The demon's voice turned cunning. 'However, young Myrren *was* magical, as I've explained. She was taken to the dungeons of the great Stoneheart of Pearlis, where she was given to Witchsmeller Lymbert for his cruel pleasure. Lymbert put her through rigorous trial and torture — I could give you details, but suffice to say that brave Myrren gave them nothing, for she knew they would burn her come what may. There was, however, one individual who showed her an ounce of compassion during her witch trial. His name was Wyl Thirsk and he was the general of the Morgravian Legion — still very much a youngster. She gave him a special gift of thanks.' Cyricus laughed inwardly and the sound of his amusement echoed horribly in Gabe's mind. 'She bestowed upon him a sinister magic, which he only learned about later, when it finally chose to manifest itself in the most harsh and gleeful manner. You see, Thirsk could not die although many tried to kill him. As they made their attempts Myrren's magic would claim their lives instead, ensuring that Wyl Thirsk assumed their thoughts, their memories, but most importantly, the soul of Thirsk would assume their bodies. He moved through several people — men or women, the magic wasn't choosy,' Cyricus laughed, 'and this was part of Myrren's cunning to topple a kingdom. Her magic only stopped when it was satisfied that Wyl Thirsk, in whoever's guise, had assumed sovereign control. Myrren's only desire, I believe, was that Celimus, who had so enjoyed her torture, didn't live long as King of Morgravia and never tasted life on the imperial throne he craved. He was her target all along.' He sighed. 'Marvellous story. I never tire of it.'

'And this is the magic you are using?' Aphra said.

To Gabe this sounded like a piece of a jigsaw fitting into place.

'Well done, my beauty. That's exactly what I'm doing. I was very impressed with Myrren's gift and the dark magic it contained. It amused me, constantly kept my attention as I watched Thirsk on his journeying in that traumatic time; the magic was a dark shadow shifting the way Morgravia's history unfolded.

'But I began this tale about a man called Elysius, didn't I? And it's his story that is relevant here. He was the powerful warlock whose talents passed through to his daughter, Myrren. She never knew him and he remained very secretive. He lived in a place called the Wild.'

Gabe was surprised to feel his body shiver as though a cold wind had swept across it, but it had been a genuine tremble prompted by Cyricus's mention of the Wild.

'What's wrong?' Aphra asked.

'You've forgotten, it seems. It was the Wild that divided us.' He pointed Gabe's arm toward a street. 'We're nearly at our destination so I'd better hurry my story.'

Gabe had been aware that they'd entered a far more salubrious part of the town. He was surprised that what had looked to be a small area from the other side of the toll-gate was a bustling town and, going by the size of the houses, it was home to wealthy residents.

Cyricus continued. 'You never knew why you were cast out of our world, Aphra. You were too young, probably not interested in learning the history.'

'You're going to tell me that it was because of this mage Elysius,' she said, leaping to her conclusion.

'Indeed I am, and all our recent sufferings are due to him. I hadn't meant to invade the Wild. It happened after one of the cyclical wars between Zarab and Lyana in the far east of Percheron. The goddess Lyana —' he paused to spit, surprising Gabe — 'had beaten our leader, Zarab, and not only reduced his powers for a long, long time, but hunted down his minions. I was one of them. I escaped her wrath but found myself weakened and cast into the oblivion of the Razors — a mountain range north of Morgravia and far from Percheron. I travelled without purpose or direction, drifting south on the winds, and that's when I felt the magic of Myrren. I found it irresistible; I watched her death and marvelled at her dark legacy. I had no time for the battles of mortals, of course, but now that Thirsk carried this demon-magic, I was intrigued by its consequences. I went in search of its origins and that led me to the Wild. I was not on guard, not at all prepared for the fury of Elysius, his manic protection of what I realised was a supremely magical place.

'It shrouded itself so well that even I did not pick up on its power until I passed through one of its great defences, known as the Thicket. My trespass was innocent — more one of fascination than anything else — but Elysius knew of my breach immediately. He hunted me as Lyana had, but he was relentless, as she was not. And when he cornered me, employing magic I was not familiar with, he used it to catapult me into a dark wilderness, where I have been for centuries, trying to find my way back through the planes. More than that, he also punished those who paid any form of homage to me. One by one he found those loyal to me and they never saw it coming. He was patient, cunning and ancient. He sent each of you into a void of your own. You were sent to another world —'

Aphra sounded indignant when she cut him off. 'Where I too have roamed for centuries trying to find my way back to you.'

Cyricus remained silent.

'But we are together now, Cyricus. We should —'

'I want revenge,' Cyricus said, and it was so quietly murmured that Gabe strained to hear, 'and I will take it now that the opportunity presents.'

It was as though Aphra was fluttering around inside his body. Gabe felt dizzied by her sudden blaze of emotion.

'How is this revenge?' she demanded.

'I know it's hard for you to understand, Aphra, but my plan is taking shape. And you must not question me.' He sighed. 'If you wish to be with me, you must follow. Nothing else.'

'I've done everything you've asked.'

'True, and if you want to remain with me then you must continue following. I will have my revenge. This is the land that Elysius loved, that he worked hard to protect. Now I'm going to have my fun with it. The best place to begin is with the Crown — exactly the way his daughter did. She didn't waste her skill or energy on the noble who began her downfall. He was nothing. Myrren levelled her fury at Celimus, who had laughed at her and conspicuously enjoyed her suffering. I might add, she didn't even bother with Celimus at the time. She possessed patience like no other. And she used a "mule", poor Wyl Thirsk, to carry her magic and unleash her vengeance long after her death, when Celimus reached the throne. She went after only what mattered to Celimus — his reign, his lands, his title, and ultimately his life. I will mimic Myrren, but the Imperial Crown of Morgravia, Briavel and the Razors is not enough for me. I want the Wild.'

'But what about Elysius?' Aphra asked, sounding awed.

Cyricus laughed. 'Elysius is dust by now; he was mortal, after all. And, while I'm sure it's still magical, the Wild can be tamed. I will find a safe way to return to it and I will raze whatever I find. I will fell its forests, drain its waters. I will kill its animals and I will destroy everything — especially and including its Thicket, which I will watch burn. And in Myrren's honour I will destroy the crown of Morgravia in the bargain.'

'Oh, what a wonderful revenge you will wreak, my lord. Are you sure no-one inherited the crown of that warlock?'

'Elysius was a freak. No-one could replace him. No mortal could wield that magic again. The Wild might scream its rage at my re-entering its region but this time it won't have its warlock. I have watched for decades, since I found my way back to this plane, and no mortal walks its paths. Only beasts have access and they are no threat to me. I will use the magic of his daughter to lay waste to the land Elysius held so dear.'

Gabe was astonished. The story he'd just heard was terrifying. It didn't matter how or why, but he was now mixed up in this battle and likely to be the only soul in this world who knew of this sinister plan … possibly the only one who knew of the existence of Cyricus and Aphra. Excitement had begun to build in him that he could play his part in not only bringing them down, but helping to warn the unsuspecting people of this world of the vengeance being levelled against them. But he must make no move yet. He had learned plenty by keeping his own counsel, hiding completely, but he must continue to learn everything he could about the demon's motive and plans.

'And then you will be content and we can leave this place?'

'Yes, Aphra. My hunger will be sated.'

'Where are we, my lord? I am yours to command.'

'Indeed, to the business at hand, the next stage of our journey. If we are going to behave as mortal — and reach the Crown — then I need the wealth to move freely and the standing to mingle with the right people. Behind these doors lives a man with just these attributes.'

Aphra laughed. 'Who is this man?'

'A wealthy merchant but he lives as a recluse. Few in the capital could claim to have met him.'

'No family? No wife?'

'Tentrell's tastes do not run to the female form.'

Aphra giggled. 'Ah, I see. And you think he will enjoy the look of Gabriel?'

Gabe's senses went onto full alert.

'I like that you catch on fast, Aphra. Yes, I think the body you brought us is precisely what Tentrell craves. Shall we?'

She laughed again. 'You're in control, my lord.'

Gabe watched his fist bang on the door, feeling helpless.

The small peephole hatch swung open. 'Yes?'

'Someone told me that Merchant Tentrell might have some work for a fit man,' Cyricus replied, a soft plea in his tone.

'Thank you, no,' the man said and began to close the hatch.

'Oh, please wait,' Cyricus said, even more pitifully. 'I was sent by a man called Easov.' Clearly Cyricus knew this would win the attention of the person behind the door.

Easov is powerful in a neighbouring town, he explained inwardly to Aphra. *I'm sure we'll get entry now.*

Cyricus waited. The door opened a short while later and a man stood before them wearing pale robes with the striped edging that attested he was a slave. He was young, almost feminine in his movement.

'Master Tentrell said you are to go around to the back,' he said in a light, breathy voice, nodding his head in the direction of the side of the house. 'He will speak to you in the grounds.' The door closed without another word.

Cyricus chuckled and walked Gabe's body down the side pathway until it opened up into a neat, formal garden. It was, in the main, a beautifully manicured small orchard. Miniature pear trees had been strung against lines so their branches acted as climbers and framed one side of the garden. Gabe noticed there was no fruit, but there were signs it had been a good crop. On the other side, citrus trees had enjoyed similar treatment, with limes and oranges hanging plump and ripe.

In between the trees, herbs and spices mixed with highly coloured flowers while small benches were strategically placed to enjoy maximum sun, or shade, or simply to revel within a cloud of perfume.

Cyricus inhaled and Gabe recognised the look and scent of lavender and mint, rosemary and thyme. There were other plants he didn't know but he could smell clove and aniseed. There was also a dark, arrow-shaped herb with a bouquet that was akin to crushed berries, but he had no idea what it was or how it might be used.

The flowers were a riot of purples and deep reds, rich pinks and chocolatey yellows. His attention was dragged from the garden beds by the arrival of a heavily built man.

'Master Tentrell?' Gabe heard his voice ask.

'Am I supposed to know you?' the man queried. He may have been handsome once, Gabe thought, but he had run to fat. Clearly his life was prosperous and sedentary.

'No, sir,' Cyricus continued, 'but Master Easov told me of your lovely garden and said you may have some manual work for me.' Cyricus made a show of looking around. 'I can see that he told me no lie of its beauty, Master Tentrell.'

'Easov said that?' Tentrell said with a smirk. 'The man despises me.'

Cyricus shrugged Gabe's shoulders. 'I don't know anything about that, sir. I can tell you that he doesn't despise your garden.'

Tentrell's hooded eyes seemed to shrink back further into the layer of flesh above his cheeks, in which was a network of broken red veins. 'And you want some work?'

'I can't remember the last time I ate, sir. I will give an honest day's work for a bowl of food and a half flagon of watered wine.'

'A very modest wage, indeed,' Tentrell remarked. 'Take off your shirt.'

'Pardon?' Cyricus said, putting on a startled tone. Gabe could tell the demon was amused, as though expecting a request such as this.

'You heard me. What's your name by the way?'

'Gabriel.'

'Well, Gabriel, I need to see that you have the, er … loins, shall we say, and a strong chest to do my work.'

Gabe could hear the innuendo in the man's words and feel the amusement from Cyricus at the same.

'So you have some work?'

'Always. This garden does not tend itself. Over there,' he pointed, 'I am keen to plant a new vegetable bed.'

'I can help with that, Master Tentrell.'

'I'm waiting to see some proof.'

Cyricus began to peel off his leather jerkin and the shirt beneath. Gabe knew the demon was relieved he'd taken the precaution of bathing Gabe's body and stealing a shirt, for Flek's had been ruined. He knew he hardly looked like a strong labourer, but it was true that he took care of himself and had worked on staying physically fit. He had nothing to be ashamed of.

He watched Tentrell's gaze alight on his torso and observe it hungrily.

'Do I look up to the task?' Cyricus deliberately baited, layering his words with innuendo as well.

'You'll do,' Tentrell said, turning away, trying to sound as though Gabe was of no further interest, but he betrayed his intention by turning back. 'You will present yourself to me at the end of your day's toil.'

Gabe could feel the pleasure that Cyricus felt warm his body at having achieved his aim.

'Of course, Master Tentrell,' Cyricus replied, nonetheless humbly. 'Should I come to the back door?'

'No, Ash will show you upstairs. I shall be spending the afternoon resting. You can come and get your coin at sunset.'

'But a meal is more than —'

'I like to pay my workers, Gabriel. You can certainly have a meal on the back porch.' He pointed to where a stool and table were. 'Then clean yourself up and present yourself … Ash will show you where.'

'Thank you.'

'You'll find all the tools you'll need in that small enclosure.' He pointed again. 'Ask Ash if you're unsure. He will bring you some water to drink and show you where you can clean up at the end of the day. Make sure you prepare my bed properly.' He stopped just short of winking, Gabe was sure. Tentrell gave a final languorous smile before waddling off on swollen ankles into the house.

'Surely you're not going to do this manual work, my lord?' Aphra asked, sounding disturbed.

'I am, because I know he will be watching from his upstairs window. We might as well go through the motions and get his excitement levels to the right peak.'

Aphra laughed. 'Gabe has a fine body.'

'I hope you didn't enjoy it too much.'

'I thought of myself as a whore when I was with him. It disgusted me to feel his touch, my lord. I am for you alone. And I permitted his slobberings only in order to reach you.'

As Cyricus's laughter boomed around his mind, Gabe felt sickened by her insult and felt it stoke the fire of his rage. He had to be especially careful. If he allowed his emotions to rise any further, his unwelcome guests might feel his fists clench against their will or sense his blood warming in anger. No, he must use all of his psychologist's skills to remain calm and silent under any insults.

He took his mind away from their conversation and focused purely on the work that soon got underway. Gabe kept himself deliberately distracted, revelling in the physical exercise, sensing the building fatigue in his shoulders and arms. He was glad of the weights he had used regularly in his apartment back in Paris and it was obvious that Cyricus was not only making very good use of that training but was now exerting his own strength somehow. The memory cut into the bubble of distance he'd managed to wrap around himself and he had to control the feelings that threatened to overwhelm him. He must not allow himself to experience any rushes of emotion.

Memories of Paris, the apartment, his former life, must be banished if he was going to survive this entrapment.

SIXTEEN

Florentyna had never felt more alone than she did right now watching Darcelle fuss over the final arrangements for the arrival of King Tamas in a few days. It wasn't jealousy, it was envy — they're different, she analysed privately. She had been betrothed once. She wondered if she would ever find someone to love. *Weeping into one's sewing just won't do, majesty*, Reynard used to tease when he caught her in a moment of self-pity. Shar, but she missed him.

'Oh, I'm so nervous,' Darcelle twittered in Florentyna's general direction.

'Formal welcome, to the throne room, meet the queen, talk with nobles briefly ... and so on and so forth,' Darcelle continued murmuring to herself as she looked over her list. It had originally held a mammoth series of tasks, which she had doggedly shortened — through canny management over seven moons — to this final list. 'Stables, cleared. Guestrooms, ready. Servants appointed ... er, Burrage?'

'Yes, highness?' he said, looking up from his desk in the queen's salon, where they were all seated.

Florentyna felt obliged to be present but was doing her best not to be involved in the final flurry of activity to organise the welcome for the arrival of the King of Cipres.

'I know it's tedious of me,' Darcelle continued, 'but I want to check again that Tamas has been appointed the best from our household staff to wait on him.'

Florentyna had to wonder why Burrage didn't fling the book of household accounts straight at her sister's head, which appeared to be empty of anything but her own inane, repetitive queries regarding her nuptials.

'Hytchen will be his manservant at all times, and Looce his maid, your highness. I have seen to it.'

'Good,' she said. 'I'm sorry to make you run through it again.'

'It is no hardship, highness. Little Venn will be his page, and I will, of course, offer my secretarial and administrative services to ensure confidentiality and reliability. Looce has picked three other of our most senior and trusted women. Meanwhile, Hytchen has assembled his special team — from stable hands to falconer, to dressers, to musicians. Essentially, though, it will be myself, Hytchen and Looce who will supervise and manage the needs of the king and his retinue. Please do not worry yourself — we will ensure a smooth and delightful stay.' He smiled warmly and cast a glance towards Florentyna, which she ignored, preferring not to be drawn into the conversation.

'Thank you, Burrage,' Darcelle said briskly. She continued checking off her list, muttering and dipping her nib into the queen's inkpot to scribble small notes to herself. 'So, we're leaving pre-dawn to go and meet him?' she cast into the silence.

This was too much for Florentyna.

There was no actual wedding ceremony yet. The visit of the king at this time was essentially to meet the sovereign of Morgravia in order to parley, to broker the right structure for this marriage between the two realms. It continued to annoy Florentyna that strict protocol had already been breached when Darcelle had made her own journey to Cipres and accepted the king's proposal so emphatically. Darcelle should have known better, which is why Florentyna continued to believe that her stepmother was behind this union. Getting a crown onto Darcelle's head was, no doubt, Saria's prime outside interest while incarcerated at the monastery.

Once Darcelle became a queen — with the power that such a title might bring — Florentyna was sure Saria would then set about chipping away at *her* through Darcelle. She'd hoped, over the passing of many moons, that Darcelle might drift away from their stepmother. Florentyna had to acknowledge to herself it was why she had acquiesced to her sister making the journey across the ocean to Cipres in the first place. It was a useful, cunning old ploy to expose a young woman to new experiences, new people, fresh interests. It hadn't worked. Darcelle's affections for Saria had remained intact; intensified if anything.

Now Florentyna's frustration spilled over. 'Darcelle, I insist upon some decorum. You will meet Tamas at Baelup. There is absolutely no need for

215

you to go traipsing across the countryside in the dead of night. Don't act so desperate. He's wooing you. He needs you far more than you him.'

'Dead of *morning*, sister,' Darcelle corrected. 'And there is every need for me to gallop at the highest speed toward the man that I love. I don't know how you managed to talk me out of being on the shore to meet his ship! This is my future husband. It is how I demonstrate my commitment and love for him.'

Burrage cut the queen a glance. His eyes urged her to remain calm.

Florentyna sighed. She was always the one who did the right thing. She could almost hear her father — and Reynard — telling her that she had no choice as sovereign but to always do what was right and correct. Florentyna put down her papers and schooled her features to look a lot less irritated than she felt.

'It is more seemly for the bride to be a little more reticent. The match is very good for King Tamas — please don't forget that. He is marrying into what is arguably the most prosperous dynasty in all the world and —'

Darcelle snorted. 'I think the Denovians might like to take you to task on that, sister.'

The queen forced herself to let her sister's rudeness pass. She hated it when Darcelle derided her in front of others, and as the Ciprean king's arrival date had drawn closer, Darcelle's confidence had grown to arrogant levels. Saria was lurking in this, but deep down Florentyna knew she had helped create the monster by being so soft on her little sister.

'Nevertheless,' she said, evenly, working to remain gentle with Darcelle, 'the Ciprean crown is the real winner in this marriage, so please —'

'Florentyna! You are determined to ruin my pleasure. I've waited so many moons to see Tamas again and you know how much I've longed for him.'

Florentyna cleared her throat and glared at Darcelle to remind her that Burrage was still in the room.

Darcelle stood. 'I just want it all to be perfect for him.'

'And it will be. You are perfect for each other,' Florentyna said, meaning it. She rose and walked around her desk to take Darcelle by the shoulders. 'You are the most beautiful bride that any king could ever possibly be

216

fortunate enough to win.' Darcelle pouted a smile. 'You're intelligent and talented, you're young and capable of giving him strong sons.'

Darcelle laughed. 'A whole army,' she quipped.

Florentyna grinned. 'Indeed. He knows you love him, beautiful child. You have nothing to prove. Just be elegant, be restrained, let him discover all there is to discover about you slowly. He's an older man ... he should and no doubt will worship the ground you walk on. But he must earn your love too, Darcelle.'

'Florentyna, you don't understand. I worship *him*. And it's too late if you want me to play the coy virgin!'

The queen gasped. Burrage cleared his throat and made some inane excuse to leave the chamber which Florentyna barely heard. She was staring uncomprehendingly into Darcelle's defiant gaze.

'You slept with Tamas?' she asked, her tone incredulous.

Darcelle gave one of her sly smiles. 'I don't think we did much sleeping —'

Florentyna looked as shocked at the sound as Darcelle was stung by the pain of the slap. The queen even looked at her hand, baffled that it was the culprit that had inflicted the strike. Darcelle covered her cheek while Florentyna's lips thinned as much in despair as in anger.

'How dare you!' Darcelle whimpered.

'Someone has to,' Florentyna bit back.

'No, Florentyna! Someone has to get on with enriching this family, broadening its horizons, bringing fresh blood into it and breathing new life into our line. It's fairly obvious it's not going to be dry old you,' Darcelle snapped. Both women were breathing heavily. 'There's about as much chance of you being bedded as me sprouting wings and flying out of that window!' She hurled the words at her sister. 'I'm a woman now and I will marry Tamas ... and I will wear his crown. And though I may nod my head towards you, sister, in acknowledgement of your crown, I will never, ever bow as subserviently to you as I've had to previously, once that crown is on my head. Do you understand me? We will be queens and we can get on as sisters ... or we can be enemies.'

And there it was. All that she'd dreaded.

'You senseless, self-centred brat,' Florentyna exploded. 'I know Saria is behind all of this.'

'My mother —'

217

'She's *not* your mother.'

'Saria is the only mother I've ever known. And I don't care if you hate her. I love her. I thought I loved you too — that's what always made our triangle so difficult. I was torn. Increasingly, Florentyna, you are making it far easier for me to choose. You have become an emotionless, isolated island of a person whom no-one can reach, least of all me. And worse, now you're jealous of me. Frankly I've done so much to promote your reign that I should be the one to feel hard done by. But I don't bear grudges. I want only what's best for you. Pity you can't feel the same sentiment towards me!'

She took a breath and before Florentyna could voice her despair, her sister continued her rant. She pointed aggressively. 'You should be revelling in the fact that we have this opportunity to bind our realm with Cipres and, ultimately, perhaps Tallinor. And you should be especially thrilled that this is not a strategic marriage with me kicking and screaming as I'm dragged away to marry an acid-breathed man I despise. He's older, yes, but I love Tamas. What's more — and I know this cuts you deeply — he genuinely loves me. You should be showering me with praise. Instead, all you do is think of yourself.' Darcelle backed away and lowered her hand.

Florentyna shrank at the sight of the welt on her sister's cheek. 'I'm sorry. I should not have done that,' Florentyna whispered, knowing she should not be apologising, knowing Darcelle was finally showing the flaws in her character and that, as queen, she was making a terrible error in condoning her sister's behaviour. The sovereign might find ways to make amends, but to accept blame was inappropriate. She could all but hear her father's voice lambasting her.

Darcelle continued her tirade. 'No, I do not accept your apology. I'll wear this bruise as a mark of pride. It's testimony to the shrivelled stick of a woman you are fast becoming that you would criticise me for crafting one of the most positive events this realm has seen in an age. We're teetering on destruction of the triumvirate but maybe … just maybe, a royal wedding, a merger of realms, a whole empire in celebration might drag us all back from the brink. The only reason you're queen is the five winters that yawn between us, sister. But we all know — including you — that I would have made a far better sovereign and that would have left you free to moon about in your enchanted garden or play with the magics that I know you believe in. You're a disgrace! Saria's right. This crown of Morgravia is rightfully mine.'

At Florentyna's horrified look, Darcelle laughed. 'Scary, isn't it, that I might even entertain such a thought. So don't push me, your majesty! I've walked in your withered shadow for long enough. I respect the role of sovereign more than you know and that's the only reason I will bow once again to you, my queen,' she said, lowering herself elegantly but her tone was poisonous. 'And be *very* grateful that I will never speak of your hand against me. I repeat my warning. Don't push me or you will have armies marching against you from across the oceans, and while Cipres might be small in comparison to this empire, it is loyal, patriotic and has the might of Tallinor behind it.

'What's more, you should be considering closely whether Briavel would support you. I doubt it, given what you've done to its beloved Saria … beware that the loyalty you have taken for granted doesn't turn on you. It won't take much for me to persuade a lot of powerful people that I would make a better queen. Let's face it, Florentyna, most Morgravians barely know you … it's me they meet at social events. You're invisible … a figurehead … a name. I am real to them. And they love me.'

She turned and flounced away.

All Florentyna could do was watch her shapely form disappear from the salon.

Burrage soon filled the space that Darcelle had left. 'Majesty?'

Florentyna was too stunned by her sister's rantings to respond.

He stepped closer. 'My queen,' he said, gravely, 'she is still a child. She exaggerates everything.'

'No, Burrage,' she said, her voice not much above a terrified whisper. 'That's just it. She's not a child. And she doesn't see herself as one either. I'm sorry you had to hear what you did.'

Burrage lowered his gaze but risked discussing what might otherwise remain a topic never to be broached again. 'She must have taken the right precautions.'

Florentyna knew exactly to what he referred. 'I have no doubt Saria made sure she was well equipped with the right concoctions to prevent pregnancy while Darcelle turned into a whore for King Tamas,' she growled.

Burrage gave a hushing sound. 'Please, your majesty. Understand this will never be discussed by me with anyone.'

'I know, Burrage. I realise now that the sooner she is married the better,' she said, the shock of Darcelle's scorn still making her hair feel as though it was standing on end. She felt the hot scald of her sister's words burn at her cheeks, while at the same time the coldness of contempt from the only person she loved was leaking into her heart. 'I will do as she wants. I will see her safely, happily married to the King of Cipres and then I will wash my hands of trying to guide Darcelle.' She felt her voice choke, could hear it too.

'Your majesty, you are upset. Please, take some time these next few days. You need to be at your sparkling best when the king arrives.'

She looked away, nodding.

'May I add on a personal note, your majesty ...?'

Florentyna met his gaze. Burrage never got personal. Her pause gave him permission.

He cleared his throat. 'I heard some of what was exchanged, forgive me. I wanted to be gone, but I didn't want any of the other staff to hear the princess's tirade,' he said hesitantly. Then he sighed. 'What I really wanted to say is that as an outsider looking in — and especially one with as many years in Stoneheart as I — it is obvious that the princess is the one with the sense of inferiority. Risking your ire, majesty, may I say that you are none of those things she accused you of being. I think it's important you know that you carry yourself with grace and are beloved by *all* of us in your household. You have more than filled your father's shoes despite your young years. We are all proud of our queen, who we feel is destined to rule as wisely and magnanimously as her illustrious forebears.' He cleared his throat again. 'Your sister covets your role, majesty. She deliberately hurt your feelings today. I hope you'll see it purely for what it was and not take any of her poisonous accusations to heart.'

She felt a sob racing towards her throat. Burrage was saying all that she needed to hear. His tender words reminded her all the more of how alone she felt without parents, without Reynard, without even a sister to count on. But if his message meant anything, it was that bleating like a lost lamb was not the path to take. Her people demanded strength and poise in all situations and that's what she would give them.

'Thank you, Burrage. May I say that you and I have both had big boots to fill and you've quietly and modestly become someone I trust and know I can always rely upon.'

Burrage regarded her with a softening expression before bowing gently in response.

'Is there any word on that man Fynch?' she asked, changing the subject and turning away to banish the emotion of the moment. Duty called and there were matters to attend to other than her silly sister's threats.

'Nothing yet.'

'There won't be either,' she replied with a tone of resignation.

'I've cast a wide net. We'll catch something in it, I'm sure. And each piece of information leads to a new one. If he can be found, I will find him for you.'

Florentyna stared out of the window into the great bailey. It was a hive of activity in preparation for her royal guest. She realised it must be a very long time since Stoneheart had greeted royalty from another household, for the cobbles of the bailey were being scrubbed, a sight she had never seen.

'When is Saria free to leave the monastery?' she asked, switching topics suddenly.

'Er, I believe that happens in three moons, your majesty.'

'She must be squirming with rage to be missing Tamas and the pomp we must accord a visiting royal.'

'The word from Brother Hoolyn is that they have an ogress in their midst.' Burrage chuckled quietly.

She turned, having made a snap decision. 'Then I think it's high time I paid a visit to Rittylworth Monastery.'

Burrage's humour fled. 'Whatever for?'

She swung around. 'I'm not going to wait for my stepmother to make any moves. Before Tamas arrives I shall take Dowager Saria by surprise and propose that she go west with Darcelle. I shall leave her no choice — either Cipres, or the equivalent of banishment to Briavel. She will not be welcome at Stoneheart. Nay, she will not be permitted to enter the borders of Morgravia or the Razors. Let her be gone with her stepdaughter to live in Cipres and trouble me no more.'

* * *

As Gabe had suspected he would, Merchant Tentrell had dismissed his single manservant, Ash, and at sunset had called for Gabe to down his tools and come into the house. Cyricus gleefully guided his body indoors and, as reluctant as Gabe was, there was little he could do to prevent the inevitable. He shrank so tightly that he hoped he might shut himself away from seeing what his eyes were regarding. He couldn't close off the sounds of Tentrell dying beneath his hands, but he felt at a remove.

It was an ugly death, for Tentrell — as flabby and soft as he'd become — was nonetheless strong, if only because of his sheer bulk. Cyricus had been patient, allowing the man to flirt, to touch and to ply Gabe's body with wine, or at least believe that's what he was doing. Cyricus acted drunk very quickly, first managing to toss the best part of two goblets of wine into the bushes below the balcony where Tentrell had planned his seduction, and latterly spilling far more than he allowed Gabe's body to consume. While Tentrell was becoming soused, as well as more bold with his hands and lewd suggestions, Gabe sensed rather than saw the moment when Cyricus picked up a fruit knife and plunged it into the tender flesh at Tentrell's throat. It took several stabs for the man's grip around him to weaken. He was sickened by the knowledge that he was surely drenched in another's blood once again.

Now laughter boomed through his body. 'There we are, my beloved,' Cyricus said. 'Now we have the means.'

'I thought you might travel in Tentrell's body. Surely he's more use in royal circles?'

'I'll worry about that later. I told you, I like Gabe's body. It attracts the right attention. I can put it to good use for just a little longer.'

'Won't they be looking for Gabe? The servant saw him, can identify him.'

'We will be gone this night. By the time anyone can hunt down Gabriel, he too will be lifeless. I plan to be rid of this body within days.'

'Good,' she replied.

'It's time to ransack the house. I know Tentrell has lots of gold, as well as jewels, and I know just the person we shall attract with them.'

Days, Gabe thought mournfully, ignoring the sound of Aphra's sinister chuckling. That's all he had to come up with a plan. He became aware of Cyricus washing his body and selecting fine clothes to wear. It seemed Tentrell was vain enough to have kept his wardrobe intact from when he'd cut a slimmer figure.

Cyricus found rings to put on Gabe's fingers and then went hunting for the man's money and other valuables. It felt like an eternity before a safebox was found in a cunning recess in the wall behind a shutter, and it was dark by the time Cyricus finally walked Gabe's body out of the house and went looking for stables. He couldn't risk using Tentrell's horse.

Here the stable master was paid handsomely from the stolen gold and silver.

'Good evening,' Cyricus said from the saddle and Gabe was surprised that he could remember how to ride. Those lessons in England when he was a child were paying off.

'Hmmm,' Cyricus pondered as he eased the horse out of the stables.

'What?' the mostly silent Aphra asked.

'Strange …'

He walked the horse out of the town, guided by the burning torches lighting the streets.

'Just for a moment,' Cyricus continued, 'I could swear I wasn't in control of this body.'

Gabe mentally held his breath.

'I don't understand,' she said.

'No, neither do I. It was odd though. When we left the stables, I wasn't moving the reins, nor did I dig my knees in to get the beast moving. It was as though …'

'As though what, Cyricus?'

'Well, as though another had done so.'

She laughed. 'It wasn't me. I have no idea how to ride.'

There was a horrible silence during which Gabe shrank back, desperately frightened at the possibility of discovery.

'Maybe there are remnants of memories left behind. And now I come to think of it, that makes sense. I know Wyl Thirsk inherited the memories of his victims when Myrren's magic went to work. I hadn't realised that we have no doubt inherited Gabriel's memories.'

'I haven't been aware of them.'

'No, that's odd too. I would assume we'd possess all or none.'

'Magic changes, my love. Perhaps what you just experienced was an echo of Gabe's memory.'

'I hope so. But search for them. Let's see if we can find any others. I want no sudden surprises that might be more troublesome than his memory of horse riding.'

'I'll do that immediately,' she said.

And Gabe forgot about Tentrell's messy death, his memory of horse riding, and his determination to strike back at the interlopers who had stolen his existence. All that remained was a desire to remain alive long enough in this strange spiritual form to see them gone. He mustn't be found by Aphra. She was hunting for memories — he didn't know how to give them to her, but he deliberately thought about the apartment, making that picture of it come to life vividly. He thought about coffee, knowing she would recognise that as one of his passions. He thought about books, about the shop, about Paris.

Would he be able to hide from her? He tried to imagine himself disappeared and immediately the nave of Pearlis Cathedral surrounded him ... and Gabe felt safe.

SEVENTEEN

The man called Wevyr stood behind the counter of an otherwise bare shop. Cassien had been told by Hamelyn that the workshop was hidden behind the walls of this area. Wevyr was as tall as Cassien but broader, no doubt due to years of pounding metal flat and making beautiful weapons; his hands looked like a pair of mallets. Grimy, with sweat-streaks cutting through the smudges of dark grey, he glanced at Cassien's sword and Cassien noted recognition flash in the man's otherwise leaden expression.

'I have no appointments,' he said flatly.

'You are Wevyr?'

'Jonti Wevyr, yes. I have a brother, Eldo.'

'Which of you made this sword?' Cassien asked.

The man considered him carefully. 'Forgive me, Master …?'

'Cassien,' Hamelyn obliged, stepping forward. 'Morning, Master Wevyr.'

Wevyr nodded at the boy, then reached for a linen and wiped his face deliberately. Finally, and without hurrying, he placed the linen down and looked at them again. 'May I?' he asked, nodding toward Cassien's hip.

Cassien unbuckled his belt and placed the weapon on the counter. As the craftsman pulled the sword clear of its sheath, it seemed to Cassien as though he was holding his breath. After a silent and lengthy pause, during which Jonti Wevyr touched the blade reverently, sighted down its length, held it in various ways checking its balance, admired its hilt and the magnificent length made up of wavy lustre of metal, he sighed out the long breath he had indeed held. 'Exquisite,' he breathed. Then he gave a wistful smile. 'I have such a long way to go.' He looked up at Cassien. 'You have come to the wrong place.'

'Pardon?'

'This is not my work, nor is it Eldo's.'

Cassien cut a glance at Hamelyn while Hamelyn frowned and began to splutter a query. Wevyr stopped him with a meaty hand in the air.

'This is the work of my father, Ferrer. I'm intrigued for he has not worked on a weapon in many years. In truth I didn't believe he had the strength left to fashion such a sword, and yet this is irrefutably his work.'

Cassien produced the smaller blades. 'And these?'

Wevyr let out a low whistle. 'I'm lost for words. When did you get these?' There was a vague sound of irritation in his voice.

'A few days ago,' he replied. 'I need to see him.'

'Master Cassien, my father is gravely ill. He is extremely old, past his eightieth summer, so Shar has been generous to him over the seasons. Even so, I doubt he'll make his next name day.'

Cassien frowned. 'Is he sick because he's old, or is he sick because something has happened to him?'

At this Wevyr shrugged. 'Both. He has paid his respects at the graveside of many friends. I suspect his own time is near. It's also true that two moons ago he seemed to be suddenly wearied. We had no warning. One day he was tending his herb garden, the next he could barely get out of his bed.'

'I need to see him,' Cassien said.

'I'm sorry, Master Cassien, but my father is really too —'

'I give you my word I will not upset him. I need only a few moments of his time.'

The sword maker nodded. 'Hamelyn knows where my father lives. He can lead you there.' He returned the blades to Cassien. 'Goodbye, Master Cassien. You are a fortunate man indeed to possess the last weapons that Ferrer Wevyr will make.'

Cassien smiled. 'I feel privileged.'

'Take care of them.'

He walked out to the back of the shop and left Cassien and Hamelyn staring at each other, while Cassien strapped on his sword and blades again.

'He's not happy,' Hamelyn remarked after they left.

'He didn't know his father did these. That's hard on any son, especially one who is carrying on his father's trade.'

'And he's head of the sword guild. Jonti is highly respected.'

'Even harder for him, then. And you did not recognise Ferrer when you were spying?'

'The Wevyr brothers are a dead spit of Master Wevyr senior in height and build. In the dark and in my fear I probably didn't see the small differences.'

'Is the sword speaking to you?' Cassien suddenly asked as he followed Hamelyn down more unfamiliar streets.

Hamelyn nodded. 'It hasn't stopped. Mostly it whispers … murmurs to itself. When you're wearing it, it's quieter. When you took it off, it began a shrill tone.'

As odd as it was to hear this, and even odder to accept that a piece of inert metal was somehow communicating with his companion, Cassien took private pleasure in knowing his sword was calm when it was at his side. This factor alone meant he had to talk with Wevyr. He had to understand what Fynch had drawn him into.

They'd moved away from the hubbub of the town; buildings began to thin and beyond the path they were moving down, Cassien could now see pastureland and further into the distance, woodland.

'Has old man Wevyr always lived here?' he wondered aloud.

'As long as I've known him, he has.'

'Hamelyn, how is it that you know everyone?'

'I never forget a face or a name. I remember everything I've ever heard or seen.'

Cassien stared at him. 'Really? That is a talent any of us would wish to have.'

Ham shrugged. 'It's always been like that for me. Did you go to school, Cassien?'

Cassien shook his head. 'Not the way you would know it. I belonged to an order of … well, I suppose you could call them monks. They taught me how to read and write. Books taught me everything else except how to use this,' he said, touching the sword at his hip.

Ham nodded wistfully. 'I used to watch the other children going to schools. Emperor Cailech set up a system for children to have five summers of schooling in this region. In the city they were given eight summers.' He sighed. 'I didn't get any schooling because I was an orphan. Orphanages usually provide workers from a young age so I was not allowed to have my five years of learning.'

227

'But you read, I gather?'

'Not well. I tried to teach myself by hiding beneath the open classroom window. I learned a little.' He gave another small shrug. 'I didn't want to be a tanner or a slaughterer. I don't eat meat and I knew I couldn't be involved with anything that required me to kill an animal.'

'But that's what awaited you?'

He nodded. 'Most of our boys were sent to the local tannery or slaughterhouse. I was fortunate, though, because around the powerful sword guild grew an industry in nearby towns and villages for saddlery, carts and wagon building, the furbishing of leather-covered seats in coaches and the like. So I taught myself other skills. I didn't know what I'd do but my good memory has helped me to live by my wits.'

'A powerful recall is a gift, Ham; not a skill you've acquired so much as an endowment from Shar upon you.'

'I'll try to remember that,' Ham said, looking pleased with the compliment. 'This is old man Wevyr's house.'

It was the last house on the last street, and the path leading to it had long ago stopped pretending it was a road. Grass and weeds provided a soft, mossy tread underfoot. A walkway had been made simply by people walking to and from the house; bulbs sprouted at the side of the path. They were not open yet, but Cassien suspected they would provide a shout of colour very soon. The house itself was modest.

He banged on the door and they waited.

'If he's unwell, I doubt he'll answer the door,' Hamelyn noted.

'We'll try once more,' Cassien said, not wanting to barge in on the fellow. He banged again.

There was no answer for the second time. 'Go around,' he suggested to Ham.

The boy skipped away to the rear of the house, while Cassien banged for the third time. 'Master Wevyr?'

He waited for a few moments in silence and then heard footsteps. The door was opened by Ham, who grinned.

'The back door was ajar. I called to Master Wevyr. He knows I'm here, but not that you are. Perhaps I should go and see him first so we don't startle him.'

Old man Wevyr was propped up in the parlour shelling peas into a bowl when Cassien followed Ham down the small passage of the modest dwelling. Wevyr was indeed a spit of his son Jonti, except his hair was white, tied neatly in a tail, and his face was lined and mottled. Cassien could believe that, in shadow, Ferrer Wevyr could have been mistaken for Jonti. Wevyr was hunched from the bone-ache and his fingers were gnarled by the ravages of the same disease. The old man looked up unhurried from his simple toil.

'I grew these. Plumper than Wife Tanny's tits of fifty summers gone.'

Ham guffawed, but reined in his amusement quickly after a glance at his companion. 'Master Wevyr, this is Cassien.'

Wevyr regarded him as Cassien undid his cloak.

'I apologise for visiting uninvited, sir,' Cassien began as politely as he knew.

'I've been expecting you,' Wevyr admitted, popping another pod and giving a gentle smile of satisfaction.

That was a surprise. Cassien said nothing but his pause asked the unspoken question all the same.

Wevyr continued. 'Ever since I handed over those weapons you're wearing to that chatty tailor, I figured you may find your way here. I told Fynch you should come.'

'Why's that?'

The sword maker shook his head slightly. 'Guilds — particularly the sword guild — are especially secretive. I'm sure you know that. Or perhaps you don't? Your young companion would. My father taught me how to keep my mouth shut as his father had taught before. It's not that we are all about secrets in our line of work, but we must always be discreet and respect our clients and their need for privacy. I have made blades for kings, and equally fine blades for assassins and ne'er-do-wells, as did my father and grandfather before me.' He laughed. 'Everyone pays with the same money. And everyone has their reasons for needing a new blade.'

'Why did you make mine?'

Wevyr snorted deep in his throat as if it were clogged. Cassien had noticed the spit bowl. He wondered if they were going to share what was in the back of Wevyr's throat, but the older man continued as brusquely as before. 'I was commissioned. I don't ask questions of my clients.'

'Some clients are certainly more intriguing than others, aren't they?'

'Why yes. My great-grandfather once made a sword for the Emperor Cailech himself. Shar, but that would have been the commission of all commissions,' Wevyr said wistfully.

'And what is your proudest work?' Cassien baited. He was sure he knew the answer.

'You already know. You wear it.'

Cassien nodded. 'The tailor is dead. Killed for what he knew.'

Now he had Wevyr's attention. The old man regarded him with a gaze that was still bright and alert.

'And have you come to kill me too? For what I know?'

Ham looked startled, whipping an anxious glance at Cassien.

'I've come to learn what you know. It's why you hoped I'd come, so you could share it before you pass. These are my weapons, given to me personally by the man who commissioned them … and we both know it wasn't Zeek. The tailor was merely the courier so he could pass through the region unquestioned, untroubled.'

'Pity he was a drunk.'

'Yes,' Cassien agreed.

'Or perhaps it would have been best if Master Fynch had simply collected the weapons himself.'

'A decision that always had a risk, I agree, but a calculated one.'

Wevyr shook his head. 'I warned him it was dangerous.'

'Why did you think that about Zeek?' Cassien asked. He still hadn't moved from the doorway and Wevyr hadn't stopped shelling his peas.

He did so now to regard Cassien dolefully. 'I'm not talking about Zeek. Those weapons, had they fallen into the wrong hands, are more dangerous than you or I can imagine.'

'Wevyr,' Cassien said urgently, dragging a chair opposite the sword maker and sitting down, 'the weapons are in the right hands, but I don't understand why I was given blades that were forged with blood.'

The old man dropped his hands and in so doing upended the bowl and scattered bright peas in a shower of green to the parlour floor. He barely noticed. His eyes were on Cassien, his mouth parted in shock, bottom lip quivering. Cassien noticed his hands shook.

'How do you know this?' he hissed. 'Master Fynch did not tell you, so don't start fashioning a lie.'

'You were seen,' Cassien admitted, although he had intended to lie and blame Fynch.

He watched Wevyr blanch. The old man shook his head. 'It's not possible. We took all precautions.' He tried to stand, but fell back against his chair.

'Not quite,' Cassien said, 'but you must not fret on this. We are fortunate that you were witnessed by a friend rather than foe.'

'Who?' he demanded. 'Who spied upon us?'

'I did,' Hamelyn admitted, looking terrified.

Old man Wevyr's huge, twisted fingers shot out and grabbed Ham's shirt. He shook the boy. 'You!' he growled.

'It was an accident, Master Wevyr,' Ham began to gabble.

Cassien had stood and now reached over and pulled Ham away. 'Leave the boy. He is innocent and, as I've just told you, he is an ally.'

'What did he see?'

'Enough that you'd better tell me the truth.'

'Master Fynch would —'

'Wevyr, the last time I saw Master Fynch he was dying.'

'Dying?' he breathed, sounding deeply unnerved.

'Likely dead, given how he looked. He banished me. Made me promise I'd come to Orkyld, to follow through and make sure we had no more loose mouths.'

The man gasped. 'So answer me. Have you come to kill me with my own blade once you learn all that you need?'

Cassien shook his head. 'Not you, although I wouldn't hesitate if you cross me. Is the blood in each weapon?' The old man nodded. 'Tell me why Fynch's blood is mixed with the metal.'

The old man shook his head. 'If he wants you to know, he would have told you.'

'I agree but he was dying before he could share anything relevant.'

'He was hale and hearty when I met him.'

'And we both surely know that can't be right. How does a man of his age remain hale and hearty? How does any man reach such an age?' Cassien said, leaning so near to Wevyr's face that he could smell the porridge on his breath.

Wevyr looked away. 'Why is he dying now?'

'I can't answer that, not because I'm withholding information but because I simply don't know. I don't understand much about him, except that he is my friend, as he is yours. He has come to both of us. He commissioned you to make a special blade and he chose me to bestow that blade upon. He has a purpose for it.'

'He never told me, Master Cassien.' Wevyr held up his hands in defence. 'That's the truth of it. You must know he's a secretive man. I have met him many times through my life so I have come to like and respect him. But it has always troubled me that he talks about my father and ...' he sighed, '... and my great-grandfather before him, as if he knew them. How else would he know about clients such as Romen Koreldy — a noble turned mercenary — who had blades made in our family workshop more than a century ago? No-one is privy to our secret accounting books. No-one but myself ... not even the boys yet, although soon I will hand them the key to the vault where our records are kept and my sons will have access to the names of the kings and villains alike who have used the services of Wevyr and Son. How does Fynch know about Koreldy? The same way he knows my great-grandfather had gout, and there is no logical explanation.' Wevyr looked away. 'So we turn to the illogical, which is that Master Fynch has outlived his peers many times. I don't understand it. I don't want to. But I do like him and I trust him more than most men. Yes, Master Cassien, he bled into the molten metal that your sword is forged with. He insisted upon it.'

'Didn't you ask why?' Cassien queried.

'Of course I did!'

'What was his reply?'

'He simply said that the wielder would need this enrichment.' He looked up at Cassien and shrugged.

'That was his precise wording? And he used "enrichment"?'

Wevyr nodded. 'Exactly Master Fynch's words.'

'And you didn't think it curious?'

The old man wheezed a laugh. 'Curious, you say? I thought it downright lunacy, young man — and in agreeing to it, as though I too had been touched by the moon!'

'Why would you permit it? Not just a master sword maker, but arguably the Grand Master of the modern age, yet you let a client drip his blood into your crucible.'

He nodded with a look of bemusement. 'You're right, of course. But Master Fynch is persuasive. He knows things, and the way he talks it ...'

'It what?'

'Well ...' He gave a long, slow sigh. 'I know we're not supposed to, but I believe in the old stories that magic once roamed our land. I used to watch my grandfather at work — now there was a master sword maker. And later, when he was taking a long draught of the chilled water flavoured with leezel that he so enjoyed, I'd sit on his lap and he'd tell me about the existence of magic in our lives. He used to say that some of us were aware of it, while others travelled through their lives never knowing of magic, even if it touched them.' Wevyr stood and hobbled gingerly to a corner where an old broom leaned.

'I'll do that, Master Wevyr,' Hamelyn offered.

'I'm not throwing those peas away,' Wevyr warned. 'Brush them into that pan and I'll rinse them.'

Ham set to while Wevyr returned to his chair and sat down carefully, nursing his aching joints no doubt.

'Anyway,' he continued, looking back to Cassien, 'Master Fynch is obviously one of those people touched by the magic that my grandfather used to tell me about. How could I deny him his wish? It was certainly odd, but it was harmless enough in the sense that it didn't hurt anyone and didn't offend me. He was paying for the weapons — a handsome sum, you should know.'

'But you kept the weapons a secret from your sons, I understand?' Cassien remarked.

'Ah, yes, that's true. It was part of the agreement between Master Fynch and myself. He paid an extraordinary amount of money to lure me from my retirement, to allow him to put his blood into my crucible and to buy my secrecy. I'm only telling you because you own them and as I said at the beginning, I've always expected the owner of those weapons to come and find me.'

'Yes, and why did you expect that, Master Wevyr?'

Wevyr chuckled to himself. 'Because of the dragon.'

'Dragon?'

Wevyr's gravelly voice turned dreamy. 'When I poured the molten metal into the crucible and Master Fynch bled — quite profusely — into the vessel, I thought I was seeing things. You know how you see shapes

233

in clouds?' Cassien nodded, just to keep the man talking. 'I saw the shape of a dragon forming as the blood bubbled furiously on top of the molten metal. And …'

'And?' Cassien urged.

'A voice, in my mind. To this day I believe it was my grandfather. He told me I was making something extraordinary and that its owner needed to know it, so now I'm telling you just that.' His voice lost its faraway tone and he was instantly alert again. 'I saw other things as well, but I didn't understand them either.'

Cassien held his breath. *Them?*

'The Triad,' came the answer, except it wasn't Wevyr who spoke, but Ham.

Both men swivelled to regard the boy, who looked to be staring through them.

'There were three people in your vision, Master Wevyr, weren't there?'

Wevyr looked astounded and could only nod.

Cassien leapt from where he sat and held Ham's shoulders. 'How do you know this?' he murmured, equally astonished. 'Was it the blades talking?' he said, vaguely embarrassed to ask in front of Wevyr.

Ham shook his head slowly, but it was as though he was no longer with them; he seemed lost momentarily. 'I looked into the crucible too. The Triad is forming and the blood of the dragon will out,' he said, then Ham's eyes rolled back in his head and he fell forward, slumping into Cassien's arms.

EIGHTEEN

Darcelle stood before Burrage with a look of incomprehension. 'She's gone to see my mother?'

'Queen Florentyna is paying a visit to the dowager at Rittylworth Monastery, yes, your highness.'

'Why wasn't I told?'

'She only left a short while ago with a few men. Forgive me, highness, I cannot say why she did not inform you,' he lied, knowing the queen expected this of him. 'I suspect she wants to discuss your upcoming nuptials with the dowager.'

She gave Burrage an open sneer. 'Now we both know you're lying,' she accused him. 'Florentyna would rather choke on her own spit than have discourse with my mother over my wedding.'

Burrage blinked at the rebuke but maintained his poise. 'I wouldn't know, your highness — that is simply a thought that has occurred to me,' he said.

'You and Florentyna discuss everything, including me. I'm fairly certain you'd know why my sister took off in the middle of the night and stole away from the palace to see the one person she despises more than any other. And the fact that you're not telling me, Burrage, confirms my suspicions that Florentyna means my mother harm.'

'Highness! Please, do not suggest such a thing. The queen would not —'

'The queen, Burrage, slapped my face only yesterday. I can still feel its sting and I know you heard the blow because as always you were probably eavesdropping.' Burrage gasped. 'Is that the action of a balanced person? Is this how we want our sovereign to behave, with her emotions out of control?'

Burrage frowned. 'What can I say, your highness, to reassure you that the dowager is not in harm's way?'

'Nothing you say could reassure me, Burrage, because you're the queen's right hand and I wouldn't trust a word from you, just like I no longer feel I can trust her. My mother said this would happen. My mother assured me that Florentyna wanted her dead and I've been the one promising her that my sister would not do any such thing. I was blinded by my own loyalty to Florentyna. But her actions yesterday, her demands that I treat Tamas with contempt, and now, taking a few men with her to Rittylworth, can only mean she is no longer trustworthy.'

'What can I say to ease your mind, highness?'

Darcelle did not respond. She simply smirked at him and Burrage couldn't help but note a sense of cunning in her expression.

Rittylworth nestled in a comfortable valley, as though hugged in an affectionate embrace by its surrounding countryside. To its north were hills and beyond that the Razor Mountains. To its less barren south were fertile pastures which gave way to soft woodland flanking the River Tague. It was this river that Queen Florentyna and her men had followed.

She had wanted to travel as quietly and as inconspicuously as possible, choosing to ride, rather than travel in a carriage. But no sovereign and certainly no titular empress could arrive in small hamlets and not be noticed, given that she travelled with a retinue of impressive-looking guards. Florentyna had haggled with Burrage, who was insisting upon an armed guard of thirty men.

She'd laughed at him. 'Let's throw in some heralds for good measure, shall we? They can trumpet my arrival through any villages and towns along the way.'

'Majesty,' he had begun again patiently.

'Burrage, I know, I know. But not this time. These are my wishes. Three guards, none in uniform. We will travel without colours — no dragon insignia of Morgravia, no imperial crest, no regal purple. No bowing and no formal greetings or meetings. I am travelling quietly. I will be plainly clothed so as to move as just another noble wife on a journey from south to north. The less attention we draw, the fewer questions are asked.'

Burrage's mouth had opened and remained open and wordless since she'd insisted on three men only. Now he just stared at her. She smiled as she watched him.

'Are you in pain, Burrage?' she'd jested.

'My heart will surely fail if you persist with this lunacy, your majesty.'

She'd cut him a wry smile. 'Lunacy, eh?'

'My queen, please, you must see reason,' he'd pleaded.

'There is nothing to see. I am under no immediate threat,' she'd said, trying to ignore Fynch's warning. 'If we do this well and with minimum fuss, then I believe it diminishes potential for any problem.'

She'd seen he knew she was right. Now she would compromise.

'Burrage, if it makes you feel more at ease, send an extra number of men to escort me home. By then, people may know that I'm in the region and certainly Saria's demented howls will be heard throughout the realms,' she'd said smiling. 'I may need some solid protection by then.'

'I will do that, your majesty. You can count on there being two dozen of our house guard to escort you home.'

'And a herald or two, don't forget,' she'd said, touching his arm affectionately. 'Thank you for understanding. Now, not a word to anyone. I will leave the palace quietly. Brief Felyx and ask him to choose his most reliable pair of companions and that will make up our quartet to travel north.'

'Understood, majesty. What about your maid and —'

'No, Burrage. I am travelling without servants.'

'But even a noblewoman would have a maidservant,' he reasoned and although he'd sounded calm, she'd been able to detect the panic underlying his even tone.

'Not this one.'

Burrage had sighed worriedly and shaken his head, but he'd hurried away to find Felyx while the queen had moved at a far less frantic pace to her chambers to pack a few essentials, including a single gown in which to meet Saria.

Their trip north had been uneventful. Certainly not boring though. Florentyna had been unable to remember the last time she'd ridden out of the palace grounds on a long trip on horseback. She'd realised with a silent groan that it was as far back as childhood, when her father had indulged her with a ride alongside him to Argorn for talks with the southern noble families. It had been a treat, before Saria had come into their lives and when Darcelle was little more than a cherubic, unbelievably pretty infant princess with only a few words to her repertoire. Her much-improved repertoire continued to burn in Florentyna's mind.

Now, as she stared at peaceful Rittylworth, she hoped with all of her heart that she could carry off this confrontation with the grace her household believed she possessed.

They had deliberately not hurried their journey, for galloping riders drew attention, but she was eager to get this discussion with Saria over and done with. Felyx ambled up on his horse from where it had been drinking from a small brook.

'Beautiful, isn't it, your majesty?'

'It is indeed. I regret that I've taken so long to visit. Burrage mentioned its history is a colourful one.'

The queen's soldier scratched his head. He looked so different out of the rich colour and heraldry of his uniform. The trio of men were well armed, of course, but they looked like hired mercenaries offering safe escort to a noblewoman. Florentyna looked the least changed because she was not one for rich brocades, silks and flounces and her courtiers were used to seeing her in more neutral colours and plainer-style fabrics. She refused to wear the face 'paint' and jewellery that Darcelle used to enhance her features. Now, in her split skirt she looked like the Florentyna they knew from whenever she went riding. She'd taken the precaution of wearing a hooded cloak just in case some wily fellow traveller made any connection, but they'd come to Rittylworth without attracting much more than a second glance, including a night spent at Dryden Vale. Felyx had deliberately chosen that hamlet because it was celebrating its annual well-dressing. All the wells and springs of the region were grandly decorated with plants and flowers, some sites so ornate and picturesque that many years previously people had begun visiting from far and wide to view the spectacle. The gathering crowds and general festivities meant that strangers passing through were not an uncommon sight at this time of year.

They'd had little trouble in gaining refuge for the night in the sprawling home of a friendly noble who was unhappily having to miss the annual fair, but had gladly given permission for one of his cottages on the property to be used by 'a friend of the queen'. Florentyna and her escort were not greeted by the family — as quietly requested — but the butler was on hand and a maidservant was provided. Florentyna and her escort were gone by dawn and were considered the perfect houseguests as a result, having left the place almost exactly as they found it, with the plentiful wine stores barely touched.

She now shivered slightly in the thin midday sun. Summer was still a couple of moons from warming the land. Their ride this morning had been short. The long haul had been the previous day but Florentyna was feeling every moment of it through her aching body.

'You should ask Brother Hoolyn; I'm sure he'll be glad to relate Rittylworth's stories,' said Felyx as they gazed at the monastery.

She nodded. She'd paid attention to her history too. 'Yes, including a blot on our own family's history.'

'Not your family, majesty. As I understand it, it is King Celimus who shoulders the responsibility for that tragedy.'

'How awful it must have been,' she remarked, remembering the tale that the men of prayer were slaughtered where they stood, their monastery burned, their senior monk crucified and torched, left to smoulder on his cross. It seemed unthinkable that a Morgravian sovereign would perpetrate such suffering upon his own. It was that murky time in the history of her forebears though, where inexplicable events occurred. They included her great-grandmother, Valentyna, marrying King Celimus, who was poisoned — and dead — within hours of the marriage by his own chancellor, who then mysteriously died. Then the new Queen Valentyna had taken everyone by surprise, declaring her love for the rogue King Cailech of the Razors, whom everyone thought had been executed, but she married him and began the new dynasty. No-one understood this clouded past, least of all the historians who had recorded what they knew and what witnesses had seen; events nevertheless remained shrouded in mystery.

'You wouldn't know it now,' Felyx continued.

She returned from her thoughts. 'No, the monastery looks so peaceful and beautiful. Soon it will have the shrieks of the dowager to contend with,' she said, with an arched eyebrow.

Felyx shrugged. 'If it pleases your majesty,' he said and they both shared a quiet chuckle.

'Lead on,' she said, and the royal quartet eased its way onto the main path that would lead them into Rittylworth Monastery, where a dowager awaited.

No-one noticed the two riders, with their horses' hooves bound in linens, steal up onto the rise behind them.

Cassien and Hamelyn departed Orkyld within moments of emerging from Wevyr's house. Cassien had toyed with the idea of seeing Vivienne once more, but it had been awkward and curiously painful to leave her that morning and it would do neither of them any good to linger on what had occurred between them. If their paths were meant to cross again, they would.

Wevyr's revelation about the dragon and Ham's subsequent statement about the 'Triad' and then his fainting were baffling. He still had no idea why Fynch had bled into the metal, but it was obviously an important element for what Fynch believed was necessary for Cassien to keep Florentyna safe and to help destroy the demon. All Wevyr had been able to say was that Fynch had insisted, that it was critical to the role of the weapons … but they remained clueless to why it was necessary.

He glanced at the boy riding alongside. Ham appeared fully recovered now and had woken from his stupor full of apology and surprise at his collapse. He couldn't recall fainting, but he had not forgotten what he'd claimed and remained as baffled as Cassien as to what it all meant.

'Nothing more has surfaced,' Ham said, aware of Cassien's study of him, 'in case you're wondering.'

Cassien sighed. 'I was. You saw three people in your vision. But my confusion is that you said you saw into the crucible. How can that be when you were looking through a peephole in the wall?'

Ham nodded. 'I know. I've been trying to work that out myself. I wasn't dreaming, I know that much. What I'd seen had been blocked from me until now; now I can remember it vividly. One moment I was staring at Master Fynch and Master Wevyr, the next I was looking into the crucible.' He shrugged. 'I know that doesn't make sense.'

'It makes it easier if you accept that magic is involved.'

Ham cast Cassien a worried look. 'I didn't want to be the one to say it,' he admitted.

'There's no other way of looking at this. As it is, I have had to accept that you can hear my sword talking when no-one else can even hear it moving. It is just the sword?'

Ham nodded. 'The other blades do make noises but nothing like the sword's range of sounds.'

Cassien shrugged. 'So, we're now both going forward on the strength of a man's word, that man being impossibly old and familiar with people and ways and events from previous centuries. More magic. He put blood into my sword because he believes I'm going to need whatever magic the blade is imbued with, through the bleeding presumably.'

'The magic of the dragon?' Ham cut in. 'Royalty?'

'Who are the three?'

Ham shook his head. 'I don't know. Cassien, what is your role? You said you're going forward on the strength of Master Fynch's word. What has he asked of you? Perhaps that might tell us more about the three.'

It was time. Hamelyn already knew too much, and besides, he was involved — Ham's vision, his hearing of the sword and his deliberately meeting Cassien were all being orchestrated, but why?

Cassien nodded. 'I'm going to tell you everything that's happened to me to this moment and perhaps together we can make some sense of it.'

'Where are we going by the way?'

'To Pearlis,' he replied.

If Ham was surprised he didn't show it; for someone so young he was impressively composed, Cassien thought.

'Then we need to make a decision now whether we skirt the woodland and head south to the capital via Rothwell, or we bear east toward Rittylworth, Renkyn and down through the foothills,' Ham advised.

'I don't mind; whichever is fastest. What do you suggest?'

'There will be more travellers on the easterly route, but via Rothwell is definitely a less direct route. And going east, there's a monastery at Rittylworth that people talk about as being very good to travellers. We can get food for ourselves and our horses, probably a place for a short rest.'

Cassien nodded. 'The horses are our priority. How long to Rittylworth?'

'We often get people in Orkyld travelling up that way. It's a few hours riding, and Renkyn is not far from Rittylworth. I gather it's a direct route from Renkyn into the capital. The best part of a day's ride probably.'

Cassien gave him a smile of gratitude. 'Whatever magic pushed you into my path, Ham, I'm glad we met. Your wealth of knowledge never fails to astonish.'

'One more thing I should probably mention,' the boy said, frowning. 'It's only just occurred to me as I've been prodding at that memory of the vision.'

Cassien looked at him expectantly.

Ham gave a crooked grin. 'The Triad. It's definitely three males.'

'Is that important?' Cassien queried, his mind racing to what it might mean.

'I can't say,' Ham replied, 'but what is interesting is that I think one of them in that crucible vision was a boy.'

Cassien's reins went slack when he turned to regard Ham with a look of surprise.

The boy shrugged. 'I'm just telling you what I saw.'

'Before you passed out you said the Triad was forming.'

'Yes, but I don't know what I meant by it.'

Cassien stared into the distance as his thoughts gathered some solidity. 'You were sent to find me. We were strangers yet here we are travelling together.'

Ham nodded, frowning. 'Perhaps what you tell me about your life will prompt something more for me. It's this way,' he said, pointing, 'to Rittylworth.'

'Let's go. My tale will help pass the journey,' Cassien said and they veered east toward the monastery just as their queen was leaving the hamlet of Dryden Vale for the same destination.

The monks tending the fields nearby waved to the quartet as they rode their horses slowly up the road leading to the main courtyard of the monastery. Florentyna smiled as she lifted her hand, enjoying the anonymity and admiring the monks' toil on the hard earth, still untilled from the winter gone; with thaw almost finished they were preparing to nourish the soil.

'What do they grow here?' she asked absently.

'What don't they grow, majesty, is more to the point,' Felyx replied. 'Rittylworth is self-sufficient and it also provides generously for the less fortunate in the surrounding hamlets. Brother Hoolyn is a firm believer in the high monastic way, whereas some leaders of the monastery in the recent past had allowed the old rules to slacken.'

'Don't expect rich pickings for a midday meal, you mean?' Florentyna jested.

'A broth if you're fortunate, majesty, especially as they have no idea that the most important guest they could imagine is strolling her horse up their path.'

'I haven't felt such freedom in many moons.' The senior soldier laughed. 'You know, Felyx,' Florentyna mused, 'I'm really enjoying seeing you so relaxed as well. I can't remember when I last saw you laugh.'

He shifted in his saddle to regard her sheepishly. 'Yes, majesty, forgive me. I have certainly been a grouchy soul of late. Being out here amongst the real life of Morgravia has —'

Felyx never finished his sentence. The arrow took him through the back of the neck. Florentyna watched with horror as the arrowhead exploded through Felyx's throat, felling him as he grinned at her. The remaining soldiers reacted swiftly, flinging themselves from their horses towards her. She felt herself being thrown back as the sound of another arrow whizzed from afar to land harmlessly in the field just beyond.

Yells erupted and monks came running as a third arrow sang its horrible song through the air.

One of the guards held her down. 'Don't move!' he growled, forgetting all protocol. 'Erle? Erle?'

Erle lay dead with an arrow in his back, they soon realised.

Without further discussion, the remaining soldier dragged Florentyna back to her feet but kept his huge frame covering her. Monks had arrived, looking at them aghast.

'What has happened here?' one of them said uselessly.

'Behind the horse,' the soldier growled to the queen, ignoring those clustering around them. 'Use it for cover.'

'I understand,' she said, not sure where her calm was coming from.

'Right, on my mark, we move. Carefully.' She nodded, knowing she looked fearful but he gave her a reassuring nod. 'I shall get you there safely, your majesty, even if it means taking a full quiver of arrows in my body.' And with little pause, he said, 'Now.'

With monks' cassocks fluttering around the horse, which also hid Florentyna, the soldier she knew to be called Brom led her slowly but steadily up the path. No more arrows landed, but two good men lay in their wake.

Brother Hoolyn had come to see what the commotion was about.

'Men are dead, these people are being attacked,' one of the elder monks exclaimed.

Others nodded mutely, pointing to the bodies. Hoolyn, shocked, but acting quickly and decisively, ushered them into the cover of the cloisters. Without tarrying for questions, he hurried them swiftly through corridors, up stairways and along tiny passages until they were high in the gods of the new bell tower of Rittylworth Monastery.

The older man looked at them both with incomprehension, but as they were breathing hard, he waited a moment or two for each of them to catch their breath.

Finally, he asked the inevitable. 'Now tell me, who has brought these deaths to a peaceful house of Shar?'

They both shook their heads mutely. Brom spoke first. 'Brother, we have no idea who has attacked. We are as shocked as you. Those were my fellow soldiers killed. My friends.'

'Soldiers? Shar's breath. Who are you?'

Florentyna pulled her hood down. 'Brother Hoolyn, forgive us bringing fear to the monastery. Brom tells you the truth. We have no idea who has attacked us. But to answer your question, I am Florentyna.' She gave a sad shrug. 'The queen.'

He stared at her in astonishment. 'Queen Florentyna,' he repeated as if he hadn't heard right. 'Of Morgravia?' he qualified.

'I'm afraid so, Brother,' she admitted with a wan half-smile.

He put a hand against his chest, as though his heart had skipped a beat. 'And we weren't told?'

'I have come to see the dowager.'

'Why the secrecy?' he demanded, forgetting himself.

'It had to be so. Again, forgive me,' Florentyna said, ignoring his improper tone.

'Wait, how can I be sure you are her majesty?' Hoolyn queried, looking between them cautiously.

Brom seemed as though he was ready to knock the man senseless, but Florentyna gave him a glance of caution. 'Of course.' She reached beneath her cloak and drew out the chain she wore around her neck, from which hung her father's ring. It bore the dragon insignia of the royal crest of Morgravia. She was supposed to wear the ring, but it was an entirely impractical size and shape for a woman's hand; the chain had been cast in matching gold and she could still wear it at all times.

Hoolyn leaned in to stare at the ring and gave a gasp of fresh fear as he bowed low. 'Your majesty, please forgive me. I don't know that you are safe, however. We must assess the situation.' He kept staring at her as though he wanted to pinch himself.

She touched his arm and smiled as she looked back to her companion. 'Brom, we must see to our friends immediately. What if they appear dead, but perhaps are only wounded? Felyx ...' She gave a sound of soft anguish. 'We were laughing ...' She gathered her wits, knowing she mustn't lose any control now. Florentyna took a deep breath and looked at the head monk. 'We have travelled in complete secret, Brother Hoolyn, so someone has clearly been following us, or has been told where to find us.'

'Who knew you were coming?' he asked.

'Brom, anyone else other than Felyx and Erle from your side?'

He shook his head. 'No, majesty. Felyx swore us to secrecy. We weren't even allowed to give any clue that we were leaving the barracks. He gave orders for us to do some chores that took us away from the palace. Others think we've gone to check on some new horses that the royal stables have purchased.'

'Yes, I knew he'd be careful. So that leaves only my side. The only person who knows I was departing the palace was Burrage and I trust him with my life.'

'Felyx wouldn't —' Brom began.

'No, absolutely, he wouldn't. I have complete faith in him.'

'Your majesty,' Hoolyn interrupted, 'if I may, right now I'd suggest we worry about keeping you safe rather than who is behind this. Brom, is it?' he said to her companion.

'It is,' Brom replied.

'Well, none of us can protect our queen as well as you can. This tower is hard to reach and arguably the safest spot.'

'We have good vision from here too,' Brom agreed, prowling around the four window openings.

Hoolyn nodded. 'Please, if you would, stay here with her majesty, and I will go to assess the situation.'

They waited impatiently as he sped off.

'Brom?'

'They're both dead, majesty. Don't hold any hope.'

She swallowed. Poor Felyx. 'How many do you think?'

'It felt like an army at the time but it would only take a couple of men with the vantage of high ground.'

'Were they just highwaymen, do you think, a random attack on a noble party?'

His mouth twisted as he thought about this, but not for very long. 'I doubt it. They were too accurate. Good archers. Well trained. No doubt excellent weapons for that range.'

She knew he was right, but not for any of those reasons. 'The arrow that killed Felyx was meant for me. If he'd not leaned forward in his saddle at that moment, the arrowhead would have been in my eye, not his throat.'

'Don't think like that,' he said quietly.

'I have to, Brom. Someone wants me dead. Professional archers were paid to ambush us. They knew precisely where we'd be when only less than a handful of us knew about this.'

'It could be anyone, majesty.'

'Yes, but it has to be someone with enough of a gripe and a sufficient purse to be able to pull off something like this.'

Brom conceded this with a slow nod. He turned to check the windows again. 'Felyx and Erle haven't moved.'

'Don't look at them.'

Hoolyn was back, this time with an angry dowager trailing up the stairs. She didn't give anyone a chance to speak.

'You!' she sneered. 'So you thought you could have me assassinated, did you?'

Florentyna's mouth opened but she didn't respond. The notion hadn't occurred to her that the attackers weren't meant for them. 'Greetings, Saria,' she began, pleased to see her father's widow looking plumper than she recalled and wheezing slightly from her efforts. 'We did not bring these men. They were firing directly on us.'

'Probably because they thought you were me!' she snapped, but a lot of her fire had burned out from the climb up the tower. 'Why are you here?'

'I thought we needed to talk … about Darcelle's nuptials. You know, mother to daughter.'

Saria gave a gust of a laugh and there was no warmth in it. 'Really? Why have you sneaked in, your majesty? Where's your entourage?'

'Saria, we can have this conversation in private. Right now we have to be sure of our safety.'

'You're not safe,' Hoolyn interjected before the dowager could stir the queen's emotions any further. 'The attackers were not the least bit interested in the monks who checked on your men. I deeply regret that they are both dead. We can't tell how many archers there are — at least two, my Brothers think.'

'Only two,' the queen murmured.

'At least two, majesty,' Brom cautioned. 'How do they know this?'

'They've had a conversation of sorts, yelling back and forth. They've allowed us to bring the dead men into the chapel. They have no gripe with us, apparently … well, not if we give them you, your majesty.'

Florentyna nodded. Her instincts had been right.

'Are they mad?' Brom asked. 'They're prepared to kill the sovereign.'

'They nearly succeeded,' Hoolyn remarked. 'I think we must be mindful that the dowager is in danger too. They wouldn't know that we have two royals in the monastery.'

Florentyna tried not to show how she bristled at being compared to Saria, but this was not a time to be sensitive. 'Of course. If they knew, they might use her as bargaining power.'

Saria snorted. 'All the more reason for you to throw me to the dogs, Florentyna. You can use me to divert their attention.'

'Oh, do stop, Saria. I'm already tired of your poisonous tone,' Florentyna snapped. It helped to have someone to direct her pain towards.

The men shared an awkward glance.

'Brother Hoolyn, what did these men actually demand?' she asked, ignoring Saria's glare.

'They seem to think we'd be prepared to meekly hand you over, your majesty.'

'Or what?'

'Well …' he began, and then cleared his throat. 'They will smoke you out. They're planning a fire for Rittylworth and don't seem to care if anyone else dies.' He gave a low sigh. 'We've survived that ravage before and will do so again.'

'That's not going to happen,' Florentyna announced. 'Brom and I will leave. And Saria, we can't risk them discovering you here or they might use you to bargain with.' She looked back at Brom and Father Hoolyn. "We'll take the dowager and our chances in the hills.'

'I'm not leaving,' Saria assured her. 'If you've got a big target painted on your back, I'm not going anywhere near you outside of these walls.'

Florentyna threw a snake-eyed glare at Saria. 'And there I was thinking you wanted to escape the monastic lifestyle, Saria. All right then, take your chances. You're most welcome to stay if Brother Hoolyn will keep you.'

'No, wait. She might be behind this!' Brom suddenly boomed.

'What?' Saria cried. 'How dare you? I'll have you lashed just for thinking that, and I'll have your tongue cut out for saying it!'

'Be quiet, Saria. And that's a command!' Florentyna turned to Brom. 'What do you think?'

'We can't stay here,' he said.

She agreed. 'So we run? What about the horses?'

'We'll be slower, but we'll find it easier to hide and react on foot.' He looked at the dowager. 'You'll have to change into more suitable clothes to go across rough terrain, er … your highness.'

'Let me tell you, soldier, I am not going anywhere today in any change of clothes.'

Florentyna leaned in close to the Queen Dowager. 'Get changed, madam, or I'll have Brom change you himself. You're coming with us. And you'd want to be quiet about it or you'll be the one without the tongue. Is that clear?'

Saria looked at her with such loathing both men stepped back. 'There'll be a reckoning for this.'

'You think I'm scared of you, Saria?' She stared so angrily and intently at the dowager that the older woman took a step back. Florentyna cut a look at her companion. 'Brom, go with her.' At his look of worry, she nodded. 'I'm fine here for the moment. Keep her on her toes and rip that gown off if you have to — you have my permission.'

Saria glowered at her before giving an indignant growl and turning on her heels. Florentyna looked at Brom and nodded in Saria's direction as if to tell him to hurry up. Clearly angry, he did as he was told and she could hear him clomping down the stairs behind the dowager.

'Your majesty, I cannot let you leave here without fighting to save you.'

'You are a man of peace, Brother Hoolyn. I do not want you to fight at all.'

'You know what I mean. We must at least protect you with our lives.'

'No. I think we just invite more death. This way we have a chance. We may need a diversion though.'

'Whatever you need is yours.'

She couldn't believe she smiled. Here she was about to run for her life and she could grin. She wouldn't admit to any sense of excitement because that would be plain madness, but there was a rekindling within her of something that had been mute for a long time. She could feel her spirit returning; all that had once made her the person her father was proud of was reawakening. It had been buried and silent since his death and she had felt like an empty shell. Now her life was threatened and she wanted to fight for it, as well as hunt down these murderers.

'Do you have livestock here?'

'Some cows, yes, a few sheep. Some horses too.'

'The cows. Can you perhaps lead them out to pasture or something?' She gave a shrug, embarrassed by her lack of knowledge of animal husbandry.

'Yes, of course we can.'

'The three of us will steal out with the cows, using them for cover as best we can, just until we can reach the higher ground,' she said, casting a glance out of the window that faced north.

'Better still, your majesty, you lead the cows out wearing our cassocks. It may just buy some extra time, whether they realise the ploy earlier or later.'

'Excellent idea, Brother Hoolyn. I might leave it to you to let the dowager know about yet another change of clothes.'

NINETEEN

Cassien and Ham emerged from the hills that overlooked Rittylworth Monastery from the north.

'It's beautiful,' Ham sighed. 'I never thought I'd see the famous monastery.'

'I'm glad we came this way,' Cassien admitted, 'I've read about Rittylworth in the history books but to see it is worthwhile, especially ...' His voice trailed off as his sharp gaze picked out a scene that looked altogether wrong. 'Ham, something's odd.'

'What?' he said, following Cassien's gaze into the distance.

Cassien squinted. 'Shar! Those are bodies,' he exclaimed.

Ham focused. 'Two men.'

Cassien concentrated, trying to make sense of the scene from this distance. 'Killed with arrows.'

Ham looked at him. 'What can that mean?'

'Search me.' They both stared again. 'Monks are walking out.'

They watched in silence now as the dead men were half-dragged, half-carried back into the building.

'What is going on here?' Cassien wondered aloud.

'What do we do?'

'We wait.'

'For what?'

'For more to be revealed,' Cassien decided. 'We need to get off this rise, though, in case we're spotted. Come on.' He jumped off his horse and Ham did the same. 'Follow me,' Cassien said, leading them down toward the wooded area that rose up behind Rittylworth. Once beneath the safety of the tree canopy, they tied their horses up. 'Right, we watch from here. We have a good vantage point,' he said.

They waited, neither talking. There was no sign of who had shot the arrows. Finally, they watched several monks re-emerge from the compound, their hands held out before them in a show of surrender. Moments later, another group of monks at the back of the monastery complex let some cattle out of a pen; three of the monks moved with the animals, walking slowly out into the pastures. Behind them, two monks lifted their hands in farewell; one held his fist and shook it earnestly. Cassien frowned. That was a sign of wishing someone good luck.

He blinked. It didn't make sense that while an attack was underway the monks would carry on normal activities like taking care of animals. But it was Ham who put into words what was nagging most on the rim of his thoughts.

'Those monks aren't very good with the cows, are they? The one on the right — the short one — looks scared of them.'

'He does, I agree. And the tallest of them keeps looking around, as though he's worried at being followed.' He chewed the inside of his lip. 'Ham, those aren't monks. Two of them are tripping over their cassocks. They have small hands, and one has long hair if I'm not mistaken. I think we have two women being pursued.' He squinted a little, couldn't see any more action at the front of the monastery. 'It looks as though we're going to get involved whether we like it or not, because they're headed our way.'

'What are you going to do?'

'Nothing until I can hear what they're saying.'

Saria pushed at a cow with a repulsed groan. Any moment she was sure it would tread on her foot or touch her with that huge wet nose.

'I have to get you away from this open pasture, majesty,' Brom said looking over his shoulder. 'You're too vulnerable.'

'You only care about her,' Saria accused. 'Why did you ever bring me?' she spat.

'So that I could strap you to the queen's back and let you take the arrows,' the man growled.

'Brom, don't,' the hooded figure in the middle admonished. 'We're going to be safer once we reach that ridge.'

'Brom. I won't forget that name,' Saria assured him. 'Between now and when you're arrested, I'm going to dream up ways to punish you long before I have you killed.'

'Be quiet both of you,' Florentyna, said, her hand resting on the back of one of the animals. 'Right now the cows are peaceful, but if you scare them our pursuers will notice.'

But their attackers were not to be fooled and were already upon them. 'Your majesty!' they yelled as one in singsong, derogatory tones.

The three cassocked fugitives halted and Saria let out a shriek of fear. The cows scattered.

Brom pushed both women behind him and pulled off the constraining cassock. In a fluid movement, he drew his sword. 'Get back, you bastards,' he warned the three men.

Their pursuers laughed behind masks as they sauntered up quietly on horseback. 'You're so terrifying, Brom. I'm sorry I didn't get to watch the light die in Felyx's eyes. I'm glad that I'll have that pleasure with you.'

Brom blinked uncomprehendingly. His shoulders slumped. 'Hubbard?'

The man who'd spoken gave an ironic shrug. 'You see, I told you masks were irrelevant,' he said to his two companions. He pulled off the helmet and visor and Florentyna judged him as having seen thirty-five summers. His face was one of those arranged with features that were neither dark nor light, neither handsome nor plain, and was lightly bearded, with hair of a nondescript colour. Even his voice had no defining timbre. Nevertheless, he looked strong and he possessed an innate arrogance, with an ironic tone that could cut to the bone. 'Greetings, Brom. Majesty.' He inclined his head. 'And whoever this shrieking haridelle is.'

'I have absolutely nothing to do with these people,' Saria announced to him.

The man regarded her with no amusement. 'Then why are you with them?'

'They captured me. Forced me. He said he'd use me as a shield for the queen.'

At this their pursuer laughed. 'Clever, Brom. You were always the creative one.'

'Who is this?' Florentyna asked, ignoring the man taunting them, allowing Saria's words to wash over her unheeded, as she addressed Brom.

'His name is Hubbard, your majesty. One of our best, clearly turned mercenary,' Brom answered, his head lowered. 'Forgive me, my queen,' he whispered.

'For what?' she said mournfully. 'We nearly made it.'

'Tell our queen all of it, Brom,' Hubbard urged slyly.

Still she refused their captor eye contact and held Brom with her stare.

'Hubbard is my younger brother and brings my family the worst shame of all. I'll at least try and kill him before he —'

'Too late, brother,' Hubbard said. The blade was expertly thrown and it sank into Brom's throat a heartbeat later.

Florentyna gasped as Brom sank to his knees, dropping his sword. She reached for him, helpless tears rolling down her cheeks, not in fear but for the senseless waste of another good man.

'I'm sorry,' he managed to choke out again as blood bubbled from his mouth.

Florentyna fell forward with the momentum of Brom's collapsing body. He was dead before their bodies touched the ground, but she felt an impotent rage ringing in her ears.

'You would do that to your brother?' she said from where she kneeled at Brom's side.

'As easily as I would do the same to you, my queen, for the right amount of gold.'

'Then do it, Hubbard, and I'll triple whatever each of you has been promised,' Saria said, her voice losing its fear, replacing it with cunning.

'There're three of them,' Ham warned, but it made no difference to Cassien if there were a dozen men. That was the queen down there he now understood.

They'd watched with shared loathing as the man who had put himself between the killers and the two women was murdered.

'Ham, I need you to stay here. It's too dangerous. They're killing without pause. We can't risk you.'

'But we can risk you?'

'Do as I say.' He fixed Ham with a hard look.

'Your weapons are awake,' Ham said dully. 'Use them.'

Cassien nodded just as the second woman offered to triple the reward if the men would hurry up and execute the queen.

Cassien moved as Romaine had taught. Against the wind, so the horses never sensed him, stealing confidently across the uneven ground as he ran fleet and silent as a wolf.

Florentyna turned slowly to regard Saria. 'I cannot believe you just said that.'

'Can't you? I thought you'd always known how much I despise you, Florentyna. Darcelle must sit on the Morgravian throne. I'm just doing what's best for our empire.'

'You vile and treacherous creature,' Florentyna whispered. 'I came here to offer you a truce … a way for you to enjoy a full and free life with Darcelle.'

'That shows just how useless you are at this role. Darcelle would never countenance such a magnanimous move and I would never permit her to be that weak.'

Florentyna felt Saria's words like blows. 'Whatever did my father see in you?'

'He saw only a younger woman and pleasures of the flesh. Like all men he could be manipulated. It's more what I saw in him, Florentyna. A crown. I was fond of your father and I grieve that Shar took him so early, but I still want my crown and its authority — and I shall have it through Darcelle.'

'Ladies, ladies,' Hubbard said, climbing down from his horse. Neither of his companions followed suit and were yet to remove their helmets. 'I hate to interrupt whatever you're both hissing about, but I have an ugly job to do.'

Saria smiled maliciously at Florentyna. 'Well, get on with it, man.'

'Thank you, I will,' he said, pulling his blade from where it was lodged in Brom's throat. It made a horrible sucking sound as he cruelly wrenched it free. 'May I, your majesty?' he asked, reaching for the voluminous sleeve of her cassock.

She didn't know how she kept her voice steady. 'Burn in hell with her!' she snarled, looking toward Saria.

He calmly took his time wiping the blade clean of Brom's blood, while he watched her closely, a wry smile mocking her.

'I've been living as a mercenary for a long time, your majesty, sailing too many seas to faraway lands. I think the last time I might have seen you from a distance was when you were still a child. But look at you now — all grown up and, you know, now that I see you up so close, you really could rival your sister's prettiness if you bothered. Why do you hide it?'

'It's a great pity you're nothing like your brother,' she snapped. 'I'm sure your parents will be proud to know that Brom served his realm with great faith. I can't imagine their despair that his brother betrayed it.'

He didn't flinch as she'd hoped. Her words didn't appear to hurt him in the slightest. In fact his grin widened. 'That's true. He was a very loyal man; very pure, while my heart is all black,' he said dryly.

'You'd kill a sovereign for a few gold coins?' she asked, sounding incredulous. 'What a sorry excuse for a man you are.'

'Not a few, your majesty. A small fortune was paid to us, just to agree to it. An even greater fortune and land aplenty if I do the deed, which I'm happy to say I will.'

'Shame on you, Hubbard,' she said with as much condescension as she could muster. 'So, get on with it. Why do you hesitate?'

'Yes, hurry. Do what you came here to do,' Saria pressed.

'All right,' he agreed, turning and, without warning, took one stride toward the dowager. When he stepped back, smiling innocently at Florentyna, she saw the blade he'd just cleaned was now embedded in Saria's belly.

Saria gave a startled moan, belatedly realising what had occurred. Florentyna rushed to cradle her as she fell. The vicious, fatal wound suggested this would be no easy death and Florentyna suspected this cruel man had known as much.

He seemed to read her thoughts. 'I thought you deserved the satisfaction of knowing at least one of your enemies died painfully, your majesty. Who is she anyway? Oh no, don't bother to even tell me. I don't care one way or the other,' he said.

'Saria,' Florentyna cried, shocked, as she lay her stepmother down.

'You win,' the dowager sighed, in obvious agony from the hideously gaping wound that seeped with every shallow breath she took. Hubbard had, in that brief flash of violence, not only stabbed his victim but gutted her. Florentyna felt a surprising flash of pride in her stepmother as Saria wrenched the ghastly knife from her belly. 'I don't want to die with his blade in me.' Her voice turned to a whisper that only Florentyna could hear. 'Bury me near your father, child. Whatever you think is the truth,

I did love him and whatever I've said to you to the contrary was only to hurt you because of my own petty jealousies.'

Finally, she somehow found the strength to press the knife secretly into Florentyna's hands. As the light was fading from her stepmother's eyes, she nodded at Florentyna and gave a final whisper. 'Don't let him ...' was all she was able to say before her head rolled to the side.

Florentyna could hear the men talking, but had ignored them while Saria had been dying. Hubbard, she sensed, had moved back towards her and she looked down at the bloodstained knife in her hands. Before she could think of how to use it, one of the attackers suddenly yelled.

She looked up at the same time as Hubbard wheeled around, and they both saw one of his companions lifeless and prone on the ground, his head at a strange angle as though his neck had been broken. His fellow horseman was already off his animal, sword drawn, facing a tall newcomer.

'And where have you sprung from, stranger?' Hubbard asked. 'I don't take kindly to my friends being set upon.'

'Then we're in agreement,' the man said. He cut Florentyna a glance. 'Your majesty. Are you hurt?'

She was stunned. 'I'm ... I'm not hurt.'

Hubbard sneered. 'Not yet. But you can count, can't you, stranger? There are two of us, one of you. One of us is going to kill you. I hope it's me. And then we'll kill her majesty.'

'One of you can try,' the tall man said, and before any of them could grasp what was happening Florentyna watched him run straight at Hubbard's companion.

It seemed unbelievable that a man could jump into the air from two strides and use the horse like a wall, bouncing off its flank and landing noiselessly. The horse was startled and bucked, but the newcomer was already leaping away and kicking out a foot with such force and speed that Florentyna could barely replay in her mind what had just occurred. The nasty snapping sound suggested the man's neck had been broken and the body slumped lifelessly to the ground next to his fallen friend before any weapon had been swung in defence.

The man landed softly and easily. 'Congratulations. It seems you are the one left who is going to kill me,' he said to Hubbard, 'because the souls of both of your treacherous companions are already being gathered up by Shar's minions. Frankly, I hope he throws them into the eternal fires of hell.'

To his credit, Hubbard's expression barely registered fear, or even disappointment, from what Florentyna could see. If anything, the traitor looked vaguely impressed.

'I detested both of them, so you've done me a kindness in ridding me of them and my need to pay them their share. And that fighting style is impressive. Where did you learn that?' He sounded conversational.

The man said nothing but simply stared at Hubbard.

'Pity, you've gone all moody on me. I was so hoping for some convivial conversation. It seems you want to fight.'

'Not really. I just want you co-Opérative, so I can take you back to Pearlis and you can wait for your execution at the queen's pleasure,' he said with a smile that didn't warm his eyes.

'Why do I get all the blame?' Hubbard feigned indignation, glancing at his companions.

The man ignored him. 'Your majesty, do you want this man taken alive and as you see him here?'

Hubbard looked over at her with interest as though they were discussing some other person. He waited patiently for her reply.

'This man must answer for his crimes.'

Now Hubbard laughed. 'You'll never take me alive,' he sneered.

'Then I shall take you dead,' the stranger said in a chillingly low, calm voice.

'You can try.'

'I'm ready when you are.'

Florentyna watched the stranger unsheathe a magnificent sword.

'Impressive, once again,' Hubbard said. 'That's a Wevyr sword. I'd stake my life upon it.'

'It is.'

'I wish I had time to admire it,' he said, also unsheathing his sword.

'You'll get your chance. You'll be on the receiving end of its keen edge.'

Hubbard laughed. 'I trust you can handle it as beautifully as it deserves to be.'

'Try me.'

To Florentyna it was a blur of moves, the sound of ringing metal and the explosion of sparks as the swords clashed. Hubbard was the attacker but it didn't matter what he did, her protector countered every move with such an economy of strokes and so little energy expended that it was as though the stranger stood still. Meanwhile, around him Hubbard danced, at first teasing but very quickly he took the stranger's measure and realised he was not sparring. The stranger's intensity was chilling and even Florentyna could sense the mood of the fight change. Hubbard was no longer amused or playful and he appeared to redouble his efforts to penetrate the defences of his opponent. As she watched, entranced, her fear leached away.

Hubbard's swagger had deserted him, and she could see him sweating with his exertions, trying to break through the solid, steady, rhythmic counters of the stranger's fluid sword moves as he defended himself, with no attacking strikes that she could perceive. Hubbard was fatiguing; he staggered back at one point.

'Fight me, damn you!'

'Why?' the man asked in a bored tone. 'You're doing a very good job of wearing yourself down.'

Hubbard's lips thinned at this. He raised his sword high. 'I'm going to cut you open from neck to navel.'

'You're not, Hubbard. You're going to be trussed like the animal you are and I'm going to fling you over your horse and take you back to Pearlis, where you will stand trial for three cold-blooded murders and the attempted murder of our sovereign.'

Hubbard paused at this. She thought he was trying to think of an acid retort or perhaps some type of distraction — Shar knew he needed it! She was ill-prepared for what happened. Hubbard didn't leap at his enemy and try another series of parries, looking for the opening that would allow him to injure, hobble or even kill. Instead, he leapt at her and had her gripped around the neck, squeezing the life out of her.

'I came here to kill you, your majesty. I think I should complete my business.'

She couldn't talk. His arm was so tight across her throat, she thought she might pass out shortly. Across the pasture, her vision blurring, she could see the look in her protector's eyes and she was sensing a similar white-hot rage to the one she had felt earlier at the killing of innocents.

'... or, I could, of course, barter for my life with this curious champion of yours.'

They could hear the voices of the monks, now stumbling across the pasture towards them. She thought she recognised Hoolyn's voice shouting.

Florentyna found the strength to growl through gritted teeth. 'Let him kill me, stranger, but make sure you do not let him keep his life.'

Florentyna could see dark spots floating in front of her eyes. She was sure she saw the stranger nod, watched him drop his sword and reach behind him.

Her last conscious thought was that the grip around her throat had loosened and she had the feeling she heard a guttural yell as she fell into darkness.

When Florentyna regained consciousness, men were bent over her and she felt her eyelids flutter open and met the concerned expression of a thin boy.

'The queen is recovered,' he murmured and she lost his innocent face to the row of monks who suddenly crowded in over her.

She was still disoriented, then it all came flooding in: the sharp daylight, the tang of blood on the wind and the realisation that she hadn't died this day.

'Majesty,' came a voice she recognised as Father Hoolyn's.

'What happened to me?' she asked, trying to sit up.

'Take it slowly, majesty,' someone cautioned.

'You passed out, luckily, my queen,' Hoolyn said.

'And as you slumped, the stranger's blade found its mark,' another voice said. 'Extraordinary. You were so fortunate, your majesty.'

She blinked, not fully understanding. 'Help me up, please.'

Florentyna felt strong arms beneath hers and she was returned gently to her feet, feeling slightly unsteady but glad to be upright and in control of herself again. Rittylworth monks, in their distinctive tan robes, immediately began to bow to their sovereign. Florentyna barely noticed, for she was looking for one man in particular, and there he was, standing off to the left away from everyone fussing around her. Before she could address him properly her attention became unhappily and helplessly riveted nearby to where he stood ... four bodies were neatly placed in a row, well away from where she'd fallen.

Their heads and torsos were covered with spare cassocks. Florentyna was instantly nauseated to recognise the feet of Dowager Saria, and the intense emotion occasioned by her stepmother's, Brom's and Felyx's deaths overtook her once again. She swallowed to steady herself.

She thought on her father's advice that people would wait on her word: 'Pause, breathe, *compose*, before you speak steadily, calmly and with confidence. That's how you win trust,' he had counselled. 'That's why men will follow you.'

Well, she needed only one to follow her now.

'Your majesty,' he said, bowing, as she approached.

'I don't know how you did this,' she said, glancing at Hubbard's corpse, 'but thank you.'

'Cassien killed him with a throwing blade,' the boy she'd seen earlier said enthusiastically, stepping forward. 'I'm Hamelyn, Queen Florentyna,' he added, with a perfectly executed bow. 'A friend of his.'

She regarded the boy with a faint smile: 'Greetings, Hamelyn.' Then she turned to his friend. 'You threw a blade that accurately at the man holding me in front of him?' she asked, incredulous. 'You were standing over there. That's an impossible throw, surely.'

'Maybe I was lucky, majesty,' the man replied, his tone modest.

'I admit that I saw it occur, my queen,' Hoolyn confirmed, 'and the accuracy of Master Cassien's throw directly into the eye of your attacker was like nothing I can imagine witnessing again, nor would I want to see such violence. He was dead before he hit the ground. Even so, I would be lying before Shar if I didn't say I was glad that this stranger happened upon you and dealt with the attackers, but the dowager … and your man, Brom …' He trailed off, looking mystified by the row of corpses.

Florentyna held out a hand. 'Cassien, is it?'

He looked at her gravely through dark blue eyes set in a symmetrical face of spare but nonetheless neat, proportionate features. His nose seemed to be in perfect concert with his mouth, leading to clearly defined lips that were generous but not thick. His hair looked freshly combed, his chin was shaved and he was wearing quality attire. It was his hands that caught her attention and made her linger; some fingers were misshapen, as though they'd been broken. And of course his piercing gaze, once she engaged it again, arrested her, held her hostage. Now that she was close enough to stare deeply into his eyes, she saw pain buried behind the calm they projected.

'Yes,' he answered.

'Of where, may I ask?'

'Of nowhere in particular, your majesty. I was born in Morgravia but I have spent a lot of time living in and around the Great Forest.'

'In the forest? Whatever for?'

'Why not? One can learn a lot when one lives in peace.'

'You sound like a philosopher, not a fighter.'

'That's because I am not a fighter, your majesty, although I was sent to protect you ... by a friend.'

Florentyna felt her pulse quicken at his words. She was suddenly sure she could guess who that friend might be. 'Father Hoolyn, perhaps we could shift these bodies. Dowager Saria must be laid out alone, please.' She immediately thought of Darcelle. 'My sister will ...' She heard her voice catching but cleared her throat. 'My sister will wish to pay her respects.'

'Of course,' Hoolyn answered and began organising his Brothers.

'Walk back with me, would you?' she said to Cassien.

He nodded, fell in step.

'Had I not lost consciousness and slipped from that man's arms, you might well have killed me with that blade throw.'

'Someone else might have, but not me.' The claim was spoken so earnestly that she couldn't help feeling vaguely charmed, rather than offended, by his arrogant words.

'You are clearly confident of your skills, Master Cassien.'

'They are the only aspects of the world I can control, I'm afraid, my queen. The rest is all extremely unpredictable.' He smiled and this time she saw the crinkling around his eyes, the light of humour flaring within them.

'How did you know we were in trouble?'

'We were coming to Rittylworth from the north. And we had a good vantage point.' He shrugged. 'We saw everything unfolding.'

'Did you know I was here?'

'No. I saw people in trouble. We guessed you were not monks. It all looked wrong ... even to Hamelyn. When you drew closer we could hear clearly.'

'I see. You said you were sent to protect me. How did you know to help?'

'I didn't know anything other than I was helping three people under attack. When I discovered it was you, your majesty, I was as shocked as anyone might be.'

261

Florentyna nodded. 'Were you on your way to Pearlis?'

'Yes.'

She was aware of the boy trailing them. 'Hamelyn too?'

'No ... and yes.'

'How is that possible?'

'No, he was not sent at the time that I was. Yes, he has deliberately joined forces with me to ensure your safety.'

Florentyna shook her head and regarded him. 'You have me intrigued, Master Cassien.'

They'd reached the monastery and Florentyna knew they would not be left alone to talk until she'd extricated herself from the monks. Nevertheless, there was a burning question demanding to be asked. 'We don't have time right now for you to answer all of my questions but there is one I feel might explain plenty.'

'I will answer whatever you ask of me, your majesty.'

'Tell me then if a man by the name of Fynch sent you to me.'

He didn't hesitate. 'Yes, he did.'

It felt as though a flock of birds had just lifted off in her chest at his admission. Fynch. He was certainly determined.

'He believes the Crown is under grave threat.'

'So I gather,' she said softly.

'Have you heard of the Brotherhood, your majesty?'

She blinked, stunned. Those words were rarely uttered outside of Stoneheart. 'Yes, of course, but I have no reason to —'

'Forgive me,' he murmured, looking over his shoulder, 'but time is short. I am of the Brotherhood. Master Fynch believes there is a sinister force at work.'

She could tell he was choosing his words with care, speaking obliquely. Florentyna opted to be direct. 'I don't believe in demons, Master Cassien.'

'Neither did I, your majesty, until I met Master Fynch ... or Hamelyn here. There is more to say but now is not the moment,' he said, noting that a fresh party of soldiers was waiting for them as they returned to the monastery's cloisters.

Florentyna remembered Burrage's promise to have more men waiting to escort her back to Stoneheart. She wished now with all her heart that she'd let him send an entire unit with her to Rittylworth and then perhaps Felyx and Brom, and even Saria, would still be alive.

'Perhaps you'll permit me to accompany you on your return to Pearlis?' Cassien suggested. 'We can continue our conversation when you're safely back in familiar and secure surrounds.'

'Yes, of course.'

She watched him bow his dark head and turn away but already she missed his quiet, strong presence.

TWENTY

Burrage regarded the man. 'It is very unusual that we should grant such an audience; I'm sure you understand,' he said carefully. The handsome fellow had been respectful, though, and earnest.

The man nodded. 'I do understand, of course. But the people of Robissun Marth are keen to present King Tamas and Princess Darcelle with an early marriage gift. Briavel is having its difficulties with Morgravia right now. A show of our respect for Princess Darcelle and the new bond with the Isles of Cipres,' he shrugged, 'could go a long way. And you cannot fault me for wanting to make new ties and friendships with the people of Cipres, Master Burrage.'

'Given that you are such a highly regarded merchant, no, I wouldn't blame you one bit. You can lay the trail for our merchants in the future,' Burrage replied.

'That's magnanimous of you, sir. Especially as my dealings have normally been eastward.'

'Indeed. Although I'm surprised you have not presented yourself at court previously.'

His visitor placed a hand on his chest in a gesture of remorse. 'It has been remiss of me, Chancellor Burrage. The truth is, even my own neighbours barely see me, sir. I am what many might term reclusive. Too many moons spent on ships crossing oceans to faraway lands perhaps. Whatever it is, I value my privacy. I have not had reason to present at court because much of what I am buying and selling is done with other merchants and conducted through my factors.'

'An exception for a royal wedding, though,' Burrage suggested, with a wry smile.

'Yes, sir. This is an occasion that insisted even Layne Tentrell air his best cloak and make a special visit with a token of the huge respect I hold for the Crown of Morgravia.'

Burrage watched the merchant sip the apple tea that had been set out not long after they'd sat down in this salon reserved for the commercial dealings of the palace, far from the living quarters of the royals. He didn't have a taste for the new concoction that had taken the people of Morgravia in its grip in recent times. He himself had taken a pot of minted tea, which he always found agreeable. He inhaled its menthol bouquet now.

'And you wish to present this gift at your expense on behalf of your town?'

'Correct again, sir.' Tentrell gave a charming smile. 'I am arguably the wealthiest person of the region — I hope that doesn't sound boastful? I am merely being objective. It is my pleasure to represent the people and show our care for the princess. We can only hope the queen finds someone equally suitable soon.'

'Most generous … most generous indeed,' Burrage said, clearing his throat uneasily at the mention of Florentyna's oft-discussed spinsterhood. 'As you can imagine, this is an incredibly busy time. Her royal highness, Darcelle, is in fact preparing to meet the King of Cipres and —'

'Why, yes, of course,' Tentrell said, apology on his face interrupting the chancellor. 'We noted all the preparations and bunting along the roads. His arrival must be imminent.'

Burrage nodded.

'How exciting. Perhaps I might be allowed to meet both of their highnesses on behalf of the west of the realm?'

It wasn't lost on Burrage how his guest kept increasing the reach of his influence. However, he didn't find him anything other than charming and knew that Florentyna — like her ancestor, Valentyna — was a genuine 'queen of the people'. Florentyna would be pleased to think that King Tamas met some ordinary folk of Morgravia, accepted their well wishes in person and so helped Darcelle to understand that being royal wasn't always about privilege and power.

Tentrell waited patiently while the chancellor gave consideration to his request.

'There is a gathering of civil dignitaries tomorrow evening. Even the mayor of your parish is expected to —'

'Oh, no, no,' Tentrell said, putting down his cup. 'I wouldn't consider it my place to be at such a gathering.'

Burrage frowned. 'But —'

'No, Master Burrage. That is for the dignitaries and I would feel entirely out of place. Is there a situation that is less formal perhaps?'

Burrage was surprised. He had thought Tentrell would leap at the opportunity to meet with the very dignitaries he was now shunning, albeit graciously. 'I shall have to consider that, Master Tentrell. We haven't finalised all of the arrangements yet.'

Tentrell reached for his cup and politely drained the contents. He stood. 'That was delicious and most kind of you, Master Burrage. I have taken up enough of your valuable time. Thank you for seeing me and perhaps you might let me know once you've had an opportunity to consider the possibilities.' He offered a neat, blunt-fingered hand. 'You've been most gracious. I'm staying at the Fatted Goose and look forward to hearing.'

Burrage allowed Tentrell to clasp his hand warmly. He smiled when Tentrell smiled and nodded when the man was ushered from the salon and, all the while, couldn't shake the feeling that he was being expertly manipulated. The merchant had been searched by the soldiers and he'd laughed at them, saying that he had never carried a weapon in his years of travelling foreign lands, so he would hardly be bringing one into Stoneheart.

What he had brought, however, was an extraordinary jewel for Darcelle. Burrage had viewed it when Tentrell had removed it briefly from a velvet pouch. He recalled how the merchant had referred to it, very casually.

'It's called the Star of Percheron,' Tentrell had explained. 'This jewel was once presented by the seventeenth zar of Percheron to his second favourite. Her name was Sheeva and she only ever clad herself in pink garments. The zar had this stone cut for her on the day she gave him his second and most beloved son. The boy went on to become zar, I gather. Anyway, can you see the tiny hole that was bored through it?' Burrage nodded, entranced by the luminous quality of the gem. 'It is reported that from the day she received this precious gift from her husband, the young wife — who was incredibly beautiful, I'm assured — wore this jewel strung around her small waist attached to a golden chain ...'

Tentrell held his finger in the air, '... and nothing else but a pale pink, gauzy wrap that she would wear loose upon her shoulders.'

'Nothing else?'

Tentrell had shrugged. 'Ever. She never left the harem, so her naked, bejewelled body offended no-one but the older, jealous women and the envious odalisques, desperate to be chosen as wives. Her nudity is legend and she has been sung about, written about, painted and sculpted by many an artist. This,' Tentrell had said, holding the jewel to the light so it threw bright spangles around the room, 'was her signature.'

Burrage was not going to ask how he'd come by such a dazzling prize. 'And you wish to give this to Princess Darcelle?'

'Who else but a princess and new bride should wear such a magnificent jewel on her wedding night for her king?' Tentrell had asked.

Burrage had stared at the glittering, teardrop-shaped gem. 'Indeed. Her majesty is going to be speechless at your generosity, Master Tentrell.'

Burrage knew Darcelle would want that stone more than anything. He had to make it possible for her to have it as a show of good will between her and her sister's authority. He must find a way for Layne Tentrell to be given the opportunity to present it as he'd asked.

Florentyna had wanted to invite the man called Cassien and his young friend, Hamelyn, to travel with her party, but she'd noticed his reluctance to mix with the soldiers and the suggestion had died in her throat. She had learned about the Brotherhood as a young girl, certainly before her first blood; that's how seriously her father regarded this fraternity. He had never told Darcelle, though; that secret was not hers to know. The sovereign shared the knowledge of the Brotherhood with his or her heir and their closest, most trusted aide, so this was a special secret between king, chancellor and princess royal. Because she'd learned of their existence so young she'd always thought of the Brotherhood in rather romantic terms, imagining courtly men with shiny armour and daydreaming of them dying for her surrounded by sighs, wistful gazes and heroic actions. The reality was cruel and ugly. There was grunting, the smell of fear and tang of sweat, the shrillness of metal meeting metal, the cry of the wounded, and the impossibly bright colour of fresh blood. She had firsthand experience now.

To her knowledge, the Brotherhood was not involved in any Crown-appointed tasks here or abroad at the present time — no spying, no assassinations required, not even stirring up trouble abroad or embedding themselves politically within other realms. The Brotherhood was under no instructions from the Crown as far as she was concerned.

A few moons after her father's death Burrage had needed to go through his paperwork and a special, rarely opened file of papers was brought before her.

'This is the correspondence between your father and the Brotherhood during his reign,' he'd explained as he put the vellum-bound sheaf of papers before her.

The new queen had touched the soft hide. 'Do I need to look at this?' she recalled asking.

'You need to be acquainted with its ...' — Florentyna remembered now how he'd searched for the right word — '... projects,' he had finally said. 'Until yesterday I was as unfamiliar with it as you, your majesty. I do hope you are comfortable that in the absence of Chancellor Reynard I took the liberty of learning more?'

She nodded. 'Of course. But it's awfully thin,' she had remarked.

'Which is a good thing, majesty,' Burrage had replied. 'The fewer dealings with the Brotherhood, the better.'

She'd frowned. 'They're not bad people, though?'

'Not at all. I've discovered they are pious men, dedicated to their work, faithful to each other, to their cause and above all, ruthlessly loyal to their king ... and now their queen. But their assignments on behalf of the Crown are, as you know, entirely clandestine.'

'Yes, I do know that. So, do we have any ... um ... projects underway?'

'None, according to this file, majesty. Nevertheless, as a matter of course I think we should give some time to going through the pages contained in it and ensuring we understand how our relationship stands with the Brotherhood.'

'Very well,' she'd replied, only vaguely interested. Now she wished she'd been more focused when she'd flicked through the pages, although the correspondence had been nothing more than polite exchanges and accounts for the upkeep of the facilities where the Brotherhood was housed. She had suggested to Burrage that they follow the same course as her father. He had agreed.

But now here was one of its members, fully engaged in his duty and talking of a threat to her Crown in the same way that Master Fynch had tried to counsel. Was the attack today a part of that overall threat? Or was it coincidence? Whichever it was, who was behind the attack? She had thought of little else during the journey and continually returned to the idea that it was someone with an ear inside the palace who had ordered her assassination.

Each time she turned the concept over in her mind and its hold strengthened, Florentyna winced internally. Few people had the influence to command such an attack; even fewer the financial clout to make the kinds of promises that Hubbard was boasting about. Surely even fewer still who may want her dead?

Florentyna took a breath and looked out of the window of her carriage into the mellowing light of the afternoon, which seemed to smooth all the rough edges of the countryside. Tree branches became outlined by a glow, leaves softened, the lines of the hedgerow were blurred and glimpses of light peeked through the spaces between the shrubs and trees. Meadows were brushed with a golden hue and the sky had lost its sharpness; its bright thaw blue had ripened into a gentle, blushing pink where the sky met the land. With the sun's passing she felt thaw's chill sneaking its way into the velvet-lined cocoon and was rocked by the rhythm of the four horses sweeping her rapidly south. In her wake and moving far more slowly were the bodies of those who had been speaking with her only this morning; she couldn't rid herself of the image of Felyx laughing as the arrow struck.

Reliving the death scenes, her thoughts fled to Cassien and she wondered if he was following at their heels or taking his own course to Pearlis. Would he move ahead, preparing to await her arrival at the gates of Stoneheart?

Suddenly she hoped he would. Maybe she could convince him to stand alongside her when she had to break the news to Darcelle about Saria. She wasn't relishing that confrontation. And King Tamas would be arriving soon.

As if on cue, a polite rapping on the roof occurred.

'Stoneheart ahead, your majesty,' the voice called.

* * *

Burrage paced outside the queen's salon. How had so much gone so spectacularly wrong in such a short space of time? Why hadn't he listened to his misgivings? His instincts had screamed at him not to permit the queen to have her way in travelling with so light a guard. Now people were dead, among them the dowager queen. Her noble family in Briavel would have to be told and the repercussions of that would surely only hack away further at the already weakened bonds between the realms. He suspected he would need to advise both stepdaughters to make the journey east to deliver the news and comfort their relatives. Florentyna's presence at the funeral too would add valuable weight to the empire's display of grief at Saria's loss. He sighed — the Ciprean king's visit took precedence, but that too only complicated how Briavel might feel sidestepped.

There was still the horrifying question of which party had designed an attack on two of the royals, one of them the sovereign. Who would commit regicide? He had never seen Florentyna so wrathful or determined. She'd already promised Burrage that as soon as Tamas had left Morgravian shores she would be devoting all her energies to hunting down the perpetrators and bringing them to account on the end of her executioner's axe. For now she had to calm her uncharacteristically high temper and go through the motions with her important foreign visitor.

Then there was poor Felyx. Every time he thought about Felyx, his hand would move to grip his forehead in pain and regret.

They'd agreed to tell Darcelle about the dowager as soon as the princess arrived back at Stoneheart from meeting Tamas. Florentyna had baulked at the suggestion to hold off until the festivities were complete.

'Absolutely not!' she'd rounded on him. 'I couldn't sleep last night. My sister is seeing me through dark enough eyes at the moment — you heard her rant, Burrage — and I'm not giving her an excuse to hate me. As it is, I have no idea how she will take this news other than badly.'

'It is not your fault, majesty.'

'But Darcelle won't see it that way. She will need to blame someone. I am the logical target.'

The queen was likely correct in this, but Burrage was hoping against hope that Darcelle's joy in seeing her betrothed might help calm her reaction.

The door to the salon opened, interrupting his troubled thoughts. 'You may go in,' the queen's private maid announced. Her tense smile said a lot to Burrage about the mood within. He entered. Florentyna looked surprisingly beautiful. Gone were the riding trews and she was now in a gown befitting a queen of Morgravia. It was too rare that her people saw her like this, though he knew she preferred not to compete with Darcelle.

Burrage bowed. 'They are moments from the city gates, your majesty.'

He watched her nod and run a hand down the bodice of her exquisite gown. It was fashioned from the fabulously rich and exclusive imperial purple — formerly known as Percheron Purple. It won this name in the west because the dye was extracted from a large whelk common only to that exotic peninsula's glittering emerald waters. Nowadays, most sovereigns had garments dyed this deep, vibrant hue and it had become known as 'royal' — or in Morgravia's case 'imperial' — purple. No-one else but the sovereign in Morgravia was permitted to wear it. Certainly, few but the sovereign could afford to in any case, given that the dye fetched its own weight in gold. He knew she would prefer to be garbed in dark mourning clothing this evening, out of respect for the fallen, but she was required to be nothing less than empress today as she received a neighbouring king.

The sumptuous imperial purple echoed the blue–black sheen that one hundred brushstrokes had coaxed from her hair. It was loosely pinned up, a few wisps allowed to escape, adding a touch of feminine whimsy to the austere line she was cutting with her tall silhouette. He noticed how slim she'd become. He would have to talk to the cook about what the queen was eating ... or not.

'Will this do?' she asked, smoothing her skirt.

'You look perfect, your majesty.'

He didn't want to say that she looked sad.

'I keep trying to find the words, Burrage.'

'They will find you, my queen. This is not a discussion you can rehearse.'

'No, I believe you. It is better I speak with all the emotion and fear that I'm feeling.'

He closed his eyes and nodded gently. 'Princess Darcelle knows what is expected of her, majesty. She will not let you down in a formal situation ... and not in front of the king.'

'You're right, I hope.'

'There's a man calling himself Cassien Figaret. I've asked him to wait in the Keep. Apparently, you've invited him to the palace?'

'Yes, I did.' Her creamy skin flushed at her cheeks and his curiosity deepened. 'This is the man who saved my life.'

'Truly,' he said. 'No doubt you wish to speak with him.'

'I do.' She checked herself once more in the long glass and walked closer. Burrage noted how the tiny beads of amethyst sewn onto the bodice of her gown caught the light and shimmered when she moved. 'There is something I should tell you about Cassien.'

'Yes, majesty?'

'He is of the Brotherhood,' she said evenly.

'Brotherhood?' he repeated, astonished.

She nodded. 'What is curious is that he was travelling to Pearlis to seek me out, but instead stumbled across me at Rittylworth.'

Burrage's mind had already begun to dart in a dozen directions but he gathered himself. 'And how glad we are he did.'

'I would be dead if not for Cassien. Please show him and Hamelyn — the boy he travels with — every courtesy.'

'Of course.'

There was a knock at the door. Burrage answered it, nodding once. He returned to Florentyna.

'We must go, your majesty.'

'Walk with me, Burrage. You'll have to brief me as we descend the stairs. I'm sorry to have left you so little time.'

He knew it was not her fault and moved straight into his briefing. 'Tonight is the official welcome, but I suspect they will be fatigued so I plan to keep the celebrations brief. It will be intimate — no more than forty guests. Tomorrow I have arranged a festive picnic with sporting activities, a hunt if his majesty would like to participate; food will be laid out down by the stream. We've brought in mummers, poets, minstrels and jongleurs to entertain. I believe Samwyl Tooley has crafted a poem in honour of the marriage —' He noted Florentyna's eyebrow lift at that news. Tooley was the most angst-ridden and overly theatrical artist in the land; at the death of the king he had declared he would never write another poem. Burrage smiled and continued. 'And Justyn Faircluff has a new ballad he would like to sing for the couple. In essence, tonight is a formality. Tomorrow is the real betrothal celebration, and in the evening we will have the formal feast — more than three hundred nobles will be arriving to pay their respects. A civic gathering first, of course. We are following the plan we set out moons ago. I saw no reason to change that structure. Festivities will end with an open carriage ride through the capital the following afternoon, your majesty, after you and the king have completed your formal talks. The people will want to see Princess Darcelle and her handsome King Tamas.'

'Everything sounds marvellous. The people will be given food and ale?' she enquired, as they began to descend the great staircase.

'My word, yes. There is to be a vast two-day street party, from what I can tell. Decorations are up everywhere, with the colours of Morgravia and the colours of Cipres flying together.'

'I look forward to seeing that.'

'Oh, and I've granted permission to a merchant called Layne Tentrell to attend the picnic and present the most exquisite jewel to her highness.'

'Jewel?' she queried.

He explained about the merchant from Robissun Marth.

'How magnanimous,' she remarked.

'My sentiment exactly, majesty.'

'The Star of Percheron,' she repeated, looking impressed. 'And it's all perfectly credible?'

'He is very well known in our west and strikes me as sincere, although I admit he is baffling.'

'In what way?' she asked, descending the stairs with more decorum than her usual stride, encouraged in this by having a number of skirts to keep out of the way of her feet.

Burrage gave a soft *moue* of helplessness. 'That's just it. I can't put my finger on it. His motives are admirable but there's something vaguely unsettling about it ... about him.'

They reached the bottom of the stairs. Staff and household guard were lining the entrance to the grand doors. Florentyna was to greet King Tamas and Darcelle outside on the steps leading onto the bailey. The heralds were ready to proclaim the foreign sovereign's arrival. It seemed as though everyone was holding a collective breath.

She turned to Burrage. 'You trust him though.' It didn't sound like a question. She stared at him intently, with a soft frown. Given recent events, he couldn't blame her for being in any way nervous of strangers.

'I have no reason to mistrust him, majesty, and he will be searched and guided in by soldiers and escorted away by soldiers shortly afterwards. He will be allowed to approach Princess Darcelle and King Tamas only with their express permission and with soldiers either side. He will have only moments with them. I have to tell you, Darcelle will want that jewel. And if you grant it...' He didn't need to say more.

They shared a rueful smile. 'You'll check for poison too?'

'Of course. The jewel will be dipped to clean it of any potentially harmful agents, his fingers and lips will be swabbed to nullify any poisons before he is permitted to so much as kiss your sister's hand. I have already sent a message that the clothes he plans to wear are brought to the palace beforehand. They will be checked by our people for hidden pockets or the presence of poison, or any form of weapon. He will only be permitted to dress in the presence of two soldiers.' He shrugged. 'I've taken this precaution because his request was unexpected and unusual. In the light of what occurred at Rittylworth, I'm very glad I have.'

'Should we do the same for all the performers?'

He sighed. 'None will be permitted to get close enough to the royals. Rigorous checking for weapons will be carried out. Household staff will be put through more stringent checks, of course. There will be food and drink tasters for everything.'

Burrage saw the signal from the gate. 'They're here, my queen.'

'Do as you see fit, Burrage. I trust your judgement implicitly. Now wish me luck, and please bring Cassien to me at the first available moment I get to myself. This is going to be a most difficult next few hours.'

'No luck required, my queen. Just be yourself.'

She gave him a wan smile and glided away, through the doorway, as the first trumpets sounded. Burrage signalled to Meek, who was standing by, along with a row of other youngsters for running errands and delivering messages.

'Yes, Master Burrage,' Meek enquired, his attention helplessly riveted on the arrival of the grandest of the royal coaches.

'Go to the Keep. There is a man waiting by the name of Cassien Figaret. He is to be escorted to the Orangerie. He is to wait under guard. Make sure he is taken there by four of our men.'

The boy threw him a glance of mystification but nodded and ran away.

From the shadows Burrage could see that the royal carriage was making a wide circuit in the bailey. Any moment, the king would step out and with him his princess. He hoped that Darcelle would keep her emotions in check when the news of Saria was shared. He wished he could have time right now to consider who in the palace had discovered and then leaked the information of Florentyna's journey to Rittylworth. There was only one person he could think of and that realisation frightened him more than Darcelle learning that her beloved 'mother' had been murdered.

He sighed in private fear. In the distance he caught a glimpse of Meek running nimbly across the bailey, barely noticed by anyone else for their eyes were on the carriage.

'The Brotherhood,' he murmured, still surprised and more than a little apprehensive that a member of that order was suddenly within their presence. Something in the back of his mind told him that he should be making connections. The arrival of Master Fynch to talk with the queen and Reynard's subsequent mysterious disappearance; the curious death of Flek with the royal sigil burned on his skin; suggestions of a force against the Crown; a direct attack on the queen … seemingly from within. And now the unexpected arrival of one of the Brotherhood. He knew he should be adding something up, but none of it amounted to anything other than a vague, underlying sense of threat.

Although he hadn't told the queen, Burrage had ordered more than a dozen senior archers to be in the bailey, positioned at various strategic locations, with an eye only on her majesty. Any person perceived to be a direct threat was to be brought down immediately. They had orders to shoot first — but not to kill — and questions would be asked later. In the meantime, soldiers out of uniform and kitted in appropriate regal clothes were already peppered throughout the household, watching everything and everyone. If this Cassien could truly live up to the reputation of the Brotherhood, then perhaps he too must be brought into the secret circle that was now ringing the queen without her knowledge.

On the other hand, if today's attack had been prompted from within the palace walls, as suspected, then she was not safe in Stoneheart no matter how much security was thrown around her. They had to get through these next few days and then Burrage would make arrangements for the queen to be whisked off to Briavel and ultimately to a secret location, no matter how much she protested. And he would personally oversee the hunt for the traitor and his or her network.

Two days. That's all he needed. He saw the carriage door open and a strapping man step out. It was King Tamas. His luxuriant golden beard was knitted through with the silver of age … or wisdom, as some liked to call it. He was grinning broadly, showing his enjoyment of the trumpets playing and the cheering of the people in the bailey. He offered his hand to help his princess from the carriage; she emerged into the evening wearing a dazzling smile and a gown of mauve. Darcelle looked enchanting, as always, but Burrage thought he noticed her falter slightly when she saw the queen awaiting them on the stairs. He would give her the benefit of doubt that this wasn't the shock of her being alive. Instead he would allow that perhaps like him, Darcelle had been surprised to see Florentyna looking so beautiful. None of them were used to seeing her in such finery.

He watched Florentyna descend the grand stairway of Stoneheart, gliding regally into the bailey proper and he felt a pang of pride for this young sovereign. She could so easily have remained at the top of the stairs, waiting for her less important sister and Darcelle's more important guest to ascend to meet her: somewhere in that stillness Florentyna could have silently reinforced her status and particularly her power. Instead she had made an altruistic gesture — welcoming without reservation.

Burrage didn't need to look into the eyes of King Tamas to know that the Ciprean king acknowledged her benevolence; it was conveyed in the way he watched the Queen of Morgravia arrive to stand before him, in the deferential bow that he gave, and in the way he touched his lips to her hand bending low as he did so.

The watching chancellor was impressed. King Tamas was far more regal and his presence infinitely more daunting than he'd imagined. Why he'd imagined a less imposing, maybe even paunchy, effeminate older man, rather than this earthy 'man's man', he couldn't be sure. Perhaps because Cipres was famed for its art, culture and the exquisite pale beauty of its royal palace. He blinked, surprised at himself for being so judgemental; King Tamas looked as though he could ride, drink and swap punches with the best of his soldiers. Darcelle curtsied alongside her betrothed and suddenly Florentyna was beyond officialdom and pulling both sister and brother-in-law-to-be toward her in the embrace of family.

TWENTY-ONE

Cassien stood quietly within the fragrant tranquillity of the Orangerie —
an inner courtyard of Stoneheart. He noticed no servants bustling
around here; the only sounds were the soft coo of pigeons beginning
their evening roost, together with the low drone of the last determined
bees of the day. Hamelyn, too, had fallen silent and sat on the edge of
a low stone wall watching a small army of ants swarming over a dead
beetle. Cassien was sure the boy must be famished and exhausted after
the ride, although he heard no complaint.

There were no fruits on the citrus trees but the thaw blossom was just
bursting and the perfume of their explosions was heady and romantic.
He was thinking about the queen and how courageous she had been,
not shrinking from Hubbard despite death lying around her. His mind
wandered, and suddenly he was considering his physical reaction to
Florentyna. At first sight he'd found her irresistible, standing there in
her oversized cassock, flushed and angry, with the hood fallen back and
her hair tumbling in strands from the tight pins she'd hoped might hide
her femininity. But the rules of the Brotherhood were clear. No emotion
was to cloud his judgement. He had to go about his business with a cold
detachment or fail in the eyes of Brother Josse and his elders. There was
also Vivienne, but he would not permit himself to dwell on her.

He had been given what was arguably the single most important task
undertaken by his fraternity. The direct championing of a monarch was
unheard of in the Brotherhood. It was a testament to the serious nature
of the present threat that the Brotherhood would sanction such a public
mission. He would not let his emotions interfere.

'Cassien?' Hamelyn said, breaking into his fractured thoughts.

He emerged from the grove into the early evening sunlight. It was
warm in the courtyard, more so than outside it, because its smallish

size and thick walls had managed to trap the sun's thin warmth through the day.

'Yes?' He saw the boy's frown. 'Is something wrong?'

'I'm not sure whether something's wrong but …'

'Say it.'

'Something isn't quite right.'

Cassien moved closer to where his friend sat. 'Tell me.' He'd become used to Ham's cryptic notions and was now fully accepting of the youngster's invisible senses. 'Is the sword making noises again?' His sword was hanging at his side, openly visible — he'd deliberately made no secret of it.

'That's just it. It has always made some sort of sound. Now there's nothing.'

This was Ham's specialty. Cassien had no idea what to suggest. 'Follow your instincts,' he offered. 'What are they telling you?'

Ham looked up at him. 'It's hiding.'

Their conversation came to an abrupt end as one of the soldiers approached. 'The queen will see you now.' Cassien nodded, threw a tight glance at Ham. 'Follow us, please. The boy is to go with this messenger.'

A sandy-haired youngster not far off Ham's age, but far better dressed and rosy-cheeked, regarded them. 'I am Meek, sir,' he said to Cassien, and nodded at Hamelyn. 'I was told to take you to the kitchens … to make sure you were given some food.'

Hamelyn's eyes lit up.

'Off you go,' Cassien urged. 'I'll see you shortly. And, Ham … keep listening,' he said carefully. Ham nodded.

The senior soldier put a hand up and gestured for one of his men to search Ham and he was duly given permission to go with Meek. Now the senior man turned to Cassien. 'I need your weapons. You cannot meet with her majesty wearing that sword.'

He understood, could tell the man was baffled that he'd got this far into the palace wearing it. 'Perhaps you'd like my blades as well?' he offered, pulling back his cloak.

The soldier's eyes widened. 'I'll need *all* your weapons.'

Cassien obliged. He unbuckled the two belts and noted the amazement in the soldier's face as he accepted them. 'These will be returned to you after your audience with her majesty.'

'Fair enough.'

He felt curiously naked without them and for the first time realised how comfortable they had felt strapped to his body.

'Your weapons will be cared for.'

He hadn't realised his concerns were etched on his expression. He brightened. 'Of course. Shall we go?'

Cassien walked between his two minders down long draughty corridors, poorly lit, and assumed they must be approaching from the back of the palace. He had not taken too much notice of his path to the Orangerie and was now working hard to make sense of which direction they were travelling in; there were no clues but he was alert for a glimpse of sunlight that would prompt him. Soon the men had him climbing a narrow staircase. They passed a small arched window and he immediately took his bearings and knew that he was facing east. By the time they had escorted him down a few more passages — these more lavishly lit, and decorated with tapestries and pieces of furniture — he was sure, despite all the twists and turns, that he could pinpoint in which direction they moved. The larger spaces, no longer bare, had taken on a sense of life with their trimmings, and the lit sconces added a deeper elegance to the dark stone of the castle, which had looked so sombre from a distance.

As they travelled, Cassien began to see carvings in the stone and he recognised the great beasts of myth whose fabulous likenesses were sculpted in huge form within the cathedral of Pearlis. He was longing to see the famous nave; yearning to test again which beast was his. He was sure that this time Lupus would call, convinced that as a child his fanciful notion of the dragon was mere whimsy.

They walked along an arcade, the open corridor linking two parts of the palace like a bridge. Cassien glanced over the balustrade and saw an orchard below with ragged trees, still in their winter nakedness, awaiting blossomtide's warmth to coax them into a fresh burst of life. He was impressed that Stoneheart defied its name; he was discovering that there was much softness around this palace, the further he walked through it. The love of orchards and fragrant shrubs was evident from the multitude of winterblossom bushes he saw beneath him. Their blooms were finished but he was sure he could conjure the vaguest hint of their gorgeous scent still lingering on the waxy green leaves.

He continued walking between his minders, who suddenly came to an abrupt halt.

'Wait here, please,' the head soldier said.

His interest was diverted, riveted on the great arched doorway over which presided a magnificently rendered dragon. It curled, serpent-like, over the sweep of the arch, but its broad head faced outward in stark relief. Presumably it was meant to instil true fear in those who stood in this spot awaiting their sovereign's pleasure.

The dragon's eyes, though fashioned from dull stone, seemed to look straight into him. There was no escaping the gaze from the king of the beasts; he thought of Fynch and how gentle he seemed and yet the man was linked with this terrifying creature. And how could he be? How was Fynch connected to the dragon unless through blood? His mind began to tease at this while the door opened in front of him and he caught a glimpse of an older man listening to the soldier.

The thought snapped into place. Fynch *was* blood. It felt like a thunderclap in his mind. He even looked around in case anyone had heard the sound of it. *Fynch had to be the son of a king?* What the —?

'Master Cassien?'

Cassien snapped out of his thoughts. 'Yes,' he said, looking into the intrigued gaze of the older man he'd glimpsed.

'I am Chancellor Burrage and I believe Morgravia … indeed, the empire … owes you a debt of thanks.'

Cassien wasn't sure how to respond to such a salutation. 'I … am at her majesty's service,' he said.

Burrage smiled and Cassien saw only kindness. 'Queen Florentyna is keen to speak with you again,' he said, gesturing toward the painted double oaken doors that between them formed the great crest of Morgravia. There was no doubting he was now in the private sanctuary of the realm's monarch. Burrage nodded at his guard of soldiers, who looked to Cassien as though they were going nowhere, and right enough, they took positions flanking the door as he followed Burrage beneath the arch, still thinking about the revelation connected with Fynch. *A king's bastard perhaps?*

Burrage closed the door. 'I'm afraid the queen has limited time. King Tamas is taking a short rest, preparing for the evening festivities.' Cassien nodded. 'Her majesty must also prepare,' he added. 'Please forgive us for hurrying you through this initial meeting.'

Cassien smiled and Burrage gestured toward the second door, which he presumed would lead into the queen's private study. As Burrage knocked, Cassien thought about his location again: If I've got it right, he pondered silently, then I should be facing in a northwesterly direction and looking straight across the bailey.

Burrage opened the door onto a vast chamber, with arched picture windows running the length of it. A fireplace at one end had a merry blaze crackling. The queen stood nearby.

Cassien caught his breath. He wasn't prepared for her to be garbed in such finery, and had ignorantly imagined she would still be dressed as he recalled, in her riding clothes. She stood so still, and so regally awaiting him, he quite forgot to glance out the windows.

'Your majesty,' he said, remembering his manners, and bowing low.

'Cassien — welcome. It is good to see you again.'

She spoke evenly. He sensed she was more confident in these familiar surrounds and had a greater sense of security and wellbeing.

'I can definitely say I feel the same way, your majesty. That you are returned to the palace unharmed is all that matters.'

Her smile was tentative, but he felt its warmth touch him. It occurred to him that Florentyna's life was very serious for the most part: most you might take for granted, aspects of life like laughter, abandon, and recklessness, but she could not. In this, they had led similar lives. He could only imagine the responsibilities and duties that rested on her thin shoulders. And she did look thin. Her riding clothes had hidden her frame but her gown, so cinched at the waist, hid no secrets.

'Are you well, my queen?'

'I am. Truly. Burrage, perhaps you might order us some refreshment. I'm sure there's a little fat in that time schedule of yours.' She glanced at Cassien. 'He is a fastidious timekeeper,' she whispered, though loud enough for Burrage to hear and arch an eyebrow at her. Cassien sensed the bond between them.

'I'm sure I can. A honeywine, majesty?'

'Please,' she said with an affectionate glance at the man.

'Master Cassien? Would you care to join the queen in the same, or perhaps we could offer you something else. A spiced gartrell, or maybe some —'

'No, no. I'm happy to take a cup of honeywine,' he said, without a clue what honeywine was or how it might taste. The best he'd had in the forest was ale and only if Loup had remembered to pack a flagon for him, which was not often.

'And Burrage?'

'Majesty?' he said turning back.

'I wish to speak with Master Cassien privately, please.'

Cassien watched her elder counsel frown, but the hesitation was brief and he quickly pasted on an even expression. 'Of course,' he said with a small bow.

He left them. Cassien returned his gaze to the queen. There was a heartbeat of awkward silence before she flashed an embarrassed smile with a brief gust of relief.

He broke into a smile to reassure her. 'He cares a great deal.'

'I sometimes think he's trying to replace the father I miss, but there's nothing cynical about it. He really does care.'

'That's his role. Counsel, protector, friend … everything a father is.'

She nodded. 'Wise words. My father's chancellor — a man called Reynard — disappeared soon after my father's death. He was the most loyal of men and I had become close to him.' She gave a sad shrug. 'Reynard had always been there since my early childhood. He was like a comfy old piece of furniture.' Florentyna gestured at a chair near the fire and they both sat. 'I think Burrage is always aware of walking in big footsteps, but also not trying to replace Reynard in my heart. It must feel like a tightrope sometimes.'

Cassien was impressed by her sensitivity. He was just about to use her mention of Reynard as a way in to discuss his presence when Burrage reappeared, with a servant bearing a tray with goblets and a flagon. The older man supervised the pouring of the goblets. Cassien noted a tiny cup on the tray and was intrigued when that was filled and everyone waited while the servant — a young man — swallowed its contents with a look of trepidation. Burrage was certainly taking no chances.

'Not the poisoned brew,' Florentyna quipped, with a wry expression directed at Cassien, who noticed Burrage's slightly pursed lips.

The chancellor sent the servant on his way. 'I shall return before the next bell, majesty. Time is short.'

'Thank you,' she said, her tone kind, but both of them knew it was a dismissal.

When they were alone again she stole another embarrassed glance at Cassien and this time they both laughed.

'I'm sorry about that. Burrage has become frantic about security since this morning's episode. He's now refusing to leave me alone. I'm sure there must be soldiers hiding behind every doorway.'

'Can you blame him?'

She sighed. 'I just hate that this is how life is going to be. It's stifling enough without more scrutiny and rules being added. And that young man — how unfair that he should risk death by poison. I'm going to insist all the tasters are paid exceptionally well; I've never taken their role quite as seriously as I do now.' She looked at him over the rim of her goblet. 'Forgive me, I have no right to complain. I must sound wickedly selfish to you.'

'Not at all. I was just thinking how constrained your life must be, what with you having to be so many things to so many people.'

A few seconds passed. Florentyna raised her goblet. 'To your health,' she said.

He did the same. 'To your health,' he echoed and they both sipped in comfortable momentary silence.

'Did your young companion make it here with you?'

He nodded. 'He's enjoying some treats in the palace kitchens, I gather,' he replied.

'Good. I asked Burrage to ensure … Hamelyn, is it?' Cassien nodded. 'That he was properly cared for. He looked far too thin.'

'So do you, majesty,' he said. It had slipped out before he could censure himself.

The queen regarded him with bemusement. 'Oh, really? Because you know how I should look.'

'Forgive me. That was indiscreet.'

Florentyna laughed. 'No offence taken. Everyone always feels they know best where I'm concerned. Now, tell me why you're here. No guile. I am depending on your complete honesty.'

He barely blinked. 'I would never give you anything but the truth as I know it.'

'I believe you.'

'You mentioned Chancellor Reynard, your majesty,' he began. She nodded and he sensed she was frightened.

'You know what happened, don't you?' she said baldly, all humour gone from her expression.

Cassien hesitated only briefly before he began his story from the moment Fynch had come into his life, and told the queen everything that he knew about the threat to the Morgravian Crown. He didn't believe it was necessary for her to know the background information on the Brotherhood, or his own curious life, or even Hamelyn's involvement, for even to his ears there was too much that sounded strange. The episode in Orkyld would surely come across as delusional, so he withheld that as well.

Florentyna had said nothing while he had spoken, quickly and quietly. One of the logs of wood snapped and a burst of sparks exploded with a crack. It broke the silence between them.

'And you believe this?' she asked pointedly.

'Queen Florentyna, I am a Brother. I have no say and it is not my place to question my duties. I have been given the task of protecting you. I could have tried to fulfil my role from a position of invisibility, which is the Brotherhood's preferred way. However, Master Fynch knew that couldn't work easily in this instance. It made sense to me that if you knew of my involvement, you might help me to play my part in this curious set of circumstances.'

'Help you?'

'By co-Opérating with my presence.'

'Doing what you tell me, you mean,' she qualified.

He watched her carefully. She was young but she had already proved to him that she was courageous and pragmatic. To all intents and purposes she was helpless against this unseen threat, but he sensed Florentyna would do everything in her power to help herself. It would not be wise to treat her with anything but the transparency she had demanded.

'Exactly as I say, in fact,' he said, as directly as he could. Then there could be no misunderstanding. He quickly added, 'Your majesty, I don't know in which guise this threat will come either ... or even if it will. But I suspect my talents are far better suited than half a dozen of your guards encircling you at every turn.' She pulled a face of disgust. 'Exactly. If you

284

will permit my constant presence, and that I might bear a weapon at all times, I believe you have the best protection any public person could have.'

He watched her take a deep breath and pressed his point. 'Fynch believed that you trusted him despite the strangeness of what he was conveying.'

She nodded unhappily. 'I didn't mistrust him — there's a difference. I just couldn't quantify, and neither could he, the threat he warned of. However, there was something compelling about him. I sensed no guile, no separate agenda. He was here for my benefit, or rather, for the good of the Crown.'

Cassien nodded. 'I believe that too. Given that he was sent away unhappy, unable to convince you to take his claims seriously, may I ask what has changed your mind enough to hear me out?'

Florentyna told him about Dean Flek.

'Help me?' he repeated, baffled by the bizarre explanation.

'I heard it. I know I did,' she said, sounding defensive. 'I can't explain the royal sigil burned on his chest, or the return of the scrivener's quill that I'd given to Reynard, either.'

'I think I can, your majesty,' he said gravely.

She bit her lip. 'Tell me please. It's been a conundrum that haunts my sleep.'

He stared into the flames, piecing together what he knew. 'On the assumption that we both place our faith in what Master Fynch has foreseen, then I believe that the threat must already be in Morgravia. The demon has arrived.'

She gasped. 'Hubbard?'

Cassien shook his head. 'He doesn't fit. He said he was being given money and landholdings. I suspect no demon is going to be persuaded by that.' He frowned. 'No, Hubbard was something else. A different threat, from a different source.'

'Which I intend to hunt down!' she promised before shivering. 'Demons. I can't believe we're giving this credence.'

'I won't let it near you, majesty,' he said, desperate to reassure her.

'We don't have any idea who he is,' she said. 'How can you protect me from everyone? He could be Burrage according to you. He could be my maidservant!'

'Yes,' he said, gravely, 'he could also be me.'

She blanched.

'It's not,' he said, smiling crookedly, 'but we will need to formulate a plan should you suspect it.'

'So he will use various bodies to reach me … hopping between them?' she asked, with a tone of disbelief.

'That's my understanding, although how he will do so and what constraints there may be I don't know. One thing I do know, majesty, is that magic exacts its price.'

'What do you mean?'

'Each time magic is used … cast … I believe that it will require the wielder to pay in some way a part of himself.' He looked down.

She waited until he looked up again. 'You sound as though you speak from experience, Master Cassien.'

This was not the time. 'I have an understanding,' is all he was prepared to say. He put the unfinished goblet of honeywine down. 'Let me add that it makes it much easier for me to protect you if you wish my presence rather than dread it.'

Cassien watched her swallow and saw a reddening of the pale skin at her neck, and he found that small glimpse behind the control of the most powerful person in the empire highly attractive. That she might desire his presence suddenly felt more important to him than anything else. There was something alarmingly sad and needy about her that echoed his life, and yet she deliberately cloaked herself with a reserve of resilience and stoicism that she wore as armour. Cassien had done the same living in the forest; his torturous physical training and tolerances were his armour against his desire for family, for love, for affection.

'Given that I've recently lost my royal champion, I would be glad of your protection in whichever shape or form you can provide it.'

Relief flew through his body. 'Then I am yours to command, majesty.'

'We both know that's a lie,' she said, lifting an eyebrow.

He smiled. 'I will gladly pretend.'

'I must leave you despite having many more questions. We are not finished, you and I, Cassien,' she said, offering a hand. Cassien moved to bend over it and his lips touched her skin. 'Thank you for being here,' she said, adopting her more imperious tone. He too had heard the door open. Burrage was back. 'Ah, Burrage,' she said, looking over Cassien's shoulder. 'I've just formally appointed Master Cassien as the Queen's Champion.'

Burrage looked astonished. 'But …'

She held a hand up. 'No buts. This is what I want and surely it is what you want, too. He has already saved my life once and I trust him. The Brotherhood has sent him to us, Burrage, and according to Master Cassien, we don't have much say in this. So you can blame Emperor Cailech of a century or more ago!' she said brightly.

Cassien knew how difficult this was for the older man to accept. He clearly wanted to orchestrate the queen's every move, for all the right reasons, and to appoint those who were permitted close proximity to her. 'Chancellor Burrage, I assure you I am not here to interfere. I will be the shadow within the shadows. I expect no privileges, I require no assistance, and I will ask nothing more than the basics of the palace.'

Burrage's mouth opened and closed silently like a fish.

Cassien hurried on. 'Where was Felyx accommodated, may I ask?'

'In the barracks, of course,' Burrage answered, finally finding his voice and sounding indignant.

'I will not be in the barracks. That offers no ready protection. Where are your chambers, your majesty?' he asked, turning to the queen.

'They're …' she began to point.

'This is preposterous! Do you mean to accommodate yourself near the queen?' Burrage spluttered, looking between them.

Florentyna said nothing, though Cassien sensed an underlying amusement.

'As close to her as I can possibly be,' he answered with a straight face. The innuendo was clearly not lost on Florentyna, but it was the apoplexy of Burrage that was silently entertaining them. He knew it was unfair to the man, who had only the queen's best interests in mind. 'Forgive me, Chancellor Burrage, but in light of yesterday's events her majesty is going to need protection day and night, in every situation.'

'I have taken measures to ensure just that,' Burrage replied, barely just managing to keep his temper.

'I am not here to usurp any authority. I will simply be nearby at all times and I will not permit anyone to get closer to our queen than you or I believe is appropriate. We are moving into a time of celebration and festivity, where anyone and everyone may be a potential threat.'

Burrage was yet to appreciate that while Florentyna had survived the recent attack on her life, Cassien was not thinking of that, but of the approach of something far more sinister. 'Perhaps if you would brief me and give me your instructions, then I can make sure that I remain entirely unobtrusive throughout the festivities, Chancellor.'

Burrage brushed a fleck of lint from his robe and seemed finally appeased. 'I can do that for you,' he said evenly.

'Thank you. I will need the return of my weapons and I must be permitted to wear them, even in the presence of the queen.'

Burrage began to shake his head but Florentyna answered. 'I am comfortable with this.'

'Your majesty, I must protest —'

'Burrage, please,' Florentyna said, her tone with a slight edge to it now, 'these are unusual times and we must bend the rules. I need you to work with Cassien and help me through whatever it is that we face. Now, it is surely time I dressed in my next gown,' she said with a mock sigh. 'I shall leave all the arrangements for Cassien and his friend, Hamelyn, to you.'

She swept out of her salon leaving both men staring awkwardly at each other.

TWENTY-TWO

Florentyna had allowed her maids to dress her while she hid her flustered state of mind behind an expressionless mask. When her head dresser had suggested the dark green gown — 'because it sets off your eyes so beautifully, majesty' — Florentyna had mumbled that she didn't mind what she was attired in.

The reality of having to face Darcelle with the news of their stepmother was now feeling like the heaviest of burdens.

Florentyna blinked. 'Pardon?' she said, realising Sharley had spoken to her.

'Are you all right, majesty?'

'Yes, I am. Please don't worry. I'm thinking about this evening and how we're going to get through it without showing the scars of Morgravia's troubles.'

Sharley smiled with relief. 'I stole a glimpse of King Tamas and Princess Darcelle when they arrived, your majesty. He is such a handsome man. I thought he was going to be old and ...' The queen looked at her in query. 'Well, I thought when they said he was into his fourth decade that he'd be —'

'Hobbling? Withered? Hard of hearing?'

Sharley giggled. 'Forgive me, majesty. I did think it sounded old, but King Tamas is the talk of the palace. Emmy says she'd let him keep his slippers under her bed any time.'

The queen gave a mock gasp, smiling. 'Shame on Emmy.' It was true; Tamas was a fine-looking man, far more impressive than she'd imagined. She sighed. Did Darcelle truly grasp that she had everything in life, and still with so much to look forward to?

'They looked very much in love,' Sharley continued. 'I feel sure the love and affections of her betrothed will get the princess through this difficult time.'

'I think you're right,' Florentyna replied, realising Burrage must have briefed her closest staff on the demise of the dowager. 'Forgive me, did you ask me something before?'

'I suggested your great-grandmother's emeralds. May I fetch them from the vault?'

She nodded. Burrage would have to oversee that too.

'Sharley?'

'Yes, majesty,' her maid said, turning.

'Send a runner to my sister's rooms. Have her meet me in my solar shortly and have Chancellor Burrage send Master Cassien to the solar as well.'

'Master Cassien?'

'He will know,' she said and turned back to the mirror, pretending to admire herself but not seeing anything, other than her sister's histrionics and knowing she needed an ally. Cassien would give her strength.

Chancellor Burrage glanced at him, but Cassien pretended not to notice. He had been surprised to be summoned so soon after his meeting with the queen. Darcelle was yet to arrive, so the three of them stood in the difficult silence of people who shared the knowledge that an unpleasant exchange was about to take place.

'Are you sure this is the right time, majesty?' Burrage ventured, almost whispering.

'I told you, I cannot get through this evening with the dowager's death constraining my every breath — as it will when I'm around Darcelle. I managed the formal greeting this afternoon, but if I withhold this news any longer she will interpret it as a betrayal rather than a kindness. And before you find another way to repeat it, Burrage, I know it will ruin her evening and probably the whole time that Tamas is here, but even Darcelle has to learn that life is rarely neat and tidy, and very often cruel. She has Tamas to comfort her and she has a new life beckoning to look forward to. I feel sympathy but I can't keep shielding her from every one of life's knocks.'

Cassien thought she sounded stilted, as though trying to convince herself of the truth of what she was saying, but he believed she was right in not postponing the confrontation. He'd caught his breath when he'd laid eyes on her in even more finery than this afternoon; from the top of her head to the tips of her toes, she was all queen tonight. A vision in silk and jewels, though he suspected she laid no store by it. Her hair had been pinned up to reveal her long, elegant neck and angular shoulders, and she wore a dress the colour of the forest. Once again she could not hide her thin frame and yet there was an elegance and quiet beauty to her gauntness. The magnificent necklace of shimmering emeralds seemed to pick out the flames from the fireplace and reflect their glow, complementing her exquisite gown and showing off her dark green eyes to their best effect. Simply, the queen was stunning.

Darcelle didn't knock. She arrived in the room in a swish of silk. Cassien blinked as a froth of buttery ivory — like freshly clotted cream — billowed and was finally still within the queen's private office. The younger sister was undeniably pretty, but in a loud, extravagant manner. Her dark golden hair flowed free and her blue eyes sparkled with indignation that made her pink-stained lips look tight. Her cheeks were glazed to achieve the smooth appearance of porcelain. He'd first seen it in Orkyld on a noblewoman and then again on the dead face of the dowager. Ham had explained that some women used egg white painted on their skin to achieve that appearance. Darcelle had followed in her stepmother's footsteps, but had added to her cheeks a soft smudge of pink over the glaze. He had to admit that her face paint achieved a look of pale perfection heightened with the blush of 'girlhood', but to his eyes she looked doll-like and fake. Her sister wore none of the paint, but he'd noticed Florentyna had been blessed with a flawless complexion and a natural blush to her cheeks.

The stiff silk of Darcelle's gown all but crackled in sympathetic anger as she ignored the men to address the queen. 'Florentyna, are you barking mad summoning me now when —'

Darcelle's complaint died in her throat when she noticed the stranger in the corner.

'Darcelle,' Florentyna said, wearily, 'this is Cassien. He is my new champion.'

Cassien felt the cool gaze wash over him like a shower of rain. Her expression took on one of slight bemusement as she appraised him.

'Oh? You don't look like Florentyna's usual choice. She prefers to surround herself with older men,' Darcelle said, not even looking

Burrage's way, but Cassien was aware of the chancellor pursing his lips. 'What, may I ask, has happened to the very dour Felyx?' she said, not quite hiding the sneer.

Florentyna took a patient breath. 'Felyx is dead, dear one.' Her voice was even he noticed and he felt a spike of pride for her.

Darcelle looked at her sister properly for the first time since arriving. 'Dead? That's unfortunate. Good gracious, sister. Where did you drag that ensemble from?'

Florentyna blinked in shock.

'Don't get me wrong. I approve. It's gorgeous. You look ... well, you look ...'

'Fit for a queen?' Florentyna offered tightly.

'You do. Don't sound so surprised.'

'I'm not the one who is surprised, Darcelle. I would suggest you're the one with the shocked expression. Did you not think me capable?' Florentyna replied, sweetening her tone.

'I'm not used to seeing you dressed so sumptuously. Normally you'd be ...' She didn't finish.

Florentyna looked down, Cassien noticed, but then she raised her gaze. 'This is a formal occasion,' she countered.

Darcelle's voice took on a slight whine. 'Yes, but one would think you were the one celebrating her engagement. I could quite convince myself that you are trying to upstage me, sister.' Then Darcelle tittered as though such an idea was ludicrous.

No-one smiled.

Florentyna sighed. 'Did you absorb what I said? Felyx is dead.'

'An accident, I suppose? I barely knew him — please don't ask me to don mourning garb on his behalf,' Darcelle replied, returning her gaze to Cassien. 'If you're looking for my approval of his replacement, you have it. Good evening, Cassien.' She held out her hand and Cassien could see how much Darcelle was annoying her sister with her careless baiting. Nevertheless, he bent over the slim, perfectly manicured hand and barely touched his lips to it.

'Your highness,' he murmured.

She smiled at him and he saw only flirtatiousness in her expression; her slightly hungry gaze left him colder than he'd felt at her arrival.

'Darcelle!'

'Yes, Florentyna,' she said, only just preventing herself from snapping. 'Hurry up and tell me what I'm doing here. You are aware that I'm about to show off my husband and entertain forty or so guests at his welcome feast.'

'He's not your husband … yet, and I believe *I* rather than you, am the host this evening,' Florentyna replied. A firm tone had crept into the queen's voice. 'The guests are mine. You merely have to look pretty, which is not hard for you. I am very aware of what you're facing, which makes it all the more hard for me to tell you what I have to. But I cannot keep this from you.'

Darcelle bristled at her sister's initial admonishment but then her expression clouded. 'What are you talking about? What do you have to tell me?'

Florentyna cleared her throat. 'Darcelle,' she began taking a step toward the princess, 'I'm so sorry, but I have to tell you that Saria is dead.'

At first Darcelle didn't look as though she'd heard the queen properly, frowning at her while she turned the words spoken over in her mind. Then her mouth moved and they barely heard her murmur, although Cassien could lip read. She repeated it. 'Dead?'

And then Florentyna was upon her, opening up her arms. 'Oh dearest, I needed to tell you before —'

Darcelle pushed her rudely aside. 'Dead? What do you mean?' she shrieked.

Florentyna didn't show any offence but continued calmly. 'There is no way to say this and make it easier on you. So here's the truth … the facts. She was killed yesterday morning … and very nearly so was I. The —'

'Killed!' Darcelle hissed, her voice breaking.

Burrage had obviously decided this was the moment for him to join in. 'Your highness,' he said, trying to exude calm, 'the dowager was inadvertently caught up in an attempt on Queen Florentyna's life. Assassins descended on Rittylworth Monastery and killed not only your stepmother, but Felyx, as well as the soldiers guarding her majesty. They almost achieved what they'd set out to do, which was to murder the queen,' he said.

Darcelle looked between them and Cassien was struck by how suddenly composed she appeared. He frowned, staying in the shadows.

The others seemed to be ready to ignore her behaviour and just hang on her words. No doubt the queen was simply relieved the truth was out. 'Why were you at Rittylworth?' Darcelle demanded.

'I had gone to see our stepmother,' Florentyna replied.

'Why?'

'About your wedding. I wanted her to be a part of it. I wanted to offer her a hand of peace.'

Darcelle gave a smirk. 'You?'

Florentyna showed no offence. 'Yes. I was offering her the opportunity to leave the monastery early, help you to prepare for your special day, witness your marriage and be able to share in your life beyond it. It is what she wanted. And I know it is what you wanted.' She shook her head. 'I wanted you to be happy and I knew that Saria and I finding some common ground would help you to start your life afresh, with no familial burdens.'

Darcelle seemed to ignore her sister's gentle and generous offering of peace. 'You tried to bribe her?'

Cassien was astonished but remained silent, stepping back deeper into the chamber's shadows, well away from the glow of the flames.

'What were you offering her?' the princess demanded.

'The chance to go to Cipres with —'

'And get rid of the thorn in your side?'

Florentyna regarded her sister. She stood unnaturally still as she did so. In the space of her pause, Cassien felt the atmosphere in the queen's solar turn frigid. 'You forget I had already rid myself of that thorn.'

'But she had nearly completed her mourning! She was on the brink of release from Rittylworth.'

'What is your point?' Florentyna asked, frowning.

'You had her killed, didn't you?'

'What?' the queen and Burrage said as one. Florentyna threw him a sharp look. 'Darcelle, listen to me now, you silly child. I have been lenient with you because this is an emotional time and no bride-to-be should learn of the death of someone she loves on the brink of betrothal festivities. However, I will no longer tolerate your attitude. You risked my anger only a day or so ago and I forgave you. No longer! I'll ask you to remember whom you address right now. Your queen, and she commands you to beware of that sharp tongue of yours. It may cut too deep and it might not be me who bleeds. I told you I would give you the facts. Here they are.

'Saria died as I was trying to keep her safe from attackers. We had no idea what was underway other than a hail of arrows that felled Felyx and another soldier as our party arrived into Rittylworth. We couldn't risk the dowager being kidnapped, or her life being put in danger if she was used as a bargaining tool, so in the little time we had we came up with a plan to get Saria and myself away from the monastery over the hills on foot. It nearly worked. Two other loyal men died trying to keep our stepmother and myself safe. I had to watch a brave guard die in front of me and Saria was cut down cruelly and unnecessarily. I held her as she died and her final words were ones of love ... for you and for our father. It only took a few moments for me to understand just how much she loved you both. She died courageously, determined I should prevail. If not for Cassien, Hubbard would have defied her dying wish.'

Cassien saw it. Had the others? The flare of recognition. Darcelle had schooled her features within a blink, but he'd seen it: she knew the name Hubbard. He was sure. She was looking at him now and he pasted on a blank expression that revealed nothing of what he suspected.

'You saved my sister?'

He nodded.

'How did you know?'

He squinted slightly. 'Know that she would be attacked?'

Darcelle nodded.

'I didn't, your highness. I happened along,' he said carefully.

'Blind luck. Not in time to save Saria, although every fibre of my being wishes it different,' Florentyna impressed, searching Darcelle's face as she reached for her hands and took them. 'I don't know why this happened but I will get to the bottom of it ... if just for Saria's sake. Someone knows something. This man was not sent by anyone with a shallow purse. He had been promised wealth for my head.'

Cassien could see Florentyna was having very little impact on her sister, whose expression had become unreadable.

'What happened to him?'

'Who?'

'Hubbard.'

Cassien was impressed that she remembered the detail of his name amidst the emotional turmoil … it was all the more obvious that she already knew it.

'Cassien killed him,' the queen replied.

Darcelle flicked a gaze around the three of them. 'So you didn't learn who was behind this attack?'

Florentyna shook her head. 'No. More's the pity. He was never going to allow himself to be taken alive. He mocked us.'

Burrage moved to practicalities. 'Your highness,' he said, addressing Darcelle. 'We must look out for your safety too. A special guard has been organised for yourself and King Tamas.'

'Tamas,' Darcelle whispered. 'He was so looking forward to meeting Saria. I can't believe this has happened.' Cassien heard the false concern. Did the others hear it too?

'We're all trying to come to terms with it,' Florentyna said gently. 'I felt you needed to know this now, in spite of the upset it causes you. Now is exactly the time when you must show yourself to be strong in the fashion of our forebears.'

They were rallying words but to Cassien, Darcelle looked unimpressed. She licked her lips and looked far from crushed by grief.

'I will be fine,' Darcelle insisted, sounding to her sister as though she was already rallying. 'We must cancel this evening.'

'Surely not …' Florentyna said, her voice trailing off with indecision. 'Is that your wish … truly?'

Darcelle nodded. 'It is. I wish to grieve. I need some time alone, maybe a quiet supper with Tamas. Will you forgive me?'

'Oh, my darling,' Florentyna said and swept her sibling into her long arms, wrapping them around her to protect and console. 'Of course, whatever you want.' She looked over Darcelle's golden head to where Burrage stood by. She nodded at him. 'Make our apologies. Everyone is to eat and enjoy the food and wine that the palace has prepared, but we should cancel the entertainment. Those coming will understand that our family is grieving.'

Burrage nodded and left the room, glancing at Cassien. Perhaps he expected him to leave as well, but Cassien was going nowhere.

Darcelle sniffed. He could see her cheeks were wet as she pulled away from the queen. 'Is my mother here?'

'She's lying in the chapel, darling. She looks very peaceful.'

'That is where I should be. I will mourn her this night and tomorrow I will be ready to face our guests.'

Florentyna shook her head and smiled. 'Shar, but I'm so proud of you. I didn't want to make any decision without you, but this is the right one. Tamas will understand too. Would you like to tell him or do you need me to do so?'

'I can tell him. He can sit with me in the chapel for a while.'

'Would you like any other company …' Florentyna asked softly, tentatively.

Darcelle shook her head, weeping slightly harder. Cassien wasn't feeling proud of himself for being so cynical, but he heard only empty tears. He had no doubt that Darcelle was sad at the loss of Saria. He was also certain this was a charade — an act for the sake of Florentyna.

'I must change into mourning clothes,' Darcelle whimpered.

Florentyna nodded. 'Just for tonight, dear one. Then I would like to see you in your finery looking splendid for Tamas. Listen to me now,' she said, putting an arm around her sister's shoulder. 'Saria wanted you to be joyful. You owe it to her to fulfil that wish. You must continue with your marriage arrangements and permit yourself to be happy.'

'But what will everyone think of me?'

Florentyna gave a scoffing sound. 'As far as the rest of the empire is concerned, the dowager willingly took herself off to Rittylworth to mourn the passing of her beloved king and husband. She has been out of sight for long enough that she has slipped from the tongues of the gossips and from the minds of most. I will make an announcement and I know everyone will understand why we do not have some days of mourning, given the distance that Tamas has travelled to present himself at our court.

'There will be time for mourning when you're married — it's how she would want it. We must ensure Tamas has a special time here with you and that the people of Morgravia and those who have travelled from Briavel and from the mountain regions can also celebrate with you.' She smiled. 'You must not allow anything to dissuade you that you are not behaving entirely as I consider appropriate. If anyone wants to complain — they can come and present themselves to me. All right?'

Cassien watched Darcelle give a wan smile before nodding. 'I'll be ready for the picnic tomorrow.'

Florentyna kissed her head. 'That's the spirit.'

Darcelle made to leave and then turned back. 'What are you going to do about the attack? I mean, do you think whoever is behind this will stop?'

The queen shrugged a shoulder. 'I doubt it. But that's why Burrage is having everything that passes my lips tasted first ...' Darcelle opened her mouth with astonishment '... and why Cassien will shadow my every move from now on.' Darcelle flicked him a burning gaze. 'I will just have to be very mindful until my enemy is discovered.'

Darcelle's eyes fluttered for moment. 'So you still plan to hunt him down.'

Cassien pushed off from the wall. 'He or she,' he said quietly.

He watched her swallow beneath his gaze. She turned back to her sister. 'Where do you begin? Do you have any clues? We're safe in Stoneheart, surely?'

'That's just it. I believe the danger comes from within.'

Cassien wished the queen had not played this card. Nevertheless, he was intrigued to see Darcelle visibly pale and raise a trembling hand to her forehead as though suddenly overcome.

'I will be in the chapel if you need me,' she said.

Cassien bowed as the princess lifted her silk gown a fraction and rustled out of the solar.

When she'd gone, he watched Florentyna take a deep breath, her hand placed against her belly as if to steady its churn.

'Can I get you a water, majesty?'

She smiled bleakly. 'No, I'll be fine. I'm just sad it took death to remind me just how much I love Darcelle. She's all I have left. We argued before I left for Rittylworth. It was the most unpleasant exchange I've ever experienced and it was over Saria, of course. I don't want to ever see my sister look at me that way again and I don't ever want to feel such loathing for her attitude either. Saria's passing has forced me to forgive.'

Cassien nodded, kept his own counsel on his suspicions for now. 'Majesty, I realise that this event has caused anxiety and upheaval for everyone, but may I urge you not to lose sight of the bigger threat. We need to be ever-watchful.'

'Yes, I understand. I had better go and make personal apologies to Tamas.'

'Forgive me if I'm overstepping my place, majesty, but how are you holding up?'

She gave him a smile and sighed. 'I've read the history books that spoke of my great-grandmother's heroics in her time. I'm keeping in mind that she must have been terribly frightened, but she never once compromised her position. I will take heart from that.' Then she added quietly. 'Besides, I have you now.'

TWENTY-THREE

Cassien was supposed to spend the night with Ham in a small chamber, normally used for storage, adjacent to the queen's suite. Servants had cleared it, made up two cots; despite Burrage's protestations and Florentyna's embarrassment, he had assured them both he would be fine.

While Ham had slept the sleep of babes with his belly full, Cassien had sat staring at a rendition of the dragon carved over the queen's bedchamber door. The floor was cold, the moonlight was fiercely bright and the regular changes of the guards that he personally had posted also kept him alert. At each change he would straighten, stretch and take a walk around the corridors flanking the queen's chamber. Twice he'd made the journey down the great staircase and gone out into the frosty night to check on the guards watching her various windows. They were a long way down from where Florentyna slept, but Cassien was taking no chances. Men encircled the wing from below, and above on the battlements, and again he was changing them each bell. The rotation would continue day and night. He'd gladly lie on the floor by her bed if he didn't think Chancellor Burrage would have an apoplectic fit.

He didn't need to look at the gently burning candle in the small alcove in the wall to know it was aevum. The middle of the night was sensed through his body, finely honed to know instinctively. It was the period trey from dawn, as the Brotherhood called it, the three hours when men were mostly still and the Brothers went about their killing, if need be. If the Brothers used trey to steal up on victims, so might a demon, he reasoned. He thought about the men on the palace's uppermost reaches. Some, he suspected, would already be leaning against the merlons and dozing, hoping not to be caught. Yes, this was the time for any enemy to strike.

There had only recently been a guard change. A whole bell before they'd rotate again. He stared at the door; the dragon stared back … and dared him.

Cassien chose.

He shifted to lean against the balustrade and used the skill he'd possessed since his earliest memories of life, and withdrew into himself. It happened fluidly. One moment he was entirely in control of his physical self, the next he was a guest of his body. He would give himself the briefest possible time; he just had to be sure nothing was approaching in a spiritual form.

Perhaps he should have woken Ham, asked him to sit next to him. Too late. Even withdrawn into the tiny kernel that was his spirit, his gaze was still fixed on the dragon. He drew some comfort from it.

Watch over me, Fynch, he cast out. And then Cassien lifted fully away from his body and he roamed.

In the Great Forest, a she-wolf looked up from her nuzzling brood. They were too sleepy to fully suckle, but were safe in the comfort of their mother's warmth, her smell, her rhythmic, reassuring breathing. She wondered what had disturbed her and eased herself away from her cubs, which moaned at the loss and tucked themselves in around each other. She nuzzled them closer, paused until they were quiet again before moving soundlessly out of the cave-like overhang of rock and trees where the pups had been born. In the clearing she could see the other wolves from the pack — some with their head resting on their paws, others lying on their sides. Her mate looked up as she emerged, but satisfied himself that she was simply stretching and settled his large dark head back onto his huge paws and closed his eyes. She knew he wouldn't sleep. He was as alert as she, determined they raise their young safely to maturity.

Romaine stretched her large, lean frame while she listened. There was nothing to hear other than the comforting, muffled sounds of the forest at night, where it was so quiet even an insect could make itself heard scrambling over leaf fall. Clearly nothing unusual had made a noise to disturb her or the other wolves would also be startled. She straightened, lowered her ears. *Cassien.* Romaine closed her eyes and listened inwardly while she cast out her senses and waited.

She heard the echo. *Watch over me, Fynch.*

301

Cassien was roaming. She hated him roaming at any time, because of its inherent dangers, but especially now when she was nowhere near to look after his cooling body. Romaine tipped back her head and howled.

In the Wild, many leagues into the far northeast, Fynch stirred fitfully and woke suddenly. He thought he'd heard a call. He swung his legs down from the modest pallet he slept on, padding across the stone floor warmed by a hot spring that ran deep below the hut in which he lived. His predecessor, Elysius, had chosen his position well, he thought absently, sighing at the small comfort on this cool night.

He stared out the window to the moon and a clear spring night sky. It would be sunny tomorrow. His gaze searched the near and far distance. Nothing stirred.

Fynch listened. All was quiet. He blinked, turned inward and heard the whisper reach him.

Watch over me, Fynch.

And then he heard in his mind the anguished howl of a wolf.

Cassien was roaming.

Trust him, Romaine, he soothed, casting the thought back to the she-wolf in the forest. *The sacrifice is his to make, his burden to bear.*

Moving as swiftly as he could he roamed Stoneheart. Seeing it from many different angles in this guise, Cassien began to appreciate its sombre, clean-lined beauty. Whimsy was permitted in its courtyards and groves, some beautiful connecting passages; they were perfectly structured to suit the inherent 'order' that was Stoneheart and yet each so creative within itself. These particular spaces ensured airflow would help the palace breathe and allow the perfume of blossom and flowers to scent its halls and occasionally catch drifts of conversation or birdsong ... harmony was one way of thinking about it. He admired it; even in the darkness, it stood proud.

Cassien was aware of the cathedral soaring up to the gods nearby. He desperately wanted to visit it, especially in this form, but he was mindful that every moment might cost an animal its life as much as threaten his own. He focused on the palace, searching for magic or anything of an ethereal power, and satisfied himself that no demon was within its walls ... not tonight anyway.

He found his body again, hating the way it stared so sightlessly at him in the form of invisible spirit. He dreaded the cost, but hesitated no longer and re-entered himself.

As he stretched his stiff limbs, feeling the first waves of nausea wash over him, he heard the screams begin.

Stoneheart woke rudely to the calls of despair. The servants had begun the panic, when those up early enough to start baking the day's bread had found the bodies of doves and swallows littering the ground outside the kitchen.

Next, two horses were found dead, along with sundry dogs and cats, as well as ducks, geese, even one of Stoneheart's cows.

The killing rampage continued. People hadn't woken from their sleep: immediate discoveries were two pages, a pair of scullery maids, a guard. One noble, who had drunk a little too much wine and had strayed out of the great hall, was found slumped by one the wells, stiff in death, as had a gong boy, one of the stable hands, one of the gatekeepers and a travelling monk.

Florentyna emerged from her rooms, still in her night attire, her expression anxious.

'What's happening?' she said, pushing away servants who ran up and begged her to go back into her rooms. 'Cassien!'

He was bending over the balustrade, desperately sucking in air.

'Go inside, your majesty,' he growled, nodding at the two servants. 'I'll find out.'

Relief coursed through him when she obeyed, although not before she pointed at him. 'In the time it takes me to get properly attired I want you back here and reporting to me. And you, Elsey, fetch Chancellor Burrage. Where is Sharley? I need to hurry.'

Cassien watched through glazed eyes as the queen, gorgeously dishevelled, allowed herself to be ushered back into her chamber. He steadied his breathing, wrestled control over the weakening nausea and opened the door of the storeroom. Ham was already washing his face in a bowl of water.

'Where have you been?' the boy asked, looking worried. 'What's all the yelling about?'

Cassien shook his head. 'I don't know,' he lied. He thought he could guess, but couldn't imagine why a few dead animals might cause so much commotion. 'I'm going to find out.'

'Cassien, you look sick.'

'I didn't sleep well,' he replied.

'No, it's worse than that. Do you want to sit down?'

'There isn't time.'

'What's happened to you?' Ham held a hand up. 'If you're about to tell me you've eaten something rotten, don't. I know you ate nothing last night.'

Cassien regarded Ham through bleary eyes. This was bad. He didn't think it would hit him this strongly. A fresh wave of nausea rolled through him. He turned suddenly and fell to his knees at the pail and retched. Ham sensibly waited, saying nothing until Cassien's heaves were done.

'You look like you're dying,' he said, dipping a cloth into the water bowl. 'Here.'

Cassien groaned, couldn't move momentarily because the room was spinning. The pain was immense. It felt like his heart was being squeezed out of his chest and that his bones were shattering like glass. He gradually became aware of Ham wiping his face with the damp cloth and its coolness was a balm.

'Stay here,' Ham said. 'Do not move.'

The boy disappeared.

He didn't know how long he sat there. It felt like an eternity until he heard his friend return. He could hear something being stirred.

'Drink this,' said a new voice.

'Who are —'

'Drink, Cassien!' Ham ordered and was suddenly pouring the contents down his throat.

He spluttered and gulped, coughed and roared his displeasure at the intensely bitter potion, but Ham got it down him and as suddenly as he'd grabbed him, he let him go.

'What in Shar's almighty balls was that?' he said, spitting.

The new voice chuckled. 'Witch's brew,' she said.

He blinked, focused and looked into the eyes of a woman he couldn't immediately age. She wasn't old but she was certainly well into her third decade, with a square-shaped face and hair of indeterminate colour piled into an untidy bun. One aspect of her was striking though … her eyes. He suspected that in his stupor he was imagining their odd colour.

'Who are you?' he groaned.

'I'm Tilda. I don't know what's happening around the palace but anyone could be forgiven for believing a plague has hit. You're the lucky ones.'

He felt the mist clearing. This was unusual after a roaming episode. 'What did you give me?' he asked, realising he was right — one of her eyes was dark like the berry of the ivy that crept up the palace walls, the other was like a golden leaf faded to dry brown.

'I met your young friend last night. We broke bread together at the queen's pleasure, in her kitchens.' She shrugged. 'Queen Florentyna likes my special teas. I make regular deliveries to Stoneheart and yesterday happened to be one of those times. Hamelyn seemed intrigued by my skills.'

'Which are?'

'Herbs.' She hesitated. 'Curatives.'

'Well, your nasty brew has helped,' he said, surprised at how rapidly the symptoms were diminishing. 'Thank you.'

'Go fetch me some fresh water, Hamelyn,' she said and he obediently ducked out with the bowl. She sat on the cot and regarded Cassien.

His eyes met hers.

'That was no upset belly,' she said quietly. 'This is an illness brought on by magic.'

He hoped it didn't show how startled he was.

'You don't deny it,' she continued evenly.

'Who are you?' he repeated.

She shook her head. 'No-one special. Be careful with that skill. I think you already know its effects.'

He nodded.

'But still you used it.'

'I had to.'

She took a slow breath as if too fearful to ask. 'And is it your magic that has killed?'

'No-one will miss a few pigeons.'

She helped him to stand. The dizziness had abated and he was further impressed with her bitter brew. 'It's not a few pigeons,' she replied, as Ham returned.

The boy's face was pinched with shock while his voice sounded dulled. 'There are people dead all over the palace,' he said, the rise and fall of his usually lively tone absent.

'What?' Cassien exclaimed.

Ham nodded, his eyes moistening. 'Meek, the boy I was with last evening ... he's one of the dead. No-one knows why. I don't even know how many.'

Cassien stared open-mouthed at him, guilt tightening in his throat like poison as reality hit. He'd never before roamed in a town or village. It had always been in the forest and it had only affected animals and birds; his roaming did not kill once Romaine had guided him to the Thicket that protected, and she also warned the forest creatures. It hadn't occurred to him that his magic would kill people or that they were so vulnerable to fall in numbers. His gaze slid awkwardly to Tilda.

'Be careful, Master Cassien,' she reiterated, and pressed a vial into his hand. 'I hope you don't need it. I don't think this is going to be as much help next time.'

'Why not?' he whispered.

'Because your skill learns,' she said cryptically. 'And so must you,' she added, staring hard at him before reaching for her shawl and twisting it expertly around her shoulders and over her head like a hood. 'I can't be caught up here, I've been told not to wander the palace. If I'm found ...' She didn't finish. 'Farewell. I'm glad I could help.'

'Wait,' he said, his mind scrambling to make sense of Ham's disturbing news. 'What will happen if you're found?'

Tilda paused. 'I've never risked finding out,' she said softly.

'Then let me accompany you,' he offered. 'At least let me see you back to the kitchen, where you are obviously permitted.' At her hesitation, he added. 'Please. If you are with me, no-one will question you.'

'All right,' Tilda said, looking grateful, 'but we must hurry.'

'Ham, find out as much as you can. And if the queen is looking for me, tell her I will be back very soon.' He left with Tilda before Ham could ask questions of his own.

'How does it learn?' Cassien pressed, without any preamble, knowing time was his foe.

'I sense it is an ancient magic. Old magics are cunning,' she replied.

'So the cure you gave me today ...'

'It wasn't a cure. It was simply a remedy for pain and the feeling of illness. What you possess within, Master Cassien,' she whispered, 'no-one can cure.'

They could hear guards. He was ready with his explanation, but would prefer not to be confronted. 'Tilda, where do you live?'

She gave a sad gust of a laugh. 'I don't live anywhere. I roam.'

At her words, he felt a chill. Was she toying with him? He frowned at her as they hurried down the passageway and decided there was no guile in her. She had not given him away to anyone — not even in Ham's presence had she been anything but cautious.

'You roam the land ... like a tinker?'

She smiled. 'Yes. I come routinely to the palace. I will not be back here now for a few moons. Queen Florentyna has her stocks.'

'Where will you go?'

'Where the wind blows me. Ah, here we are,' she said, relief evident in her tone.

'Which direction are the winds blowing?'

Tilda regarded him and he was struck by the intensity of her odd gaze.

'Northeast, perhaps,' she said with a vague shrug.

Cassien disguised his surprise with a frown. 'But that's the Great Forest.'

'And beyond,' she qualified, 'toward the Wild.' There was a message there; he sensed it, even though her words were spoken casually enough. 'I and my donkey cart will take the most direct route.' She smiled.

People were running past them now and the tension was palpable. Much as he wanted to question her more, it was inappropriate. Besides, he needed to reassure Florentyna.

'Thank you, Tilda.'

'Learn from your experience,' she added as she turned, echoing her previous caution.

A wide-eyed serving girl darted by. She was a pretty young thing who was so startled by all the sudden and early activity that she still hadn't taken the rags out of her curls. Stoneheart was in panic.

As he moved through the palace, retracing his steps, he gathered that more and more people were being found dead at their station or in the immediate surrounding fields. It seemed to him that the majority of victims were outside Stoneheart's walls though, and perhaps that was a clue. He hoped he was right.

Cassien took the stairs two at a time and when he arrived back at their shared room, Ham was waiting for him, his expression solemn, direct.

'It was you, wasn't it?'

Cassien glared at him. 'Whatever makes you say that? Tilda has no —'

'It wasn't Tilda. It was the sword. It knew.'

Cassien took a slow breath. 'What?'

'It woke me. It seemed to call, although to explain it that way seems too simple.'

'What did it want you for?' Cassien said, forcing himself not to grab Ham and shake the answer from him.

'To be close.'

He swallowed. 'What do you mean?'

Ham shrugged. 'I don't know what I mean. And the wolf said I had to keep you safe.'

'The wolf?'

'I think I dreamed her ...'

Her. Romaine!

'... but even so,' Ham continued, 'I obeyed her.'

'And what did the wolf tell you?'

'She simply said I must watch over you. Let no-one interfere as you —'

'As I what?'

'Roamed,' Ham finished awkwardly, with a worried gaze.

Cassien had closed his eyes.

'So it was you?' Ham asked again.

He nodded, hanging his head. 'Yes. In the past it has damaged me, and initially caused the death of animals. I had no idea it was powerful enough to kill on this scale.'

Ham gave a shrug. 'Now you do.' He said no more about it.

They parted and Cassien went in search of the queen, found her dressed and with a mix of frustrated concern in her expression. 'There you are.'

'Forgive me,' he said bowing and, as he pulled up to attention, realised he was now in her bedchamber. He turned away.

Florentyna didn't seem to care. 'This is no time for modesty, Cassien. I really thought I'd lost you too, the way you were sickening.'

'No, majesty,' he said over his shoulder, 'I believe I ate something that disagreed with me.'

She let it go. 'What is happening?' she exclaimed, turning on her heel. 'Can someone explain it? And where is Burrage?'

'He must be busy with all the problems, majesty,' her maid said.

'Thank you, Sharley. Leave it, it's fine,' she said, as the girl reached to tidy her hair. 'Today is not a day to be worrying about how I look.' The maid curtsied and left. 'What in Shar's name is happening?' she asked again.

'Perhaps the physics can tell us if it's a case of poisoning or ...' He didn't know what to say.

'My sister is fine. I've had word back. So is Tamas, thank Shar!'

If only she knew the relief flooding his body at her reassurance.

'And you are safe, majesty.'

'Well, I'm not staying here, Cassien. Come on, I have to do my best to relieve the confusion.' She strode out of her rooms and guards snapped to attention, ready to follow her. Cassien held up a hand to tell them to wait there, that he could handle her safety for now.

Darcelle met them at the stairs, ignoring his bow and launched straight into her private complaint.

'Florentyna, please don't tell me we have to cancel the festivities.' She must have realised how callous she sounded, particularly as she had been so grief-stricken the previous evening. 'I mean,' she hesitated, 'I'm having to be strong over my loss, but for the sake of Tamas and what we're trying to achieve between our realms it's important we don't let the problems of Morgravia spill over into his visit. You do agree, surely?'

Florentyna took a breath. 'Darcelle, people have mysteriously died through the night ....'

'None of them important,' Darcelle countered, censuring herself when her sister gasped. 'That came out wrong. I mean none are important to the future of Morgravia's critical relationship with Cipres. I want you to keep your promise. We have to put on the right face. No-one needs to know, not even Tamas.'

'You don't think word will get out?'

'We can contain it. Just for as long as he's here.' She grabbed Florentyna's hands. 'Let me marry him now.'

'What?'

'Let's turn his visit into wedding celebrations. The sooner it happens, the better.'

'Darcelle —' Florentyna began.

'I know you think I'm young and impetuous and no doubt that's how you'll always see me! The fact is, I'm going to be married whether it's this blossomtide or next. I won't change my mind either. We have a king in our midst as keen to marry me as I him and in doing so we will bind our realms. Why wait?' She searched her sister's face. 'This is something our father wanted.'

'I can't agree to this,' Florentyna replied, despite her sister's pleading. 'I'm sorry but —'

The princess rounded on her. 'This is all about jealousy, Florentyna. Are you so warped by your own loneliness that you can't let me have my happiness? Just because no-one wants to become your king shouldn't mean that I can't have mine.'

Cassien watched the queen's face cloud. A storm was gathering within. He wondered whether to distract the two women, but Florentyna spoke before he could act.

'I don't need a king to be queen … or are you forgetting that?' Florentyna's tone cut sharply. 'You really are the most self-centred brat. You shame the Dragon throne.' Darcelle's eyes had narrowed to slits, but Florentyna hadn't finished. 'I have no doubt that marriage, and the plans you've so ably made, are taking an emotional as much as physical toll, but affairs of the state do not play second fiddle to your personal ups and downs. Our private sorrow aside, people have dropped dead around us. And while I agree that we will contain this information as best we can within Stoneheart, you should be as concerned as I am about the need to comfort and reassure our staff. That's our job.

'Darcelle,' she said, her voice dropping lower, becoming more intense, 'the Crown is not a right without cost. Everything in life has a price, little sister, and your fancy silks, the cringing courtiers, the wealth, the status, the power you wield, has a price of duty.' She stood tall over Darcelle as she took a step closer. 'And now you must pay it.' Cassien held his breath. For all her reticence, Florentyna had spine and her sense of responsibility to her people was palpable. Darcelle should not have pushed her sister this hard. 'I am cancelling further festivities. Tamas is welcome to stay on, but there will be no further formal celebration in the immediate future. Is that clear?'

Darcelle's face was colourless save two high spots of bright pink, as though her cheeks had been pinched. 'So, you'd do anything to prevent me having the status of queen, because then we'd be equal. That's your nightmare, isn't it Florentyna? The prettier, more talented, more socially adept, more beloved sister on an equal footing ... your last little bastion of power removed.'

Florentyna shook her head, barely noticing that Cassien was moving along a pair of serving girls who were staring at the arguing royals. 'You really are empty-headed, aren't you, Darcelle? All you want is to use the Crown, to take from it. You disgust me. Go to your rooms or I'll have you taken there and put under guard.'

Darcelle's mouth opened in horror. Fortunately, no sound issued forth.

'Go!' Florentyna said. 'I don't think I can bear to look upon you right now. I have dead people in my palace and no explanation.'

'How I wish you were one of them!' Darcelle snapped and turned on her heel.

Florentyna also turned away, leaned her weight on the banister rail and drew a deep, steadying breath. Cassien felt momentarily helpless. His inclination was to hold her, but he resisted.

'I've managed to turn the only member of my family left to me entirely against me,' she growled. 'I know you and Burrage are thinking it — and I'm fighting it — but perhaps Darcelle was behind the attack at Rittylworth. There was real venom in her attack just now. She wishes me dead.'

He could hear how angry she still was and as he reached for the right words to reply a young woman skittered up.

'Your majesty,' she warbled. He could see she had been crying now and her eyes were still moist and red.

Florentyna straightened, breathing deeply. She turned, composed. 'Yes?'

'We've found Chancellor Burrage.'

'Thank Shar's mercy,' she said, relief obvious in the slump of her shoulders. 'Now, I can —'

'He's dead, your majesty,' the woman cut across the queen's words, forgetting herself.

Florentyna sucked in a breath and this time Cassien did step forward with helping hand.

'Are you sure?' he demanded of the servant.

'His body is already stiffening,' she said.

Her words brought a fresh gasp from Florentyna. 'This can't be happening. I must see for myself.'

Before he could stop her, the queen was running.

TWENTY-FOUR

King Tamas frowned. He had been given a suite of chambers in one of the wings of Stoneheart that clustered around a charming courtyard dedicated to herbs. From where he was now sitting, it looked to him like a work of art, a living sculpture in green. He was enchanted by the well-tended and clearly constantly replenished garden, for even the hedrill looked young, with tender leaves. At home the hedrill in the kitchen herb gardens turned woody within a season.

He found it intriguing that this palace, known for its imposing mass and dull, dark stone, was innately feminine at its heart. It was a lovely discovery, given that his own capital was pale and beautiful, often compared to a nymph. He was thoroughly enjoying some quiet time, made all the more pleasant by the fact that he had banished the ever-present retinue of servants and counsellors from his side.

So now he sat in the thaw sun of a Morgravian morning and inhaled the scent from the herbs; together they formed a new fragrance, with wafts of rosemary and shirl twisting around hedrill and thyme, jessamy and mint. He looked at the small posy of colourful flowers he'd picked and wondered why herbs were not used more often in the more lavish floral displays around Cipres.

He'd grown up learning about herbs and food, having spent a lot of his days lurking around the Ciprean palace kitchens. His closest friend in those childhood years had been Lacey, one of the scullery maids, so pretty she made most others appear dull. And despite her natural radiance she seemed to possess a limitless grasp on all things practical and worldly — from finding herbs in the garden to knowing how to bring out a bruise quickly. Lacey could run as fast as Tamas, sling a punch as quickly and take a black eye without more than a whimper. Whenever he could slip away from weapons and fighting drills, or horse training, or the dreaded academic studies, they were together. She was the first girl to kiss him and the last one he had truly loved. At ten summers his parents had thought it time he leave behind his childhood friends, especially those not of the same social standing, and he was removed to live in Tallinor.

When he returned fourteen moons later, Lacey was gone from the palace and he had no doubt his mother had made sure it happened. His father expected him to make his own way while he, something of an adventurer and learned man, travelled constantly on long voyages, leaving much of the raising of the three boys to their mother. The queen was a powerful figure, possessing a drive and ambition that their quieter father fed off. His mother essentially ran the realm while the king disappeared on his adventures. One couldn't criticise the king too loudly, since his travels yielded advances in so many areas of knowledge that Cipres, despite its size, seemed to be at the forefront of everything from farming methods to education, as well as creating new industries in varied fields such as perfume and fruit preserving; and in developing its famed blue paint, toolook — with a lustre like no other — and also a pure and iridescent green known as ferge. These became so eye-poppingly expensive that the Crown had to take control of production as people killed each other for the right to collect the raw material.

And then the plague had come. It was believed to have arrived with the flotilla of ships that had sailed his father back to Cipres in Tamas's eighteenth summer. The king's gift to Cipres included far more than the silver pearls, a raft of new medicines and a beverage called dinch.

None of the medicines he'd acquired could touch the disease, which had travelled with the insects that made their way off the ship on the backs of the rats they infested, as well as in the hair and beards of the men who then carried them into homes, taverns, even the palace.

People had begun to die at a chaotic, tragic rate. Each day yielded a hundred more corpses. Royalty was not immune. The 'Venturer' plague, as it became known, claimed the lives of his mother and both brothers; he was spared, although he never understood why.

His sensitive father had died not long after from what was officially recorded as a fall. Tamas suspected, however, that King Wurt could not bear the guilt and had thrown himself from the cliffs.

Despite the depth of his grief, Tamas had risen to the challenge of taking charge of the realm. Cipres was small but advanced, and Tamas knew that he must work to the kingdom's strengths to lift it out of grief. Education was the key and Lacey was his motivation; he could only imagine what she might have achieved if she'd had the benefit of his teachers to complement her ability to absorb information and extend her practical skills. Maybe their love could have been kindled rather than destroyed. Tamas implemented a new system to teach the young to read, to write, to calculate in their heads — no matter their family's position in society.

Cipres had been right in its forward-thinking approach and, as a result, even its farms used methods that were ahead of their time, and yields from smallholdings soon tripled the grain harvests achieved by much larger pastures in neighbouring lands.

The young king had also travelled to every town, village and hamlet to comfort, offer support and generally see to the wellbeing of his people. He opened up the palace coffers to give aid to those in serious need — to families who'd lost their livelihood, to children who'd lost parents, to convents and monasteries that were taking care of the sick, lonely, needy, heartbroken. He built three new centres of medicine, strategically placed up and down the realm so their restoratives and knowledge were accessible to most people within a few days' ride. And he built another wing to the learning academy specifically for physics. His schools — perhaps his greatest achievement and modelled on those of Cailech, when he was a young king in the Razors — were established in every major town over a certain size. He implemented a new system of rewards to families whose children achieved seven full cycles of consistent attendance at school — summer to summer. Cipres now had a new generation of educated farmers, smiths, bakers, millers.

Change was catching up with Tamas too; he was reaching the end of his fourth decade. He was nearly thirty-nine summers, more than twenty of them given to a feverish commitment to the Ciprean cause. In doing so he'd overlooked the most important aspect of what it is to be the sovereign: he'd neglected to take a queen, to give the Crown heirs, to give his people what they probably needed most … the future that children alone could provide.

As if in answer to his realisation, Princess Darcelle had arrived in his life like a breath of fresh, golden promise, brought to him under sail for a gathering of monarchs, but he was sure she was actually delivered to him by benevolent gods. He'd been charmed by her on sight for her beauty, but he appreciated her far more for her strength.

He'd since learned that there were sides to Darcelle's personality he had to overlook. She was wealthy beyond most royals' dreams and was addicted to having only the best; she took power for granted, revelling in the attention it won her, and she liked to use it to manipulate people. Darcelle was used to getting her way as the highly indulged youngest royal of Morgravia.

Thinking strategically, he was convinced she would make a fabulous Queen of Cipres. She was young and could bear him children for many years; a special bonus was that she was surprisingly politically astute, despite her delight in frippery, as he liked to call it. If he could use her manipulative skills for the benefit of furthering the Ciprean good, all the better. And if she were used to getting her way then he should put her in charge of some of his duties where her charm, beauty and skills could persuade people to support the Crown, where perhaps they might be criticising it.

What surprised him most about Darcelle was her affection for him and his sense that it was genuine. He had always believed the better-looking Ciprean princes had perished with the plague. His serious, handsome elder brother would have made a fine king, while the dashing younger brother would have charmed everyone into doing anything he asked of them. Tamas smiled at their memory — even so many years later, he missed them.

He was not so naïve he didn't appreciate that Darcelle's fondness for him was partly fuelled by the crown he would place on her head at the same time as he put his ring on her finger. This didn't matter to him — or so he'd convinced himself — as long as she cared enough for him that they might be good friends, good partners, a good royal team. The Cipreans were demanding a royal family, some even questioning his leanings. Did he love Darcelle? He didn't know. Apart from Lacey and one other — a child he had no right to love from afar — he'd never felt anything for any woman other than lust, and he could do so much worse than beautiful Darcelle. Besides, there was no question that to marry Darcelle and link Cipres to Morgravia and the great empire that stretched beyond her boundaries would be a dream come true in every respect.

As if she knew he'd been thinking about her, the double doors into the courtyard burst open and the weeping bride-to-be flung herself into his arms. Tamas waited, knowing the tears would dry and she would explain herself. He was right and realised he would have to get used to this theatrical behaviour from now on. Not every girl had Lacey's attitude.

Tamas listened, filtering her scorn through his own more balanced view. The drama, it seemed, was that Queen Florentyna had cancelled all festivities relating to the engagement. True, the news of so many curious deaths was deeply troubling and brought memories of the plague that had hit Cipres. He made a mental note to do a head count of his soldiers. He didn't believe anyone from his retinue within the palace had suffered.

Darcelle calmed. 'I could sail with you today and we could elope.'

He stroked her hair, which looked and felt like it was spun from golden silk. 'You don't mean that —'

'I do, Tamas, I —'

'Stop, my love. Give an older man some credit,' he jested. 'You would always live to regret such a decision, and besides, why cheat your people of their rightful celebrations?'

'I'm not! She is!'

'She has good reason … certainly I can see it from Florentyna's point of view. If this was Cipres, I too would put this matter ahead of celebrations. She is entirely within her rights to pursue what is killing her people.'

'Putting off our events will not raise the dead.' He gave her a look of mild admonishment at such a heartless comment and Darcelle shrugged. 'Tamas, I'm furious!'

'I can see that and I understand it.'

'She's so angered me. Talking to me like I'm a servant.'

'A servant of the Crown, perhaps?'

She slapped him — not hard, but not playfully either. 'You know exactly what I mean. I deserve more respect. I'm not a child, but she still treats me as one. Florentyna should censure her haughty attitude. What's more, she attacked me publicly. It was humiliating.'

'Would you like me to talk with her?'

'She's being unreasonable — her usual obstinate and superior self!'

She hadn't said nay to him having a word with Florentyna. 'It was only a picnic … a feast or two,' he reasoned, shrugging deeply to make her smile. 'On the journey of life, it's not that important.'

But Darcelle was not amused. 'You're not understanding, are you, my love? It's not the celebrations to which I refer. She has effectively cancelled the marriage.'

Tamas's humour left him. He blinked at her while the words sunk in. 'I don't understand.'

Darcelle became more animated the moment she sensed his confusion. 'No, I didn't think you had. Listen to me, Tamas. You and your Ciprean contingent will likely be told to climb aboard your ships and sail home. She brooks no discussion on when or where any wedding will take place — if at all. She's claiming she's too busy with matters of state, but is too short-sighted to take care of something that's going to do more for Morgravia in the wearing of one small golden ring than she might achieve in a lifetime.' Darcelle gave a bitter smirk. 'She's never been comfortable with me marrying before she does. Let's face it, I don't see a tower of marriage betrothals on her desk. If Florentyna's not careful, our children are all she'll have to pass her precious crown on to.'

'That would suit me,' Tamas thought, not realising he'd expressed it aloud.

'And me,' Darcelle echoed. 'She can't take this away from us.'

Tamas felt on shaky ground for the first time. It had not occurred to him that his happiness could be taken away on Queen Florentyna's whim. Still, he tempered his mood; even in their brief conversation he'd found the queen to be level-headed and charming, and surprisingly beautiful, despite her sister's claims of plainness. 'Let's not jump to any wrong conclusions, my love. I promise you,' he said, taking her hands and kissing them gently, 'nothing will stop me making you my queen.'

She nestled herself into his arms and kissed him hard. 'I know,' she said, 'and I want it more than anything.'

'Be patient then. Let me talk with Florentyna.' As she opened her mouth to interject, he placed his fingertips to her lips. 'Sovereign to sovereign,' he said, with a knowing smile. 'Be still for a while. Wait here for me. I've sent my people away, so I could have some peace. You will not be disturbed, although guards will be posted outside. Listen to the song of birds, the hum of busy bees and enjoy the sunshine. I shall be back shortly with good news. You will have your ring, your crown, your very own realm — that I promise you.'

Darcelle embraced him, and he felt her trust in him. He would not let her down.

Florentyna stared, ashen-faced, at the body of Burrage. He had died on his balcony. It was only on the second search that people had discovered the chancellor slumped outside the windows of his chamber, and had laid him out on his bed.

He looked younger, now that his expression was no longer pulled into its permanent frown of worry.

'... As though his heart just gave out, your majesty. Same as the others. Master Clem, who helped me to move him to the bed, took the liberty of closing his eyes,' a servant prattled.

'Thank you, Fay,' the queen said. Florentyna dabbed at a helpless tear and sniffed. 'Forgive me. He will be missed. I wish I understood what has happened to us. Struck down like this; no sign of disease or struggle.' She noticed Cassien, who had been standing silently by the door observing. 'Leave us, please,' she ordered and the three other people in the room gladly departed.

Cassien presumed she wished the door closed and obliged. He waited.

'Is this the demon's work?' she mused unhappily. 'Is this how he plans to hurt the Crown? Is he going to pick us all off one by one?'

'No, your majesty. This is not the work of a demon,' he answered truthfully.

'How can you know that?'

'I know.'

He said it with such quiet force that she took a step away to scrutinise him. 'Then what is this? Disease? Do I have to cordon off Stoneheart?'

He shook his head.

'And you know this for sure as well?' she said. Her tone was bitter, rather than mocking.

'Your majesty, it will not occur again.' He didn't believe Florentyna would ever trust him if she knew he had caused this through carelessness. 'I trust my instincts implicitly. I'm asking you to do the same. What has happened here is not an attack in any traditional sense.'

'Then what is it?' she demanded in such an agonised voice that he felt her pain.

'An aberration,' he offered.

She stared at him in stunned disbelief. 'Oh, that's going to sound convincing when I have to stand before my people to reassure them.'

'Then don't,' he said. 'Follow the plan to contain it. No-one on the outside of Stoneheart need know. Burrage died of a heart attack, some of old age, the rest of poison from the filligo greens cooked last night and not boiled long enough to take away their toxicity.'

Now she looked at him in undisguised horror. 'Lie?' she said baldly.

'Not entirely a lie if you don't know what the truth is.'

She folded her arms and the set of her mouth told him that his reasoning was not going to wash.

He sighed. 'Offer an explanation to appease the worry and prevent panic. Gather up your staff, hunt down anyone who is aware of the deaths and find out if they only know about isolated ones. If so, let it be. Anyone aware of multiple deaths, counsel them. Do it directly. They will be in awe that the queen is addressing them. Assure them you will find out what caused this, but that you need their silence until you do. Appeal to them, your majesty ... tell them their quiet tongues will prevent panic and more deaths, and that's exactly what you're facing if word begins to get out.'

She nodded. He despised himself for making his lie sound so sensible, when he knew the true culprit.

'Cassien, here lies my chancellor. A very good man. I can't even spare the time to grieve for him because lots of other very good men and women, and some children, have also died equally mysteriously. And he is the second chancellor I have lost in a short period, and both have left me under mysterious circumstances. Something is happening here. I don't understand it and I don't know what to do. I'm under siege. My counsel is dead, my sister suddenly hates me, I have a king under my roof — to whom we're not giving proper respect — and an attempt was made on my life yesterday morning. Can you appreciate how unravelled I am feeling?'

He nodded.

'And you're here, calm as cake, suggesting this is all an aberration, when you yourself are perhaps the strangest of the bizarre happenings.

You arrive out of nowhere, save my life, take charge, speak about demons and have knowledge I need yet you won't share because you belong to a secret society.' Her voice had risen but not become louder.

'My queen, I come to you with only your safety and the preservation of the Crown as my single duty. I will not let you down, but you have to listen to me above any other, and perhaps even against your instincts. Burrage is dead. I am sorry for you, but let him go. Let the dead go and do as I say, for a greater threat is coming.'

'I do trust you, Cassien. Curiously, you seem to be the only bit of sanity I can cling to.'

'Thank you,' he said, glancing over at the desk. 'May I?'

She nodded. Cassien read out a list that Burrage had obviously been swiftly scrawling before he died. The chancellor must have been working into the early morning on this, for Cassien knew his roaming had only begun in the hours before dawn. Burrage had just finished presumably and had gone out onto the balcony. He was convinced now that only those outside of Stoneheart's walls at the time of his roaming were affected by it.

The queen joined him, sighing as she read her chancellor's notes.

'Burrage worked tirelessly for the Crown. I don't think I recall ever asking him about his family or his early life. How selfish of me. And how sad that his last thought was "visit by Merchant Tentrell with Princess Darcelle and King Tamas at fifth bell",' she read. 'It doesn't do him justice that he was concerned with such minutiae while his life was in the balance.' She sounded bereft.

Cassien scanned the list again and focused the queen. 'This is a checklist he was making for today's picnic, I gather?'

She shrugged. 'Looks like it. He dropped dead while working. He was so loyal.'

'Who is Tentrell?' he said, pointing again to the final entry.

'A wealthy merchant from Robissun Marth, as I understand. He has a wedding gift to present. Why? Is it important?'

He gave a small shake of his head. Burrage had died because of Cassien; there was no reason to be looking for clues here. And still something nagged. 'Not important. However, everything on his list relates to the picnic arrangements, except this last entry. Presumably lots of people will be presented to them. Why is this man special?'

She gave a small frowning shake of her head. 'It's not that he is so special. More that his gift is extraordinarily generous. Darcelle would cut off a limb to own it.'

'So Tentrell's personal presentation is considered important,' he qualified.

Florentyna nodded. 'It was important enough for Burrage to write it down. Which meant the request came through him. Burrage is … was,' she corrected in a voice laced with sadness, 'always thorough. Always worried he wouldn't live up to how well Chancellor Reynard took care of us all.' She turned to look at the body again, noting his ink-stained fingers, which she held, as if in farewell.

Cassien could see her mind was turning to maudlin thoughts. 'Let's get Burrage moved to the chapel, majesty. You'll feel better to know he's in Shar's house.'

Nevertheless, having left Burrage to the servants, Cassien still had a nagging feeling that he had missed something.

TWENTY-FIVE

Darcelle was still fuming in the king's courtyard, when she heard someone clear his throat.

'Your highness, please forgive my interruption.'

She leapt up, startled. 'Who let you in?'

The man before her didn't move, clearly not wanting to frighten her. 'The guards permitted me, your highness, and I was told to come by at fifth bell to meet with the king.'

Darcelle looked at him confused. 'Fifth bell?' she repeated. 'The king said nothing to me — in fact I got the impression he was expecting no-one. You absolutely should not be here. I am calling a guard.'

'Please wait, Princess Darcelle. Either King Tamas might have forgotten, or perhaps was never told of the arrangement.'

'Arrangement?'

'I have royal permission,' he said, shaking a small roll of parchment at her. 'It's signed by Chancellor Burrage, delivered to me early last evening. I ... I'm here to see King Tamas. It's about a jewel for you,' the man said hastily, bowing and backing away. 'Please forgive me. I shall leave. I want no trouble.'

'Wait!' Darcelle commanded. 'A jewel, you say?'

'For King Tamas,' the man repeated. 'I was told you would be here as well. I was to expect both of you so I'm sure it's not wrong of me to mention the jewel ...' His voice trailed off.

'Your name?' she demanded, but Darcelle's voice was far less shrill now. She was intrigued. Tamas had failed to mention the visitor, had explicitly said she'd be left in peace. Perhaps this was meant to be a surprise for her from her betrothed. And Burrage ... odd that he hadn't arranged for this man to present his gift to them at the picnic. Even odder that he be given access to the royal rooms. However, she couldn't pass up the chance of a jewel from her beloved.

'I am Merchant Tentrell.'

She frowned, only now registering how good-looking he was, with that dark hair and smoky, dark blue eyes that seemed to hold amusement. He carried himself tall and was dressed in fine clothes, she could see. 'Your name is familiar. You're Morgravian?'

'Oh, through and through, highness,' he said, flashing a bright smile, although he lowered his eyes once more. 'I'm not seen often in Pearlis. I do all my trading in the exotic ports ... cities like Percheron.'

'Oh yes, I'm sure I've heard of you now. Merchant Tentrell ... of Robissun Marth, is that right?'

'It is. But we have not met, surely?'

'No, your reputation precedes you, sir,' she giggled, choosing to flirt now with the handsome merchant. Why she held an image of an older, paunchier man, she couldn't recall. 'Percheron. My sister has a horse from there.'

'Does she?'

'A gift from its zar. The most magnificent *Pearl* mare. She's beautiful. I often wish she were mine. Florentyna has been generous to lend Pearl — as she was predictably named — to King Tamas for his stay. He loves to ride, you see.' Tentrell smiled broadly and she noted his white, even teeth. A truly handsome man. Darcelle sighed. 'It has been a long-held dream of mine to visit the wondrous city of Percheron.'

'Perfect, your highness, because the jewel I bring for King Tamas is called the Star of Percheron.'

She sucked in a breath. 'You jest, Master Tentrell.'

'Not at all, your highness. But forgive me, I thought you knew. Where is the king, may I ask?'

'He is with my sister. An unexpected meeting.'

'Well, as I say, perhaps he's forgotten. Or maybe he hasn't been told of our meeting. Chancellor Burrage was to arrange it. Oh dear, I feel embarrassed now for it must feel like trespass.'

'No, no, Master Tentrell. Please don't feel badly,' she said. 'The truth is Master Burrage is ...' She hesitated. He looked at her in enquiry and she couldn't help herself but admit that this Tentrell was disarmingly attractive; she felt vaguely guilty for thinking it on the brink of her engagement. He watched her with intensity, almost hungrily, which was confusing because something in the back of her mind suggested that this man's tastes did not run to women; the rumours must have been wrong. Probably jealously. Perhaps like all men he was helpless in the face of her beauty. 'Please, join me,' she said, gesturing for him to walk deeper into the garden. 'I was enjoying this long-awaited spring sunshine while the king is absent.'

He obliged but kept his distance. 'Your highness, you were going to say something …?' he queried.

'Yes … yes, that's right,' she said. 'The truth is, Chancellor Burrage died through the night, and that's likely why I hadn't been told of your meeting. I don't believe the king is aware of it either.'

'Shar's breath! Burrage looked hale yesterday.'

'Indeed, it is a shock for all of us.'

'Heart?' Tentrell wondered.

She shrugged. 'I'm sorry, I don't know. I was only told on my way here. May I offer you some refreshment, Master Tentrell? Or perhaps some cherries? They are the violets — the best Morgravia's southern orchards can provide.' She gestured at the untouched plate of fruit that had been provided for Tamas earlier. The cherries gleamed plump and ripe, shining beneath the soft sunlight, vividly violet.

'I haven't tasted cherries in centuries,' he said, winning a smile from her at his exaggeration. 'And the violets have such a short life. I always seem to be on a voyage in this season and this time is no different. I'll be leaving shortly. But how lucky you are to have them so early.'

She grinned. 'One of the rights of being a royal is the end-of-thaw, early-blossomtide fruits. I tasted some when I broke my fast this morning. They are sweet and tender. Please, help yourself or perhaps you'll miss out again.'

He did sample a handful, she was glad to see. 'My, so juicy,' he said, eating three at once and licking the telltale liquid from his fingers. He politely blew the stones into his hand before tossing them into the bushes.

Darcelle giggled. 'And now your lips are blue. You know it can linger, don't you? I had to virtually scrub mine clean this morning.'

He tittered with effeminate affectation. It sounded false but, even so, this is what she'd expected the Tentrell she'd heard about would be, and yet it contradicted that hungry look of earlier. 'I shall proudly wear it,' he teased. 'My royal violet lip balm.' She grinned, liking his uninhibited way; around Stoneheart this was refreshing behaviour. 'Well, your highness. As you've given me a special treat of prized Morgravian cherries, perhaps I might be permitted to show you this glorious jewel. I may have misled you. King Tamas is not buying this jewel.'

'Oh?' she said, mystified and deeply disappointed.

'No, it is from the people of Robissun Marth as our wedding gift. We can't think of a more beautiful person to show off this magnificent gem than our own Princess Darcelle as she becomes a queen in her own right.'

She gave a small gasp of pleasure. He was certainly speaking to her heart. 'But how did ...?' she began.

He laughed, producing a velvet sack. 'Your highness, this stone is mine. I acquired it and have had it a long time. I owe a lot to the Crown — your father was always generous to me — and this is one way of showing my gratitude, and I am also doing this on behalf of my fellow townsfolk. This is a gift that I can afford to give from us to you. I hope you'll wear it with pride when the Cipreans first glimpse the beauty of their new queen.'

She held her breath as he tipped the magnificent teardrop-shaped gem into his palm. Even from that distance it looked to be on fire.

'The Star of Percheron was worn by the favourite wife of the zar many centuries previously. While it was once worn by the famous royal woman around her belly, I have had it fashioned to be worn on a gold chain hung around the forehead,' he said, miming placing it around his own.

Darcelle could only watch, fascinated.

'I've taken the liberty of having a special golden loop provided, so should you prefer, you may wear it dangling from a circlet, your highness. Then it can be worn as part of a crown or alone, as you choose.'

He held it up so its fire caught the sunlight and danced for her. Darcelle's eyes grew wide with intense pleasure. She was already imagining herself naked in the king's bed on their wedding night, wearing only this jewel. She would need nothing else.

'Master Tentrell, you've taken my breath away.'

He looked pleased. 'That was my intention,' he said. 'The Star of Percheron deserves to be worn on the most beautiful forehead in the empire.'

She giggled as he stepped forward, the huge, heavy jewel glittering as the light bounced off its facets and sent rainbow rays arcing against a mirror set into the courtyard wall.

'May I, your highness?' he asked, his manners gracious. He bowed.

'Why not?' she said, turning and allowing Tentrell to clasp the chain around her head.

'There,' he said and stepped back as she turned once more to face him. He gave a soft sigh of what sounded like disbelief. 'Princess, someone should paint you just as you stand there, in this garden, more radiant and gorgeous than any woman alive, I'd wager.'

She felt herself blush. She was used to flattery but it had been a long time since it could affect her. Darcelle felt a fresh energy beneath his praise.

'See for yourself, your highness,' he said, gesturing at the bird fountain, where the still waters would show her reflection. 'King Tamas is going to catch his breath to see it on you. You'll need no other adornment on your wedding night,' he confided with a knowing wink.

She felt the heat rush to her cheeks again, wondering if he had dropped in on her thoughts. 'You're very kind, Master Tentrell,' she said, stealing a glimpse of herself. She had to admit, it looked far more glorious than she'd imagined.

'On behalf of the people of Robissun Marth, may we wish you our love, our blessing on your marriage and only happiness for all your days and your new life in Cipres. Come visit us sometime and wear the Star of Percheron for us.'

Darcelle stepped forward. 'Master Tentrell, can you not wait to meet Tamas?' They were close enough now to embrace. He seemed aware of this, she sensed, and she liked him for being so careful in her company. He was superbly handsome, she thought again, in spite of his blue lips. What a senseless waste if he did prefer men.

'Forgive me, highness, but I am leaving on a ship tomorrow, bound for faraway lands, beyond Percheron. It's why Master Burrage permitted me this special appointment, or I might have had to queue with all the other well-wishers. I know you will pass on to King Tamas my respectful felicitations.'

'Pity.' She was genuinely sorry that Tamas would not meet Tentrell. Besides, she would have liked his company a little longer. She was also feeling vaguely irritated; having admitted to herself that Tentrell was handsome, he suddenly reminded her of that stranger, Cassien, who was hanging around Florentyna like a constant cloud of darkness.

'Well, beautiful princess,' he said, sketching the lowest and most elegant of bows just a breath away from her, 'perhaps you will allow me to kiss your hand in farewell. I will treasure the memory throughout my long and no doubt arduous voyage. But frankly, Princess Darcelle, should the great water serpent rise up and take my ship, I shall be able to die happy because of this moment.'

'Oh, you wicked flirt, Master Tentrell,' she joked, waving a hand at him. She wished she'd met him a long time ago, for she was sure he would have provided her with lots of interesting trinkets.

'Please, you must call me Layne,' he offered.

'Well then, Layne, you must promise to come to Cipres. Spend some time at our court, as our guest, on your return,' she urged.

His eyes widened with pleasure. 'I won't even bother to come home with that invitation waiting for me, highness. I shall sail straight for Cipres, bringing with me all the treasures of the east so you can view them first.'

She gave a smiling nod to show she was impressed, then held out her hand with an even broader smile. 'Farewell, dear Layne. I am in awe of your gift and will wear it on my wedding day with pride.'

'You do the people of Robissun Marth a great honour,' Tentrell said, reaching for her hand, bending over it and laying his lips against her skin.

She shivered at his touch, and then he was no longer kissing the back of her hand as she felt his mouth on her palm and his tongue licking it and she'd never felt anything so lustful. Now his warm lips moved up her arm, making the hairs on the back of her neck wake up in tingling response to a new sort of awakening deep within. He was rapidly working his way up to her face and she was helpless to stop him.

'Master Tentrell,' she murmured, scared but at the same time lost in the moment of passion. She had lied to Florentyna about lying with Tamas. He was far too correct to have taken advantage of her presence or her youth and naïvety. She had just wanted to shock her conservative, stuffy sister … and had. She knew that Tamas wanted both her youth and virginity. He had been prepared to wait for it and would give her a realm for it.

She loved Tamas, but she'd never had a lover. Now handsome Layne Tentrell, who clearly was not a half-man, was kissing her in an intimate way she had never experienced. She'd truly never felt anything so sensual. Suitors had been part of her life, but while the ardour had been there, the kisses were perfunctory as there had been chaperones at every turn. Here she was, for the first time truly alone with a man who obviously had no inhibitions about what may or not be regally prudent, and she was all but melting beneath him like a bitch on heat. His warm breath on her neck was making her gasp, the way he bit at her ear made her see sparkling lights beneath her closed eyelids and all the while she felt a throb of need ... of desire.

Tentrell pulled away. 'Your highness,' he began, his voice throaty and full of longing.

'Don't stop,' she uttered, horrified and yet unable to help herself. 'Kiss me,' she begged.

Cassien had withdrawn to stand some distance from the two sovereigns. Tamas had only just managed to corner Florentyna in her solar for a brief private meeting when a messenger ran in wide-eyed, not bothering to knock or present himself properly.

The queen looked appropriately mystified at this break in protocol.

'Your majesty, forgive me,' he blurted, 'but I was sent in all haste. It's Princess Darcelle.'

'Shar, no!' Florentyna exclaimed, her mind clearly winging to the worst scenario. 'Not dead, please Shar. Not the magic on her.'

Cassien gave her a frowning look. When had she made the leap to magic? Her remark, however, had been lost in the chaos of the moment.

'She's fine, your majesty,' the messenger assured her. 'It's her visitor. He dropped dead before her. She says she needs you.'

'Oh, my precious girl,' Florentyna uttered. 'Tamas ...'

But the king was already moving. 'I told them no visitors when I left,' he growled, and only just managed to stop himself pushing the queen aside. Cassien realised Tamas wasn't used to anyone going before him.

'Where is she?' Florentyna demanded of the servant.

'In my suite?' Tamas roared, and the servant nodded.

Cassien blinked. It wasn't possible for someone to die after the roaming. This didn't make sense. 'Let's go,' he said and, with the queen between himself and Tamas, they ran after the servant through the twists and turns of corridors. They seemed to gather people along the way — guards followed and so did other servants. Cassien left everyone else waiting in the king's entrance chamber while he, Florentyna and Tamas continued through the suite into the herb garden. They found Darcelle sitting beneath a mosaic set in the wall, a linen handkerchief dabbing at her nose. Her two senior maids were with her, offering comfort. They stood and immediately dropped into low curtsies on sighting the two sovereigns. Darcelle didn't bother to even look up.

'I'm all right, I'm all right,' she said, holding up a hand.

'Thank Shar's blessings,' Florentyna said and Cassien could hear the tightness and terror in her voice. She sat on the bench beside Darcelle and put her arms around her sister and hugged her, all previous offence forgotten. 'What happened, dear one? Why were you alone?'

Over the top of the queen's words, Tamas was demanding to know about the corpse at his feet. 'Who in hell's flames is this?' he demanded of his own personal guards, standing by the doorway, shocked and embarrassed.

'The man had papers, my liege,' his senior guard said. 'Chancellor Burrage had granted him access. The queen's seal was upon it.' They pointed to where the parchment lay on the ground, near Tentrell's corpse, which lay face down.

'I wasn't here,' Tamas roared at the man.

The guard shrank and Cassien felt sorry for him. 'We changed watch, my king, from Morgravian to Ciprean. I was not told that you'd left. I was simply informed that Princess Darcelle was within. We doubled the guard as a result. Her own servants waited alongside.'

Tamas's shoulders dropped. Cassien reckoned the king had wisely decided to cool his rage and not create a scene when more important matters were at stake. 'My princess is safe. That's what matters,' Tamas said. The king turned back to Darcelle. 'Did he touch you, my love?'

She shook her head, emerging from Florentyna's embrace. 'No, no, not at all,' she said, now dabbing at her eyes. She pointed at the jewel in her hand. 'But he did give me this.' At everyone's noises of surprise she explained all about Tentrell's visit. By its end, her somewhat forced tears had dried and her sniffs were getting less frequent, Cassien noticed. 'He was kind and funny,' she added.

'And what actually happened, Princess Darcelle?' Cassien said, speaking for the first time. As was usual for him he stood aside from everyone.

'What do you mean?' she said, frowning at him.

Her eyes were not even red, he noted. 'Did he make a sound, clutch his heart, call out to you for help?'

'All of those,' she answered, growing haughty at having to answer his questions. 'His eyes grew wide as if in pain and then he put his hand here,' she said, mimicking the motion by touching her chest. 'He groaned and then he cried out for help.'

'And then he fell here?' Cassien pointed.

She nodded, frowning. 'Why is he asking these questions, Florentyna?'

The queen stood, giving Cassien a glare to halt his questions. She moved to the entrance of the courtyard, where it led into the king's guest rooms, and beckoned. Two maids emerged.

'Take my sister to her chambers and wait for me there. Make up a warm bath for her. She is in shock. Tamas, will you send some of your guards with ours, please? It might reassure you to have some of your people around Darcelle,' she offered. It was a kind gesture, Cassien thought. 'No-one is to go in or out of Darcelle's rooms without my permission other than you two,' she said to the maids, both of them senior, and taking in the guards with her glare as well. 'Understood? No-one. I don't care if they're waving a paper with my personal signature on it.'

They both dropped obediently into a low curtsey in answer and the guards bowed low to show they understood too.

'Go now, dear one,' she urged Darcelle gently.

'Aren't you coming?' the princess whimpered.

'Soon enough,' Florentyna assured her. 'We have a few things to sort and find out. But you'll be safe now.'

Darcelle looked to her king. 'Tamas?' she asked wearily, expecting him to follow.

'King Tamas,' Cassien said quietly. 'Er, forgive me, your majesty, but it may be helpful if you stayed.'

Tamas frowned, glanced at Florentyna, who shook her head, unsure. Cassien added. 'Please, your majesty. We should get to the bottom of this.'

The king shrugged. 'Of course, however I can help. Go on, my love. Your sister's quite right. This has been a shock and you need to rest; have some quiet time.'

Darcelle threw Cassien a sharp glance he couldn't decipher but she allowed herself to be led quietly away.

Cassien asked everyone else to leave the courtyard, save the three guards. Word had obviously got around the palace that his orders should be obeyed.

Florentyna looked at him as he closed the doors and walked back into the garden. 'What's going on?'

Cassien sighed. 'Something's not right.'

'Something?' Tamas mocked. 'Nothing's right! Anything could have happened to her. People have been dying in the palace overnight from some strange phenomenon, including your own chancellor, plus festivities have been cancelled ...' He held up his hands in defence. 'Believe me, Queen Florentyna, I would do the same under the circumstances but these are strange times.'

'Cassien?' she urged.

'Let's have the body moved to the chapel and have it put somewhere separate. I want to look at Tentrell properly. But not here.'

'I've had all the dead taken to the crypt of the cathedral. There were too many for our chapel; only Burrage is there, together with the dowager.'

'Then there's room for Tentrell.'

She nodded at the remaining men. 'Take this man to Stoneheart's chapel. No-one is to go in or out until Master Cassien gives permission.'

They bowed and silently removed him. Cassien picked up the fallen parchment, glanced at it.

'Tamas, I've just realised you haven't been properly introduced. Forgive me. This is Cassien Figaret, my champion, or more rightly, my shadow.' She smiled faintly at her jest. 'He's now entirely in charge of my security.'

'That's wise. I think you should do the same for Darcelle.'

'Perhaps that will be your role, sir, soon enough,' Florentyna said gently. 'I'm thinking it might be best for her to sail with you to Cipres on the morrow.'

'But ...' His gaze narrowed. 'What about the Pearlis wedding?'

'I realise this is a hasty decision but in light of what's happening, I think it will prove unwise. Better she be married in Cipres. Morgravia is not a safe place at present.'

'Do you really mean that? Not about the safety … about the wedding being held in Cipres?' Tamas asked, astonished.

'I do,' she said. 'I just want her to be happy and I think you can do that for her. I know she would love to be married as a queen in front of her new people. It makes sense.'

'But your tradition, Florentyna?'

She made a soft sound of dismissal. 'Tradition should be broken every now and then … for the right reasons,' she said and treated him to one of her rare smiles.

Cassien watched the exchange between the two monarchs. It looked effortless and sounded honest. They were going to make a sound strategic 'marriage', given that both were keen to find solutions. It was a pity that they weren't the betrothed.

'You make me proud to call you sister, Queen Florentyna. I'm sorry that Darcelle painted you in such a poor light — she said you'd cancelled the wedding plans.'

Florentyna sighed. 'My sister is wound rather tight at present, sir. Forgive her, as I do.'

He nodded. 'Such pragmatism is rare.' She dipped her head at the compliment, although both of their gazes lingered a little longer on each other than Cassien thought politic.

'So, Cassien,' Tamas said, clearing his throat and turning from the queen, 'I sensed an undercurrent earlier. Why don't you say what's on your mind?'

Cassien was impressed. He found himself liking Tamas more by the moment, but the king would not like him shortly. He took a breath. 'Forgive me, both of you, but I don't believe that what Princess Darcelle told us is what actually occurred here.'

He felt the former warmth chill around him as though blossomtide had forgotten her place and sneaked back behind her cooler cousin.

'You think my sister lied?' Florentyna said.

'Let me just tell you what I saw. Forgive me, please, if I offend.' He didn't wait for their response for there was no easy way to say what he wanted and not offend both royals. 'I saw a mark on her forehead and through her hair. She had worn that heavy jewel he'd brought. I doubt very much that she could have put it on easily without help, and she would have needed to ask and give permission for him to approach. I think Tentrell did touch the princess at her behest. When he fell, I suspect she pulled the jewel and its chain off, which might explain the telltale strands of hair that had come loose from her otherwise perfect styling.'

Florentyna was as still as ice and looked at him with a gaze to match. 'Go on.'

'Her lips, your majesty.'

'Stained with cherry juice,' the queen finished, looking unimpressed by this observation.

'She ate the cherries, man!' Tamas growled. 'What's your point?'

'Perhaps. Your guest did too,' Cassien said. 'I noted his lips and fingers were stained as well. I'll wager his tongue is blackened from the juice.'

'So?' Florentyna said.

'Your sister's tongue was clean, her teeth white, her fingers unstained. If she ate cherries, she swallowed them whole. Did you see your sister's neck?'

'No ... I —'

'Oh, this is preposterous,' Tamas said, losing patience. 'What are you suggesting?'

Cassien cleared his throat again and forced himself to say it. 'Forgive me, your majesties, but I believe Tentrell kissed Princess Darcelle, or so the telltale cherry juice suggests.' He expected howls but he was given only frigid silence. 'I'm sorry,' he added.

Tamas growled and launched himself at Cassien, but fell into the yielding softness of air; the champion had leapt nimbly, dancing back silently.

'I'm going to flay the very skin from your frame for that accusation.'

Cassien shook his head. 'And pigs might fly, your majesty. You won't even get close enough to reach me with that Ciprean sword.'

Tamas yelled and drew his sword with a rasping sound of iron. He looked astonished to see a magnificent sword, already drawn, already poised to strike, just a hair's breadth from his throat.

'I serve the Queen of Morgravia. I have no duty to the King of Cipres, so put your blade away, majesty. I alone have permission to draw a weapon in her company.' Cassien's tone was chilling.

'Stop! Both of you!' Florentyna commanded. 'Kill each other later. I have more important matters than watching you two making each other's hackles rise. We're all on the same side here. And Cassien, you'd better be prepared to back up your alarming claim with fact. Why would Darcelle lie for Tentrell? And what has that got to do with his death?'

The men stared angrily at each other. It was Tamas who sheathed his sword first, which again impressed Cassien. Only a confident king would do so in service of the common good. So he apologised, bowing low to the sovereign of Cipres. 'Forgive me, your majesty. As you say, these are strange times and if I'm overly protective of our queen, you can surely understand why.'

'Answer Florentyna's question.'

'I sense Darcelle's protecting him.'

'He's a stranger. I can say with all confidence that she has never met the man previously. Please, Tamas, believe me,' Florentyna offered.

The king glanced at Cassien. 'Be very careful.'

'Let's go to the chapel,' Cassien said. 'I'll show you what I saw. Make up your own minds. One more thing.' They both looked expectantly at him. 'This permission from Burrage,' he waved the parchment, 'makes it very clear that it was for the picnic only.' He looked between them. 'Tentrell took it upon himself to ease his way past the guards and into this courtyard.'

In her bath, Princess Darcelle allowed the warm suds to soothe away her fears … at least that's what she conveyed to her maids, begging them to leave her alone so she could have just a few moments of peace to gather her thoughts.

They agreed, but said they would be standing on the other side of her chamber door. When the door latch clicked and she heard the key turn in that lock — for they were taking no chances on this strange day — a smile stretched across Princess Darcelle's cherry-stained mouth.

And her smile was heavy with old cunning.

I didn't know you could do that, my love, Aphra said, her voice full of awe. *The magic has evolved.*

Not really, Cyricus replied, amused. *It's taken my knowledge to change it. You don't give me enough credit, Aphra.*

Change it? Then why did my form as Angelina have to die? I rather liked it and I know you would have.

You're not thinking, are you? We couldn't have a disturbance in the worlds. The body of Angelina belonged there, not here. I'm more likely to grieve the loss of Gabriel's body. I don't like being female — makes me think of Lyana,' Cyricus said and spat at the bathwater.

But the kiss. How did you do it? It's so clean; no messy death.

Cyricus chuckled, his hate for the goddess instantly set aside. *Well, you see, in Myrren's view, when she first cast this spell, she was so full of anger, her need for vengeance so raw, she designed her magic to be spiteful. In every way it was harmful … to its host and to the victims it worked on. It was such a cynical magic, I continue to be impressed by it. But I've had centuries to lick my wounds, Aphra. My anger is so cold, it has turned white in my mind. It's now a thing of pure, hard beauty. It feels nothing but the satisfaction of seeing itself coming to fruition. And it is patient. My revenge will be taken slowly, painfully and without the mistakes that anger prompts. Myrren's magic demanded pain and blood. I don't need to hurt people like Darcelle … she's irrelevant — nothing more than a host. I just want her dead — her spirit gone. Did you feel her fright?*

I did, my love. I revelled in her fear.

And she fled to her god, allowing us to enter her body — so much neater, don't you think, than how we entered Gabe, or you entered Angelina, leaving our former hosts bloodied? This way is neat, painless, soundless. And imagine, the last physical sensation she felt was a kiss … infinitely more subtle than a blade.

I wonder what they'll make of Gabriel's death? Aphra remarked. *What if someone knows he's not the real Tentrell?*

It was time to leave Gabe's body. I had hoped to hang on to it a little longer, but I have a grander plan about my ultimate host, so I can wait. I suspect Gabe's body will be laid out somewhere and hopefully forgotten about for the time being as the queen has much to deal with. The news of Tentrell's death will still be filtering through and it will be assumed the gardener killed him. Now we have a beautiful new host. It's odd to be a woman, I'll admit, but it makes the cunning of this magic so much more fun. They have no idea who is among them!

That bodyguard of the queen was suspicious.

I noticed. Cassien is his name. I won't forget it either. But he's suspicious of only things mortal, my love. He has no idea what has come to visit Morgravia.

He laughed and Aphra joined him as Cyricus dipped Darcelle's beautiful body even deeper into the warm depths of the bath.

TWENTY-SIX

King, queen and Cassien arrived at the chapel. There was a ring of stern-looking Morgravian guards around it, who stood to attention at the sight of the trio.

'Is Father Cuthben here?' Florentyna asked the most senior of the men who approached.

Cassien noticed that she looked relieved when the soldier who greeted them said that the priest had left his apologies. 'He felt it necessary to accompany the, er … the others to the cathedral, your majesty.'

'I understand. So the three corpses are laid out?'

He nodded. 'As you instructed.'

'Let us in, please,' she said and the guard unlocked the door, holding it ajar while the queen and her companions filed in.

'Send word,' Cassien told the man, 'for the boy called Hamelyn to be brought here. The queen's servants know him.' He could use Ham's insightful observations right now and he needed to know if the sword was talking. The idea of a fit man dropping dead in front of Darcelle was not acceptable to him.

The door closed solidly behind them.

Inside, the stained glass was of rich, deep colours, which allowed only a small amount of daylight to leak in. The candles burned steadily and gave off a comforting glow. It was dry and cold — very cold. Convenient for the corpses, Cassien thought, and noticed the queen shiver.

She had moved to stand over Saria's body, reaching to touch the woman's hand. It must feel like ice by now, Cassien imagined. They would have to bury her tomorrow as his keen sense of smell told him it would be hours only before everyone would smell the same bouquet of decay.

'This is the Dowager Saria,' Florentyna explained to Tamas and as she spoke, Cassien stopped listening to her, looking around.

He saw Burrage, fully robed and bedecked in his chancellor's finery, hair tidied, hands placed neatly across his middle. Cassien looked for the third and most recent corpse and turned to search in the other direction, frowning.

'Cassien?' the queen queried.

'Where's Tentrell?' he said. He could now see where the body must have been placed. The pallet was in place, set away from the two more important chapel guests, but it was empty.

'They said there were three,' Tamas added, swivelling to check he wasn't mistaken.

There was a knock at the door. Florentyna nodded at Cassien. He opened it. Saw Hamelyn waiting with a guard dwarfing him.

'Come in. Er, Fend, is that your name?' he called to the man who'd first spoken to them, as Hamelyn pushed inside, looking unsure of why he'd been called.

'It is, sir,' the senior man said.

'Three corpses laid out, you say?'

The man looked at him as though he were mad. 'Yes,' he said, reaching for patience. 'I checked the merchant's laying out personally.'

Cassien closed the door, every muscle on alert and glanced at Ham. 'Is it talking?'

'Very disturbed,' the boy said, 'especially right now.'

Cassien drew the sword.

'Shar! What are you doing?' Florentyna asked.

'Behind me, majesty,' he growled, 'now!'

She quickly moved to his back. 'Cassien?'

'Hush,' he cautioned. 'Tamas?' he said, ignoring protocol.

He knew the king was drawing his sword as quietly as he could, but the sound of the metal echoed off the walls with a piercing ring.

'Behind the queen. Watch her back,' he ordered and heard the king step into place.

'What in the name of gods are we looking for?' Tamas murmured.

'Cassien!' It was Hamelyn.

His gaze swung to the boy, who nodded his head up and into the darkest shadows at the back of the chapel.

Cassien followed Ham's line of sight and although fear was not a word that held many connotations for him, he felt it now, like a cold wind blowing through him, forming itself into a mass to settle in his gut. Staring back at him from the shadows, suspended on a ledge, where he'd presumably hoped to remain hidden, was Tentrell.

Cassien hissed with the anxiety that suddenly released itself. How had he missed the demon's presence in the palace when he'd roamed? 'Show yourself, demon!' he snarled.

The man dropped to the floor, stumbling. The queen gave a low, short cry and Cassien was aware of Tamas pulling Florentyna behind him.

'What the —?' the king breathed.

Tentrell took a stumbling step forward, his hands held up in defence. 'Wait!' he said.

'I will strike you down, Cyricus,' Cassien promised. 'And send you back to —'

'Cassien, listen to me!' It was Hamelyn. He must have been yelling at him, but he hadn't heard. Cassien only had eyes for the demon, who was babbling. All he could hear was the sound of his pulse pounding and the slower rhythm of his heart and breathing as he prepared himself.

Ham shook him. 'Listen!'

He glared at the boy.

'The sword is not frightened of him,' Ham must have repeated. He looked vaguely exasperated.

'What?'

'It's welcoming him, like it welcomes you. This is not the demon.'

Cassien's gaze narrowed as he let go of the urge to hurl himself at the resurrected body.

'I am not Tentrell,' the man yelled at them. 'Hear me out. I know this is frightening, but I'm just as frightened. Please put away that sword.'

'It stays right where it is,' Cassien promised.

The man nodded, swallowing hard. 'Then, please, just listen to what I have to say.'

The queen emerged from behind her keepers. 'Speak, I will listen.'

'Thank you, your majesty.' The impostor staggered. 'Forgive me, I am very weak. I have much to explain. Do not let us be interrupted.'

'By whom?' Tamas joined in. 'No-one is —'

'By your betrothed, King Tamas. Your sister, Queen Florentyna. She is now one of the damned … My name is Gabriel.'

At the queen's recognition of the name that Pel had mentioned, she permitted him to begin his tale. He told them a story of such incredible breadth they each stared, incredulous, until he finished, his head hung low. He was visibly shaking from the retelling and the cold, and what seemed to be the powerful magic he'd used to not only keep himself alive, but to reinvigorate his body.

They were so silent with shock that Cassien could hear the flames of the candles burning and the sigh of the oaken doors that settled now and then against the chill.

It was Hamelyn who broke the stillness and smashed through the frigidity of the four others gathered there. He stood up from where he'd crouched to listen and wrapped a blanket that had been folded at the feet of Burrage around the shoulders of the shivering man.

'You need this more than Chancellor Burrage,' he said kindly.

'You say you're not from this place,' Florentyna repeated, frowning, 'but a land called Paris.'

He nodded, gave a wry smile. 'So very far away, majesty.'

'But magic brought you here,' she qualified.

'Evil, trickster magic. As I explained, I have been a host for two demons. I brought the swan quill, which was given to me by a man called Reynard.' The queen gasped. 'Good, I'm glad you know him. I hoped it would make you curious and try and learn more because I didn't know how to reach out to anyone from the secrecy of my own body. But this man who calls himself Cassien seems to know exactly what I'm talking about.'

Cassien took a breath. 'I can't lie. What you say rings true.'

'Then you must know that they think I'm dead. They've killed to get here. They'll keep on doing it.'

'Is Reynard dead?' the queen asked.

Gabe shook his head. 'Not when I last saw him.'

'Shar's grace,' she whispered and wiped a tear. 'Thank you.'

Tamas's deep voice came from the back of the chapel, where he'd sat brooding. 'They've killed Darcelle. Is that what you're telling us?'

Gabe nodded, and spoke softly but firmly so neither Florentyna nor Tamas would hold out hope that Darcelle might resurrect as he had. 'Yes, your majesties. I can confirm it. She is as dead to you as Burrage over there. I am sorry for you.' Florentyna sucked in a breath of shock, and Cassien hated to see that no matter how she fought it, she couldn't contain the mewling sounds of grief. He wanted to comfort her, but she naturally leaned toward Tamas — almost family — who immediately and equally naturally put an arm around her, he too looking ashen. 'She did not wish it, sire. Cyricus is so persuasive; he seduced her, and in kissing her was able to move into her with his loathed companion, Aphra.'

Through her tears, Florentyna pointed at him. 'But if you're alive, why not —'

Gabe shook his head helplessly. 'For whatever reason, I have been granted a skill. It's hard to explain, but it's as though I can hover within myself. I was able to withdraw, hold myself back from them. They had assumed I died when we first entered this world.' He shook his head as though unable to accept that he was here.

Florentyna wasn't listening and Cassien wasn't sure if Tamas was either. They stood in each other's arms, drawing whatever solace they could.

Cassien felt a prick of envy but pressed on. 'Why did they need to go to the trouble of a host? Why not come in the guise they were in? We would not have known.'

Gabe looked up in puzzlement. 'Yes, I've queried this repeatedly. They needed my body for a reason I don't grasp. Or at least she did. She couldn't come as Angelina. Angelina belonged there.'

'And you belong here,' Hamelyn finished.

Gabe looked even more confused. 'No, I don't mean ...' and then he stopped, considering the words of the boy.

Ham pressed. 'It has to be so. If bodies from the other world are dangerous to this, how come yours isn't ... unless it belongs here?'

'That can't be,' Gabe railed. 'It doesn't work. I've lived a whole life before this.'

'Enough,' the queen said, rallying and wiping her tears. 'Cassien, I'm entirely confused. We need clear thinking. You know more about this than any of us here.'

He stared back at her vacantly. 'The demon is among us, your majesty. And, fortunately, we know in whose guise. You cannot stay here. I can't permit it. We must get you away, but we must also watch Darcelle. She is our only clue to his next move.'

'Which is?' she asked.

'I think I can answer that,' Gabe said. 'He spoke of destruction. He wants to tear down all that a person — whom I know only as Elysius — holds dear.' At this the queen and Cassien shared a glance.

'Fynch mentioned Elysius to me,' the queen admitted.

'And Fynch is now the keeper of the Wild, as Elysius was before him,' Cassien explained, although Tamas frowned with lack of understanding.

'Then Cyricus will destroy the people Fynch cares about and the land he loves, but most of all, he will lay waste to a magical force known as the Thicket, and what I gather are hallowed lands beyond that he called the Wild.'

'Magical?' Florentyna repeated. 'The Wild in the far northwest of Briavel is just that … a wild place where nothing flourishes. People hate it, speak of it feeling wrong.'

'That's the magic they're feeling,' Cassien counselled. 'I have learned about this place from Fynch. It repels most.'

'You know the man and the place that Cyricus speaks about,' Gabe said. 'So you know I am telling you the truth. I now realise Reynard was telling me the truth as he knew it.'

Cassien saw the queen sag. She looked as though she'd been punched and all the wind in her body had been expelled.

'Poor Reynard,' she whispered.

'He warned me. And yet, I still get the feeling that he wanted me to come here. He pushed me into it but at the same time needed me to understand the danger. I can't explain it. I still don't understand the quill. He called it a scrivener's quill, because he knew I liked history and also to write.'

'No,' Florentyna said, 'that's not why he gave it to you. It was a message to me. I gave Reynard that quill, because he always told me the old stories from when I was very young. He was a great storyteller. I begged him all of my life to write them down and I gave him the swan quill with the royal sigil on it and told him it was a royal order.' She laughed mirthlessly. 'I was eleven. He knew I'd notice it had disappeared, knew I'd notice if it came back in the wrong hands. He was sending me that message from far away. Why couldn't he just come back?'

Gabe shrugged. 'I don't know.'

'Because he needed magic to travel,' Ham said, understanding quicker than any of them. 'He probably didn't have access to that magic once Fynch had sent him.'

Before anyone could ask more, the door hammered.

'Queen Florentyna, we have an urgent messenger from Princess Darcelle.'

Cassien shook his head at them and moved to the door, opening it slightly. 'We are not to be disturbed.'

The guard had a frightened-looking maid alongside. 'Forgive me, sir,' she mumbled. 'The princess said I was to bring either King Tamas or Queen Florentyna, or both, in my wake.' She curtsied. 'Sorry, sir, that's what I was ordered to say.'

'And you have, thank you,' Cassien said. 'Tell your mistress they will be along shortly. Oh, and can you send the queen's private maidservant, please, with her majesty's warmest riding clothes.'

The maid frowned.

'Just give her the message.' He dug a coin from his pocket and handed it to her. 'And that's between us alone. The queen wants a little time to herself. Don't tell anyone at all.' He beamed her a bright smile.

She thanked him, shyly curtsied, and ran. Cassien eyed the guard. 'You can move all the guards now, Fend. We're done here.'

'Very good, Master Cassien. All of them? What about the personal guard for their majesties?'

'Send everyone away. The queen wishes some private space. I will escort her the short distance back into the palace.'

The man frowned but nodded. 'I'll attend to it.'

'Thank you.' He closed and bolted the door from the inside.

Everyone looked up expectantly, but Tamas. The king looked dark and Cassien recognised the storm gathering.

'King Tamas —'

'Let me kill him,' Tamas said.

'That would require you to kill Darcelle,' Cassien said bluntly, 'and I doubt you could do that. Besides, you are not dealing with a mere "him", your majesty. You are confronting a demon. He doesn't die on your order or necessarily beneath your sword, although I'm not fully sure of the latter. I suspect he is vulnerable in a body.' He looked at Gabe, who nodded.

'That makes things interesting.' He began to pace. 'We could drug Darcelle, possibly.'

'Wait. I'm not having my sister slaughtered in her sleep.'

'It's not her, your majesty,' Cassien said.

'Yes, but Darcelle the impostor will walk, talk and act like the princess you know,' Gabe warned. 'No-one who loves her should attempt this.'

'No-one is going to until I'm absolutely certain that my sister is not buried deep within herself. If *you* can, Gabriel, she might be able to emerge as well,' Florentyna said, ignoring the appeal in Cassien's eyes that begged her to believe the opposite. 'Will he tire of her body?'

Gabriel considered this. 'Definitely, if he senses that anyone suspects she is acting strangely. If you want to keep her under watch, then she has to be watched either clandestinely or by someone she implicitly trusts and thus has full access to the princess.'

That made sense to Cassien. 'We're getting you away from here, Florentyna. And I suggest you come with us,' he said to the king. 'We must work from a position of safety. It is not safe here. I don't know who he might become next, but the palace has myriad hosts to choose from.'

'Except the princess gives him power,' Ham reminded them. Cassien was glad he'd brought this youngster along. His advice was sage counsel.

'I've gone along with this talk of magic and mayhem since I can't explain it any other way — especially because I saw your dead body,' Tamas replied, looking at Gabe but including the group. 'But do you expect me to just give up everything I've worked toward?'

Florentyna shook her head. 'Tamas, Cassien is right. We're trapped here. We need to go somewhere that the demon doesn't know about. Right now, he can only know what Darcelle is being told. Soon she will start exerting herself and not care a whit about protocol. Let's get away before that begins.'

'No, leave me behind to find out more,' he said. 'I have to see this with my own eyes. I am the one who has access to her and whom she trusts. More importantly, I can keep her occupied and give you long enough to get Florentyna away to safety.'

The queen looked to be in pain.

'But you are the very one she can compromise,' Gabe warned.

'I will be on my guard, I promise you, Queen Florentyna,' Tamas said, taking her hand and surprising everyone by putting it to his lips for a heartfelt kiss.

Gabe stood up, looking a little stronger. 'Your majesty, please, if you're going to do this do not let her become intimate. And remember, the demon can become anyone. I'm not sure how the magic has evolved. I thought I had it worked out, but the possession of Darcelle broke the rules as I understood them. The most important thing is that he doesn't know that we know anything. Cyricus is moving around in the smug belief that he is the one springing the surprise. Best we keep it that way.' He looked around at the small group.

Cassien nodded. 'King Tamas, we cannot tell you what to do. I would prefer that we stick together, but I'm also grateful for the time you'll buy us. Please heed Gabe's warning.'

'Believe me, I have no intention of being possessed by the devil.' He shot a glance at the queen. 'Forgive me, Florentyna, that was clumsy of me.'

She put a hand on his arm in silent forgiveness and the king absently reached and covered her hand with his own. Cassien noticed the intimacy, as he said, 'I have asked the guard to leave. We are going to slip out of here and hope to move unnoticed. I don't know how yet, but I plan to get the queen well away from Stoneheart. We will use Ham as a go-between. He can move far less obtrusively than any of us, masquerading as anything from a page to a —'

'Gong boy,' Ham finished for him, looking excited. 'Where will you head?'

Cassien shook his head. 'I'm more worried about getting out of the complex. We'll head north and we can all meet up in a couple of days. Any suggestions?'

'Majesty?' Tamas asked. 'You know Morgravia best.'

Florentyna frowned. 'Farnswyth is logical.'

'We want the least logical,' Cassien suggested.

'There's a hamlet called Tyntar in the north,' she offered.

'I know of that place,' Ham remarked. 'Isn't it where people go for their health?'

She nodded. 'Yes, it's famed for a spa.'

'We don't want anywhere famous,' Cassien frowned.

'No, but it's only known to Morgravians. I doubt that the demons will know of it,' the queen replied. 'And it's tiny, on the southwestern edge of the Great Forest.'

'Be careful,' Gabe said. 'The demons may not know but they have access to Darcelle's knowledge. Presumably she knows of it.'

'Yes, Darcelle knows of it, but she doesn't care for the place. It's too remote for her. I'm suggesting it only because we can get supplies there and if I choose somewhere entirely unknown then Tamas and Ham will have a hard time finding us.'

Cassien nodded. 'All right. Let's go with Tyntar. Buy us one day's ride, Tamas, and then get out of Stoneheart. Use whatever excuse you can, but put distance between yourself and Darcelle.'

'Cyricus will swap bodies. He's looking for a male,' Gabe said, glancing at Tamas.

'Well, he can't have me!' the king snarled.

Gabe gave a sympathetic shrug. 'I say this only so that everyone is under no delusion. We won't know who he becomes so we have to mistrust everyone. And you must believe me when I say he has the most cunning of minds, so he will not be obvious and he is patient … he will use many bodies if he has to, especially as I know he wants to get rid of Aphra sharing the same body.'

'Let me get this straight, Gabe. His intention is to topple the imperial Crown?' Florentyna pressed.

He shook his head. 'No, that is merely for his amusement — part of his revenge is because of this man I mentioned called Elysius, who ruthlessly protected the land you preside over. His real target is the Wild.' He shrugged again. 'I think he wants to lay waste to your realm, to Briavel, to do whatever he can to raze all that Elysius held dear.'

'Well, it is Fynch who is now his enemy,' Cassien reminded them. 'Fynch brought Ham and myself together.'

'And that same man paid me a visit too,' Florentyna reminded them. She shook her head in disbelief. 'The Fynch of legend?' she asked, pointing to the ceiling, where a boy rode a dragon. She glanced at Cassien and caught his nod. Florentyna swallowed, said no more.

'Let's get on with this,' Tamas said, becoming impatient. 'The sooner we move, the better our chances are of keeping the imperial Crown safe. We shall meet up at Tyntar in two days. Until then …'

Cassien smiled inwardly at the way Tamas had taken charge, every inch the king, and perhaps a born leader — even though he believed Tamas would dispute that.

'I am now officially your personal messenger, your majesty,' Hamelyn said and bowed.

'Excellent. I'll have you kitted out in Ciprean colours in no time. But for now, let's go take our first look at this demon.'

'Don't jest, Tamas,' the queen said. 'I'm worried enough about you.'

'Don't worry. I plan to see you again,' he said and, surprisingly, hugged her close. 'Cipres is a small place but breeds its royals tough.' He smiled sadly and then turned to Cassien. 'I know you'll keep the queen safe.'

Cassien bowed to the king and took a moment to kneel in front of Hamelyn. He took him by the shoulders, privately wondering at how small and thin the boy was for his age. 'I know your skills mean you can remember everything we've shared. They have none of the background we've learned. Stay watchful and careful.'

'I always am,' the boy said. 'I suppose it hasn't occurred to you that you and Gabe look alike?'

The queen turned and regarded them. 'It has occurred to me, but I thought I was imagining it. If Gabriel's hair were longer …'

'And if he were not so scrawny,' Tamas offered.

'You could be brothers,' Ham finished.

Gabe frowned. 'I have no siblings.'

'I have lived alone most of my life but I did have family once,' Cassien replied. He felt awkward as a forgotten memory nipped at his subconscious, but time was drifting on. 'You'd better go,' he said to the king, who was anxious to leave. 'We don't want to make Darcelle too angry. Say the queen is speaking with the guard, has gone to the barracks. That should give us sufficient time to get out of Stoneheart's immediate reach.'

There was a knock at the door again. Cassien put a finger to his lips and everyone was silent as he answered.

'Ah, thank you. I'm taking the queen out for a quiet ride. She —'

Florentyna suddenly appeared. 'Hello, Sharley.'

'Majesty. I hope these will do.'

'Perfect,' she said. 'Please don't tell anyone. I just need a little while on my own. I'll be in the palace grounds, but if they ask, shrug!' They shared a conspiratorial grin. 'Thank you, Sharley.'

'That was well done,' Cassien said to her as they bolted the door. 'Hurry, get changed.'

'Help me, Ham,' she said, pointing at the laces behind her bodice.

The men turned away politely, but Cassien thought Hamelyn had drawn the lucky straw.

They heard a swish of silk and a few moments later, Florentyna returned to them looking far more comfortable. 'I'm ready.'

The king nodded at Cassien and Gabe, squeezed Florentyna's shoulder and then, together with Ham, walked out of the chapel.

'They're brave,' Gabe murmured.

'Our turn to be brave,' Cassien said. 'We'll go into the bailey and make for the barracks, but then we can —'

Florentyna gave a small gasp. 'Oh, how dim of me. I know how to get us out.'

'There's only one door,' Cassien remarked wryly.

'Ah yes, but that's because you're not a royal of Morgravia, nor are you related to the Briavellian royal family, which believed utterly in secret passages. If I had time I'd explain that. But over there,' she said, pointing, 'behind the altar and that huge tapestry hung against the wall, is a passage. No-one but the sovereign ever knows of it.'

The two men looked impressed.

'How come no-one's opened it?'

'Because no-one has the means.'

'Not even your sister?'

'Not even Darcelle,' she said. She dipped into her shirt, between her breasts and withdrew a chain. Hanging from it were several small items, one of which was a tiny peg of stone. 'I have worn this since the day my father died. Darcelle thinks I wear it out of sentiment. She has no idea that this is a key.' She walked up to the tapestry. 'Pull this aside, would you?'

They did as she asked. 'My father showed me this once only, so I hope I remember how.'

'I see no door,' Gabe remarked.

'Cunning, isn't it? The great Empress Valentyna had it made.'

'To where?' Cassien said.

'It splits, goes two ways,' Florentyna explained. 'One path leads into the palace,' she said, slotting the peg into a hole that looked like a random pockmark in the stone. She held her breath; they heard a soft click and then a sigh as the stone seemed to let go. And with that sound, the shape of a narrow opening became visible as its door relaxed from whatever tight hinges kept it in place.

'Brilliant!' Gabe said. He hauled it back. It swung easily and without the groan that Cassien had anticipated.

'Where does the other path lead?' he asked the queen.

'To the cathedral. Once there we will be in the midst of the city,' she said.

'Does this door close with no sign of ever being opened?' Cassien asked.

'Invisible,' the queen assured.

The passage was low and narrow. Although it was dusty, Cassien could feel a soft breeze against his skin. 'Close it,' he said to Gabe. And when it was done, he nodded. 'Right, your majesty. Lead us to Pearlis Cathedral.'

TWENTY-SEVEN

The trio ran through the tunnel, Cassien privately marvelling at the Empress Valentyna's foresight to have built this passage. If only she could have known how one day it might save her great-great-granddaughter's life.

'My father told me that she famously quipped to Emperor Cailech, when asked about her folly, that she didn't want her hair getting wet when she visited the cathedral,' Florentyna explained. She gave a wry smile. 'Although everything I've learned about her suggests she was not in the least bit vain, despite her beauty.'

Cassien believed Florentyna took after her ancestor and might have ventured to say so, but she put her finger to her lips before he could.

'We're close now,' she whispered.

'Will there be a service on?' Gabe wondered.

'A service?' the queen repeated.

He looked lost momentarily. 'Will the cathedral's priest be holding a ...' He couldn't find the word.

'Ritual, do you mean?'

Gabe smiled awkwardly. 'Perhaps I do.'

Florentyna squeezed his arm sympathetically. 'I can't imagine what you've been through, how strong your conviction in yourself must be. But we're the lucky ones that you defied his evil magic, Gabe. After that, learning our language will be —'

'A piece of cake?' he finished for her. And when Florentyna stared at him bemused, he smiled more confidently. 'Perhaps I can teach you some new expressions too, your majesty.'

She regarded him alongside Cassien for a moment. 'Hamelyn's right. You really do resemble each other. I've been puzzling at it ... there's something in the lilt of your voices, and the way you stand.'

'With respect, you are definitely away with the fairies now, your majesty,' Gabe said, adding, 'because it's just not possible.'

'And until today, I would have said it's just not possible to travel between worlds. But you've proved me wrong.' She gave a small smile. 'The cathedral is only used for important official events of a religious nature,' the queen continued, changing the subject. 'Otherwise, it's always open for pilgrims coming to find their beast and for followers of Shar who simply wish to pay their respects.'

Cassien was intrigued by the newcomer. Like Florentyna he admired the man's tenacity and courage in thwarting the demon. He'd not sensed any guile in Gabriel; believed the man was in shock, but had told them the truth as he'd understood it. The magic surrounding him was baffling and the notion that they looked alike was nagging at him. He could see it now that it had been mentioned; something in the way Gabe held his head when he was listening was rather familiar. He'd tried to ignore it, but now he was searching for mannerisms that echoed.

'I can't tell you how I've dreamed of this place,' Gabe continued in a whisper. 'Years and years of seeing it in my mind's eye, using it as a crutch, fleeing to it for safety when life challenged me. I even dreamed of having a brother, I think. I hear his boyish voice sometimes.' He shrugged. 'Dreams are filled with confusing images at the best of times.'

'Extraordinary,' the queen replied. 'Did you know it was Pearlis?

He shook his head. 'I thought it a place of my own imagination. It was Aphra who showed me I had been dreaming of this place.'

Florentyna looked to Cassien. 'There has to be a reason for Gabe dreaming the cathedral.'

He nodded. 'I wish Ham was here. He's young but he sees things in different ways, from different angles. He's got a talent for seeing everything as a whole.' She looked at him quizzically. 'I'm not explaining it well, I know! He can pull in unrelated facts and tie them together to form the truth.'

Florentyna was thoughtful. 'So he might make something of the fact that Gabe has come from a different land but dreams of Pearlis, while you have a vague recollection of family but were raised outside normal life in a monastery of sorts. You both act rather similarly despite being worlds apart and you both clearly have a fortress mentality that can defy even the biggest of tests. Gabe flees to the cathedral and you draw upon the forest ... nevertheless it is a highly developed mind trick — a shared skill.' But it was her final words that had the most impact. 'He can roam in his body like a spirit.'

He felt her reasoning like a slap. Gabe roams? Not identically, but similarly, so their magic could surely be linked.

The queen continued, oblivious to Cassien's sense of revelation. 'And do you think that, given all of these observations, he might surmise that you are brothers?'

They both stared at her with startled expressions. She gave a small, satisfied rise and drop of one shoulder, her mouth twisting in a crooked half-grin. 'Given that we're having to accept the presence of magic and strange phenomena, why is being related so far-fetched?' She tapped Gabe's arm. 'I hope our cathedral lives up to your dream.'

Queen Florentyna moved forward, leaving behind her shocked companions.

Hamelyn walked alongside Tamas with a heavy heart.

'Are you frightened, Hamelyn?'

'Yes, sire.'

The king gave a short burst of laughter. 'I like your candour. Well, if it consoles you, so am I. But we're going to keep each other safe, you and I.'

He'd only just met the king and yet the man was treating him as an old friend.

'You sound so brave.'

'It's an act, young man. I have to sound like this. I'm the king. Responsibility stops with me.'

'You could have left with the queen. No-one would have blamed you and it would have made more sense.'

'The truth is I couldn't. I have to prove to myself that Darcelle is lost.'

'You really love her.'

The king gave a small sigh. 'Love is a difficult thing to understand, Ham. This marriage was highly beneficial to two realms. Darcelle is ...' he cleared his throat '... a prized young beauty with a fine mind for politics. I've watched her in action and her skills in diplomacy would render most other counsellors impotent. She would be like a weapon — her charm, her looks, her intelligence. She would have been a magnificent asset to Cipres and to me personally. But ...' he hesitated 'I think you're actually asking me about whether my heart turns somersaults for her?' He smiled and didn't wait for Ham's reply. 'I'm too realistic for that. What does amaze me is that she could look forward to a life with me. That makes me very fond of her and thus makes me believe I should be with her, give her everything I can.'

'But what about your heart, your majesty. Doesn't it need to be filled?'

The king laughed. 'What a curious child you are, Hamelyn. I like you. You ask such deep and relevant questions. Most wouldn't. They stay with surface politeness around a king.'

Ham's expression grew grave. 'Forgive me, sire, I didn't —'

'No, I know you didn't. I'm not at all offended, boy. I find you refreshing and interesting and intelligent. And provocative. Let me be honest because we both could be dead by next bell. Do I love her? I thought I could learn to love her, but I'm comparing it to how my heart felt about a childhood sweetheart. Grown-up love has evaded me. I've had my share of women, mind, but I rotate them — if you understand me. These are not women to fall in love with … they are women who give their affections freely.'

'I understand, sire,' Ham replied, earnest in his expression.

'Darcelle … well, she made sharing a crown with me seem sensible. I could have made her happy and she would have given me a fine royal family. I have never looked for butterflies in my heart, child.'

Hamelyn nodded. 'There's still time,' he assured the king.

Tamas clapped him on the back and chuckled. 'Indeed.'

'You've promised you'll be careful,' Hamelyn began, and felt surprised when the king took his hand briefly and squeezed it.

'I always keep my promises,' he replied. 'Now walk tall, Ham. Look as though I'm giving you lots of instructions. You're my personal messenger now.'

Ham nodded. He hoped he would be as brave as King Tamas. As they ascended the vast staircase of Stoneheart he wondered at how his life had changed. A few days ago he'd been an orphan, with nothing to his name but the few coppers thrown to him by nobles who needed directions or assistance with their bags, horses, errands. Now he walked alongside a king.

He remembered the image of the boy and two companions that he'd seen in the trembling white heat of Master Wevyr's crucible. At that moment, he knew the three were Cassien, Gabriel and himself.

They were the Triad.

The knowledge had been nagging at him since he'd first seen Gabriel and Cassien standing near one another. He just hadn't been able to pull his thoughts together. Now his heart surged; it felt as though a piece of the puzzle that he'd been fiddling with had clicked into its rightful position, and as they crested the flight of stairs his eyes were drawn to the head of a wolf sculpted into the newel post nearest him. The wolf was looking at him ... and then, impossibly, it spoke to him.

You are the heir, he heard in his mind, and it was the voice of a she-wolf.

'Ready?' Tamas said, breaking into his thoughts.

'Yes, sire.'

'Into battle then, brave Hamelyn.' The king squeezed his shoulder and sighed at the harried maid who saw Tamas and ran toward them, dropping into a curtsey.

'How is she?' he asked in a wearied but conversational voice, betraying none of his fear.

Hamelyn admired Tamas for this moment. And decided that if Tamas could act so well, he could too.

We are going to hunt you, Cyricus, he swore silently. He cast a prayer to Shar to keep them safe in the face of evil, long enough to work out how to send the demon back to the void he'd come from.

'Wait here,' the maid said to Hamelyn.

'He comes with me,' the king ordered and stared her down when the maid began to protest. 'Hamelyn, I'll need you to run a message to Captain Wentzl shortly, so stick close, boy,' he instructed in a gruff voice, different to his reflective tone earlier.

Act! Ham reminded himself. 'Yes, sire,' he mumbled as he'd seen Meek do.

'And straighten up, boy! You're in the presence of a princess and soon to be your queen!'

Ham straightened his bearing, looking up at the top of the door as they entered the chamber. The sculpture of a dragon stared down at him.

I am here, Hamelyn, said a familiar voice. The dragon had spoken in his mind now.

Master Fynch! He wondered if he were going mad through fear.

Guide the king, child. Remember, you are now in the presence of evil. And evil is cunning.

Ham took a deep breath and followed the king into the chamber where the puppet princess awaited them.

'We're here,' she said, pointing to the end of the tunnel.

'Another hidden door?' Cassien asked.

She smiled. 'My trusty key,' the queen said, reaching for it again. 'We're fortunate this doesn't lead directly into the crypt because Father Cuthben is there, laying out the dead of Stoneheart.'

'So where do we enter?' Gabe asked.

'You'll see,' she said mysteriously.

Florentyna went through identical motions as before, and soon they were entering the cistern of the great cathedral. Gabe gasped.

'Amazing!' he whispered. 'It's huge!'

Cassien wanted to take the time to look around. He hadn't mentioned to either of his companions that visiting the cathedral was one of his most persistent ambitions. He was distracted by Florentyna, who was busy pulling her hair from its pins and pulling off the jewellery she was wearing. She stuffed it all in the pocket of her cloak.

'There,' she said. 'No more queen. Do I look like a pilgrim?'

'You'll do, your majesty,' Cassien smiled. He didn't think she'd ever looked more beautiful than with her hair untidy as it was now, unfurling over her shoulders.

'Don't call me majesty,' Florentyna warned. 'Just call me Florrie or something.'

'Tyna?' Gabe suggested.

She smirked. 'I can cope with that for a bell or two. Let's not get noticed by Father Cuthben. Move quickly once we get to the top of the stairs. We'll have to go past the crypt, but it doesn't have a view of anything but legs passing on the stairs from memory. It's so deep, you see. The stairs lead into the back of the cathedral by the great altar. Don't run,' she whispered. Then smiled. 'We're pilgrims remember. Saunter down the nave — separately. I'll meet you at the front doors.'

They nodded.

'Hey!' said a voice from the other side of the pool of water. 'Who are you?' He began to call to men above.

'Oh, Shar. It's the cathedral guard. I'd forgotten,' Florentyna hissed.

'How many?' Cassien growled.

'Six permanent.'

'I hope they're expendable.'

'What?' she said, looking at him in alarm.

'No-one can know we've come through here. No-one. Gabe, as soon as you can, get the queen up those stairs.'

'How? They're —'

'I'll make it possible. Just do it. They mustn't see her face or make any connection. Understand? Now behind me, you two. Florentyna, hide yourself. *No-one* must know the queen is here.'

The man was coming towards them and other men followed behind him.

'Cassien, don't kill,' Florentyna urged.

'Too late,' he murmured. 'It's what I'm trained to do when your life's threatened.'

Gabe dragged the queen into the shadows. The cistern was huge and they had the advantage of the pond of water that separated them from the cathedral guard. However, the stairway to safety and freedom was blocked by the guards.

'Who are you?'

'No-one,' Cassien said. 'Lost pilgrims.'

'No-one's allowed down here. I don't know how you even got here through our security.'

'It was a mistake,' Cassien replied. 'We will leave.'

'You're coming with us.'

'I don't think so. I want no trouble, sir, but you will force it, if you persist.'

The guard laughed. 'You're no pilgrim. You're hiding something. Take him.'

Cassien drew his sword and everyone paused.

'There are six of us,' the man reminded him. 'Are you sure you want to die?'

'Do you?'

The guard sighed. 'Do not hurt the woman unless she draws a weapon. The other two can be killed if they resist.'

'Wait!' the queen said, stepping forward.

'She can die too, if she doesn't submit. I might even let you have some time with her,' the guardsman joked with his companions.

'I take it back, Cassien,' Florentyna said, her voice sounding like ice splinters. 'Do what you must.'

Cassien leapt. They were not expecting such a daring move. He swooped among the rafters of the low roof, swinging agilely in a disorderly pattern so none could pin him down. He took out the first man with a heel to his jaw before any of the guards had even drawn their weapons. The man dropped like a stone into the water. The second was felled by a circular swing of the sword as he landed, cleaving the man almost in half. He heard Florentyna gag in the distance, but he was losing himself now. He had trained for this. Flesh felt different to straw, but he would ponder that later.

Two men surged towards him. Cassien spun one way high; that man blocked, but Cassien then spun so fast and low that he took him at the knees and the man went down screaming. The other was already swinging, but Cassien had anticipated this and had reached for the blade at his back. The blade buried itself into the man's groin. Cassien stood, wrenching away his blade. Two remained. They backed up a little. He took the opportunity to finish off the guard, who'd near enough had his legs chopped off at the knees. The moans stopped. He wanted no further help to come running.

Four were now dead. He wiped his blades clean on one of them.

'I would have spared your lives if you hadn't threatened rape. What would your queen think?'

'Frigid Florentyna?' the head guard said. 'She could use a good seeing to.'

Cassien blinked. He didn't need to look the queen's way to know how well that crude remark must have gone over.

'Let's not waste time, gentlemen. I'm now between you and the stairs. There's no getting away, so you might as well chance your arms. Gabe, take her.'

He could hear his friends shuffling around the walking ledge that surrounded the waterway, towards the stairs.

'Over my dead body,' the guard threatened.

'That would be a pleasure,' Cassien said and stepped into the man's swinging blade arc.

He fought them both at once, aware that Gabe and Florentyna had disappeared up the stairs safely. This pair was a better outfit. They were putting up a good fight; Cassien knew he must finish them fast. The sound of clanging swords would surely come to some sharp ear. He wanted to be gone from here.

'Go around, Jof,' the head guard growled, parrying another blow.

He readied himself to perform a challenging move that he'd nicknamed 'the crux'. Loup had approved. It required inordinate strength and he'd spent many moons perfecting it, developing the core power required to explode with energy in two opposing directions. It needed precision, so these cramped, low-roofed spaces, where he had to duck stone pillars and water, made it a less than ideal place. Now, the two men were both stepping back and circling him. He had no choice and the crux could kill two at once.

'You are good,' the leader said, 'but you are going to die. We'll find your companions. I know what he looks like; are you brothers, perhaps? The girl will follow him. We'll punish her properly.'

'Well, then, I'll just have to kill you like the others,' Cassien shrugged, dropping his sword, leaving only one of the blades held ready. He centred. Focus!

Both men laughed, assuming it had been an accident the blade slipping from his sweaty hand. 'Not like that you won't,' Jof baited.

They pounced as one, and in a fluid action that to an observer might have appeared to be a dance movement, Cassien crouched and drew his second short blade and using the power that his bent knees gave him, he thrust himself up and out, his arms and legs forming the crux shape.

It was a cruel, powerful, athletic move. Cassien's intensive training had prepared him better than any others to perform it and, despite all the conditions that said otherwise, he formed a low but perfect cross. His feet kicked out so hard and so perfectly positioned that both connected with the bellies of the rushing men, their swords held high, their bodies open to such punishment if the timing was exquisite ... and it was.

They were both predictably winded by the blow to their guts, but the moment of agony was lost to a new sensation when their collapsing bodies brought them closer to Cassien's knives — he seemed to hold himself longer in the air than seemed possible. The vicious blades punched into the exposed throats of his two attackers.

Wet, gurgling sounds of death accompanied his soft, balanced landing. Cassien took a moment to draw breath, surveying his horrible work as he murmured the Prayer of Sending. He was not proud of it, but he nodded to himself, acknowledging that he had lived up to the promise of his training and to his duty as a member of the Brotherhood. He had kept his sovereign safe.

He wished six bodies were not around as clues for the demon, but the waters were not deep enough and he had no time to plan how to conceal them. Getting away cleanly had always been a wish, rather than a given. A last breath was heard being sucked in and expelled … the sixth died. Cassien was satisfied. They may be clues — but to what, the demon would not know.

Cassien took a few more moments to wash himself of the blood that he could feel spattered on his face and hands. He was glad of the dark clothes he wore — Fynch had chosen well, it seemed. He dampened his hair, running his hands through it to be sure no telltale blood spots had been trapped, before he tore a sleeve from the shirt of one of the fallen. Again he took the extra time to be meticulous in drying his face and hands. He cleaned the blades and returned them to their sheaths, all the while calming his breathing, his heartbeat. He must walk upstairs looking composed and hope the dead were not found until he and Florentyna were long gone. He took a few more moments to take the breeches, plain shirt and cloak from one of the dead men. Gabe would need them.

He was aware of the majesty of the cathedral as he stepped into its enormous space. Beautiful soft light filtered in through magnificent, huge windows of stained glass, with one immense, dominating rose-shaped window above the northern end of the nave. Cassien desperately wanted to linger, feeling the pull of this spiritual centre of Morgravia, but he could see a figure in grey at the entrance. She looked small in the distance and he could sense she was fearful and tense beneath the hood of her cloak; perhaps she was mindful that it was unusual in this place for a person to keep their hood up. He must hurry. But where was Gabe?

A new sensation began to crowd within him. Not a voice, yet it called to him. He felt suddenly helpless, began to walk, as if no longer in control of his actions. He walked dumbly, slowly, drawn down the nave to its centre, where aisles led off to meet other corridors that flanked the central nave.

He could see Gabe sitting in the pews, looking up at a pillar. Even from this distance, he could see which beast Gabe was staring at.

Cassien, he now heard in his mind. The voice sounded as though it was coming from a long way off. It was a whisper, carried on the wind. He wasn't imagining it. It called only to him. And as he finally paused beneath the stone pillar that soared into the gods, he felt his heart give, and an outpouring of emotion flood his body. It weakened him, forced him to sit alongside Gabe and follow his line of sight to the great flying serpent ... the king of all the beasts looked down upon them with a benevolent gaze.

Cassien, he heard floating on his mind. *My son.*

He realised his mouth was gaping and he felt teary — something he hadn't experienced since childhood. Gabe turned to him, damp-eyed. 'I ... I don't understand. It called me by name. It compelled me to be here.'

Cassien squeezed Gabe's shoulder, handed him the clothes. 'Compelled both of us. Do you understand the nature of the Pearlis Cathedral creatures? That one alone will single you out and call to you; that is your magical beast for life.'

Gabe shook his head. 'So mine's the dragon?' he said innocently.

'It can't be,' Cassien murmured, his breath coming sharply. He was confused, more frightened by this than by any number of swords being thrown at him.

'It called to me, I tell you. It ... it knew my name.'

Florentyna had obviously seen them and given up waiting. 'New plan?' she asked, arching an eyebrow.

'Forgive us,' Cassien said. 'Get dressed, Gabe. You're too recognisable in Tentrell's clothes and this is something of a disguise. Hurry.'

'What are you doing here?' Florentyna continued. 'Admiring the scenery? Of course, this is the first time in the cathedral for both of you, isn't it? I can see how emotional this is for you, Gabe. It is for all of us the first time.' She smiled kindly. 'Which beast called to you?' she asked, a slight wistfulness in her tone.

Cassien's breath caught. It didn't make sense but either way they couldn't admit the truth. 'The, er ... the winged lion is mine. Gabe's is the unicorn.' Gabe stared at him. 'Isn't it?' he urged, hoping his companion saw the warning in his eyes.

'Er, yes,' he said, tying up his new breeches. 'The unicorn.'

She nodded. 'I'm pleased for you. Both such magnificent creatures. Mine, of course, is this one.' She gestured to the pillar that dwarfed them. 'I can't blame you for admiring him — the royal dragon. King of the Beasts. He is magnificent. I remember the day he called my name as though it was yesterday. I was three summers old, and he knew me and I knew him. I wept too.'

Cassien stood. 'We must go.'

'I'm staying here,' Gabe said, looking as mystified as they did by his words. He shook his head. 'It told me to wait.'

'What did?' Florentyna asked.

Gabe glanced at Cassien. 'The, er … the unicorn.'

'It definitely spoke to you in this way?' Cassien asked, not disbelieving Gabe but certainly surprised. Gabe nodded.

'My creature has never spoken to me, beyond his initial summons,' Florentyna admitted, sounding envious of him.

'Darcelle knows you. It's highly likely she'll come into the cathedral. It's too dangerous. I will bring you back, if it's your choice to be here.'

'It's not my choice. It's the creature's,' Gabe said. 'I trust it, I trust the cathedral. I always have. You need to know that I've been searching for this place for most of my life. I found it now … I can't leave it.'

Cassien nodded. He had to let everyone follow their instincts, especially now magic was at work … in curious ways. His job was to protect the queen alone. He frowned. 'Why would it want you to stay?'

'It's my role, it said. There are three of us. He didn't say more. Just that I must stay in the cathedral.'

It was the Triad that Ham had spoken of, Cassien was sure of it. 'Well, then, you have to stay out of sight.'

'I will, I promise.'

'Can I talk with Gabe a moment, your majesty?'

'Of course. I will wait just over there.'

'Are you sure?' Cassien pressed when the queen was not in hearing distance.

Gabe nodded. 'About this, yes. About whether we see one another again, no.'

Cassien gave a mirthless chuckle. 'If for any reason you ever visit Orkyld, make sure you meet a woman called Vivienne. Tell her I'm glad she tried to trick me … that I have fond feelings for her and I was sad to have to leave.' And that she should use the gold I left to better her position in life; I have no need of it.'

'Tell her yourself. Unless you want to start finding your way to a place called Paris to pass on messages to my friends.'

They both grinned.

Cassien surprised himself by giving Gabe a firm hug. 'I don't understand much of what is happening, but we are certainly brothers in spirit, at least. Be safe, Gabriel.'

There was something achingly familiar about the way Gabe felt in that moment of embrace; the way he tipped his head, the way he naturally wrapped an arm around Cassien's neck and particularly the words he whispered: 'Safe trails, Cass.' It sounded so familiar, so effortless.

Cassien shrank back to stare at him. Gabe stared back.

'What?' the man from Paris asked.

'Why did you say that?'

Gabe shrugged, looked bemused. 'I don't really know. It felt like a memory,' he said, with a crooked smile. 'Nothing's normal for me here. I can't separate what's real or dreaming, what's this life or my previous. Forgive me.'

Cassien joined fists with his new friend. 'I will see you again, Gabe.'

'You can be sure of it,' Gabe replied. He bowed now to Florentyna. 'Your majesty. As we say where I come from, "Take no shit from anyone."'

Florentyna exploded into a helpless laugh, quickly censuring herself as she looked around the nave, but it was quiet. 'I don't even know what that means,' she whispered, leaning forward and kissing Gabe on both cheeks, 'but it sounds deliciously wicked. And remember this, you are my brother too. I will see you again, dear one.'

Gabe beamed. 'Go!'

With a reverent touch of the dragon's pillar, and one final glance at their friend, Cassien took the queen's arm and ran her to the front doors. 'Hurry, Florentyna, those bodies could be found any time.'

She pulled the hood of her cloak over her face and allowed Cassien to walk her quickly out into the streets of her city, where they immediately fell into stride with the flow of traffic, dodging horses, carriages and the general to and fro of people going about their daily life.

'I'm going to buy a pair of horses and then we head for Tyntar.'

'And after that?' she murmured.

'To another cathedral I trust.'

'Where is that?'

'To the one place I know where I can keep you safe, your majesty,' Cassien whispered. 'We're going to the Great Forest.'

TWENTY-EIGHT

Ham held his breath as he watched King Tamas meet Princess Darcelle emerging from her bedchamber. She looked flushed from her bath — or was it excitement? Over the top of a pale-blue knitted shift, she wore a cream lace dress, studded with pearls. The attire was 'fussy' in Ham's opinion but it certainly showed off Darcelle's exquisite shape as though it had been painted on her.

She reached out her hands to the king. Ham was impressed that Tamas didn't hesitate but grasped them warmly and held them against his cheeks.

'You've never looked more desirable,' he said.

'Tamas,' she exclaimed in a more breathy voice than he was used to hearing. 'You took your time, you had me worried.'

'You must never worry about me, my love.'

Ham watched her cut him a glance.

'Why is the boy here?'

'There's a lot going on, Darcelle — my retinue is understandably concerned for me, for both of us. This is Hamelyn. He's been appointed my personal messenger and I've given my word to my guard that he will rarely leave my side. I cannot linger either, my dear. Forgive me, but there is much to do. Obviously all the formalities have been cancelled and we must make arrangements to return to Cipres.'

Hamelyn watched the queen's sister shift her attention fully to him and he realised all of their suspicions were surely confirmed. Cyricus had not seen him previously, and thus could not know him. If Darcelle had still been present perhaps he would have seen a flare of recognition in her eyes; instead, he fancied he could see the evil spirit lurking behind the cold gaze that felt like winter on his skin.

'You are obviously seeing more of my betrothed than I, Hamelyn of Cipres.'

'Your highness,' Ham muttered deliberately, lowering his gaze to show deference, but really not wishing to look upon the cruel eyes.

'Tell me why a visiting merchant's death is so important to our proceedings, Tamas. The man was barely known in the court so his absence is not going to create any large disturbance.' Ham watched her observing the king's surprised reaction to her words and noted the way she covered her callous response. 'What I mean is, Tentrell dropped dead. It could have happened to him at any time and anywhere. It was inconvenient that his heart chose that moment to give out but we shouldn't let his demise disrupt our nuptials ... surely.'

'It's far more serious, though, Darcelle, and it's not only Tentrell. Have you already forgotten that your chamberlain died through the night, not to mention so many other inexplicable deaths around the palace? I believe there is danger for all of us.'

Darcelle adopted a peeved expression. 'I haven't forgotten, Tamas — don't talk to me as though I'm a child.'

'Oh, forgive me, my love,' Tamas said and pulled her close. Darcelle moved to receive his kiss, but Ham noticed that the king cleverly avoided contact on the lips, making soothing sounds and hugging her, 'but you are as precious as a child to me and thus too valuable to risk.'

Ham moved cautiously and slowly into the shadows in order that Darcelle could forget his presence and he could observe her without being too obvious.

She appeared comforted by this. 'Where is Florentyna?'

The king shrugged. 'I left her at the chapel. She'd gone to pay her respects to Burrage. Quite a shock for her, I gather.'

Darcelle lifted a shoulder, gave a careless smirk.

'Do you remember that beautiful river journey we took together when you visited Cipres?'

'Yes, of course,' she replied, smiling lazily. 'Why do you mention it?'

'Well, there was a tiny island with that chapel I showed you?'

She nodded encouragingly. 'Go on ...' Darcelle said, turning away to stare out the window.

'It was built by my great-great-grandmother for the burial of her daughter, who died suddenly, far too young.'

'Yes, I recall it. It was a beautiful spot.'

'High on a cliff,' he said.

'That's right.'

'And you saw the eagle, said it reminded you of me.'

She giggled. 'I can be fanciful at times, my king. And what did you want to tell me about this chapel?'

'I thought it might make the perfect place to take our vows. It's just that Florentyna mentioned in her distress that so much has ruined our nuptials —'

'And she's suggested we sail for Cipres as soon as possible and get married in your realm for expediency?'

Ham watched the king's eyes narrow. 'I wouldn't put it quite so bluntly — as though it is a devious move — but yes, in essence that's precisely what she's suggesting. We could leave tomorrow. I will ready my men, the ships. We can be prepared by tonight if I push hard.'

'Tamas, don't you see this is playing directly into her hands? She wants me gone. I'm a thorn in her side and —'

'I have never got that impression, dear one,' Tamas cut in. Ham could see he didn't want to allow Darcelle to get worked up. 'She simply made the offer. Look, humour me. I will ready the Ciprean retinue for departure and we shall take a few days to consider our position. If you wish to remain, so be it. We can reorganise the festivities. But if you choose to sail, we can slip our moorings in a blink … if that's your choice.'

'So … it's up to me?' she flirted.

'It will always be up to you, my love,' he responded in kind. 'Now,' he put a finger in the air and then touched his lips, with a grin, as if correcting himself, 'Ham, hunt down a man called Menster, and also Captain Wentzl. Tell Wentzl to meet me in the bailey.'

Ham frowned. He didn't know Menster or where to find him. 'Yes, your majesty,' he said gravely, and bowed before making for the door. Obviously the king wanted him to leave, but Ham didn't want to walk out of the door without Tamas in tow.

'And Ham?'

He looked back. 'Tell Menster that the homing pigeons need to be sent. He'll know what to do.'

'Yes, my king.' Ham had absolutely no idea what it all meant but he turned sombrely and bowed to the princess. 'Your highness.' She barely spared him a glance, but Ham felt he had to do something to help the king extricate himself. 'Er, your majesty?' Tamas turned his way. 'You asked for a reminder that you had to give some instructions directly to Felder Goring. I gather it was urgent. Forgive me for presuming,' he said, lowering his eyes.

'Felder Goring?' Tamas repeated looking at Ham. 'Ah yes, of course. Well done, boy. Off you go now.' Ham deliberately turned, but moved slowly. He heard Tamas make a soft groan of suffering. 'Forgive me, my dear one. I must beg your leave. I am going directly to make provisions for our departure and once I have set that in motion, I intend to find us two horses and we are going to ride away from this nonsense and have some quiet time together.'

Ham could hear the excitement in Darcelle's voice. 'Truly?'

Ham opened the door.

'Truly. Give me until next bell and be ready. I shall come for you. And I plan to banish my bodyguards,' he teased. 'I want time genuinely alone with you,' he chuckled.

Ham heard Darcelle give a pleasurable tinkle of laughter. The sound was chilling and he imagined Cyricus thinking that time alone with Tamas would provide the opportunity for transference into the king's body.

'Don't make me wait too long, my ...' Ham lost the last few words as he closed the door, praying that Tamas would get out of there fast. The king had managed to get Ham out of the room and Ham figured Tamas would not want to find him still lurking, so he began to trot away from the palatial quarters of Princess Darcelle, hoping to hear the sound of her chamber door opening.

Tamas was upon him before he knew. 'What are you still doing here, Ham? Run! Run now for the stables. Look like you can't spare a moment for anyone, but to deliver my message and I want two nondescript horses saddled immediately.'

'What about you, majesty?' Ham spluttered, still shocked at the speed with which Tamas had caught up with him.

'Don't worry about me. Just get there and be ready.'

Ham ran, taking the grand steps two at a time even though he knew he should be using the back stairs of Stoneheart. This was the quickest way and anyone would struggle to keep up with him if they wanted to catch and punish him. He threw a glance over his shoulder and saw Tamas moving swiftly, but toward the wing where his chambers were.

'Hurry, King Tamas, hurry,' he breathed, swerving to avoid two guards passing by at the bottom of the stairs and then he was hurtling into the bailey, running as fast as he could toward the stables, his mind reeling with the memory of Fynch's voice in his head, a wolf talking to him, the concept of the Triad and an odd notion about himself, Cassien and Gabe that he wasn't yet prepared to explore.

Tamas was moving as quickly as he dared too, relief flooding through him that he'd got Hamelyn out of harm's way for the time being and that he'd also made it out of Darcelle's chambers without having to kiss her. His promise about their sharing some private time later, without minders, was a barefaced lie concocted on the spot.

The ruse had appeared to work, appeasing her for the time being, but he knew two things for sure, and the first was that Darcelle, the young woman he'd chosen to be his queen, was dead. At no time during their brief conversation was there so much as a flash of the Darcelle he knew, only mimicry of who she'd been. It still looked like Darcelle, had her voice, moved in her graceful manner, showed glimpses of her petulance and self-absorption, and it even laughed in that particularly gleeful tone of hers. But he was grateful that he'd taken the risk, for now he understood that his beautiful wife-to-be was dead; her soul fled to a safer place with her god ... for there had never been a trip on the river together, there was no chapel on a cliff built by his great-great-grandmother for anyone. He'd fabricated a memory and the demon walking in Darcelle had gone along with it. If he possessed her memories, he hadn't bothered to refer to them.

Beyond having to accept now that Darcelle was dead he was also sure that the monster using Darcelle's body would not trust him. Darcelle may have been smart, cunning even, and more than capable of intrigue, but what he knew they'd also shared from their first meeting was a mutual trust. For the moment, the demon would give Tamas the benefit of the doubt so the King of Cipres had given himself a slight head start to get away from the Morgravian palace and hopefully the capital.

Sending his young sidekick off to find Menster was a ruse. Menster didn't exist and Tamas was sure Hamelyn would work it out and head, as asked, for the stables. He burst into his rooms and found Captain Wentzl awaiting him, worry deeply etched in his face as he swung around at the king's arrival.

'Majesty!' he said, relief now smoothing out his expression.

'I know. Wentzl, hear me now,' Tamas said, peeling off clothes and rapidly moving around his chamber as he spoke, gathering up items into a sack. 'We are leaving. All our men are to assemble in the bailey and I want you to get them galloping hard for the western harbour and our ship. Send word ahead to the men we left behind to ready her sails.'

Wentzl frowned, watching the king, now almost naked.

'We're leaving, your majesty?'

'Indeed.'

His captain baulked. 'King Tamas —'

Tamas shook his head, pulling on his favourite leathers and riding garb, instantly transforming him from king to noble. 'I wish I had something even less obvious,' he muttered. 'I'll find it along the way.'

'Along the way?' Wentzl repeated. 'Your majesty, please, what is happening?'

'It's too long in the explanation, other than to say that we are in danger here and if you value your king's life, you will not fight me on this and you will carry out my instructions without querying me further. I know it flies in the face of everything you know you should be doing for me, but I am attempting to save our lives. If we do this any other way, I will surely die and so will a lot of Cipreans.'

Wentzl looked at his king, baffled, as Tamas pulled on his old worn and much loved boots. 'Ah, that's better,' he said, thrilled to be out of the regalia of royalty. 'Now where is that prized bow of mine?'

'It was put in this chest, your majesty,' his companion said. He fetched it for the king. 'I'm afraid there are only two arrows. We were going to have more fletched for the hunt when we got here.'

'One is all I'll need.'

Wentzl frowned, unsure of what his king was referring to but he waited, appreciating that Tamas was on a mission and clearly had a plan.

'Wentzl, you and the men are to set sail for Cipres as fast as your horses can get you to the ship. Is that clear?' Wentzl nodded, wanting to speak but clearly too confused to form the questions exploding in his mind. 'Here, take these clothes,' he said, gathering up his discarded finery and reaching for his sword. 'Run with me, I'll explain as we go. Do you know how to get out of this part of Stoneheart through a back or side entrance?'

Wentzl, still too confounded to speak, nodded. Then he cleared his throat. 'Forgive me. Yes, of course, your majesty. Follow me.'

'Bring everyone. Leave no-one here,' Tamas said, pointing to the door where he'd passed guards as he'd entered.

'But your belongings ...' Wentzl queried, looking around the suite.

Tamas knew the man was in shock, but couldn't help smiling. 'Forget about them, Captain Wentzl. I'm sure my life is worth more than some formal wear. This is all I need,' he said, grabbing his distinctive fur-lined coat. Tamas finished buckling on his sword and reached for his riding gloves and bow. 'Let's go,' he said, physically pulling the stunned captain with him. 'Lead the way and pay attention because I'll only have time to explain my plan once.'

Hamelyn had never run faster. Menster was surely a ruse to get him out of Darcelle's clutches. He ignored it and made for the stables. His mind was scattering in various directions. Was he being pursued, or more likely was King Tamas being pursued? In his mind's eye he saw Darcelle suddenly develop fangs and fly, swooping after the king to kiss him or kill him, but either way to claim him. He was worried for Cassien too — could he keep the queen safe and smuggle her out of Stoneheart? He had no idea how that was going to be achieved but he felt that if anyone could, it was Cassien. And Gabe. Coming back to life as he had! It was terrifying, but thrilling, because it meant Gabriel was alive and the Triad, whatever it was, was complete.

'Where will we all meet?' he murmured to himself as he slid into the stable and the new problem of how he was to access horses arose.

'Hey, you boy, what's your name?' a deep voice yelled.

'Er, Ham.'

'You don't belong in here,' the voice arrived. It belonged to a youngish man, who towered over him. Nevertheless, he wasn't that much older, Ham reckoned; definitely less than a decade between them.

'Not usually, no,' he said, rallying his confidence. 'I'm with Master Cassien, who is the queen's newly appointed champion.'

'Ah, I'd heard rumours this morning. A little bird said he was sleeping with the queen.'

Ham eyed the man and decided he was slightly simple-minded rather than disrespectful. 'Not sleeping with her, just sleeping outside her chambers for the time being. You know odd things have been happening around the palace, right?'

The man nodded. 'Aye. Animals have died. Broke the stable master's heart this morning when he found them. Cook wanted to butcher them for the meat, but Master Cole won't hear of it. They were fine horses, those. He's having them put on a pyre. It's where he is now.'

'I see.' Ham seized his chance. 'I've come to get our pair of horses,' he said. 'You wouldn't happen to know where they are?' he asked, looking down the length of the impressively large stables.

'Of course I do,' his companion said. 'Master Cole insists on a detailed inventory of every animal we keep and it's listed against its owner.'

'Perfect. Can you get me our horses and saddles, then?'

'I could if I could read the list,' he said and grinned innocently at Ham.

Ham smiled back. 'Or better still, I can point them out.'

'No, that means I'd have to take your word for it,' the man said, taking off his cap to scratch his head slowly. 'You need your mounts urgently?'

'I'm afraid I do. Master Cassien won't be pleased if I keep him waiting.'

'I know every horse here. I know the visiting animals, but we have a lot of them at present because of the king's arrival.'

Time was moving on and Ham could feel his fears gathering and sounding a distant alarm in his head. He had to be ready; that's what Tamas had conveyed. Tamas was clever with his ruse, but it would all come to naught if he didn't have horses at the ready.

Ham closed his eyes and pictured himself riding with Cassien on their way to Rittylworth. He knew he could do this, knew his mind absorbed every detail of the landscape around him at any given moment. At the next bell, if he were asked to describe this stable in detail he knew he could, even though he'd barely given it more than a cursory glance. It was simply how his mind worked.

'What is your name?'

'It's Clef.'

'Clef, perhaps they'll be stabled nearby to each other?' Ham suggested, hoping he could lead the stableman where he needed.

Clef nodded obligingly. 'They may even share a stall, as we're crowded right now.'

'Good. Then shall I describe Master Cassien's horse?'

His companion laughed but not unkindly. He scratched his head again. 'You could try. Horses are horses,' he said, not sounding helpful.

'I can be accurate in my description and then, if you recognise the one I tell you about, mine will logically be the one with it or next to its left or right and I'm sure you'll know which.'

Clef frowned, clearly not grasping such obvious reasoning. Ham didn't pause to explain but drew on his skill. 'It's a mare. She stands this high,' he said, gesturing with a hand. 'She's a grey, but her tail is a lovely soft golden colour,' he began, glad the horse's light colouring would set her apart quickly from the predominantly chestnut horses.

From the window of her chambers, the gaze of Princess Darcelle absently wandered over the bailey while Cyricus and Aphra plotted.

'We should stay together,' Aphra argued.

'No. I need the body of a male. I regret losing Gabriel. I was too hasty.'

'But in Darcelle you have the power you need,' she pressed.

'Not entirely, Aphra. As the princess we have some power to command, but at the queen's word, everyone bows, including Darcelle.'

'Stick to your plan, my beloved,' she cooed. 'I'll be your Darcelle and you be my Tamas. Then we have power.'

He yawned as Darcelle. 'Yes, I suppose you're right, although you seem very trusting of the king.'

'He has no reason to mistrust his bride-to-be. I thought he was very tender toward her just now,' she soothed.

'Did you?' She didn't reply. 'I was sure I detected a false note in his words.'

'No,' she said, firmly.

'You didn't get the impression that he was eager to be away from Darcelle?'

'I didn't,' she admitted. 'Besides, what possible reason could he have for being suspicious of her? He was distracted if anything, by his concern when they found Gabe's body ... or what they thought was Tentrell's body.'

'Yes, I do have to agree with you. Tamas was shocked and profoundly concerned for Darcelle in that courtyard. I also agree that unless Gabe sat up and spoke,' he jested, sounding amused now, 'I see no possibility that Tamas could know about any other threat.'

'That's right. And Gabe was *very* dead, my love. We got rid of him long ago,' she assured him.

He hesitated, allowing Darcelle's eyes to scan the bailey, where there seemed to be an inordinate amount of activity. He knew Darcelle's pretty face was frowning while he absently pondered Tamas and what he was looking at.

'And yet, still I had this sense that the king was being careful.'

'In what way?'

'Do you not think that a man would at least wish to kiss the woman he intended to marry when he had her alone in a room?'

'I suspect he is being highly respectful of the Morgravian Crown's as its guest.'

'He's a man, Aphra! Men have needs.'

She giggled. 'So do you, my love. I can't wait to service them when you are flesh again.' She sighed. 'He wouldn't have been intimate in front of the boy.'

'The boy … yes, indeed, the quiet child with the steady focus and all-seeing gaze,' Cyricus mused.

'He was a servant, nothing more,' she said dismissively.

'But I sensed a lot more. I sensed scrutiny from the shadows. I sensed knowing. I sensed …'

'What?'

Cyricus gave a soft groan. 'Ah, it was the child … the child! I had all my concentration on Tamas.'

'What are you talking about?'

'I'm talking about that stealthy, quietly spoken, bowing boy, who said the right things in the right places but he was gathering information. He knows!'

'What?'

'You heard me. It's his knowledge that my instincts were sensing. Nothing to do with Tamas!'

'I don't understand,' Aphra bleated.

'No, I know you don't, which is why you are my slave and I your lord. And why, if I decide to move out of Darcelle's body, I will not need your permission. The boy knows, believe me in this. Oh, I can't imagine why

I was so slow to realise it. I've been duped into feeling safe. Who is he? How can he know anything about me?'

'Cyricus, I think Tamas is —'

'Don't, Aphra! Don't placate me. I follow my own intuition and it is growling that the child who came with Tamas was far more than a simple messenger boy.'

'But, the king —'

'I said, don't,' he murmured so quietly it was definitely a threat. 'Don't even speak just now.'

He made a low, growling noise of frustration — which issued as a mewl from Darcelle — as he gave his attention in a more focused way to the bailey. To his astonishment he saw Tamas, sitting in the saddle of the beautiful pearl-coloured horse that Florentyna had donated from her personal stable for the king's use. Although Cyricus could ride, he barely knew a smattering about horse husbandry, but even he could appreciate the glowing beauty of the pale horse, whose coat shimmered with two colours beneath the sunlight. And though he knew so little, there was no doubting that horse, and certainly no doubting that glorious fur-lined cloak of King Tamas, brightly flashing azure blue in its silken lining against the gold of the horse's flank.

For a couple of Darcelle's heartbeats he was struck silent and still as a statue. And then he moved, his voice emerging as Darcelle's shriek. 'No!' he cried, forming the lips of the princess into a helpless snarl. 'No!'

'Cyricus, it's what I've been trying to tell you. The king is leaving!' Aphra said, stating the obvious and enraging her demon companion.

'Ride!' Wentzl roared to his men. 'As fast as the wind. Protect our king!' he yelled, standing up in the saddle as his horse, leading the charge from Stoneheart, reacted to the knee dug into its side.

The men of Cipres rode, kicking up dust, scaring the women servants who happened to be crossing the bailey, scattering chickens and dogs in their wake. They didn't leave by the road either. Wentzl led them cross-country, determined to cut many hours from the journey by going over the rougher terrain. He would not spare the horses that way, but clearly that was not his intention, Stoneheart's gatekeepers mused between themselves as they watched the fast-flowing column of men disappearing, the king in their midst.

Those same gatekeepers heard shattering glass, and when they looked up they saw Princess Darcelle with fists bloodstained from battering at the windows and, like her, they had wondered why King Tamas was riding away from Stoneheart in such frenzy.

Darcelle spun on her heel, flushed, furious and heedless of the blood spattering her fresh gown. Servants rushed in, having heard her cries. They gasped and wanted to fetch water and bandages, but she swatted them away like gnats. Darcelle ran, heedless of who she bumped into or offended in her hasty passage to the stables.

She arrived, breathless, her unpainted lips pale and thin. 'Who are you?' she demanded of the man who approached, doing his best to effect a bow but managing to achieve only an awkward stoop. He looked awestruck by her presence. 'I said …' she screamed at him.

'Cl— Clef, your highness. I am the stableman.'

'Where's the stable master?'

'Burning two horses,' he replied baldly. 'Er … your highness.' He pulled his cap off, realising too late he'd forgotten his manners. He lowered his eyes, but Darcelle barely registered him.

'The king just rode out,' she said, her breath ragged and angry. 'Did he say to where?'

'They said to the harbour, your highness. That's what I was told,' Clef replied.

'Harbour?'

'Where the ships are,' he said uselessly.

Darcelle let out a groan of despair. 'Get away from me, you simpleton. Fetch me a horse!'

'A horse?'

'Are you deaf as well as dumb?'

'No, your highness.'

'Then saddle my horse this moment or I will have your ears cut off and your tongue cut out so you might never offend me again.'

Clef looked ready to weep. He began to stammer but somehow rallied his nerve. 'Please, your highness. If you'd wait out there,' he gestured to the hitching rail, where a step was positioned for riders to mount their horses easily. 'I'll bring your Gold immediately.'

Darcelle stomped from the stable entrance, her resident's rage making him careless. Consequently, Cyricus didn't notice the hooded rider ease a grey from the side and emerge into the sunlight leading a second horse — a chestnut — toward the gate. At the gate, he raised a hand to the gatekeepers, who barely paid him more than a glance, their attention still riveted on the cloud of dust the Ciprean party was kicking up as they disappeared over another hill, heading to the west of the realm.

The hooded rider walked both horses onto the main road, ignoring the hustle and bustle of the endless human traffic, carts, animals that flowed into and out of Stoneheart's great bailey. Once he'd cleared the bottleneck and had taken the bend that would lead him north, he leaned down to mutter to the lad who sat in front of him hiding beneath the old, dun hooded cloak that the rider had pulled around him.

'Ready, Ham?'

'I am, your majesty,' he said, clambering down to take the reins of the second beast. 'Nicely done.'

'It may buy us some time,' Tamas said. 'On your horse, then. We must ride until our backsides are numb,' he said and winked at his young companion.

TWENTY-NINE

Cassien had ridden hard for as long as he could keep pushing the horses. He'd deliberately drifted east and brought them into the town of Micklesham, northeast of Farnswyth, whose three roads all led up the winding gradient to a small convent built at the hill's summit. On the way they threaded through streets with tall houses leaning precariously inward, and yet it seemed a light-filled town.

'I've not heard of this place,' he admitted, choosing not to address Florentyna by her new nickname, but knowing he could not even think to utter her title.

'Really. Where have you been living, Cassien?' she replied. 'My father was always very proud of Micklesham.'

'Is that so? What's it famed for?'

She smiled wearily. 'For being planned. He designed it.' She shrugged. 'Oh, he had lots of help, of course, but he wanted to leave behind a plan for future towns in Morgravia. It's his legacy.'

'I appreciate the broad lanes.'

She nodded. 'He wanted carts, wagons, animals and people to be able to share the streets of towns without clogging them. He wanted lots of light and he hated to chop down trees.' She gave a sad twist of her mouth. 'It's why you'll see they've left these grand plane trees intact,' she said, pointing to the side of the street. 'Father said that in his dreams he could hear the trees screaming their protest over the centuries as forest gave way to towns.'

Cassien smiled. 'I wish I had met the king.'

'You and he would have got along famously, I suspect.'

'I'm glad you think that.'

'Why is that important?'

'Because I know how much your father meant to you.'

She eyed him, controlling her horse expertly with a light touch on the reins. 'You mean because he would like you, that means I like you?'

Cassien blinked. 'That wasn't really what I was getting at, but it sounds reassuring.'

Florentyna grinned. 'You're a strange one, Cassien.' She looked around. 'It is a quiet town,' she said, easily returning to their previous conversation. 'It's probably most famous for its kite festival.'

'Kites. As in things that fly?'

She giggled deliciously. He'd never heard her laugh like that before. 'Yes, I do. Truly, where have you been living? Or, let me guess. You're going to say the forest, aren't you?'

He gave her an intense glance. 'Yes. It's been my home for a while now.'

'And you came out of the Great Forest for me?'

'I came out because Fynch urged me to protect you with my life.'

'Fynch,' she pondered. 'I wish I'd listened to him.'

'Fortunately for us, I did,' he replied. As he watched the queen frown and the next obvious question forming, he continued. 'Don't ask me how he knows what he knows. I know so little about him other than that he is deeply committed to the realms that you now preside over.'

He could see the queen bite back the question that he'd neatly dodged. 'So we're going to just live out in the forest?' she said brightly, but he could hear the dry note of bemusement. 'I'll rule from a secret camp somewhere perhaps?'

He couldn't help the look of scorn that he knew was ghosting into his expression. 'That isn't my plan, no. The forest is safe and we shall go there as a precaution and to give us time to organise our thoughts, plan what is the next best step. Your sister has become a demon — we must never lose sight of the ever-present danger to you.'

'No, forgive me, Cassien, if I sound in any way ungrateful.' He shrugged. 'Everything has been happening so fast, I have scarcely drawn breath. In fact, I can barely think, almost trying not to … it's so painful when I consider what has been lost this day.'

He nodded understanding.

'And King Tamas. What if he has succumbed too?'

'I will be warned,' he said, thinking of his wolf, of Fynch … of Ham. *Be safe, Hamelyn*, he cast into the void.

'By whom?' she asked and he wished he hadn't sounded so mysterious.

'By my instinct,' he replied, a tad too fast to be convincing he thought. He relaxed his expression. 'We'll both know, your majesty, I'm sure of it.'

She straightened in the saddle, a mood of resignation showing in the thinning of her lips. 'It won't come to that. Tamas was fully warned. I know he would be very careful in that thing's presence.' She frowned and then sounded beaten. 'Cassien, how are we ever going to beat the demon?'

'That's why I need the forest … it helps me to think.'

'All right,' she said. 'If giving you a clear mind means I sleep on the forest floor tonight, lead the way.'

Cassien smiled dryly. 'Not tonight, your majesty,' he said, glancing up at the sun that was lowering itself behind one of the tall houses.

'Don't hesitate on my account,' she warned.

'I'm not,' he said. 'We'll overnight here on account of the horses. They need rest and watering as well as feeding.'

'Get new ones. We have no reason to … Oh!' she said, sounding understandably surprised when Cassien suddenly leapt off his horse.

'Don't move!'

'What?'

'Stay with the horses. Tie them up to that post and stand between them. Keep your head low.'

'Cassien …'

But Cassien was already moving. He knew he shouldn't leave the queen alone, but he was sure he'd just spotted someone in the street ahead who might help them. He broke into a run.

Florentyna eased out of her saddle, made very aware of the many hours spent on it when her back protested with a twinge of pain. It wasn't wise to stand between the horses — they could cause her injury if they were spooked by someone or something and crushed her between them. Even so, she didn't want to defy Cassien, who expected her to obey him without question; he was all that stood between her and a demon, so she told herself to behave graciously and do as he said. It was unnerving watching him run away as he had — after what or whom?

People passed her by and barely gave her a second glance. This felt strange. She was used to gazes being riveted on her, not just because she was a queen, but because she was the queen that everyone was very curious about. It was her fault. She was far too remote. She'd let Darcelle usurp her in public show, and she could hardly blame her sister for such …

'Oh, Darcelle,' she muttered, faltering. She hadn't lied to Cassien; until they'd stopped their mad dash away from Stoneheart her mind had been empty of everything except alarm.

Gabe's emergence; the guards in the cathedral; the blood she'd noticed on Cassien's shirt; and then the way they'd had to thread a path to a local stable, where he'd insisted she hide beneath the hood of her cloak while he bought the horses. She'd moved through that time in a stupor of fear … no, not fear … it was shock. Everything from the moment she'd woken had been a shock. All those people dead in the palace. Why?

Burrage! Florentyna gasped, covering her mouth for fear of crying out and drawing notice to herself. The horses shifted at the low sound, but mercifully didn't move toward each other and threaten to crush her. Burrage was dead. And now Darcelle. Florentyna swallowed. It was her fault. Her instincts had told her to listen to Fynch, but she'd been persuaded to ignore him — persuaded by two who were now dead and needn't be. Even Saria was dead, along with two other brave, loyal men.

Reynard had tried to counsel her otherwise in his gentle way, and her belief that Master Fynch's warnings were not a genuine threat had forced him to take matters into his own hands.

Too many deaths. She had no one to turn to.

Florentyna's breath turned ragged. Her cheeks were wet with tears and she felt herself crumbling under the burden of knowing all this loss and destruction rested on her shoulders and her poor judgement. She began to struggle to breathe and her vision was turning misty. Strong arms were suddenly beneath hers and she was aware of being lifted as she rallied, became more aware of her surrounds again. She looked up and could see Cassien's worried face. He was carrying her and with such ease.

He looked down and gave her a crooked grin. 'Forgive me, I was gone just a few moments,' he said.

'You swooned, nothing serious,' another voice said.

Florentyna turned as Cassien released her to stand unaided.

'You remember Tilda?' he said.

Florentyna frowned and then opened her mouth in surprise. 'My infusions woman?' Tilda laughed and the sound was warm and earthy, like a full barn in leaf-fall. 'Tilda, of course!' she said, trying not to sound weak or teary. She gathered herself swiftly. 'I'm pleased to see a familiar face. How do you two know each other?'

'Come, I shall explain more but first I think you need some food, some rest. Here, Tilda,' he said, pushing coin into the woman's hand, 'could you get some rooms in that guest house you mentioned? I'll see to the horses.'

'No, wait,' Florentyna said. 'The forest is where we need to be, isn't it?' Cassien gave a slight nod that was almost a shrug. 'Can we make it by nightfall?'

'We can make it there during the night,' he confirmed. 'Three hours.'

'Then I'd rather keep moving. I agree, a rest and something to eat would be helpful, but we are not to stop pushing onward on my account. Stable ours and buy new horses if you must.'

Cassien stepped closer. 'Florentyna, this is all on your account. There is no point if you are not safe.'

She smiled sadly. 'I know. All the more reason for me to make this easier for you. You can offer better protection in the forest, you said.'

'I can.'

'Then let's eat and move on.'

He studied her for a moment longer before he nodded at Tilda. 'Where do you know that's quiet for food?'

'Mistress Falc offers soup and bread for a few coppers at her dinch-house. There's nothing elegant about it, I'm not sure we could take her maj—' she looked at Florentyna and corrected herself '— take our guest. Well, it's not what you'd be used to,' she said, looking uncomfortable.

'Tilda, this is going to be a struggle, I know. Why don't you call me Florrie, as my father did? You too, Cassien,' she said, 'or neither of you will ever finish a sentence.'

The both smiled back at her awkwardly.

'It's fine, really … I insist. And I always rather liked it,' Florentyna said, as though bringing them both into her secret. 'Now, a bowl of soup sounds good, Tilda. Then you can both tell me more about how you know each other.'

Tilda glanced at Cassien. 'Ask anyone the way to the stable and back to Mistress Falc's. They will know it. I'll take … Florrie,' she said, looking at Florentyna with an enquiry of permission in her expression to which the queen smiled. 'And I'll order the food.'

Cassien glanced at the queen and nodded encouragement. He left her with Tilda, leading the horses away.

Florentyna could hear the dinchers' conversations well before they'd reached the dinch-house itself. It was as simple a dwelling as Florentyna had ever stepped into. Yet the atmosphere was warm and cheery. Mistress Falc had whitewashed the timbers and, as evening was drawing in, her girls began to light the lamps hanging from the house's eaves and from the tall spokes driven into the earth to form a bright pathway. The dinch-house was at the end of a lane and while it had no formal gardens, the land around it had been left to grow wild. Sprawling cleaver plants, which appeared to glow as darkness fell, created pretty, luminous drifts of flowers that trailed away from Mistress Falc's into the meadows beyond.

'I've never understood cleaver flowers and their glowing petals,' Florentyna remarked as they waited for the girls to clear one of the small outside tables for them. 'But they're very beautiful. My father used to say it was the magic of the moon that lit their internal lights.'

Tilda seated herself, giving a soft groan. 'I must stop doing that. Makes me feel older than I am,' she said with a grin. 'It's not the flowers that glow. I like your father's notion though. It's romantic.'

Florentyna fiddled with the largest drip of beeswax oozing from a small channel at the lip of the fat candle in front of her. She snapped it off, feeling the stinging but not unpleasant burn of the clump of hot wax, still molten in the middle. She thought of her father and how, if he could see her, he would be frightened on her behalf, yet he would expect her to set aside her fears to be decisive and courageous, come what may. 'So what makes them glow?' she asked, massaging the wax like putty until it hardened. She wanted to talk about anything else but demons, death, destruction.

'There's a worm inside each flower.'

'A worm?' she repeated, astonished. 'You jest.'

Tilda grinned. 'My old pappy used to say we learn something new each day. The worms are female; they use their glow to attract their mates and they use the flowers as warm, safe cups in which to lay their eggs.'

'Do the eggs glow as well?' Florentyna asked, pushing the solid ball of wax back into the heat of the candle near the wick.

'No, only adult females and only at mating time.' She grinned. 'Just like us, really,' she said in a wry tone. Florentyna smiled shyly. 'I use the eggs for my potions.'

'Really?'

'I only take one or two from each flower. As you can see, there are thousands in each drift.'

'Plenty to go around,' Florentyna smiled, as one of the serving girls arrived. 'Anyway, Til—'

'Soup for three,' Tilda said, cutting across the queen's words. 'What is it for tonight?'

'Mistress Falc is doing a sweet farl and creamed chivarac this evening. It's delicious.'

Tilda nodded her approval. 'And some of her sunflower bread?'

'I shall organise that for you. Dinch for you both … and your other guest?'

Florentyna nodded, feeling a thrill of excitement — despite the danger — to be doing something so common and so very normal as being out at nightfall in a dinch-house. Even better, she was doing it without a host of guards and the usual pomp and ceremony. Darcelle would turn in her grave — if her body hadn't been stolen by a demon, Florentyna thought bitterly. She abruptly pushed Cyricus away from her thoughts, determined to appear composed and strong, as her father had always counselled her so that everyone around him — or her — would have a model to follow.

'The best thing,' Florentyna said, taking Tilda into her confidence, 'is that this is so very normal for everyone. Look around. People are chatting, having a good time, solving the problems of the land over a hot cup of dinch.' She sighed. 'I don't get to do anything remotely like this. Whatever I do, I have people minding my every move.' She looked out across the tables of dinchers. 'I envy you.'

'Don't. Most of them here would pull out their own teeth with pliers to have your life, your lands, your money, your power.'

Florentyna frowned. Tilda spoke evenly, but there was an edge to her words. They sounded like wise counsel but there was also an underlying note of scorn. She tried a different tack. 'That's how it is, isn't it? We always want what the other person has,' Florentyna admitted with a sigh.

They both looked out across the fields. 'So is this a regular watering hole for you, Tilda?'

'Yes. I always take a bowl of dinch and soup here when I leave Pearlis. It's my routine to head north after seeing everyone in the city.'

'How do you come to know Cassien?' Florentyna asked, determined to be direct.

Tilda hesitated and the queen noticed. 'Is it a secret?'

'No, although it is a sensitive topic.'

'I see,' Florentyna said, but she didn't.

Their bowls of soup arrived then, the steam rising enticingly enough to make the queen's belly grind with anticipation.

Cassien chose this moment to enter the garden. He threaded his way to their small table and she was amazed that no-one felt threatened by the weapons she knew he wore, but then as she watched him approach, she was aware there was no giveaway clank of metal; in fact he never 'clanked' like other men who carried weapons. Cassien seemed to move in silence and yet she knew he wore a fine sword, carried blades. 'Something smells good,' he admitted.

'I'll bring the dinch out shortly,' said the serving girl, staring at him. 'I'll be back in a moment with the bread,' she said to Tilda, stealing another glance at Cassien, in which Florentyna saw only invitation.

The queen joined Tilda in a shared dry look that they then directed his way.

'What? Did I miss something?' he said, his eyes darting between them, his brow creased in enquiry.

'You're not even aware of it, are you?' Florentyna said with a grin.

'It?'

Tilda laughed aloud. 'That's what makes him bearable.'

He frowned deeper, but they shook their heads. Florentyna was hit suddenly by a novel notion … why wasn't she as heartstruck as the serving girl? Or the palace servants, for that matter, whom she had overheard talking about Cassien? He really was extremely easy on the eye, and his strapping frame meant he would have won attention even without his handsome features. She blinked as he seemed to note her attention and then looked away. It was obvious, even to her slightly detached approach to the world around her, that Cassien liked her. And he was clearly fighting liking her in a way he was undoubtedly not permitted to by the Brotherhood. She too had restrictions on her friendships, but even so … why didn't she respond?

'Shall we?' Cassien said, breaking into her thoughts.

She smiled and began to eat. Florentyna noticed she was the only person in sight who was tipping their bowl away to scoop up the soup. Some patrons, she observed, dispensed with the spoon altogether and picked up the bowl to tip the contents directly into their mouths. She could imagine what Burrage might have to say about that. *Might have said*, she corrected, feeling a fresh wave of sorrow wash over her.

'Feeling better?' Cassien enquired.

'I felt overcome with grief and became dizzy. My sister, Burrage, the deaths at the monastery, the deaths within the palace,' she murmured, becoming quieter with each word.

'Perfectly understandable. Eating will make you feel stronger — capable of facing anything.'

She gave him a wan smile. 'Food does not solve a single problem,' she counselled more dryly than she'd meant to sound.

'It would if you'd ever had to spend a day hungry … or a day and night. Or a few,' he countered and then looked away, appearing self-conscious. 'Forgive me …'

'No, you're right, of course. I haven't got a clue really about everyday life and yet I yearn for it,' she whispered, her apology written in her expression. 'I have no idea about how to live through hardship,' she added, 'other than the emotional kind.'

The bread arrived and it was warm, oozing with chunks of golden butter.

'Don't let your soup go cold,' the girl said and was quickly gone, but not before casting Cassien another silent invitation.

This time the two women sighed.

'I didn't say a word,' he muttered, biting off a chunk of his bread.

'You don't have to,' Tilda said. 'That pretty young thing has already said yes to your question.'

'Be assured I'm not asking,' he replied.

Florentyna stifled a grin. She picked up her wooden spoon again and began ladling the broth into her mouth without observing the courtly customs she'd been raised in. It felt wicked to do so, but Burrage — if he were watching — would forgive her, she was sure.

'So, Tilda, you obviously know about the problems in the palace with the deaths …?' She took her cue from Cassien as he was clearly at ease with the herbwoman.

'I do. It's good to see you have an appetite,' Tilda said, not giving a specific response to the queen's query. 'People think you've been looking very thin and frail.'

The queen didn't like being sidetracked but went along with it for now. 'Poppycock,' Florentyna admonished. 'I've always been this size. It's just recently I've had to wear gowns that annoyingly accentuate waists and busts and those bits usually covered by my everyday clothes. Now, Cassien,' she said. 'Tilda preferred you to tell me how you two know one another.'

Cassien stopped eating and put his spoon down. Florentyna sensed his discomfort.

'I see,' she said. 'So there is a secret?'

He shook his head. 'No, more to the point a difficult epiphany, that's all.'

'An epiphany, I recall from my long and intense education, suggests something divine, certainly something supernatural, which has come to you from the outside and opened your mind to encompass a far bigger comprehension of your world,' Florentyna said, matter of factly, chewing on a thick slice of the bread.

'Then I chose the right word. It was exactly that,' he said.

She looked between her companions. 'And still you don't explain anything to me. You both look tense. Scared even.'

'That's because it is unnerving,' Tilda admitted.

'Try me,' Florentyna urged.

Cassien glanced at Tilda and nodded to indicate he would tackle this. 'Your majesty,' he whispered, only for her hearing, 'the reason I have been sent to protect you is, I believe, not just because of my skills with weapons.'

Florentyna stopped chewing. She watched him intently, waiting. 'Go on.'

He took a breath and placed his spoon down. She noticed his soup was finished; not a drop wasted. 'Fynch sent me to you because of my ability to roam.'

'Roam? You mean cover great distances?'

He shrugged. 'You could say it like that but the meaning is, perhaps, shrouded.'

'Why don't you explain? Say it simply to me. Why do I get the feeling this is a struggle for you?'

'Because it is painful,' he said. 'My roaming is not of the earth.'

She blinked. 'I don't understand.'

'You're not meant to,' Tilda chimed in.

'I roam on an ethereal plane,' Cassien continued. Florentyna knew she was looking at him as though he was speaking gibberish while he tried to enlighten her. 'It's a skill like wielding a sword, or running faster than others.'

'A magical skill,' Tilda qualified. At Cassien's glare, she returned it with one of supplication. 'Say it how it is, Cassien.'

'Yes, why don't you?' Florentyna added.

He did. His roaming episode at the palace was explained baldly and clearly. She stared at him in shocked silence before she licked her lips, buying another few heartbeats to gather her thoughts.

'So if I understand you right, you killed Burrage?'

'Not directly or intentionally, but yes I did. And I have not yet come to terms with the deaths I caused, including his. I had no idea of the effect of my roaming. All I had in my mind was protecting you.'

She shook her head in silent despair. 'But surely you've roamed previously?'

He nodded. 'In the forest.'

'And?'

She noted he struggled with how to phrase his reply. 'Well … the first time animals died. After that, I went to a place where animals were … um, where they were scarce and I could roam without hurting any.' He was speaking carefully, seemingly choosing his words as though couching the truth neatly behind them.

'So you knew if you roamed at the palace it could cause death?'

'I thought only that it might kill a few dogs, cats, rats.' He shrugged. 'I am honest with you when I say I had not even the slightest idea that it could hurt a person.'

'How does it choose?' she said, aware vaguely of Tilda's awkward silence but too determined to understand Cassien's magic to worry about their companion.

388

'I don't know,' he said, running a hand over his face. 'I wish I did. It's one of the reasons I had to get you away from Stoneheart,' he murmured. 'In the forest I can protect you properly with my skills. I have worked out, however, that it only killed anyone who was outside of Stoneheart's palace walls. Everyone within the palace was kept safe.'

She frowned. 'Burrage was —'

'On his balcony,' Cassien interrupted softly.

Florentyna blinked in consternation; Cassien was right. The animals, the people who'd died had all for some reason been moving or sleeping outside of the palace proper.

'This is clearly a heavy burden for Cassien,' Tilda finally said, eyeing him. Florentyna wondered what her intense look meant. Cassien hadn't noticed and the queen couldn't read the nuances dancing around her. 'He has been charged to hold your life as the most precious in the realm … and at the expense of others. He should not be blamed.'

'So any of us could have died?' Florentyna pressed.

They nodded together.

'How did you think your roaming might protect me?' she demanded. 'I mean, explain to me how the risk of killing was worth it.'

He nodded, understanding entirely her sense of despair. 'In that magical plane, I would have seen the one who hunts you.'

Tilda sat back and stared at Cassien in wonder. Florentyna privately wondered at so much being revealed in front of a stranger. It was obvious Tilda knew about Cassien's skill before Florentyna was told, but even so, surely Cyricus and his threat were to be kept secret.

Cassien shook his head, easily reading her thoughts. 'Tilda knows that we are moving you away from the palace and that there is someone who wishes death to the royals.' There was a hidden message in his words. So, he hadn't told Tilda about the demon, but was letting the herbwoman think the threat was a person.

Florentyna glanced at Tilda and could see her eyes narrowing as she considered Cassien. 'I didn't know you could use your roaming magic to find this killer. If you know who it is, why do you need an ethereal plane to see him?'

Florentyna didn't know why her instincts were screaming at her to assist Cassien in keeping their real purpose secret, but she interjected to help obscure and distract. 'Shar, but this is beyond my ability to reason. My sister always said magic was dangerous.'

'And she's right,' Tilda said. Again Florentyna saw her regard Cassien speculatively.

He looked up. 'Are you coming with us, Tilda?'

The older woman shook her head. 'You can move quicker and with less notice as a couple. I must go now. Please,' she said, standing and holding a hand up, 'don't disturb yourselves. I promise our paths will cross again. You trust me, don't you, Cassien?'

He looked surprised to be asked. 'I'll look for you.'

She nodded, turned to Florentyna. 'I'd like to kiss your hand, but dare not. Be safe.'

'How can I be otherwise with Cassien at my side,' she replied, and threw him an affectionate glance.

Tilda left and the dinch was served. Florentyna suggested they drink the spare cup that Tilda would not be taking. She was surprised the woman hadn't at least remained for that. She noticed Cassien didn't meet the serving girl's gaze on this occasion.

'Odd,' she remarked to herself, then looked up brightly at her companion. 'Do you know, I've never had dinch before,' she admitted, giving a satisfied sigh. 'It's wonderful.'

He smiled. 'I have tasted it only rarely.'

'You are a strange one, Cassien.'

'I'm sure of it. Forgive me.'

'Don't be silly.' She reached to touch his hand and he moved it as if scalded. Florentyna frowned. 'I meant that you engage my curiosity because you have led such a different life to mine and to everyone I know.'

He looked away, back to the path that their companion had recently left by. 'What did you mean about Tilda?'

She blinked. 'Tilda. What did I say?'

'That it was strange.'

'Ah, no, I didn't say strange, I said "odd". I simply meant it was curious that she seemed so friendly — and informed. She joined us for soup and dinch, then disappeared suddenly before the dinch was served.' She shrugged. 'Odd.'

'You know her better than I.'

'No, not really. I've met her on two occasions. I have always liked her brews but I don't know anything much about her.'

'I see. I was under the impression that you and she were friendly.'

Florentyna shrugged. 'I take her infusions and that's it. I pay a premium and she makes up one especially to my taste. She seems to know when my supplies are low and delivers my leaves to the kitchens. Burrage's orders.' Florentyna frowned. 'You knew she would be here?'

He shook his head. 'At the palace she mentioned that she would take a direct route north. She made me press her for the information but I did feel she wanted me to ask and then her reply felt like an invitation, but nothing so clearly stated.'

'Do you doubt her?'

She watched Cassien thinking deeply. She allowed the silence between them to lengthen as his eyebrows knitted in thought. 'Not until you just asked me.'

Florentyna leaned forward. 'What does that mean?'

His gaze snapped up to meet hers. 'Until moments ago I would have considered Tilda an ally.'

'And now?'

He shrugged. 'I also think it odd that she left so abruptly.'

'Cassien, speak plainly. My impression is that we're running for our lives, so it's best we are clear with each other.'

He shook his head. 'I have nothing to say about her. She knows nothing, only that we are running for your life.'

She finished her dinch and wanted to drink Tilda's, but decided that might be greedy. She gestured at it to Cassien. He shook his head.

'You're so restrained, Cassien,' she said, referring to everything about him.

But he believed she meant his appetite. 'The forest taught me to eat and drink only what my body needed. It's habit now,' he said softly.

'Do you believe your life is not important?'

He straightened to dig in his pocket for some coins. 'I believe it has a purpose, certainly. But no, it's not important.'

She looked at him bemused, shook her head. 'I've been raised in the opposite manner, to believe my life is of the highest importance.'

'It is. But I'm glad it hasn't made you indifferent to others.'

'My father would not have permitted that.'

'He did with Darcelle.'

She eyed him. 'Darcelle is ... was ... indulged. We are all at fault there. However, for all her spoilt ways, she was an asset and no-one could question her loyalty to the Crown. Have you registered how everyone is suddenly eyeing you differently?'

He nodded. 'Since they noticed my sword, you mean?'

'So you do know.'

'I take in everything about my surrounds.'

She smiled and frowned at the same time. 'I'm not sure whether you're immodest or honest.'

He looked wounded. 'I state only what I know to be true.'

Florentyna put her hands up in mock defeat. 'We should go. I think we're making the other patrons feel uncomfortable.'

'I am not the first swordsman who has sat down to a pot of dinch.'

'The first perhaps who looks as you do.' When he looked back at her in query, she shrugged. 'You are intimidating, Cassien, on a number of levels.'

'Good. If everyone keeps away from you, I am happy.'

She grinned. 'That sounds very possessive.' It was meant as a jest to lighten their conversation, give them the right moment to stand and glance over at the others with a smile before they left. Instead, his expression only deepened in its seriousness.

'If you were the only person I could ever speak to, it would be enough,' he said, his gaze grave and intense.

She held her breath, for as he'd spoken — his careful words making her feel suddenly awkward — she understood why she didn't react to him as others seemed to. And the reason was so shocking, she'd caught that single breath and was now too fearful to let it go ... and with it the acceptance of what she'd been hiding from.

'Florentyna?' he murmured, suddenly concerned by the way she fixated on the pot of dinch and was silent.

'Forgive me,' she said, gathering her scattered thoughts and trying to find a smile. 'I ...'

'No, I'm sorry for speaking so plainly. I thought ...' he stammered, unsure for once. 'I thought candour is what you demanded of me.'

'Oh, Cassien, the fault is mine. It's just ... I've realised something and the honesty of it is painful.'

'Can I help?'

She gave a small gasp of a laugh. 'Shar, no!'

He guided her away from the dinch-house, toward where he'd tethered two new horses. 'You spoke of honesty. Perhaps it is your turn?'

She cut him a look of reprimand but then realised he was right. This man was prepared to lay down his life for her, not even question why or when, simply that he would give it should that need arise. Florentyna swallowed. 'It's Tamas.'

'The king will be careful. I'm sure —' He stopped at her horse and looked at her with an unreadable expression. 'Ah, you meant something else, didn't you, your majesty?'

She nodded. 'I thought I'd put it behind me.'

'You have feelings for Tamas?'

'They frighten me. I've had them under very strict control. I really didn't think they'd burst through the defences,' she said, with an embarrassed smile. 'I'm sorry …'

'Don't be. He has no bride to consider anymore.'

'That sounds so heartless.' She looked away, hating herself.

'It's honest. I didn't mean to make you feel in any way ill at ease. You should know that I could not and would not permit myself to let my feelings go any further. There is another woman.' He shrugged. 'I was simply stating the truth. If you were the only person left in the world, it would be enough to converse with you. You are wise, calm, amusing when you want to be and you are educated. Besides, any interest I showed in you, my queen, defies the law of the Brotherhood.'

She frowned. 'Celibacy?'

Cassien found a smile. 'No, thank Shar! No wives, no permanent relationships. No family. We are not permitted to have long-term distractions, and women and children are precisely that; they compromise our emotions and ability to act decisively, swiftly.' He helped her up onto her horse and handed her the reins before climbing easily onto his mount. 'You're still happy to ride through the night?'

She nodded as he guided his horse to the path that would lead them out of the hamlet. Florentyna followed. 'It looks daunting,' she said, nodding toward the blackness stretching beyond the soft glow that the hilltop town threw on the path for a short way.

'We will have to pick our way slowly,' he said, looking up. 'But with luck, the moon will come out from behind those clouds and smile her light our way. Then we can move faster.'

She moved her horse into step with his and they set off companionably, winding their way down the hill.

'Cassien, if it's any consolation, you make me feel safe … you give me confidence.'

He gave her a rueful smile. 'That is a rich compliment to a member of the Brotherhood. And, strangely perhaps, it is enough for me to know I have achieved this. You and I, as long as I live, will always be friends, I hope.'

'We shall. I give you my word.'

'Then that will keep my heart full … and Tamas is a lucky man.'

She blushed in the dark furiously. 'Tamas has no idea.'

'How long have you known?'

'Since I was a child of about eleven.'

He cut her a sharp look of surprise. 'Truly?'

She nodded, glad he couldn't see how hot her cheeks must look, for they felt like they were burning. 'He didn't come to Stoneheart. He wasn't even meant to be visiting Morgravia, but his ship was in trouble and had to limp into the Grenadyn Islands. My father and I happened to be in Racklaryon at the time — that's in the Razors. We got word that Ciprean royalty was on our doorstep unannounced. My father was a gracious man, Cassien, and often didn't stand on ceremony. He stopped his meetings, cancelled his tour of the Razors and raced to the islands to see what help could be given to the stricken ship. Tamas barely noticed the shy daughter of the king who greeted him. But I noticed him; I even sat on his lap once,' she confided with an embarrassed giggle. 'And my candle has burned for him ever since, you could say,' she finished, sighing. 'We met once more, when I was about fourteen, but I was so cringingly shy of my feelings that I found it easier to ignore him. I couldn't even look upon him for fear of disgracing myself. I've always felt sad about that, because Tamas has always been so kind to me. There, now we've each swapped our dark secrets!'

'How did you face him on this trip?'

'There's something about becoming a ruler that instils confidence, or at least one learns very quickly how to school one's features into obedience. He can't guess because I've become adept at hiding and managed to adopt an easy, sisterly approach. Just standing next to him, though, makes me feel weak,' she admitted. 'Forgive me for burdening you but it does feel good to admit it to another.'

'Nothing to forgive. I sensed there was something between you both but it is not my place to ponder it. But he doesn't know? I mean, when Darcelle —'

'No!' She knew her expression was horrified. 'Absolutely not. Darcelle never knew about my feelings and Tamas certainly has no idea.'

'But when she told you … I mean surely you —'

'No. I didn't … couldn't. She was in love with him. And he with her, by all accounts. Plus, it was a perfect union for Morgravia.'

'I don't understand. Why didn't you pursue him?'

'I was fourteen summers, Cassien! And I was a shy child to boot. I became more introverted and Darcelle was so extroverted she seemed the perfect ambassador for the Crown. She begged me to let her go to Cipres and represent Morgravia one year. I wanted to go, desperately … I wanted him to see me as a woman rather than a stammering mooncalf. You have to understand that I had been promised to another and I was fond of him. I could never tell my father that I loved the Ciprean. Don't ask why. It was all too complicated at the time. My feelings were torn but I had learned to control them entirely, to bury them.'

'Darcelle never suspected?'

'Darcelle,' she gave a mirthless chuckle, 'wanted to go more than I did on that occasion, or at least our stepmother wanted her to. Darcelle could be so persuasive and — oh, what does it matter?'

'It matters that even in something as important as love you permitted Darcelle to usurp your heart's desire. Imagine what could have been if you'd gone to Cipres instead of her.'

'She didn't do it deliberately. And she had no idea of my feelings. She met Tamas and they found enjoyment in each other. It seems both sisters were stricken with the pleasure of loving an older man.' She smiled sadly in the dark, knowing he couldn't see it.

'There is nothing in your way now.'

'Don't, Cassien. Tamas does not think of me in this manner.'

'I wouldn't be too sure of that,' Cassien advised.

'I can't think of it,' she dismissed, eager to banish talk of her heart and its love for one man. 'It's too painful from every angle. My sister …' She stopped. There was no point in traversing old ground. 'All I care is that he remains safe and free from the demon's touch. That we *all* do.'

They left Micklesham behind, soft candlelight from its dwellings feeling far more cheery than the landscape stretching out before them. As if it could hear their prayers, the moon chose that moment to emerge and instantly the way ahead was cast into a ghostly road.

'The forest awaits; let's ride, your majesty,' Cassien urged.

He kicked his cantering horse into a gallop and Florentyna followed suit, a thought nagging on the rim of her mind. It felt as far from her grasp as the moon that lit their way.

THIRTY

Princess Darcelle caught the Cipreans just past Hynton, a neighbouring hamlet of Harpers Riding and its tithe barn, where Gabriel had made his entry into Morgravia. Behind her raced three dozen well-armed, hardened soldiers from the famed Morgravian Legion, who had been ordered to follow the princess. She'd given Stoneheart's gatekeepers a fright the way she'd suddenly taken off from the bailey — alone and in pursuit of the Cipreans, who had also left mysteriously swiftly and with no prior warning.

The senior commander happened to be in the gatehouse at the moment of Darcelle's departure and when he had asked why the princess had no minders with her and received no satisfactory explanation, he had acted on his instincts. Without waiting to find out more he gave orders for three stems of the Legion to follow the princess and bring her back safely. He sent Lieutenant Tyle as his representative.

Tyle had tried but failed to slow the princess enough to discover the reason for her hellish pursuit … she refused to converse with him on the gallop. With no other choice he'd had to keep up, urging the men to do the same. They had their orders and their role was to protect Princess Darcelle.

She arrived at the Ciprean camp, with Tyle on her heels, galloping so fast she could barely stop the horse, and shocked the Ciprean Guard as much as Tyle by carelessly leaping from the slowing beast into the area where the soldiers were congregated. Men dodged out of the horse's way and two gave chase to prevent the animal harming itself or the men. Darcelle clearly couldn't care whether the animal lived or died.

Tyle was off his own mount just as fast while the princess was grabbing a man who wore the giveaway gold buttons on his cloak, suggesting he was a senior member of the Ciprean guard. He reared back from the snarling expression on her face.

Tyle came up behind her, loathe to interrupt until he could gain her attention and follow the right protocols. She ignored him.

'Do you know me?' she demanded of the Ciprean.

The man bowed. 'Your highness, Princess Darcelle.'

'Then tell me where I can find King Tamas.'

'The king is …' He looked around, seemed embarrassed. 'He's —'

'Where?' Cyricus boomed in the man's face, using Darcelle's voice as best he could to inflict fear.

'He's in Pearlis, your highness.'

'Pearlis?' she snarled. Cyricus didn't understand. Aphra sensibly remained silent, although he could feel her tension skimming through Darcelle's body. 'I saw the king leave with you,' Darcelle continued.

He shook his head. 'No, highness. We were sent ahead.' He glanced Tyle's way and nodded. 'Let me take you to Captain Wentzl.'

'Do that!' Cyricus snapped, his mind racing. Back in Pearlis? That couldn't be right. He saw it … clearly saw the king mount the pearl-coloured horse and ride with his men.

'Your highness?'

Cyricus turned and eyed the Morgravian officer standing before him. 'Yes?'

The man blinked. 'Er, Lieutenant Tyle, your highness.' He said it in a way that suggested Darcelle should know him.

'Well?'

'My orders are to accompany you. Is there … um … anything I can help with?'

'Unless you can help me find King Tamas, I doubt it.'

'Let me stay with you, your highness,' he said and Cyricus could see the officer carefully eyeing her with confusion.

'As you wish,' Cyricus said and stalked away. He let Darcelle's body follow the Ciprean officer, who led him to the shade of a tree where a man with a neatly trimmed moustache and grey, intelligent eyes gazed at him. The man quickly stood politely from where he'd been crouching to take a drink from a ladle. Cyricus watched the man wipe his lips hastily and immediately sweep into an elegant bow.

'Princess Darcelle.' Cyricus noted the man's eyes dart behind him. 'Lieutenant Tyle,' he said in greeting and nodded.

'Captain Wentzl,' Tyle acknowledged and Cyricus observed that the Morgravian drew level.

'Your highness, your arrival is most unusual.'

'Your man said the king is not with you?' Cyricus said, ignoring the pleasantries.

Wentzl nodded. 'Yes, your highness, he gave you the truth. King Tamas ordered me to take the men back to the ship. I was given no further information. I anticipated that he would join us.'

'Did you?' Cyricus snapped, his mind reaching to the possibility that he had been tricked. Darcelle's gaze settled on a familiar cloak, worn by someone standing close by and listening to the conversation. Its wearer, who should have been Tamas, was clearly not; Cyricus accepted now that he had been outwitted by the Ciprean king. Wentzl was still talking, apparently responding to Darcelle's last query.

'... with so much death in the palace, he thought it best, your highness.' He stopped, cleared his throat, glanced at Tyle.

Cyricus knew he was wasting his time here. He felt the violence erupting, certainly wanted to answer its call even though it was pointless.

Ham rode unhappily alongside King Tamas. 'Your majesty, please, we should not do this.'

'We must.'

'Cassien would not —'

'Hamelyn, my boy,' he said gently. 'I am a king. Kings make their own decisions, are answerable to no-one but their god. If I don't do this, our future — especially that of Florentyna — is even less certain than it already is.'

Ham sighed audibly. 'I think you like our queen.'

'Of course I do.' And when Ham eyed him, it was the king's turn to sigh. 'More than I should, perhaps. One daughter of Morgravia is lost. We cannot risk the only other member of the imperial Crown's family. I would never forgive myself.'

Ham sighed resignedly. 'Then let's ride, your majesty!'

'Lieutenant Tyle?'

'Highness,' he replied, snapping to attention.

'Seize that man over there.' Darcelle pointed.

'Er …' Tyle looked torn.

'Don't look at Wentzl for permission, lieutenant. You were sent to escort me, keep me safe, I presume?' Tyle nodded and looked to be holding his breath. Cyricus liked it when people were unnerved, and even better when they were fearful like Tyle, who was trapped between duty and a clear desire to bundle the princess back to Pearlis and let someone else sort out what must look to be an emotional explosion. 'Well then, lieutenant, I presume also in those orders was the inherent instruction to obey your princess. Am I not right?'

'You are right, highness,' he murmured. 'But we —'

'Have your men seize that man now!' Cyricus roared in Darcelle's voice.

Tyle took a long slow breath through his nose. Cyricus could see his nostrils flaring with anger and confusion.

'There is no need for this, your highness,' Wentzl said. 'Ranker! Over here,' he called, and the man who Cyricus could now see shared a similar build and colouring to Tamas, limped over. 'Why do you need to see him?'

'Because, Captain Wentzl, I believe this man wore the king's cloak when he rode out of the Stoneheart bailey.'

'As you can see, your highness, this is not who you seek,' he said, ignoring the point Cyricus was making.

'Tyle?'

'Yes,' he answered unhappily.

'Have your men draw arms.'

'Your high—'

'Do it, Tyle, or I'll have your neck swinging from the palace gallows faster than you can stammer out an apology.'

The Ciprean guard murmured as one, many reaching for weapons, but Wentzl put a hand up. 'Cipreans, stay your hands. Remember, we are guests in Morgravia and our king is here. Ranker?'

'Sir?' the man stood to attention.

'As her highness demands, man,' Wentzl said, not taking his gaze from Darcelle. It glittered defiantly and Cyricus couldn't fail to be impressed by the man.

Ranker stepped forward, knelt, and bowed his head before Darcelle.

'Cyricus, my lord,' Aphra finally murmured, 'this would not be a wise move.'

'Do not presume to tell me what I should or shouldn't do, Aphra!' he growled, knowing almost one hundred men were watching Darcelle, holding a collective breath.

'It's just, if you —'

'Quiet!' he roared privately at his acolyte. He regarded the lieutenant. 'Tyle,' he said aloud in Darcelle's voice, 'draw your weapon.'

The Morgravian's expression told Cyricus that he knew it was hopeless to object any longer or further. Tyle drew his weapon and the ring of the metal resonated around the camp, which was quiet enough that Cyricus could hear a lone bird chirruping nearby. A moment later, though, that sound was drowned by the jarring ring of thirty-five other swords being drawn. The Morgravian men stood ready and armed. But on Wentzl's order not a single Ciprean drew his weapon.

'Did the king ask you to deliberately trick me?' Cyricus asked.

Wentzl shook his head. 'I don't know what this man is doing with the king's cloak, to be honest, your highness.' Cyricus — and probably every other Ciprean, he assumed — knew that Wentzl was lying.

'Let's ask him, shall we?' Darcelle offered, her words polite, but her tone as acid as lemon juice on a wound. 'Ranker, explain to us why you are wearing the cloak of King Tamas? Please don't deny its ownership. I know it is his, because he wore it only this morning when I was with him. It is far too distinctive to be any other cloak than his.'

Ranker did not change his position or raise his head. 'I do not deny it, your highness. King Tamas asked me to carry it for him as he no longer required it.'

'Really?'

The man said nothing.

'Why would he do that, Ranker?'

'Your highness, I am a simple soldier. When the king of my country bids me carry something, I do it without question.'

'You did not think it curious?' Cyricus pressed, his fury at being tricked intensifying. He needed to take his rage out on someone.

'I do not think much at all, your highness,' he said, and even though it was a humble response, Cyricus felt it like a slap of sarcasm.

'I know you are lying, Ranker. I suspect your captain is lying too. But here, let me give you something that you, he and your whole company can think about ...' Without pausing for breath, Cyricus reached out

Darcelle's arm and snatched the sword that Lieutenant Tyle held unhappily at his side. With the inordinate strength that Cyricus piled behind the action, the sword was raised in the hands of the princess and with a hammering, double-handed blow it was brought down on Ranker's unprotected, bowed head.

It split like a soft, vasha melon but first made the noise of a nut cracking. A sound like the distant roar of a wave moved through the Ciprean Guard but Wentzl had raised his hand again and they obediently followed his silent order to do nothing.

Ranker had looked up, wearing an expression of total confusion, before his body slowly toppled, crumpling to Darcelle's left as blood spumed from the mighty blow. His body writhed while his heart caught up with what his brain already knew. And then Ranker began to convulse but Cyricus was already moving Darcelle's attention away from the spasms of the dying soldier to focus on Wentzl.

'Your sword, Tyle,' she said, without glancing his way as she held out the bloodied blade to her offsider, needing both arms to do so. Cyricus knew every man present was wondering how a woman of Darcelle's stature could wield a blade of that size. He didn't care. He didn't care about a single one of them or what they thought — he would gladly kill them and enjoy watching each suffer his death throes … if he'd had the time. But he had a king and queen to catch, for it seemed someone, somehow, had informed both that their young princess was not all that she seemed.

'Fetch me a horse,' Cyricus snapped.

'Would you not prefer to take a —'

'You surely aren't deaf, captain Wentzl, and I'm surely not so stupid that I can't make my own decisions. I will return to Pearlis and I will find King Tamas on my own. You and your men had better weigh anchor as soon as you reach the port at Ramon. I am sending Lieutenant Tyle and twenty-five of our men to ensure your departure.'

'We cannot leave without —'

'Without Tamas? Fret not, Captain. I will provide a ship for the king, should he require it. Either you leave Morgravian soil or our countries will be at war. I can have ten times the number of men hunting down your small force within hours. Leave, captain, and leave by nightfall or I promise you, more Ciprean blood will be spilled.'

Wentzl's face twitched in anger. 'As you wish, your highness,' and still Cyricus knew he lied. Wentzl would not leave Morgravia until he had his king safely on his ship. So be it, Cyricus thought. He had a new idea forming.

'Tyle, ten of your soldiers may ride back with me. The rest will escort the Cipreans to the docks and see them onto their ship — every last man. If anyone defies my order, you have my authority to kill him and I demand you do just that. Wentzl, you've heard my orders. Do not defy me.'

'Your highness, with respect, I take my orders from the Ciprean sovereign alone. However, I respect your wishes and will leave peaceably with my men. May we take Ranker's body?'

Cyricus looked over at the still-twitching man. 'No, there's life in him yet. I think he can travel back with us.' He'd made his point and yet still his rage wasn't sated. 'Tyle, tie him to my horse's backside,' he said, with as much scorn as he could load into Darcelle's tone. Then he gave a cruel laugh as a fresh idea occurred. 'Oh, and Wentzl …'

The captain's gaze slid angrily to the princess from where it had been fixed watching Morgravian men hauling the almost-dead Ranker toward the waiting horse. 'Your highness?' he said and Cyricus imagined how he must be gritting his teeth to remain as polite as he sounded.

'Approach,' the princess said, beckoning.

He frowned, cast a quick glance at Tyle, who Cyricus knew was likely giving a surreptitious shrug in response, before stepping forward.

'I'd like to give you something to remember not only Morgravia by, but especially me,' Cyricus said, and without giving the man a chance to say anything, Darcelle pulled him forward and kissed him on each cheek before shocking him with a kiss on his mouth.

Captain Wentzl pulled away, blinking, could hear his men murmuring softly behind them. They were confused; Cyricus understood this. He'd felt Wentzl's surprise, as much as his fear, when Cyricus had arrived into his body and caused the man's spirit to flee to Shar. Wentzl was dead, but his body stood and gazed around in a well-disguised sense of smugness.

'I have a better idea, your highness,' Cyricus said, in the mild voice of Wentzl. Resisting the urge to wipe his lips, he inclined his head politely. 'Why don't I return with your party and help to find King Tamas?'

He waited. Princess Darcelle looked momentarily baffled and Cyricus knew Aphra hesitated as she considered what he required of her.

'This is something I would want to do for you,' he pressed, needing Aphra to understand.

'Thank you, Captain Wentzl,' Darcelle finally said for everyone to hear. 'That would be permissible. Tyle, I've changed my mind. Release that man and give his body back to the Ciprean Guard. They can cast him to the seas when they hit Ciprean waters.'

Cyricus watched Tyle look at the princess as though she really was out of her mind. The Morgravian lieutenant threw Wentzl a look of exasperation as much as sympathy.

'Your men can take him,' Tyle said to Wentzl.

'Thank you,' Cyricus said, uncaring, but he went through the motions of looking over his shoulder to nod permission at the man standing nearest. 'Accord Ranker a burial that is fitting. I am returning with Princess Darcelle to Pearlis and I will accompany our king back to Cipres when he is ready. You are to board our ship and return to Cipres as instructed. Is that clear?' He wanted to be rid of all Tamas's loyal supporters.

The men murmured as one. A man stepped forward and Cyricus had to assume this was the next officer in line to him.

'Captain, is this wise? I thought you said we had direct orders from our king for *all* of us to leave as instructed.'

'I am not leaving King Tamas to this madwoman,' he whispered. 'Do as I say. We are outnumbered, we cannot win any fight with the Morgravians. We will have to use diplomacy to extricate King Tamas if he becomes trapped. And diplomacy is best without weapons. Go now.'

The man frowned, then nodded. 'Yes, sir.' He turned and began barking orders to the Ciprean Guard.

'Your highness, shall we?' Wentzl was seen to say to Princess Darcelle, but only Cyricus saw the gleam of amusement in Darcelle's gaze.

Now he could walk in a man's body again; a not unreasonable one. Wentzl was in good shape. Most importantly, King Tamas would trust Wentzl when he appeared.

Cyricus was now of the opinion that the champion — Cassien was his name — who had kept such a close watch on the queen at Stoneheart when she and Tamas had come rushing to Darcelle's aid — was far more than he appeared. He, and the boy, were now marked men in the mind of Cyricus.

In case they were overheard he adopted a formal approach. 'Do you remember that man who accompanied Queen Florentyna to King Tamas's rooms, your highness?' he asked Darcelle as he accompanied her to her horse.

'Yes, the quiet one in dark clothes.'

'Did he strike you as in any way special?' he whispered.

Aphra shook the princess's pretty head. 'No,' she said, barely taking time to think. Cyricus accepted this. Aphra was servile but she was sharp and he trusted her insights. He nodded Wentzl's head and helped the princess onto her horse. 'One thing, perhaps,' Aphra added as though it was barely worth mentioning. 'He reminded me strongly of Gabe …' She shrugged. 'Something in his manner maybe. Perhaps I'm being fanciful,' she corrected.

'Ready, Princess Darcelle?' her own man asked.

'Lead the way,' she said, casting a glance at Wentzl standing by her horse. 'Captain Wentzl?'

But Cyricus wasn't paying attention. He was thinking about how glad he was now that he'd taken the precaution of setting a spy up in the palace.

'What are you doing?' Ham said, from where Tamas had instructed him to remain, flat on his belly, overlooking the shallow valley where their attention had been fixed. He watched now as Tamas reached for the bow he had strapped to his horse. Ham hadn't paid much attention to it earlier because they had been in such a hurry to leave Pearlis, but now he frowned, unsure.

'We haven't had much time together, have we, Ham? But if we had, you'd have learned that there isn't an archer in Cipres who can outshoot Barbary here.'

'Barbary?'

Tamas threw him a grin, but there was no humour in it. Ham sensed anger, and fear, but not directed at him.

'I was given this bow by my eldest brother. It was carved for him by a master bow maker called Barbaran, a man whose work most Cipreans revere and who is long dead, but his legend lives on. Both of my brothers were hopeless at archery and yet I showed a rare affinity for this weapon,' he said, stroking the shaft of one arrow. 'No-one in Cipres could match my range or accuracy.' He shrugged as though embarrassed to be caught talking in this way about himself. 'The bow is made of kisten — flexible and stronger than ten men. The arrow is from the matten branch; it flies straighter than anything the empire has, I'll wager.' Ham touched the fletched tip. 'Pingara feathers,' Tamas said reverently. He gave a wink that reassured Ham somewhat.

He was worried about Tamas, but how much could a boy say to a king before it became inappropriate and insubordinate? He wasn't sure, although they were friends and they were both running for their lives. Ham could see Tamas intended to use his skills as an archer and his precious bow and it worried him.

'King Tamas, we are a long way from what I believe is your intended target.'

'And you're frightened I'll only alert people to where we are, I know,' Tamas finished what Ham hadn't wanted to say.

'Not just that. There is a light breeze and undulating terrain and bushes. Have you ever shot to kill before?'

'Yes, of course.'

Ham's expression tensed. 'I mean a person. Have you ever killed a person in this way?'

Tamas grinned and once again it was mirthless. 'Man, beast … what does it matter?'

'It matters.'

'Hush now, Ham. Soon you'll see why we're so far away. Now let me focus.'

Ham obeyed, feeling his chest constrict with the tension of what he now understood King Tamas was about to attempt. He heard Tamas begin to mutter instructions to himself, perhaps unaware that he was saying them aloud.

'Allow for the wind, up … no, a bit higher, Tamas … picture it in your mind, imagine it soaring, hitting the target,' the king muttered. Ham was straining to hear as the gentlest of gully breezes shifted his hair.

He looked down below and held his breath.

* * *

On the plain outside Hynton, Cyricus, in his new guise, was feeling released from the increasing sense of entrapment he'd begun experiencing as Darcelle. It was a pity. He had wanted to be a Morgravian royal, had anticipated its many benefits, but the reality was that travelling as a woman had too many pitfalls ... and travelling as only the second-most-important woman in the land was not good enough. He needed to be Florentyna ... although Tamas would do, if he could catch him.

When he found Tamas — and he would — he knew the king would trust his closest military advisor, and Cyricus would then give Cipres a monarch to be proud of ... especially when he married Darcelle and set about annexing Morgravia.

'Captain Wentzl, are you coming with us?' Darcelle repeated to him. She was seated on her horse with a lovely straight back and her head upturned to the sun. 'Shar, but it's a glorious day. It should be a pleasant ride.' Aphra said this in a tone that probably only he understood was filled with the smugness of their new bodies and her anticipation of the coupling that would surely take place as soon as they could be left alone.

She laughed, raising her head and enjoying their private amusement.

'Yes, your high—' He didn't finish his sentence.

Like an avenging storm, it seemed to come out of nowhere and with no warning. No-one heard it, not one of them suspected anything untoward ... least of all Darcelle.

It dropped from the sky in a precisely calculated arc. One moment Cyricus was thinking about how hard he was going to work Princess Darcelle's body tonight, admiring the coquettish laugh that Aphra was giving him, the next he was staring, impossibly, at an arrow embedded in her eye, passing easily through the middle of her head with its flinty point puncturing the soft tissue at the back of her neck.

Darcelle tried to say something, but a word or two of nonsense was all that issued forth before she toppled ungraciously from her mount and slammed to the ground like a sack of potatoes, one foot still trapped in the stirrup. The horse took fright and bolted, dragging the body of the Princess of Morgravia alongside it, doing to her what had been intended for the Ciprean soldier, Ranker.

Inside Wentzl, Cyricus felt blood rage. He knew he must show none of his fury or despair as he watched Darcelle's body, with Aphra dead no doubt before her host hit the ground, bouncing behind the horse like a rag doll.

The Ciprean guard watched with shock — albeit tinged with a collective and helpless glee — that the woman who had treated them with such disdain had just been seen off in a wholly appropriate manner. One among them, an older man called Fyffe, turned to his neighbour with a frown and whispered: 'Unless my eyes deceive me, that was the king's arrow.'

'What?' his companion said, startled.

Fyffe shrugged. 'No-one has striped Pingara fletching like that except King Tamas.'

'I didn't notice,' his neighbour admitted. 'I was just glad to see the bitch die.'

'Hush,' Fyffe warned. All the men in the Ciprean Guard had sensibly drawn their weapons to discourage the Morgravians from retaliating. One of the senior officers was assuring Wentzl and the Morgravian officer that every Ciprean was accounted for. The shot had to have been made by a Morgravian with a grudge, he reasoned.

Nothing was so much as breathed by a Ciprean about the fletching on the arrow.

Far away, well out of sight, Tamas took a long, slow breath. It would have taken another archer of his stature to know which direction the arrow had come from.

'That's the end of the demon and his minion,' he growled. 'Mount up, Ham. Let's go find Florentyna before a pack of her soldiers have our hides drying out in the sun. They'll want blood.'

Ham could only peek over the top of the mound that he had been hiding behind, open-mouthed. It had been an impossible shot, surely, and yet his eyes had told him only the truth. He had watched Tamas stand and take the deepest of breaths, which he then held tightly; he had seen the king close his eyes briefly and focus his thoughts before he'd suddenly snapped them open, pulled back the string of his bow; Ham had heard the soft creak of the kisten, the wheezing strain of the hemp becoming taut; Tamas had raised the bow, the arrow menacing as it had waited to be released into the air. In that heartbeat, as Tamas had paused in that position, becoming so still he looked to be part of the landscape, Ham had imagined the arrow as a living creature, eager to be let loose to fly. It only had one flight in its life, Ham had thought, and it wanted to be the best it could be. It wanted to fly faster than any before it; smoother and straighter than all the arrows that had been shot from this same bow. It wanted to land more accurately and with more force than its predecessors had ever been able to on their targets, so the king and his fletcher could be proud of it. It wanted to be known as the arrow that had killed a Morgravian royal.

Tamas had released the bowstring and the arrow had been catapulted toward the clouds, creating a sinister farewell hiss as it left its still-thrumming bow and began its first and only journey. Ham did his best to follow its flight, but lost the arrow in its ascent because of the glare of the sun. Immediately, he'd dropped his gaze to Princess Darcelle sitting atop her horse, talking to the king's man — laughing, in fact, her chin lifted in her amusement. Ham had watched in a state beyond amazement as death met Darcelle's laughing expression in the most daring and impossibly accurate arrow shot that Morgravia had surely ever witnessed.

Her death had been instantaneous and shockingly ugly, even from the distance of five hundred strides. Her corpse had fallen from the horse and was immediately dragged by her startled mount, but Hamelyn had smiled, for Gabe had told them that if the host was destroyed, then the demon and his hideous minion were destroyed also.

'We're done here, Ham,' Tamas urged, pulling his arm. Ham came out of his state of wonder, blinking at the king. Tamas nodded his head toward the valley, back to where men were glaring in their rough direction and pointing. 'They'll chase us down if we don't leave now. But we've got the head start we need and I intend for the Morgravian men never to find us, never to know who shot that arrow. Come!'

They jumped onto their horses and fled as fast as their animals could gallop.

THIRTY-ONE

'Are you all right, my son?' the kind voice asked.

Gabe stirred awake. He hadn't realised he had drifted into sleep. He stammered a response.

'No need to apologise. You've been here a while. I just want to know that you are not sick or in trouble? After those terrible deaths in the cistern, I'm worried about everyone.'

Gabe cleared his throat and rubbed the sleep from his face. 'Forgive me. I am a traveller,' he said. 'Very tired. My name is Gabriel.'

'Welcome, Gabriel. I am Canon Petrus. This beautiful vessel of Shar's love is my responsibility,' he said, gesturing to the cathedral's nave. He smiled warmly in the low light and Gabe realised suddenly that it was night and the oil in the cressets on the pillars had already been lit. 'First visit to the Pearlis Cathedral?' the man asked.

'Yes, it's overwhelming,' Gabe admitted. 'But in a good way.'

Petrus smiled. 'That gladdens me. You have not eaten?'

'You've been watching me, father.'

'Indeed. Would you care to share some bread and cheese? It is only a light supper but I'm happy for you to join me. It seems we are the only supplicants this eve.' He lifted a small bundle from the pew where he sat and watched Gabe. 'Shar will not mind if we munch in his beautiful nave.'

Gabe grinned. 'Shar is a modern thinker, then?'

Petrus gave him a quizzical smile in return, and Gabe reminded himself of where he was and the times he was now living through.

'Help yourself, young man. I eat very little these days but Mistress Lyme, who looks after us clergy of the cathedral, seems to believe we all need endless fattening.' He tapped his small paunch. 'I have more than enough.'

Gabe stood gingerly and stretched. His spine gave a satisfying click and he sighed.

'That should tell you how long you've been in that one spot,' Petrus said, gesturing at the food and for Gabe to help himself. He did, taking a hunk of the bread and a wedge of the cheese. There were two apples, another linen filled with nuts and dried fruit, and he noticed only now the small flagon of wine with two beakers. He didn't think that Mistress Lyme had set up supper at all. He suspected that Petrus had prepared his own and included Gabe in his calculations, but he sensed no guile.

'Thank you, that's kind.'

'I admit I've been keeping an eye on you, Gabriel. You looked a bit lonely. You're not lost?'

He shook his head and gave a rueful smile. 'I've never felt more at home,' he admitted.

Petrus regarded him with another frown, more bemused this time. He turned and poured them each a wine. 'I told you a fib. I did ask Mistress Lyme to include enough for two.'

'I guessed,' Gabe said, as he took the proffered beaker and raised it. 'To spiritual release,' he said, not really understanding why he said it.

Petrus gave a low chuckle. 'Yes, I'll drink to that,' he agreed and they touched beakers. Gabe watched his new friend take the first sip. Satisfied he was not to be poisoned he began to sip companionably.

'So which is your beast?'

'The unicorn,' Gabe answered quickly, looking away but careful not to appear or sound suspicious. 'It called to me the moment I set foot inside the cathedral,' he lied.

Petrus shrugged. 'That's the thrill of the first visit,' he admitted. 'I remember mine like it was yesterday.'

'What's yours?'

'Canis.'

Gabe tried not to look unsure. He waited, hoping the priest would clue him in.

Petrus sighed. 'Yes, the humble dog,' he replied and grinned.

Gabe shrugged, relieved to know to which beast he referred. 'Everyone loves dogs,' he said.

'Nicely said, Gabriel. And you're right. When I was young, I wished it had been Lupus who had chosen me. A wolf — wild and dangerous — appealed so much more. As a child I tried to convince myself it had been Lupus who'd called my name, but it was Canis who knew me.'

'Dogs are faithful. Dogs are loyal. Dogs are true because a dog doesn't lie,' Gabe said, smiling. 'Its tail gives it away every time.'

'I like you, Gabriel,' Petrus said, lifting his chin with a sense of pride. 'Thank you.'

'It's the least I can do for someone who shares his supper.'

They sat in a friendly silence, chewing on their food and listening to the soft splutters of the burning oil.

'If you're Unicornia, why were you sitting beneath the king?'

Gabe was ready for this, having guessed the wily canon might ask. 'I suppose, like you, I was pretending for a moment. I wished the Dragon had chosen me. I wanted to see what it felt like to touch him. I really didn't mean to fall asleep.'

'You looked very comfortable in his embrace. And he looked ...' Petrus searched for the right phrase, '... very protective of you.'

'It's always helpful to have friends in high places, don't you think?'

At this remark, Petrus laughed and the sound of his amusement echoed around the cathedral.

'Petrus, would you mind very much if I remained here for a while ... I mean, in the church?'

'Why should I mind, son?' the man said, his dark eyes twinkling with humour.

'I don't see anyone else remaining after dark.'

'Oh, you'd be surprised. This is just a quiet night. You are welcome to stay. Everyone is welcome. No traveller is ever turned away. Where are you headed ultimately?'

'Salvation,' he said and immediately wished he hadn't at the way the canon's eyes widened.

'Gabriel, have you a troubled soul? Can I help?'

He shook his head. 'Not troubled. I have felt trapped. In here, I feel safe but not imprisoned.'

'You are looking for release?' the older man asked carefully.

Gabe realised what the man suddenly feared. 'I am no danger to myself. I simply want quiet time away from others, alone with my thoughts, a time to reflect and be close to my spiritual beast.'

His companion visibly relaxed. 'Stay as long as you wish. I must leave you now to attend to my duties.'

'Thank you for the food.'

412

'Commune with your beast, Gabriel. Find peace,' Petrus said, standing and sighing as his hip creaked. 'I'll look in on you from time to time.' He left Gabe with an avuncular smile after gathering the linens, flagon and beakers into the small basket he'd brought in.

Gabe watched him leave, returned his attention to the dragon and remembered how it had welcomed him as his son. He was confused, needed to understand more. If the beast could speak with him, then surely he could in turn speak with it … if he could find the way.

And then it occurred to Gabe that he already knew the way. He left where he was and sat in a pew close to the dragon but not on it as before. When he reached out he could still touch the dragon, which was comforting. He stared at it. And its stone sculpted eyes appeared to stare straight back at him … almost daring him to try.

He dared.

Gabe closed his eyes, as if in prayer, and reached for his mental haven. This was not for an exam. It wasn't for escape from the darkness of losing his family. It was to learn.

He easily saw it in his mind's eye. There was the nave of the cathedral from his vision, and it was identical to the architecture of where he sat … down to the pattern of the flagstones his feet were upon. He took a deep breath and privately marvelled. How could he have known this place?

Suddenly he felt as though he were travelling but not moving anywhere. The image in his mind shifted, became skewed and suddenly he was in a place he didn't recognise.

He wasn't in it physically. He knew his body was anchored to the pew in Pearlis Cathedral, but his spirit seemed to have found a very strange plane. There was nothing around him … just a neutral space that was neither misty nor clear, neither dark nor light. It was devoid of colour and he could not describe the hues — black, white or grey — that surrounded him. It was nothing. It wasn't air. It wasn't water. It had no smell, no taste. It had no sense of distance, but it wasn't claustrophobic either. It was baffling.

'Where is this?' he asked nervously. He didn't anticipate an answer.

But a voice did answer. 'You are in the Void, Gabriel, but you are protected. Do not be afraid while you are with me.'

'Who speaks?' he demanded, not frightened but not feeling entirely comfortable. 'Please … show yourself.'

He hadn't known there were shadows until the man appeared, walking slowly but purposefully, gradually acquiring definition. He wore a grey robe. His hair was silvered, and though Gabe sensed he was old, he had a genial quality about him.

'Who … who …?'

'I am Fynch,' the man said.

'Should I know you?'

He shook his head. 'More's the pity.'

It was an odd response. 'I don't understand.'

'Why should you? It's me speaking in riddles to defend myself against something you will understand soon enough. Suffice to say I am not your enemy, Gabriel. Far from it. May I call you Gabe?'

'Yes. How do you know me?'

'I knew your mother.'

Gabe had to repeat Fynch's words in his mind to fully grasp the enormity of what he'd just said.

'My mother? She had this skill?'

'No.'

'Then how does a mother who lives in the village of Poynings in Britain come to know a man called Fynch from another world … another plane, it seems?'

Fynch chuckled softly, but the sound seemed sad to Gabe's hearing, as though regretful. 'The woman who raised you and the woman who birthed you are different, Gabe. I'm sorry, I'm sure this will shock.'

Gabe was certain his heart skipped several beats.

'How can you say that so heartlessly?'

'There was nothing but heart in what I've just told you, son. You were loved, but you had a role. I had to take the precaution of sending you far away from Morgravia. You were taken to a place we could trust you would never be found.'

It felt like a jigsaw piece slotting into the right spot in his mind. 'Until the right time,' Gabe finished, his mind scrambling to catch up with his instinctive response.

Fynch nodded. 'I knew you would be found.' He shrugged. 'Time moves differently here.'

'I was born here?' Gabe exclaimed, the shock beginning to sink in. Fynch nodded gravely.

'Because of how time moves, I had to hold you back in the Wild, where I live — it's complicated. If I'd let you go immediately, you would have returned too old. The Wild kept you safe and ... hibernating, for want of a better word. It has immense magic that I don't question.'

Gabe felt like he'd been punched in the softest part of his belly. He felt sick.

'When the time was right, you were still so young. You were given to a lovely family as I understand it, with parents who loved you deeply. Did you not know you were adopted?'

'No. I bore an uncanny resemblance to my mother. It was never questioned.'

Fynch sighed. 'You do bear an uncanny likeness to your birth mother too, so your adoptive parents were chosen well. There's never a good time to tell a child something like that. Maybe they just found it easier to live life with the secret intact.'

'Who is my mother ... my birth mother?' he demanded.

'A truly beautiful woman by the name of Jetta. As her name suggests she was dark haired, dark eyed ... like you.'

'Why did she give me up?'

'Because your father asked her to ... no, because he insisted.'

'Tell me about my father.'

'Little is known of him. He was a traveller, rarely seen. People thought your mother invented him. She became labelled a whore.'

Gabe blinked as if slapped.

'She was no such thing,' Fynch continued gently with affection in his gaze. 'She loved your father fiercely and did not question his motives. She did as he asked.'

'Did she know where I was taken?'

Fynch shook his head. 'It was thought best she didn't.'

'Who thought this?' he snapped. 'My father?'

'That's right. It was his choice alone.'

'So my father knew I would one day return like this, my body stolen, my life threatened, my whole existence turned upside d—'

'Gabriel, he knew only that you would return and that you would bring strength, power, skills ... and goodness to the war against Cyricus.'

'He knew! How? Tell me how he knew about Cyricus or that any of this would occur?'

'He didn't. He suspected the threat existed —'

'So on a whim … a hunch … a vague feeling that Cyricus may take an interest in Morgravia, my father — a traveller — ripped me away from my family and sent me to a new world?'

Fynch didn't blink at Gabe's rising tones or the steps that he'd taken toward him, almost in threat. 'He was right, though. Cyricus always had a need for revenge against the empire. It was just a matter of time before he directed that revenge. You had to be the innocent party. Your father had to believe that Aphra would find you.'

'When, in fact, it was the other way around.'

Fynch nodded. 'The man you knew as Reynard was Chancellor Reynard, who trusted me and knew that you existed. He gave his life to find you and send you back, but he needed Aphra's magic to make it happen. He was clever and brave and above all, he was a loyal man of Morgravia. Don't think badly of him.'

It seemed Fynch had the answers he had sought then. 'The raven?' Gabe asked, suddenly remembering how unnerved he'd been made to feel by the silent, staring bird.

'Another friend of our world, loyal and brave. In a way, he gave his life for our cause. He will be irrevocably changed through it, but he will survive because of his magic.'

Gabe felt the weight of years, of never quite feeling he belonged, crushing on his chest. 'Fynch … who am I?'

'You are one of Morgravia's precious sons and, together with Cassien and Hamelyn, you may save many lives and the land itself.'

It was too much. His voice cracked as he spoke. 'Fynch, whoever you are, you know so much. Perhaps you know this. Is Cassien my brother?' Ever since their likeness to each other had been mentioned, it had been playing on Gabe's mind. Cassien was probably just as disarmed by the suggestion.

He noticed that Fynch hesitated, but only briefly. 'Yes, you are brothers. But he barely knew you.'

Gabe let out a groan of pain — he felt it physically, as much as emotionally. 'I dreamed him.'

'Yes, I have no doubt. You are connected to this world, Gabe, and you possess a magic that allows you to roam.'

'Roam?'

'Your mind is an incredibly powerful tool. You have memories of the cathedral. Am I right?'

He nodded dumbly.

'It was the last place you saw, your last stop before you were sent away. It is burned into your memory. Your memory is your power, Gabriel, because your mind is so strong. How else would you have been able to survive possession by Cyricus and Aphra if not for that robust mind of yours?'

'How do you know about that?'

'I know because I watch you and protect you as best I can.'

'I want to understand the roaming that you speak of.'

'Roaming magic is rare and can show itself in different ways. Cassien roams too, but his magic takes his spirit out of his body. It is very dangerous for him and equally dangerous for those around him. Each time he roams, he kills. It chooses the victims, not him. It is random and ruthless. Luckily, if it chooses not to kill you, it never will.'

Gabe was not paying attention. 'And mine?'

'Your magic is contained within you. By not pushing it beyond yourself, no-one suffers the consequences of the power. You have more constraints on you than Cassien, as a result. You have taught yourself to roam in your mind to one place only — the cathedral. It was a safe place for you. Your memory told you it was home.'

'Has my roaming created this place?' he said, looking around.

'This place, as you call it, is real. It is the Void. It offers nothing. Your roaming skill is powerful enough to lock onto the Void. Most people, even sentients — as those with magic are called — would not be able to touch it because it is so secret, but you reached it easily. Remember its trace now so you can recognise it and move away when you have to. I need you to remain here, in the Void.'

'Why?'

'Because this is where the battle with Cyricus will be fought and you are its facilitator.' Gabe groaned but Fynch quietened him with a soft sigh. 'Hear me now, I have things to tell you. Things about you and about me that we must share.'

'Cassien, am I imagining it, or is there a wolf flanking us? And did you lift your hand in acknowledgement to it a moment ago?'

417

'You're not imagining it, your majesty. She is a friend — more than that in fact. Her name is Romaine.'

'She has a name?' she said, slightly breathless from the gallop they were now slowing from. 'My life gets stranger by the moment.'

He nodded with a grin. 'Shar, but it's good to be back here. I wasn't sure I'd feel that way,' he said, smelling the forest that loomed ahead. Thin woodland had been their neighbour on either side for a while, gradually thickening into the dark blur of true forest. 'I feel as though I've come home,' he added.

'And in contrast, I feel entirely out of my depth and scared by the lack of buildings,' Florentyna admitted. 'Plus a wolf with a name is following me.'

'Romaine is my wolf. She would not hurt you — she is protecting us, guiding us in.'

Florentyna smiled. 'You seem so much more carefree now you're here.'

'Carefree?' he shrugged. 'I don't think I've ever felt that way, but I feel much safer.'

'Can I meet her?'

'Only Romaine will answer that question. She may be my soul mate, but she is also a wild beast.'

'Is that what you are, Cassien? Wild?'

He shrugged. 'That's a valid question, your majesty. I possess a wild magic and I like being in the Wild of Morgravia. I essentially grew up alone. Yes, I'm wild,' he pronounced with a grin.

'Tell me how you came to be in the Brotherhood,' she asked, hoping it would help pass the time and take her mind off her insecurities.

So he told her what he knew of himself.

'You have no memory of parents?'

'Not really, no. I often feel there was a sibling … an elder one, but I lose that feeling as soon as I lock onto it.' He shrugged. 'I'm told I look very similar to my mother, other than my eyes. Hers were dark.'

'So you get your very blue eyes from your father.'

'I suppose. I know even less of him. They say he was a traveller.'

'A merchant?'

He shrugged. 'I don't really know.'

'And yet we all agree you look so similar to Gabriel. You could easily be his younger sibling.' Their horses had slowed to a walk. Romaine was nowhere to be seen. 'Do you really believe that you were taken from your parents and raised, first in all-male monastic life, and second, thrust into the forest to raise yourself, amuse yourself, teach yourself for the past decade? And then, with no warning, you are wrenched away from that strange life by an even stranger man called Fynch and told you were the one would save the realm?'

Cassien opened his mouth to speak, but Florentyna continued, cutting him off.

'What's more, you have a powerful magic at your disposal. You meet Hamelyn, who seems to have an array of skills equally baffling. He himself is an enigma, don't you agree?' She paused only to take a breath, not waiting for his response. 'Along comes Gabriel into the fray in the most extraordinary manner, I'm sure you won't deny. And although he hasn't demonstrated his magics to us, I'm sure they are there ... or tell me how in Shar's bright light that man could not only travel here from another world — or so he says — but carry with him a demon's servant? Beyond that, he gets himself possessed by the true demon, and in the process has the wits about him to not only return me my quill, letting me know he is not an enemy, but somehow hide within his own body in a spiritual form, only to resurrect himself and his body, which the demon believed was dead.' She stopped and let out a snort of disbelief, pulling on the reins to pull up her horse. 'Now I ask you, Cassien. Can you honestly look me in the eye and say this is all coincidence?'

It was the first time Florentyna had put everything she knew into one series of events — as best as she could. It was daunting and she rather wished she hadn't done so. Nevertheless, she held Cassien's gaze in the moonlight and awaited his answer. 'Well, can you?'

He shook his head. 'No. It is implausible that these events are unrelated coincidences.'

'Then you can accept that Gabe's similarity to you may not be a coincidence also ... especially as he's involved. He's been "orchestrated" to be here at the same time as you were "orchestrated" to keep me safe. You have been brought together to use your skills against Cyricus by Fynch.'

'Brothers.' He rolled the word in his mouth. To him that meant his family at the abbey; blood family was a stranger to him.

She was frowning. 'Fynch knows so much more than he let on to me.'

'Or to me,' Cassien admitted. 'Although in his defence I heard that he did not have a willing audience in you, your majesty. And I was more interested in my role when I met him, rather than knowing his.'

Florentyna knew Cassien was right. She nodded. 'I didn't sense any dishonesty. I'm sure if I'd asked more questions he would have answered them candidly.'

'Yes. We just didn't ask the right questions.'

'What would you ask him?'

'Who my father is. The problem begins there. Why would a mother give up her son?'

'Both her sons,' Florentyna corrected and gave him a smug smile.

'That only makes the situation more intriguing and baffling. If you're right and we are brothers, she gave us both up to a cause.'

'The same cause, Cassien,' Florentyna said, confident now. 'There is no way that Fynch is not pulling the strings and you are both his puppets. I don't mean that to sound as cruel as it does. I'll tell you what, I wouldn't be at all surprised if Fynch didn't convince your mother to give you both up. He is behind this.'

'For the right reasons,' Cassien said, and Florentyna was sure he was trying to convince himself of this fact.

'Well yes, you've saved my life. Gabe saved it again by telling us what we needed to wary of, or I would now be under the control of Cyricus through my sister.'

'My head is spinning, your majesty, and even though you seem to have found a second wind, I would like to get you into the cover of the deep forest before daybreak.' He nodded to where the trees formed a perfect gateway and before it stood the huge she-wolf. 'Romaine awaits us.'

Florentyna blinked in surprise. 'It looks like a mouth waiting to swallow me into the dark.'

'Nothing to fear in the forest,' he assured her.

They come, she said softly over their link.

Fynch had his back to the forest entrance, thinking deeply about what was ahead. *Mmm, I know. I can feel Cassien's presence like an ache. And the others?*

Gabriel ... yes. Hamelyn most of all.

Hamelyn is more than worthy, the Dragon had whispered sadly into his mind.

The she-wolf seemed to sense his thoughts shifting to the dragon.

I hope our king does not believe I have defied him by letting you come back into the Forest. You are not meant to leave the Wild.

No, Romaine, the Dragon King would never believe such a thing of you. He is clear that it is I who defy him.

You will pay a hefty price. Why must you do this?

Because I was once mortal. He knew it was not a helpful answer but it was all he had. Instinct was driving this and somewhere deep and visceral, he knew that while he was disappointing his twin soul, the dragon, this was the right way to proceed.

He turned to greet the sovereign of Morgravia, leading her horse alongside Cassien. Fynch emerged out of the darkness of the trees to stand beside Romaine, whose fur was silvered beneath the moonlight.

Cassien saw him first.

'Fynch!' He ran to him. 'I am relieved to see you well.'

'Hello, Cassien, my boy,' he replied, his spirits lifting as Cassien pulled him into a bear hug. 'I could say the same to you.' He shifted his gaze to the tall, slim woman who held herself back while the men enjoyed their reunion. 'Your majesty,' he now said, bowing, 'it gladdens my heart to see you safe.'

Florentyna stepped forward and held out her hand. He took it and kissed it gently. 'Master Fynch,' she said and he heard the slight tremble in her voice. 'It is I who am the more glad. Forgive me for not paying your warnings enough heed.'

'That is the past, your majesty. Don't look to it now. Worry only about staying safe while we rid the land of the curse that has come upon it.'

'No, but if I'd listened, Chancellor Reynard might still be —'

'Even if you had taken my warnings to heart, I believe Reynard would have followed the pathway he took and it is only because of Reynard that we have Gabriel with us, my queen.'

'You know Gabriel?' Cassien chimed in, looking up from where he knelt by Romaine, stroking the wolf.

'He and I have spoken.'

'Spoken?' the queen and Cassien repeated together.

Fynch smiled. 'I will explain. Come. You have made a long journey. Let us return to your old hut, Cassien, and give the queen a place to rest her head for a while.'

He turned and his companions fell in step, following the wolf into the forest.

'Ride like a demon is chasing you,' Tamas roared over his shoulder, laughing bleakly at his own dark humour.

Ham was grateful for it, though. It made him feel more secure if Tamas presented confidence. He'd seen death before but not like that: not cold, calculated and so very cruel. But as the wind tore at his hair and turned his horse's mane into a wave of undulating gold, Ham was reminded that the woman who had died was not Princess Darcelle but merely the puppet of a demon that had stolen her corpse. It had to be done and he admired Tamas for his resolve; the courage it took for him to destroy Cyricus and Aphra and give Darcelle's body to Shar's keeping, where it belonged. He wished the corpse had not been dragged behind its horse, but there was no point in worrying over that now, especially with Morgravian riders giving chase in the firm belief that the heir to the throne had just been murdered.

Tamas had been right. The men had no idea where the arrow came from and had scattered in various directions, including theirs. If Ham's last glance had been correct, three had headed their way, which was easier to stomach than thirty-six angry legionnaires. No doubt the Cipreans had been forgotten and left to get to their ship without another moment's thought.

He urged his horse forward. 'Where are we going?'

Tamas shrugged in his saddle theatrically. 'I'm just trying to get us away. You get to choose where we go.'

Ham was not as familiar with his realm as perhaps the king presumed, but he knew Tamas couldn't be expected to make the most informed decision either.

There was only one direction to ride. 'We head north, back the way we came.'

'Where in the north, though? Not that it matters to me ... I have no idea where I am even now,' Tamas admitted.

Ham wanted to say the Forest. But the Forest was huge. He wouldn't have any idea where to start looking for Cassien even if they did make it to the Great Forest. He frowned and it occurred to him that apart from Orkyld, there was one other place that he and Cassien had shared and that Cassien may think to go to as a meeting point.

'We'll head for Rittylworth Monastery,' he finally yelled as they galloped, knowing he sounded more confident than he felt. 'It's a direct route northwest. We can avoid Pearlis too.'

'You're in charge, Ham. Lead the way,' Tamas said.

Gabe was holding to the Void as instructed but was relieved that he could still sense the familiar grey stone of Pearlis Cathedral. He knew he was sitting by the great dragon and that his hand was still placed against one of the huge toes of the beast's clawed foot and it reassured him.

What Fynch had told him had been startling, but there was no time to reflect on his past, the discovery that he had family in this world, or the identity of his real parents. He was now part of a triumvirate of power that had to link together in order to destroy Cyricus and he wouldn't let his companions down.

'Everyone will be counting on each other, none more important than the next … but you, Gabe,' Fynch said, fixing him with a stern look, 'you're the eldest brother and without you we have no means of fighting Cyricus. We need your skills alone to entice him into the Void. You must commit to memory how to get here, how to stay here and how to design the architecture in your mind to allow others to travel to it. You will have to be strong — you will be tested like never before.'

'Eldest,' Gabe murmured. 'Tested like never before,' he added. Surely the loss of a child and a wife was more than proof of his mental strength? Maybe that's why he had been chosen. 'No,' he whispered, alone in the nave, 'you were chosen long before then.'

It was all coming back to him now. Memories that had been so deeply buried that he'd needed the shock of learning that his father wasn't dead to retrieve them.

THIRTY-TWO

Florentyna had reluctantly agreed to rest. She'd fought it, but Cassien had joined forces with Fynch to insist and she'd eventually lain down. A check by Cassien a moment earlier had seen her fast asleep in his old cot, her mouth slightly open. Cassien had smiled; he was glad that this place was the safest for the queen. He'd never felt anything but secure here.

He stepped outside the hut, knowing time was short. 'She's asleep although I doubt it will last,' he said to Fynch, who was seated on the stump of a tree that Cassien remembered felling to make his small clearing.

'And you?' Fynch asked.

Cassien shrugged. 'I can go without sleep for days, but then you know that.'

'I do.'

'There's something I want to ask you before Florentyna wakes.'

Fynch smiled, but it was awkward. 'Mmm, well, there's something I need to tell you before she wakes.'

'All right.' Cassien was aware of Romaine padding up to sit beside him. He buried his hand affectionately in the ruff of thick fur at her neck. 'Tell me.'

'I'm wondering whether I should pre-empt it by suggesting that you're not going to be very happy by what you learn.'

Cassien looked at him quizzically. 'And you just did.'

'I did, didn't I? At heart I'm a coward, Cassien.'

'I doubt that very much. I can tell whatever you wish to say is hard.'

Fynch looked away. 'Painful is a more appropriate word. Anguish is also another that comes to mind. And perhaps even fear.'

'Fear? Of whom?'

'Of you, Cassien,' Fynch said, raising his head to meet his gaze.

'Me? Nothing you say could —'

'Make you despise me?' Fynch cut in.

Cassien stilled, his mouth open as though robbed of the words it had wanted to say. He frowned.

'Despise you?' he repeated in disbelief. He shook his head. 'No, nothing you say could make me despise you. I revere you.'

Fynch nodded with resignation as though he'd expected Cassien to say something like this.

'Just tell me,' Cassien urged.

'Your mother's name is … was Jetta.'

Cassien blinked with confusion. Of all the topics that Fynch could have raised, the furthest from his mind would have been his mother. He swallowed, immediately feeling defensive. 'Jetta,' he repeated.

'She was exquisitely beautiful. Her hair was raven and she possessed huge, dark, searching eyes that looked like depthless caverns when she was upset, or black sparkling jewels when she was happy.' Fynch looked away again, but this time it didn't seem to be from self-consciousness; rather, it was him focusing his gaze on a distant point, searching back through memories … or it seemed so to Cassien. 'Her complexion was like the palest rose you can imagine and just as velvety.' Fynch touched a spot on his chest. 'Here, just above her heart, she had a tiny mark of the gods; it looked like a crescent moon. She once laughed and told me that although she'd known many men she had not loved a single one. And when she did fall in love she was going to ask him to ink the corresponding and opposing half-moon on his chest.' He sighed and laughed to himself. 'She said it would form a loose heart shape that would bind them.'

'How did you know my mother?' Cassien asked, sounding fearful.

'I met her by chance on a visit to the Pearlis Cathedral. She lived in the city and loved the cathedral. She told me it humbled her and she liked to clean the feet of the dragon.'

Cassien swallowed. 'Why?'

'Jetta said the dragon was the king's beast and it was her way of honouring Florentyna's father. Later I learned more. She admitted one day that she felt a strange kinship to the dragon himself.'

'Surely she wasn't —'

'No, she wasn't, son. Her beast was the blackbird. Appropriate. Mysterious, busy, good mothers, and the females not even black.' The last one Cassien could see was added for levity, but he wasn't feeling it.

'Good mother? Really? I couldn't agree with that.'

Fynch glanced at him. 'You didn't know her.'

'That's my point. She gave away an infant.'

'Your father made her give you away.'

'Then my father's a bastard!' Cassien snarled, hurling the word as an insult.

'He is indeed.'

Cassien shook his head, looking perplexed. 'What?'

'A bastard, but I use it in its original meaning. Your father was never claimed by his father. Although he suspected he knew him. The truth is the man he knew as his father liked him and was liked back in return.'

'Are you saying my grandfather didn't know his own son?'

'Yes. That's what I'm telling you.'

'Then my father's a fool for forcing my mother to give me up.'

'Yes, he's that too. A fool in many respects.'

'Fynch, you speak about my father as though you know him, as though he is alive.'

'I know him. He is alive,' Fynch replied, meeting Cassien's angry gaze.

Cassien stood in shock. 'What?' he whispered. 'You know him? You can name him?'

Fynch nodded, grief reflected in his eyes. Cassien watched as Fynch began to fumble with the neck of his robe. The man never took his eyes from Cassien, but Cassien shifted his to stare at the flesh that Fynch revealed. Inked onto his chest just above his heart was a crescent moon. Cassien felt a choking pain at the back of his throat and the animal sound that issued had Romaine on her feet and growling back at him.

In a blink, she stood between the men. Cassien wasn't sure whether she was defending Fynch against potential attack, or warning Cassien.

Fynch moved. 'I deserve it, Romaine,' he said, standing with effort and moving stiffly to where she stood, no longer snarling, but hackles raised. He stroked her. 'I know,' he said.

'What did Romaine say?' Cassien demanded, his words sounding as choked as he felt.

'She repeated what she'd said earlier to me ... that I should not be here.'

'Why are you here, Fynch? Or should I call you father? What's the protocol now?'

'Call me Fynch. I don't deserve to be called anything but that. And I'm here to finish what I began and to be truthful about it. No more intrigue.'

'You gave me up to the Brotherhood; why?'

'For this role. I knew you would possess certain skills that came from my magic. I needed you to learn about them in safety and over time. I needed you to prepare yourself for the fight that is coming. Only you can fight him, Cassien. You have the power. You are what stands between Cyricus and the desecration of everything we hold sacred. He wants the Wild. If it is breeched, there is no more magic that can protect our land. Our animals will be powerless. The Dragon King will die. Our world will wither.'

Cassien held his head. 'I don't know how to fight him. This is too much responsibility on my shoulders. I barely know real life. You took it from me.'

'There's no point in turning away now,' said a new voice.

Romaine had heard her, because the wolf had moved to the entrance of the hut, but neither Fynch nor Cassien, both more than capable of sensing someone's approach, had even noted her silent arrival from her cot to the doorway.

'Your majesty,' they said together and bowed.

'How much did you hear, Florentyna?' Fynch said.

'All of it. I'm sorry, I had woken. I hated eavesdropping, so thought it best to show myself.'

'It's best you know it,' Cassien replied, throwing a glare toward Fynch.

'Cassien, isn't this what you wanted? When we spoke on our journey, I heard only longing in your voice to know where you belonged, why this special task had been placed on your shoulders, why you were sent to the forest to learn. Now, you know. And it is not a blot on your life, but surely an acknowledgement of just how important you are to us, to this land, to the Crown and its wellbeing and continuation. I know about duty. And that's what you're in the midst of … doing your duty. It doesn't mean you weren't loved by either parent.'

'It's the lie, my queen. You've not been lied to.'

'Oh, I think I've had my share. Seeing only the darker side of this will be a poison in your heart, believe me. You can't undo what has been done, Cassien. Fynch has given you the truth. Can't you see how painful this is for him to tell, just as it is painful for you to hear it? I suspect he would like to tell you that he loves you.' Florentyna turned her gaze on Fynch, who looked instantly mortified, as though reprimanded.

'Cassien,' he said, his voice suddenly raspy with emotion, 'I held you as a newborn and I wept for your perfection. Both of us did. Your mother understood me. She accepted me and all of my burdens. She possessed no magic, but she revered mine.' He swallowed. 'Jetta, your beautiful mother, was glad to shine the feet of the dragon in the cathedral long before she met me, but perhaps long before she met me she felt me in her heart. Your mother knew me and loved me as instantly as she loved you. Giving you up was one of the hardest tasks she'd ever had to face.'

'One of the hardest,' Cassien sneered. 'What were the other hardships that she could compare to giving away her son?' he snapped, feeling churlish and wishing he could be understanding in this tense moment. But years of loneliness were driving this despair.

'Two others compare,' Fynch answered. 'Giving up Gabriel and Hamelyn to similarly lonely fates.'

Cassien's head snapped up, shocked. Fynch didn't wait, pressing on. 'She'd had to face relinquishing Gabriel before she gave you up, and by the time it was Hamelyn's turn, she'd hoped it would be easier, but that was not the case. Your mother took her own life the day she handed me Hamelyn, the day he was weaned, and I took him north. She couldn't face life a moment longer, and while others believe she succumbed to the disease that was ravaging folk, she ended her life. It was from heartbreak, not from the poison brew she drank.'

Cassien could hear a ragged sound. It took him a moment to realise it was his own breath, shallow and difficult to draw, making the noise. 'Brother Josse said —'

'I know what he said. He believes your mother was a whore as well. Everyone thought she gave birth to three boys from different fathers. No-one knew of me, or our love and faithfulness to each other. Josse knows none of the truth. I alone am telling you the truth. Gabriel is your elder brother, sent to a different world for reasons perhaps you can now piece together. Hamelyn is your younger brother. He has a special role to play that he is not aware of yet. He does not know about my connection to each of you, but it will be my task alone to explain as I have to Gabe first and now you. You should also know that I will not permit Hamelyn to face Cyricus, even though he sees things and has such deep knowledge. He will be the one to connect you all.'

'We knew it!' Florentyna said, unable to help her excitement. 'Not about Ham, but we could see the undeniable likenesses between Gabriel and Cassien.'

'Gabe's dark eyes reflect his mother. Cassien, my colouring affected yours.' He shrugged. 'Your eyes were always such a deep blue. But Hamelyn ...' he grinned softly to himself. 'I believe I looked very similar to him as a youngster. He does not resemble Jetta so much as a gong boy called Fynch. It was long long ago ...'

'You brought us together. We are the Triad?' Cassien asked.

Fynch nodded. 'You each had a role. I hoped I'd never have to use you, but the mere fact that I took the precaution means I knew in my heart that you would be needed.'

'Use is the right word.'

Fynch shrugged. 'I love each of you. I'm sorry that I am your father because any child of mine was going to have burdens as I did ... as I have.'

Florentyna stepped between them now, just as Romaine had earlier. 'Stop this! Cassien, your *father* stands before you. This is the man you have surely longed to meet, to embrace. I could hear the longing in your voice to know family — Fynch has just given you three blood kin. Grab them and hold on! Fynch, I am beginning to gather you have had very little choice. It seems that you, too, have had a life of duty to Morgravia. I am sorry that you two have not known one another in the way you would wish, but life is not known to be terribly fair. I can vouch for that.'

Cassien felt her words sting. Everything she'd said was right. If he could only push himself past the pain of learning the truth, then all that she suggested seemed perfectly reasonable to ask of an intelligent person and especially someone who had known loneliness for so long. *Why push my father away?* he asked himself silently.

'Hamelyn's so young.' He realised he'd spoken aloud.

'True, but he has enormous untapped power. He can speak with Romaine,' Fynch said. Cassien blanched.

'But he doesn't know her.'

'Romaine can reach out to him. We're waiting for him, in turn, to initiate contact, and then he will accept his power. Once he knows how, he will be able to speak to you and Gabriel as well. Hamelyn is still scared. He dismisses his power in his mind as simply being knowledge he has accumulated, but it's so much more, Cassien. Hamelyn's knowledge is coming from a far more ancient source than he can begin to believe.'

Cassien swallowed. So the strange happening in the cathedral was true then. 'From the dragon?'

Fynch smiled in wonder. 'You know?'

Cassien put a hand up in defence. 'I don't understand though. Forgive me, your majesty. I lied because I thought it was a mistake.'

She frowned, sat on the stoop of the hut and hugged her knees. 'What lie?'

Cassien watched Fynch lean against a tree, noticed how concerned Romaine was. She padded over to sit by Fynch in case he needed her. Cassien squatted down to make everyone feel easier. 'In the cathedral,' he continued, 'both Gabriel and I were called to the dragon pillar.'

'What?' she said, an odd smile of disbelief in her expression. 'That can't be right. It's impossible,' she added, cutting a glance at Fynch and then back to Cassien.

'He named us both,' Cassien pressed. 'We were both unnerved, as you can imagine. It was easier to lie than to face it.'

She shook her head. 'But ...'

'It is possible, Florentyna,' Fynch said softly, 'if the three boys have the blood of Morgravia passing through their veins.'

'Wait,' Florentyna begged, 'I need to catch up. Explain to me how my father is somehow father to Cassien and —'

'Not your father, child. My father,' Fynch said.

They both looked at him with lost expressions.

'It's high time I said this aloud and admitted it myself,' he said. 'My father was King Magnus. My mother was no-one — a farmer's wife. She was very beautiful, far too loose with her affections and inordinately fey. He was lonely; she made him laugh, she wanted nothing from him, and even from the moment I quickened in her womb she never let on that I was his child. I was born into a humble family. A good man believed me to be his son. I had no reason to doubt it until I began working at the castle as a gong boy. Then I, too, began to feel the attraction to the dragon and began to piece together what must have occurred.' He waved a hand. 'That's all history. The fact is, I am the bastard son of

King Magnus of Morgravia, half-brother to the hated Celimus and kin to your ancestors,' he said to Florentyna. 'I am soul-twin to the dragon king, who chose me and with whom I have remained bonded through centuries. He knows what I do today is ...' He trailed off and looked sadly at Romaine.

'What?' Cassien asked, his tone suspicious.

'It has inherent dangers,' Fynch replied, 'for all of us.'

'Will you forgive me?' he then said suddenly, taking Cassien by surprise.

Cassien was stumped for words momentarily, although he was well aware of Florentyna's glare burning the side of his face.

The pause lengthened and Cassien saw Romaine lift her head and fix him with a penetrating stare that felt like a knife into his heart.

'It ...' he began and Fynch looked up and at him with a sad expression. 'It has been lonely. But it has not been unhappy or unworthy,' he said and knew he was speaking from his heart. This was no brave face, no words of a martyr. The truth was that his life, though strange, was not without pleasure or merit. 'I could have done without Loup's punishment,' he admitted, 'but then I also couldn't imagine life without Romaine, or the forest. If you asked me to choose, I would choose Romaine and the forest again and put up with the beatings and loneliness.'

Fynch nodded. 'Thank you for your grace, Cassien. It is more than I deserve.'

Cassien glanced at Florentyna, who slumped her shoulders in a frustrated sigh. 'Cassien, what wouldn't I give to hug my father. Don't waste it.'

In three strides he had the small man in his arms and both wept with joy at finally being father and son in name, as well as in knowledge. And they wept especially for the simple physical pleasure of their embrace. Nearby, Florentyna shed happy tears for their reunion, although she seemed blatantly unaware that, at the same time, she was stroking an enormous she-wolf.

Later, over a small picnic of fruit, nuts and a soft goat's cheese that Fynch had thoughtfully provided — but did not himself partake of — they gathered their thoughts for the pressing matter that had thrown them together.

'We can't let the queen remain here, Cassien. I know you feel you can protect Florentyna in the forest and in any other circumstance you would be right, but not where Cyricus is concerned,' Fynch advised.

'Why?'

'Because the forest is too large. The creatures are at risk, as you will need to roam.'

'What do you mean? I don't understand.'

'I've asked Gabe to use his skills to open up the Void to you.' Fynch shook his head slightly at Cassien's frown. 'Let me explain. Gabe possesses an extraordinary ability to create a scenario, for want of a better word. In his life in another world he could re-create the Pearlis Cathedral with such authority, ease and accuracy, that he believed, firstly,' Fynch said, holding up a finger, 'that it was a place of his own design because he knew it so well. As it turns out he was building this cathedral in his mind from a childhood memory. Secondly,' he continued, holding up another finger, 'he can access his "destinations",' Fynch said, loading the word, 'in a heartbeat and maintain them for as long as he chooses.'

'How do you know he can do this … and what is the Void?' Cassien asked, receiving a nod of approval for the questions from Florentyna, who was clearly finding it hard to follow the conversation.

'I'll answer the second part of your question first. The Void is emptiness. It is where the Wild catapulted Cyricus centuries ago. It sent Aphra elsewhere, not taking any chances with the two of them. Gabe can reach the Void. Better, he can create it.'

Florentyna gave a small gasp, sounding awed, and shrugged at Cassien's wry glance. 'You've had the presence of magic in your life. I'm having to accept everything that's been going on around me in the last few days without question. That's hard, Cassien. Even so, without being told, I'm presuming that what Gabe can do is impressive.'

'It is indeed, your majesty,' Fynch confirmed, 'and let me tell you why. Gabriel thinks that I showed him the Void and I've let him believe it, because he hasn't yet put faith in himself. Understandably he feels like the interloper we can't help but see him as. However, I have told him the truth about his birth and his parents, that his real beginnings are here in Morgravia.'

'How did poor Gabriel take it?' Florentyna asked, sipping on some sweet wine that Cassien had rustled up from the hut.

'Shocked. He felt wounded, as you did,' Fynch said to Cassien. 'Most understandable. Unlike you, though, he didn't ask lots of questions. He listened. He's a deep thinker. I think Gabriel will turn it over in his mind and know that I speak the truth because he has felt like an outsider all his life. Now he knows why. He has experienced Cyricus and Aphra for himself, so I am not asking him to take leaps of faith as I ask you. He already knows the truth. He is already primed and determined to destroy Cyricus … except he can't do so without his younger brothers.'

'Are you telling us that he created the Void?'

'Not created, no … I'm saying he can re-create it in his mind. He has seen the Void in his nightmares but has never remembered the detail of the dream when he wakes, only that it frightened him. Why? Because it is where he will place Cyricus.'

'He's going to do what the Wild did,' Florentyna breathed, catching on.

'Yes, your majesty!' Fynch said, sounding delighted that she was following his thoughts. It was obvious she'd made the connection faster than Cassien had. 'I cannot allow Cyricus to get close to the Wild. His destructive powers are vast. I don't really know what he is capable of with his magic and I'm not prepared to test his abilities. I do know that he is far wiser this time. His first visit to the Wild was made so innocently, although I can hardly bear to speak in such terms about Cyricus. He simply wandered over to explore because he sensed its magic and beauty.' He looked at Cassien. 'As I've told you, it shunned him, knowing before he did that he would want to harness its power, certainly make it his realm. Elysius before me urged the Wild to rid itself of Cyricus. Now as the present Keeper of the Wild I have taken a different approach.'

'Outwitting Cyricus with the placement of your empowered sons,' Florentyna finished.

Fynch nodded, with a smile for her. It was obvious he enjoyed her agile mind, able to quickly embrace and follow new thoughts.

'How does Gabe know he can do this … I mean, put Cyricus into the Void?' Cassien asked, throwing the crumbs of their food into the undergrowth for foraging birds to discover.

'He can't put him there. Only Cyricus can do that. Gabe's job is to entice him … lure him there for you. He can put you there; you can use Gabe, through your blood connection, to reach the Void when you roam.'

It all seemed to make sense now. Both Cassien and the queen sat back, as though dawning had hit.

Fynch continued. 'Gabriel has immense power, enabling him to preserve the Void for the length of time you will need to face Cyricus and defeat him. He believes that I was waiting for him in the Void to show it to him, when in fact he understood the Void — and embraced it without being aware of it — as soon as he laid his hands on the claw of the Great Dragon in the cathedral … his beast. The King of the Beasts showed him the Void and Gabe can now conjure it up, reaching out to it as though dragging it close to himself. And without even being aware of it, he called to me. He included me in the Void — I cannot get there alone. He will conjure it and bring you to the Void as well.'

'And my younger brother?' Cassien asked, clearly getting used to the notion of having family.

Fynch shared a glance with Florentyna. 'He sees things, hears things that others miss.' He smiled. 'He's like me in that regard. I was a wealth of what seemed to be useless information until, one day, I was required to start putting together all that I had seen, heard and experienced. It's how I worked out that King Magnus was my father, that Celimus was planning to kill my friend Wyl Thirsk … and other things that are of no relevance to you,' he said, cutting his thoughts deliberately short. 'Ham's role will be to warn you and Gabe, for he will know when Cyricus is close. He has another role that hasn't fully shown itself but I'm sure it will.' He smiled at them both as if concluding all that he wanted to share. Cassien knew it was pointless asking Fynch more about what he wasn't saying.

He looked at Florentyna, who clearly also had a question in mind. 'He won't tell you. He'll speak in riddles. He only shares what he thinks we need to know,' Cassien said.

Florentyna glanced at Fynch, who laughed.

'Cassien seems to have my measure. I may be old but you might like to tell your champion, your majesty, that my hearing remains sharp.'

She looked from one man to the other with a bemused expression, but Cassien was already moving on.

'If we can't stay in the forest, where do we go?'

'Somewhere we have the advantage of seeing people approach — remember, we don't know what guise he might be in. Somewhere that can feed and house a queen with slightly better quarters than a one-man hut.'

434

'All right,' Cassien said, looking only slightly hurt. 'Then how about Rittylworth Monastery? It won't take us long to reach it and it has everything you demand for Florentyna.'

'Including stuff that I don't want to confront again so soon,' Florentyna murmured, although her remark was ignored by her two companions.

'Brother Hoolyn is a friend,' Fynch went on, turning the idea over in his mind. 'He would lay down his life for the Crown.'

Cassien nodded. 'That's settled then.' He sighed. 'Fynch, there is one thing I want to ask.'

'Go ahead.'

'I was told that my power … magic … call it what you will, can learn.'

Fynch's gaze snapped back from Romaine, who he was stroking, to Cassien. 'You were told?' Cassien nodded. 'By whom?'

'By a hedgewitch, I think you'd call her. Her name's Tilda.'

'When was this?'

'At the palace,' Cassien answered.

'He doesn't know about the killings,' Florentyna prompted. 'Fynch, Cassien's magic caused a lot of deaths,' she confided to the older man. 'Was it yesterday or the day before?' She looked to Cassien, but he was so unhappy to be remembering, she pressed on alone and told Fynch all that had occurred.

Afterwards, Fynch's expression was clouded. Cassien couldn't tell what his father was thinking.

'I thought you might have known,' Cassien lifted a shoulder with a rueful expression, 'you seem to know so much.'

'I have my ways of observing,' Fynch replied without telling them more. 'But I didn't know about the deaths. Poor Burrage.'

Florentyna closed her eyes briefly, and Cassien quickly leapt in. 'I came out of my roaming trance with a sickening like I've not experienced previously. Ham immediately fetched a woman he'd met in the palace kitchens who supplies Florentyna with herb teas. We met with her in Micklesham.'

'She organised to meet with you?'

Cassien scratched his head. 'No. She told me she was heading north. I don't think she expected to see me again, although she did look at me in a way that suggested I should follow, maybe catch her up. The point is, she gave me a curative which helped my headache and nausea, but Tilda warned that my magic learns.'

Fynch stared at him for several long moments. 'I can't see how. It is what it is. You control where you roam, when you roam, how you roam, if you roam and why you roam. The roaming magic is there for you to use or not. What is she suggesting it learns?'

'I don't know. She didn't have time to explain.'

'She did, over our supper, Cassien,' Florentyna chimed in, then shrugged an apology at him for the interruption.

He didn't seem to mind. 'That's true.'

'She had the perfect opportunity because we were discussing the roaming magic.'

'You discussed it?' Fynch asked aghast, looking at Cassien in horror. 'With a stranger?'

'Not really a stranger, Fynch. She already knew about my skill, my roaming, my murderous ways. She was helping me.'

Florentyna was frowning, picking at invisible lint on her riding clothes. 'Cassien, I want to say this and I'm not going to try and say it carefully. I think I'll just air my thoughts.' Both men looked at her. She swallowed. 'I could be wrong, but I sensed something was slightly amiss with Tilda.'

'Why do you say that?' he asked, aware that Fynch was fixing the queen with a wintry stare.

'Just a feeling, call it womanly intuition. I thought she became curiously quiet and watchful at one point and then when I thought it likely she would travel on with us, she seemed to be in a hurry to leave us.'

'Yes, I noticed her eagerness to depart,' he admitted slowly, then frowned. 'I didn't feel startled or surprised, though.'

'She cut me off a couple of times when she sensed I was going to ask a pointed question. I'm her queen, let's not forget, so what she did was unusually rude. I didn't react to her impropriety but, even so, she took the risk of offending more than once.'

'What are you saying, majesty?' Fynch urged.

Florentyna shook her head. 'I don't know. The fact is, I don't know Tilda at all well. She seemed very friendly — too friendly — with Cassien and with me, given that she barely knew us and that I, her sovereign, was sitting down to break bread with her. She seemed neither surprised nor cowed. It was odd, that's all. I don't enjoy provoking the reaction, but most ordinary people find it hard to speak in my presence simply out of respect for the Crown.'

'Does everyone have to be scared, your majesty?' Cassien reasoned.

She threw him a sharp look. 'No, not scared. But it's fair to assume that most people are going to be shocked, surprised or unnerved, if their sovereign suddenly takes supper with them. But Tilda seemed to take our presence in her stride as if …'

'As if what?' Fynch pressed.

'Well, as if she was expecting us. There, I've said it. It's been nagging me since we met her.'

Cassien slowly shifted his gaze to Fynch. 'What are you thinking?'

Fynch gave him a look of uncertainty and then shrugged lightly. 'She could be innocent. She was drawn into your life by Hamelyn and she offered help. She obviously hasn't pursued you, but she knew what your magic was, you say?' Cassien nodded. 'So it's little wonder she was interested to see you again when you found her at Micklesham.'

Cassien nodded, relieved, and looked at Florentyna as if to say she shouldn't be so suspicious. Nothing was said for a moment while Cassien and Florentyna digested Fynch's summation.

'And then again, she could be a spy,' Fynch offered baldly.

THIRTY-THREE

Tilda waited where the man called Tentrell had instructed. He was a strange one. So handsome and charming, but there was something odd about him. He looked at her with intensity, and as though he knew something that she didn't. Except she did. Her own weak magic picked up that this was no ordinary individual. She sensed power in his manner and also hidden power of the magical kind. He'd surely sensed hers ... or why had he approached her?

Tilda went over their original conversation in her mind. He'd found her at a dinch-house selling her own brand of infusion which claimed therapeutic properties for people with fatigue and another remedy for those who suffered from headaches.

He'd been seated at the counter, nursing a pot of dinch. She could see the curl of steam rising gently from his pot but she also saw that he didn't drink. He watched people around him but spoke to no-one. She'd been waiting to make her delivery and had found him irresistible to observe simply because he was such a handsome man — tall and dark with matching eyes and long ebony lashes. She'd also noticed she was not the only woman who was sneaking glances at him but, while he observed his surroundings, he hadn't made eye contact with anyone. Not even her.

'Ah, Tilda.' Loos Francham had broken into her thoughts.

'Loos, nice to see you again. You're very busy?'

'Always busy although it helps that the King of Cipres is coming in tomorrow. Everyone wants to catch a glimpse.'

'Ah yes, of course.'

He had smiled. 'Come on up here to the counter. I need to keep my eye on things.'

She'd followed Francham. He went behind his bar and she stood nearby while he gave a couple of instructions to his staff.

'Forgive me, Tilda. Now, you've brought how much for me? I want both teas and some of your lavender infusion.'

Tilda became aware that the handsome man had shifted his gaze to their negotiations; she'd suspected it was an absent gaze but, even so, she'd hoped her cheeks did not burn. She was too old for this sort of self-consciousness!

She'd lifted the small sacks and smiled when Loos smelled them. 'Lovely. Very fresh. I'm impressed.'

'You should be. I'm very fussy about the flowers and herbs I use.'

He'd grinned. 'And you won't sell me any of her majesty's brew?'

She'd waggled a finger. 'Now, now, Loos. You know I can't. It's designed for our queen alone. Can't have the peasants drinking the regal brew,' she said, grinning archly.

'You can't blame me for trying. Are you going up to the palace now?'

Tilda had nodded. 'Yes, I have a delivery for the Crown. Can't have our queen running out of her preferred tea at such an important time, what with visiting royals and so on.'

Loos Francham had tapped his nose. 'You might even get your brews noticed by the Cipreans. Then we "peasants" won't be able to afford your teas anymore.'

'Oh, go on with you, Loos,' she'd said, giving him a friendly push.

He in turn had counted out some silver coins. 'Thank you, Tilda. Next moon, we may increase each by one bag, if that suits.'

'Easily done,' Tilda had said. 'Right, I can't tarry. The palace kitchens are tetchy about who is coming and going, as you can imagine. Apparently I have to get a special clearance from an officer of the Legion just to get into the complex.'

'How long are you staying?'

'Oh, just overnight. I've got a couple of new infusions for the palace to try, as well as supplies of her majesty's favourite one.'

'There's not many can say they're spending the night at the palace, Tilda,' he replied, sounding impressed.

'It's not as grand as it sounds, my cot being next to the kitchens, Master Francham,' she'd cautioned in an affectionate tone. 'See you next moon.'

She had walked away from the dinch-house and crossed the main square that was teeming with people and horses, dogs and carts. Pearlis was always frantic, but it seemed totally chaotic as it prepared to welcome Princess Darcelle's new husband-to-be and his entourage. She remembered how she had just been thinking how happy she was for the royal family, when someone had tapped her shoulder.

Of all the people she might have thought it could be, the handsome customer from the dinch-house would have been the last person on a list of dozens. She recalled how she'd gasped.

'I didn't mean to startle you,' he'd begun in a voice that she would compare to the warm, spicy tones of the cannoda honey of this region — dark, mysterious and mellow. All of that had struck her in the moment he'd spoken and had beamed her a bright, heart-fluttering smile. 'My name is Layne Tentrell,' he'd said. 'I'm a merchant, not from around here.'

She'd shrugged, too taken aback to speak immediately.

'Most people are visitors at the moment,' she'd finally said, sounding stuck for words. 'I am.'

'Yes, I overheard, I'm sorry. I was at the dinch-house bar,' he'd said gesturing over his shoulder.

'I remember you,' she'd admitted and wished she hadn't, because it had prompted a knowing smile. That smile was different to the one he'd given her moments before, and it was in that moment that she'd first sensed that she was in the presence of magic.

She'd frowned.

'Is something wrong?'

'No, not at all. You know that saying about someone walking over your grave?'

He'd shaken his head, but she'd thought at the time that he'd not told the truth.

'Oh, well, it was like that. Hard to explain.' She'd chuckled, embarrassed. 'Tilda, isn't it?'

She'd nodded, not trusting herself to say anything as she felt she was making enough of a fool of herself already.

'I couldn't help overhearing that you make deliveries into the palace.'

She'd baulked at this. 'Well, Loos Francham should not have said what he had so freely. It's not secret, Master Tentrell, but it's also not something I promote. Her majesty is a modest person, from what I can tell. She probably wouldn't like it if I traded off her name or her choice of brew.'

'You know her?'

'I've met her a couple of times. I doubt she'd remember me, although yes, she spoke directly to me when she first tasted my infusions.'

'That must feel very rewarding, to know that the Crown approves of your products.'

She'd nodded. 'It is.'

'May I be frank with you, Tilda?'

Tilda remembered that she'd not known how to answer that question. She had not been sure she wanted to and nodded dumbly instead.

'Will you walk a little way with me? Just over toward that park.'

'I'm due at the palace in —'

'This will only take a moment of your time,' he'd pressed and had smiled so disarmingly that she'd melted.

When he'd told her what he wanted she had been confused.

'I'm spying?'

'No, no, no, Tilda. Not at all. I am meeting Master Burrage, the queen's chamberlain, shortly to discuss security around the royals during this busy time.'

She'd frowned. Not understanding. 'I thought you were a merch—'

'A merchant, yes. I am, or at least that's my cover. I'm actually working on behalf of Master Burrage clandestinely. You see, Queen Florentyna refuses to be surrounded by men-at-arms. She has enough of that in her daily life but Master Burrage has intensified security because of …' He'd shaken his head, looking perplexed.

'Because of what?'

'Tilda …' he'd begun again, and sighed. 'Forgive me, but I believe you may have a magical sense about you?'

She'd given a small sound of surprise. 'How do you know?'

He'd looked smug. 'I can tell. Perhaps because I have some wits of my own that I don't promote. They can be useful. Master Burrage knows of them and contacted me. He wants to add an element of security against any sort of magical attack against the Crown.'

She remembered how she'd looked at Tentrell aghast. 'Why would there be one?'

'Oh, it wouldn't be the first time,' he'd replied loftily. This tone didn't suit the man she was looking at. There was definitely something slightly amiss about him, but he'd admitted to having 'wits' as he called them and she appreciated his honesty. It was probably this aspect of him that her weak magical sense had locked onto.

'My magic is meaningless in that sense, Master Tentrell. I brew teas. I imbue them with healing — some might call me a hedgewitch. Nothing more.'

'Even so, Tilda, I wonder if you'll help me to keep the royals safe. I need other people, even those with weak skills who can, nevertheless, sense "otherness".'

She'd smiled. 'I've never heard a sentient talked about in that way, Master Tentrell.'

'Call me Layne. I prefer it,' he'd said and the charm was back. 'Master Burrage has charged me to find people like you and pay them handsomely, but so far everyone I have found — and there are four others — can only watch from the outside. You and I can get into the palace perfectly legitimately without raising any eyebrows or alarms.'

'I see. Who am I spying upon?'

'No spying. Just keep your senses alert. If you feel that magic has found its way into the palace and is close to the queen, I simply want you to warn me. Don't do anything, don't confront anyone, don't even follow the magical trace. Simply register it and find me.'

'How?'

'Come back to this spot and I will find you.'

'How often?'

'Daily, until you leave the palace and are on your way.' He'd smiled, looking deep into her eyes as though no-one else in the world mattered to him. 'That's not too hard or intrusive, is it?' She'd shaken her head. 'And for this, the palace will give you gold. Here,' he had said, pressing two glinting gold coins into her palm, 'let this be a down payment and a show of goodwill between us sentients. We're going to make a good team, Tilda.'

'But ...' She had felt confused.

'I don't want you to do anything except what you would normally do,' Tentrell had emphasised, a hand lifted to forestall any objections. 'I'm presuming you deliver to the kitchens?' Tilda had nodded. 'Then stay where you normally would. Keep your senses alert for the presence of magic and you just have to meet me here and let me know. Master Burrage pays very well for the protection of the queen and Princess Darcelle.'

'I don't understand who might want to hurt them?'

'Neither does he. He's being very cautious. Cipres is a place that pays homage to the old ways. Tallinor, its huge and powerful neighbour, is renowned for its magic — I've been there. It has an academy to teach magic and encourage the use of it, so I believe Master Burrage is being wise and simply making sure that nothing untoward enters the palace. It's easy money, Tilda. I will give you quadruple this amount when we next meet.'

Her eyes had widened in shock. She'd never seen so much money in her life, let alone held it. Owning it would be beyond even her brightest, most fanciful dreams.

'What will you do with it, Tilda?' he'd said then, as if reading her thoughts.

She remembered how she'd smiled, embarrassed. 'I want to open my own shop. I'm tired of being a wandering seller. I'm getting too old for the cart and horse. I'd like to settle down with a cottage and a shop and have my own large garden that grows everything I need for my teas. I'd also branch out into herbal tonics.'

He'd given a shrug. 'And now you can. That dream you hold in your heart can be a reality. You'll have more than enough gold to settle down immediately. No more harsh winters on the road for you, Tilda.'

So now she waited, having been seduced by Layne Tentrell into spying on the queen. She hadn't expected anything to occur, of course, and once she'd left him, the two gold coins clanking with a happy heaviness inside her robe, she'd begun to feel her spirits soar. This was going to be the easiest way to make money.

What she didn't foresee was Layne Tentrell's prediction and Master Burrage's fears coming home to roost. She had not sensed any magic being used in the palace and yet, with all the deaths the next day, she could all but smell the trace of magic that had caused them. When that lovely young Hamelyn had found her and begged for her help, she'd gladly gone with him to assist his companion. Nothing had prepared her for the reek of magic that swirled around Hamelyn's friend.

She hadn't told Layne Tentrell — it was something she never admitted to anyone — that she could smell magic. That was her real talent. Her own magic was weak as she readily admitted, but she could smell magic on others — like Tentrell, just like Ham and like the boy's good-looking friend. She'd been intrigued by the man, Cassien, and his power to kill. If he'd wanted to harm the royals he would have done so. Therefore, he was no enemy. Then what was he?

From what she'd gathered, no-one knew about Cassien's magical skills — not even Hamelyn. Presumably, the chancellor and Empress Florentyna had been unaware of his skills when they'd appointed him champion. Tilda had decided to ignore Tentrell's instructions and try to learn more about Cassien. He'd pressed her for directions and she'd simply said she might head north, which was the truth. Then she'd used all her money to take a carriage north to Mickelsham, where she knew he would come through on horseback. What she hadn't expected was to see the queen in his company. While not in disguise, the queen was certainly doing everything in her power not to promote her identity, even though most people wouldn't know what she looked like in everyday clothes. Darcelle was unmistakable, but Florentyna kept herself to herself.

An even greater shock had been to discover that Cassien was using his powers to aid the Crown. She needed to assure Layne Tentrell that the queen was in safe hands; that the magic, which had come to the palace, was working for the benefit of the royals.

And so here she sat beneath the walnut tree, awaiting Layne Tentrell to give him the good news and hopefully to earn some gold that would secure her future. She could never have anticipated soldiers bearing down on her. She could not outrun them and her mind was too slow to catch on that they had come for her.

'I'm meeting Layne Tentrell,' she'd bleated, 'and I'm helping Chancellor Burrage,' she'd added, breaking Tentrell's rule to not mention the Crown's involvement.

'Burrage is dead. So is Tentrell,' the hard-faced man who gripped her arm said. 'And we were told by her highness, Princess Darcelle, before she left the palace, to meet with you. She wishes to speak with you about the disappearance of her sister.'

And something in Tilda's sharp perceptions told her she would likely not live to see another sunrise.

'It doesn't pay to dance with the devil,' she said to them but they couldn't understand her meaning nor did they pay her much heed.

* * *

'But why would he have a spy?' Florentyna asked as Cassien was dumbfounded by Fynch's words.

'We are not dealing with a criminal, your majesty,' Fynch said evenly. 'We're not even confronting a person as you might recognise one. We are trying to outwit an ancient mind that has already seen much cunning, and has watched Morgravia for centuries. Not only is he intrigued by the magic of Myrren that came from the Wild and so profoundly affected your forebears, which he is now using to his advantage, he also has a grudge against the empire because of the Wild itself and what it did to him.'

She frowned.

'Cassien can tell you all about it on the next part of your journey. Suffice to say that, because of his interest in its magic and his grudge, he is levelling his wrath at the imperial Crown. It wouldn't matter if your father sat on the throne, or Darcelle ...' He shrugged. 'He wants to hurt the empire and the best way is through its figurehead. Killing is not his intention, I realise. Possessing you — as he did Gabriel, or more recently your sister — is his aim. His ultimate revenge would be to then use the Crown to turn Morgravia against Briavel and the former Razor Kingdom and incite wars between neighbours, destroying the empire from within.'

'What about the Wild?' she asked. 'I've never known much about it, only that no-one goes there and most Briavellians fear it.'

'Wisely so. It is not a place for people. It is beautiful, but it is magical and dangerous, erratic and powerful. It's a strange marriage, you could say. It protects your realm and those of the empire, but the people, in turn, must respect its privacy. It is available to the animals and the forests and is full of magic so ancient that I am still discovering much of it. You have no need to enter its territory — no-one does — but it will fiercely fight to protect the land it neighbours.'

'What a strange phenomenon,' she murmured.

'It is. I don't know why it came into existence. I suspect the Wild has always existed, long before inhabitants came to the surrounding regions.'

'You're from the Wild, Fynch, aren't you?' she said, beginning to piece together the puzzle.

'Yes. I am simply the keeper ... a caretaker if you will.'

'How are keepers chosen?' Cassien wondered.

'By the dragon and his filial mortal. Before me it was Elysius; before him I do not know.'

'And after you?' the queen said and then checked herself. 'Forgive me, Fynch, that was unfair of me.'

'Not at all. It is a valid question,' he said with a disarming smile. 'There will be someone chosen. The point is the keeper's role is simply to observe the ebb and flow of magic beyond the Wild in order to keep it safe ... and thus keeping our land safe. Magic exists everywhere, most of it harmless and used for the good of others — healing, herbals, farming, teaching ...' He shook his head. 'Rarely, something sinister comes along and that's when the keeper's role becomes more important. It's why I have paid a lot of attention to Cyricus and why his putting a spy or two in the palace does not surprise me in the least. His mind is far more complex and capable than you can imagine.'

Cassien stood. 'So, if Tilda is a spy, she would be telling him that we're headed to the Great Forest.'

'I would imagine so.'

He paced. 'She knew of my power, and now, Shar strike me, she knows that I can see him when I roam. I was too open with her.' He gave a growling sound and Romaine's ears pricked.

Dawning appeared in Florentyna's expression. 'Cassien, I remember now, she looked shocked when you admitted that. Don't you recall how she sat back, looking surprised. She covered it well but I was already slightly suspicious of her because she wouldn't answer any of my questions easily. I mean ...' Florentyna searched for how to explain what she wanted to. 'It was a feeling I had, that she was constantly deflecting me.'

'Your feelings might have served you truly, my queen.'

Cassien scratched his chin. 'Wait, Fynch! Although I agree that I've probably pointed Cyricus toward us, is that really such a bad thing?'

Florentyna looked at him askance, and Fynch frowned.

'Hear me out. There's going to be a confrontation, come what may. You say Gabe is in place and ready to lure Cyricus into the Void?'

'He is. But he's going to need Cyricus to feel threatened enough and angry enough to leave Darcelle's body for the Void. As a royal, Cyricus is now in a position to command the Legion. You need time to hatch a plan to isolate him, and then force him to cast aside the body of the princess.' He glanced with a grave expression at Florentyna. 'Forgive me, your majesty. I know this is painful for you and must sound cruel.' She nodded but her expression told him she understood. He returned his attention to Cassien. 'You can hide and wait, but I think you should stay one step ahead. He will find you, make no mistake. He's after Florentyna and has no reason to give up, for he is in no hurry — he's probably enjoying himself and feels no sense of threat, although he knows now that we are aware of him. This will only intensify his pleasure of the game. He will employ more cunning, behave in a more outrageously vicious way to draw his enemies to him.'

Cassien nodded. 'Yes, you're right, it's too dangerous. Tilda may be back at the palace already. Cyricus could be on his way. We need a bit more time.'

'A wise precaution,' Fynch echoed. 'As I say, she may not be a spy, but trust those instincts of your queen. Go to Rittylworth. I suspect Ham will make for there, too.'

Cassien seemed to agree because he nodded. 'What about you?'

'I shall remain here,' Fynch said, 'or at least for the time being.'

'But why? Surely —'

'Cassien, my son, do not question me,' he said. It was a reprimand, but said so gently that Cassien's expression reflected no rancour. 'I have my path to follow. You have yours.' He directed Cassien's gaze to Florentyna. 'The queen is your total responsibility now. Do not think on me.'

'How will I know what to do?' Cassien asked, looking vaguely unnerved.

'You and your brothers will know exactly what to do. I cannot tell you how events will come to pass. I can only tell you that you are each equipped to play your part. I can do no more. It is up to the Triad of my sons to best Cyricus.' He pointed at the sword resting silently at Cassien's hip. 'Remember that was made for you.'

'Beautiful, but I've had little need to draw it.'

'Don't ignore its presence,' Fynch said, sounding cryptic.

'When will we see you?' Florentyna queried, knowing this was what Cassien really wanted to ask.

Fynch smiled and shuffled over, although it looked to be painful for him to do so. He took her hand in his and she felt his palm, dry and warm. The old man surprised her by kissing it. 'Empress Florentyna, thank you for trusting me.'

'I didn't show it enough, did I?' she said, wishing she could turn time back.

'You were open to my concerns though, my queen. I know what I said resonated within you. If not, you wouldn't have paid heed to Cassien, to Gabe, even Ham, and had enough faith to entrust your wellbeing to them.'

'I hope to see you again under less anxious circumstances,' she said.

'I look forward to it, your majesty,' and as his pale eyes sparkled, she thought she saw the gleam of a secret … and instinctively knew, and accepted, that he was avoiding the truth, perhaps for Cassien's sake.

She nodded. 'Take care, Master Fynch. Morgravia … indeed the empire owes you a debt of gratitude.'

His brief, intense gaze spoke his thanks, knowing she understood.

'Cassien,' he said, turning to hug his middle son again, 'our reunion as father and son has been short-lived but heartfelt, child.' He held Cassien at arm's length, looking up to the towering figure, who looked back with a deeply sad expression. Florentyna suspected that Cassien was hiding his emotions and likely also understood this was a true goodbye. She had to look away, made herself busy tying on her cloak and moving toward her horse. She heard their words of farewell.

'You've made me proud. You have one more confrontation to face. Think of Cyricus as Loup. He can be bested if your mind remains strong. And you are the one who can rid the empire of his blight. Trust Gabe. Trust Ham. Trust me. Above all, trust yourself and what's in here,' he said, touching his son's chest above his heart.

Florentyna glanced around in time to see Fynch pull Cassien's face down and kiss him on each cheek, lingering on both.

'I have loved you from afar and now I've had the opportunity to love you up close, Cassien. Thank you for forgiving me my secrets and your isolation.' He looked over at Romaine. 'Stick to the forest for as long as possible. She will protect you. Do not roam. Don't even be tempted. Not yet, or you will give yourself away.'

Again Cassien nodded. He pulled Fynch into a bear hug. 'I will see you again,' he said, his voice tight, 'when this is done.'

'Shar willing,' Fynch said. 'Now go, you two. Be safe.'

As they rode away with heavy hearts, Romaine flanking them, Cassien gave a deep sound of anguish. 'He's lying.'

'Why do you say that?' Florentyna said, although she didn't add that she agreed with him.

'Because he's dying, your majesty. He was dying when he first showed himself to me. It's why he collapsed the last time he and I were together. He seemed rejuvenated when he met us at the mouth of the forest, but just in the course of these past hours he has become frail. I don't think he can leave the forest, I don't think he should ever have left the Wild.' He gave a sad laugh. 'Let's be honest here. We are talking about someone who is centuries old. It has to be the Wild's magic that sustains him. When he's beyond it, maybe it cannot keep him alive.'

'He can go back, he can —'

'No. I don't believe he can,' Cassien said, thinking it through as they walked the horses away from Fynch. 'It's why he's released Romaine to me. It's why he told us to leave the forest. He doesn't want me to suffer his death.'

THIRTY-FOUR

Hamelyn and King Tamas had ridden through the day, preserving their horses as best they could. When Tamas sensed the horses could not carry them further, he paid for a new pair at Tooley Marsh, northwest of the capital.

'It's not really a marsh. Hasn't been one for centuries, 'specially not since the river dried up,' the stableman said, as he looked over their horses. 'Yes, they've done enough. I'll fetch a couple of fresh ones. You can pay Master Flegon over at the inn. It's where you'll find him at this time.'

They paid Flegon, whom they'd found gambling in a corner of the inn over a game of racks. He didn't seem to be winning and Tamas was certain that the coin he was handing over for the horses would go down on the table for the particularly chaotic and probably dishonest game of dice.

'You'd better check for drops of mercury in those cubes, Master Flegon,' Tamas warned. 'Won't be the first time a man's lost his fortune over loaded dice.'

Flegon's opponent glared at Tamas. 'Which wind blew you in, matey?' he demanded, casting a glance at Ham. 'You all right, son, or is he planning to buy a room and give you a thorough going over?' He laughed cruelly. Tamas cleared his throat, nodded at Ham for them to be on their way. The men's laughter followed them.

'Cut some meat from the haunch,' Tamas ordered a woman working behind the inn's counter, 'pack it with bread, some cheese if you have it.' He looked back at the men playing.

'Could you add some chutney too, please?' Ham asked politely, with a disarming grin and the young woman smiled at him.

'Well, someone has good manners,' she said, cutting Tamas a sharp look.

The king glanced at Ham with an expression of confused innocence. When her back was turned Ham gave a shrug.

'You can't treat every stranger like a servant, your majesty,' he whispered. 'In here, and dressed the way you are, you're simply another well-heeled traveller.'

Tamas nodded. 'Sage advice, Ham.'

The woman had given their order to a younger girl, who scurried back into the kitchen. 'Anything else?'

'What is your name?' Tamas asked.

'Arly,' she replied, sounding guarded.

'Well, Arly, forgive my brusqueness. I just don't like cheats much.' He looked over his shoulder toward the men playing dice. 'We'd like two ales, please, and his should be a small watered one,' he said, thumbing at Ham, who remained silent.

'Don't let him get you drunk, boy!' the man, clearly still resentful of the king's warning to Flegon, yelled across the tavern.

Arly sighed. 'Take no notice of him.'

'I'm not,' Tamas said, grinning fiercely. Ham noticed that Arly had warmed quickly to the king's charm. There was no doubting that women found him attractive. 'He's fleecing the stable owner,' Tamas continued.

She shook her head gently in frustration. 'Flegon's been fleeced for years. We've watched him lose money so often he's like a piece of the furniture in here. He doesn't seem to care ... not since his family died of the green fever. All of them, sir. Five healthy sons and a wife he was true to. He's a broken man, but he was once a good man in the community.'

Tamas sighed. 'Pity. Here, take a tankard of ale over to him from me.' He tossed an extra coin onto the counter.

Arly smiled. 'I'll do that. Here's your food,' she said as the younger girl set a small linen bundle on the counter.

Hamelyn hadn't realised how famished he was. His belly rumbled at the smell of the roasted meat wafting from the package.

'Drink this,' Tamas said, handing over the small tankard.

'I don't —'

'Drink it. You need its sustenance. We'll eat as we ride.'

Ham swallowed it down as instructed, his eyes watching as Tamas downed his own tankard, twice the size and twice as potent. The king smacked his lips, but not with pleasure. He gave a small belch. 'Done?'

Ham tipped the bitter-tasting dregs into his mouth and thanked Arly again. The king simply smiled at her.

'Safe travels,' she called to their backs.

'Here,' Tamas said, handing him the largest share of bread and tearing off a hunk of the meat. 'Get this down you.'

'I don't eat that much, ki— er, sir.'

Tamas smiled. 'A growing lad needs a lot more than you think. Eat.' He pushed the food into Ham's hands once he'd saddled up.

They chewed silently, walking the horses out of the village and back onto the main road north.

'Better?'

'Much,' Ham replied. 'You?'

'Food isn't going to help the pain inside.'

Ham was glad they'd finally touched on the topic that had moved like an uncomfortable, awkward beast around them. Their fast ride had prevented conversation, but it hadn't taken away the ugly image.

'It was necessary,' Ham offered.

'And still you were shocked, surely.'

'By its swift brutality, yes,' he admitted. 'Also by your courage, sire.'

'It was easier to watch Darcelle's body being dragged behind a horse than to see her being moved like a grotesque puppet by the demon.'

'It was a breathtaking shot, your majesty.'

Tamas gave a mirthless bark of a laugh. 'My best ever, I'd say. Pity I pulled it out for the execution of my betrothed and not for the Ciprean Finals in the Contest of the Realms,' he moaned, trying to make it sound light, but it came out grief-stricken.

'King Tamas, you have likely killed the demon and his partner. You've saved countless lives and the realms. Empress Florentyna will forgive you. She knows her sister was lost.'

'Are you sure she will? I keep imagining that she held hopes that Darcelle might re-emerge as Gabe did.'

Ham shook his head. 'I think the queen saw in Gabe and Cassien what I did.'

'That they're brothers?'

'Ah, you think so too,' Ham replied.

The king nodded. 'The resemblance is strong. I didn't realise I'd noticed until you mentioned their likeness, and then it made such sense.

I'd probably been thinking the same the whole time we were in the chapel.'

'I think there's more, King Tamas.'

Tamas frowned. 'More to them?'

'In a way. I think there are three brothers.'

'Three? Why would you think that? Do you know him?'

'I know him well. He is myself.'

King Tamas was chewing but he stopped mid-mouthful. He blinked and swallowed. 'You?'

Ham nodded. 'I think so. I could be wrong but I doubt it. There are too many signs. I won't bore you, sire. But I have a happy knack for being able to carry a lot of information around in my mind and bring it right upfront,' he said, tapping his forehead, 'at the oddest times. I've made the connection. I know I'm not wrong.'

'How can it be?'

'Magic has its part to play. But I suspect we each have our role in this fight.'

'Yours?'

Ham shrugged. 'I'm yet to learn.'

'This strangeness we're involved in just gets more tangled,' the king moaned. 'Shall we ride?' he challenged.

'After you, sire.'

Tamas tossed away the tiny knuckle of bread in his hand, slapped the reins against the flank of his horse and growled a whoop that kicked it into action. Soon they were galloping over a path that cut through the heath of the mainly deserted region of the northwest. They rode without exchanging words until the horses began to flag. Tamas gradually slowed until his beast was blowing hard but down to a measured trot. Ham had done the same, and now brought his horse alongside Tamas.

'We've made good ground,' he said, dragging in deep breaths. 'I saw a marker for Rittylworth about a mile back. We're just three miles east of it now. We should be there by dusk.'

'Excellent,' Tamas said. 'The horses couldn't have maintained that pace for much longer. We'll just cool them down and keep up the trot. They'll need some watering, but I can see a stream ahead so we'll stop when we can.'

They trotted on. 'I've been thinking, sire,' Ham said, finally deciding to air something that had been nagging him since they left the killing fields.

'Yes?'

'Well, you know how a thought skims around the back of your mind? It's there and it's irritating but you can't fully grab it?'

'Of course, it's like when you have a name on the tip of your tongue. But you just can't say it. It's frustrating.'

'That's it! And you just have to be patient until it comes back.'

The king grinned. 'And?'

'Well, sire, this thought was just out of my reach but I knew to let it sit, to wait for it to get bored of teasing me and that it would finally come into my mind fully.'

'You've a wise head on a young body, Ham. Go on. What's this notion of yours?'

'It concerns your man, Wentzl, sire.'

'Captain Wentzl? He's a good man. He stood up to the demon well enough from what we could tell.'

'Yes, here's the thing, sire. I think Wentzl was one of the men I glimpsed who headed in our direction. I didn't register that at first. It's taken me a while to realise I recognised someone and that it was him.'

'Really?'

'You seem delighted.'

'Why wouldn't I be? A fellow Ciprean and all that?'

'But why would he follow?'

Tamas chuckled. 'I'll tell you why, Hamelyn, and I'm thrilled your sharp eyes picked up that information. I'm feeling better for knowing that he didn't head to the ship with the rest of the men.'

Ham waited, uncertain.

'You see, only a Ciprean would have known who shot that arrow. And Captain Wentzl would have not only recognised the fletching, he would have known that shot could only have been made by me.'

'Ah,' Ham said, understanding. It also explained why Wentzl would have stuck with the Morgravians rather than the Ciprean soldiers.

'Excellent, that means Wentzl — who is a brilliant tracker by the way and too loyal for his own good — can follow me. If we can rid ourselves of the Morgravian legionnaires, then Wentzl can help.' The king surprised Ham by removing his white kerchief. He took the blade from the holder that sat neatly on the side of his leg and without pausing dug its tip into his forefinger. He wrote *Rittyl* in blood onto the kerchief and without saying a word tied it around the highest branch he could reach by standing up in the saddle. 'Old Ciprean trick,' he said, tapping his nose. 'Wentzl will see it.'

'Are you sure that's wise, your majesty?' Ham asked evenly.

'Wise? We'll go to Rittylworth, hopefully meet up with your companion, Cassien, and Empress Florentyna. Take a slow breath and congratulate ourselves on having rid the land of the evil that was threatening it and —'

'It's just that telling you that Captain Wentzl is following us is not the thought that's been nagging me, your majesty.'

Tamas had blinked at Ham's interruption, but now frowned. 'What else do you have to say, then?' he said, his tone tighter than previously.

Ham swallowed, feeling uncertain that he should share it.

'Come on, Ham. You can't stop a man mid-sentence with what is clearly an unpleasant idea and then leave him sweating. What is troubling you, boy?'

'I'll say exactly what I'm thinking, majesty, because I don't know how to make this sound in any way easier for you to hear.'

Tamas gave him a look of sheer exasperation. 'Say it!'

'I'm deeply troubled that Captain Wentzl is not who he might appear, sire.'

Tamas stared at him, confused for a few moments. Then his expression relaxed into dismay, and then changed to despair. 'You can't be serious.'

'I'm not very adept at jests, your majesty.'

'What makes you say such a thing, Ham?' Tamas said, his voice raspy with anguish. 'I didn't see …'

'You didn't see what I did, no,' Ham said. 'I didn't want to believe it and I thought it happened too fast, so I pushed the notion away. But it won't go away. You were readying your bow for its shot when Princess Darcelle briefly kissed Captain Wentzl.' Tamas gave a keening sound, like an injured animal. 'Darcelle was seated on her horse, speaking with the captain and was even laughing when your arrow felled her.'

'I remember,' Tamas groaned. 'Wait! If Darcelle was moving, surely that means …' His words and excitement trailed off when Ham began to shake his head. He pulled on the reins until the horse stopped.

Ham followed suit and faced the king, turning in his saddle to sigh softly. 'Your majesty, I could be wrong, but I suspect that Cyricus is one step ahead of us. I believe he transferred into Captain Wentzl, leaving his companion, Aphra, in Princess Darcelle. Meaning that it was Aphra who perished with your arrow, not the demon himself.'

He watched as the king slid off his horse and stomped away. Tamas said nothing, approaching a tree that was one of the first to suggest they were entering a region that might loosely be termed as within the outlying reaches of the Great Forest. Ham winced as he saw Tamas punch the tree, yelling his utter desolation. He looked down and waited for what felt like an eternity before the king returned to saddle up.

'Forgive me,' Tamas said. 'Well, we can't be sure one way or the other so I suppose it's best we proceed with caution and follow the assumption that Captain Wentzl is now possessed by Cyricus. Is that Rittylworth?'

Ham stole a glance to see the king's knuckles were bleeding profusely. He nodded. 'Yes, sire. Um, you may need your kerchief for your hand.'

Tamas wrenched the stained linen from the overhanging branch and wrapped it around his bleeding knuckles. 'What are we waiting for?' Tamas growled and kicked his horse into motion.

They arrived at the small valley in which Rittylworth sat, unaware that the hill they'd crested before directing their horses down its slope had been, only days earlier, the vantage point of the archers who had begun firing upon the guard that surrounded Empress Florentyna.

'It's a fine-looking monastery,' Tamas admitted, as they approached its outlying buildings, although Ham could hear sadness in the king's voice. 'I hope you're right, and that the queen is here, because I don't think I can —'

'She is here, your majesty,' Ham interrupted and pointed.

Tamas looked to where figures were spilling out from the shadow of the cloisters. Amongst them was the unmistakable figure of Empress Florentyna.

'Thank Shar's merciful stars,' Tamas breathed and was suddenly leaping off his horse and running towards her; and she towards him just as eagerly, it seemed.

Bemused, Ham and Cassien watched as the two royals stopped before each other, and after an awkward heartbeat of silence were suddenly hugging hard.

'You made it!' Ham heard Florentyna say and her voice had the shaky sound of someone relaxing from intense worry.

'I'm lucky to have had Hamelyn for a companion. He suggested we come here. But you are a wonderful sight for sad eyes, your majesty,' he said, taking Florentyna's hand and kissing it, his lips lingering against her skin.

Ham looked away to where Cassien stood watching him intently. He raised a hand and the man of the Brotherhood saluted him with a hand to his heart. Ham slid off his horse and Cassien was with him in several large strides, picking him up and hugging him.

'Brave boy, Ham. Brave, clever boy!'

When Cassien put him down, Ham could see that the other man's eyes looked misty. He shrugged. 'It made sense that you'd bring the queen back here.'

'Only in your mind,' Cassien said, grinning. 'And in Fynch's. He knew you'd come, urged me to journey here.'

'Now then, who are our newest arrivals, pray tell? Ah yes, I know you, child. Hello, young Ham,' said the monk in charge of Rittylworth.

Florentyna was smiling, still wiping away tears of relief. 'Brother Hoolyn, may I introduce the King of Cipres, his majesty, King Tamas.'

'Shar's light! I think my heart is going to stop with all these shocks. Your majesty,' Hoolyn said, bending low, as did all the monks behind him. 'Be welcome to our humble monastery.'

Cassien bowed to Tamas as well. 'We have a lot to discuss, majesty,' he began and the king began to nod, but Hoolyn interrupted.

'Firstly, eating and resting is what I insist upon. Come along, Brothers, we have mouths to feed and beds to make up for important visitors.'

Tamas was muttering about no fuss but Ham noticed how tenderly he took Florentyna's arm and guided her behind Hoolyn.

They'd been left alone by the monks after a simple, hearty meal of chicken stewed with vegetables and aromatics from the monastery gardens. Only Brother Hoolyn had remained to hear the quartet share their news with each other.

He stood up. 'Well, this is a tale to curl my hair ... if I had any,' he said, with a tight smile. 'I must attend prayers now and I suspect you would appreciate some private time. If you need anything, you know where to find me, Cassien.'

Cassien nodded. 'Thank you, Brother Hoolyn.'

They all murmured their thanks.

The old man smiled. 'Your majesties,' he said, bowing his head and taking his leave.

When the door closed, a silence fell like a pall around them.

'Will you forgive me, Florentyna?' Tamas finally asked.

She looked up from her lap, her face tear-stained, and laid a hand on his. 'You released her. Forgive you? I worship you for making that heroic shot and giving my sister to Shar.'

Cassien wished he could give them longer to grieve. However, time was not their friend. 'Ham, you're sure … about what you saw?'

Ham nodded. 'I'm sure of what I saw, yes. Whether transference occurred I cannot tell you, but my instinct says that Cyricus breathes in the form of Captain Wentzl.'

Tamas gave a sound of disgust. 'I'll kill him too,' he offered.

'I think you and Ham should rest,' Cassien said. 'Meet back here; one of the Brothers will fetch you. The repose will be brief, but it is necessary for you.'

Hamelyn couldn't sleep. He was tired, but the sensation of letting go and drifting into unconscious rest eluded him. Cassien had insisted he put his head down in the small dormitory that Brother Hoolyn had provided, and he'd obeyed mainly to ease Cassien's anxiety. He lay on the cot, staring at a spot on the wall, playing a game he knew from the orphanage, making pictures out of stains on the walls and the ceiling, or from clouds or spilled water.

He cocked his head to wonder what the stain on the wall looked like. His eyes felt suddenly drowsy and the stain began to shift, rolling and changing until he could clearly make out the head of a wolf.

Hamelyn?

Am I dreaming?

The king comes, the wolf said and Hamelyn watched the stain shift its shape again. This time it turned into the head of a dragon.

Ham blinked, trying to shake the drowsiness that had overcome him. When he focused again, standing before him was a man, shimmering in a mist. Behind him Ham could see forest, and an enormous wolf was sitting by the man's side.

'Master Fynch. I am glad to see you again,' he said, and sensed a great warmth infusing him. 'Thank you for visiting me here.'

'I have so much to say to you, Hamelyn, and plenty has passed since our first meeting in Orkyld. However, time is against us. You have a very big and dangerous task ahead. I am sure you have worked out that you are brother to Cassien and Gabriel.'

Ham nodded.

'Yes, I knew you would with that smart mind of yours. It will be up to you to keep your brothers safe.'

'I'm not sure I have the —'

'Listen to me, Hamelyn. Your eldest brother has skills beyond even my imagining for creating stories, images, scenes. He is a scrivener of sorts, although he uses his mind to bring his stories to life. He has no need for the quill. He can place people involved in his stories wherever he wants them.'

Ham frowned. 'What is his role?'

'He can call up and tap into wherever and whatever he wants. We're only interested in the Void, which is where Cyricus must go and where Cassien will await him.'

'And Cassien?'

'If Gabe is the creative brother, Cassien is brawn. He is powerful, his mind is impenetrable. He will be the one who will fight Cyricus and if it's possible, he will destroy him.'

'What is my role?'

'Gabe is the creator, Cassien is the fighter … you, child, you are the power. Your mind can wrap itself around anything. Trust yourself. Trust your ideas.'

'What is in the Void that might tempt the demon?'

'Nothing. That is our biggest hurdle. We must get him into the Void in order to have any chance at destroying him once and for all. But, he has experienced the Void and will have no desire to return to it. You must enrage him, taunt him, trick him back to it.'

Ham saw the wolf stand. It nudged Fynch's hand.

'I must go now, child. Forgive me, this has taken a lot of my strength to reach you.'

'I have questions, Master Fynch.'

'I know, Hamelyn. We will meet if the Triad succeeds … and I will have answers to those questions for you.' He smiled and the figures blurred into the mist and disappeared, leaving behind a stain on the wall that resembled nothing.

Ham was wide awake and his mind was already reaching, teasing at an idea.

They drank a thin broth quietly together in a small room near the kitchens. Brother Hoolyn had insisted, and seen to it, that the monks gave their quartet a wide berth.

'Did you sleep, Ham?' Florentyna enquired.

'Yes, your majesty. I feel much rested,' he lied.

'Do we have a plan?' Tamas asked into the gloom. He looked around at them with frustration in his eyes.

Cassien spoke up. 'King Tamas, facing Cyricus is something that we now acknowledge is what Gabe, Ham and myself were brought together for. You have done your bit, your majesty: you've rid us of Aphra,' he said, glancing at the queen with apology in his expression, 'and now it's up to us to rid Morgravia of Cyricus.' He paused. 'Ham and I have things we must discuss.'

Florentyna nodded, understood what he was asking. 'Come on, Tamas, walk with me. I need some air.'

Tamas frowned. 'It's cold, your majesty, you risk —'

She gave him a wry smile. 'I have a cloak,' she said and gave him a hard look.

He stood, seeming to understand that the brothers needed privacy. 'It would be an honour,' he said, offering an arm.

THIRTY-FIVE

The sovereigns had departed the chamber leaving Cassien and Ham seated opposite one another at the refectory table.

'You were right,' Cassien said.

'That Gabe is your brother?' Ham replied.

He nodded.

Ham gave a soft sigh. 'And that we are brothers too. We are the three ... the Triad I saw in Wevyr's crucible. I just can't work out how.'

'It will be explained,' Cassien said, standing to walk around the table. 'You know?'

He arrived to seat himself next to the boy and looked into those bright pale eyes that he now realised echoed Fynch so closely. Is this what Fynch had looked like as a youngster ... he felt sure he did. Spare, small, wide-eyed, reserved, full of intelligence and ideas, but so quiet at times that he could forget Ham was alongside. He was a good listener and had courage in spades.

He was his baby brother.

Without pausing to analyse his intensifying emotions a moment longer he pulled the boy close and hugged him hard.

'I'm so glad we met, Hamelyn.' He didn't know what else to say.

Ham pulled back, grinning. 'Now we both have family. Who are our parents?'

'I promise you will find out.' At Ham's quizzical look, Cassien put a hand up in defence. 'I am not being deliberately opaque. Trust me.'

The boy nodded. 'I should tell you that Master Fynch spoke to me while I was resting. I can't tell if I was dreaming but we talked.'

Cassien looked surprised. 'What did you learn?'

'Only what I already know. That it is up to you, Gabe and myself to work out how to rid the land of Cyricus.'

'Fynch has manipulated us into the position we find ourselves now.'

'Tell me again about Gabe.'

'There is only what I've already told. He remained at Pearlis ... in the cathedral,' Cassien began and told Ham everything he had learned, except who Ham's father was.

'I'm the key?' Ham said, looking and sounding both baffled and frightened. 'Master Fynch said as much but how can that be?'

'Ham, do you know Romaine?'

His brother shook his head.

'She's a wolf.'

Cassien saw the spark flash in Ham's pale eyes before his brother bit his lip frowning. 'Yes, I know her. A wolf spoke to me ... in the palace. And she appeared to me with Fynch. She's very beautiful.'

'She's my wolf. My dearest friend for the years of loneliness in the forest. She's special ... enchanted, I suspect, although every hair of her is a wild beast.'

'She protects you, Cassien. She told me to watch over your body. That's how I knew you were responsible for the deaths in the palace. I watched you slumped ... there, but not really there. The wolf didn't say but I was able to piece together what was happening.'

Cassien gave a sad smile. 'She's always protected me. And now she protects you. But more than that, little brother, she talks to you. She has never communicated with me as she has you. I don't understand her fully. She is of the dragon; one of his watchers, I suppose. But she's there for us and we must make use of her presence.'

'How?' Ham said, getting up to pace.

Cassien decided it was a family trait. He shrugged. 'Work it out. You will know how if you search your heart.'

'This is what I understand, Cass, frightening though it sounds. Gabe deliberately stayed behind at the cathedral claiming the dragon king demanded it of him.' Cassien nodded. 'You have also been told that Gabe can conjure and lure Cyricus into this emptiness called the Void.'

'Why, though?'

Ham frowned. 'I understand,' he said, chewing his lip. 'It's because we have to get Cyricus to leave the mortal body he inhabits. Because once he's in his spiritual form, then we can trap him in the Void.'

'Why not just kill this Captain Wentzl and be done?' Cassien said. Ever since King Tamas had angrily explained what Ham had pieced together, he'd been considering the ease of finishing Cyricus once and for all. 'I will find it a great deal easier to kill a man than a spirit.'

Ham shook his head. 'That would be a mistake. It's why Master Fynch has planned so meticulously. Otherwise he could mobilise an army after Wentzl.'

'I don't understand.'

His younger brother paced and something in the way he held his head reminded Cassien of Fynch. He felt a rush of sadness that all of them had missed out on their parents, on each other. He pushed the grief aside.

'I think I do,' Ham was saying, waving a finger, staring at a spot on the wall while he spoke. 'Aphra was a spiritual being but with none of the powers of Cyricus, as I understand it. She was his servant and so her possession of Darcelle was always fraught with the knowledge, I think, that she could die in Darcelle's body. Perhaps not Cyricus, though. Maybe Master Fynch knows this, or he's taking the precaution against it.'

'That he can't trust Cyricus will die, you mean?' Cassien said, working it through in his mind.

'Mmm, yes ... Master Fynch may not trust that Cyricus will die if we kill his host. He wants to make certain of it and the only way to do that is in the Void, which Cyricus cannot escape easily.'

'Right ...' Cassien murmured. 'So he's lured from the host so we know he's free and we trap him in the Void.'

Ham nodded and shrugged. 'And you destroy him.'

'Why not leave him in the Void? Why fight at all?'

The youngster blew out his cheeks. 'That's what was done before. It didn't contain him for eternity. I suppose Master Fynch is going to make sure that the demon is destroyed, not just banished.'

Cassien took a deep breath. 'You do see things clearly.'

Ham gave a crooked smile. 'So our plan is that Gabe conjures the Void and you destroy Cyricus.'

'I'd like to know with what though?'

Ham shrugged. 'Oh, that's obvious.'

'Really?' Cassien looked at his smaller brother with awe. 'Not to me.'

'You know how, Cass. Think through what has gone before. In all the strangeness of the days since we met, which of the strange events is the most curious, the most secretive, the most powerful? And don't say your roaming. I'm talking about something only very few people know.'

Cassien's brow creased in thought. He didn't like being made to work like this. 'Just tell me.'

Ham shook his head. 'Come on, work it out. You're going to be alone in the Void. What are you going to use to destroy Cyricus? You know what it is!'

Cassien blinked in consternation and focused, closing his eyes. Everything had been strange since Fynch had accompanied Loup into the forest. Nothing had been the same since. He reached, deciding to let go with his thoughts and try for Ham's sake to open his mind … perhaps what had shocked him the most had been …

And then it happened.

It was freakish and sublime in the same instant. Suddenly, like a doorway yawning to let in a blinding light, he felt his mind opening, as though beyond his control, and within that moment of loss he realised he was not alone.

Cassien, spoke a voice he instinctively knew.

Romaine!

He could feel her pleasure in his mind. *I am honoured to serve you*, she said, the grace he knew she possessed as a creature so evident in her thoughts.

How …?

My fault, said another familiar voice.

Ham. You did it.

I don't know how. I felt your mind straining to reach out and it felt easy to latch on to it. The moment I did, I felt connected through Romaine.

Hello, brothers, said Gabe into their sense of wonder.

Gabe! they replied as one.

And now the Triad is connected. It won't be long now, Romaine warned.

Where is Fynch? Gabe asked.

I am with Fynch, she answered. *Gabriel. I hope we will meet.*

What about the Void, Gabe? Cassien asked.

Ready when you are, he replied.

Cassien was impressed. *Ham, you will have to be my eyes on the land. I suspect once in the Void I see only the spiritual world.*

I will be the one watching over you. Cassien, keep in mind that Cyricus is not your only enemy. Time away from your body can hurt you as badly.

I won't forget, he promised. *I think I know how I must destroy him, Ham.*

He sensed the smile from the youngster.

It's the sword, forged with the blood of the dragon.

Yes, Cassien, yes! Ham's voice was full of congratulation. *The sword is made of Fynch's magic — wild, royal, ancient. It is singing to me now. It senses that its purpose draws close. He is near. I feel him ... the sword does too. Romaine?*

Evil comes, she said.

Gabe, Ham said, *can Cassien hear us when he's in the Void?*

No. But we are all connected through you, Ham.

Ham paused and Cassien wasn't sure whether this was surprise or simply the boy realising he must shoulder the burden of keeping them safe, keeping them connected, keeping them strong. Cassien waited, knowing to trust him. Gabe, though the eldest, seemed comfortable to defer to his younger sibling too.

All right, then. Ham finally said. *Romaine?*

Yes, Hamelyn.

Would you please tell Master Fynch that we are ready, although I just need some private time to think something through.

Cassien nodded. *I'm going to take a walk up the hill. I can get a better view of who is coming.*

See you on the other side, brothers, Gabe said and although neither understood the expression, they grasped the nuance of his words.

Ham watched Cassien leave and let his mind wander down the path it had been itching to explore.

At the top of the monastery, in the same tower where she had stood petrified only days previously, Florentyna smiled at Tamas before looking back to the lush landscape of the valley. It was still cool this far north, and the green of the surrounding hills was vibrant and punctuated by drifts of wildflowers. Below them, monks toiled in the small patchwork of fields, growing herbs, flowers and vegetables, although as she watched it looked as though they were packing up their tools. Chickens pecked and clucked and scratched around the men, while a few goats chewed lazily in the distance. She noticed the monks unharnessing a donkey from a small plough. Word had obviously gone round to stop their work for the day. Even so, it was a peaceful, gentle scene — the typical picture she held in her mind of rural Morgravia … the one that felt safe and comforting. Reality, of course, was very different. 'It's hard to believe when you look out here that we're running for our lives, isn't it?'

She sensed rather than saw Tamas nod. He had been extremely quiet as they'd strolled around the cloisters and finally up to the tower, where she'd promised a fine view.

'Apart from the obvious, Tamas, what is troubling you? I give you my word, you helped me when you took what was left of Darcelle's life. I can grieve now in private, and properly, knowing she is in Shar's keeping.'

She laid a hand on his arm to reassure him. He covered it with his own.

'No, it's not Darcelle. I did what I did for all the right reasons and will not anguish over that arrow shot. I'm sad for Morgravia, who should not have lost one of its brightest so young.'

She nodded, appreciating his gracious sentiment. 'Then if not Darcelle, what? We are all in this together. Master Fynch believes he has put everything into place, as I explained moments ago.'

Tamas sighed. 'No, it's not that either. If we're all going to die, Florentyna then, as strange as it sounds, I'm comfortable that it will happen here, with you, and among loyal friends of Morgravia.'

She turned, fixed him with a dark, penetrating gaze and tipped her head to one side. 'Curiously, I agree with you. But if not impending death at the hands of a demon,' she continued dryly, 'then what? I'm not enjoying your pensive mood and feel obliged to fill the silences.'

Tamas surprised her by raising her hand from where it rested lightly on his arm and kissing it. She felt a guilty thrill.

'It's you, Florentyna,' he said, meeting her eyes.

She blinked, hardly daring to believe what he'd said.

Tamas cleared his throat. 'Do you remember when we first met at Grenadyn?'

'I have never forgotten it,' she said, finding it difficult to talk easily. He still held her hand, was scrutinising it, as if unable to look her in the eye.

'You were such a funny little child. I was charmed by your serious approach to life.'

'I was the heir, on foreign soil, trying to make my father proud.'

'And you did. He was very proud of you. And I was enchanted by you. You sat on my knee and told me in great detail — and with much gravity — about the new foal that had been born recently to your father's favourite mare.'

'Stella,' she said and gave a low chuckle. 'She gave us many foals of her own since.' Then she took a breath. 'Um, on your knee?'

He looked up at her, and gave a crooked smile, full of mischief.

'That's rather … mmm …'

'Corrupt?'

She giggled. 'I was going to say improper.'

'Your father was present. Full of smiles.'

'That's all right then,' she said, archly, remembering it vividly even though she pretended otherwise.

'He had no idea what you were doing to my heart.'

She looked at him perplexed. 'You jest.'

Tamas shook his head. 'I was completely enchanted. The next time I saw you — at Cipres — you didn't sit on my knee. You were really very distant. I … well, I thought you found me repugnant.'

'What?' she said, aghast. 'If only you knew.'

'Knew what?' he said, holding her hand against his chest now.

Florentyna felt her heart begin to stutter and then thump far too loudly. *Could he hear it?* 'I was so frightened by my feelings for you. I thought you'd laugh,' she admitted. 'I felt intensely uncomfortable around you, petrified my heart was on show for all to view.'

It was the king's turn to look dumbfounded. 'Truly? I thought I disgusted you. You wouldn't even look at me.'

'A stupid young girl, unsure of how to behave around a man she loves. And let's not forget I had been promised to another.'

'Loves,' he repeated as though the word was foreign to him.

She nodded, holding his gaze. 'Forgive me, Tamas. It's wrong of me to share this now. Darcelle was your true love, and although it wounded me to learn of her feelings toward you and yours for her, I was strangely happy.'

'Florentyna, I —'

'No, wait. Let me say this. I bore no ill will. I loved Darcelle enough that I could feel only happiness for her in her choice of husband and a deep pleasure that she had chosen so well … for her, for her realm … for the empire.' She smiled sadly, risked touching his cheek. 'I couldn't have chosen better myself.' Then she sighed. 'I'm only saying this now because I'll never forgive myself if something happens and I didn't share with you that I have loved you for years, and now meeting you as an adult and sovereign to sovereign has only deepened my admiration for you. I believe if we survive what is coming, Tamas, then you and I will be close friends despite whomever we both end up marrying, if we marry. What's more, I would like to formally associate our two realms in honour of Darcelle. I've been thinking, we could call a stretch of water between our two lands after her — her name and memory will forever link our shores. What do you think?'

Tamas took both of Florentyna's hands now and turned her away from the view to face him fully. 'I will tell you what I think,' he said, his voice thick and gentle. 'This is what I think,' he continued and leaned close to tenderly kiss her.

At first Florentyna was startled, but not enough to frighten Tamas away; if anything, he leaned in closer, his lips searched hers longer, harder, until Florentyna was lost in his kiss, loving the soft scratch of his beard against her skin, feeling the surge of years of pent-up attraction roaring into that kiss and deepening it, letting him know she loved him, always had, always would.

When he pulled away, she was trembling. 'It was always you, Tamas. I was betrothed to another man — a lovely man — and dutifully I had resigned myself to being his wife. If fate hadn't stepped in and sent him to an early death, I would be married to him now, bearing his children, being a good, loyal wife but harbouring the secret that the man I loved with all of my heart belonged to my sister.'

'Oh, Florentyna, my dear one,' he said, pulling her close, stroking her hair. 'We were both trapped. I thought I disgusted you. I had no intention of wooing Darcelle. She seduced me. She was so determined that we wed. I won't deny I found her attractive and amusing. She made me feel young, she gave me hope, she made me realise that Cipres had plenty to offer a powerful realm from across the seas.' He took her face in his hands. 'But you need to know this. I never loved her, not as I have loved you. I have loved only one other girl and I was a child and so was she. We were playmates. My mother disapproved of our deepening relationship and saw to it that it was cut short before it turned into something adult and serious. You remind me of her — you reminded me of her when you were little. Brave, strong, a match for any man.'

'Tamas ...'

He kissed her again. This time for a long, loving while. Their lips felt pleasantly bruised when they finally parted and they grinned helplessly.

'Are we mad?' she said. 'I feel so guilty.'

'Madly in love perhaps,' he offered, giving her a way out of her guilt. 'No demons. We have enough of those in our midst — you don't need them in your mind. Darcelle is dead. You did nothing to provoke her death. And I find myself helpless in your presence. I fought it, Florentyna. When you glided down those stairs outside Stoneheart, I thought my heart would stop from the pain of seeing you again — so composed and gracious ... and generous to a neighbouring sovereign. I had to mask my feelings, frightened that Darcelle would guess how I felt about you.'

Florentyna put his hand against her damp cheek. 'How silly we are, both avoiding each other. If only I'd known.'

'I could say the same. Maybe fate has stepped in again.'

'I don't want to think like that. I loved Darcelle and I wanted only happiness for her.'

'It showed. You were magnanimous toward both of us. Never doubt that.'

Florentyna threw her arms around her king. 'Tamas, I love you. Hold me, promise me we're going to be safe. I want a life with you.'

He buried his head in her neck and kissed it gently. 'I promise you, Florentyna, with all of my heart — which now belongs to you — that when this is done, I am going to marry you ... make you my queen and, if you'll allow, I shall proudly be your regent.'

She searched his genial face, loving that she was in the arms of the man whom she had always dreamed of holding this close. 'I love you.'

Before Tamas could respond, a cry went up. They both swung around.

'Riders!' Tamas said. He squinted. 'It's Wentzl. Well, no time was wasted in our pursuit, your majesty.'

They heard running up the stone stairs.

'Ready?' Florentyna nodded, not taking her eyes from his. 'I love you,' he whispered to her as Cassien and Ham burst into the tower.

'It's him, your majesties,' Ham said, his eyes wide, his stare piercing. 'I can feel it. Cass, the sword is screaming at us.'

Cassien turned to the royals. 'You've just got to trust us now. Listen to Ham. He will know what to do.'

Florentyna nodded, frightened out of her wits and yet surprised by the calm that was flooding through her. She suspected it was the culmination of finally being able to tell Tamas how she had felt for most of her life, and especially to learn that he felt the same way. Whatever happened now, she wouldn't die wondering or miserable in unrequited love.

'Wait.' Tamas looked beseechingly at Ham. 'Are you sure it's him?'

'It's him, your majesty. The sword tells me so. You have to trust it — me, Cassien, Gabe.'

Tamas nodded, hung his head.

'One more thing,' Florentyna said, a finger in the air and look of fear on her face. 'If Cassien does this — I mean his roaming magic — won't it kill?'

'The monks are now closeted in the refectory. They should be safe as it seems my magic does not pass through stone. It may kill animals.'

She glanced into the valley and noted the chickens had been put away in their coop, the goats had disappeared. No men worked the fields. 'And us?'

Cassien shrugged. 'Strictly speaking, you are within the walls of the monastery, and stone, I suspect, repels the killing nature of the roaming. However, you were immune last time. I asked Fynch. He said that since you survived it, you were invulnerable to the roaming magic's killing way.'

'Oh, that's a relief,' Tamas said wryly. 'Just the rampaging, soul-snatching demon to worry about then.'

Ham grinned, enjoying the gallows humour that Tamas seemed good at.

'Ham — ready?' Cassien urged.

Florentyna watched the youngster nod gravely, heard him say 'I am', and then she saw Cassien draw the magnificent sword and heard it for the first time. It made a shrill ringing as it came free from its scabbard, as though eager to be loose, and she felt goosebumps on her skin at the sound. He kissed the blade before returning it to its sheath and then he shocked her by sitting down, his back against the stone of the tower.

She looked at Tamas, confused, back at Cassien and Ham. 'Cassien, what —'

'Your majesties,' Ham interrupted, 'everything we do now is about protecting you, your crowns, the lives of your people, so let us do what we've been sent to —'

Wentzl's voice cut across Ham's words. 'Well, well, well. Queen Florentyna? King Tamas?' he roared. 'I hope you don't think you can hide from me. I'm also sure you know this isn't pathetic Captain Wentzl, although I think his body is very fine indeed … a lot like a man called Gabriel, whom you'd know as Layne Tentrell.' Cyricus laughed in Wentzl's familiar voice and it proved too much for Tamas to bear. He leapt forward to hang out over the tower's window and brandish a fist at the man taunting him.

'We know you, demon, and we will destroy you.'

Wentzl was laughing with pure delight. 'Destroy me? Oh dear, King Tamas. I'd love to know how you found out about me, but perhaps whoever your informant is hasn't explained how incredibly strong I am. Combine that with Wentzl's formidable fighting skills and this is the result. Sorry, Florentyna, I hope these men weren't special in your life.'

Florentyna joined Tamas at the window and saw the bodies of two men, one hanging upside down beside his horse's legs, still trapped in the saddle, and the other splayed lifelessly on the ground. 'They're all special, Cyricus,' she snarled, determined that her voice, her expression would not betray her despair. 'You'll pay for their lives.'

His evident joy broadened. 'Ah, your lovely majesty, there you are. I did enjoy being your sister but I had to leave her. I wonder, has Tamas mentioned that it was he who was the one who killed her?' He made a tutting sound. 'It was so vicious!'

She didn't blink. 'And I thanked him for his courage, demon. Now she can rest in peace.'

'Perhaps. If you can find the tattered remains of her corpse, your majesty, I'm sure they can be bundled into the family tomb. I'll tell you what. I promise I'll see to that when I take over your body — I'm not without my kindnesses.'

'Go burn in Shar's flames, Cyricus!' Florentyna hurled down.

Her rage appeared to thrill the demon. Wentzl leapt down from his horse. 'I am so going to enjoy possessing you, your majesty, and using you to destroy your realm and your empire. Then we'll take ships and go hunting the Cipreans, shall we?'

'Over my dead body,' Tamas roared.

'That's my intention, Tamas,' Cyricus promised. 'Now, let's get this death and possession started, shall we?'

THIRTY-SIX

Cassien had looked at Ham, who'd given him a sad but reassuring nod. 'We will tempt him, I promise. Go now, I will watch over you.'

Ham leaned down and kissed his cheek. 'I've opened the link. We're all connected.'

Cassien closed his eyes. *Gabe?*

Let's do this, he heard his elder brother say in his mind.

Romaine?

Here, Cassien, she said, and he knew she used Ham as a channel. For a moment he felt a twinge of jealousy that it was Ham who could speak to his wolf, but he let the petty thought go, as he also let go of his body.

I love you. Look after Ham. He'll need the forest.

I know, she replied and then the link he felt with her became blurred as his link with Gabe intensified.

It's time, Cassien. Come into the Void now.

His spirit soared; he didn't know how to do what was being asked of him but he trusted Fynch. He hovered in the familiar weightlessness of his roaming magic and let his senses reach out.

Now! he heard Gabe call and felt himself being dragged at speed. Colours, sounds, even smells hurtled by him in a dazzling rush of images. He was disoriented, nauseated … as though the roaming sickness was already attacking him, but he told himself he was imagining it.

In this form he felt no pain, no raging emotions, no … His thoughts halted. No pain? No raging emotions? Is that what Fynch had set up all along? He had made him immune in the flesh to most of the other weaknesses of man, so that he would be ready for this moment. Cassien didn't need to ponder it to know this notion was true. He didn't even feel sad for himself.

473

Cassien could now feel a soft breeze; he could smell a familiar and not unpleasant aroma of slightly damp earth overlaid by a drifting scent of bitter almond, which he recognised as the sap of the colincal tree. Suddenly, the sense of movement stopped and his surrounds snapped into sharp focus.

The forest! How could it be?

Gabe?

Hamelyn's idea, came the answer, but not from Gabe. It was Romaine who spoke as she padded into the clearing where he stood.

I have my body?

Your younger brother is extremely clever ... and cunning, she said. *Meanwhile, your elder brother is an extraordinary talent.*

Gabe created this?

Yes. Hamelyn worked out how to let him see the forest through my eyes. He only needed to view it once and he has re-created it.

But where is the Void?

You're in it, Cassien. You see, Hamelyn reasoned that the Void, according to what Gabe told him, is an emptiness so dark, so mind-numbing that persuading Cyricus to revisit was a near impossible task. Fynch was counting on his arrogance and the Triad's persuasiveness, but Gabe has been touched by the demon and he agreed with Ham that Cyricus was having far too much fun to want to return to the Void and risk entrapment. He's too clever.

Why will he come then?

Hamelyn believes he can still be tricked, but we have to be cleverer than he can imagine us to be. Your brother feels that Cyricus will not consider that anyone has a more cunning mind than himself, so Hamelyn is counting on him making presumptions. If he doesn't see the Void — as he knows it — he will not for a heartbeat suspect that we have access to it or have re-created the forest in the Void.

Cassien was dumbstruck momentarily. Romaine waited, sensing that he was considering everything that she'd just revealed.

You look real enough to touch, he said in wonder.

I am. That's the point. Gabe's brilliant skill at re-creating means that I am 'real enough' when here. And so are you.

I know, he said, awe in his tone.

Gabe has reproduced you to perfection. Wherever you roam, this image moves with you.

Can Gabe hear me?

Yes, but I doubt he's listening. It is taking almost all of his mind power to maintain this. Your brothers must bring Cyricus to us.

Does Fynch know about this magical forest?

No. Cassien, you realise Fynch is dying?

He waited a moment to permit what he already knew — but had allowed himself to deny — to resonate. *Yes.*

We can't fail him.

We won't.

Fynch might have believed Hamelyn's idea to be too daring, too risk-laden. But Hamelyn insisted that unless we take the more daring path, the real risk is that we fail to entice Cyricus out of his mortal body at all.

I agree.

I won't ask if you're ready. You have been ready for a long time, Cassien.

Bring Cyricus to me, he growled.

And Romaine winked out of existence from the Void that masqueraded as the Great Forest.

Ham watched Wentzl approach the monastery walls.

'It's now or never, your majesties. Are you sure, King Tamas?'

'Tamas, don't!' Florentyna pleaded.

'Florentyna, everyone is putting their life on the line. There's no point in me cowering here, waiting to be cut down later rather than sooner, hiding behind monks. I'm a king. I lead.'

'You speak as if we're already dead,' she said, angry tears flowing. She dashed them away. 'Whose idea was this?'

'Mine, your majesty,' Ham said, looking contrite. 'I feel it's the only way.'

'Listen to me, my queen. It's easier to accept death than to fear it. If I don't fear it, I will find more courage. Let me go. Let me play my part.'

'Now, your majesty, if you're ever going to do it,' Ham warned, his eyes imploring. 'We can't let him in.'

Tamas kissed Florentyna's hands holding them to his lips for a few moments. Then he turned to Ham and hugged the boy. 'Brave lad. Now it's my turn.' He didn't wait for them to say more, but hurried away down the stairs.

'Your majesty,' Hamelyn said. 'Please go with Brother Hoolyn.' When she began to protest, he frowned. 'This is for you, Queen Florentyna, for your people, for the empire. Please let us help you.'

She bit back on her words. Nodded. 'Lead the way, Brother Hoolyn.'

He shooed her down the narrow stone staircase to a secret place. Hamelyn hoped keeping her out of sight might buy some time. He hung out the window, just in time to see King Tamas burst from the monastery.

'Cyricus!' Tamas yelled, feeling himself possessed with a fury he had never experienced previously.

'Tamas!' the demon said in Wentzl's amused voice. 'What fun. Do you plan to cross swords with me?'

'I wasn't planning on asking you to dance.'

Wentzl's face erupted with glee. 'Excellent, your majesty. Should I be frightened? I can't be bothered to search your man's memories. You probably know about Myrren's magic by now, don't you?' He didn't wait for Tamas to answer. 'Her magic was so clever that whenever a body was possessed it handed over its knowledge too. Sadly, that's not happening easily for me. Having tampered with the magic, I think it's punishing me. I do not have access to Wentzl's former knowledge unless I hunt for it.' Cyricus drew Wentzl's sword with a flourish. 'That said,' he continued conversationally, 'I'm sure, as your right-hand military man, his skills would be second nature and will occur without me having to think too hard. You should also know that I have had some previous experience with sword —'

Tamas gave a growl of boredom, lunging at Wentzl, who managed to block the hammering blow just in time. 'You talk too much, Cyricus. Wentzl was a man who kept his thoughts to himself. I suggest you shut his mouth and get on with trying to kill me, because I know I can kill you in his body … just like I killed Aphra.' He grinned maliciously.

Wentzl looked shaken. 'Don't threaten me, Tamas. You are nothing!'

'You look unnerved, Cyricus. You hadn't counted on having the fight brought to you, had you? Now your servant is dead, you are alone. I won't let you get to her, you need to know that.'

Cyricus laughed. 'I will feast on your body when this is done.'

'When this is done, Cyricus, you will feel Wentzl bleeding out from the wounds I plan to inflict. And you will die in the body of a Ciprean soldier.' Tamas laughed. 'A nobody,' he added, knowing Wentzl would forgive him the insult.

Cyricus roared his anger, swung with Wentzl's sword and the fight was on in earnest.

In the tower, Ham stole a glance at the slumped figure of Cassien. He wondered what his brother had thought of his surprise in the Void. He also wondered what Cassien would think of his idea to throw Tamas into the fray. He would know soon enough; it was simple, but fraught with danger. The king had to best Wentzl. Then Ham was going to be the one who would lure the demon — give him the choice of certain death or a chance to fight a different sort of battle.

Time was slipping away. Cassien's body would cool inwardly and no longer accept him back if they left it too long. Even blankets wouldn't help, although he had considered it briefly.

He shifted his attention to the fight. Tamas had been doing well; clearly, he was the better swordsman and obviously far too modest because he'd never mentioned his ability. But he was the elder man by a decade. In Captain Wentzl's body, Cyricus was stronger, faster. Tamas looked to be wearying.

He watched the king feint and strike. He caught Wentzl a slashing blow on his fighting arm and Wentzl shrieked with pain. Blood flowed easily. Good, that would slow him … in fact, that was the way to win this fight. Ham checked again on Cassien and then took the risk, hurtling down the staircase two at a time until he rushed out into the main yard, emerging from the shadow of the cloisters.

'Your majesty,' he yelled.

'Busy right now, Ham,' Tamas yelled back, blocking and swinging, missing a nasty hack at his calf, dancing out of the way just in time.

'Wound him, your majesty. Make him bleed any way you can.'

'Who in the devil's bright blood is this, Tamas? You take advice from a boy now?'

'You should too, Cyricus,' Ham said, beginning the ruse, 'because I would advise you to give up this mortal body.'

Tamas, not yet bleeding, but visibly slowing, sneaked in a crushing blow that damaged Wentzl's shoulder.

'You'll pay for that, Tamas,' Cyricus groaned, but Ham could see that the king had gone into the fighting trance that Ham had heard spoken of when he looked after swordfighters in Orkyld. He'd had it explained by several different men as they talked of the curious 'space' they fell into when fighting. *You go within yourself*, one had said, *in order to stay focused and not be distracted.* Another had likened it to wearing blinkers: *You are simply not aware of anything around you, other than your opponent's blade and where the weight of his body is shifting.* And that's how Tamas looked now. Completely absorbed and dedicating himself to parrying the sudden flurry of blows that his younger, stronger opponent was pressing. Tamas was holding, twisting and turning his sword with skill and courage to ensure the flat of the blade met the blows and deflected them, although his shoulders were likely burning by now. In fact, Ham could see he raised his hands slightly lower with each parry. Time was getting away. Was it already too late?

Even so Ham urged him again.

'Make him bleed, sire!'

'Shut up!' Cyricus roared, turning his blade on Ham, which was a foolish error, for Tamas — in his 'space' — saw the opening and took his chance. Like a viper striking, he moved, throwing his last reserve of energy into a hacking motion that brought the keen edge of the Ciprean sword into Wentzl's unprotected side. Wentzl staggered, still facing Ham.

And Ham cheered inwardly. *He's ready, Gabe.* Ham opened a new link — they came easily now. *Cyricus, do you know that Wentzl is already dying?*

Shut your filthy mouth, boy. How are you speaking this way to me? Wentzl's body crumpled to his knees.

The king doesn't know, Ham continued, as if unoffended by the demon's insult, *and what you don't know either, is that I am on your side.*

What? Wentzl's expression was a mask of pain and confusion as he doubled over, but Cyricus sounded strong if perplexed. *What are you talking about?*

Ham cut a glance at Tamas and nodded. The king staggered back in fatigue. He had sustained one wound to the body, but although it bled, it did not look life threatening. Ham's peripheral vision told him that Florentyna and Brother Hoolyn were making for the king but he had eyes now only for Wentzl. He turned his mind back to Cyricus.

Cyricus! I can save you.

The demon laughed in Ham's mind, cruel and mocking.

Trust me, he continued calmly, *we can do this together.*

Cyricus raised Wentzl's head. The gaze was fading, but Ham knew the demon inside was as strong as ever.

Your host is failing, but you needn't die.

I won't die. I can remain dormant.

Not if they burn the corpse, Ham followed up quickly.

Ah, now he had the demon's attention.

They don't cremate in Morgravia, Cyricus sneered.

They do in Cipres. Tamas will ensure the captain's body is accorded full honours. Besides, no Morgravian will protest; they're not taking chances with this one. Wentzl is going on a pyre.

The silence that followed his reveal was loud and horror-filled.

Still Cyricus rallied. *That doesn't mean I'm finished. I can move through the spirit world again. But I'm interested. You said you could save me?* His amused tone belied the way the body he inhabited was crumpling in on itself, wheezing to its death as blood bubbled around a sucking wound.

I can.

Why?

You tell me.

Power?

Yes. Power. Wealth. Lands. Women. I am an orphan, Cyricus. I have known only poverty. I have no skills but this curious talent to engage in mindspeak with other sentients. I have no magic, other than my mind. But I am clever. I see opportunities that people see as dead ends.

Cyricus actually laughed. *How old are you?*

Far older than I appear, Ham said lightly, but not masking the truth. *You'll need to make a decision now, Cyricus, for Wentzl's body is not going to last beyond another fifty heartbeats.*

I know what I must offer you, boy, but what are you offering me? You speak of saving me. How?

It was the moment.

Like this, Ham said and opening up his mind he drew Cyricus in and showed him a vision of the forest. *I can take you here.*

How?

Magic.

You don't have any.

I told you I had some, not as much as you. Use me. Harness what I'm showing you, take yourself to the forest.

Where is this forest?

No ordinary place, my lord. In Morgravia and Briavel, it is known as the Wild, he lied.

Another deafening silence.

They both heard the roar. It was Tamas again, hauling himself back to his feet, and brandishing his sword.

'Not finished yet, Cyricus. Let me help you on your way, demon!'

Choose, my lord. The Wild is a place of fierce magic.

I know of it, Cyricus snarled, but Ham could hear the hunger in his voice. *Tell me again, who are you?*

I am … Myrren, my lord, once known as the Witch Myrren of Morgravia.

Myr— he stopped and Wentzl coughed.

Ham glanced up at Tamas and shook his head, to stay his hand a moment longer. Tamas obeyed making a show of finding it difficult to raise his heavy sword, muttering and growling obscenities.

Myrren, Cyricus repeated. *It's not possible.*

It is. I will explain how later. I walk in the form of this young boy now, but tomorrow I can be Florentyna. I can be your queen. I can be anyone I want to be.

You died! I watched it happen.

Ham shook his head and gave a sly smile. *People believe what they see. My spirit escaped and hid. My magic made a mess of Morgravia and Briavel for a while, didn't it? But I got bored. Centuries have passed. You've livened things up a bit, Cyricus. I'd like to join your vengeful mission. But,* Ham made a show of looking at the wound again, *a dozen heartbeats and you'll never know what you've missed.* Ham intensified the image and the forest glowed dark and green. *And that's only one entrance to the Wild, Cyricus. You should see it on the other side.* He paused, took a breath — this would be his last chance. He didn't think he could stop Tamas now even if he begged.

The king's towering figure stood over Wentzl and the Ciprean blade was being raised for the final time.

'Die, Cyricus!' Tamas growled, animal-like.

Cyricus! Ham urged. *Let go!*

Tamas brought the sovereign sword of Cipres down onto the neck of his beloved captain and severed the man's head from his body.

THIRTY-SEVEN

Ham whispered across the private link to his brothers, relief evident in his voice. *He's back in his ethereal form.*

The demon was still slightly stupefied from the transference. He groaned from where he crouched and Cassien, waiting in the shadow of the trees, was intrigued that he took the form of a man.

But he wasn't ready for the familiar face or voice when the demon looked up.

'So this is the Wild?' he murmured in Fynch's voice.

It was shock enough that Cassien, who had been stepping forward, shrank back. Fynch! How could it be? His mind raced. Fynch was the demon? Surely they hadn't all been duped. Why?

Cassien! It was Ham. *It's not Fynch.*

I … he hesitated.

Gabe's mellow voice joined Ham's. *Brother, listen now. If it were Fynch he would know where he was. He would not have said, 'So this is the Wild.' He's just adopted a form.*

But why walk as Fynch? Cassien demanded, his ethereal heart pounding. *He doesn't know him.*

Cass, there's no time for this, Ham urged. *Think of your body.*

Ham, you don't understand, Cassien said. He didn't want to say anything about Fynch being their father, but how could he explain to his brother how confronting it was to know in the next moments he was going to attempt to kill this man who walked as Fynch.

I understand this. Your body is cooling fast. We have Cyricus where we need him to be. You know what you have to do. He's Cyricus, just tell yourself that. I suspect, Ham began, thinking hard, *it's an echo. He's adopted the form of someone the forest knows well and whose paths he has oft trod.*

Cassien couldn't tell whether Ham was just placating him, but the concept of the echo resonated with him, felt right, and Gabe's point about the man's easy belief that this was the Wild did reassure him.

Fynch looked around. 'Well, come on, Myrren, where are you? Show yourself, girl! We can have a little fun together. It's been a long time since I've squeezed a bright, firm, young —' He stopped, looking thunderstruck.

He doesn't recognise me, Cassien said. *It's not Fynch.*

Keep telling yourself that, Gabe whispered across their link. *Hurry, Cassien. I don't know how long I can maintain the forest.*

Cassien took a breath and stepped out from beneath the low-hanging branches.

'Myrr—' Cyricus stopped. 'You! It can't be. Cassien, the Queen's champion?'

'I am your destroyer, Cyricus.'

The demon sighed. 'And Myrren?'

'Dead, burned as the witch she was.'

Fynch's expression changed from bemused to sombre to frowning, and Cassien could feel the rage building.

'I was tricked?'

Cassien nodded. 'Twice now. This time in a brilliant ploy by the lad. His name is Hamelyn, I don't know if you recall. He's my brother.'

'I knew I recognised him,' Cyricus said, shaking his head. 'I just didn't pay enough attention; although, in my defence, Wentzl was dying at the time. And his ploy about Myrren sounded so plausible. Yes, I remember now, the wretched messenger boy who came with Tamas into Darcelle's chamber.'

'Very good.'

Fynch spun around. 'This isn't the Wild?'

Cassien laughed. 'You're about as far away from the Wild as we could bring you, Cyricus. Welcome back to the Void.'

Fynch's face darkened, all humour fled. An animal-like growl sounded distantly and it took Cassien a moment to realise that it wasn't some creature bearing down upon them but that the noise was coming from the small man who replicated his father. Fynch began to tremble, and then he began to shake uncontrollably; the whole time a roar was gathering, growing in intensity around him.

Any ideas? Cassien threw at his brothers. *Can you sever the forest illusion, Gabe?*

I'd leave you stranded where you are. Your body with Ham, your spirit in the Void. So no, that's not an option.

Cassien watched in bleak horror as Cyricus suddenly reached up to his head and, as though he were peeling the skin off a ripe, juicy finula, tore away the flesh that encased him. Unfolding out of the dark space within was a monstrous, forbidding shape. It was huge, troll-like, with a head as big as a boulder and a body that looked far too large, making that massive head appear like a pebble on a cliff top. The hirsute body shifted and blotted out the pretend light that was dappling through the pretend trees of Gabe's creation.

Cyricus stood to his full height and cast aside the shell of Fynch like an empty husk. It looked tiny and pathetic by comparison with the creature that stood before him.

The voice belonged to the same, sly Cyricus that he knew.

'Well, Cassien, brother of clever Hamelyn and no doubt brother also to Gabriel, it appears to me that I shall have to take out my rage on you.'

Cassien drew his sword and for the first time he heard its voice. It was female and she screamed her joy at being drawn in the Void and her fury at who stood before her. 'The sword knows you, Cyricus.'

'Knows me? Could I care any less, brave Cassien? Do you really believe a blade frightens me? You can smite me a hundred times and I won't feel it.' And the troll-like creature leapt.

Cassien swiftly retreated behind the trees. He could hear Cyricus laughing. Cassien dodged one way and then spun back the other. He thought he'd given himself enough clearance, but he underestimated again how swiftly the demon could move. He felt a vice-like grip and he was thrown into the air. Then his training took over and he twisted to land lightly before rolling, never letting go of his sword, which was now singing, and he could hear her beautiful voice.

The boldly drawn face of Cyricus, with its heavy brow and pouting lips, formed a frown. He hadn't expected Cassien to be so acrobatic. 'Tell your blade to stop its incessant song so we can focus on killing one another.'

'Are you finding it annoying?' Cassien taunted. 'Wait until it cuts you.'

'I could take a thousand cuts from that needle and barely feel a sting,' Cyricus retorted.

Cassien leapt forward, but the troll was ready for him and swept a hand in a big arc. The connecting fist felt like a tree hitting him and Cassien was punched back. He felt bones splinter somewhere as he broke his fall and he registered the annoyance of pain but didn't so much as pause. He was back on his feet.

'You are tough, Cassien.'

'I told you. I am here to destroy you. If it requires my final breath, I'll give it.'

Cyricus exploded with laughter before bearing down on Cassien, but Cassien was quicker to react this time, rolling beneath the clubbing fist. He was behind the troll within a heartbeat and, holding the hilt of the sword like a spear, he plunged the blade into the creature's great calf muscle.

Cyricus roared with pain.

Cassien. End it. Your body ... it just convulsed. Ham's worried voice pressed into his mind.

This had happened the first time he'd roamed, he was sure. He had trembled for days afterwards. Romaine had nearly attacked him she had been so angry with him. He'd promised her he would never push to such a limit again, and he hadn't ... until now.

'Ooh, that hurt me, little mortal,' Cyricus jeered.

Cassien noticed that although the wound barely bled because the creature's hide was so tough, there was a distinct blue-black welt snaking its way up the demon's leg, like a trace of poison. Cyricus was unaware and thought of it as barely more than a scratch, it seemed.

He couldn't follow the thought and should not have hesitated as he had. Cyricus flung him again and this time Cassien couldn't break his fall as well as he had on the previous occasion. He found himself wrapped around a tree, ribs smashed, coughing up blood.

'That's real blood. The Void doesn't spare us,' Cyricus sneered. 'You are certainly courageous. Not so much as a groan of pain. What are you?'

'I'm your destroyer, Cyricus,' Cassien said again, ignoring the immense pain as he hauled himself slowly back to his feet. He had not let go of the sword and he leaned on it now.

Cyricus laughed mirthlessly. 'Yes, you look like you could really hurt me, mortal. What is in your mind to make you think to hunt me?'

'It's not me who hunts you, demon. I'm merely the one who will deliver your death blow,' Cassien said, through halting breaths.

'Really? Who hunts me?' Cyricus asked, sounding genuinely intrigued.

'Fynch, Keeper of the Wild, will rejoice in your destruction.'

'The keeper,' Cyricus repeated and his voice had taken on a dead tone.

Cassien. It was Gabe. *Ham is panicked. Florentyna is weeping. Please, brother, come back now. Leave it. We will watch him in the Void. He can't escape us. Whatever he's doing to you there is happening to your body in our plane. I didn't know that would occur. He is killing you. Maybe I should change you back to the spirit.*

No! Then I can't hold this sword. Let me be, Gabe. I let you be at the cathedral when you knew it was the right decision. I'm going to finish this, Cassien sent back over the link. *I can make it.*

He heard the hesitation.

Ham's voice came into his mind. He sounded as though he too was weeping. *Please, Cassien. Please.*

Be strong, little brother. My turn to be the hero.

Cassien snapped off the link, realising that Cyricus had him again and there was nothing gentle about the way the troll was handling him, rolling his body between his fingers as though he were preparing fingen weed to smoke. He grimaced with the agony, but let out no sound.

'Impressive, Cassien. How do you bear it as I shatter your tiny skeleton?'

He could hardly speak and knew time was short. His body would let him down, but not before he finished what his father had charged him to do, what in his life of loneliness — albeit in ignorance — he had been raised for.

He pretended to whisper.

'I can't hear you,' Cyricus teased. 'The fun's gone out of you, Cassien. You're dying. That's the sad thing about mortals. You die. But you see, we demons, we live on. I found my way out of this forsaken place once before, I'll do so again. I hope the forest remains for eternity.'

'It will be gone the moment I am,' Cassien choked out.

'What are you saying? I didn't quite catch that?' Cyricus taunted, holding Cassien's limp, broken body in a curled fist close to his ear.

It was his one chance. Cassien summoned every ounce of his remaining strength and more, from reserves he didn't know he possessed. In a fearless, killing arc he swung himself up and forward, using the motion to swing Wevyr's sword around over his head and plunge it into the cheek of Cyricus, where it stuck like a needle embedded in the face of the giant, demonic creature.

Cyricus flinched angrily and flung his attacker down, this time succeeding in breaking Cassien's back as easily as if he'd snapped a twig.

Gabe, Cassien struggled to whisper, ignoring the pain that passed quickly into a numb sensation; he was sure that life was nevertheless draining from him. *It is done. Release me, I beg you … let me go. Let me float free and painless.* His brother heard and in a blink he was free of his body and mortal sensation. *Thank you … I'm sorry I did not know you.* He rose helplessly, invisible, cast weightlessly adrift. He would have one more pleasure before all that he knew winked out of existence.

'Cassien … oh, mortal,' he could hear Cyricus saying in between his laughter. 'Your "death blow" is like a pinprick!'

Cassien hovered close to the ear of Cyricus. 'That's the dragon sword, Cyricus.' The demon swung around, swatted at the mist he alone could see.

'Dragon sword?'

'Forged in magic, demon. Magic more ancient and powerful than you.'

Cyricus frowned. The words were having their effect and so was the wound. Cassien could see the telltale path of the poison creeping across the demon's ugly face. If he could have smiled in his ethereal form he would have.

'The sword was made with the ancient blood of a dragon and the ancient blood of a king. That blood is in you now, Cyricus. It is the blood of Fynch, Keeper of the Wild, and his magic will do the killing. I merely brought the death blow as I promised.'

Cyricus began to scream. There was no doubt he understood what the blood of the dragon king and especially the magic of the Wild meant.

'I hope you die very painfully, Cyricus. This time the Wild has rid every world of you.'

The poison was working swiftly now. Cyricus was making gasping, choking noises, leaning against a tree. Cassien smiled as the demon creature slumped to his knees.

'As well you might bow your head to the power of the dragon and the Wild,' he whispered for the last time into the ear of Cyricus, and then Cassien of the forest, son of Fynch, let go of everything that mattered except a final whisper to his elder brother.

Kiss Ham for me ... and go visit that woman I told you about, Gabe. Her name is Vivienne. You will like her. I'm going to look at the forest light one more time and then I want you to tear down your creation. I want Cyricus to take his last breath looking into the Void.

Cassien lifted his spirit's gaze and in that last sweep revelled in the light filtering through leaves, the shadows and the colour green against the rough bark of the trees, and the soft browns and greys of leaf litter.

Farewell, Romaine. I have known the love of a mother through you ... and I thank you.

The Void absorbed Cassien as he died, while Cyricus wheezed his last breath, poisoned with the proud blood of the dragon king, and the demon winked out of existence.

Ham. He's gone. He said it is done. And that he loves you, Gabe said across the link to his younger brother.

At Rittylworth Monastery, the small frame of Hamelyn shuddered in the arms of Florentyna, who wept with him, while Tamas cradled Cassien's previously convulsing body against his chest. Now it lay slumped and lifeless against the king, who glanced at Florentyna and shook his head.

'The demon is destroyed,' Ham said, sounding choked.

She sniffed, gathered her emotions up. 'Ham, he's peaceful now.'

The boy gulped. 'That's because he's dead, your majesty.'

'I know,' she soothed. 'He was heroic.'

'He shouldn't have stayed there.'

'I wish I understood everything that has happened this day and where Cassien had to go,' Tamas admitted. 'All I know is that his name will never be forgotten by the Morgravians ... or the Cipreans.'

'He saved our world,' Hamelyn sobbed.

'The three of you did,' Florentyna said. She hugged the boy closer and kissed his soft sandy-coloured hair.

'I'm taking his body to the Great Forest. It is where he would want to remain.'

'We will help you,' Tamas said. 'Come. We shall take him today and honour him.' He stood, offered his hand to Florentyna and then helped Ham to rise.

The boy wiped his eyes, sniffing. 'We need Gabe to be there too.'

'I agree,' said Florentyna. Can you reach him, Ham?' The boy nodded. 'Then I will help Brother Hoolyn prepare Cassien for his journey. Would that be all right?'

'You, your majesty?'

She smiled sorrowfully at him. 'It would be a true honour. He is a proud son of Morgravia. And I have lost too many of those in too short a time. The empire is in mourning.'

EPILOGUE

A ring of legionnaires stood to attention, flying the colours of Morgravia at the entrance to the Great Forest on its southern rim. They were not permitted to follow the mourners into the depths of the forest, but the queen assured her men that she would emerge, unscathed, for she had the protection of wolves.

No-one understood her jest, but none were going to argue with the huge she-wolf that awaited their majesties, who were accompanied by a lad and a tall, dark-haired stranger whom someone had fetched from the cathedral. The beast, with her distinctive silver-tipped fur, glared at the men, who lowered their gazes, before she turned to pad softly ahead of the burial party.

Cassien's broken body was wrapped in a linen sheath and set on a hollowed tree trunk, according to Ham's wishes, before being lowered into the ground. Only four people and the wolf were present. After each of the quartet had quoted a prayer, Romaine had howled and her companions had been stunned when a pack of wolves answered in mournful echoes.

One by one the wolves emerged, each carrying a leaf in their mouths. Gabe held his breath in wonder, watching the majestic animals take turns to weave their way around each of them before dropping their leaf into the grave of a man they had respected. When all were done, the adult wolves, of which Gabe counted twelve, sat back on their haunches, lifted their heads and let out a chilling and searing howl, which raised the hairs on the back of his neck.

The wolves melted away, leaving only one. She stood in the clearing and beside her stood a man. He looked featherlight and frail.

'Master Fynch,' Florentyna said in welcome.

'Empress Florentyna.' He dipped his head. 'King Tamas.' He smiled and it was wan. 'Thank you for bringing Cassien back to his beloved forest; the wolves will always watch over him now.'

The king and queen murmured their gladness.

'Will you forgive me, your majesties, if I am brief? I wish to speak with Gabriel and Hamelyn.'

Florentyna nodded. 'Of course. Should we wait …?' She looked uncertain.

Fynch beamed her a bright smile, despite how ill he appeared. 'No, your majesty. I will take Ham home. And it looks to me as though Gabriel is set to travel.'

Gabe nodded. 'Yes, I'm going north.'

'Is there anything we can do for you, Master Fynch?' Florentyna asked.

'Give us a royal marriage to celebrate, perhaps, your majesties,' he said, looking from one to the other.

There was a moment of awkward silence and then Florentyna laughed. 'Is it that obvious?' she said, stepping closer to Tamas, who took her hand and held it close to his heart.

'Screamingly so,' Fynch said warmly. 'It's what the empire needs; it's everything Cassien gave his life for. Mourn by all means, but get on with your lives. Make sure Morgravia and Briavel, the Razors and now Cipres flourish. Make a good life for your people. Give us strong sons and beautiful daughters.'

Florentyna's eyes were misted as she stepped forward and gently clasped the little man to her. 'Thank you, Fynch, for having faith in me.'

'We are kin, majesty. How could I not?'

Their farewells were brief.

'Don't get lost in the north, Gabe,' Florentyna warned. 'Lots of loose and lusty women up there,' she joked.

'That's what I'm hoping for, your majesty,' he grinned, raising a hand as the king led Florentyna from the clearing.

The three men of the dragon watched until the royals had disappeared.

Fynch sighed. 'My time is short. Gabriel, you were magnificent … your creation stunned me when I heard.'

'It was Ham's idea. Everything we did was Ham's inspiration.'

Fynch nodded. 'And you're headed north ... why?'

'There's a woman there. I promised Cassien I would visit her.'

'Vivienne,' Ham said. 'You will like her.'

Gabe sighed, getting the strong impression that it was time to take his leave too. 'That's what Cassien assured me. I know you have things to discuss with Hamelyn, so with your permission, I will bid you farewell ... um ... Fynch.'

'You'll come back, won't you, Gabe?' Ham urged.

He grinned. 'Of course, little brother. We have a lot of years to catch up on, but I made Cassien a promise and I must fulfil that. He gave his life for us ...' He couldn't finish, merely shrugged. Ham jumped into Gabe's arms and Gabe squeezed him hard, kissing his head. 'We have a link. Something that no other family has, so talk to me. In the world I come from we have a contraption for that, but it's more of a nuisance than it's worth. I like having you in my head, Ham. Anytime, give me a call.' He grinned.

Ham nodded, echoed the grin and slid back to the ground. 'Don't be gone too long, although once you meet Vivienne, I doubt you'll be in a rush to leave Orkyld.'

Gabe chuckled and ruffled his brother's hair. 'Don't you be so sure.'

'Wait here with Romaine, Ham,' Fynch said. 'I would walk a few steps with your brother.'

Away from Ham, they paused.

'I will tell him now,' Fynch said, before Gabe could say it. 'It has to come from me.'

He nodded. 'Will I see you again?' he asked, already knowing the answer.

The little man shook his head. 'My time is done.'

Gabe hardly knew him and yet he felt instantly choked. He bent low and hugged the man, kissing the top of his head as he had Ham. 'I'm glad I found you, have known you.'

'I'm glad I have been able to tell you in person that I love you, Gabriel. And that I am proud of you.'

Gabe nodded, suddenly overcome with emotions that felt similar to the loss of his wife and child. 'I ...'

'No need. I understand, son. Sometimes it's better to leave things unsaid.'

491

Gabe swallowed, knowing his father to be right.

'Good luck on your travels,' Fynch continued. 'May they be bright.'

'Good luck on yours too. May they be restful … you deserve it.'

Despite his fragility, Fynch appeared to light from within. 'Go, my son.' He kissed him once more and then Gabe couldn't bear to look upon the father he scarcely knew or he was sure he could not leave. He raised a hand to Ham, turned away and forced himself not to glance back, not to slow, but to keep his stride steady and long until he'd cleared the forest, to where a horse waited patiently tethered. He did not allow himself to pause even then; he untied the horse, immediately hauled himself into the saddle and guided the animal toward the road that would take him north into Orkyld.

When he saw the milestone that told him how far the journey ahead was, he realised he had been weeping without being aware of it … still he kept the horse firmly headed in the same direction.

A wolf from Romaine's pack watched him until he was a dark smudge and until even that was lost. Only then did the young wolf turn and blend back into the darkness of the Great Forest.

Ham was scared. Everyone he loved had gone, although it was evident that Master Fynch wanted to speak with him alone. He glanced with trepidation at Romaine.

Be at peace, Hamelyn, she pressed into his mind.

A young she-wolf trotted up and sat at the edge of the clearing beneath the dappled light filtering through the canopy of leaves.

Fynch smiled at Ham from where he stood, steadying himself against Romaine. 'Gabriel has gone,' he said, 'and now we are truly alone, Hamelyn.'

Ham held his breath, not sure what was wanted of him.

'I'm wondering if you can guess why I wanted to speak with you alone?'

He shrugged. 'Do you have another task for me, Master Fynch?'

The elderly man chuckled. 'Oh yes, indeed, young Hamelyn, I do have a task for you. It is both a burden and a joy. I have chosen you for it.'

'Then I am honoured, Master Fynch.'

'I will tell you your new role if you would be kind enough to sit with me against that tree. I fear, Hamelyn, that my strength is rapidly deserting me.'

Hamelyn helped Fynch to be seated and sat beside him, stroking Romaine. The younger female had not moved, barely twitched a whisker in fact, although Ham was aware of how closely she watched them.

'I have another favour to ask of you,' Fynch said, his breath sounding laborious.

'I am happy to do whatever you ask of me.'

'Good. You may find it difficult, but it is a word I wish you to say, just once.' Ham looked at him quizzically. 'The word is father and I would gladly hear you utter it in my presence,' Fynch said, his skin taking on a terrible pallor suddenly.

Ham stared at him. His thoughts scattered. He knew he'd heard right. He knew he'd not reacted, but inside he felt as though he was in turmoil.

'Would you do that for me?' Fynch asked.

His son swallowed. 'You're my father?' Fynch nodded, regarding Ham carefully. 'And Cassien's and Gabe's?' he added, incredulous. Fynch nodded again.

'How did I miss that?' Ham said, his voice tiny.

'Because you were not looking for it. Both of your brothers were troubled by their parentage … their lack of knowledge. But you, Hamelyn, you simply accepted your lot and got on with life as each day presented itself. It's one of the reasons I've chosen you for this task I speak of. Gabriel and Cassien are both too emotional, whereas you are perceptive, inquisitive and indeed conclusive, thus more up to the challenges that may be ahead.'

'Who is my mother?'

'Her name was Jetta,' Fynch began and told Ham everything he could about the beautiful woman who had birthed him.

'That's so sad,' Ham said, unable to help the large tears that fell heavily into the leaf litter where he sat.

'It was her deep and abiding love for her children, but especially for you, that made her believe she couldn't face life without you, Ham. You were a calm, sweet, beautiful infant … and I suspect the man who is growing within you will be no different.'

'What do you want of me?' he asked.

'It is not what I want of you. But what he desires,' Fynch said.

'He?' Ham repeated, and then a blinding light forced him to look up and then away as something huge began to descend into the clearing.

He was speechless, knowing from the glimpse of the shape of the great head that this was a dragon ... the most famous of Morgravia's creatures of legend.

'Am I dreaming?' he murmured.

'No, son. Here is the dragon king, to whom your father is bonded. We are flesh and blood together. He has come to collect you.'

'Why?'

'Because I am dying, Hamelyn. In fact, I believe it is only moments before my strange and long life will breathe its last.'

'No!' Ham yelled.

Romaine was in his head in a heartbeat. *Calm, now, Ham. You are becoming one of us. You are chosen. Accept the mantle that your father bestows. It is an honour.*

'What is asked of me?'

Fynch reached for Ham's hand, clumsily let it fall against his chest. 'Oh, my beautiful son, you are to be the next Keeper of the Wild. You will ensure the safety of Morgravia and Briavel, of the Razors, and now of Cipres, once I am gone. You will be the king of the beasts; the forest will be your home when you are not in the Wild. The forest creatures are your friends. Romaine will guide you, but she too is becoming an old girl, eh?' he said, reaching out his other hand to the wolf, who licked it. 'Romaine is giving you her daughter. She is your wolf and she will defend you with her life and be a companion always for that life she protects.' His voice had become so quiet that Ham was straining to hear.

Ham turned to regard the young wolf that had padded up. She was pure light grey, with the palest of blue eyes. He offered his hand, which she sniffed, and then she stepped forward and without warning licked his face.

Greetings, Hamelyn. I am Sylvan.

Hamelyn bowed his head, at first lost for words. *Hello, Sylvan. You are magnificent.*

He felt her pleasure trill through him.

Hamelyn, boomed a new voice in his head like a mountain shifting.

Ham stood and bowed. 'My king.'

Your king and father. Fynch has given me his son and I am honoured to accept you, the dragon king pushed into his mind. *Come to me, Hamelyn.*

Hamelyn walked over to where the brilliance of the dragon glinted in a dazzling array of colours which winked and sparkled with an internal luminescence they seemed to possess. Ham imagined that Florentyna and Tamas could see the light from Stoneheart but the dragon seemed to hear his thought.

Only the forest creatures see me … and the Keeper of the Wild, of course.'

Is that where we're going?

The Wild is our home, but you may visit here and the realms as you choose.

Why is Fynch dying?

Because he is old, son, and because he has defied the rules of the Wild. He needed its strength and power but he was determined to finish what Elysius began with Cyricus. It meant we could not keep him safe from the ravages of his own mortality. And I suspect Fynch is tired. He has watched over the empire faithfully … protected the Wild and been a good son of Morgravia.

And now it's my turn.

Yes, child. Say farewell to Fynch. It is his time.

Ham ran in a daze back to where Fynch was breathing so shallowly that Ham couldn't be sure he was breathing at all. His father opened his pale eyes to his son once more.

'I have loved you boys with all my being. Each of you has made me proud, but none more than you, Hamelyn. Now you will kiss me and wish me Shar's speed. I go willingly and with a pure heart.'

Hamelyn did not reach to wipe away the tears but bent low to kiss his father for the first and last time. 'I love you, father.'

Fynch died with a soft smile and a gentle sigh.

It was only then that Ham became aware of the rustling and shuffling; he was astonished to see a crowd of forest creatures gathered around him. He wasn't sure whether they were paying homage to Fynch or to him, but each had bowed its head.

Bring beloved Fynch to me, Ham heard the dragon say.

Together with the wolf pack, Ham carried Fynch's feather-light corpse to the dragon and placed him on the great clawed foot. His father looked tiny, and although Ham knew he shouldn't be shocked, he gasped when the King of the Beasts lowered his enormous head and swallowed Fynch of the Wild.

Now we are truly one, he said, softly. *Come, Keeper, ride and let me show you the Wild, your new home.*

Ham glanced at Sylvan. *I will see you, my wolf, from time to time.*

I will be waiting, my king, she said.

From the dragon's foot, he raised a hand to Romaine.

Be safe, Hamelyn, she murmured and then the animals bowed their heads once again as the great winged serpent lifted itself from the ground, beating powerful wings.

The horse ride had taken just a few hours. He'd found Orkyld without a problem, had left his horse with the stables, and was now making his way to a brothel, where he was assured a beautiful whore called Vivienne worked. As he approached through the small alley Gabe felt the link slice open in his mind.

Ham? You already?

Are you in Orkyld?

Yes. Just arriving at Vivienne's. Where are you?

Look up.

What?

Look up.

Gabe did and blinked. He laughed over the link. *If I didn't know better I'd say I could see a dragon.*

And if I didn't know better I'd call you a liar, Ham replied and Gabe heard a joyous whoop of childish laughter. He frowned. Looking up he saw nothing but cloud. Had he imagined it?

'Look where you're going!' someone snapped.

'Oops, pardon me,' he said to the offended passer-by whose toes he'd trodden on.

The vision had brightened him, banishing the memory of how he had screamed in despair in the cathedral at the foot of the dragon pillar when he knew he had to let Cassien go. That had been part of his dream — the man in agony in the cathedral nave; he had been seeing himself.

He looked at the doorway. He'd never been to a brothel, not even in his wayward youth. The timber-framed, slightly ramshackle house was how he'd imagined an old French brothel should look. He took a breath and pulled on the cord, hearing a bell ring distantly on the other side of the door. Gabe waited what he felt was an inordinately long time and was about to pull the cord again when the door opened and he was met by an older woman, who filled the doorway without a crack to spare. Her white hair was neatly groomed into a high bun with a jewelled clasp and her plump fingers dazzled him with their gold and sparkling stones.

'Greetings, I'm Mistress Pertwee,' she said, eyes sparkling. 'I want to ask you if you're in the right place. A strapping and handsome man like you should have no trouble finding a woman without having to pay for the pleasure,' she said, looking him up and down.

'Er, I'm here to see Vivienne.'

'Vivienne? Of course, oh Shar save me, you're the fellow she keeps hoping would come back for her.'

'No, I ...'

'We met, remember?' she said, holding out her hand, which he took, not wanting to give offence. 'Cassien! That's right.' She managed to somehow swivel her bulk in the doorway. 'Elkie! Go fetch Vivienne. Quickly, girl!'

She turned back. 'Come in, come in.'

He followed, wondering if it was worth trying to explain.

Beautiful girls crowded around him — at least eight of them. They touched his clothes and oohed and ahhed at his fine skin, his hair shot through at the temples with silver, his beautiful dark eyes. He squirmed and smiled, made excuses for not wishing to touch the products on sale or sample the wares for a special price.

Still wriggling out of a particularly determined set of hands that clutched his, he caught sight of a tall, voluptuous woman with strawberry-coloured hair and skin that made him think of ripe peaches in a summer orchard. She looked flushed and confused.

'Cassien ...' She shook her head, her bright and lovely smile faltering. 'No, forgive me. I ... I am mistaken, sir.' He could see she was breathing deeply as if her heart were pounding.

He smiled crookedly, stepped forward. 'Vivienne?'

She nodded, her expression suggesting he'd just dashed her hopes.

'The apology is mine,' he began.

A tear escaped. 'Oh, I'm so sorry,' she said, quickly reaching for a linen and dabbing at her eyes. 'I've been expecting ... er, well, hoping to see someone. He ...' She trailed off to a silent shrug. 'You remind me of him.'

'Cassien?'

Her mouth opened in surprise. 'Yes,' she said, shocked.

'Vivienne ...' he looked around and realised he could hear a pin drop in the room. Everyone was hanging on his next words. He was determined. 'Vivienne,' he began again. 'I am Gabriel. Brother to Cassien ...'

She searched his face and knew. 'Cassien is not coming, is he?'

He shook his head slightly and the other girls gave a sigh of regret for their friend. Mistress Pertwee shooed them from the room. 'You need to be alone, I suspect,' she said. Then whispered to Gabriel, 'You can buy Vivienne tonight if you need. I'll do you a good rate.'

He looked at the woman, startled, but didn't answer and she mercifully continued on out of the door. Gabe returned his gaze to Vivienne. Ham was right. He could easily fall for this woman on sight.

'He's dead?' she said, her intuition serving her well.

He didn't know how to explain that Cassien's spirit had been separated from his body and was lost. It was easier just to think of him as dead. 'Yes. His last words to me were that I should find you.'

It impressed him that she didn't shriek or dissolve into sobs. Her tears were silent and calm. 'Thank you for coming. It is alarming how alike you both look. I'm sorry if I have upset you.'

'You haven't. I've travelled a long way and I'm very glad that I could meet you.'

She straightened at the news of his journey. 'He left me plenty of money and a small heart-shaped wreath. I don't have to live like this — but I hoped he might return for me. Where are you staying?'

'I came directly here. I've never been to Orkyld before. I've not been to Morgravia since I was born.' She frowned. 'Cassien and I have only recently been reunited. We were separated when he was an infant.'

Her face fell. 'That's sad. I'm glad you found one another.'

He nodded. 'I think you know our youngest brother too. His name is Hamelyn.'

'Ham?' she said giving a moue of shock. 'Shar's breath! You are full of surprises.'

He shrugged. 'I'm sorry. They both send their love. I wish Cassien could have delivered it in person, but I hope I'll do.'

Maybe it was his choice of words, or maybe it was just her private grief, but Vivienne's expression softened as she regarded him. 'Yes, I think you'll do,' she said, almost in a whisper. 'You can stay here if you wish.'

He hesitated. 'Ham said if I met you I would never want to leave Orkyld.'

She found a shy smile. 'What do you do?'

'I'm hoping to be a scrivener at the cathedral in Pearlis. But for now, I am simply a traveller, looking to belong, and hoping my journey will help me come to terms with my recent losses.'

Vivienne stepped forward and he smelled perfume like freshly mown grass envelop him. She took his hand. 'Come, Gabriel. Let's help soothe each other's sorrows.'

Acknowledgments

For a decade now I've maintained it was unlikely I would return to a previous landscape. However, when the opportunity arose to write a single-volume fantasy, I knew page-space to build an imaginary world would be limited, so it was a happy homecoming to the familiar realm of *The Quickening*. I hope you enjoy your return to Morgravia as much as I have.

My thanks to Voyager around the world for allowing me to go back and play in the land I have held a soft spot for, and especially to my editor, Stephanie Smith, who went along with the curious idea to set a story in the contemporary, real city of Paris and the imaginary, medieval capital of Pearlis. Special thanks too to Anne Reilly and Deonie Fiford for wrestling the manuscript through its various phases. I have to thank Darren Holt for his gorgeous artwork and the hardworking HarperCollins sales team that is relentless and upbeat in its efforts to preserve sellers of fantasy books in the 'high street'. My gratitude is extended to booksellers around the world — now more than ever — as the complexion of our industry changes. Thank you for recommending my stories and for your determination to keep the traditional book moving through welcoming hands.

To family and friends who are always so supportive — thanks for being there, especially you Mum and Dad. Draft readers — Pip Klimentou, Judy Bastian, Steve Hubbard, Nigelle-Ann Blaser ... thanks for having my back. Walking buddy, Marianne D'Arrigo ... thanks for all the weekend kilometres that helped to clear my mind for storytelling. Baking has been a quiet escape from work but became a passion during the writing of *The Scrivener's Tale* and I must thank my baking muse, Belinda Jeffery for her recipe books and her wonderful friendship this past year.

Ian ... first reader, harsh critic, best friend ... love always.

Will and Jack, forever crazy about you two ... xx

Fiona McIntosh left the U.K. at twenty to travel, discovered Australia and fell in love with it. She has since explored the world working in the travel industry but now writes novels full-time and roams the globe for her stories. She lives with her husband and twin sons in Adelaide.

Read *The Scrivener's Tale* blog:
http://scrivener.fionamcintosh.com

You can find out more information
about Fiona on her website:
www.fionamcintosh.com

Visit the Voyager website —
www.voyageronline.com.au
— for lovers of science fiction and fantasy.

Turn the page to see where it all began, in

Myrren's Gift
The Quickening Book One

Fiona McIntosh's first adventure set in Morgravia, a dazzling

and remarkable epic fantasy of loyalty, love and eveil, of

savage adventure and dire magic.

❖ ❖ ❖

"A 'just one more chapter' sort of book. Don't start reading
Myrren's Gift in the evening if you have to get up early the
next morning."

— ROBIN HOBB

PROLOGUE

He knew the injury would be fatal. Accepted it at the very moment he caught the sword's menacing glint as it slashed down.

Fergys Thirsk, favorite son of Morgravia, began the last part of his journey toward death as a gray dawn sluggishly stretched itself across the winter sky. He faced his end with the same courage he had called upon for all of his life as General of the Legion.

It had been the King's idea to attack the Briavellians gathered on an opposite hillside under the cloak of night. To Fergys it had seemed somehow ignoble to interrupt the traditional night's peace in which men sat quietly around small fires, some singing, others deep in thought as to whether they might live through another day of battle. But the King had fixed his mind on this bold plan to take his enemy by surprise on a night where dark, brooding clouds eliminated the moonlight. The River Tague, which bisected the realms of Morgravia and Briavel from the mountains in the north to their midlands, had already run red with the blood of both armies earlier that day and Fergys had been reluctant to put the men to the sword again so soon. But his sovereign had persisted and Thirsk had accepted the challenge.

There had been no sense of foreboding as he carried out his monarch's wishes and led the attack. He simply did not like the plan. Fergys was a man of honor and tradition. War had a code that he preferred to observe rather than flout.

Nevertheless he had fought ferociously but had been disturbed when Magnus, his friend and king, going against his wishes, had joined the fray. Without further thought Fergys had planted his feet and grimly dispatched three Briavellians before he was able to make a move toward protecting his sovereign.

"The white cloak's suitably inconspicuous?" he had yelled above the din toward his oldest, dearest friend.

Magnus had ignored the sarcasm and even had the audacity to wink back. "Got to let Valor know I was here when his army was beaten into submission."

It was a reckless act and more dangerous than the King could have suspected. They were fighting on Briavel's side of the river and once the element of surprise had passed, both armies had gotten down to the business of slaughtering one another. Valor's men were no cowards and had worked with a newfound passion to repel Morgravia.

Fergys had noticed Briavel's standard—signaling that Valor too was in the thick of the fighting—and remembered now, as lifegiving blood leaked from him, how he had feared for both Kings.

With Briavel having the advantage of higher ground, Fergys had made the decision to pull back. His army had already inflicted a terrible price on its enemy; no need for either of these sovereigns to die. He knew by daybreak and the inevitable clash that would come later that day Morgravia would overcome its enemy once again. So he had given the order and his men had obeyed immediately.

All except one.

And it was that one man whom Fergys Thirsk had sworn to protect. The one he would give his life for.

As with the Thirsk Generals who had gone before him, Fergys had lived long, so the only regret that surfaced as the killing blow came was his absence from the family he loved. Fergys was not at all used to losing but it seemed Shar had asked more of him on this occasion; his god had asked for his life and he had given what had been requested without hesitation. He had fought so many battles and rarely returned with more than surface wounds.

And this battle had looked to be no exception until he had seen the danger, heard the man's battle cry, and deliberately stepped in front of that slashing sword. Up to that fateful moment only a thin line of dried blood across one cheek marked the closest a blade had come to threatening him. Duty, however, came first.

Fergys had not even paused to consider the implications of pushing aside King Magnus, knowing he would have no time to block the inevitable blow. The only thing standing between the King and certain death was Fergys's own body. The blade struck, fate guiding it ingeniously beneath the breastplate.

He cried out at the pain from the sucking wound in his abdomen but did not falter, too intent was he on dispatching the Briavellian and ensuring the life of his King. Only then did Fergys Thirsk fall, not yet dead but commencing the longest journey of all.

As they had hurried him from the battleground and back over the Tague, he was still calling orders to his captains. Once he had heard the full retreat sounded, he lay back on the canvas that would bear him back to Morgravia's camp. This journey seemed endless and he now used the time to reflect on his life.

There was little to complain about.

He was loved. That in itself should be enough for any man, he reasoned, but then there was so much more. He commanded respect—had earned it too—and he had walked shoulder to shoulder with a King whom he called friend. More than friend . . . blood brother.

That brother now walked in shock by his side, giving orders, fussing for his care, whispering to himself that it was all his fault; his stupidity and recklessness had seen the great

General felled. It was all pointless. Fergys tried to tell the man this but there was insufficient strength in his voice to speak above the din of the retreat. If he could have he would have hushed his blood brother and reminded him that Shar's Gatherers had spoken and whether any of them liked it or not he must now answer that call. No regrets. Duty done.

Men were bowing their heads as the stretcher passed by. Fergys wished he could somehow convey his thanks to each. The Legion produced exceptional soldiers, loyal to a man to his command. He spared an anxious thought for how they would accept the new General, yearned for a last opportunity to beg their tolerance. "Give the boy a chance," he would beseech. "He will be all that I am and better still." And he hoped it would be true.

He thought of the youngster. Serious and a firm follower of tradition. Tarred by the same brush, as they say, especially in looks. They were plain, stocky, fearless men, the Thirsks, and this boy was already shaping up as a leader. The Morgravian Legion followed a curious tradition of handing down leadership from father to son. Fergys wondered if it could last. The lad was so young. Would he have time to sire his own heir to continue the Thirsk tradition or would a new family vie for the right to lead the army? Thirsks had led the Legion through two centuries now. It was an extraordinary history for one family that bred sons with warrior capabilities, tempered with intelligence.

The dying man's bearers were nearing the tent that he knew would be his final resting place. Once he was laid down he would have to concentrate on his King for as long as his heart held out. He wanted time to think about his beautiful wife, Helyna, of whom so much lived on in their son. Not her looks, mind. Those exquisite features belonged to their daughter alone. Fergys grimaced, not from pain so much as grief. His daughter was so young . . . too young to lose both parents.

How would his family manage? Money was no problem. They were the wealthiest of all the nobility, perhaps barring the Donals of Felrawthy. He would have to rely on Magnus. Knew he could. What his family needed now was time. Time to grow into their new lives. Peace must be achieved with Briavel until the young Thirsk was ready to lead into battle. That peaceful time would have to be bought and he hoped his life would suffice as raw currency.

They laid him down. The King had insisted he be settled in the royal tent. Physicians hurried to Thirsk's side. He ignored their probing, knowing it would ultimately be followed by a shaking of heads and grave glances. Fergys closed his eyes to the sudden frenetic activity and returned to his ponderings.

The old hate. It all seemed so pointless now. Valor of Briavel was a good King. He had a daughter. Little chance now of a son. Valor had shown no inclination to remarry after the death of his wife; it was rumored that theirs had been a love gifted from Shar. And he was probably too old now, at seventy, to bother himself with trying to sire a male heir. He too needed peace for Briavel's Princess to grow up and grow into her role. The wars had been a tradition in a sense. Their forefathers had fought each other when they were little more than feuding families. Initially it had been a case of maintaining the balance of power between two small factions suspicious of one another. But when the two strongest families established their own realms, and kingdoms were born, the battles were fought to increase power, gain more land, greater authority. Over the centuries, neither managed to claim domination over the region and so their animosity degenerated into squabbles over trading rights or merchant routes—any petty excuse, in fact, until by the time Magnus and Valor had inherited their crowns, neither was sure exactly why the two realms hated one another so intently.

Fergys shook his head. If truth be known, he rather admired Valor, and lamented the fact that the two Kings could not be neighbors in spirit as well as location. United in friendship and mutual respect, the region would be rich beyond dreams and near-invincible to any enemy. Now he would never see that dream come to fruition. He sighed.

"Talk to me," his King beseeched, voice leaden with guilt.

"Send the physics away, Magnus. We all know it's done."

The King bowed his head in sad acceptance and gave the order.

All except his friend had now been banished by Thirsk. No emotional farewells would he tolerate from his captains. He could bear neither their sympathy nor their despair. They had filed out in silence, stunned by the notion that their General might not even see this day's sun fully risen.

Thirsk asked for the tent flap to be left open so he could see across the moors to the smoke from the distant fires of the Briavellian camp, where soon the sounds of dying men and beasts would be heard again should the battle resume today. In his heart Thirsk knew the two armies were bleeding and wearied; all of the men were now keen to acknowledge the outcome of yet another battle between these ancient enemies and return to their towns and villages. Many would not be going home, of course, and their widows and mothers, sisters and betrothed were mostly from Briavel.

And yet, as Fergys Thirsk slipped further into death's cool embrace, most from his side knew it would be later argued in the taverns that it was the great realm of Morgravia that had suffered the loss on this occasion.

The General looked wearily back at his oldest and closest friend.

"It's over for them," King Magnus of Morgravia finally said.

Thirsk tried to nod, relieved that Magnus had navigated his way out of the shocked stupor; there were things to be said and little time. "But Valor will try to fight on," Fergys cautioned. "He will want Briavel to salvage some face."

The King sighed. "And do we allow him to?"

"You always have in the past, your majesty. Pull back our men completely and let him have the news of my injury and subsequent passing," his dying companion replied, shivering now from pain cutting through the earlier numbness. "It will be a proud moment for them and then we can all go home," he added, knowing full well he would go home shrouded in black linens and tied to his horse.

The battle was won. Morgravia had prevailed as it usually did under General Thirsk. It had not always been so, however. There were centuries previous when Briavel had triumphed. These nations had shared a long and colorful hate.

"I wonder why I give him quarter—a weakness, do you think?" Magnus pondered.

Fergys wanted to tell his King that it was not weakness but compassion that saw today's Morgravia resist the temptation of out-and-out slaughter. That and the fact that Magnus had never had to watch his best friend die before— suddenly the battle had taken second place in the King's priorities. And if compassion was a weakness, then Fergys loved his King for the contradictions in his character that could see him willingly pass sentence of death on a Morgravian criminal while, on the battlefield, sparing the lives of his enemies. It was this enigmatic mix of impulsiveness and honor, stubbornness and flexibility that had drawn Fergys to Magnus from childhood.

Thirsk noticed his own breathing was becoming shallower. He had witnessed this many times previously on the battlefield as he held the hands of the dying and heard their last labored words. Now it was his turn. Death was beckoning but it would have to wait just a little while longer.

There was more to be said even though it hurt deeply to talk. "If there is weakness in this, then it is shared equally among us all," Fergys responded. "Without it, Briavel and Morgravia would not enjoy this regular opportunity to send their young men thundering on fine steeds across the moors to kill each other."

Magnus nodded. Fergys Thirsk never willingly went to battle; he cared too much for the sanctity of peace and the preservation of lives, particularly those of Morgravian men. But history attested to Fergys Thirsk being the most successful of the campaigners to lead Morgravia. He was legend amongst his men.

Through a haze of pain Thirsk scrutinized the grieving man before him, noticing for the first time how gray his King's hair had become. Once lustrous, it framed a strong-looking face, a determined jaw, and eyes that somehow reflected the man's extraordinary intelligence. The King's tall bearing suddenly gave the impression of a vague stoop, as though his big body was getting too heavy for him to carry around. They were getting old.

The General suddenly rasped a laugh. He would grow no older than this day. The King looked up sharply at the unexpected sound and Fergys shrugged, sending a new wave of agony through his ruptured body.

"We've always managed to laugh at most things, Magnus."

"Not at this, Fergys. Not at this." The King sighed again.

Fergys could hear the pain in that deep breath. They had shared their childhood. Their fathers had raised them to be close but the friendship was not forced. Fergys had worshiped the heir and then the King, and for his part, Magnus considered his General a brother in all but birthright. He loved Fergys fiercely and relied on his counsel, had done so throughout his long and flourishing reign. They were as wise together as they were wily.

"What must I do?" the King whispered.

With his last reserves of energy, the soldier squeezed the hand of his King.

"Your majesty, it is my belief that you would no more celebrate the death of King Valor of Briavel than you do mine.

Morgravia has nothing to fear from him now for perhaps as much as the next decade—make it so, my King. Call a parley, sire. No more young men need lose their lives today."

"I want to. I have no desire to prolong this battle, as you well know, and if it had not been for my own stupidity, you wouldn't—"

Thirsk interrupted the King's outpouring of guilt with a spasm of coughing, blood spattering his shirt. Death would no longer be patient. The King began to reach for linens but his General pushed the monarch's fussing hands away.

"My death should suffice—it will be seen as a major blow for Morgravia," he said matter-of-factly before adding, "Valor is proud but he is not stupid. He has no male heir, sire. His young Princess will be Queen one day and will need an army of her own, and for Briavel to breed the soldiers of the future, they need peace. But their men, and ours, would do well to dispense with the ancient quarrel altogether. The threat from the north is very real, my King, for both our realms. You may need each other one day."

Thirsk spoke of Cailech, the self-proclaimed King of the Mountain People. In the early days Cailech had merely been the upstart and impossibly young leader of a rabble of hard Mountain Dwellers who rarely left their high ground among the imposing sprawl of ranges that framed the far north and northeast. His kind for centuries had kept their tribal squabbles to themselves, contained within the Razors, as the range was called. Back then, fifteen or so years ago, this young warrior, no more than eighteen summers, had begun to stamp a brutal authority across the tribes, uniting them. Thirsk had believed for several years now that it was only a matter of time before Cailech would feel confident enough to look beyond the mountains and out toward the fertile lands of Morgravia and Briavel.

"I will continue your strengthening of the Legion to the north," the King said, reading his thoughts.

"That will help me rest easy."

Both men could hear Thirsk's increasingly rapid breathing.

Magnus had to push back all the emotion welling inside him. "And so for you, my dearest friend. What can I do for you before you leave me?" They clasped hands for the last time in the Legionnaire manner.

"A blood pact, sire."

The King's eyebrow raised. He remembered the first time they had mixed blood. They had been lads and permitted to witness the ritual being performed between the former dukes of Felrawthy and Argorn—a special linking of Morgravia's most powerful duchies in the north and south of the realm. The two boys had watched the rites wide-eyed, impressed at the solemnity of the occasion and the deep commitment between the participants. It had been Magnus's idea for them to do the same. "We'll commit to each other," he'd said to Fergys. "You will love me as your King and I will love you as my General, but we will be blood brothers above all else."

They had found the courage to cut each other and hold palms together as the two nobles had done. They had not been even ten years old.

Thirsk coughed violently again. His passing into the dark was just moments away. They could sense it.

"Name it, Fergys!" the King growled, his anxiety betraying him. "Whatever you ask is granted. You know it."

Thirsk nodded, exhausted. "The children. My boy, Wyl. He must return from Argorn immediately. He is already General of the Legion and does not know it. He must finish his training in the palace." A new fit of coughing interrupted him. "Bring Gueryn with him, sire. Keep them close. There is no better teacher for him."

"Except the one who leaves him now," the King replied grimly. "And Ylena?"

"All I ask is that you make a good marriage for her." Thirsk looked toward the table where his dagger lay.

Magnus moved without a word and fetched it. He sat down again beside his friend. The King passed the blade over his palm and did the same to Thirsk. They rejoined hands, mingling their blood.

The King spoke softly as he made his promise. "Ylena will want for nothing. Your son is now my son, Fergys Thirsk."

"A brother for your Celimus," Thirsk rasped as his breathing turned ragged.

"They will be blood brothers, as we are," the King said, fighting back tears. His grip on his friend's hand tightened. "Go now, Fergys. Struggle no more, my friend. May your soul travel safely."

Fergys Thirsk nodded, the light already dying in his eyes. "Brothers in blood," he whispered, breathing his last.

King Magnus of Morgravia felt the clasp of his friend's hand slacken as death claimed Thirsk. "Our sons will become one," he echoed gravely.